P9-AOM-045

Thanks for your pure excitement whenever we talked about the characters and stories. This is for you, Joelle and Jill. —M. Y.

SIMON SPOTLIGHT
An imprint of Simon & Schuster Children's Publishing Division
1230 Avenue of the Americas, New York, New York 10020
This Simon Spotlight hardcover edition August 2020
© 2020 Mark Young and The Jim Henson Company
JIM HENSON'S mark & logo, FRANKEN-SCI HIGH mark & logo, characters, and elements are trademarks of The Jim Henson Company. All Rights Reserved.
All rights reserved, including the right of reproduction in whole or in part in any form.
SIMON SPOTLIGHT and colophon are registered trademarks of Simon & Schuster, Inc.
For information about special discounts for bulk purchases, please contact Simon & Schuster Special Sales at 1-866-506-1949 or business@simonandschuster.com.
Designed by Ciara Gay
Manufactured in the United States of America 0720 FFG
10 9 8 7 6 5 4 3 2 1
ISBN 978-1-4814-9143-3 (hc)
ISBN 978-1-4814-9142-6 (pbk)
ISBN 978-1-4814-9144-0 (eBook)

3 9547 00462 3067

Jim Henson's FRANKEN-SCI HIGH

THE CREATURE IN ROOM #YTH-125

CREATED BY **MARK YOUNG**
TEXT WRITTEN BY **TRACEY WEST**
ILLUSTRATED BY **MARIANO EPELBAUM**

Simon Spotlight
New York London Toronto Sydney New Delhi

CHAPTER 1

Half Brothers, All the Time

"Attention, students! Today our lunch staff accidentally used the recipe for interdimensional meatloaf instead of international meatloaf. If your meatloaf has disappeared from your plate unexpectedly, you may choose another lunch special."

The loud chatter in the Franken-Sci High cafeteria died down during the announcement, and rose again to a dull roar when it had finished.

Newton Warp looked down at the square of gray meat on his plate. He picked up his fork and attempted to stab the loaf, but it shimmered and disappeared because it could.

"Rats!" Newton cried.

Next to him Higgy, his roommate, burped loudly. "I ate mine before it could escape to another dimension," he said.

"How do you know it won't still escape?" Newton asked.

"What do you mean?" Higgy asked.

"Well, you might have absorbed it into your—your goo," Newton began. (He'd been going to say "stomach," but Higgy Vollington was made of green protoplasm, and Newton wasn't entirely sure his friend *had* a stomach.) "But it could still move to another dimension once it's inside you, right?"

"You may be right," Higgy agreed. "Then I'll just be hungry again! Better get something else to eat." He slid off the bench and made his way back to the lunch line, making a *pffft, pffft, pffft* sound as he moved.

Across the table Newton's friend Shelly Ravenholt pushed her plate toward him. "Want to share my salad? It's pretty good."

"That's okay," Newton replied. "I'm not that hungry anyway. Those protein pancakes at breakfast filled me up."

At the end of the table, a brain in a jar trained its eyeballs on Newton.

"I don't know why everybody makes such a fuss about eating," said Odifin Pinkwad. "It seems like such a bother. And you have to do it three times a day, every single day."

"Five," corrected Rotwang Conkell, a tall, skinny boy who had just sat down at the table. His plate was piled with a mountain of nuggets.

3

The robot student sitting next to Shelly frowned. "Well, I don't eat either, but I'm glad we get a break three times a day," said Theremin Rozika. "Otherwise we'd just have three more classes."

"Didn't I hear that your dad was working on artificial taste buds, Theremin?" Shelly asked. "That would be cool. Then you could see what you're missing. You too, Odifin."

"I can assure you, I'm not missing anything," Odifin said.

Higgy came back and slapped a tray of purple gelatin onto the table. "It helps to be nice to the lunch ladies," Higgy said. "They gave me extra helpings!"

"They prefer to be called 'dining engineers,'" Shelly reminded him.

A feeling of happy calm came over Newton as he looked at all his friends.

Just a few months ago, Shelly and Theremin found me in the library Brain Bank, with no memory of who I was or where I'd come from, Newton thought. *I thought I'd never fit in or find out what my story was. But now . . .*

But now Newton was closer than ever to learning the truth. First he and his friends had discovered that Newton had special abilities. He could instantly grow gills if he jumped into water. He could camouflage himself if he was in danger. He could change his appearance

to mimic others. His sticky hands and feet allowed him to climb up walls and stick to ceilings. And he was discovering new things all the time.

Newton had done his best to keep those special abilities a secret. At the same time, he had tried to find out the truth about his past. Headmistress Mumtaz seemed nice, but whenever he questioned her, she'd say she couldn't tell Newton anything, which was strange. Then a mysterious green-haired man had started following him around. The man had turned out to be Professor Flubitus, who said he'd come from the future to protect Newton, because Newton was somehow—in a way he did not yet understand—very important to the future of the school.

This was interesting, but Newton didn't necessarily want to know about his future—he wanted to know about his past. Finally Flubitus had revealed that Newton had a relative at Franken-Sci High. After an intense search, and some DNA testing, Newton had discovered who that relative was: Odifin the brain in a jar, was his half brother!

Newton gazed over at Odifin, who was talking to Rotwang. Odifin thought about what he wanted to say, and then his words came out of a speaker attached to his jar.

"I hear they're showing a movie called *The Thing with Two Heads* in the gym tonight," Odifin said to Rotwang. "We should go!" Then Odifin looked at Newton. "Want to come, Bro?"

"Thanks, Odifin, but I need to check my schedule," Newton replied. "I think I have a homework assignment to do."

Theremin's eyes flashed red. "'Bro'? Aren't you guys half brothers? Or is it more like *quarter* brothers?"

Newton heard an edge in his robot friend's voice, and suspected that Theremin was a little bit jealous about the fact that Newton and Odifin were brothers of any kind. Newton understood where Theremin was coming from. Until recently Odifin had been a rude, mean kid who wasn't particularly nice to Newton and his friends. Newton and Odifin had only become friendly right before the big news.

On the other hand, even though Newton and Theremin's friendship had gotten off to a rocky start, they'd already formed a stronger bond than Newton and Odifin. Newton guessed that Theremin's jealous side was showing through, and maybe this time it was for a good reason. All Newton had wanted since the moment he'd woken up in the school library's Brain Bank was to have a family, and now he had found a

family member. It didn't matter to him that Odifin was a brain in jar, or that they weren't related as much as brothers with shared parents would be. Odifin was family, and the first family member Newton ever had.

"You obviously need to brush up on your genetics, Theremin," Odifin snapped at the robot. "Newton and I share the amount of DNA you would expect of half brothers. And Professor Flubitus supported that conclusion himself. So Newton and I are half brothers, all the time!"

Shelly took out her tablet. "That reminds me. We haven't finished our brother similarity survey," she said. "We're on question twenty-one. Can we do a few more before the next class?"

"More questions, Shelly?" Odifin asked. "They are getting a bit tiring."

"Well, I can't get accurate results without at least a hundred questions," Shelly pointed out.

Newton was getting tired of the questions too, but Shelly had helped him so much with everything that he wanted to make her happy.

"It's okay," Newton said. "Let's do a few more, Bro."

"Fine," Odifin said. "Continue, Shelly."

"Okay," Shelly said, scrolling through the questions. "Do you prefer sleeping late or waking up early? Are you a night owl or an early riser?"

"I prefer sleeping late, I guess," Newton replied.

"I wake up at precisely five fifteen every morning," Odifin replied. "I don't have superfluous limbs and organs that need cellular regeneration every night, so I don't need much sleep."

Shelly nodded. "Mmm-hmm. Next question. What is your favorite color?"

"Well, I like gray because of my gray matter, of course," Odifin answered quickly. "But green is my favorite color."

Newton thought about what color made him the happiest. Maybe it was the color of Shelly's eyes, or Theremin's shiny silver arms, or maybe the blue of the sky outside? Then he thought of all the leafy green plants on the island, and how lately he had taken to going outside and, when nobody was looking, practicing camouflaging with them. It felt really peaceful to him to be in nature.

"Green," Newton replied.

"A match! I was wondering if it would be another difference," Shelly remarked, pressing her tablet screen to document it.

"Can't brothers be from the same family but like completely different things?" Odifin asked.

"Yes, indeed," Higgy piped up. "Take my little brother, Wellington, for example. He's always polite, he never breaks the rules, and he keeps his room clean, unlike me. Can you believe it? It's like we're not even from the same planet, let alone the same parents!"

"I'm just collecting data," Shelly said. "Maybe finding out what Odifin and Newton have in common can help us figure out more about how they're related. I'm not sure it will help, but it's worth a try."

"It's a good idea," Newton assured her, and then he paused. He spotted something out of the corner of his eye—an ear!

The ear was all by itself, and not attached to anyone's head. It had tiny feet stuck to the bottom of it. It hopped off the bench of their lunchroom table and began to walk across the floor.

"Does anybody else see that ear?" Newton asked, pointing.

Shelly zoomed in closer on the object using the magnifier in her glasses. "That's not a real ear! That's a remote spy speaker from the Junior Mad Scientist toy line! I had one when I was a kid."

"Who would be spying on us?" Newton wondered.

"Do you really have to ask?" Shelly replied, and she stood up and followed the ear. Newton and the others followed her.

The ear led them right to the table of Mimi Crowninshield. Mimi scooped up the ear and shoved it into her pocket.

"What gives, Mimi? Why are you spying on us?" Shelly asked.

Mimi innocently blinked her blue eyes. "Why would I want to spy on you and your friends? I've got better things to do."

Shelly pointed to Mimi's pocket and said, "We saw your remote spy speaker. Admit it. From the day Newton first showed up here, you've been convinced that he's some kind of spy, trying to steal your family's secrets."

Mimi smiled. "I might have been suspicious at first, but not anymore," she said sweetly. "And we all know that this little spy speaker is just a kid's toy. Besides, if you had anything to hide, you wouldn't be talking about it in the cafeteria, would you?"

"Um, no," Shelly answered hesitantly.

"Great," Mimi said. "Then it's okay if I let everyone in school know that Odifin and Newton are brothers, right?"

"Half brothers," Theremin corrected her.

"Half brothers," Mimi repeated. "Although, I knew all along. I mean, you look practically identical."

The kids at Mimi's table laughed.

"Very funny, Mimi," Newton said. "Sure, you can tell everyone that Odifin and I are related."

Why not? he thought. Flubitus hadn't told him to keep it a secret.

"You tell her, Bro," Odifin said, and they all turned away and walked back to their table.

"I don't care what she says," Shelly said in a low voice. "She's always been suspicious of you, Newton, and she still is. We'll have to be more careful where we talk about your . . ."

Her voice trailed off, but Newton knew what she meant. They'd have to keep hiding the fact that Newton had special abilities. Abilities that meant that maybe he wasn't exactly human, or at least not fully human. That he was some kind of—

The holographic head of Headmistress Mumtaz appeared in the middle of the cafeteria, interrupting his thoughts.

"Good afternoon, Franken-Sci High students!" she said. "I've got a special announcement for the freshman class!"

CHAPTER 2

The Future Is Now

The noise in the cafeteria died down as Ms. Mumtaz spoke.

"Thanks to a generous donation from the Crowninshield family, the entire freshman class will be going on a very special class field trip," she announced, "to the newly opened Museum of the Future in New York City!"

A holographic image of the museum appeared in place of Ms. Mumtaz's face: a five-story building with no straight sides, but with walls that rippled like waves. The structure gleamed with polished steel, and glass windows. The students began to chatter and buzz with excitement.

"There's a new exhibit called *The Future Is Now*, which highlights ideas from science fiction that have become science fact," the headmistress continued. More images popped up: robots, a submarine, a

nuclear power tower. "This exhibit should inspire our freshmen for the Idiosyncratic Inventions course that is required next semester. And I'm told that some of the inventors featured in the exhibit are actually graduates of Franken-Sci High."

A cheer went up from the students.

"The trip is one week from today," the headmistress continued. "More details will be sent to you all on your tablets tomorrow. This is a wonderful learning opportunity for our freshmen, and I know I'm looking forward to it!"

The holographic face disappeared, and everyone began talking loudly.

"Where is New York City?" Newton asked his friends.

"It's in the US," Theremin said. A red 3-D map projected from his chest. "Our island is here," he said, and an X appeared on an island in the ocean. "And New York City is here." Another X appeared on the coast of a large landmass.

Newton stared at the map. "Wow," he said. "I didn't realize the world was so big!"

"I forgot that you've never left the island," Shelly said.

"He's not the only one," Theremin reminded her. "My

dad created me in his lab here, and I've never left. Dad doesn't believe in vacations. He says only weak-minded people need to take time off from doing nothing with their lives, so that they can do more nothing on a beach somewhere."

"The only two places I've been are here and Mom's house," Odifin added. "Mom always said the world wouldn't be able to appreciate someone as unique and special as me. But as I got older, I realized she was trying to protect me. Mad scientists are only a small portion of the world's population. We're different, and people can be cruel about things they don't understand. I wish it wasn't true, but it usually is."

Odifin sounded a little sad, and Newton felt for his half brother. At least Newton could hide the things that made him different. To everyone else in the school, he was just another ordinary human . . . unless they saw him do something strange by mistake. Odifin, on the other hand, didn't look like anyone else in school.

"I don't think that's true everywhere," Shelly said. She turned to Higgy. "You and your family live in London, right? And nobody there gives you a hard time about the way you look."

"That's because we live a nocturnal lifestyle," Higgy

replied. "We all cover up our goo, but in the daylight it still freaks people out. Every time I go out, people stare at me. I hate being stared at so much! That's why I still cover up here at school. I know that the school is different from the outside world, but I didn't want to risk being stared at again."

Higgy was referring to the usual getup that he wore every day: rubber boots, a trench coat, a scarf, bandages wrapped around his face, goggles over his eyes, and a winter beanie covering the top of his head. The outfit hid all of his green protoplasm, but the end result was a not-quite-human-looking boy. The only time Newton had ever seen Higgy not covered in clothes was in their dorm room, or when Higgy roamed the school's underground tunnels at night.

"We mostly only go out after it gets dark," Higgy continued. "Dad and Mum do their experiments in our lab at home, and run errands at night. That's easy to do in a big city like London, where a lot of shops stay open late. And Wellington and I go to Miss Ravenwood's Night School for the Perpetually Pale. That is, I *used* to go there, until I got kicked out. Then I came to Franken-Sci High."

"I'm glad you're here with us," Newton said.

"So I'm going to tell Mumtaz that I can't go on the trip," Higgy said.

"Really, Higgy?" Newton asked. "It'll be more fun with you there."

"Being stared at is *not* fun," Higgy said.

Theremin looked at Odifin. "What about you? Aren't you worried you're going to get a lot of unwanted attention?"

"Maybe, but I'm really excited to see New York City!" Odifin cried. "The skyscrapers! The subway! Broadway! The Big Apple!"

Newton frowned. "You mean they grow mutant fruit there?"

"No. It's just a nickname, because . . . actually, I don't know why," Odifin admitted. "But I don't want to miss out on this trip!"

"Maybe you could wear some kind of disguise," Shelly suggested.

"Yeah. Rotwang could put a lampshade on you, and you'll look just like a lamp," Theremin said.

"Very funny, Theremin," Odifin said with sarcasm in his voice. "Anyway, you shouldn't talk. You're going to stand out too!"

"Didn't you see the holograms?" Theremin asked. "There are going to be robots at the exhibit. If

anybody asks, I'll just say I'm wearing a robot costume. Get it? They'll think it's a costume but it'll just be me."

Shelly wasn't sure that would work. "I'm sure Ms. Mumtaz will have a plan so everyone can go on this trip, regardless of how they look," she said. "The school rarely goes on field trips, because we work so hard to keep this place a secret from the outside world."

"Yes, I'm sure it will all work out," Odifin said hopefully.

"I don't care if it works out or not," Higgy said, sulking. "Have a—*buuuuuuuurp!*—good time without me. I'm not going."

Then the bell rang, and it was time to head to class. Newton watched Higgy walk away. Normally the fart noises coming from his goo squishing in his boots sounded joyful and upbeat after he ate: *pffffFFFFT! pffffFFFFT! pffffFFFFT!* But now they sounded sad: *pfffffffft, pfffffffft, pffffffft.*

"I never realized that Higgy was so self-conscious about how he looks," Newton remarked as he, Shelly, and Theremin headed to Genetic Friendgineering class. "He always seems like he's happy. He loves to joke around!"

"Yeah, poor Higgy," Shelly agreed.

Suddenly the hallway in front of them became very

crowded—too crowded for them to move ahead. Newton stood on his toes and realized that a group of kids had surrounded Mimi.

"I am so excited to go to New York City," Minerva Kepler was saying. "Thanks, Mimi."

Mimi smiled. "You're welcome," she replied. "I mean, Crowninshield Industries is paying for everything, but it was my idea."

"Well, that's really nice of your family," Debbie Danning said.

"Crowninshield Industries loves to give back to the mad-scientist community," Mimi said proudly.

"EXCUSE ME," Theremin said loudly. "Some of us are trying to get to class."

Mimi rolled her eyes. "Weren't you programmed to say 'please'?"

"In seventeen different languages," Theremin replied. "I just didn't feel like saying it."

The bell announcing the start of the next class rang, and everyone scattered before Mimi could respond. Newton, Shelly, and Theremin slipped into their seats in class late, but lucky for them, Professor Wells was distracted.

"Aim for the thorax!" he was yelling. "No, not the spiracles!"

It wasn't unusual for Professor Wells to be yelling out unusual things in class. He had a round face and a thin mustache, and the left half of his body was in this dimension, but the right half was in another one. His right side looked fuzzy and constantly flickered in and out. An interdimensional portal accident had resulted in the professor being permanently stuck in two dimensions at once, and his attention was constantly torn between the two of them.

Suddenly he stopped yelling and focused his left eye on Newton's class.

"Students, my class in the other dimension is being attacked by a giant grasshopper, a matter that requires my immediate attention. Please keep yourselves busy by reading chapter four of your textbooks! RUN, I SAY! RUN!"

Confused, everyone stood up.

"CORRECTION. ONLY RUN IF YOU ARE BEING CHASED BY A GIANT GRASSHOPPER!" Wells yelled, and everyone in Newton's dimension sat down, following the professor's instruction.

Newton tapped his tablet screen and scrolled to the fourth chapter in his *Genetic Friendgineering* textbook.

CHAPTER FOUR:
A LITTLE OF THIS, A PINCH OF THAT

What do you want in your genetically engineered friend? Unfortunately, many genetic friendgineers do not consider this question carefully before beginning their experiments. If you're going to go to all the trouble of genetically engineering the perfect friend, then you'd better be sure you know what you're looking for in a friend.

This step is helpful if you've ever had a friend before. Ask: How did that friend make you feel? In what ways did that friend help you?

Newton stopped reading and thought of Higgy. At first Newton hadn't been sure what to think of his roommate, who'd started off their friendship with one of his trademark practical jokes. But Higgy had proved himself to be a very loyal friend who would do anything for Newton. Higgy had helped Newton sneak into Mumtaz's office once to try to find out information about his past. And once, when Newton was sad, Higgy cheered him up by shaping his gooey form into human shapes—shapes that looked like they could have been Newton's mom or dad.

Higgy had always been there to help Newton, and make him laugh when he needed it most, and Newton realized that he'd never really done anything to help his friend in return. He thought of Higgy's sad *pfffffffft* after he'd announced that he wasn't going with the others on the field trip.

It's not fair that Higgy feels like he can't go on the trip, Newton thought. *If there's a way to help Higgy, I'll find it!*

CHAPTER 3

It's Not Easy Being Green

The next night, Newton asked all his friends to meet up in room #YTH-125, the dorm room that he and Higgy shared. Half the room was taken up by Higgy's giant computer (and giant mess), so Shelly, Theremin, Odifin, and Rotwang squeezed in on the other side, which was clean because Newton didn't have many possessions.

"Are we having some kind of party and you didn't tell me?" Higgy asked. "I was just getting ready to go out on my nightly food run. Does anyone want anything? Pudding? Chips?"

"I really want you to go on this trip to New York, Higgy," Newton said. "So I thought we could put our heads together and come up with a disguise for you that would work."

"You're wasting your time," Higgy said. "There's no way to make me look like a human. And I don't want to go anyway."

"Can't we at least try?" Newton asked.

Higgy sighed. "If I say no, you're going to keep bugging me, aren't you?"

"I might," Newton admitted. "I really want to help you."

Odifin piped up. "Perhaps it would help you to see the disguise that Rotwang and I have worked up. Rotwang, please!"

Rotwang pulled a backpack off his back and opened it up. He took a metal hanger and hung it under Odifin's rolling table. Then he hung a beige trench coat on the hanger so that the coat covered up everything below Odifin's jar. Rotwang placed sunglasses on the jar, where Odifin's eyes were, and topped off the jar with a baseball cap. Rotwang smiled, looking very proud of the costume.

"We're still working on it," Odifin said. "What do you think?"

"I think you look...stylish," Shelly said diplomatically.

"Yeah. A stylish scarecrow," Theremin said.

"Yes, the whole look needs a bit more padding," Odifin said. "I'm also considering a wig."

"Well, clothes don't do much to disguise me," Higgy said. "People always stare at me when I wear my usual getup. I don't look human. I look like a squishy blob wearing clothes."

"Well, I had a thought about that," Newton said. "I know you can move your green stuff around into different shapes. You did it for me once, remember?"

"I can," Higgy said. "But I can't keep the shape for very long."

"Can you show us, Higgy?" Shelly asked.

"All right," Higgy replied. He shed his coat, scarf, bandages, and hat, leaving on his goggles and boots. Then his green blobby shape wiggled and jiggled and he transformed his green goo into the shape of a chubby human boy with a friendly face and a shock of wavy hair on top of his head.

Shelly clapped. "Oh, Higgy, that looks good!" she said.

"But I'm still green," Higgy said as he looked at his gooey hands.

Shelly opened one of Newton's drawers and pulled out a button-down shirt. She slipped it over Higgy's wobbly arms.

"That's not bad," Theremin said. "Except for the fact that humans aren't green."

"I've got an idea," Shelly said. "Stay just like this. I'll be right back."

Shelly dashed out of the room. Higgy turned to

Newton. "It takes a lot of concentration for me to stay like this," he said. "Is it easier when you do your mimicking thing?"

Theremin's eyes flashed. "Higgy, be careful what you say!" He nodded toward Odifin and Rotwang.

"It's okay, Theremin," Newton said. "We can trust them." He looked at the other human in the room, Rotwang. Then he closed his eyes and concentrated on what Rotwang looked like—tall, thin, pale, with black hair that covered his eyes. Newton took a deep breath and continued to focus until . . .

He heard Rotwang gasp. "Whoa, you're me! I mean, you look just like me, but you're not me!"

Newton opened his eyes and turned to the mirror. Rotwang's reflection stared back at him. He'd done it! He still didn't know how it worked, but he was able to change his appearance.

"That's pretty amazing, Newton," Odifin said. "But as far as I know, that's not a human ability. It's more octopus-like."

"It's kind of a long story," Newton said. "But I know I can trust you and Rotwang now. Basically, I just woke up at the school here one day with amnesia. I have weird memories of emerging from some kind of pod. With some help from Shelly, Theremin, and Higgy, I've

realized that I can do things that humans can't do."

"Cool origin story," Rotwang said.

"Thanks," Newton said. "Higgy, Theremin, and Shelly have also been trying to help me find answers about who I really am. That's how we ended up discovering that you and I are brothers, Odifin."

"I always knew there was something strange about you," Odifin said. "But don't worry. Your secret is safe with us."

"Yeah," Rotwang echoed.

"It had better be," Theremin said.

"Sorry to spill the beans," Higgy said. "Odifin and Rotwang are part of the gang now, so I thought it was fine to tell them."

"It is fine," Newton assured him.

Higgy glanced at the door. "Where is Shelly? It's taking a lot of energy to maintain this human form. I'm going to need an extra gallon of pudding just to replenish. I don't see how I'd be able to keep this up for the whole museum trip."

"Maybe you could practice," Newton suggested. "Or, you know, eat a lot right before the trip to keep your energy up."

"I don't know, Newton," Higgy said, and then Shelly came through the doorway.

"All right. I've borrowed some makeup from Tabitha Talos," she said, and she pulled out a little jar of pinky-peach liquid. "Let's see how it looks on Higgy. Come here, Higgy!"

She poured some onto the fingertips of her left hand, and then she rubbed it into Higgy's cheeks. He giggled.

"That tickles!"

"Hold still," Shelly told him, and she spread the liquid makeup over his face. It streaked the green goo with peachy pink, but it didn't cover it up.

"You kind of look like a watermelon," Theremin remarked.

"Wait. Maybe the powder will be better, or will make it look more natural," Shelly said. She opened up a compact container and took out a round cloth pad. She pressed it all over Higgy's face, but that just made the makeup look splotchy.

Shelly frowned. "This isn't working like I thought it would," she said.

Newton stepped back and studied Higgy. The makeup did make him look less green.

"We're getting close, though, I think," he said.

Higgy let go of his human-boy shape, and the makeup absorbed into his protoplasm.

"Don't worry about it," he said. "It's too hard to keep

that human shape. I'll just stay here. It won't be so bad. I'll have less competition at the cafeteria with all of the freshmen on a field trip."

"It looks like I'll be staying here with you, Higgy, unless Rotwang and I can come up with a better disguise," Odifin said.

"We'll keep thinking," Shelly promised. "It's getting late, and I've got to go feed the crew."

By "the crew" Shelly meant the group of monsters and injured animals that she took care of in a special room in the basement.

"Come through the tunnels with me," Higgy offered. "You'll get there faster."

"Sure," Shelly said, and she followed Higgy through the opening beneath the bunk beds that led to the basement.

Theremin, Odifin, and Rotwang said good night, leaving Newton alone in the room. He changed into a T-shirt and shorts and scrambled onto the top bunk.

That didn't go like I thought it would, he realized.

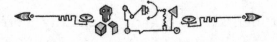

The next morning Newton met Shelly and Theremin in the main hallway of the school building.

"Remind me again why we signed up for this extra class?" Newton asked Shelly as they walked on the yellow-and-green-tiled floor.

"Because Professor Leviathan is teaching it, and we like her," Shelly said. "Besides, I think Transmogrification of Common Flora sounds like it's going to be fun."

"'Flora' is plants, right?" Newton asked. "What's 'transmogrification'?"

Theremin's eyes flashed green as he accessed his data banks. "It means 'the act of transforming in a surprising manner.'"

They entered the school library. Drones flew overhead, making sure students kept quiet and stayed away from the section of restricted texts.

Shelly led Newton and Theremin through the stacks of books to a glass-walled greenhouse attached to the library.

Inside, there was a lot to take in. The room was filled with shelves of green plants and colorful flowers. Some of them were glowing, spinning, or shooting out puffs of gas.

The students who'd arrived already were gathered around a metal lab table. At its head stood Professor Leviathan, a friendly tower of a woman with curly pink hair. She wore a leopard-print lab coat.

One of the students grinned when she saw Newton and his friends.

"Hey, guys!" Tootie Van der Flootin called out loudly and happily.

"Tootie, shhhh!" Professor Leviathan warned. "The greenhouse is under library rules. We've got to keep quiet or the drones will be on our case."

"Sorry, Professor," Tootie said, but she didn't lose her smile. She motioned toward Newton, Shelly, and Theremin, and they sat down in the seats closest to her. Newton glanced around the table and saw a few kids he didn't know yet—and Mimi.

"It looks like everyone is here," Professor Leviathan began. "Welcome to Transmogrification of Common Flora! I am excited that Ms. Mumtaz has given me the opportunity to teach this class. I've been studying the works of Phineas Broccolini for years now, and while my main passion is monster creation, I love the idea of creating monstrous plants."

Professor Leviathan placed a small potted plant on the table. Bright red, spiky flowers grew inside a cluster of long, thin green leaves.

"This is a bromeliad, a plant common on this island," she said.

Then she put another plant next to it. It looked just like the first.

"This is a bromeliad that has been transmogrified," she said, and she picked up a tiny watering can and sprinkled the plant. The red flowers began to open and close, looking very much to Newton like birds' beaks. Then they began to sing!

Twee, twee, twee! Twee, tweeeeee!

Shelly gasped. "A singing plant!"

Professor Leviathan beamed. "It's magnificent, isn't it?" she said. "This is the kind of fun we'll be having in this class. But before fun comes work."

She pointed to a shelf filled with very old, very thick books. "Everyone, take a copy of Professor Broccolini's book, *Leaf It to Me: A Compendium of Plant Transmogrification Techniques*. Today I'd like everyone to read chapter one and take notes."

There were a few grumbles as everyone got up to take a book, but Newton didn't mind. Thanks to his having woken up with amnesia, he always felt like there was a lot for him to learn. He liked reading about new things.

The greenhouse was quiet for a few minutes as everyone began to read. Then . . . *SCREEEEEETCH!*

The horrible, grating sounds of nails on a chalkboard interrupted the silence.

SCREEEEEETCH!

A drone whizzed into the room and hovered over Mimi.

"Quiet in the library," the drone warned in a robotic voice.

Mimi, who had been tapping her fingernails on the table, sat up straight. "Oh, sorry."

The drone sped away, and Professor Leviathan nodded to Mimi. "Miss Crowninshield, what was that racket?"

Mimi grinned and held up her hands. Her fingernails were painted bright pink. "It's my new invention," she said. "I call this color "Piercing Pink". It's nail polish that makes nails sound like they're scratching on a chalkboard no matter what surface you tap them on. I started tapping my nails on the table when I was reading, without thinking about it."

"That's very . . . creative," Professor Leviathan said. "But please try to keep your nails quiet. I am not a fan of these library drones! Once they ejected me just for sneezing."

"Yes, Professor," Mimi said, and she looked back down at her book.

Newton started thinking about the first time he'd met Mimi. She had sprinkled Shelly with a makeup powder that had made Shelly sing an annoying song over and over. Mimi seemed to have a talent for inventing unusual cosmetics.

Maybe she could invent something for Higgy, Newton thought. He wanted to tell Shelly and Theremin his idea, but didn't want to risk upsetting Professor Leviathan. So he waited until after class.

"I have an idea," Newton said as soon as they exited the library. "I'm going to ask Mimi to invent some kind of mad-science makeup for Higgy that will make his goo look more human. She's really good at makeup inventions. I bet she'll come up with something great!"

Shelly stopped. "Newton, asking Mimi for help is a waste of time."

"Why?" Newton asked.

Theremin answered. "Because Mimi doesn't like helping anybody but herself."

"It can't hurt to ask," Newton reasoned. "The worst she can do is say no, right?"

Shelly shook her head. "No, it's *not* the worst she can do," she replied. "Last year Percival Aubergine asked Mimi for help with a concept for a shrink ray he was working on. Mimi was convinced that he was only asking her because Crowninshield Industries was working on a shrink ray too, and he was trying to steal her ideas."

"I remember that," Theremin said. "She sabotaged his shrink ray, right?"

"Right," Shelly said. "Percival hated broccoli, and he was trying to shrink it down so it would have the same nutrients but he could eat less of it. And Mimi engineered the ray so that he ended up with a seventeen-foot-tall stalk of broccoli! It trapped Percival in his dorm room and he had to eat his way out. On the plus side, he learned to like broccoli after that, believe it or not."

Theremin laughed. "Poor Percival. But that was kind of funny."

"It's an example of why you should never ask Mimi for help, Newton," Shelly said, and then she looked around. "Newton?"

But Newton had left midway through Shelly's story and had run to catch up with Mimi. He caught up with her in the hallway and tapped her on the shoulder. She spun around and raised her eyebrows.

"What is it, Newton?" she asked.

"I need your help, Mimi," he began, and her eyebrows raised even higher. "I need something special—makeup that will make Higgy look human for the school trip. You're so good with inventing stuff like that, so I thought I'd ask."

"Hmmm," Mimi said, frowning thoughtfully. "You

came to the right person. That might be something I can do."

"Really?" Newton asked hopefully.

"Really," Mimi replied. "But if I do this for you, then I want you to do something for me."

That sounded fair to Newton. "Sure. What do you need?"

Mimi stepped closer to Newton. "Ever since you came to this school, I've been trying to find out who you are," she said. "I'm still convinced you've been sent to spy on me, to get information about my family's company. We've hired the best private detectives to give us information on Newton Warp, and they've come up with nothing. Nothing. So if you want my help, then come clean, Newton. Who are you? Where did you come from?"

Newton stared into Mimi's blue eyes, which seemed to bore right into his mind.

"I—I don't know, Mimi," he stuttered. "Honestly. I've had amnesia ever since I first came here."

"I don't believe you, Newton," Mimi said. "You and your friends are always sneaking around. You're hiding something. And now there's this whole thing that you and Odifin are brothers."

"Half brothers," Newton said. "And Odifin was

adopted, so he doesn't know where he's from eith[er] swear, I still don't know."

"You must know something," Mimi prodded him.

Newton did know some things—like how he ha[d] superhuman abilities and how he was somehow important to the future of the school. But his skin started to tingle like it did when danger was near, and he got the feeling that he shouldn't tell Mimi—*especially* Mimi— any of this.

"Nothing," Newton repeated.

Mimi stepped back from him. "Well, then, I can't help you," she snapped at Newton, and she continued down the hall.

Newton felt a sense of relief as she left. Shelly and Theremin approached him.

"Let me guess," Shelly said.

"You were right. She won't help," Newton said.

"Come on. We need to get to our next class," Theremin urged.

He zipped off on his rocket robot legs, and Newton and Shelly jogged to follow him. Newton kept thinking about his conversation with Mimi. He still wanted to help Higgy, but something else was weighing on his mind.

After everything that had happened, he *still* didn't

know who he was. And he wanted to know. Until he knew, there'd be an emptiness inside him, one he could never fill.

It's finally time I got some answers, Newton thought. *And I know who can give them to me!*

Ten Fingers!

At lunchtime Newton didn't head to the cafeteria. Instead he went to the office of Headmistress Mumtaz.

He'd been practicing a speech inside his head all morning.

I'm not asking you to tell me who I am. I'm demanding it! It's my right as a living being!

Then he remembered that Theremin hated the term "living" because technically he was a machine and not alive. Newton tried to remember the word Theremin had said robots preferred.

"*Sentient*" popped into his head. That meant you were capable of thoughts and feelings. Theremin had plenty of those, and so did Newton!

He found Ms. Mumtaz's door cracked open and knocked on it.

"Come in, Newton," she said.

Newton stepped inside.

"Ms. Mumtaz, I am a sentient being, and so I'm, um, well, I'd like to know, if um . . ."

He quickly lost confidence in the face of the headmistress's piercing gaze.

"Is this about your identity again, Newton?" she asked. "You know I can't tell you more than you already know. The future of the school is at stake."

"But I don't understand how me knowing who I am affects the future of the school," Newton countered. "I really need to know who I am. I feel empty all the time. Like something's wrong with me. And when I asked Mimi for help today with a makeup invention, she wanted to know who I was, and I couldn't tell her. And now she won't help, and Higgy won't be able to go on the trip, and everything . . . everything just stinks!"

He sank down into the chair in front of Ms. Mumtaz's desk. Her gaze softened. "What's that about Higgy? Why can't he go on the trip?"

"Because he doesn't look human enough," Newton replied. "Neither does Odifin. And it's not fair that they have to miss it."

"Well, who says they have to miss it? That's one thing I *can* help you with, Newton," Mumtaz said. "I've been working with some of the other professors on a device that will allow Higgy and Odifin to travel freely in the world outside the island. We've been putting the finishing touches on it, which is why I hadn't mentioned it yet."

"Really? That's good news," Newton said. "Can you let them know soon? Then Odifin can stop online shopping for clothes at the Tall and Skinny Guy store. And Higgy will be happy, even though he says that he doesn't really want to go."

"I can call them in right now," Ms. Mumtaz said.

She opened the top drawer of her desk and pulled out two tiny robot flies.

"Higgy Vollington," she told one, and to the other she said, "Odifin Pinkwad."

The two bugs flew off.

"Are you really not going to tell me who I am?" Newton asked.

"No, and as I've told you, it's—" But she was interrupted by a ringing sound. The lenses in her eyeglasses flickered, then brightened, and then transformed into translucent screens. Words began scrolling on the screens, and she sighed.

"It's Professor Yuptuka, of course," she said as she read the screens. "It seems that while teleporting her senior class to the San Diego Zoo, she miscalculated and they have landed in the lion habitat."

Mumtaz blinked and started speaking again. "Edith, can't you teleport right out of there?"

There was silence as Mumtaz read the response. "Oh, I see. Well, then, I would suggest learning how to communicate with lions very quickly. We've recently updated the translators so it should work quite well. Give it a try, and good luck!"

The glasses flickered again and returned to normal as Higgy and Odifin entered the room.

"I swear those industrial-size cans of pudding were right out in the open! I thought they were up for grabs!" Higgy said to Ms. Mumtaz.

"Don't worry, Higgy. You boys aren't here because you're in trouble," she said. "I have something to show you."

She stood up, walked over to a shelf, and opened up a metal case. She took out two small domes, each about the size of half a tennis ball.

"Newton here tells me that you two have been concerned about going on the field trip," she began. "Well, some of the professors and I have been working on a solution to that. Making sure all our students look like typical humans is a key safety measure for this school. So we've created these umbrella hologram devices."

She lifted up Higgy's beanie and placed one of the devices underneath it. Then she balanced the other on top of Odifin's jar.

"When the holograms activate, each of you will be surrounded by a hyper-realistic hologram that completely changes your appearance," she said. "Higgy, we've based your look on a compendium of boys from London who are your age. Odifin, we took the liberty of using some of your DNA to determine what your appearance will be."

"How do we activate them?" Higgy asked.

"We've calibrated each one to your own specific voice," Ms. Mumtaz answered. "To activate it, you can just say the word 'incognito.'"

Higgy spoke up first. "Incognito!"

Instantaneously his appearance changed. He looked a lot like the chubby boy he had transformed himself into the night before, except 100 percent human.

"I don't feel anything," Higgy said. "How do I look?"

"Oh dear. I don't have a mirror in here," Ms. Mumtaz said. "But here, let me take a picture."

Her eyeglasses flashed, and a photo of Higgy popped up on her computer screen.

"Wow!" Higgy said. "This is amazing. I look totally human!" He looked down at himself. "Wow,

five fingers!" He flexed them on both hands. "Five more fingers! Ten fingers!"

"This umbrella hologram technology also contains physio-sensory enhancement," Ms. Mumtaz explained. "You can touch and feel things with those fingers. Odifin, you'll be able to do that too."

"My turn!" Odifin said. "Incognito!"

In an instant Odifin too was transformed. Newton stared at the boy Odifin had become. Odifin was taller than his height on his rolling table. His hair was sandy blond. And he and Newton had the same button-shaped nose, and the same big ears. Not exactly like looking into a mirror—but Odifin looked more like Newton than anyone else in the school.

Newton slowly walked up to Odifin and held up his right palm. Odifin held up his left palm. Then Newton held up his left palm, and Odifin held up his right. Cautiously Odifin pressed his palm against Newton's, quickly pulled his hand back, and smiled.

"Cool," Odifin said. "This is a high five, right?"

"I think those are faster," Newton responded. "But basically, yeah."

Ms. Mumtaz snapped a picture of Odifin, and he broke away from Newton and stared at himself on the screen. He didn't say anything for a minute.

"So that's what I would look like," he said in a soft voice. "If I weren't just a . . . a brain."

"That is what your DNA suggests, yes," Ms. Mumtaz agreed with a quick, birdlike nod of her head.

"Wow," Odifin said.

Newton felt excited. "This is great! Now you guys can come on the field trip and not worry about anything."

Ms. Mumtaz reached for Higgy's device, but he backed up.

"Wait," he said. "Why can't I wear this everywhere? Why can't I look like this all the time?"

"These are still prototype devices," she answered. "The field trip is sort of a test. We still don't know the long-term effects of using the umbrella hologram all the time."

Higgy sighed and took the device off his head. He immediately transformed back into his familiar green and gooey self.

"Here you go," he said, handing it to Ms. Mumtaz. Odifin handed his over too.

"Well, that was interesting," Odifin said. "I can't wait to tell Rotwang."

"I think this brief test went very well," Ms. Mumtaz said. "You three may go now. Unless you still had something you needed to say, Newton?"

Newton thought about it. He still hadn't gotten the answer he wanted. But it was clear that Mumtaz wasn't going to budge.

"I guess not," Newton replied. "Come on, guys!"

He left the room with Higgy and Odifin.

"Well, I'm glad we can go on the trip," Odifin said. "But I have to admit, it was kind of weird to see myself that way. I've always been happy being myself. What kind of place is New York City if I have to look like somebody else to fit in there?"

"A city without mad scientists, I guess," Newton said.

"I hope the test when we're on the field trip goes well," Higgy said. "It would be cool to look like that hologram all the time."

"I don't know if I could get used to that," Newton said. "I like you the way you are."

"You're just saying that," Higgy replied.

"No, I mean it," Newton said sincerely. "So what if you don't look human? You're green, my favorite color. And you can do lots of cool things that humans can't."

"So can you," Higgy pointed out.

"Yeah, but—" Newton didn't know what to say. Higgy was right. But doing superhuman things made Newton feel like a monster—not cool at all.

Is that how Higgy feels too? he wondered. *At least*

Higgy knows why *he can do those things. If Mumtaz has her way, I'll never know!*

Odifin interrupted his thoughts. "I'm starting to feel excited about this trip again. I can't wait to see someplace new!"

"Whoot!" Higgy cheered in agreement. "New York City, here we come!"

CHAPTER 5

Through the Portal

"All right, freshmen, please quiet down and line up!" Ms. Mumtaz said.

Ms. Mumtaz's voice echoed through the Franken-Sci High gym. She stood in front of the gathered students, flanked by the other chaperones for the trip: Professor Juvinall, a six-year-old girl with red hair in ponytails, and Professor Phlegm. He wore a black sweater and pants instead of his usual black lab coat, and he'd shed his rubber gloves, but his shiny bald head and black eyepatch still gave him a sinister look.

Newton took his place in line between Higgy and Odifin. Both boys had activated their umbrella holograms.

"You know, I wanted to look human so that people wouldn't stare at me," Higgy said. "But now *everybody* is staring at me!"

"I think it's weird for everybody to see you looking so different," Newton said.

"I don't mind the attention," Odifin said. "It's kind of fun mixing things up like this. As a brain in a jar, I don't get to accessorize much. Hats always make my brain look chubby. But now . . ."

He looked down at his feet. "Red sneakers! They're so cool! And look, I can kick!" He kicked with his right foot.

Newton glanced down at his own white sneakers. He'd always thought it was weird that he had a bar code on his foot, and that his feet were sticky and extra grippy.

But at least I have feet, Newton thought, suddenly appreciating them.

"NOW I NEED EVERYONE'S COMPLETE ATTENTION!" It was Professor Juvinall. Newton always marveled at how loud she could be, considering how small she was.

Everyone stopped talking.

"Finally," she said. "Now listen up. We've installed a portal in an abandoned warehouse in Queens, a few blocks away from the Museum of the Future. Ms. Mumtaz is going to open a portal here in the gym, and she and Professor Phlegm will go first. The rest of you will enter one by one, and I will go last. When you land, remain in the warehouse until further instructions. Got it?"

The students all responded affirmatively, and Ms. Mumtaz held up a brochure of the school to begin using it to make a portal. She opened it fully, into a big square. Then she folded it into smaller and smaller squares. Finally she folded it diagonally so that the top left and bottom right corners touched.

The tightly folded brochure began to spin, and floated out of her hands. As it spun faster and faster, it created a rotating column of air. The whirling air caused the hair on the students' heads to whip around their faces. Even Odifin's physio-sensory holographic hair fell over his eyes.

Then the whirling stopped, and a human-size black hole with a halo of glowing light appeared where the brochure had been.

"Proceed in an orderly fashion!" Ms. Mumtaz instructed, and then she gracefully stepped into the portal and vanished.

"All right, let's keep it moving!" Professor Juvinall yelled.

Professor Phlegm stepped into the portal without a word. Then Professor Juvinall started calling out last names.

"Atomico! Azerath! Bacon! Conkell! Let's do this!"

Rotwang waved good-bye to Odifin and the others and stepped through the portal. The students disappeared into the portal alphabetically, one by one. Soon it was Odifin's turn. He looked down at his new, real-looking legs.

"Pinkwad, why are you lollygagging?" Professor Juvinall asked him.

"Well, normally Rotwang pushes me into a portal," he explained. "I've never stepped into one before. I've never taken any steps at all, actually."

"There's no time like the present, Pinkwad," Juvinall snapped. "Move it."

Odifin cautiously walked to the portal and jumped in.

"At last!" Juvinall said. "Okay, Ravenholt and Rozika, you're next."

Shelly looked at Newton and grinned. "See you in New York City," she said.

"Yeah," Newton replied, and he watched his friends disappear. Higgy was his only close friend who remained.

"I'm a little nervous," Newton admitted. "The last time I used a portal, I went nowhere. What if it doesn't work this time too?"

When Newton and his friends had won the school's Mad Science Fair, Newton had won a portal

pass that would allow him to go anywhere in the world. Newton had asked it to take him home, but it hadn't worked. He'd stayed right in the office of Ms. Mumtaz, where he'd started.

"I'm sure it'll be fine," Higgy assured him. "It's working for everyone else. That must have been a funky portal you opened last time."

Newton nodded, hoping his friend was right.

"Vollington!" Juvinall yelled.

Higgy ran across the room and jumped into the portal.

"*Wheeeeeeeeeeeeee!*" he cheered, and then he vanished inside the black hole.

"You're next, Warp," Juvinall said.

Newton nodded and stepped through the hole.

Please work! he thought.

Just as before, the blackness engulfed him. He felt his skin tingle and his hair stand on end.

Brightly colored lights swirled around him as his body, which now felt weightless, somersaulted through space.

Then . . . *Whomp!* Newton's feet landed on solid ground.

As he gained his bearings, he heard the chattering of excited voices.

Then Higgy's human face popped up in front of him. "You made it!" Higgy cried.

"I . . . I guess I did," Newton said, looking around. They were in an enormous rectangle-shaped empty building with high ceilings. *This must be what a warehouse is,* he guessed.

Then Higgy pulled Newton aside as Saffy Zastruga popped out of the portal.

"Gotta keep moving once you get here," Higgy said. "You don't want to get knocked over."

Professor Juvinall jumped out of the portal next, knocking over Saffy. Then the professor turned and yelled at the portal.

"Portal, close!"

The black hole immediately shrank and transformed back into a school brochure, which dropped to the ground. Professor Juvinall picked it up and put it in her pocket for the trip home.

Ms. Mumtaz clapped her hands. "Well done, freshmen!" she congratulated them, and her voice echoed around the empty building. "Phase one of our trip is complete. The Museum of the Future is five blocks away from here, and we're going to walk there in an orderly manner."

"Don't forget the ice cream!" Mimi called out.

"Thank you, Mimi," Ms. Mumtaz said. "The Crowninshield family has arranged for all of us to have ice cream at a shop on the way to the museum. Isn't that so generous of them?"

"Wow, your family is so awesome, Mimi," Tabitha Talos said, and Mimi smiled.

"I know," Mimi said.

"What's everybody standing around for? Get moving!" Professor Juvinall yelled.

The students began to shuffle through the open warehouse door into the late-morning sunlight. Ms. Mumtaz approached Newton and his friends, who were all standing together.

"Higgy, Odifin, how are your holograms working?" she asked.

"Great!" they responded, showing off with a high five.

"Excellent," Ms. Mumtaz said. "If you have any problems with the technology at the museum, report to me immediately."

She turned to Theremin. "And you, Theremin, are you sure you can convince people you're in costume, instead of being a real robot?"

"I'm a natural actor," Theremin responded. "Didn't you see my performance in *Frankenstein: The Musical*?"

"Brief, but memorable," Mumtaz said with a nod. "Please take caution, Theremin. It's very important that we keep our school a secret."

"You can count on me!" Theremin said, and Mumtaz walked away.

"This is going to be great!" Theremin said. "Out in the world, for the first time!"

Newton started to feel excited. Like Theremin, he'd never been anywhere except the school and the island. Now he was in New York City, and he could barely contain his excitement.

"Theremin, what if *this* is where I'm from?" he asked in a low voice. "What if this sparks a memory?"

"This is just one city in a big world, Newton," Theremin said, and then he saw his friend's face fall. "But you never know!"

They stepped outside and walked along the sidewalk. Across from the warehouse was another warehouse, but when they turned the corner, the street was lined with shops, restaurants, a bus stop, and apartment buildings.

Newton gazed around in amazement. *Everything* was new to him. The mom pushing a baby stroller, the cars whizzing by, the delivery woman on her bicycle. Nothing sparked a memory, but he was so excited that he didn't care.

Mimi, on the other hand, was not as impressed.

"Where are the skyscrapers? Where are the bright lights? Where are the Broadway theaters?" she complained loudly.

"Mimi, those are in Manhattan. This is Queens," Ms. Mumtaz explained. "The two boroughs are very different."

Mimi frowned. "I should never have asked Daddy to sponsor this trip."

"It's going to be fun, Mimi, really. You'll see," Tabitha told her. "Besides, we haven't even gotten to the museum yet."

Professor Juvinall blew the gym whistle that hung around her neck. "Ice cream place, fifteen meters on the right! Everybody file in!"

The ice cream place was a large room with big windows at the front and lots of metal chairs and tables. In the back was a counter and a freezer with all the ice cream flavors.

"Vanilla, chocolate, strawberry," Shelly read from the flavors on the sign board, and she gave a happy sigh. "I haven't had just normal ice cream in a while. Everything at the school is scientifically enhanced somehow. Sometimes it's nice to just eat plain old food and simple, regular flavors."

"Line up!" Professor Juvinall barked, and she and Ms. Mumtaz led the line to the counter.

"We're here from Franken-Sci High," Ms. Mumtaz told the young, ponytailed server at the counter. His name tag read PABLO.

Pablo nodded. "Sure, the Crowninshield party. Order whatever you want."

"Nothing for me, thank you," Ms. Mumtaz said. "It's savage to eat ice cream in the morning."

"Suit yourself," the server said. Then he leaned down toward Professor Juvinall and began to talk in a sickly sweet voice. "And what would you like to order, little girl?"

"I'd like you to stop patronizing me and make me a unicorn sundae with extra rainbow sprinkles," Juvinall told him. "Got it?"

Pablo blinked. "Yeah, sure."

More servers came to assist them, and the line started to move quickly. Odifin and Rotwang ordered vanilla cones dipped in a hard blue candy shell. When a server with orange braids tried to hand Odifin his cone, he backed away.

"My assistant will take that, please," he said, nodding to Rotwang.

Rotwang nudged him and whispered, "You've got hands now, remember?"

"Oh yes, that's right," Odifin said, and he took the ice cream cone from the startled young woman. "Thank you!"

Higgy ordered a bucket of pistachio ice cream, and the woman server raised both eyebrows. Higgy nodded to Pablo. "That guy said we could order *whatever we wanted*," he told her. She shrugged, reached into the freezer, and pulled out the whole bucket for him.

"I'll have the vegan coconut milkshake," Shelly requested when it was her turn. Then Pablo nodded to Theremin. "What'll you have?"

"Nothing. As you can see, I'm a robot, and robots don't eat," Theremin shot back, his eyes flashing red.

Oh no! Newton thought. *Theremin forgot to pretend to be in costume.*

But Pablo just smiled. "You must be headed to the Museum of the Future. That's a great robot costume, dude. Seriously, though, what kind of ice cream do you want?"

Theremin laughed nervously. "Ah, nothing, actually. I had a big breakfast."

Newton breathed a sigh of relief.

"What about you?" Pablo asked.

Newton had been so distracted by his surroundings—and Theremin—that he'd forgotten to study the board. So he ordered the first thing on the list.

"Vanilla," he said.

"Cone or cup?" Pablo asked.

"Cone, please," Newton said.

A minute later, cone in hand, he and Theremin sat at a table with Shelly, Higgy, Odifin, and Rotwang. Rotwang had an ice cream cone in each hand and was licking both of them.

Newton laughed. "What's going on?"

"It seems that I got too excited about my ability to hold things when I ordered that ice cream," Odifin said. "I still can't eat or taste things, which is disappointing. But Rotwang is being very helpful."

"Well, for a second I forgot I was supposed to be wearing a robot costume," Theremin confided. "Luckily, the ice cream guy didn't get suspicious."

"You know what, guys? I think you're all doing a great job of blending in here," Shelly said. "This is going to be an awesome trip! Even if it was all Mimi's idea."

Newton licked his ice cream cone. It was delicious! He looked around at his friends laughing, and made a promise to himself.

Today I'm not going to even think about where I come from. I'm just going to have fun!

Professor Juvinall's whistle pierced the air.

"Hurry up and finish that ice cream!" she yelled. "The Museum of the Future awaits!"

CHAPTER 6

WELCOME TO THE MUSEUM OF THE FUTURE!

A digital sign flashed across the entrance to the museum, the same gleaming metal-and-glass structure that Mumtaz had shown them in a hologram. Dozens of visitors funneled through the entrance. Most of them were students with school groups, just like the kids of Franken-Sci High.

"Look, Theremin, there are kids in actual robot costumes," Shelly said, pointing to three students. They'd fashioned their costumes using cardboard boxes painted silver, aluminum foil, coat hangers, and metal pots and pans.

"Crude, but nice," Theremin remarked.

Higgy started taking photos with his camera. A woman in a security guard uniform quickly walked over and approached him.

"Excuse me, young man, but you're not allowed to take photos in the museum," she said. She pointed to a sign on the wall.

"Well, that's not fair, now, is it, Justine?" he asked, reading her name tag. "How am I supposed to remember this trip without photos?"

"There's a souvenir booklet available at the gift shop, or an exhibit catalog you can buy," Justine replied, and then she walked away.

Higgy sighed and slipped his phone into his pocket. "Too many rules in this place," he muttered. "I really dislike rules. Rules are the enemies of fun."

"All right, students, we've got some rules to go over before we start exploring!" Professor Juvinall announced loudly. "One: stick together. We're touring this museum as a group. Two: don't touch anything. Three: don't take pictures of anything. Four: behave yourself, or you'll be transp—" She looked around at the regular humans in the lobby and stopped herself from saying "transported."

"I mean, sent back to the school," she finished. "Got it?"

The students nodded silently.

"We'd better be careful," Shelly whispered to Newton. "Juvinall can be really mean if she doesn't have her afternoon nap!"

"Time to move!" Juvinall shouted, and they followed her through the lobby into the first room in the museum.

The circular space was dark, with glittering lights that twinkled like stars above. Hanging from the ceiling was a large globe-shaped moon with a face—and a rocket ship stuck in one eye.

Suddenly a glass case illuminated to the left of them. Inside, a hologram of a man in an old-timey suit and bow tie appeared. He had white hair and a white beard and mustache.

"Greetings, visitors," the hologram man said with a French accent. "I am author Jules Verne. I was born in Nantes, France, in 1828. I became known as the father of science fiction after writing several adventure novels. Some people say that my books forecasted the future of science, but that is only partly true. I performed a great deal of scientific research before writing each of my books, and coupled that with my imagination. If my creations inspired innovations in the future, I must humbly state that I am proud to have played a role."

Ms. Mumtaz nodded as he spoke. "Jules Verne's novels are very inspiring to all future ma—scientists," she said. "This is a very fitting place to start the exhibit."

The students followed her around the circular room. The next case held a cutaway replica of a metal ship that reminded Newton of a fish, with a window where an eye would be and a fantail at the other end.

Another hologram appeared, this time of a man wearing a suit similar to the one Jules Verne had worn. His hair, mustache, and beard were brown.

"I am Pierre Aronnax, the protagonist of Jules Verne's novel *Twenty Thousand Leagues under the Sea*," he said. "In the novel, my servant and I are searching for a sea monster when we discover the *Nautilus*, an underwater ship piloted by Captain Nemo. This is the first appearance in fiction of a submarine vehicle powered by electricity."

"Submarine," Newton repeated. It was the first time he had heard the word. "That's cool. Imagine all the things you could see underwater!"

Another display was all about the novel *From the Earth to the Moon*, in which Verne had written about space suits and lunar modules before they were invented, and a rocket landing on the moon a hundred years before it happened.

Other displays credited Verne with writing about video conferencing, holograms, and solar-powered sails used by spacecraft.

"As a young child I found the works of Jules Verne to be very inspiring," Ms. Mumtaz told the students. "Such a brilliant creative mind!"

"That was really awesome," Newton remarked as they left the Verne exhibit.

"I guess," Theremin said. "Compared to stuff that we see every day at school, it's pretty tame."

They all followed Mumtaz into another room. A sign over a metal archway read: THE WONDERFUL WORLD OF ROBOTS.

Theremin's eyes widened with excitement. "Now we're talking!" he said.

They stepped through the archway into a long, narrow corridor. As they walked, the voice of a narrator explained what they were seeing.

"Two thousand years ago ancient Greeks told stories of their god Hephaestus, who created mechanical assistants out of gold. In these early myths the concept of the robot was born."

Newton stared in awe at the sight of the golden robot in the display, and his mouth dropped open. "Wow!" he said.

"Sure, he's shiny, but I bet he can't do quadratic equations," Theremin said.

As they walked along, they saw more robots. Robots from cheesy science fiction movies. The first robots made in labs, which looked like boxes on wheels. The first widely used household robots— wheeled, disk-shaped machines that vacuumed or served snacks to your guests.

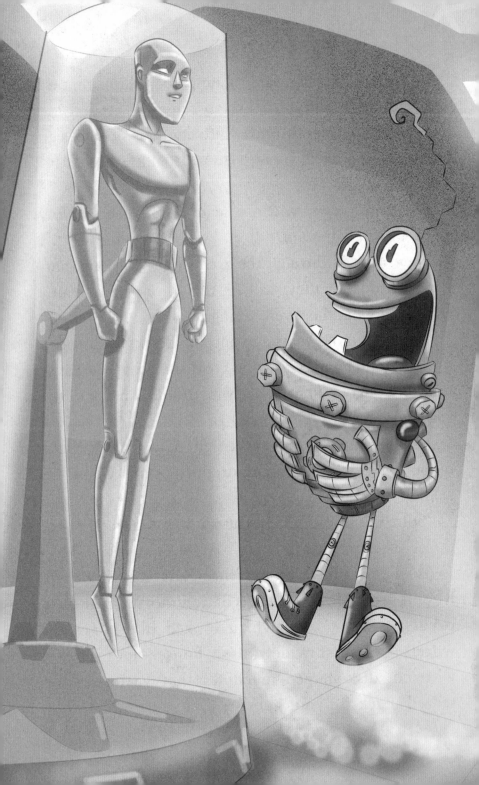

Then the robots started to look more like Theremin again, humanoid machines with arms and legs.

Finally, the last robot in the display looked like a typical human—with humanlike skin stretched over a metal frame, eyes that blinked, and a chest that moved up and down like it was breathing.

"As robotic technology progressed, the imaginations of writers and filmmakers kept pace," the narrator continued. "They dreamed up androids, robots who looked and acted like humans so convincingly that it was impossible to tell them apart from humans. These androids had one thing that early mechanical robots did not—advanced artificial intelligence."

The corridor opened up into a large, dark room. Lights flashed erratically. Lit-up words scrolled across a big screen in the room's center.

ARTIFICIAL INTELLIGENCE: THE FUTURE OF ROBOTICS . . . AND OF EARTH?

"The future of Earth," Theremin said.

"Within the last one hundred years, science fiction authors have imagined humanoid robots with the ability to think, reason, and feel like humans," the narrator began.

"Just like you, Theremin," Newton whispered.

"Scientists are using artificial intelligence to

accomplish much more than was ever imagined before," the narrator went on. "AI technology powers the world's first self-driving cars. In the future, AI might create vaccines, solve the climate crisis, and come up with new methods for clean energy. With AI the future is bright!"

"That's right!" Theremin cheered.

The lights in the exhibit room flashed on. Then a sound like thunder rumbled in the room, and the lights went dark again.

"AI may save humanity, but will AI also destroy humanity?" the narrator went on. "That is what some writers imagine, and what many humans fear. For when machines can think and reason and feel like humans can, they may join together and attempt to take over . . ."

Images of robots attacking humans filled the screen. The thunder rumbled again. Then the sound stopped and the lights came back on.

"Please enjoy the rest of the AI exhibit," the narrator said calmly."

Most of the students from Franken-Sci High remained staring at the screen, frozen in fear. Then they all slowly turned and looked at Theremin.

Mimi spoke up first. "Wow, Theremin. Are you part

of the robots' plan to take over the world? I didn't think you had it in you . . ."

"You know there's no plan like that," Theremin shot back. "But just in case, maybe you should try being *extra* nice to me."

Mimi rolled her eyes and walked away.

"That was certainly intense," Higgy remarked.

"Yeah, it was great!" Theremin said. "You know, when Professor Flubitus came back from the future, he said that Newton and Shelly played an important role in the school. But he didn't say anything about me. So I got kind of worried, you know, that maybe robots weren't going to be important in the future. This exhibit makes me feel a lot better."

"I think it's silly to be afraid of AI," Shelly remarked. "Humans are only afraid because they know that humans are the scariest things on the planet, and they think robots will be just the same. But robots might be a lot better."

Newton's head was starting to fill up, with so much new information to take in. He thought about asking one of his friends to say the words "noodle noggin," which somehow allowed him to be really smart for a short period of time. But when that happened, he sort of got lost in his head and lost focus on everything else.

And Newton didn't want to miss anything in this amazing museum.

They toured the AI exhibits, and then moved on to the next room.

"Blimey!" Higgy exclaimed.

In the center of the space was a large statue of a being made of green protoplasm. It looked a lot like Higgy did in his original form.

"What is this?" Newton wondered out loud.

In this exhibit, comic-book-style lettering on the walls told the story of the green guy. A comic book artist named Bettina Ramirez had created the superhero, Goo Guy, who was made of super-advanced protoplasm and could change his form, squeeze into small places, and do other cool stuff.

Higgy stared at the words, then stared back at the statue. He kept looking back and forth in awe.

"Check it out, guys," he said, pointing to one of the comic book panels on the wall. "In this one, Goo Guy single-handedly saves the planet from aliens! And in this one he stops a nuclear accident by sneaking into the control room of the power plant. He is the coolest! A gooey superhero!"

Higgy handed his camera to Newton. "You've got to get a photo of me next to the statue. Mum and Dad and

Welly are going to flip when they see this!"

"I thought we couldn't take pictures," Newton said.

Higgy looked around. "I don't see that guard any-where. Come on!"

Newton took Higgy's cell phone from him, and Higgy ducked under the rope surrounding the statue and posed in front of it. Newton clicked away as Higgy tried different poses, flexing his arms, waving, and making funny faces. Newton was laughing when he felt a tap on his shoulder.

He turned to see Justine the security guard there, and the sight of her startled him so much that he almost camouflaged—but he caught himself in time. It was a really close call.

"I told your friend no photos," Justine said. "That goes for all of you. If this happens again, I'm going to have to confiscate your phone."

"Um, sorry," Newton said.

Higgy scrambled away from the statue and ducked underneath the ropes. "No need for that," he said, and he quickly tucked his phone into his pocket.

Justine's eyes narrowed, and she leaned closer to Higgy.

"There's something strange about you, kid, but I can't put my finger on it," she said. "I'm going to be keeping my eye on you."

Higgy smiled sweetly at her and spoke in his most polished British accent. "Sorry, ma'am. I just couldn't contain my excitement about this wonderful exhibit. I promise to behave moving forward. You have my word, and that's a promise."

Ms. Mumtaz walked up. "Officer, is there a problem with these students?" she asked.

"Not anymore," Justine said, but she frowned and kept her eye on Higgy as she backed away.

"Higgy, Newton, I certainly hope you're obeying the rules," Ms. Mumtaz said.

"We are," Higgy said, and at the same time, Newton said, "We will."

"Good enough," Ms. Mumtaz said. "Come. We're moving on to the next exhibit."

The headmistress hurried away, and Newton and Higgy moved quickly to catch up with everyone. Newton breathed a sigh of relief.

"That was close," Newton said.

"It's okay," Higgy said. "I don't care if I get sent back to the school now. I've seen everything I need to see." He glanced back at the statue. "I'm a hero," he said softly, and Newton smiled.

"Come on, Goo Guy," Newton said. "Let's go see what's next!"

The Invincible Man

The enormous museum seemed to have no end of exhibits. The students walked through another room about a popular sci-fi television show from the 1960s and the scientific advances that it predicted. The next group of displays was about advances in medicine that had come from science fiction.

By that time, everyone was hungry again, and Professor Juvinall announced that it was time to go to the museum cafeteria.

"I wonder if the food will be anything like the food at the school," Shelly said as they walked down a corridor lined with huge windows. "You know, scientifically enhanced."

Newton sat down at a table with his friends, and a tablet-type device with screens on both sides rose up from the center. A menu listing all the food in the cafeteria popped up on the screen.

"'Halley's Comet Hamburger,'" Shelly read out loud. "'Mars Rover Mac and Cheese.' It looks like regular food with science-y names, and you press the screen to order."

She reached out and touched the screen. "One Vetruvian Vegan Burger and one order of Sci-Fi Sweet Potato Fries."

"That sounds good," Newton said, and he pressed on the circle next to the burger. His finger stuck.

"Uh-oh," he said. "My finger's doing that grippy thing again."

"Just relax, Newton," Shelly advised him. "There's a lot going on here at this museum. It's probably making it harder for you to control your"—she looked around, and then lowered her voice to a barely audible whisper—"abilities."

Newton nodded. "Relax. Right." He took a deep breath and pulled his finger away from the screen. Then he pressed the button for the fries, and everything went smoothly.

Rotwang and Higgy placed their orders next—Theremin and Odifin, as usual, weren't eating.

"How do you guys like the museum?" Higgy asked, looking around the table.

"It's fun, but I mean, none of the inventions here

are as cool as the stuff we have at Franken-Sci High," Odifin pointed out. "I'm not sure exactly what we're going to learn here."

Mumtaz had been walking past the table, and she stopped. "What we are learning here today, Odifin, is inspiration!" she said. "Inspiration is the basis for all great inventions, in every field, including mad science. The creative minds of writers and filmmakers have come up with ideas for things that even mad scientists haven't invented yet. This is a reminder that we can't ignore great literature in our studies. The next exhibit is all about ideas in fiction that haven't become reality yet. I'm very excited for that one."

Mumtaz moved on.

"She has a point," Odifin admitted. "Maybe in this next exhibit we'll get some ideas for next year's science fair."

Rotwang grunted in agreement.

At that moment a metal box on wheels rolled up to the table. On top of the box was a tray with the drinks that everyone had ordered.

The box spoke to them through a speaker in the front. "Your beverages are ready," it announced.

"Cool, a robot waiter!" Shelly said.

"Hey, dude," Theremin greeted him. "How's it going?

How do you like working here?"

"Your beverages are ready," the robot repeated mechanically. "Please remove your beverages of choice from the tray."

"I don't think he's very artificially intelligent," Odifin remarked.

"He can't help it if the world outside Franken-Sci High hasn't caught up to my father's work yet," Theremin said. He patted the robot's head. "Don't worry, buddy. Soon we'll be ruling the world."

"Your lunch will be ready shortly," the robot said, and then wheeled away.

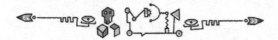

After lunch everyone lined up behind the professors once more and made their way to the next exhibit.

A digital banner announced that this one was called FANTASY OR FUTURE? The displays scattered about the area each held a different book. When you pressed a button, a hologram appeared on top of the display, showing the science fiction idea in that book.

Newton and his friends walked to a random display.

"*Between the Worlds* by Ferdinand Hargrove,'" Shelly read out loud, and she pressed the button.

The hologram showed a person walking through a shimmering field from one room into another room that looked identical.

"In his book, Hargrove imagines that humans will be able to travel between dimensions," the narrator said. "Is this something we can look forward to in the future? What do you think?"

Odifin snorted. "Ha! Professor Wells already *lives* in two dimensions."

They moved to the next display.

"'*The Invisible Man* by H. G. Wells,'" Higgy read. "I've read this book. It's great!" He pressed the button, and a hologram of a man in a trench coat and hat, wearing sunglasses and with a bandaged face, appeared. His outfit looked a lot like Higgy's regular clothes.

"H. G. Wells imagined a chemical process that could render humans invisible," the narrator said. "Scientists have come close with cloaking technology, but do you think chemical invisibility is possible in the future? Perhaps you will be the one to invent it!"

Odifin snorted again. "Professor Snollygoster has already pioneered that!"

They moved on to a third display.

"'*The Invincible Man*,'" Shelly read out loud.

"We already did that one," Higgy said.

"Not *invisible. Invincible,*" Shelly corrected him. "By some author I've never heard of. His or her name is Zoumba Summit."

She pressed a button, and a hologram appeared of a human-size pod with wires sticking out of it. Newton froze.

"Though not widely known, the works of Zoumba Summit have a small and devoted following. In *The Invincible Man*, Summit imagines the creation of a human with superhuman powers—a human with extra abilities that enhance his potential for survival."

Whooooooooosh! A memory flooded back into Newton's mind, like it had once before. He was inside a pod filled with water. He couldn't see through the pod; it was foggy. But then a bright light came on, and he could see the shadows of people around the pod. A scream rose in his throat.

"Newton, are you okay? Newton?" Shelly said, her voice sounding frantic. Shelly's voice broke through his memory, and he slowly came back to reality. He looked down, and realized Shelly was ten feet below him.

"Shelly?" Newton asked.

A crowd was starting to form. Newton looked up and realized that he was hanging from a light fixture,

holding on to the metal with his grippy fingers. His legs dangled below him.

"Newton, the security guard's coming!" Shelly warned. "Can you jump?"

Newton glanced to his side. He saw Justine walking through the exhibit entrance.

"I—I think so," he said.

Higgy stood underneath him, his arms wide open. "I'll catch you, Newton!"

"I don't think that's a good idea, Higgy," Newton said.

"Trust me. I can do it!" Higgy said.

"What is going on in here?" Justine's voice echoed through the exhibit.

Newton jumped down. He crashed into Higgy, who slid across the floor, knocking over Ms. Mumtaz. Then Higgy's umbrella hologram fell off his head! The chubby blond-haired boy disappeared, and in his place was a boy made of green goo!

Newton scrambled to his feet. He was about to reach for the umbrella hologram disc when Justine marched over to them. Newton stepped in front of Higgy, who froze.

"You, kid!" Justine pointed to Newton. "Did I just see you hanging from the ceiling?"

"I—um—wanted to get a better view of the exhibit?" Newton stammered.

"That's the last straw. You and your friend are officially banned from this museum," Justine said. She looked around. "Where is your friend? The one with the blond hair?"

Newton shrugged.

Justine peered around him. "What is that?" She stepped around Newton and examined Higgy. "Since when did they put a Goo Guy statue in this room?" She poked Higgy, and her finger sprang back. "This one's pretty lifelike."

"Yeah, it sure is," Newton said. "I guess you'd better be escorting me out about now, right?"

Ms. Mumtaz approached them, sounding calm in spite of the recent commotion. Newton spotted Higgy's hologram disc in her hand. "This young man is my student. If it's okay with you, I'll take him outside while the rest of our group visits the gift shop."

"Thank you," Justine said, and she looked around. "I'm happy to see that the rest of your students are behaving themselves."

Justine turned and walked away. As soon as she was out of sight, Mumtaz put the umbrella hologram back onto Higgy's head. He looked like a boy again, but his whole appearance was a little fuzzier than it had been before the crash.

"I think you'd both better come outside with me," Ms. Mumtaz said.

Newton and Higgy followed her out of the exhibit, past the gift shop, and through the exit doors that led to the outside.

"Ms. Mumtaz, you know I didn't mean to do that!" Newton burst out. "I—something freaked me out, and I must have jumped straight up in the air, like an escape instinct or something. You know that weird stuff happens to me sometimes."

Mumtaz nodded thoughtfully. "What freaked you out, Newton?"

Newton thought about his answer carefully. He'd never told Ms. Mumtaz about his strange pod memory, and he wasn't sure if he should do that now.

"It was something in that display about *The Invincible Man*," he answered vaguely.

Her eyebrow shot up. "*The Invisible Man?*"

"No, *The* Invincible *Man*, by this author with a weird name," Newton replied. "Zoomie Muppet, or something like that."

Ms. Mumtaz shook her head. "A terrible author. I'm surprised they'd allow such trash in a museum like this, and among such brilliant minds as Jules Verne, too."

She looked at Higgy. "And you, Higgy. Why did you attempt to catch him?"

Higgy shrugged. "I guess I was feeling pretty confident. You know, like Goo Guy."

Ms. Mumtaz started to smile, but stopped herself. "I understand, Higgy, but that was very reckless of you."

"I know," Higgy said. "Are we in trouble?"

"I think missing the gift shop is punishment enough, to be honest," Mumtaz answered. "It's a pretty awesome gift shop."

Higgy's umbrella hologram flickered on and off.

"We'd better get back to the warehouse and wait for the others," the headmistress said. "I think your device is broken, Higgy."

They walked the five blocks back to the warehouse. By the time they got inside, Higgy's umbrella hologram had completely failed.

"You're back to your green gooey self," Newton told him, "but I think I like you better this way. Goo and all, you know?"

"Thanks, Newton," Higgy replied.

They passed the next thirty minutes talking about the museum exhibits, and then the rest of the freshman class came into the warehouse. Shelly and Theremin

broke away from the group and rushed up to Higgy and Newton.

"What happened back there?" Shelly asked.

"It was that hologram of the pod," Newton answered, and he explained how that buried memory of his had come flooding back.

"Wow," Shelly said. "Well, sorry you missed the gift shop."

She thrust a bag into his arms. "I got this for you to help you remember the trip."

Newton looked inside and found a Museum of the Future T-shirt, with a drawing of the museum on the front.

"Hey, thanks!" Newton said. Most of his clothing came from the school Lost and Found, so it was nice to have a shirt especially for him.

Odifin handed Higgy a bag. "I thought you might like this, Higgy," he said.

Higgy pulled out an issue of the Goo Guy comic book. "This is awesome! Thanks, Odifin! I can't wait to read it and give it to Welly. He's going to love it so much, too, I just know it."

Professor Juvinall blew into her whistle. "Line up! We're going to open the portal!" she yelled.

They lined up, and Shelly turned to Newton. "I'm

sorry that pod hologram triggered your memory. But you know, Newton, maybe it's a clue."

"A clue?" Newton asked.

Shelly nodded. "If that pod is the same as the one in your memory, then we need to find a copy of that book!"

CHAPTER 8

Gooey, Green, and Ready to Be Seen!

Back at Franken-Sci High the students stumbled out of the portal and into the gym. After a long day of walking around, everyone was tired.

"I'm so glad tomorrow's Saturday and we can sleep late," Higgy said with a yawn. "I might take a nap right now."

"Robots don't need naps," Theremin said. "Anybody want to power through it and play nuclear Ping-Pong in the rec room?"

"I'll play," Rotwang said.

"I'll play too," Odifin added. "I can do that now, with my arms."

Ms. Mumtaz appeared. "Sorry, Odifin. Today was just a test of the umbrella hologram. Until we're sure it's safe to use long term, I'll have to ask you to hand it over."

Odifin sighed. "Here you go."

The tall boy with Newton's nose and ears disappeared, and Odifin was a brain in a jar again.

Newton felt a tiny twinge of sadness. It had been kind of nice having somebody around who looked like him. Actually, it had been amazing.

"I guess I'll just watch you guys play," Odifin said sadly.

"I've got to go check on my animals," Shelly said. "Want to come, Newton?"

Newton yawned. "Nah, I'm gonna chill with Higgy. But maybe you guys can all come to the room later. I need your help with something."

"Sure," Theremin said. "Later, gator!"

Newton and Higgy left the gym and walked across the campus to their dorm building, and went up to their room. Once inside, Newton climbed into the top bunk and Higgy slid into the bottom.

Newton folded his arms under his head and stared at the ceiling. He closed his eyes, but the image of the pod returned. Not just the image but those feelings— everything he had felt when he'd first opened his eyes inside the pod. Fear, confusion, the feeling of being cramped inside the strange pod—

He opened his eyes again, and whispered to Higgy on the bunk below. "Higgy, are you napping?"

"Not yet," Higgy replied. "I guess I've got a lot on my mind."

Newton sighed. "Yeah. Me too."

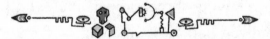

"Pizza party in Newton and Higgy's room!"

Newton's eyes opened groggily as Shelly, Theremin, Odifin, and Rotwang burst into the room. He had fallen asleep after all, a deep, deep sleep with no dreams of the pod.

Higgy leaped out of the bottom bunk. "Pizza! Thanks! I'm ravenous."

Theremin put two boxes of pizza on top of Newton's dresser. Newton jumped down and opened one of the lids. "Wow, that smells delicious," he said. He read the box top. "Fizzy's Pizza. What's pizza?"

"Bread with tomato sauce and melted cheese," Shelly answered.

"Pizza is the best," Rotwang said.

"So, what does it do?" Newton asked. "Does it sing? Or float like the food in the Airy Café? Or will I speak another language if I eat it?"

Shelly shook her head. "Nope. The mad science isn't in what's in this pizza but in how it's made. Fizzy is a physicist who measures the precise water content of

the cheese. He rolls out the dough to the perfect size—thirty-five-point-five-six centimeters. Then he bakes it for precisely four minutes and seventeen-point-two seconds at a temperature of three hundred and thirty-two degrees Celsius. The result is the most perfect pizza on Earth."

"Since you've never had pizza anywhere else, you'll have to take Shelly's and Rotwang's word for it," Theremin said to Newton.

"I wouldn't care if it was the worst pizza in the world. I'm so hungry right now," Higgy said, and two slices disappeared down his gooey gullet.

"So, Newton, what did you want to talk to us about?" Odifin asked.

Before Newton could answer, Higgy burped loudly. Then he spoke up.

"If you don't mind, Newton, I have an announcement I'd like to make," Higgy said.

"Sure," Newton said.

Higgy pointed to the pile of dirty clothes on the floor—his coat, boots, scarf, hat, and goggles.

"I'm not hiding behind my bandages anymore!" he announced. "I want to be seen for who I am: an awesome, green gooey kid who can do cool stuff, just like Goo Guy. I've been hiding myself because I

was scared. But I'm not scared anymore!"

His friends all cheered for him.

"That's awesome, Higgy!" Shelly said.

"Yeah, dude, you go for it!" Theremin added.

Odifin chimed in. "I've never tried pretending I'm not a brain in a jar—well, not until today," he said. "I think you're going to be fine."

Newton nodded. "I'm happy for you, Higgy."

His friend looked happy—at peace with himself. *Will I ever feel like that?* Newton wondered. *Or will I always be searching to find out who I am?*

After Higgy finished high-fiving everyone, he turned to Newton. "Thanks for letting me get that off my green gooey chest," he said. "What did you want to talk about?"

"It's something Shelly said earlier," Newton answered. "That the book in the museum, *The Invincible Man*, might be some kind of clue about where I came from. Maybe it could even be a clue about where Odifin and I *both* came from."

"I mean, it could just be a coincidence," Shelly said. "But that pod from the book really triggered you, so I think it's worth checking out."

She took out her tablet and searched for the book. "Here it is," she said. "*The Invincible Man* by Zoumba Summit. It says here that Summit wrote two other books two decades ago: *The Bird Women of Planet Avia* and *The Immortal Administrator*. They were published by an independent book company and not many copies were printed, but her works are legendary among science fiction fans. All her books are out of print and hard to find."

"Maybe *The Invincible Man* is in the school library?" Odifin suggested. Shelly tapped on the screen. "Nope. It's not in the library database."

"Does it say anything else about the author?" Newton asked.

Shelly read from the screen. "It says Summit is a mysterious recluse. Nobody knows where she lives or even if she's still alive."

Newton sighed. "I guess it's a dead end, then."

"It doesn't have to be," Shelly said. "We should find a copy of the book and read it. There might be answers in there somewhere."

"If you give me some time, I can try connecting my database to the inventory of every used-book store in the world," Theremin offered. "If we find a copy somewhere, then we'll figure out how to get it."

"I'd like that," Newton said. "Thanks."

"It's a plan!" Shelly said. "How long do you think it will take, Theremin?"

"I'm not sure," Theremin said. "But I'll work on it overnight. I'll give you guys a report at breakfast."

"Are you all done talking, I hope?" Rotwang asked. "I'd sure like to eat that pizza before it gets cold. It looks so good."

"Oh, sure," Newton said. He opened the first box—and it was empty. "I think Higgy finished this one, but we can hit the next box."

The second box still held almost-piping-hot pizza, and Newton took a slice and bit into it. His eyes widened. "Wow! That tastes better than chocolate-covered crickets."

Higgy's stomach rumbled. "I'm still hungry," he said. "Newton, do you want to go on my night raid of the cafeteria with me?"

Newton thought about it. He wasn't tired, and hanging out with Higgy sounded like fun, even if it did entail crawling around in dark tunnels.

"Sure," Newton agreed.

After they finished the pizza, Shelly, Theremin, Odifin, and Rotwang all said good night and left.

Higgy opened up the trapdoor in the floor and motioned for Newton to follow him. Newton took off

his socks and crawled through the hole. He knew that his grippy feet and fingers would come in handy when following Higgy.

The hole dropped them into a dark tunnel that led to the main school.

"What are you going after tonight, Higgy?" Newton asked as they walked through the tube-shaped space. Pipes snaked along the tunnel walls, some of them dripping water. Lacy spiderwebs hung in the corners.

"I think a tub of peanut butter would be nice," Higgy replied. "Maybe with one of those giant jars of grape jelly."

The tunnel opened up into the school basement. Higgy pushed open a vent and slithered down the wall. Newton used his grippy hands and feet to climb down after him.

"I think I discovered a new shortcut," Higgy said. "Follow me."

They moved through the basement, sticking close to the wall. Stubbins Crouch, the school custodian, slept down there, and he was the one person they didn't want to encounter.

Suddenly Newton felt the hairs on his body stand on end. He froze. Up ahead he could hear what sounded like muffled voices.

"Do you hear that?" he hissed.

"Don't worry," Higgy whispered back. "We're about to pass under Mumtaz's office. She's probably just talking to somebody in there, and we can hear them through the vent."

They slowly tiptoed forward, and the voices got louder. Newton recognized the male voice of Professor Flubitus, the green-haired professor who had come from the future.

"It's inevitable, Mobius," he was saying. "He's a bright boy. He's going to figure it out on his own, and when he does, that could be dangerous."

Is Flubitus talking about me? Newton wondered. *And who is he talking to?*

"I need to think about this, Hercule." It was Ms. Mumtaz—Newton had totally forgotten that "Mobius" was her first name. "After what happened today, I agree that we at least need to give him some guidance. He needs to learn how to control his abilities."

Newton's heart started to pound quickly. They *were* talking about him. They had to be.

"Newton, come on! Peanut butter, remember?" Higgy hissed.

Newton hurried ahead, his heart still pounding

fiercely. The hairs on his body stood up again.

I feel like I'm closer than ever to learning the truth, he thought. *But I can't count on Mumtaz or Flubitus to tell me. I hope Theremin can find us a copy of that book!*

CHAPTER 9

There's No Place Like Home

"Thanks for ruining the class trip, Newton," Mimi said the next morning at breakfast.

Newton's eyes widened in surprise. "What do you mean?"

"I *mean*, hanging from the ceiling like some kind of joker," she said, folding her arms in front of her.

"Come on, Mimi. It's not fair to say he ruined the whole trip," Shelly pointed out.

"He embarrassed the entire Crowninshield family. From now on he's barred from any more Crowninshield trips," Mimi said. She leaned toward Newton and whispered, "I've got my eye on you." Then she looked at Higgy. "What's up with you today? Are your clothes in the laundry?"

"I'm green and gooey and proud of it!" Higgy replied loudly, and the kids in the cafeteria who hadn't already been staring at him turned to stare.

Mimi shrugged. "You do you," she said, and walked away.

Newton shook his head. "I don't get her. Sometimes she acts like she wants to be my friend, and other times she's mad at me."

"Don't worry about Mimi," Shelly said. "Theremin was just about to tell us what he found out."

Newton, Shelly, Theremin, Higgy, Odifin, and Rotwang had all met up in the cafeteria that morning to get Theremin's report.

"Right," Theremin said. "Well, I found five hundred and six used copies of *The Invincible Man* at used-book stores around the world."

"That's great!" Newton said. "How do we get one?"

"Some of the shops let you order online," Theremin said.

"Hmm," Higgy said. "All the incoming mail gets scanned and examined before it's distributed. If that book has something of interest in it and Mumtaz is trying to keep it from you, you might never get a copy. Maybe it's safer to go to one of the bookstores in person."

"The nearest one is in Florida in the US," Theremin said, "but we have no way to get there."

"Is there one in London?" Higgy asked.

Theremin's eyes flashed as he scanned the down-loaded data. "Yes. At the Dusty Shelf Bookshop on Larchmont Street."

"That's just a few blocks away from our flat!" Higgy said. "This is perfect. I'll ask Ms. Mumtaz for a portal pass for a visit home next weekend, and then I'll get the book while I'm there."

He took out his phone. "Let me text Mum right now. She's been begging me to come home for a visit."

He typed, and then a few seconds later he looked up from his phone. "Newton, Mum wants you to come with me! She says she's anxious to meet you."

Newton brightened. "Really? Am I allowed to go home with you?"

"We'll have to ask Ms. Mumtaz, but Mum says she'll put in a good word," Higgy said. "Let's go ask Mumtaz after breakfast!"

"Sure!" Newton said happily. Whenever he'd seen other kids use portal passes to visit home, he'd felt a tiny sting of jealousy, knowing he didn't have a home to go to. But now he might be going home with Higgy. It wasn't *Newton's* home, but it was still something.

After they ate, Newton and Higgy made their way to the office of Headmistress Mumtaz. Even though it was the weekend, they knew they'd find

her there—she seemed to rarely leave it.

Newton knocked on the door. "Ms. Mumtaz, it's Newton and Higgy!"

"Come in!" she answered.

Mumtaz was perched behind her desk, studying a holographic screen in the air in front of her, filled with numbers and figures. She swiped it away with her hand and motioned for them to sit down.

Newton eyed the nameplate on her desk: HEADMISTRESS MOBIUS MUMTAZ. There was that name again. Mobius. Seeing it tickled a distant corner of his brain. But what could it mean?

"Ms. Mumtaz, I'd like a portal pass for next weekend, please," Higgy said. "I haven't made a visit home yet this semester, and Mum is anxious to see me. And she said to bring Newton, too."

Mumtaz gazed at them through her cat-eye glasses. "Yes, your mother has contacted me, Higgy. I'm happy to give you the pass, but I'm not sure if it's wise to send both you and Newton, after what happened at the museum."

"But that wasn't my fault!" Newton protested, his heart suddenly sinking. "And anyway, remember when I won that portal pass to anywhere, from winning the Mad Science Fair? I tried to go home with it, and it didn't work, and you said it was a glitch. So maybe this could count toward that."

Mumtaz frowned, thinking. "You make an excellent argument, Newton. And, Higgy, your parents are some of the most respectable mad scientists in the community. I'm sure they'll keep you two out of trouble."

"Does this mean you'll let us go?" Higgy asked.

Mumtaz opened a drawer in her desk, and after a bit of rifling pulled out a brochure of the school. "This will get you both to London. You may leave at eleven a.m. next Saturday and return at precisely eleven a.m. on Sunday. If you are late, or there is any trouble, your portal privileges will be revoked for next semester. Got it?"

"Got it!" Newton and Higgy answered at the same time.

"Thank you, Ms. Mumtaz," Higgy said, sliding off his chair.

"One more thing, Higgy," Mumtaz said. "You're going to be returning to the outside world. Please dress appropriately."

Higgy frowned, but he didn't object. "Okay."

The two boys left the office and high-fived as soon as they got into the hallway. For Newton it was a soft and jiggly high five, but it was a high five all the same.

"This is perfect, Newton," Higgy said. "One week from today we'll have a copy of *The Invincible Man* in our hands! Well, your hands, actually. I'd just get goo all over it."

"Thanks for doing this, Higgy," Newton said, and Higgy grinned.

"Sure. That's what friends are for!"

CHAPTER 10

The Dusty Shelf

For Newton the week dragged on as slowly as a sloth crossing a street on a hot day. To take his mind off the upcoming trip, Newton dove into his schoolwork. For History of Mad Scientists he wrote a report on Ignatius Nakamura, the father of Heretical Electricity. In his Genetic Friendgineering class he worked on a chemical formula that would make your friend smell like pizza. In Physics of Phys Ed, he scored six points in a game of antigravity basketball.

Finally Saturday morning came. Higgy got dressed in pants, a blue plaid sweater, and a matching cap with a small brim.

"Ugh!" Higgy complained. "These clothes are so confining!"

"No bandages or goggles or gloves or anything?" Newton asked.

Higgy shook his head. "This is good enough. This

portal will take us directly to my flat anyway."

He looked at his phone. "It's eleven. Ready to go?"

"Ready!" Newton replied. He'd filled a backpack with his toothbrush, a clean shirt, clean pants, and clean socks and underwear. He wasn't sure what else you were supposed to bring when you were visiting somebody, but that seemed like enough.

Higgy folded the brochure, and just like in the gym, the brochure flew out of his hands and a swirling wind whipped up, and then the portal appeared. Higgy motioned to Newton.

"Friends first," he said.

Newton nodded and stepped into the black hole. There was spinning and flashing lights, and then suddenly he was in Higgy's flat, face-to-face with Higgy's dad, mom, and little brother.

Higgy's dad was a foot taller than Newton. He wore a cap and a plaid sweater like the ones Higgy had put on back in the dorm, and his goo was tucked into a pair of navy-blue pants and brown loafers.

Higgy's mom wore a white lab coat and glasses with thick, black frames. What appeared to be a wig of red hair topped her head.

Wellington, Higgy's little brother, wore a red-and-white-striped shirt with a collar, red sweatpants, and

red sneakers. On top of his head was a baseball hat with the word RUGBY on it.

"Newton, so nice to meet you finally!" Mrs. Vollington said, embracing him in a squishy hug. "And where is my Higgy?"

Higgy popped out of the portal. "Hello, Mum!"

Mrs. Vollington gave him a big squeeze too. "Higgy, it's been too long! Look at you!"

Mr. Vollington patted Higgy on the back, and then hugged him too. "Hello, Son! Did you have a good *trip*? Hope you didn't *fall*," he joked.

"Good ones, Dad," Higgy said.

"Hi, snotface," Higgy's little brother said.

"Wellington! What kind of way is that to greet your brother?" Mrs. Vollington scolded.

"It's okay, Mum. I deserve it," Higgy said. "Before I left for Franken-Sci High, I kind of pranked Welly by filling his favorite sneakers with shaving cream. Sorry about that, Welly."

"Apology not accepted," Welly said, turning away from his brother.

Mrs. Vollington shook her head, but then turned to Higgy and Newton and smiled. "I'm so glad you boys are here. Newton, as Higgy may have explained to you, we're a family of night owls, and we just woke up a short time ago. We made a big breakfast to celebrate your visit. Let's sit down and eat and catch up."

"I made the scrambled eggs," Higgy's father said. "I think eggs are so funny. You know why? Because they really *crack* me up!"

Higgy groaned. "Hope you don't mind 'dad jokes,' Newton. My pop's got a million of them."

"I like them," Newton said. He'd heard kids talking about dad jokes—corny jokes that fathers sometimes made. Since Newton didn't have a dad, he'd figured he would never hear one. Mr. Vollington's jokes weren't hilarious, but they made Newton smile—and they were helping Newton feel at ease in this new place.

"I need to freshen up in my room before I eat," Higgy announced, and he left the living room.

"*Our* room," Wellington corrected him.

"Don't be long!" Mrs. Vollington said. "Come, Newton, let's eat while everything's hot."

Newton followed Higgy's mom, dad, and brother into the kitchen, a room painted a cheerful yellow. The round table in the center was piled with food: an enormous bowl of scrambled eggs, a tower of pancakes, and a bucket of sausages.

"Take a seat and help yourself, Newton," Mrs. Vollington instructed.

"Yes, take a seat but don't take it too far away," Mr. Vollington said. "We need it here in the kitchen."

"*Take* a seat. Ha! I get it," Newton said.

"Newton, please help yourself to food," Mrs. Vollington said.

Newton gingerly placed a pancake on his plate, and Mrs. Vollington topped it with syrup.

"Dig in, everyone," Mr. Vollington said. "And please, Newton, eat while it's hot."

Newton began to eat as Higgy's family piled food onto their plates.

"Newton, we want to thank you for being such a good influence on Higgy," Mrs. Vollington said. "Higgy used to get into trouble almost every day at Franken-Sci High. But after you became his roommate, his grades improved, and he became active in school programs. There was that role in the play, and then your team's excellent performance in the trivia tournament. It has been wonderful to see our dear boy deciding to participate."

"Higgy's always been a bit of a jokester, like me," Mr. Vollington explained. "And I know that sometimes you just need a good friend to set you straight." He looked at his wife and smiled.

"And we're quite pleased that Franken-Sci High is working out for Higgy," Mrs. Vollington continued. "He's gotten kicked out of every other suitable school. I don't know what we'd do if he got expelled from Franken-Sci High as well!"

"Higgy's the best roommate I could have asked for," Newton said. "When I first came to school, I didn't have many friends. And Higgy didn't care where I came from. He was nice from the beginning."

"That's my Higgy," Mrs. Vollington said proudly. Then her eyes got wide. "Higgy?"

Higgy had entered the kitchen without any of his clothes on.

"Higgy, what are you doing?" his mom asked. "Newton is our guest!"

"It's no big deal, Mum," Higgy replied. "I've made a decision at school not to hide myself anymore. I'm proud of being made of goo. Newton's cool with it."

"I am," Newton agreed.

Mrs. Vollington gasped. "Do you mean you've been going around school like this?"

Higgy nodded. "For a whole week, and nobody minds."

Higgy's mom turned to her husband. "Rollie, what do you have to say about this?"

"Well, Molly, *we* did the same thing when *we* went to Franken-Sci High, don't you remember?" Mr. Vollington replied.

"I know," Mrs. Vollington said. "But that was before we knew any better. When we dress up in clothing, we look like more than just globs of goo. For better or worse, clothing gets us more respect in the mad-scientist community. Do you want to go back to the days when we were looked at as gooey experiments instead of as legitimate scientists?"

"Why does a costume have to define who we are?" Higgy shot back. "We are goo, and we are awesome! We can do so many things that other mad scientists can't, just by being ourselves."

Newton noticed that Wellington hadn't spoken at all during the argument. His eyes moved back and forth from Higgy to his parents as he shoveled pancakes into his mouth.

Mrs. Vollington sighed. "I need to think about this, Higgy. You can stay like this for now, but you *will* get dressed properly when we go out tonight."

"Can't we go out earlier?" Higgy asked.

"Come now, Higgy, you know better than that," Mr. Vollington said. "Sunset is at seven twenty-three, so we'll head out around eight. Mum thought you boys might want to see a movie."

Wellington finally spoke. "Yeah, I want to see *Rocket Racers*!"

"Actually, I was hoping we could go to the Dusty Shelf bookstore," Newton said.

"My, you're a studious young man," Higgy's mom said. "You're our guest. If that's what you'd like to do, we're happy to take you."

Wellington groaned.

"Until then, you boys can do some sightseeing," Mrs. Vollington said.

Newton looked at Higgy, confused. "But I thought we couldn't go anywhere until tonight?"

Higgy dumped a plateful of sausages into his mouth and burped loudly before he replied. "Come on. I'll show you what she means."

"Thank you for breakfast," Newton said to Higgy's parents, and then he followed Higgy into the living room. Higgy pulled aside the curtains to reveal a large window—and beyond it, the city of London.

"Wow!" Newton cried. There were so many buildings, and streets filled with cars, and in the distance was a giant wheel!

"Does that wheel power the city?" Newton asked.

"Nope," Higgy replied. "It's called a Ferris wheel, and it's just for fun. People sit in it, the wheel turns, and then they get a great view of London."

"You have a pretty good view from here," Newton remarked.

Higgy motioned to a telescope to the right, and Newton looked through it. All of a sudden, he could see people on the Ferris wheel, too, but they looked teeny tiny.

"This is really the only way we get to see the outside world during the day," Higgy said. "Sorry if it's a little boring."

"It's not!" Newton assured him. Everything was fascinating to him—even Higgy's flat. He'd never been inside a real home before, and he was fascinated with how cozy it was, compared to the big rooms that everyone shared at the school.

"Sightsee as long as you want," Higgy offered, and Newton stared through the telescope for hours, finding something new to watch in every corner of the city that could be seen from the window.

Then a delivery man arrived with Chinese food and it was time to eat again, and Newton decided that he liked lo mein noodles, spring rolls, and soup dumplings almost as much as he liked pizza.

The Chinese food was followed by a board game with the Vollingtons.

"Come on. Let me show you my room," Higgy said when they'd finished.

"*Our* room," Wellington corrected him again, and he followed Higgy and Newton.

The room definitely looked like it belonged to two people—two completely different people. Higgy's side was a mess of clothes and electronic equipment, just like at school. Wellington's side was clean and neat. Posters of rugby teams adorned the walls.

Higgy spotted something on Wellington's organized bookshelf and grabbed it.

"Hey, put that down, Higgy!" Wellington yelled.

"It's Goo Guy!" Higgy said. "I love Goo Guy."

"You do?" Wellington asked.

"Sure," Higgy said. "Newton and I saw a cool statue of Goo Guy at a museum just last week. Here. I got a picture of it."

Higgy handed the comic book back to his brother and picked up his cell phone. He scrolled to the photo and showed Wellington.

"Wait, who's that kid?" Wellington asked.

"That's me, using a special kind of hologram," Higgy said. "It helped me blend in."

His little brother's eyes got wide. "You mean you could go outside and walk around during the day?"

Higgy nodded. "Yeah, it was pretty cool."

"Why can't you do that every day?" Wellington asked.

"The technology isn't ready yet," Higgy said. "But

I don't know if I'd want to. I'd rather be Goo Guy. Wouldn't you?"

Wellington didn't answer right away. His eyes traveled to the window and the view outside, where the sun was setting.

"I don't know," he said.

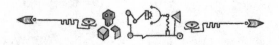

Finally it was time to venture out to the bookstore. Higgy reluctantly got dressed again, and the Vollingtons all wrapped their faces in bandages, added thick glasses, and put gloves on their hands.

"The bookstore is only a few blocks away, and it's a nice night," Mrs. Vollington said. "Let's walk!"

They took the elevator downstairs and stepped out into the cool night. Back on the island, solar-powered lights cast a glow over the plant-lined paths between the school and the dorms. But in London there were lights everywhere. There were flashing signs in store windows and bright headlights on cars.

The streets were crowded with people heading to restaurants, clubs, and shops, and when the people looked up from their phones, they did stare at the Vollington family, just as Higgy had said they did. But

the stares were brief. After a moment people looked back down at their phones and kept walking.

Soon a smell filled the air, and it was even more wonderful to Newton's nose than pizza or lo mein noodles. Newton's eyes followed the scent to a small shop, the Salty Sailor. People were walking out of it holding cones made of newspaper, with fried food inside.

"Fish and chips," Higgy told him. "Or fish and 'French fries,' as they say in the US. These are the best in London. We can stop for a snack after we get the book."

Newton's stomach rumbled. "I can't believe it, but I'm hungry again."

"Just like a Vollington," Higgy's mom said, with a smile in her voice.

Newton couldn't see her actual smile, because of her bandaged face, but he knew it was there. He kept thinking about it as they continued moving. *Just like a Vollington.* He liked the sound of that. He'd only known Higgy's family for a few hours, but they made him feel like he belonged. And that was nice.

"Newton, watch out!" Higgy yelled. He grabbed Newton's arm and pulled him to the side.

"What happened?" Newton asked, confused.

Higgy pointed to the sidewalk, where a traffic cone sat in front of an open hole. "The top to the catch basin

is missing," he said. "You could have fallen in."

Mrs. Vollington shook her head. "It's been weeks, and they haven't fixed it. It's dangerous!"

"We're here!" Mr. Vollington announced. "The Dusty Shelf. I haven't been here in ages! I hope the dust is still the same."

"Look, it's Goo Guy!" Wellington said, pointing to the shop window.

The bookshop had a cardboard display of Goo Guy wearing a red superhero cape. *The Adventures of Goo Guy* comic books were spread out beneath it.

"The new issue is out. Can I get one, Mum?" Wellington asked excitedly as they walked into the store.

"It's your allowance," his mom said.

Higgy pulled Newton by the arm. "Come on. Let's go ask about the book."

They walked over to the counter, where a young guy with dyed black hair was perched on a stool, reading.

"Excuse me sir, but we're looking for a book," Higgy said.

The guy looked up and waved his hand around the store. "Take your pick," he said.

"It's a specific book," Newton chimed in. "*The Invincible Man* by Zoumba Summit."

The store clerk's eyes widened. "You're Summit fans?

Awesome. Her work is really amazing. Follow me and I'll take you to the right section."

He jumped off the stool and moved quickly among the shop's dusty bookshelves. Then he stopped and took a book from the shelf.

"Here you go," he said. "*The Invincible Man*. Although, I don't feel that it's her best work. I prefer *The Bird Women of Planet Avia*. That one is nonstop action."

"This is the one we want," Newton said, and the clerk handed him the book. He stared at it in his hands. On the cover, scientists wearing lab coats and masks stood around a pod. Newton started to sweat. Suddenly, his hoodie felt very warm.

"Don't stare too hard," Higgy warned him.

"Right," Newton said, and he looked up. Then he turned to the clerk and said, "Um, we'd like to buy this, please."

He held out his student ID, which was how he paid for things at the school, with digital credits. The clerk looked at him quizzically.

"I've got it," Higgy said. "Shelly, Theremin, Odifin, Rotwang, and I all chipped in to buy it for you."

Newton sighed with relief. They went to the counter, and the clerk slipped the book into a crisp paper bag. Newton held it to his chest and breathed deeply. *The answers to all my questions just might be in my hands!* he thought.

Wellington approached the counter and bought the latest issue of *The Adventures of Goo Guy*. Mrs. Vollington bought a cookbook, and Mr. Vollington bought a joke book.

"This was a splendid adventure," Mr. Vollington said as they stepped outside. "What should we do next?"

"Movie! Movie!" Wellington cried.

"It's not too late," Mrs. Vollington said. "Higgy, Newton, what would you like to do?"

Before the boys could answer, a girl's cry filled the air.

"My dog! She's fallen into the catch basin!"

A small crowd was gathering around the hole in the sidewalk. A teenage girl peered down the hole, with a panicked look on her face.

"Somebody help my dog!" she wailed.

Higgy stepped forward. "I got this," he said confidently.

"Higgy, no!" his mother warned.

In a flourish Higgy stripped off his coat, hat, boots, and bandages, as people in the crowd gasped. Cell phone lights flashed.

"Goo Guy to the rescue!" Higgy yelled, and he dove into the hole.

What Does It All Mean?

The crowd started to chatter excitedly.

"Is that guy made of green goo?"

"Is it really Goo Guy?"

"I didn't know Goo Guy was *real*!"

"How did he move so fast?"

Then a green, gooey hand reached up from the hole and gripped the sidewalk. Higgy pulled himself up. In his other arm was a tiny dog with shaggy brown hair.

"Nigel!" the girl cried, and she took the puppy and hugged it. Then her eyes took in Higgy, and she backed up. "Monster!"

Higgy's parents and Wellington stood next to Newton and watched the scene, frozen with fear. The gathered crowd started to talk more loudly.

"Monster."

"Monster!"

"MONSTER!"

Newton's mind flashed back to the museum, when Higgy's hologram had fallen off. The security guard had thought he was a Goo Guy statue. . . .

Newton stepped forward and started clapping.

"Great Goo Guy costume!" he said. "You look just like Goo Guy!"

Higgy hesitated, then nodded. "That's right. It's a costume!"

Wellington bravely stepped forward. "It's a promotion for the new Goo Guy comic book! Available in the Dusty Shelf!"

The crowd started clapping. Mr. Vollington draped Higgy's coat over him and ushered him away. Newton followed the family as they hurried back to the apartment building.

They rode the elevator back to the flat in silence. When they got home, Mrs. Vollington exploded with emotion.

"Higgy, what were you thinking?" she cried.

"That a dog was in danger, and I wanted to help!" Higgy yelled.

"That's what the police are for," his mother said. "That was too risky, Higgy. You put yourself and all of us in danger of being found out."

"Maybe I *want* to be found out!" Higgy shot back.

"Maybe I'm tired of hiding all the time!"

His father put a hand on Higgy. "Calm down, Higgy. Your mum's making a good point."

"I don't WANT to calm down!" Higgy yelled, and he went into his room and slammed the door.

Newton was confused, and it showed.

Mrs. Vollington sighed. "I'm sorry you had to see this, Newton. I know this is your first time being with a family. Families fight sometimes. It doesn't mean they don't love each other."

"I think I understand," Newton said.

Higgy didn't come out of his room, and Newton stared through the telescope while Higgy's parents talked in low tones and Welly read his comic book. *The Invincible Man* felt heavy in the pocket of his hoodie, but he didn't want to open it yet. Not without his friends.

When Newton started to yawn, Mr. Vollington suggested that he go to sleep. Newton tiptoed into Higgy's room, and Wellington followed. Higgy was on the floor in a sleeping bag, staring at the ceiling.

"You can have my bed, Newton," Higgy said.

"Thanks," Newton replied. "You know, I thought what you did today was really brave."

"Yeah," Wellington said. "Just like Goo Guy! You're a real hero, Big Brother."

"It's not fair," Higgy said. "The world loves Goo Guy as long as he's not real. But when they see a real-life guy made of goo, he's a monster."

Newton didn't know what to say. Higgy was right. Newton was starting to realize that the world outside Franken-Sci High was just as complicated as the world inside.

The boys drifted off to sleep, and were awakened the next day by Mr. Vollington.

"Rise and shine, boys!" he said. "Breakfast is ready, and it's *egg*-cellent!"

A few minutes later Newton and the Vollingtons were gathered around the kitchen table, eating mounds of fried eggs and something called bangers and mash. Newton thought it was delicious.

"So we've been talking, Higgy," Mrs. Vollington said. "And we're not angry about what you did last night."

Higgy put down his fork. "You're not?"

"It was brave," his mom admitted. "And it's brave of you to want to be who you are and not hide it."

"Thanks, Mum," Higgy said. "But I don't think the world is ready for that."

"It isn't," Higgy's dad agreed. "But we think it's okay for you to keep being you at the school, for now. And in the meantime we'll try to figure out how to change the world—together."

"Can I help too?" Newton asked.

"Of course you can, dear," Higgy's mom replied. "You're an honorary Vollington!"

Newton smiled. "Thanks for letting me visit with Higgy. It was fun."

After breakfast they hurried to pack up and return through the portal. Newton received lots of gooey hugs, and as Higgy opened the portal, Newton tapped the package in his hoodie pocket to make sure the book was still there.

"Have a nice trip, and see you next fall!" Mr. Vollington called after them as they disappeared into the portal.

After some swirling and whirling, the boys landed back in their dorm—and found Shelly, Theremin, Odifin, and Rotwang there.

"Did you get the book?" Shelly asked.

"It's nice to see you too," Higgy said jokingly.

Newton took out the book and handed it to Shelly. She gave it to Theremin. "All right. Theremin, Start scanning!"

"On it!" Theremin said, and he opened a door in his metal body and placed the book inside.

"Um, what's happening?" Newton asked.

"While you were in London, we came up with a

plan," Shelly said. "Theremin's going to scan the book and send it to everyone's tablet. Then we can all read it at the same time and look for clues."

"Thanks," Newton said. "I know it sounds weird, but I didn't want to have to do this all on my own, you know?"

"That doesn't sound weird at all," Shelly told him.

"Scans ready!" Theremin said. "Check your tablets and get reading."

"Can I read the actual book?" Newton asked.

Theremin opened the door on his chest. "Sure."

Newton took the book from Theremin, scrambled to his top bunk, and settled in to read. The story was about a scientist named Felicity Morningstar whose world was in danger. So she tried to create a superhuman by combining human DNA with animal DNA.

"Animals have developed valuable survival mechanisms," Felicity explained to the gathered scientists. "For example, Thaumoctopus mimicus *can change its coloration and the shape of its body to mimic predators, thus protecting itself from them."*

Newton's mouth dropped open. He could do that too, and Shelly had guessed that it was the same as an octopus's camouflaging ability.

Felicity went on to describe many other "animal

enhancements." The ability to change color, like a chameleon. The grippy hands and feet, like a gecko. It all sounded very familiar.

Newton put down the book and looked at his friends. Everyone was staring at him.

"This book is describing me!" he said.

"I know, dude," Theremin said. "It's weird."

"But I still don't get it," Newton said. "This is just a book. A story. Did somebody read it and actually make me? Or is this just a weird coincidence?"

"Let's keep reading," Shelly urged.

Newton read on, and the similarities kept coming. The enhanced human was created in a pod. He was born as a twelve-year-old human and then encoded with superior intelligence. Then his memory was wiped clean and a code word was embedded in his subconscious to awaken his intelligence. The code word was "brain gain."

Then the story started to differ from his. The scientist named the boy Ollie and raised him as her own. When a villain rose up and tried to destroy the world, Felicity triggered Ollie's intelligence by saying "brain gain," and he used his superpowers to save everyone.

Newton closed the book. "I'm more confused than ever," he said. "There's a lot in this book that sounds like me. But there's no school for mad scientists in it. Ollie lives in the regular world and thinks he's a regular kid."

"Until he hears the words 'brain gain,'" Odifin chimed in. "Just like when you hear the words 'noodle noggin'!"

As Odifin said the words, Newton's brain felt like it was opening up.

"Odifin, you have to be careful when you say those words!" Shelly reminded him.

"It's okay, Shelly," Newton said. "Maybe it will help me figure out what this book really means."

Newton stared at the cover of the book. *The Invincible Man* by Zoumba Summit.

Zoumba Summit. The letters started to dance and shift around in his mind.

Bazoum Timmus . . .

Tuzims Moumba . . .

Musibo Tazmum . . .

Mobius Mumtaz . . .

"Mobius Mumtaz!" Newton cried. "If you rearrange the letters in the name 'Zoumba Summit,' they spell 'Mobius Mumtaz'!"

Shelly gasped. "Newton, if Ms. Mumtaz wrote this book—"

She didn't have time to finish her thought, because one of the headmistress's fly drones zipped into the room.

"Higgy Vollington and Newton Warp, report to Ms. Mumtaz's office immediately!" the drone shouted loudly.

Time for the Truth

Newton and Higgy left their friends and hurried over to the school building.

"What do you think she wants?" Newton wondered as they walked to Mumtaz's office.

"Beats me," Higgy said. "Unless it's about our trip to London."

The boys stopped and looked at each other.

"Do you think she knows about the Goo Guy incident?" Higgy asked.

"Maybe," Newton said. "Don't worry. I'm sure it will be all right."

When they walked into Mumtaz's office, the headmistress was reading a newspaper. She held it up, and there was a giant photo of Higgy handing the puppy to the teenage girl on the street in London. Newton was next to him.

"'Guy in Goo Guy Costume Rescues Puppy,'" she

said, reading the headline out loud. "Looks like you boys made the front page."

"We can explain," Higgy said. "This puppy fell down a hole, and I had to rescue it. So I took off my clothes so that I could move more easily, and—"

"And we told everybody he was wearing a Goo Guy costume, and they believed it," Newton piped up, trying to help. "They even say it in the headline."

"I understand that your heart was in the right place, Higgy, but your behavior put yourself and Franken-Sci High at risk," Ms. Mumtaz said. "The faculty is considering expelling you."

"You can't do that!" Newton blurted out. "That's not fair!"

"It's okay, Newton," Higgy said sadly. "The fact that I've been able to stick it out here for this long is a miracle anyway."

Newton shook his head. "No, you can't do this!" he said. He slapped the book down onto the headmistress's desk. "This only happened because Higgy brought me to London to get this book. I recognized the pod in the story from my buried memories from before I woke up in the Brain Bank that day. And today I realized something else. The author, Zoumba Summit, is *you*, Ms. Mumtaz! You are Zoumba Summit, aren't you?"

Guy in
Goo Guy Costume
Rescues Puppy

The headmistress froze. Then she blinked.

"Higgy, please leave Newton and me alone right now," she said.

Higgy looked at Newton. "Are you going to be okay?"

Newton wasn't sure. But at least Mumtaz hadn't told him to leave too. He thought that seemed like a promising sign.

"I'll be fine," Newton said, and Higgy reluctantly left the office.

Ms. Mumtaz pressed a button on her desk.

"It's time," she said.

"Time for what?" Newton asked.

"Time to tell you the truth, Newton," Ms. Mumtaz said. "You are right. I am Zoumba Summit. In my younger days I wrote science fiction for fun. I didn't care if I sold books, and I found a small company who wanted to publish them. I used an assumed name because, at the time, fictional pursuits were frowned on in the mad-scientist community. But I went ahead with it anyway, and the ideas in *The Invincible Man* led to the creation of my greatest work, Newton."

Newton felt a chill run through his body. "What do you mean?"

Mumtaz didn't answer, and at that moment professors started to file into the room. Professor

Flubitus entered first, his green hair standing on end. Professor Leviathan ducked to get through the doorway. Professor Phlegm wore his usual frown, and Professor Wagg wore his usual colorful suspenders and bow tie. Professor Juvinall entered holding a teddy bear, and Professor Wells came in shouting "Grab the monster by the tail!" out of the right side of his mouth as he instructed students in the other dimension that he lived in. Soon, all of the professors Newton knew were there.

"Does this have to happen now, Mobius?" Professor Juvinall asked. "It's teddy bear teatime!"

Ms. Mumtaz nodded toward Newton. "He knows too much already," she said. "I think we need to tell him the truth."

Newton felt like he couldn't breathe. Was he finally going to find out where he'd come from? And why were so many professors gathered here?

"Telling him could alter the future, Mobius," Professor Phlegm warned.

Professor Flubitus spoke up. "He's a smart young man, and he's not going to stop until he gets the answers he wants. If we tell him, we can retain control of the situation."

Nobody else objected.

"Fine," Mumtaz said. "This is the truth, Newton. You already know that you play a significant role in the future of the school. What you do not know is that you were expressly created for that future."

Newton took this in. "Created . . . like the character in your book."

"Exactly," Ms. Mumtaz replied. "Everyone in this room had a hand in creating you. We pooled our talents and skills to combine the components of the best human DNA with DNA from animals with remarkable abilities so that you would have some of their amazing aptitudes."

"Why would you need a human with special abilities?" Newton asked.

"In the future, Franken-Sci High is in terrible, terrible danger," Professor Flubitus said. "So we got together and created you to save it, Newton. But for our plan to work, we knew we had to send you back here, to the past."

A bunch of emotions flowed through Newton. This was the truth. The truth he wanted to hear. But it didn't make him happy. There was no mom and dad in this story. No family to return to. And there was something else that was even worse . . .

"So you just made me because you needed me to

do something?" Newton asked.

"I know that sounds harsh, Newton, but we gave you life," Ms. Mumtaz said. "We wiped your memories of your creation, or at least we thought we did, so that you could live a normal life with other children. A happy life, we hope."

"In the future we never imagined that you would be so curious about where you came from," Professor Flubitus said.

"We should have imagined it," Professor Leviathan said. "But our future selves must have forgotten what it's really like to be human."

More questions swirled in Newton's mind, and he wasn't sure which one to ask first.

"How am I supposed to save the school?" Newton asked.

"That is something we still can't tell you," Professor Flubitus answered. "It would endanger the future too much. But you finally know where you came from, my boy. We owe you that, at least."

"What happens after I save the school?" Newton asked, his eyes filling with tears. "Will the experiment end?"

"Of course not, Newton," Professor Leviathan answered.

"And what about Odifin?" Newton asked. "If he's my half brother, then was he part of the experiment too? Or did our DNA just come from the same place? How does he fit in?"

Ms. Mumtaz and Professor Flubitus looked at each other.

"I think we've told you all we can," Mumtaz replied. "And, Newton, you mustn't share this knowledge with your friends. It could jeopardize everything we've worked for."

"Why can't you just tell me everything?" Newton's voice was rising. "This isn't right. It isn't fair. And I should be able to tell my friends!"

"Perhaps we should sedate him now," Professor Snollygoster suggested.

"Or another memory wipe," said Professor Phlegm.

"NO! Leave me alone!" Newton yelled, and he raced out of Ms. Mumtaz's office.

He didn't know where to go, but he knew one thing. He wanted to see his friends, and he wasn't sure he could keep this inside.

As Newton left the office, a tiny eyeball on feet followed him. The eyeball walked down the linoleum hallway, out the door, and through the jungle path to the girls' dorm. It entered the door, hopped up a flight of stairs, and entered a room with the door cracked open.

Mimi picked up the eyeball. "There you are," she said, and she plugged the eyeball's feet into a port on her tablet. "All right. Let's see what Newton Warp has been up to!"

How will Newton save Franken-Sci High? What does Shelly have to do with it? And what wacky food will they serve in the cafeteria next?

Don't miss the next book about

Jim Henson's

FRANKEN-SCI HIGH

Newton Warp stared up at the tall, brick dormitory surrounded by palm trees and colorful tropical flowers. It was a typical day on the island—sunny, hot, and humid—but Newton didn't mind. He'd always liked hot weather, but now he suspected it was due to his lizard-DNA.

Newton had been staring at the building for fifteen minutes, afraid to go in. Because when he went in, he knew he'd have to either tell a big truth or a big lie to his best friends, and either way, it was going to be bad.

A fly landed on his nose, and his tongue instinctively lashed out. He almost pulled it into his mouth when he realized what he was doing, and he flicked it away.

They did this to me, he thought. *I'm a monster, created in a lab, to do a job. I'm not human, like them.*

He gazed around the courtyard, at the other students at Franken-Sci High. Boris Bacon was bouncing across the lawn in his anti-gravity boots. Rosalind Wu was circling the courtyard in a jet pack. And Tootie van der Flootin was walking a fluffy yellow monster with three eyeballs on a leash.

How nice it must be, to be a normal human. To know not just who you are but what you are. To only be worried about what's for lunch in the cafeteria and whether you'll pass your next teleportation test.

Newton had never known that feeling of being normal. The first feeling he could remember was being confused and a little scared, when he had appeared in the library of the school for mad scientists with no memories of where he came from and a strange bar code on his foot. Luckily, Shelly and Theremin were the ones who found him, and the animal-loving girl and her robot buddy had become his good friends.

He'd met more friends, too, like his roommate, Higgy, who was made of green goo. And Odifin, a talking brain in a jar, and his assistant, Rotwang. And lots of other kids were nice to him, even Mimi Crowninshield, who was usually mean to other people. In most cases, having friends would be enough to make somebody feel like everyone else. But not Newton.

Newton's first friends, Shelly and Theremin, had quickly realized there was something different about him. He had abilities that normal humans didn't have. He could blend into the background when he was afraid, sprout gills that let him breathe underwater, and change his appearance to mimic others—and those were just some of the special things he could do. Newton had uncovered memories of being born in a pod, with scientists gathered around him. Did that have something to do with his weird talents?

Shelly and Theremin, along with Higgy, had promised to help Newton figure out where he'd come from, who his family was, and why he was different.

After some digging, smart thinking, and sneaking around, they'd learned a few things. Time-traveling Professor Flubitus had admitted that Newton and Shelly played an important role in the school's future. And Flubitus had also delivered the news that Odifin and Newton shared some significant DNA, basically making them half-brothers.

Then, today, Newton and his friends had made the biggest discovery of all. They'd found a science fiction book called *The Invincible Man* about a scientist who spliced human and animal DNA to create an indestructible, human-looking creature in a pod. The character in the book sounded just like Newton! But that wasn't the most mind-blowing part. The author's name was Zoumba Summit, and Newton had figured out that when you scrambled the letters, they spelled Mobius Mumtaz—the name of the Headmistress of Franken-Sci High.

Armed with that information, Newton had confronted Ms. Mumtaz, Professor Flubitus, and the other professors in the school. And he'd learned some truths. Yes, Mumtaz had written the book. And years in the future, the book had inspired her to create Newton in a lab. The professors had worked to gather to splice animal DNA and human DNA and made Newton in a pod so he could save the school. Then they'd wiped his memory of being created and dumped him in the past, in the library.

Not a real human. No real family, Newton, thought, still staring up at the dorm.

And after dropping that bombshell, Mumtaz had refused to say anymore. She couldn't tell Newton how he would save the school because that could change the outcome of the future.

"And Newton, you mustn't share this knowledge with your friends. It could jeopardize everything we've worked for," Mumtaz had added.

Now, Newton didn't care one lick about what those professors had worked for. He had been fully prepared to tell his friends everything. But then Professor Phlegm, with his shiny bald head and sinister eye patch, had thrown out a threat: A memory wipe.

The more Newton thought about it, the more his part-reptilian blood went cold. The professors had wiped his memory before dumping him in the library, and he'd made a lot of memories since then—good ones as well as bad ones. Was Phlegm threatening to take away all of his memories? Without them, he'd lose his friends. And what if they wiped his friends' memories too? Or kept them away from each other, so they couldn't become friends again? The worried thoughts swirled through his mind.

Newton sighed. He knew what he had to do, and it wasn't going to feel good. He walked across the courtyard and into the dorm. He stepped into the glass transport tube and said, "Freshman Floor."

Whoosh! The tube shot up four floors and then opened up. He stepped out and made his way to the door marked YTH-125. He paused a moment before opening the door. Then he took a deep breath and entered.

"Newton!" Shelly, with her wild curly hair, leaped off

a chair and pounced on him in a hug. "Higgy said that Mumtaz called you to her office because of what happened in London, and then she kicked out Higgy as soon as you mentioned Zoumba Summit. What did she tell you?"

"I wanted to stay and listen through the door, but the drones carried me back here," Higgy said. He was sitting on the bottom bunk, with no clothes on his body which was made of green protoplasm. Higgy had recently decided to stop hiding his gooey self in layers of clothes and bandages, which is why they had gotten in trouble in London.

"Like always, Mumtaz didn't tell me anything," Newton lied. "She said it was just a coincidence that her name is an anagram of Zoumba Summit."

Odifin wheeled up to him. "And you believe her?" he asked, his voice crackling from the speaker attached to the jar of liquid that held him.

Newton shrugged. "I don't know. But she made it pretty clear that there's no point in asking any more questions. All we really know is that the future of the school depends on me and Shelly. We're going to have to wait for the future to get answers."

"That's not fair!" yelled Theremin. The robot's eyes flashed red. "We need answers. You need answers! I say we go to her office and demand them."

"Yeah," agreed Rotwang. Messy black hair hung down over his eyes, as usual.

Newton held up his hands. "No!" he yelled, and his friends all looked at him, surprised. Newton hardly ever yelled. "We've wasted too much time searching for answers that we're never going to get. I just want to have a normal life."

"But don't you want to find your family?" Shelly asked.

"No," Newton said, and it was easy to sound convincing, now that he knew he didn't have one. "No, not anymore. I have you guys. That's enough."

Shelly hugged him again. "That's so sweet, Newton."

"I'll always be your bro, bro," Theremin said. "But are you sure you don't want to keep looking?"

"I'm sure," Newton said, and he looked at his friends, one by one. "Let's just put all this behind us, okay?"

"Okay," everyone answered, although Shelly was avoiding Newton's gaze.

"Isn't there some big event coming up?" Newton asked. "Let's just have fun doing whatever that is."

"As a matter of fact, Founder's Day is coming up," Odifin replied. "It's a big celebration honoring the founding of Franken-Sci High."

"See, that sounds like fun!" Newton said. "So let's all get ready for Founder's Day and try to forget all about the future and that other stuff for now. Okay?"

Shelly frowned. "Okaaaaay," she said slowly. "I need to go check on my animals in the basement. See you all at dinner?"

"Certainly!" Higgy said. "In fact, I might head to the cafeteria right now for a snack. All this excitement has made me hungry."

"Since when have you needed excitement to make you hungry?" Theremin teased. "You're always hungry!"

Higgy patted his green belly, which jiggled. "I need a lot of energy to keep this protoplasm in top form."

"I'll go with you, Higgy," said Rotwang. Over six-feet-tall and skinny as a test tube, Rotwang could eat more than anyone not made of green goo.

"I suppose I'll join you," Odifin said. "I can people-watch while you eat."

Theremin turned to Newton. "What do you say, bro? Want to maybe play some laser hockey?"

Newton yawned. "Not right now. I'm kind of tired from London and everything. I'll catch up with you later."

"Sure, bro," Theremin said, and the room emptied out. He climbed up onto his top bunk and let out a long breath. He hated lying to his friends, but at least they would all be safe now. And he could wait a few decades to find out why the professors had created him, right?

Bing! The tablet in his sweatshirt pocket made a notification noise, and Newton took it out. A holographic envelope projected from the screen, and Newton touched his finger to the seal. The words popped out and hung in the air in front of him.

NEWTON,
YOU ARE INVITED TO A TOUR OF CROWNINSHIELD
INDUSTRIES NEXT SATURDAY AT 10 AM. A PORTAL
PASS WILL BE PROVIDED FOR YOU.
MIMI CROWNINSHIELD

Newton stared at the invitation. Mimi had always puzzled him. He'd seen her be super mean to Shelly, but she'd been polite to Newton and seemed interested in him. He had no idea why she wanted to invite him to her family's company headquarters, but it would give him something to do besides worry about the future. He pressed the YES button on the hologram, and holographic confetti popped out. Then the hologram disappeared.

Mimi, what are you up to now? Newton wondered.

"Mimi, what are you up to now?" Shelly asked Mimi the next day in the hallway, after Newton had told her about Mimi's invitation.

Mimi's blue eyes widened, making her look like an innocent angel. "Why on earth would I have something up my sleeve?" she asked. "My family's company is preparing some very special surprises for the Founder's Day celebration, and Newton is my friend, so I thought he'd like to see him. He didn't get to go on the tour with the freshman class like everyone else did this summer."

Shelly frowned. "Seriously? I'm supposed to believe that you have no ulterior motives for this nice gesture?"

Mimi sighed. "Shelly, I know you and I haven't always gotten along, but you have to admit that I've never done anything bad to Newton, right?"

"Well . . ." Shelly's voice trailed off.

"Anyway, Newton already said he wants to come," Mimi pointed out. "And when he comes back, I'm sure he'll tell you he had a great time."

"Hmpf!" was all Shelly could respond, and she turned on her heel and walked away, her crocheted snake scarf flapping behind her.

Mimi grinned. "So trusting, Shelly," she whispered. "So trusting . . ."

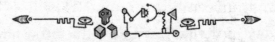

The week passed by quickly, and Newton was surprised at how normal everything felt compared to everything that had happened since he came to the school. Well, normal by Franken-Sci High standards.

Every day he licked his locker security panel to identify the flavor so he could open it. The week's options had been hot licorice, liverwurst, chocolate-covered-mushroom, garlic, and banana-blue-cheese.

Every day he went to class. In Physics of Phys Ed, he swung on ropes over a pit of hybrid shark-crocodiles. In Quantum Emotional Chemistry for Non-Chemistry Students, he worked on a "Beautiful Sadness" formula—the kind of sadness you feel when you watch a movie about a heroic dog or when you see a sunset and are sad that the day is over even though the sky looks beautiful. And in Retro Robotics class, he actually had fun making an old-school mini wind-up robot.

Every day he ate in the cafeteria. He tried new dishes invented by the cafeteria cooks. Peanut butter balls with so much protein in them that they came to life and bounced up and down on their own. A kale salad that tasted like pepperoni pizza. Chicken wings that flew right into his mouth.

Yes, it was a normal week at Franken-Sci High

all right, and Newton settled in and began to enjoy himself. Sure, the knowledge that he was a genetically-engineered being was always in the back of his mind, poking at his brain cells, but he pushed it aside.

Then Saturday came, and Newton reported to Ms. Mumtaz's office at 9:55, five minutes earlier than Mimi had asked him to. He knew Mimi didn't like lateness. The door was open, and Ms. Mumtaz was sitting at her desk. She stared at Newton through her cat-eye glasses.

"Hello, Newton," she said. "How's everything going?"

"Just fine," he said, staring right back at her. "Everything's perfectly normal. Like nothing weird ever happened."

She nodded, bobbing her head like a bird, which wasn't surprising. With her long, thin, neck and slim, pointy nose, she had always reminded Newton of a bird.

"Glad to hear it," she said. "I'm glad to see you've calmed down, Newton. Nothing to do now but look forward to the future."

"Sure," Newton replied, although inside he was thinking: *You mean the future that's going to be a disaster unless I somehow stop it with my freaky powers!*

"Good morning, Newton!"

Mimi entered the office, neatly dressed in a denim

skirt, sneakers, and a white collared shirt with a blue vest over it. Her blond curls bounced on her shoulders.

"Uh, hi, Mimi," he greeted her.

Mimi held out a hand to Ms. Mumtaz. "We're ready for the portal pass, please," she said.

The Head Mistress handed a paper brochure of the school to Mimi. Mimi opened it all the way into a big square. Then she folded it into smaller and smaller squares. Finally, she folded it diagonally so that the top left and bottom right corners touched.

The tightly-folded brochure began to spin, and floated out of her hands. As it spun faster and faster, it created a rotating column of air. Newton's wavy hair whipped in front of his eyes. Then the whirling stopped, and a black hole of glowing light appeared where the brochure had been.

"Ladies, first," Mimi said, and she stepped through the human-size hole and disappeared.

"Have fun, Newton!" Ms. Mumtaz called out, as he stepped through the portal behind Mimi.

Newton blinked. They had emerged into the bright sunlight. The portal closed and Mimi caught the brochure before it hit the ground, and tucked it into her skirt pocket. Then she gestured in front of her.

"Come on! We can take the funicular to the top of

the mountain," she said, and she ran ahead.

Newton looked up and saw a gleaming, white building on top of a tall mountain in front of them. A sign with large, black letters announced: CROWNINSHIELD INDUSTRIES: The Future Is in Our Hands.

Newton wasn't sure what a funicular was, but he guessed it might be the thing that looked like a white train car that Mimi was running toward. It was rectangular, with large windows on all sides. He followed her inside, where she announced "Main gate!" and the door slid shut behind them. Then the train car made its way on a track, winding toward the top of the mountain.

"I've always thought we should put a teleport pad down here—it would be so much faster," Mimi said. "But mom and dad insist that we keep the *mad* scientist stuff we do top-secret. To the rest of the world, Crowninshield Industries is just a top company in technological innovation—like the low-emissions auto fuel we've been perfecting." She sighed. "Maybe one day, we won't have to hide our real genius. But I guess the world isn't ready for us yet. . . ."

Illustrations, Maps, and Figures

Acknowledgments

I have benefited from the help of many people in preparing this second edition of *The Rise of Modern Business*. Conversations and work with Professors James Bartholomew, William Childs, and K. Austin Kerr in the History Department at The Ohio State University have sharpened my thoughts about business history. I want to thank Professors Philip Brown of The Ohio State University, James Kraft of the University of Hawaii at Manoa, and Michael Dintenfass of the University of Wisconsin at Milwaukee for reading and commenting on an earlier draft of this edition.

I owe great thanks to Lewis Bateman, of the University of North Carolina Press, for his constant encouragement and thoughts as I prepared this edition. I remain, of course, solely responsible for any errors this study may still contain.

The Rise of Modern Business
in Great Britain,
the United States,
and Japan

Introduction

This book grew out of the needs I encountered in teaching comparative business history to mixed groups of undergraduates—history majors, business majors, and many others—at The Ohio State University. No text on this subject was suitable for that purpose, and I found myself in perennial difficulty when selecting readings for the course. I originally wrote this book, first published in 1988, to try to fill that void. Over the past decade interest in comparative business history has greatly increased, as has my own involvement in the field, resulting in the preparation of this second edition.

As a work in business history, my study examines the history of the business firm and its management. By focussing on the firm, business history differs from economic history, which looks more at the entire economy of a nation, at the big macroeconomics picture of economic booms and contractions. Nonetheless, the external environment—politics, culture, social norms, and law—has influenced the firm; and this book deals with the evolution of business in relationship to the environment within which business has developed.

This book compares historical developments in Great Britain, the United States, Japan, and, though to a much lesser degree, Germany from preindustrial times to the present. There are compelling reasons for studying the history of business in these nations. Industrialization and the changes it caused were *big* events in the economic and business history of the world. With industrialization, the rate of economic growth soared dramatically. Great Britain was the first country to industrialize. It makes sense, then, to examine British firms as the first to be affected by industrialization. A study of Great Britain also permits an investigation of European business. So does the study of Germany, which successfully industrialized later than Great Britain. Sev-

eral reasons call for an examination of the history of American business. Even though the United States, like Germany, industrialized somewhat later than Great Britain, it was in the United States that many new forms of company structures and management methods were first worked out. American business people were the first to develop big businesses in a major way, along with new ways to run them. Some American business structures and methods were later dispersed to other nations. Moreover, studying the United States offers a chance to examine a New World country. Japan deserves investigation as a latecomer to industrialization and as a nation with a culture very different from those of Western nations. Looking at Japan permits an examination of the first Asian nation to successfully modernize its economy.

I hope this study will prove valuable to several audiences. History students will, I think, find business history a major key to understanding the past; and comparative business history can be especially useful. Through comparative business history we can begin to uncover what has been universal and what has been specific to the development of business in different nations and cultures. Business students will also, I hope, find this sketch of the evolution of some aspects of world business valuable. Today's business scene is an international one, and to work effectively in it business people need to understand business practices beyond their nations' boundaries. Comparative business history can lend an international perspective to business developments.

Business errors resulting from uninformed views of foreign cultures and histories abound. In the mid-1960s the Japanese were purchasing lots of Western-style cakes from bakeries, because few Japanese stoves possessed ovens. Executives at General Mills thought that they had an ideal new product for the Japanese market, a Betty Crocker cake mix that could be baked in the electric rice cookers found in every Japanese household. However, the cake mix did not sell well and was soon withdrawn from the market. The most fundamental problem was cultural. Historically, the Japanese placed an almost religious value on the purity of clean, white rice. They did not want to risk the contamination of their rice by cake crumbs that might be left in their rice cookers. By the same token, a lack of knowledge of foreign cultures sometimes hindered the Japanese in opening up overseas markets. Even language could be a problem. When the Japanese tried to export a soft drink with the name Calpis, that name killed sales. Similar problems resulted from efforts to export a coffee creamer called Creap and a snack named Krap.

While world history, a discipline rapidly growing in importance, encompasses much more than business history, comparative business history can contribute significantly to the study of that field. Students of world history often ask somewhat different questions than those interested in business history; they frequently take a world systems approach to the examination of economic growth, an approach stressing the interplay between areas of greater or lesser industrial development across the globe. Business historians have not probed the relationships between rich and poor nations of the world as deeply. Nor does this book. Still, there are areas of mutual concern, especially for history students working in the modern period. In particular, comparative business history can help uncover similarities and differences in business practices around the world and can begin to speak to the impacts of these practices on world civilizations.

In a large sense, this book is a comparison of capitalistic evolution in four different nations. In capitalistic societies people produce and sell goods and services through privately owned businesses and means of production. They invest in factories and stores, hoping that their sales will generate profits for themselves. In capitalistic economies people interact through markets—most obviously through the markets in which business people sell their goods, but also in labor markets through which workers often arrange with management the terms of their employment. Capitalistic business systems reduced the roles of custom, royal decrees, and arbitrary decisions characteristic of earlier feudal business systems in determining how exchanges of goods, services, and labor would occur. Far from uniform or static, capitalism, this book shows, varied from nation to nation and from one time period to the next.

This book argues that similarities in the development of businesses in Great Britain, Germany, the United States, and Japan resulted mainly from certain economic and technological imperatives that all four nations shared. Thus, industrialization led to the rise of big businesses in some fields in all four nations. Conversely, this study also argues that many of the differences in the businesses of the four nations were the results of the different political, social, and cultural environments of the countries. Those differences—within a general capitalistic framework—could be marked. The big businesses that grew up with industrialization developed at different paces and assumed different forms in each nation. Moreover, smaller firms played different roles in different nations. No nation can escape its history, and national business forms

remain varied up to the present day, despite the development of an international economy.

The general organization of this book remains the same as in the first edition. Chapter 1 looks at the world of preindustrial business. Stable political frameworks allowed the growth of thriving commercial economies, those dominated by merchants, even before industrialization. However, when compared to what would come with industrialization, the pace of business was slow, and the output of business was low, permitting merchants to conduct business by time-honored, traditional methods. Industrialization, the topic of Chapter 2, changed this situation. As shown in Chapters 3, 4, and 5, industrialization accelerated the speed of doing business and increased the output of business firms, changes that led some executives to alter their ways of doing business. Yet, as these three chapters also illustrate, not everything changed in the business world of industrializing nations. Newly formed big businesses did not sweep away all the institutions and practices that stood before them, even in the United States. Chapter 6 examines alterations in the political environment of business in the years between the First World War and the Second World War and the impacts of those changes upon the nature of business. The final two chapters look at the development of business since the Second World War, a time of growing international trade, and assess whether businesses around the globe are becoming more and more similar or increasingly different.

Within the same general framework that existed in the first edition, the second edition contains important alterations. There has been an explosion of writing in comparative business history over the past decade, and the second edition incorporates the most recent scholarship in the field. Above all, this edition seeks to capture more fully the complexity and diversity of the business experiences of Great Britain, the United States, and Japan; and the second edition also provides limited coverage of the course of business evolution in Germany, a topic not dealt with in the first edition. Small firms, as well as their larger brethren, are examined in much more detail than in the first edition. Unlike the first edition, the second edition contains full coverage of the history of nonmanufacturing companies, that is, firms in the service and sales sectors of national economies. The second edition also speaks more clearly to the contributions of labor and government to business development. Then, too, the second edition focuses more sharply on differences

that distinguish business environments. The second edition looks at business developments more through non-American eyes, recognizing that there are many paths to business evolution and economic growth, no single one of which is correct. Extended coverage in the second edition of the years since World War II makes this point abundantly clear.

Finally, a note on my use of Japanese names. In the Japanese language, the names of people are presented with the family name first and the personal or given name last. To conform with the practice in the English language, I have reversed the order. In this study all Japanese names appear with the given name first and the family name last.

SUGGESTED READINGS

Specific suggested readings appear at the end of each chapter, mainly books and articles in English that should be available at university libraries. However, several particularly important studies deserve mention at the outset. Alfred D. Chandler, Jr., *Scale and Scope: The Dynamics of Industrial Capitalism* (Cambridge, Mass.: Harvard University Press, 1990), has stimulated tremendous interest in comparative business history through its examination of the development of industrial firms in Great Britain, the United States, and Germany. The many volumes of essays collected in *The International Conference on Business History* (the Fuji Conference), edited by various Japanese scholars (Tokyo: University of Tokyo Press, and Oxford: Oxford University Press, the mid-1970s to 1996), offer a solid introduction to major topics in comparative business history. Thomas McCraw, ed., *Creating Modern Capitalism* (Cambridge, Mass.: Harvard University Press, 1997), is a valuable collection of case studies.

Most comparative business histories look at the evolution of firms in developed economies. For an account that is truly global in scope, see Dennis P. McCarthy, *International Business History: A Contextual and Case Approach* (Westport, Conn.: Praeger, 1994). For an introduction to recent world history, see Carter Findley and John Rothney, *Twentieth-Century World*, 3rd ed. (Boston: Houghton Mifflin, 1994). An interesting introduction to some aspects of world-system thought is Immanuel Wallerstein, *Geopolitics and Geoculture* (Cambridge: Cambridge University Press, 1991).

National studies remain important as building blocks in comparative busi-

ness history. Leslie Hannah, *The Rise of the Corporate Economy*, 2nd ed. (Baltimore: Johns Hopkins University Press, 1984); Barry Supple, ed., *Essays in British Business History* (Oxford: Oxford University Press, 1977); Maurice Kirby and Mary Rose, eds., *Business Enterprise in Modern Britain* (London: Routledge, 1994); and John Wilson, *British Business History, 1720–1994* (Manchester: Manchester University Press, 1995), examine the development of business in Great Britain. Chandler, *The Visible Hand: The Managerial Revolution In American Business* (Cambridge, Mass.: Harvard University Press, 1977), is an excellent study of the rise of big business and the development of modern management in the United States. For a survey of the development of small business in America, see Mansel Blackford, *A History of Small Business in America* (New York: Twayne Publishers, 1991). Mansel Blackford and K. Austin Kerr, *Business Enterprise in American History*, 3rd ed. (Boston: Houghton Mifflin, 1994), provides an overview of American business history. Johannes Hirschmeier and Tsunihiko Yui, *The Development of Japanese Business, 1600–1981*, 2nd ed. (London: G. Allen & Unwin, 1981); and Mark Fruin, *The Japanese Enterprise System* (Oxford: Oxford University Press, 1992), are valuable surveys of Japanese business history.

1 [Preindustrial Business

Directions to clerks in the London merchant house of Herries & Company in 1766 instructed them to "put down in the address book where they lodge, and as often as they happen to change their lodgings, likewise where they generally eat, or are to be found in the evenings, lest in case of fire or any such accident their presence at the Counting House be found necessary, although at untimely hours." * As this directive suggests, the world of the preindustrial merchant—in whatever land—was a world of personal business. Merchants, their clerks, their competitors, and their customers were bound together by personal and kinship connections. At Herries & Company clerks had to make themselves available whenever needed.

Merchants like those at Herries & Company were the leading business people of preindustrial times. Through their control of foreign and domestic trade the merchants provided much of the direction for the economic growth of their nations and regions. In many ways, the preindustrial business world was vastly different from the business world of industrial and modern times. In the preindustrial era the pace of business activity was relatively slow, and the volume of goods produced and distributed was relatively low.

In this situation traditional business methods, based on ties of friendship and family, dominated the business scene. Such ties were needed to overcome the tremendous risks of doing business in preindustrial years. With communications generally slow and unreliable, merchants had to rely on connections of blood and friendship to do business, especially if they sought to conduct

---

* Jacob M. Price, "Directions for the Conduct of a Merchant's Counting House, 1766," *Business History* 28 (July 1986): 141.

trade beyond their localities. With market information spotty and uncertain, they had to rely on the judgment of friends and relatives beyond their local regions to make decisions on the buying and selling of goods.

Yet, the preindustrial economies of Great Britain, North America, and Japan were anything but stagnant. They were commercial economies whose expansion prepared the way for further economic changes during industrialization. Government policies and actions were important in this economic growth. Throughout the world, economic, political, and cultural changes have long been intertwined. Business has never, and does not today, exist in a vacuum. Rather, business has always been influenced, and has influenced, its external environment. Thus, the development of preindustrial business can best be understood by first examining the political and economic frameworks within which it grew up, frameworks favorable to business development.

THE POLITICAL FRAMEWORKS

Great Britain, North America, and Japan were all characterized by growing degrees of political unity and domestic tranquility in preindustrial times, and this situation stimulated economic growth and business development. While most advanced in Great Britain, political unification and centralization began in Japan and North America as well.

Great Britain: The King and Parliament

Great Britain has had a long existence as a unified nation ruled by one crowned monarch. Civil wars, however, shattered this political unity on several important occasions in preindustrial times. Most divisive was the English Revolution, a civil war in the mid-1600s. This major conflict had both religious and political origins, pitting the king against Parliament and the Anglican (the Church of England) against the Nonconformist (Puritan). The English Revolution was a long and bloody conflict that sorely divided Englishmen. The Restoration Settlement of 1689 finally ended the conflict and reunified England. Never again would England be divided by civil war. The Restoration Settlement had several major terms. First, at the invitation of Parliament, William, Prince of Orange and the leader of the military forces of the Dutch Republic, became King of England, and his wife, Mary, became the

queen. Thus, England acquired political unity under one set of monarchs. However, a Bill of Rights clearly subordinated monarchs to Parliament. The king now ruled "in Parliament." Second, the Toleration Act of 1689 began healing religious differences. Religious toleration, the right to hold one's own public services and so forth, was given to Nonconformists by this law.

Great Britain also began building an empire in the late 1600s and early 1700s. By an Act of Union in 1707 Scotland became part of Great Britain (England already controlled much of Ireland). England acquired the origins of an overseas empire as well. British control of this empire was either direct, as in the case of many of the North American colonies, or indirect, as in the control the British East India Company exercised over India.

North America: The British Colonies

In North America, too, there existed some political unity, though not true national unity. The British colonies possessed the unity that derived from their membership in the expanding British Empire. Only later, with the American Revolution of 1776 and the adoption of the United States Constitution in 1789, would real national political unity be achieved.

British merchants and investors established some of the most important colonies as profit-making enterprises. However, because of unexpected problems the colonies faced (none made a profit initially) and because of a desire by the British government to increase its power, most colonies had become royal colonies with governors directly responsible to the king and Parliament by the late 1600s and early 1700s. Or, they were proprietary colonies in which the English crown gave large grants of land in North America to various Englishmen in return for their friendships or favors. Of whatever type, the colonies were integrated into the British Empire.

The most important political mechanism unifying the British Empire was the Navigation Acts, pieces of legislation passed by Parliament in the mid-1600s. The goal of the acts was to regulate trade—indeed, the entire economy—of the British Empire. The major terms of the Navigation Acts, which applied to all of the empire, not simply North America, were fourfold. First, most trade between England and its colonies had to be carried in English or colonial ships manned by English or colonial crews. Second, most goods going to the colonies had to pass through England, even if they originated

elsewhere. Third, many goods exported from the colonies had to pass through England, even if bound somewhere else. Finally, many forms of manufacturing were restricted in the colonies, for the colonies were supposed to act as sources of raw materials for British industry and as markets for English manufactured goods. The object of the acts was to build up the economic and military might of the British Empire, at the expense of its rivals, France and Spain.

Japan: Unification under Ieyasu Tokugawa

Like Great Britain, Japan has long existed as an independent nation. The Japanese traditionally date the origin of their nation to 660 B.C., with the accession of their first emperor Jimmu, reputedly the great-grandson of the Sun Goddess. By the third century A.D. the Chinese, who received tribute-missions from Japan, reported that the Empress Pimiko was unifying Japan from her base in Kyushu. By the sixth and seventh centuries much of Japan was unified under one emperor, who ruled as both the religious and political leader of the nation. Yet, as in Great Britain, this was a fragile unity. Different families or houses struggled against each other for control of Japan, and in doing so reduced the real power of the emperor, so that the emperor ruled in name only. After 1185 the real power rested with the leader of the most powerful military family, who became known as the shogun. Civil strife, common from the fourteenth century, reached an extreme during the Sengoku period, the years 1468 through 1573.

It was from this conflict between warring noble houses that Japan began to emerge as a unified nation. Three Japanese leaders in succession contributed to this process of unification. Oda Nobunaga began as the ruler of Owari, seized Kyoto in 1568, and took Osaka in 1580, only to be assassinated in 1582. Hideyoshi Toyotomi began as Nobunaga's ablest general, went on to win the submission of all of Japan by 1590, and died in 1597. Most important was Ieyasu Tokugawa. Tokugawa had been Toyotomi's major vassal in eastern Japan and had installed himself in a castle in Edo (later renamed Tokyo) in 1590. In a climactic battle he defeated his rivals in 1600. Tokugawa assumed the title of shogun in 1603, and the years 1603 through 1868 are called the Tokugawa period: a time of relative unity and peace in Japan. In theory, the shogun was the military ruler of Japan, acting on behalf of the divine em-

peror, who lived in Kyoto. In practice, the emperor remained a figurehead with little political power.

The type of government established by Tokugawa is termed the *baku-han* system. Under this system the Tokugawa family ruled all of Japan. All of the local lords, called daimyo, owed allegiance to the Tokugawa family. The daimyo, in turn, ruled their provinces, called *han* (or domains). There were about 260 domains. Both the Tokugawa family, which owned outright about one-quarter of Japan, and the daimyo depended upon a rice tax amounting to about 40 percent of the crop for most of their income. To gather the rice and administer their lands the Tokugawas and the daimyo relied on their former warriors, called samurai, now turned into administrators.

Throughout the Tokugawa period, there existed a tension between the centralizing tendencies of the ruling Tokugawa family based in Edo and the decentralizing tendencies of the many daimyo striving to protect their autonomy in their domains. Many of the stronger daimyo were able to maintain a high degree of independence from the shogun, and much of the political and military power of the nation continued to reside in the daimyo. Each daimyo maintained his own local government, his own army, and sometimes his own currency. Domain governments often promoted economic development in agriculture, crafts, and early-day industry. The Saga domain in southern Japan pioneered in the development of modern iron-smelting, used in making guns for the defense of Nagasaki, by introducing the reverberatory furnace to Japan. Centralization of government, while under way in the Tokugawa period, progressed slowly and was far from complete.

The *baku-han* was a personal form of government, based on bonds of allegiance and controls imposed on the personal behaviors of the daimyo more than upon institutions. The daimyo were required to take personal oaths of allegiance to the shogun and had to spend every other year living in Edo, where the shogun maintained his court and could watch over them. When the daimyo were absent from Edo, they had to leave family members as hostages. Only in the late Tokugawa period did a national government begin developing, as the shogun took responsibility for expanding regional coordination of flood control, putting down peasant revolts, and resolving regional disputes.

Unlike the situation in England or the North American colonies, Tokugawa

Japan did not favor foreign trade. Japan had long had a flourishing trade with the Asian mainland and, from 1543, a growing trade with the West. However, worried about outside political interference in Japan, the Tokugawa government ended Portuguese trade by 1640. Combined with an earlier expulsion of the Spanish and a withdrawal of British traders, trade declined dramatically. Nagasaki was the only major port open to foreign trade (conducted with the Chinese and the Dutch) for two hundred years.

Political Unity and Regionalism

By the late 1600s and early 1700s preindustrial Great Britain, North America, and Japan were either themselves becoming unified political bodies or, as in the case of the North American colonies, parts of such a body, characterized by domestic tranquility. The growing political unity of the three areas had important economic consequences, for it provided a stable framework upon which economic growth and business development could be based. Yet, there were differences in the degree of unity: political unity was most pronounced in Great Britain. In America, and especially in Japan, local regions maintained considerable freedom from control by the central government, with attendant economic results.

THE ECONOMIC SETTING

One major point stands out about the preindustrial economies of Great Britain, North America, and Japan: they were commercial rather than subsistence economies. That is, people lived to a significant degree by buying and selling goods in markets, not by simply consuming what they grew or made. Only on the farthest frontiers, such as the Kentucky country in America in the 1750s and 1760s, were subsistence economies dominant—and then only until political and transportation developments allowed localities to be linked into larger regions.

Several elements characterized these commercial economies. First, agriculture was becoming market-oriented. Second, both domestic and (except in Japan) foreign trade was growing. Third, this trade both resulted from and stimulated regional specialization. Fourth, urbanization, the growth of cities, was proceeding. These four characteristics were related to the development

of political unity, for political unity and stability stimulated the spread of the commercial economies.

Commercial Agriculture and Regional Specialization

Agriculture was becoming increasingly commercialized in all three areas. No longer did farmers simply raise food for their own consumption. They sold significant portions of their crops in markets, and they were able to raise larger crops for their markets because of increases in land and labor productivity.

Some forms of commercial farming — raising sheep for wool, with the wool being used in trade with continental Europe, for example — had existed in England from the Middle Ages. By the late 1600s and early 1700s wheat and livestock were being raised for consumption in Great Britain's expanding cities. Improvements in agricultural techniques — continued drainage of swamps, increasing crop rotation, the use of manure for fertilizer, land enclosures that made land parcels larger and easier to farm, and the introduction of mechanical devices such as seed drills — increased the agricultural output of Great Britain fivefold between 1400 and 1700.

In the North American colonies the story was similar. The use of horses and improvements in agricultural implements boosted output. As in Great Britain, much of this growing output found urban markets — either in colonial cities and towns, such as Philadelphia, New York, and Boston, or abroad, with 10 to 20 percent of all of the crops grown in the colonies finding overseas markets.

Japanese agriculture also became more and more market-oriented. The daimyo needed funds to cover their many expenses, especially their attendance on the shogun in Edo, and they sold the rice collected in their rice taxes through merchants in Osaka. Related to this point, the growth of cities as consumption centers stimulated the commercialization of agriculture. As in Great Britain and North America, productivity increases allowed agricultural development to proceed in Japan. Particularly important were the development of new strains of rice seeds, which allowed multiple plantings of rice each year in many areas, the spread of new farm implements, the use of night soil, plants, and fish cakes as fertilizers, improvements in irrigation and flood control techniques, and the development of better ways to plant rice.

In Great Britain and North America agriculture developed along the lines

of regional specialization, as would industry at a somewhat later date. In England regional specialization was noticeable in agriculture as early as the years 1450 through 1650. Grain grown in Kent or East Anglia found markets in London, while cattle raised in the North and West were driven to fattening areas in the Midlands and South. This trend became more pronounced over the next century, 1650 through 1750. The West Country became famous for apples and pears, Kent for apples and cherries, Lancashire for potatoes, and the area around London for vegetables. Colonial American farmers also engaged in regional specialization. The southern colonies grew rice and indigo (a plant from which blue dye was made), the Chesapeake areas of Virginia grew tobacco, the middle colonies like Pennsylvania grew wheat, and New England specialized in fishing, shipbuilding, and producing naval stores.

Regional specialization also occurred in Japan. Rice was the main crop grown throughout much of the country. However, from the mid- to late 1600s peasants also grew mulberry bushes (whose leaves were food for silkworms), tea, lacquer trees, paper mulberry bushes, along with hemp, safflower, and indigo plants—according to the part of Japan in which they lived.

As regional specialization occurred, each nation's economy became more efficient and productive, and standards of living rose. Accompanying the commercialization and regional specialization of farming was the growing employment of farmers in nonagricultural tasks. For instance, Japanese peasants increasingly earned a considerable proportion of their income from making handicraft products, the forerunner of some forms of later industrialization, such as the weaving of tatami mats. In some areas small village enterprises with five to twenty employees were common in the sugar, salt, oil, silk reeling and weaving, and cotton textile industries.

Trade

An increase in trade accompanied regional specialization. Trade permitted regional specialization and was, in turn, stimulated by it. Great Britain, North America, and Japan were all fortunate in being able to carry on trade via coastal shipping, for until the coming of canals and railroads inland transportation was very expensive (and in Japan was always constrained by mountainous topography).

Britain's domestic commerce and foreign trade increased as time passed. Between 1720 and 1749 some 130 turnpike companies were established to build new roads, spurring the inland transportation of goods. Harbor improvements invigorated the coastal trade, which grew in volume and diversity. Foreign trade went beyond Europe, as English merchants joined in a general expansion of European trade with other parts of the world. As Great Britain's trade became oriented away from Europe, the commodities making up the trade changed. Raw wool declined in significance. Exports of manufactured goods — metal products, cotton textiles, and woolen textiles — to the colonies rose in importance, as did imports of raw materials from the colonies.

In the North American colonies internal trade was less important than in Great Britain, largely because of the poor state of inland transportation facilities. Even in the late colonial period there was four times as much trade between England and the American colonies as there was trade among the colonies themselves. Trade went overseas. In the 1760s Great Britain took 55 percent of all the exports of the North American colonies, and the British West Indies (British islands in the Caribbean) took another 27 percent. In return, Great Britain supplied the colonies with 80 percent of their imports. This situation was just as the framers of the Navigation Acts had intended.

In Japan, by way of contrast, foreign trade was not very important after the early 1600s. More important was an increase in trade across domain boundaries, commerce facilitated by internal transportation improvements. Trade in rice, silk, and cotton developed, along with some commerce in sugar, indigo, and specialty fruits and vegetables, stimulated by the growth of consumption centers in Edo, Osaka, Kyoto, and domain castle towns. Throughout the Tokugawa period efforts were made to improve short-distance inland waterways, and from the mid-1600s coastal shipping routes around Honshu were greatly improved. A national road system converging on Edo was established. Most importantly, the Tokaido Road connecting Kyoto to Edo was improved; by the early 1800s private messenger companies provided two-day service for letters and documents carried over the 300-mile-long route. In addition, local roads were improved substantially in many areas. However, political considerations prevented the full economic integration of Japan in the Tokugawa period. Fearing the development of rival political power bases by leading daimyo, the shogun did not press for the complete development

Totsuka, one of the fifty-three way stations on the Tokaido Road linking Kyoto to Edo, as depicted by Hiroshige Ado (1797–1858) in a wood-block print. The Tokaido Road improved internal transportation in Tokugawa Japan. (Author's collection)

of internal commerce. Wheeled vehicles were not allowed for commoners in Japan, and as late as the 1860s road inspection stations and guardhouses impeded the flow of trade between the domains on national highways.

The Growth of Cities

Urbanization characterized all three preindustrial economies. Cities and towns grew in importance, though their significance varied by nation and region. In terms of economic growth, the towns and cities were important as markets for agricultural goods, thus stimulating the commercialization of agriculture and the expansion of trade. Cities also became the locus for some early industry.

In Great Britain London was *the* city: the seat of government, the residence of the court, the head of England's overseas empire, the financial center, the location of much industry, and a social resort during the winter season.

London's one million inhabitants, 11 percent of England's total population, in 1801 made it a world-class city. However, as the 1700s progressed, the growth of regional market and manufacturing cities challenged London's supremacy; between 1750 and 1800 fourteen cities with a population of 10,000 or more doubled in population. By 1801 Manchester had 90,000 inhabitants and Liverpool 83,000. Great Britain as a whole was becoming more urbanized. People living in towns and cities of 2,500 or more made up 19 percent of the nation's population in 1700, and 30 percent one hundred years later. By 1801 Great Britain possessed sixteen cities with a population over 20,000, thirty-three with a population of 10,000 to 20,000, forty-five with a population of 5,000 to 10,000, and ninety-four with a population of 2,500 to 5,000.

If urban areas were important for Great Britain's economic growth, so were smaller villages and towns, especially as centers of early-day industry. Close to supplies of water and raw materials, small towns were, in fact, the backbone of nascent industrialization in that nation. Typical was Burslem in north Staffordshire, an area soon to be known as the Potteries. Already in 1730 two-thirds of the wage-earners in Burslem, which had a population of about 1,000, made their living in nonagricultural pursuits. Pottery production was most important, with about sixty small workshops, each employing a dozen or fewer men and children. In the shops master craftsmen and their assistants turned out butter-pots, pitchers, and mugs made of clays available locally. From these beginnings, Burslem would emerge as a larger industrial center in the later 1700s and 1800s, and the home for pottery made by Josiah Wedgewood.

Japan was also a land of towns and cities, as well as countryside. There were three major cities in Tokugawa Japan. Edo, the new political capital, became a city of one million in the early 1700s, and was a major consumption center. By this time Kyoto and Osaka had about 300,000 people apiece. They, too, were consumption centers. They also were centers for some of Japan's early handicraft industry. Kyoto's Nishijin area had about 7,000 of Japan's finest textile looms, each requiring two operators. Altogether some 100,000 people—spinners and dyers, as well as weavers—were involved in textile production in the city. There were, as well, about forty substantial port towns lining Japan's coastline. In the domains, castle towns of the daimyo served as political and economic administration centers and in time became consumption centers like Edo on a smaller scale. About 200 castle towns dotted the landscape of Tokugawa Japan, some thirty to forty of which had populations of 10,000 or

more. In 1707, for example, Okayama in southern Honshu possessed 38,000 inhabitants including 10,000 samurai. As a result of this urbanization, about 22 percent of the Japanese lived in towns or cities of 3,000 or more by 1750.

Even so, by the mid- to late Tokugawa years the castle towns and other urban centers were losing ground to smaller villages as the locus of much of Japan's economic activity. In fact, in the regions where economic development was most rapid, the large centers, primarily castle towns, lost population—contrary to what was occurring in Great Britain and America. A desire to avoid taxation and regulations easily imposed in urban centers combined with a quest for raw materials, water power, and cheap labor, led handicraft manufacturers to spring up in the countryside. For example, the Izumi district near Osaka developed into a center for the production of cotton cloth. In 1843 nearly half of the households (127 of 277) of Uda-otsu, one of the towns in Izumi, were engaged in weaving, with only 14 percent still working in agriculture.

Colonial America was less urbanized than Great Britain or Japan. In 1742 about 5.4 percent of the population lived in urban centers. Boston had 16,000 people, Philadelphia, 13,000, New York, 11,000, Charleston, 6,800, and Newport, 6,200. By 1820 the United States possessed one city with a population over 100,000, two in the 50,000 to 100,000 range, two in the 25,000 to 50,000 range, eight in the 10,000 to 25,000 range, twenty-two in the 5,000 to 10,000 range, and twenty-six in the 2,500 to 5,000 range. At that time about 7 percent of all Americans lived in towns or cities of 2,500 or more people.

Much early trade and economic specialization in America involved cities and the areas surrounding cities. The evolving relationship between Philadelphia and the area within about fifty miles suggests the importance of such connections. As canals and, to a lesser extent, roads linked Philadelphia to nearby regions, the city became less reliant on trade overseas and commerce with distant American cities for its growth and more dependent on trade with nearby areas. Hinterland exports to Philadelphia tripled between the late 1810s and 1830. As trade back and forth between Philadelphia and nearby localities exploded, economic specialization occurred. Rural residents gave up handicraft manufacturing to people in Philadelphia, who worked in small shops or in early-day factories. More and more residents purchased industrial goods from Philadelphia with money earned in selling an increasingly varied range of specialized nonindustrial products—coal, iron, and many

agricultural goods (not simply their earlier major product, wheat)—to Philadelphians. By the mid-1830s an integrated, growing regional economy had enveloped Philadelphia and its surrounding area.

Politics, Economics, and Society

Preindustrial Great Britain, North America, and Japan developed commercial economies within regional and national political frameworks. A major indication of the viability of their economies was that each supported increasing populations at rising standards of living. Great Britain's population rose from 2.1 million in 1430 to 3.8 million in 1603, to 6.9 million in 1700, to 7.8 million in 1760. Between 1700 and 1760 Britain's income per capita rose from 6.7 to 9.4 pounds. By 1776 the thirteen colonies that later comprised the United States had a population of about 2.5 million, including 500,000 blacks and 100,000 Native Americans. By this time the standard of living of the white colonists probably surpassed those of Englishmen, with their annual per capita income coming to about 13 British pounds. Precisely comparable income figures are not available for Japan, but that nation's population rose from roughly 18 million in the early 1600s to about 30 million a century later, at which level it remained into the mid-1800s, probably due to the widespread adoption of population controls, including infanticide, as well as the catastrophic effect of three major famines.

A rough estimate of per capita income, expressed in 1965 American dollars, in various nations at the onset of industrialization is: Great Britain, $227 (1765–85); the United States, $474 (1834–43); Germany, $302 (1850–59); France, $242 (1831–40); and Japan, $136 (1886).

Moreover, these people were commercially oriented and well educated by the standards of their days. In Japan nearly 50 percent of the men and 15 percent of the women received some type of education in literacy, mainly in Buddhist temple schools. Most samurai and almost all merchants were literate. Literacy improved in America throughout the eighteenth century; by the time of the American Revolution, a majority of Americans could read and write. In Great Britain perhaps 50 percent of the men and about 25 percent of the women were literate in 1780, at least to the extent of being able to sign their names.

THE MERCHANT

The preindustrial period was, in business terms, the age of the merchant. Merchants were the business leaders in preindustrial Great Britain, North America, and Japan—and for good reason: their control over trade was the linchpin holding together the economies of their nations and regions. Moreover, as later chapters of this book show, it was merchants who often built up and dominated much of early industry.

British Merchants

Great Britain has often been labeled "a nation of shopkeepers," but the country could just as aptly be called a nation of merchants. It was merchants who, as much as explorers and the military, built the British Empire, and it was merchants who were most important in developing Great Britain's domestic economy. These merchants operated in a variety of ways: as members of joint-stock companies, as partners, and as single-owner proprietors.

Much of the expansion of Great Britain's overseas trade between 1550 and 1650 resulted from the actions of newly formed joint-stock companies. In chartered joint-stock companies the king as the head of state granted a charter to a group of merchants to engage in trade in a certain commodity or region. The charter often granted the company of merchants monopoly privileges in order to attract merchants into risky ventures. As investors, the merchants bought shares in the joint-stock companies and expected to earn dividends on their shares. London merchants were the most important investors, and London was the center of England's overseas trade. Elected directors and a governor ran each company. Joint-stock companies permitted the pooling of capital for risky ventures and served the twin goals of expanding English power and increasing private profits. The most important were the Muscovy Company (1555), the Eastland Company (1579), the Africa Company (1588), the Levant Company (1592), the East India Company (1600), and the Virginia Company (1606).

The Muscovy Company was typical of these joint-stock companies. After financing several profitable voyages to Russia in the early 1550s, London merchants set up the Muscovy Company in 1555. Shares in the company cost 25 pounds originally, and then 200 pounds from 1564 on. Sebastian Cabot,

a well-known explorer, served as the governor of the company, and 28 of the 200 to 240 investors worked as his assistants in running the company's affairs. The Muscovy Company received monopoly rights to trade with Russia from the British government, and for some years the Russian government permitted the company to handle all of its foreign trade with Europe. The company exported tallow, furs, felt, cordage, ships' masts, and hemp from Russia and imported various English products into Russia. The company also opened a profitable trade with Persia in the late 1500s. In later years, however, problems—competition with the Dutch, the loss of the trade with Persia, and difficulties in controlling company representatives in Russia—mounted, and the Muscovy Company disbanded in 1620.

While first set up to develop foreign trade, joint-stock companies soon engaged in a wide variety of enterprises. Between 1660 and 1719 fifty-four major joint-stock companies received charters—twenty-three in mining and manufacturing, eleven in overseas trade, and twenty in banking, insurance, fishing, and other fields of endeavor. However, many of these later companies were fraudulent, set up by their organizers simply to fleece investors of their money. Finally, in 1720, fraud in the sale of stock in the South Sea Company led Parliament to pass the Bubble Act, legislation that placed severe restrictions upon the formation and operations of joint-stock companies. Already in decline, they became unimportant in the British economy. The demise of joint-stock companies did not retard Great Britain's economic development, for merchants found other ways to raise the funds they needed and were sometimes able to protect themselves from personal liability for their debts through a variety of legal stratagems.

Many British merchants operated in partnership agreements, typically based on family ties; and, as markets expanded, many of these merchants specialized in the goods they handled and the services they offered. In contrast to Colonial American merchants, who usually handled a wide variety of goods, the British merchants were more apt to deal in only a handful of products.

The experiences of the Perrys of London illustrate well how British partnerships operated. From 1690 through about 1720 the family firm—known first as Perry & Lane, later as Micajah Perry & Co.—was the leading importer of tobacco from the Chesapeake area of America to Great Britain. Micaiah Perry, founder of the merchant house, came from a family long interested in trade in the New World (he was himself born in New Haven in 1641, before mov-

ing to England at the age of ten), as well as in Great Britain. After receiving training at a leading merchant guild in London, Micaiah Perry began trading in a partnership with Thomas Lane, an arrangement that lasted until Lane's death in 1710 (like Perry, Lane had family connections in British America).

Beginning a limited trade in tobacco in the 1670s, Perry & Lane became the leading importer of the Chesapeake product to London by the late 1690s, a position it maintained into the 1720s. By the time of Micaiah Perry's death in 1721, the firm was probably the largest private importer of tobacco in the world. In part, this success came through the firm's willingness to use a wide variety of methods to trade with all types of tobacco growers in the Chesapeake—from engaging in direct buying from very small growers to taking the output of large planters such as Robert "King" Carter on a consignment basis. This flexibility in buying methods served the firm well. So did flexibility in its shipping operations. Perry & Lane usually sent its tobacco to England in ships carrying the tobacco of other merchants as well; thus, the firm did not have to wait to fill an entire ship before sending tobacco to London. In part, success also came from being at the right place at the right time: demand for tobacco boomed in Europe in the mid- to late 1600s, with tobacco imports to Great Britain rising from 350,000 pounds per year in the early 1630s to 28 million pounds annually by the late 1680s.

Upon Micaiah's death, control of the firm passed to his grandson (his son had died), Micajah Perry, then twenty-six years old. Trained as a clerk in a Philadelphia merchant house, Micajah proved unable to compete with incursions of Scottish merchants into the Chesapeake tobacco trade. Under Micajah's leadership, the firm declined. Dealing more and more just with leading planters, the merchant house suffered from the growing debt problems of the planters. In addition, Micajah came to prefer sending tobacco to London in his own ships, which proved an expensive mistake, since the ships often sailed half-empty. Moreover, a decline of tobacco prices from 1725 bit into the firm's profits. Noneconomic factors hurt the firm as well: Micajah diluted his energies by embarking on political careers. By the early 1730s the Perry house had slipped to fourth place as a London importer of tobacco, and two decades later Micajah died in poverty.

An inability to adjust to changed market conditions was hardly unique to the Perry firm. Of the 177 firms or individuals importing tobacco into London in 1719 only eleven remained active in 1747. Ups and downs in economic

standing characterized businesses in both the preindustrial and industrial eras. Risk was always present.

Important though it was, overseas trade was less vital than domestic commerce in the British economy. Domestic commerce was roughly three times greater in value than foreign trade by 1700. Domestic commerce was run not by joint-stock companies but by merchants operating on their own as single-owner proprietors or by merchants linked together as partners. These merchants were sedentary merchants who lived in cities, where they had their offices called countinghouses, the places where they kept their accounts. Some of the British merchants were general merchants engaged in all types of trade.

However, as their markets became larger and better integrated through transportation and financial improvements, more British merchants could specialize in a manner similar to the Perrys. Merchants in Leeds, for instance, became famous for handling the cloth trade, building White Cloth Hall in 1755 to move their market indoors. It was in London, the largest city, that mercantile specialization went farthest. About two-thirds to three-quarters of Great Britain's foreign trade passed through London in the early to mid-1700s, and this volume of trade allowed merchants to specialize by commodity and type of trade.

Many London merchants even left trade to specialize in providing services. Some went into banking; marine insurance grew up around Lloyd's coffeehouse; and stockbrokers, who also first met in a coffeehouse, later set up business in the London Stock Exchange in 1802. By the 1770s a London money market was developing, along with a group of specialist bill brokers. Here may be seen the origins of what became known as the City of London—an area of banks, insurance companies, and other businesses providing financial services located within the heart of London. Serving primarily firms involved in overseas trade, the City would develop somewhat independently of British industry, and in the twentieth century would, in fact, be accused by some of not providing enough financing for their own country's manufacturers.

To handle their growing volume of business, English merchants refined business techniques first developed by Italian merchants in the Middle Ages. While some merchants continued to rely upon single-entry bookkeeping, an increasing number used double-entry, in which every transaction is recorded twice, in one place as a debit, in another as a credit. By periodically balancing

their accounts, merchants could determine their financial situation. Merchants also used bills of exchange, written agreements between the buyers and sellers of goods, as financial instruments by which they could handle transactions with each other. The seller drafted a bill for the goods telling when and how the goods would be paid for and sent the bill to the purchaser. The purchaser, in turn, wrote on the bill that he accepted its terms, thus endorsing it. If endorsed by a reputable merchant, a bill of exchange might pass as currency through the hands of many different people before being redeemed and paid off. Promissory notes, written promises to pay a sum of money at a fixed time to a certain individual, were similar. Samples, as in wheat and woolen goods, helped rationalize trade by allowing merchants to know ahead of time the exact nature of goods they would receive in trade. All of these methods were important, not just in England but in the New World as well, and they have remained important to the present day.

English merchants did not have social status fully commensurate to their economic importance. Because of their feudal past, which associated power and prestige with the ownership of land, Englishmen held landed nobles and country squires in higher esteem than merchants, an attitude that carried over into politics. Landed wealth controlled Parliament until well into the nineteenth century, while trade and manufacturing were underrepresented. However, too much can be made of the division between land and trade, for the line blurred as the 1700s progressed. The landed gentry engaged in commercial activity, mining coal and iron on many of the great estates, and cutting forests for charcoal for use as a fuel. Moreover, merchants could mingle with some of the gentry by buying land and country homes. It was a reasonably fluid situation, with a fair amount of intermarriage between the different groups. Only at the very top of British society did strict social divisions remain intact.

Colonial American Merchants

As in England, the merchant was the most important business leader in the North American colonies. The economies of the colonies were closely linked to those of Great Britain and Europe. The Atlantic Ocean acted as a bridge linking the Old World to the New World in a trans-Atlantic economy, and the

colonial merchants, together with their British counterparts, held this trans-Atlantic economy together.

The Colonial American merchants were similar to English merchants in important ways. Most of the wealthiest merchants were sedentary merchants living in urban centers where they had their countinghouses. Most operated by themselves or more commonly as partners with each other. Joint-stock companies were not important in trade, though some did exist in other fields. Like their British counterparts, American merchants used bills of exchange, promissory notes, some double-entry bookkeeping (though most Colonial American merchants got by with single-entry bookkeeping), and samples in their work.

There was, however, a major difference between British and Colonial American merchants. Colonial American, more than British, merchants were general merchants, not specialists. Colonial American merchants handled many different types of goods and took part in a wide range of commercial activities. Despite the growth of a commercial economy in North America, markets were still too small and too fragmented to allow much in the way of mercantile specialization. Only in the late 1700s and early 1800s, and even then only in the largest cities, did American merchants begin to specialize. In Philadelphia, for example, the most important merchants became increasingly specialized from the 1750s.

Most Colonial American merchants worked both as exporters and importers. In selling products in the colonies they acted as wholesalers and retailers: they imported goods from abroad and either resold them to smaller country merchants and peddlers or sold them directly to consumers through their own city stores. Colonial American merchants also engaged in many other business activities: owning ships (often as partners), loaning money to each other (Robert Morris, a Philadelphia merchant, started America's first bank in 1781), marine insurance (the merchant Thomas Willing formed America's first insurance company in 1757), real estate speculation, and, as in England, investing in mining and manufacturing.

Aaron Lopez was one such general merchant. He came to the colonies in the early 1750s to escape the persecution of Jews then occurring in Portugal, settling in Newport, Rhode Island, where other family members were well established. From the outset, ties of family and friendship helped Lopez get

ahead and allowed him to reduce his business risks. Using capital borrowed from other Jewish families, he sold soap to New York merchants and candles to Philadelphians; and he soon reached out by dealing in pewter, indigo, sugar, and tea. In the 1760s and 1770s Lopez added rum, textiles, naval stores, hardware, slaves, and many other goods to his list of exports and imports. As more of his trade went to England and the West Indies, rather than to Colonial America, Lopez came to rely on foreign agents, often family members, whom he sent abroad. While this approach to business—a trust in friends and family to overcome poor communications—usually worked well, it occasionally backfired. In 1767 Lopez sent his son-in-law to handle business in Jamaica, only to recall the man, who proved incompetent, two years later.

Nonetheless, most of Lopez's ventures prospered, leading him to diversify further his interests. His trading establishment at Newport came to include his privately owned wharf, a large warehouse, a retail store, and his business offices. Lopez owned thirty ships, either by himself or as a partner with other merchants, and controlled a large whaling fleet. He entered early forms of manufacturing—candlemaking, rum distilling, and shoemaking. By the time of his death in 1782 he was one of the leading business people in America, a veritable merchant prince.

Colonial American merchants were among the most important social and political leaders of their day, in sharp contrast to the lower status of British merchants. Most colonists held the large sedentary merchants in high esteem and deferred to them as the natural leaders of society. Several factors accounted for the high social status of Colonial American merchants. America did not have a feudal tradition emphasizing landed wealth. Moreover, Puritanism, and more generally Protestantism, placed a high value upon hard work and, within reason, the acquisition of wealth. Many colonists viewed material success on earth as a sign of God's favor, an indication that a person was destined for heaven rather than hell in the afterlife. Finally, most colonists viewed the wilderness condition of the American continent as an obstacle to be conquered in wrenching a living from the earth, and so they looked upon business activities and farming favorably, because they viewed them as tools by which nature might be subdued.

Building upon the high esteem in which they were held, leading Colonial American merchants sought to set themselves apart as a social elite by wearing expensive, stylish clothing, living in luxurious homes, having their por-

traits painted by European artists, and wearing swords as a mark of gentility. Their high social status often involved them in politics, for farmers and artisans (skilled workers) looked to them for leadership. Merchants were active in town and city politics as members of boards of selectmen (city councils), colonial assemblies (legislatures), and advisory bodies to colonial governors.

The Tokugawa Merchant

Like Great Britain and North America, Japan possessed a commercial economy before industrialization; and, once again, it was largely merchants who knit this economy together. Tokugawa Japan had a wide variety of merchants: peddlers, rural merchants serving local trade, and big city merchant-financiers in Kyoto, Edo, and Osaka handling interregional commerce.

Osaka had long been one of Japan's leading commercial centers, but in the Tokugawa period it emerged as the undisputed center of wholesale trades in the nation. By 1715 there were 5,655 wholesale merchants in Osaka. The daimyo sent rice collected as taxes for sale in Osaka and then for shipment to consumption centers like Edo. As trade routes became better established, the Osaka merchants began handling a wider variety of goods—salt, cotton, and tea. With large, ever-better connected markets, the Osaka merchants were able to specialize. Merchants who had originally dealt in many different products at wholesale and retail concentrated on the wholesale trade in only one product. While specializing, the Osaka merchants also loaned money to the daimyo, first as advances on rice sales but soon as long-term loans. In conducting their businesses, the Osaka merchants were similar to their English and Colonial American counterparts in that they used bills of exchange and samples. Few, however, employed double-entry bookkeeping.

Even more than in Great Britain or Colonial America, business was organized around merchant houses in Japan. Japanese merchant houses were more than simply business arrangements. They were also kinship matters. Merchant houses included people related by family ties: the househead and his wife, the elder son and his wife, and any younger unmarried sons and daughters. Sons might also be adopted into the merchant house. Those working in the merchant house progressed up a ladder of promotions from apprentice to clerk. As merchant houses developed, the more successful ones came to consist of a main house in Osaka and branch houses throughout

Japan, all woven together by personal family ties. As in the West, the personal ties helped reduce risks in doing business—blood relatives and close friends could be trusted, a necessity in a time of slow communications. Reinforcing the family nature of the merchant houses were their rules and constitutions, which were commonly written down in the 1700s. These gave the houses an identity and sense of historical continuity beyond that of their individual members.

Today one of Japan's leading companies, Mitsui, began as a merchant house in the Tokugawa period. Sokubei Mitsui, a samurai uprooted by the conflicts of the late 1500s and early 1600s, renounced his family's samurai status in 1616 to become a merchant and the founder of the House of Mitsui. Moving to Matsusaka, a town to the east of Kyoto, he and his family entered the brewing and money-lending businesses.

Expansion began when Sokubei's eldest son moved to Edo to open a clothing store called Echigoya. Hachirobei, Sokubei's third son, also moved to Edo with his own six sons in the early 1670s and provided the impetus needed to turn the clothing business into a success. He did so by emphasizing a rapid turnover on his stock, for which he allowed only cash payments, a new concept in Japan. Hachirobei also broke new ground in his insistence upon selling at fixed prices and his willingness to sell in small quantities. The Echigoya store, located where today's main Mitsukoshi Department Store stands in Tokyo, soon became the most fashionable and successful clothing store in Edo. Beginning his company's long-standing ties with the government, Hachirobei became a supplier of cloth to the shogun in 1687. He also soon opened prosperous shops in Kyoto and Osaka.

From these mercantile origins, Hachirobei took the Mitsuis into the business of money exchanging with the establishment of an exchange brokerage in Edo in 1683 and with similar exchanges in Kyoto and Osaka within another eight years. By 1691 the House of Mitsui had also become an official money exchanger to the Tokugawa government's treasury.

His successors built upon Hachirobei's foundations to expand Mitsui's operations. By 1740 the House of Mitsui had a well-developed structure. Members of the main, or headquarters, house, the eldest son's establishment, held regular meetings to set company policies and to distribute operating funds and capital to the branch houses and stores. The eleven branch houses, in turn, made regular payments to the headquarters house. An elaborate

Mitsui Dry Goods Store, Tokyo, forerunner of the Mitsukoshi Department Store, as shown in a wood-block print from the late 1800s. (Courtesy of Mitsukoshi, Ltd.)

fifteen-step hierarchy of advancement from beginning apprentice to the highest levels of management provided a road to the top for members of the House of Mitsui. Promotion to the sixth rank depended on seniority, but beyond that level personal performance became important. Apprentices, who started at age twelve, had to sever all ties with the outside world and were brought up according to the rules of the house.

Diversified in its business interests and fortunate in possessing shrewd managers, Mitsui prospered. The government recognized Mitsui's success by allowing the company to establish a shop in Yokohama to trade with Western merchants in 1859, and, as we shall see in a later chapter, the House of Mitsui successfully weathered the opening of Japan to the West and made the transition from preindustrial to industrial times.

Yet, despite their business successes, the Mitsuis, once they had relinquished their samurai status, dropped in social esteem. Even more than was the case in Great Britain, merchants failed to participate fully in politics

and society in Tokugawa Japan, for orthodox thinking relegated merchants to positions subordinate to other groups in society. Confucianism, as developed by Chu Hsi of China in the years 1130 through 1200, dominated social thought and relations in Tokugawa Japan. This Neo-Confucianism held that the physical world was based upon an inherently perfect order. Only when people lost sight of the order of things did disorder appear. Rulers, in particular, were supposed to prevent disorder. Social harmony was seen as depending upon the maintenance of proper relations between four different groups—the samurai warrior-administrators, peasants, artisans, and merchants. Merchants were looked down upon because, unlike the samurai, they sought private profits rather than the public good, and because, unlike the peasants or artisans, they produced no tangible crops or products.

The Japanese view of society was—compared to those in Great Britain and America—a relatively static one. How did the merchants deal with it? There was a considerable amount of crossing of the line separating samurai from merchant, especially in the 1590s through the 1640s, and much of it was done through intermarriage. The Mitsuis voluntarily gave up samurai status to become merchants. On the other hand, Yataro Iwasaki, who began life as the son of a peasant, purchased samurai status and went on to found Mitsubishi. Nonetheless, there was not as much social mobility as in Colonial America or Great Britain.

The merchants, joined by samurai, developed their own distinctive urban culture. In certain districts in Japan's leading cities there developed centers of entertainment, "floating worlds," called *ukiyo*. These were places where merchants and samurai could temporarily mingle almost as equals, places where social distinctions based upon birth or status meant little. The most famous were Yoshiwara of Edo, Shinmachi of Osaka, and Shimabara of Kyoto. The floating worlds abounded in theaters, teahouses, public baths, restaurants, and brothels. New art forms and types of entertainment were developed for the merchants. The kabuki theater, which featured more action than the traditional Noh drama, began in the 1600s. Puppetry that told stories was very popular in the 1700s. Woodblock prints pictured all sorts of scenes from daily life. One famous series of prints illustrated life along the Tokaido Road from Kyoto to Edo. A new type of poetry, the seventeen-syllable haiku, evolved from earlier forms of verse.

Other Types of Business People

While merchants were of prime importance in knitting together localities, regions, and nations in preindustrial times, other types of business people were also significant. Local storekeepers, often tied to the larger merchants by credit arrangements, sold goods at retail. They bought the goods displayed on the shelves of their shops from the merchants at wholesale, paying for them with agricultural products taken in trade from farmers, who lacked money with which to pay for the goods they wanted. Even the larger merchants found themselves accepting payment in-kind. Thomas Hancock, the leading Boston merchant of the 1750s, accepted honey, wheat, whale oil, and lumber from shopkeepers with whom he did business. The shopkeepers, in turn, had accepted those goods from their customers in payment for their shop purchases.

Artisans were important, whether making pottery in Burslem or cotton textiles in Izumi, to the economies beginning to make the shift from preindustrial to industrial times. The artisans produced a growing variety of consumer goods, and fully developed industrialization would soon evolve from these beginnings. Artisans often became early-day manufacturers, especially in the United States, but in Great Britain and Japan as well.

Artisans often worked long, hard hours; but the rhythm of that work differed from that of industrial work. Artisanal work was more episodic than industrial work. Artisans might labor twelve or more hours per day for four or five days and then take several days off on what they called Saint Monday or Saint Tuesday. By contrast, industrial work was more uniform, more disciplined, with the demands of machinery setting the pace.

Finally, there were the farmers of each nation. Except in frontier areas, where poor transportation limited their access to markets (as in northern Honshu or parts of the American West), most farmers were commercially minded. In a very real sense, more and more they were acting as business people. Thus, Okura Nagatsune wrote twenty-eight books advising Japanese farmers how to be more productive in the early to mid-1800s, stressing the monetary advantages of higher yields, lower costs, and higher prices. In fact, the market-oriented farmers in all the nations we are considering in this book were ready for the demands of industrialization. Consumer-oriented and used to the discipline of time, they were well prepared, in most cases, to become industrial workers and the consumers of industrial products.

SIMILARITIES AND DIFFERENCES
AMONG PREINDUSTRIAL NATIONS

This examination of the preindustrial economies of Great Britain, North America, and Japan must close with a word of caution. Even at the end of their preindustrial periods, no nation or region possessed a fully integrated and developed economy. Regional specialization and domestic trade, well under way, would develop much more in later years. So, too, would urbanization and industrialization. Despite the development of commercial economies, the pace and volume of business were still slow and low, when compared to what would soon come with industrialization. Hancock was able to run his business with the aid of just a handful of clerks, and he sent out only about sixty-two letters each year.

For the preindustrial merchant, business was a very personal affair. Merchant firms—especially in Japan, but also in Colonial America (as in the House of Hancock) and Great Britain (as in the House of Baring)—were houses. Relatives were important in the establishment of branch houses by Japanese merchants and in the establishment of overseas agencies by British and Colonial American merchants. Personal trust was more important than business organization or managerial hierarchies in the conduct of economic affairs. This was a world of face-to-face personal contacts. Only through family and personal ties could the risks of doing business be limited. Communications and transportation, while improving, were still so primitive that merchants could not directly oversee ventures beyond their immediate locales. They had to trust others in distant markets, and so relied on friends and family members to assist them in their business enterprises.

Similar economic situations led to similar business responses, but there were differences as well. These differences resulted from the differences in the cultures and societies in which the business people operated. Possessing fewer opportunities for the investment of their surplus funds, really only the purchase of farm land and the making of loans, and having more routine businesses than their British or American counterparts, many of the larger Japanese merchants became conservative in their outlook, an attitude that left most of them ill-prepared to make the transition to industrialization. Lacking high social status, Japanese merchants did not take part in social or political affairs to the extent that Colonial American or even British merchants

did (though some Japanese merchants staffed town and city governmental offices). Instead, Japanese merchants developed floating worlds, to which there existed no real counterparts in Great Britain or North America.

SUGGESTED READINGS

D. C. Coleman, *The Economy of England, 1450–1750* (Oxford: Oxford University Press, 1977), and Richard Grassby, *The Business Community of Seventeenth-Century England* (Cambridge: Cambridge University Press, 1995), offer valuable insights into changes occurring in Great Britain's preindustrial economy and business practices. Edwin Perkins, *The Economy of Colonial America*, 2nd ed. (New York: Columbia University Press, 1988); Gary Walton and James Shepherd, *The Economic Rise of Early America* (Cambridge: Cambridge University Press, 1979); and John J. McCusker and Russell R. Menard, *The Economy of British America, 1607–1789* (Chapel Hill: University of North Carolina Press, 1985), do the same for Colonial America. The essays comprising John Hall and Marius Jansen, eds., *Studies in the Institutional History of Early Modern Japan* (Princeton: Princeton University Press, 1968); Marius B. Jansen and Gilbert Rozman, eds., *Japan in Transition: From Tokugawa to Meiji* (Princeton: Princeton University Press, 1986), and Chie Nakane and Shinzaburo Oishi, eds., *Tokugawa Japan: The Social and Economic Antecedents of Modern Japan* (Tokyo: University of Tokyo Press, 1990), examine alterations taking place in preindustrial Japan. For a detailed look at economic, social, and political change in one region, see Philip C. Brown, *Central Authority & Local Autonomy in the Formation of Early Modern Japan: The Case of Kaga Domain* (Stanford: Stanford University Press, 1993).

Robert Brenner, "The Social Basis of English Commercial Expansion, 1550–1650," *Journal of Economic History* 32 (March 1972): 361–84; Jacob Price, "Directions for the Conduct of a Merchant's Counting House, 1766," *Business History* 28 (July 1986): 134–50; Ralph Davis, *English Overseas Trade, 1500–1700* (London: Macmillan, 1973); William Scott, *The Constitution and Finance of English, Scottish and Irish Joint-Stock Companies to 1720*, 3 vols. (Cambridge: Cambridge University Press, 1912; reprint, New York: Peter Smith, 1951); Price, *Perry of London: A Family and Firm on the Seaborne Frontier, 1615–1753* (Cambridge, Mass.: Harvard University Press, 1992); and Kenneth Morgan, *Bristol & the Atlantic Trade in the Eighteenth Century*

(Cambridge: Cambridge University Press, 1993), examine British merchants from different perspectives. Bernard Bailyn, *The New England Merchants in the Seventeenth Century* (New York: Harper Row, 1964); Frederick Tolles, *Meeting House and Counting House* (New York: W. W. Norton, 1963); and Thomas M. Doerflinger, *A Vigorous Spirit of Enterprise: Merchants and Economic Development in Revolutionary Philadelphia* (Chapel Hill: University of North Carolina Press, 1986), look at Colonial American merchant groups and the roles they played in society and politics. W. T. Baxter, *The House of Hancock* (Cambridge, Mass.: Harvard University Press, 1945), and Stanley Chyet, *Lopez of Newport* (Detroit: Wayne State University Press, 1970), present case studies of two leading Colonial American merchants. John G. Roberts, *Mitsui: Three Generations of Japanese Business* (New York: Weatherhill, 1973), examines the development of the House of Mitsui.

2 [The Many Paths to Industrialization

A worldwide Industrial Revolution beginning in the 1600s and 1700s in Great Britain, and spreading to America, Germany, and Japan in the 1800s and 1900s, reshaped business around the world. Industrialization marked a major divide in the history of the world, for a very important result of industrialization was an acceleration of economic growth. Even in Western Europe before 1700 per capita income growth had been slow, about one-tenth of one percent per year, at which rate it doubled only every 630 years. Between 1820 and 1990 income per capita increased eightfold in Great Britain, fifteen times in Germany, seventeenfold in the United States, and twenty-six times in Japan. A broad-based change, industrialization affected numerous forms of production and distribution. In Great Britain the production of toys in Birmingham, everything from buttons to trinkets, was as affected as the making of cotton textiles in Lancashire. In Japan changes in silk reeling were as significant as those in steelmaking.

Industrialization so fundamentally altered key business practices that the history of business can be divided into two basic time periods: preindustrial business, which was dealt with in Chapter 1, and industrial business, the topic of much of the remainder of this book. Still, business changes rarely occurred overnight, and new ways of doing things almost never completely replaced traditional production methods in just a few years. Older ways of conducting business long coexisted with the new, and in some cases they still do to the present day. In fact, industrialization was a complex process that worked itself out in different ways in different regions and nations. There was no single, uniform path to industrialization.

Nonetheless, over time certain changes occurred as industrialization took

hold and spread, especially changes in the nature of the work process and the ways by which laborers related to their jobs. Machines—tireless, regular, rapid, and precise—supplemented and replaced human labor in making products. Moreover, labor was often concentrated in central locations called factories, and in these factories the tasks of workers became more and more specialized. As these alterations took place, workers lost some of their control over work processes to those who owned the factories. Machines and factory owners came increasingly to set the pace of work and to determine how jobs would be performed. Yet even so, considerable differences existed, and they continue to exist, from nation to nation and from industry to industry.

THE POLITICAL FRAMEWORK: POLITICAL UNITY

As we have already seen with regard to preindustrial economic growth, political and economic developments go hand in hand. So it was with industrialization. The governments of Great Britain, the United States, and Japan spurred industrialization by removing barriers to economic growth, what might be called a permissive or indirect role, and by taking actions to stimulate industrialization more directly, what can be labeled a direct role. All three governments indirectly encouraged economic development and industrialization by providing stable political frameworks within which economic growth could occur. The political apparatus needed for the development of local, regional, and national markets was especially important. In terms of direct aid, the governments differed considerably, and the differences were related in a general way to the order in which each country industrialized. The British government provided the least amount of direct aid, the Japanese the most, with the United States government in the middle of this continuum.

Great Britain

Great Britain possessed a strong national government by the early 1700s, whose existence meant that Great Britain had a standard currency, legal system, and system of taxation. It also ensured that the country had no internal customs barriers or feudal tolls. Strong regional markets, and later a national market, could develop, and these domestic markets were more important than foreign markets to England's industrial growth. By way of comparison,

France was still divided into three major areas by customs barriers. Germany was not even one nation. The Prussian monarchy tried to introduce free trade among its royal lands in 1797, but it failed. Only in 1834 did three dozen states form the first German customs union, and only in 1871 did Germany become a unified nation.

Parliamentary action spurred economic growth and industrialization indirectly in Great Britain. Laws ensured that taxation fell mainly upon landed wealth, not accumulated capital that could be used to build up industry. The Bubble Act of 1720 outlawed most joint-stock companies, but capital accumulation remained possible through the formation of unincorporated joint-stock companies. Moreover, various types of trust agreements permitted stock to pass from one generation to the next. New limited liability laws passed in 1856 and 1862 reversed the Bubble Act and made capital accumulation easier. Even so, most British companies remained partnerships, not limited companies or corporations. The British government did much less in terms of direct aid than did its American and Japanese counterparts. For instance, it did little to finance canals or railroads, as did the American and Japanese governments. Nor did it set up model factories, as did the Japanese government.

The United States

The United States, of course, did not exist before the American Revolution. Each colony had been part of the British Empire, a situation that had economic as well as political repercussions. Until the 1750s and 1760s there had been relatively few economic or political ties between the colonies; stronger ties existed between the colonies and England. With the Declaration of Independence in 1776 and the American Revolution (ended by the Treaty of Paris in 1783) this situation changed abruptly. The colonies were no longer part of the British Empire. Now as states they had to devise a national government.

Americans set up their first national government under the Articles of Confederation in 1781. Under these articles the national government was weak, reflecting the fear the colonists harbored against the strong British Parliament and king. There was no president or federal court system. The national legislature could not levy taxes, regulate trade, or deal with general welfare measures. Soon, however, some Americans, especially merchants and other business leaders, came to think that this type of government was too weak

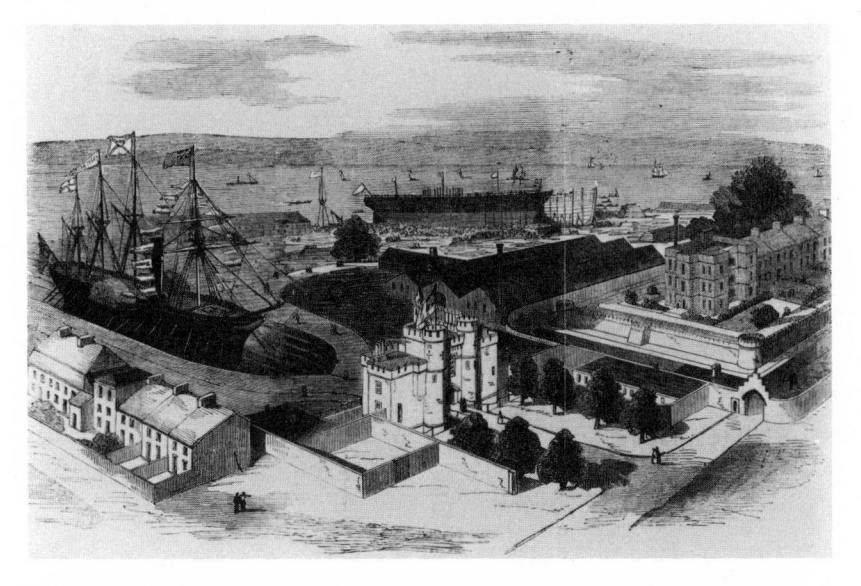

British shipyard of the nineteenth century. The possession of a merchant marine made it possible for Great Britain to expand its foreign trade. (*Illustrated London News*, 24 May 1851)

and that its weakness was retarding the development of their businesses. Merchants wanted a stronger national government to regulate trade and to settle land disputes between the states. Merchants wanted help in expanding overseas trade, including a navy supported by taxes. Manufacturers wanted tariffs to limit the importation of foreign, especially British, goods.

As a result of these and other desires, a convention was called to revise the Articles of Confederation in 1787, but instead of simply revising the articles, the delegates wrote the Constitution, which was adopted in 1789. The Constitution provided for a strong national government, broken only once during the Civil War of the 1860s. The Constitution created the presidency and a federal court system, which in the early 1800s became superior to the state courts. The Constitution increased greatly the powers of Congress. Perhaps most important for business was the commerce clause, which empowered Congress to regulate interstate trade. This clause prevented state governments from setting up internal barriers to the movement of goods within the United States, something very important for business people trying to develop more than local markets. For the first time, too, Congress had the power to tax. Congress used taxes to support, among other things, a navy; and the navy,

in turn, defended American trade around the globe. (While significant, the foreign market became less and less important than the domestic market, however. If 1790 is taken as the base year and assigned the value of 100, the value of foreign trade per capita was 55 in 1800, but only 30 by 1825.)

But not all of the legal changes affecting business occurred at the national level, for the United States possessed a federal system of government, with powers divided between the national and the state governments. Sometimes there was conflict between the two levels of government; but, for the most part, legal changes occurring at the state level also aided the development of business. State incorporation laws, like Britain's limited liability laws, gave investors insulation from the debts of the corporations in which they invested, thus encouraging them to pool their capital for business ventures. The laws also gave corporations longevity, for unlike partnerships, corporations did not have to be dissolved if one investor left. New York passed the first general state incorporation law in 1811, and by 1860 all industrial states had some sort of general incorporation law. By 1904 corporations accounted for 75 percent of all industrial production in the United States.

Unlike in Great Britain, in America all governmental bodies—federal, state, and local—offered direct aid to stimulate business growth. Most important was governmental financing of transportation improvements. Conflict between the North and South prevented the development of a truly national system of transportation, except the post office, before the Civil War. Nonetheless, the federal government financed the building of the National Road across the Appalachian Mountains, funded the construction of several canals, and provided much of the financing for pathbreaking railroads—the Illinois Central in the 1850s and the Union Pacific–Central Pacific, America's first transcontinental, in the 1860s. Local and state governments provided even more aid, as they sought economic advantages over each other. New York financed the very important Erie Canal, completed in 1825, for example. The city of Baltimore provided much of the funding for the Baltimore & Ohio Railroad. Altogether, between 1815 and 1860 about 60 percent of the total investment in transportation facilities in the United States came from governmental sources. All of this was needed for the growth of large regional markets and later a national market.

Japan

As we have seen in Chapter 1, Tokugawa Japan possessed a decentralized military government, the *baku-han*. As the leader of his nation, the shogun, acting in theory on behalf of the emperor, provided Japan with some sense of unity. However, the *baku-han* was not a modern national government. It was based more upon personal bonds connecting the shogun, the daimyo, and the samurai than upon institutions. This situation changed with the Meiji Restoration of 1868 and with the formation of a new governmental system in the 1870s, 1880s, and 1890s.

Much of the initial impetus for change came from outside forces. Americans and other foreigners had desired for years to trade with Japan, and in 1853 and 1854 Commodore Matthew Perry steamed into Tokyo Bay with his "black ships" of the American navy to force open Japanese ports. In 1854 two ports, and in later years additional ones, were opened to trade. Foreign merchants gained additional advantages. A 5 percent limit was placed on the tariffs the Japanese were allowed to charge on goods imported into Japan. Moreover, foreign nations demanded and received the right to extraterritoriality, according to which their citizens were governed by foreign, not Japanese, law while they lived in Japan.

This forced opening of their nation sorely troubled many Japanese. To them, especially to those in some of the domains on the fringes far from the shogun's seat of power in Edo—Tosa, Choshu, and Satsuma—it appeared that the shogun had failed to defend Japan in his military duties to the emperor. Samurai in these regions united against the shogun around the twin slogans of "honor the emperor" and "expel the barbarians." Shogunal forces failed to win military victories in battles in the mid-1860s. Then, in 1868 in the Meiji Restoration, the rebels deposed the shogun and, in theory at least, returned the emperor to power. Thus, the Meiji period in Japanese history, the years 1868 through 1912, is named after the Emperor Meiji who reigned during those years.

Once in power, the young, relatively economically humble samurai from Choshu, Tosa, and Satsuma realized that the only practical way to achieve their goal of ridding their land of foreigners lay in building up the economic and military might of Japan. Their new slogan became "rich country, strong

army." This aim, in turn, could, they thought, be accomplished only by borrowing from the West. Western naval bombardments of two Japanese ports in 1863 and 1864 showed that the West was too strong to be excluded immediately by force.

As part of their effort to transform Japan, the Meiji leaders set up a new system of government. The creation of the new government took place step by step. In 1871 the old domains ruled by daimyo were abolished, and the country was instead divided into prefectures directly controlled by Tokyo (Edo became known as Tokyo in the early Meiji period). The daimyo, replaced by governors, were given lump sum payments in government bonds, and these payments became an important source of capital for new businesses. Universal military service began in 1873, and a national army based upon the German model was formed. In 1876 the stipends of the samurai were abolished, and, like the daimyo, the samurai were paid off in lump sums of government bonds. In 1885 a cabinet system of national government under a prime minister came into being, and in the same year a modernized civil service was put in place. Finally, in 1889 a constitution was promulgated as a gift to the people from the emperor. The constitution emphasized the prerogatives of the emperor and that the emperor was the source of authority in Japan, thus stressing the duties of Japanese subjects to their nation. The constitution created a two-house assembly called the Diet. The lower house, the House of Representatives, was elective; an upper house, the House of Peers, was appointed.

Japan's new national government gave indirect aid to industrialization and business growth. In contrast to the United States, where state and local governments were as important as the national government, in Japan most of the aid came from the new national government. In 1868 the Japanese government abolished the road inspection stations and guardhouses separating the domains, thus ending political barriers to internal trade. The government provided for population mobility in abolishing the four-class system of samurai, peasant, artisan, and merchant in the same year and allowed peasants to grow whatever crops they desired in 1871. Certain laws stimulated business enterprise. In 1872 and 1876 the government made laws allowing the establishment of joint-stock banks, and by 1879 some 153 were in existence. The government also set up the Bank of Japan in 1882 with the sole privilege of issuing money and acting as a central bank. The passage of the General In-

corporation Act of 1893, which was similar in its intent to the British limited liability laws of 1856 and 1862 and the American state incorporation laws, led to the formation of joint-stock companies worth one billion yen by 1916.

Direct aid, under the slogan of "develop industry and promote enterprise," took more forms than in Great Britain or the United States. In the 1870s the national government built the first railroads so necessary for internal trade, a Tokyo-Yokohama line and a line connecting Kyoto, Kobe, and Osaka. Most lines built in the 1880s and 1890s were constructed by private companies, but in 1906 much of Japan's railroad system was nationalized. The government also provided subsidies to ocean shipping companies and to shipbuilders. In 1896 state subsidies were given to Japanese shipyards to produce vessels for foreign trade. Then, too, the government encouraged Japanese to study abroad and brought foreigners into Japan, 500 by 1872, to help modernize the nation.

Most different from the situations in Great Britain or the United States, in the 1870s the Japanese government built and operated pilot or demonstration plants or factories in fields ranging from mining to shipbuilding to cotton spinning to cement making and to the production of glass. Just how important were these ventures? In silk reeling the government's model factory at Tomioka was a failure. In cotton spinning a large Osaka mill set up with private capital in 1883 was more important as a model than the smaller government plants of the 1870s. Financed by ninety-five shareholders, 60 percent of whom were Osaka and Tokyo merchants, the Osaka mill showed a profit from its first year of operations. Thus, while significant in some fields, such as iron- and steelmaking, the importance of the government's pilot enterprises should not be overstressed.

In the pilot factories and other matters the Japanese government overreached itself, and in the 1880s the government entered a period of retrenchment in its economic activities, the "Matsukata Deflation," named after Finance Minister Masayoshi Matsukata. By 1896 the government had sold nearly all of its pilot plants, keeping only several arsenals, naval shipyards, a military woolen factory, and Yawata Iron and Steel.

The Meiji government's modernization efforts strengthened Japan in her dealings with other nations. In 1899 Great Britain relinquished the right to extraterritoriality for her citizens in Japan, and other nations soon followed suit. In 1911 Japan won back full control over her tariffs on imported goods. Japan also began building a commercial and territorial empire in Asia. In

1879 Japan gained clear recognition from China of her claims over Okinawa and the Ryukyu Islands and turned them into a prefecture. In 1876 the Japanese navy forced Korea to open her ports to trade, a move that brought Japan into conflict with China, and in 1894–95 Japan defeated China in the Sino-Japanese War. China ceded Taiwan to Japan, along with some other territories. Further expansion occurred in the twentieth century. Japan defeated Russia in the Russo-Japanese War of 1904–5 and as a result acquired control over Korea, the Liaotung Peninsula of China, Russian railroads in southern Manchuria, and the southern half of Sakhalin Island. In the First World War Japan took over many of Germany's possessions in China and the Pacific: Tsingtao in Shantung, the Pacific island groups of the Marianas, the Carolinas, and the Marshalls, and economic rights in Manchuria, Shantung, and Fukien.

Government, Business, and Industrialization

The establishment of strong national governments provided political frameworks conducive to economic and industrial growth. Either indirectly or directly the national governments stimulated industrial growth and business development. As latecomers to industrialization, when compared to Great Britain, America and Japan found it necessary to rely more on government to aid in economic growth. (In Germany, another nation to industrialize later than Great Britain, organizations aided businesses as they industrialized. Large universal banks and trade associations or cartels were of special importance.) Both America and Japan used government funding to build much of their infrastructures, especially mechanized transportation networks, needed for the creation of domestic markets. The Japanese government of early Meiji times tried to go farther through its model factories, but the government's actual accomplishments should not be overemphasized. In terms of its achievements, the Japanese government was not much more important than the governments—federal and state—in the United States. The national governments of all three countries were also active in opening overseas markets for industrial goods, especially in the cases of Great Britain and Japan (foreign markets became important for America's industrial goods only in the 1890s and later).

THE INDUSTRIAL REVOLUTION

"It is clear that an almost total revolution has taken place and is yet in progress, in every branch and in every relation of the world's industrial and commercial system," observed the well-known American economist David Wells in 1885.[*] Sometimes spurred by government aid, the Industrial Revolution was, as Wells noted, well under way across the globe by the late nineteenth century. The Industrial Revolution had begun much earlier in nations in which a confluence of factors, ranging from the possession of raw materials to the availability of markets, favored its development.

There was, in fact, more than one industrial revolution. The First Industrial Revolution, in which Great Britain led the world, involved making relatively technologically simple products such as cotton textiles, iron hardware, and the like. In the late nineteenth and early twentieth centuries a Second Industrial Revolution based on more scientifically and technologically complex industries as alloyed steel, chemicals, electrical equipment, and automobiles developed. Even later in the twentieth century a Third Industrial Revolution, and what is sometimes called a Fourth Industrial Revolution, both grounded in changes in communications and information handling, blossomed.

The Timing of Industrialization

There were signs of industrialization in Great Britain with regard to the use of new types of machinery and new sources of energy in the late 1600s and early 1700s. As early as 1705 primitive steam engines were pumping water out of coal mines, and four years later coking coal was being used to smelt iron at Coalbrookdale. On the other hand, some forms of handicraft production continued with industrialization. The cotton textile industry was one of the first British industries to industrialize, but handloom weavers continued to be very important in this industry as late as the 1840s.

The consolidation of work in factories—which, along with the use of new types of machinery and sources of power, is often taken as one of the hallmarks of the First Industrial Revolution—took decades to accomplish. Facto-

---

[*] David Wells, *Recent Economic Changes* (New York: D. Appleton and Co., 1899), 111.

ries appeared in some sectors of the economy well before they did in others, and even within a single field regional variations were substantial.

The centralization of work in factories offered employees and investors several advantages over older systems of production. Factories cut transportation costs associated with an earlier production method called the putting-out system. In the putting-out system merchants had distributed, or put out, raw materials to skilled workers who made them into finished items in their homes. The merchants then collected the finished goods, such as shoes or cotton or woolen cloth, and found markets for them. Gathering workers in factories allowed business people to better supervise employees, thus permitting improvements in scheduling work processes and the quality of goods. Above all, from about the 1780s on factories allowed the use of new technologies — especially water-powered and steam-powered machinery — too big, too complex, and too expensive to be installed in a single cottage. Over time these advantages outweighed the disadvantages of factories: the tremendous expense of providing the fixed plant and its equipment, which increased fixed costs and correspondingly decreased manufacturers' abilities to respond quickly to market changes. Even so, large factories did not quickly sweep across Great Britain. Two-thirds of the nation's cotton textile mills of the mid-nineteenth century still employed fifty workers or less.

In the United States and Japan, as in Great Britain, industrialization was an uneven process, requiring many years to complete. Some industry existed in colonial America, the production of pig iron for example. By the 1820s and 1830s factory production was coming to dominate the making of cotton textiles in the United States, but not until the 1880s and later did mass production develop in many fields of manufacturing. In Japan, too, industrialization took many decades to mature. It is worth noting as well that for many years traditional industries such as silk reeling were among the mainstays of the Japanese economy.

In short, industrialization was a complex and lengthy process. No single, brief five-year, ten-year, or even twenty-year period can be singled out as that time period in which Great Britain, America, or Japan achieved sustained industrial growth. Nonetheless, industrialization was achieved over long periods of time, even as traditional methods of production lingered.

Nineteenth-century industrial advances were most pronounced in Great

Britain. Great Britain led the world in the First Industrial Revolution. By 1850 the British produced eight times as much iron, five times as much coal, and six times as much cloth as they had fifty years before. In 1830 the British mined 70 percent of the world's coal and produced 50 percent of its cotton cloth and iron. Yet, while industrialization was rapidly growing in importance, it was not fully developed even in Great Britain. In 1851 Britain's leading industry, cotton textiles, employed 292,000 people out of a population of 17 million, considerably less than the 390,000 employed in the traditional building trades.

The British made further industrial advances in the late nineteenth and early twentieth centuries. However, Great Britain fell behind the United States and Germany in the Second Industrial Revolution based on the production of more technologically complex goods. By 1913, for example, 90 percent of the dyestuffs, 35 percent of the electrotechnical goods, 30 percent of the pharmaceuticals, 29 percent of the machine tools, and 27 percent of the chemicals traded in world export markets were made in Germany.

Americans had made considerable industrial progress by 1860. Between 1810 and 1860 the value of manufactured goods produced in the United States rose from $200 million to $2 billion. Yet, agriculture was still more important than industry to America's economy. It was in the late nineteenth and early twentieth centuries that America emerged as the world's leading industrial nation, especially in the products of the Second Industrial Revolution. Between 1869 and 1919 the value added by manufactures rose from $1.4 billion to $24 billion, a seventeenfold increase, and industry became more important than agriculture to the American economy.

Japan's industrial accomplishment was also marked. The proportion of Japan's workforce engaged in manufacturing rose from 4 percent in 1872 to 17 percent in 1920, and the capital invested in Japanese industries tripled in the same time period. By 1920 the manufacturing sector contributed nearly as much to Japan's economy as agriculture, and ten years later manufacturing contributed more. Yet, for all of the changes that had occurred in Japan, heavy industry was just really beginning to grow rapidly in 1920, fifty-two years after the Meiji Restoration. Japan was far from being the industrial superpower it would become after World War II.

Raw Materials

Many factors—including, as we have seen, some government aid—contributed to economic growth and industrialization. The possession of raw materials, capital, labor, and markets all speeded the development of industry in Great Britain, the United States, and Japan. It was the interaction of different elements, not one single factor, that led to the rise of industry in these nations. While all of the nations were similar in some of the elements favoring industrialization, there were significant differences as well; and those differences helped shape varied approaches to industrialization.

One reason Great Britain was the first nation in the world to industrialize was that it was endowed with or could easily trade for the raw materials upon which the First Industrial Revolution was based. England's cotton textile industry acquired raw cotton from America. Great Britain had iron ore and could purchase additional supplies from Scandinavia. Water power was used by the early cotton textile mills, and charcoal was used in early ironmaking, but coal grew in importance as an energy source, because of the deforestation of parts of Great Britain. The chemical industry was important for industrialization, for it supplied the detergents, bleaches, and dyes needed to finish cotton textiles; and England was fortunate in possessing the necessary chemicals. A final raw material the British had was food. Due to productivity gains in agriculture, Great Britain was self-sufficient in food production in its initial stages of industrialization.

An abundance of raw materials allowed the United States to catch up with and then, by 1900, surpass Great Britain as the world's leading industrial power. Cotton grown in the South; iron ore, first from eastern deposits and later from the Mesabi Range near Lake Superior; coal, especially Pennsylvania anthracite first put to use in the 1830s; and water power, which was more important than steam power into the 1850s, were among the most significant. Above all, the United States had wood, and wood was more important for initial industrialization in America than in England: to make the frames and some parts of engines, as a fuel in ironmaking (more iron was made with charcoal than coking coal into the 1860s), and as a fuel for some steam engines. Like Great Britain, the United States had a climate that supported varied agriculture, and America was self-sufficient in food production.

The use of charcoal made from wood rather than coking coal as a fuel

in smelting iron helps explain why America's iron industry was more dispersed than Britain's until the late-nineteenth century. Charcoal was fragile and could not easily be transported long distances without breaking, thus rendering it useless as a fuel. Consequently, America's iron-smelting furnaces were for decades located across the Northeast and Midwest, where there were large stands of hardwood forests. By comparison, Great Britain's iron industry, which used more easily transportable coal, more quickly became concentrated in just a few areas, especially in the Midlands.

Japan was not as well endowed with raw materials as Great Britain or the United States but did possess enough of the materials to start and sustain industrialization. Coal mines on Hokkaido and Kyushu were developed by the Meiji government and then sold to private enterprise. Japan also possessed iron mines, some of which the government sought to modernize and then sold to private companies. The government set up Yawata Iron and Steel in Kyushu in the 1890s. Japan possessed plenty of copper. The Sumitomo Besshi Copper mines had a long history, and Sumitomo modernized them with the help of French engineers in the Meiji period. A second source of copper lay in the Ani Copper mines, partially modernized by the Meiji government and then sold to a private entrepreneur. However, traditional industrial products were more important than coal, iron, and copper for industrial and economic growth in Meiji Japan. Silk, a product of the silk reeling industry, made up 40 percent of Japan's exports in the years 1868 through 1893. Tea was another major export of the Meiji period. Japan, like the United States, depended heavily upon water power, readily available from many rivers, in the early stages of industrialization.

Capital

The availability of capital, the possession of funds to build the factories and machinery so necessary in putting raw materials to work, as much as her endowments of those materials, ensured Great Britain's nineteenth-century primacy as an industrial power. Early industrialization did not require as much capital as might be imagined. Much of the machinery, as in the cotton textile industry, was simple in design. Great Britain's capital supplies were adequate for these needs. Merchants often acted as partners to industrialists, as occasionally did commercial farmers with money to invest. Local banks

were significant sources of capital, growing in importance from the 1840s by offering loans and extending overdrafts to nascent manufacturers. The number of such country banks rose from just a handful in 1750 to over 600 by 1810. Networks of kinship and friendship, often based on localities, were of prime importance in lending and investment. (By way of contrast, German industrialists depended more on a handful of large universal banks for their capital, which, in turn, played active managerial roles in the enterprises they funded. As a latecomer to industrialization, Germany simply did not have capital sources that were as fully developed and as diverse as Great Britain's.) Retained earnings, profits kept in a company and not paid out to investors as dividends, also became an important source of funds, especially for larger firms, as industrialization progressed.

Capital for American industry came from similar sources. Merchants in the Northeastern cities who had made their way in foreign trade invested directly in manufacturing and railroads. Then, too, as in Great Britain, local networks of family and friends were important. Families and friends often invested through banks they controlled in industrial ventures they owned. Entrepreneurial groups—similar to investment clubs in modern-day America—relied on funding from the sale of bank stocks from which they granted themselves generous loans, investing the proceeds in new plants and equipment. Retained earnings also fueled capital improvements, especially after the Civil War. For instance, by 1899 Carnegie Steel was making an annual net profit of $40 million, most of which was reinvested in the business. In at least one respect America differed from Great Britain: by the mid-1800s foreign investors, especially the British, were important sources of capital. About 20 percent of American railroad securities were foreign-held.

Industrial capital in Japan came from varied sources. The government set up pilot plants and then sold them to private business at prices much lower than their costs of construction. Government revenues to pay for these industrial projects came from an agricultural land tax started in 1873, a tax that provided over half of the government's tax revenues into the 1890s. So, indirectly, some of the capital for industrialization derived from agriculture. However, most of the capital came from private sources. Former daimyo and samurai invested funds granted them by the Meiji government in banking and other business enterprises. Wealthy landlords and merchants invested in banking, industry, and transportation projects. Leading merchants were,

however, less important as a source of capital for industry in Japan than in Great Britain or the United States. Many of the major merchant houses of the Tokugawa period lacked the flexibility to survive the disruptions of the Meiji Restoration and make the transition from preindustrial to industrial times. It was lower-level, smaller-scale merchants, operating in rural areas and former castle towns, more than members of the great merchant houses, who invested most heavily in industry.

The Role of Labor

Workers were needed to man the new factories, and each nation was fortunate in possessing an adequate labor supply. A combination of a rising birthrate and a falling death rate more than doubled the population of England and Wales from 7 million in 1770 to about 18 million in 1851. This natural increase, plus immigration from Ireland, provided England's industrial labor force. Blessed with an ample supply of practically minded, skilled workers, many British businesses came to have factories in which workers controlled shopfloor activities. Management generally delegated to these workers decisions over how goods were to be made. This system worked reasonably well during the First Industrial Revolution, when industrial products were relatively technologically simple. However, as the products became more scientifically complex during the Second Industrial Revolution and later, the skills of the practically minded workers proved inadequate. More knowledge of science was needed in newer fields such as chemicals. When Great Britain's educational system failed to provide such knowledge to either workers or managers, parts of the nation's industrial establishment began falling behind those of some other nations.

Industrial labor came from several sources in America. There was a major farm-to-city movement from the 1820s on, with New England farmers' daughters providing much of the initial labor force for America's cotton textile mills. There was immigration from abroad: in the mid-1800s from northwestern Europe, and from the 1880s into the early 1900s from southeastern Europe. In the mid- to late nineteenth centuries immigration from China and Japan provided workers for the West Coast, until it was shut off by legislation and informal restrictions. Even with these varied sources, there was often a shortage of labor in America, especially of skilled workers. Faced with less-skilled

workers than their British counterparts, American managers tended to impose more controls on them. There was, especially from the 1880s, less delegation over the work process to industrial workers in America than in Great Britain.

This control over labor, which most workers were willing to accept in return for relatively high wages, worked well as long as most of the goods being produced were standardized items turned out in long production runs; and that is exactly what the large domestic market in America demanded from the mid-nineteenth century into the mid-twentieth century. (Unlike the case in Great Britain, research laboratories, controlled by management, provided American companies with the scientific knowledge so necessary for the Second Industrial Revolution.) As a global demand for specialized industrial products made for niche markets mounted after World War II, and especially after 1970, better-educated workers who could play more active roles in determining production processes for shorter and more flexible production runs were needed. An unwillingness of many American executives to utilize fully the capabilities of workers—for to do so would have meant relinquishing some control over work processes to them—came to hinder America businesses in global industrial competition.

In Japan, as in America and Great Britain, industrial labor came from varied sources. Initially, the daughters of samurai and farmers composed the workforce of the silk reeling and cotton textile mills, in a manner similar to the importance of women in early textile establishments in England and America. Women made up 60 percent of Japan's industrial labor force as late as 1910. However, as heavy industry—metals, chemicals, shipbuilding, and the like—rose in significance, men entered the workforce in growing numbers, until in 1920 they composed over half of the workforce in Japanese industry, a shift in composition that was paralleled in the United States and Great Britain. Increasingly well educated and involved in determining how goods were made, skilled and knowledgeable workers—especially those employed by big businesses geared to export markets after World War II—proved to be one of the major strengths of Japan's industrial system. Suggestions and actions by Japanese workers were particularly important in improving the quality of Japanese goods.

The Importance of Markets

On the supply side, raw materials (including power), capital, and labor were needed for industrialization. On the demand side, growing markets, domestic and foreign, sustained industrial expansion.

For Great Britain both domestic and foreign markets were significant. Most importantly, the same population increase that provided the work force helped create a growing domestic market. Moreover, because income was fairly equitable in its distribution—at least more so than in France, for example—people had money to spend on industrial goods. Transportation improvements linked this nascent consumer market. In the 1780s and 1790s turnpikes began joining localities and regions, and at about the same time a mania for canal building swept Great Britain. By 1800 navigable water routes and good roads were connecting emerging industrial centers of the North to those of the Midlands, the Midlands to London, and London to the Atlantic. Still later came railroads. Railroad trackage increased from a few miles of mining lines in 1825 to 6,300 miles twenty-five years later.

Even so, local and regional markets long remained of great importance for British merchants and manufacturers, certainly much longer than in America. Of the world's manufacturing nations, Great Britain alone industrialized substantially before completing the building of a national railroad network, a circumstance that encouraged regional rather than national developments. Then, too, regional preferences and tastes simply lingered longer in Great Britain than in some other nations.

Europe and the British colonies formed an overseas market, which, while less important than the domestic market, was significant. Most of Great Britain's exports came to consist of industrial goods, while they had earlier been agricultural products. Overseas markets were especially important outlets for cotton textiles, but not just for textiles: well into the twentieth century foreign markets took about a third of Great Britain's industrial output.

In the United States the development of domestic markets was of utmost importance. In the nineteenth century transportation improvements helped create regional markets and, from the 1850s, a national market that was the largest single free-trade area in the world. Turnpikes like the National Road were of minor significance. Of more importance were canals, 3,000 miles of which had been built by 1840. Still more important was the railroad:

30,000 miles by 1860, 166,000 by 1890, and 250,000 in 1916. Even more than in Great Britain, America possessed a market-oriented population eager to buy the industrial goods made available by the transportation improvements. America's population rose from 4 million people in 1790 to 31 million in 1860 to 106 million by 1920.

Both domestic and foreign markets took Japan's industrial products. Japan's population rose from roughly 36 million people in 1878 to 56 million by 1920, furthering the creation of regional markets and beginning to form a national market for industrial goods. As in the United States and Great Britain, transportation improvements began linking Japan's domestic markets: by 1906, 6,000 miles of railroads had been constructed. However, a fully developed domestic market for a broad array of consumer goods would not develop until after World War II. In addition to domestic markets, foreign markets were significant. In the early Meiji period Japan's exports amounted to a sum equal to about 7 percent of the nation's GNP, but they rose to 15 to 20 percent in the late Meiji period, a level maintained into the 1930s. This importance of foreign markets contrasts with the experience of the United States. By the 1850s American exports came to a sum equal to only about 5 percent of the nation's GNP, a level at about which exports remained through World War II.

As we shall see, differing markets for industrial goods influenced the nature of industrial production in the different nations. Facing a wider variety of local, regional, and international markets than their American counterparts, British and Japanese industrialists less often emphasized long, standardized production runs of homogeneous products made by unskilled or semi-skilled workers. Instead, they often stressed making a variety of goods by skilled workers for different market requirements. In this situation, the moving assembly line—introduced to America and the world by Henry Ford in the making of his Model T in 1914—was less important in Great Britain and Japan than in the United States.

The Process of Industrialization

By the mid-1700s Great Britain possessed an environment conducive to industrialization, but the mere existence of a favorable environment does not explain why and how industrialization occurred.

Two phenomena merit stress in explaining the course of industrialization

in Great Britain. First, industrialization evolved as a challenge and response process—that is, an innovation in one stage of manufacturing brought forth an innovation in another stage as a way of removing a production bottleneck. Second, industrial advances were interrelated, as can be seen in the development of innovations in metallurgy and steam power, for example.

The cotton textile industry provides a classic example of how innovations occurred in a sequence of challenge and response. In the mid-1700s the problem lay in supplying cotton cloth weavers with enough cotton yarn. Inventions removed this bottleneck in production: carding machines to prepare the cotton fiber for spinning and, most importantly, a host of spinning machines which replaced the spinning wheel in making thread—Hargreave's spinning jenny in 1765, Arkwright's water frame in 1769, and Crompton's spinning mule in 1779. These spinning machines produced better yarn and much more of it than the spinning wheel. The water frame could, for instance, do the work of several hundred spinning wheels. These advances in spinning thread created a bottleneck in weaving, as handloom weavers failed to keep up with the outpouring of thread. The power loom, invented in 1787, removed this bottleneck, and by the mid-1820s a power loom could perform the work of seven and one-half handlooms. Andrew Carnegie, who founded the largest steel company in nineteenth-century America, immigrated to the United States from Scotland with his family in 1848 after his father lost his position as a handloom weaver. The development of a chemicals industry removed bottlenecks in the bleaching and dyeing of cottons.

Something of the same process occurred in the iron industry. The switch from charcoal to coking coal in smelting iron created pressures for innovation in the refining of iron, a bottleneck removed with the development of puddling in 1784 and the hot blast in 1829. The expansion of the iron industry also demonstrates well the interrelatedness of Great Britain's industrial advances: iron was used in making steam engines, many of which, in turn, powered pumps that emptied water out of coal mines, and the coal was used to power the pumps and to make iron.

Even more than their British counterparts, American manufacturers sought to achieve high-volume, low-cost production. They took steps in this direction before the Civil War. As in Great Britain, industrialization meant using machinery to produce manufactured goods. High-volume, low-cost production could not be attained through hand labor and craftsmanship. Faced with

British horseshoe-making machinery. Nearly all aspects of ironmaking were mechanized as industrialization occurred. (*Illustrated London News*, 4 January 1873)

a shortage of skilled workers, American industrialists aimed at the standard-ization or interchangeability of parts in such industries as clockmaking, small arms, and farm machinery—a goal partially achieved in the 1830s, 1840s and 1850s. Standardization was favored as a way of cutting labor costs and con-trolling workers. America's industrial progress caught the British by surprise. In the 1850s the British government sent commissions to the United States to study the secrets of America's industrial success, which the British called the "American System." Even so, much remained undone. High-volume, low-cost production had been achieved in just a handful of fields before the Civil War.

It was with technological breakthroughs in three major fields of indus-trial production that the United States fully achieved high-volume, low-cost production in the 1880s and later. In liquids and semi-liquids—oil, distilled liquors, and drugs—new processes using heat greatly increased the speed and volume of production. Catalytic cracking speeded the refining of oil, for example. In the processing of agricultural or semi-agricultural goods into consumer products—flour, soap, matches, and cigarettes—new pieces of ma-chinery came into use. The Bonsack machine, adopted in the mid-1880s, pro-

duced over 100,000 cigarettes in one day, the same time in which a team of ten men could roll at most only 20,000. In the steelmaking and metalworking industries two types of changes were important. Technological breakthroughs, the Bessemer and open hearth processes, combined with new, more efficient plant layouts to greatly increase America's iron and steel production.

As a latecomer to industrialization, Japan was able to benefit from the earlier experiences of both Great Britain and the United States. Just as Americans borrowed from the British, as in the cotton textile industry, the Japanese borrowed from other nations—Germany, as well as Great Britain and the United States. Technological transfer or borrowing was especially important in the establishment of Japan's cotton textile industry. Technology, technicians, and machinery all came mainly from Great Britain, but the Japanese soon adapted the technology to their own uses. The adaptation was so complete that Japanese mills using British machinery were soon outproducing British and Chinese mills similarly equipped in China. In 1929 the Japanese company Toyoda Automatic Loom was so technologically advanced that it leased rights to manufacture and sell a new type of power loom to Platt Brothers, a leading British loom maker.

One circumstance that set Japanese industrialization and economic growth apart from that of Great Britain or the United States was the importance of war as a stimulatory factor. The Sino-Japanese War of 1894–95 was especially important: the number of factories in Japan rose from 2,746 in 1892 to 7,640 four years later, and the number of industrial workers climbed from 396,000 in 1894 to 454,000 in 1896. Japan's wars spurred the development of heavy industry, such as Yawata Iron and Steel and shipbuilding firms like Mitsubishi. In 1906 a Japanese shipyard launched a 10,000-ton warship that was technologically on par with those of Western nations.

THE MANY PATHS OF INDUSTRIALIZATION

As already suggested, there was no single correct path to industrialization. The role of the state differed from nation to nation, as did the ways in which raw materials, capital, and labor were combined. Differing markets could also lead to different approaches to economic growth and industrial development. Even within a single nation there were often marked regional variations, as a glance at the initial industrialization of the United States illustrates.

In America four major regional variations to industrialization developed. In the Northeast, from Maine south through Pennsylvania, mill villages using water power sprang up, some 400 by 1820, to produce textiles, milled lumber, ground grain, and sometimes iron and paper. Entrepreneurs founding the villages provided living quarters for families as a way to try to hold on to a stable supply of workers in a time of labor shortage, and industrial work was often done by entire families. Bigger one-industry cities and towns—such as Lowell for large corporate cotton textile factories funded by merchants, and Lynn for centralized and mechanized shoemaking—also grew up. Here, increasingly de-skilled workers made longer and longer production runs of homogeneous products. More diversified industrialized cities, such as New York and Philadelphia, offered a third variant. In these cities many smaller and medium-sized businesses employing mainly skilled workers made a wide range of goods, including cotton textiles, in successful competition with larger counterparts in the one-industry towns such as Lowell. Frequently started by artisans and usually family-owned or owned by just a few partners, many of these smaller firms proved successful well into the twentieth century. Finally, in the South, industrial slavery developed; by the 1850s about 5 percent of the region's slaves, some 150,000 to 200,000 people, labored in textile mills, iron works, sugar refineries, and other industrial enterprises.

However hesitant and gradual in its onset and development at times, industrialization altered forever some parts of the world's business systems and business practices. By vastly increasing the speed of production and the volume of output—what the business historian Alfred D. Chandler, Jr., has called the "throughput" of business—industrialization created new challenges for business leaders. In some nations, most notably the United States, business people formed larger firms as they sought to control and channel this growing throughput. However, the impact of the economic and technological forces of industrialization upon the business firm varied considerably from place to place and nation to nation. Social, cultural, and political factors also affected the timing of the development of new business methods and helped determine the shapes new industrial companies assumed. Even within nations differences appeared, leading to the formation of varied sorts of companies. Thus, in the United States, which pioneered in the development of big business, and even more so in Great Britain and Japan, smaller firms remained very important in manufacturing as well as in other fields of endeavor. The

story of industrial business is, therefore, one of complexity, diversity, and unevenness.

SUGGESTED READINGS

David Landes, *The Unbound Prometheus: Technological Change and Industrial Development in Western Europe from 1750 to the Present* (London: Cambridge University Press, 1969); Sidney Pollard, *Peaceful Conquest: The Industrialization of Europe, 1760–1970* (Oxford: Oxford University Press, 1981); Maxine Berg, *The Age of Manufactures, 1700–1820*, 2nd ed. (Oxford: Oxford University Press, 1994); and Pat Hudson, *The Industrial Revolution* (London: Edward Arnold, 1992), examine industrialization in Great Britain and Europe from various perspectives. Thomas Cochran, *Frontiers of Change: Early Industrialism in America* (Oxford: Oxford University Press, 1981); David Hounshell, *From the American System to Mass Production, 1800–1932* (Baltimore: Johns Hopkins University Press, 1984); and Walter Licht, *Industrializing America: The Nineteenth Century* (Baltimore: Johns Hopkins University Press, 1995), investigate industrialism and economic growth in nineteenth-century America. G. C. Allen, *A Short Economic History of Modern Japan* (New York: St. Martin's Press, 1981); Takafusa Nakamura, *Economic Growth in Prewar Japan* (New Haven: Yale University Press, 1983); and Thomas C. Smith, *Native Sources of Japanese Industrialization, 1750–1920* (Berkeley: University of California Press, 1988), offer valuable introductions to the economic and industrial changes occurring in Japan.

On the roles labor and education played in industrial development, see especially William Lazonick, *Competitive Advantage on the Shop Floor* (Cambridge, Mass.: Harvard University Press, 1990); Sanford Jacoby, ed., *Masters to Managers: Historical and Comparative Perspectives on American Employers* (New York: Columbia University Press, 1991); Robert Locke, *The End of the Practical Man: Entrepreneurship and Higher Education in Germany, France and Great Britain, 1880–1940* (Greenwich, Conn.: JAI Press, 1984), and *Management and Higher Education: The Influence of America and Japan on West Germany, Great Britain, and France* (Cambridge: Cambridge University Press, 1989); and S. P. Keeble, *The Ability to Manage: A Study of British Management, 1890–1990* (Manchester: Manchester University Press, 1992).

3 [British Business during Industrialization

Industrialization affected the nature and structure of British firms less than it did companies in the United States or Japan. Nearly all British manufacturing ventures remained small family firms organized as single-owner proprietorships or partnerships, and kinship connections continued to be of utmost importance in the operation of those firms. Like Britain's pre-industrial merchants, most British manufacturers specialized in what they did; few sought to control all steps in making and selling goods. Instead, they devised alternatives to direct controls, ranging from regional groupings of smaller, specialized firms to the extensive use of subcontracting. These methods of business management and organization succeeded, and as a result Great Britain was the workshop of the world well into the nineteenth century.

THE CONTINUING DOMINANCE OF SMALL BUSINESS

Small family firms, usually organized as single-owner proprietorships or partnerships, accounted for most of Great Britain's industrial and economic growth during the eighteenth and nineteenth centuries. Their development took place in a volatile business environment, with many firms failing each year, only to be replaced by new ventures. In the eighteenth century some 33,000 businesses declared bankruptcy in Great Britain (and still others failed without legally becoming bankrupt). Britain's national income rose 0.87 percent annually, but the number of bankrupt firms climbed 1.15 percent per

Great Britain, around 1800

year. Moreover, rates of bankruptcy rose considerably in the mid- and late 1700s, as industrialization picked up speed.

The Family Firm

In Great Britain's unstable economic situation, partnerships based on ties of family and friendship made sense. British industrial companies often developed as parts of local and regional networks of trust, as had their preindustrial antecedents. Despite the existence of laws protecting bankrupts, most of these smaller family enterprises had unlimited liability, meaning that their owners were personally responsible for any debts the companies incurred. Far from being seen as a hindrance, unlimited liability was often viewed as an ingredient essential in instilling trust in those who might be interested in new manufacturing ventures, for it showed that the owners would stand behind their firms. Beyond providing networks of trust that could be tapped for capital, families and friends were valuable to nascent enterprises as sources of labor and business information. Extended families, including cousins and in-laws, were especially important in providing businesses with knowledge of markets.

Reinforcing the tendency toward smaller family firms was the nature of those markets. The contrast to the United States markets was striking. Despite its continuing growth, the domestic British market was smaller and less prosperous than America's. By 1880 the United States possessed a population of 50 million people with a national income of $7.2 billion. In the same year Great Britain's population stood at 35 million with a national income of only $5.2 billion. By 1920 the United States had a population and national income nearly triple that of Great Britain's. Moreover, Great Britain's national market was more divided by regional tastes and preferences than was America's. Foreign markets were more important for British business than for America's. The ratio of British foreign trade to national income was about 27–30 percent in 1860 through 1913, while for the United States the ratio was only about 5 percent. Throughout much of the twentieth century, overseas markets took about a third of Great Britain's industrial output.

Britain also possessed a better established system of wholesalers and retailers than did the United States, a legacy of Britain's long existence as a commercial nation. These marketers were able to sell successfully the expanding output of Great Britain's factories. Because Great Britain is much smaller

than America (in terms of geographic size Britain is smaller than the three contiguous states of New York, Pennsylvania, and Ohio), markets were more geographically concentrated in large cities.

In short, when compared to many of their American counterparts, British industrialists faced segmented markets, not one large homogeneous market. This circumstance meant that British manufacturers tended not to turn out long production runs of identical goods, something for which big businesses with large factories were well suited. Each regional and overseas market demanded variants. That British industrialists could dispose of their goods through a well-articulated system of independent marketers meant that they did not have to own or control directly their sales outlets, thus also allowing them to keep their firms relatively small.

Political factors also encouraged the reliance on small firms. Again, the comparison to the United States is marked. As we shall see in the next chapter, in the United States the Sherman Act of 1890 outlawed cartels; that is, the law forbade industrialists or other companies to get together to divide up markets or set prices for their goods. Ironically, this legislation encouraged formerly independent companies to merge and form big businesses in a quest to stabilize their business environment. However, no such legal prohibition against cartels existed in Great Britain. Small British firms could gain many of the benefits available to American companies only through merger by simply joining cartels, and those cartels helped preserve small industrial businesses in Great Britain.

As a result, regionally oriented small family firms spurred much of British industrialization. Even after the passage of the Joint Stock Acts of 1856 and 1862 permitted the formation of limited companies, the equivalent of incorporated businesses in America, most British enterprises remained partnerships. As late as 1885 limited companies accounted for only 5 to 10 percent of the total number of important business organizations in England. Only in the 1880s and later was there a significant decline in the use of partnership, and even with the rise of publicly held companies family influence on British business long remained important.

In these typically small industrial firms there was little separation of ownership from management. Throughout the nineteenth century and into the twentieth, ownership and management remained united, with business long remaining a personal, not a bureaucratic, affair. Business bureaucracies re-

The Crystal Palace at the Great Exhibition of 1851. This building and the machinery displayed within showed the world some of Britain's achievements during the Industrial Revolution. (*Illustrated London News*, 31 May 1851)

plete with divisions between top and middle management, sophisticated accounting systems, and the like were slow to spread in Great Britain, for they simply were not urgently needed.

Britain's business system worked, certainly into the late nineteenth century. As late as 1880 British manufacturers controlled 41 percent of the world's trade in industrial goods, and in 1913 they still controlled 30 percent. The system succeeded because many British firms found effective ways to cooperate. Sometimes small manufacturers worked in relative isolation, selling their products through manufacturers representatives. More commonly, however, two other methods emerged, both of which would also be used extensively in Japan as that nation industrialized.

Small companies often complemented the work of each other by locating in a particular region and then sharing the stages in making and selling a product, with no single company controlling all of the steps. For instance, Great Britain possessed 1,200 cotton textile factories by 1834, most comprising independent companies nearly all of which were single-owner proprietorships or partnerships. These companies usually performed just one step of the manu-

facturing process. In 1884 about 41 percent of the firms engaged in spinning only, 33 percent took part in weaving only, and a mere 27 percent integrated spinning with weaving. Financial services, market exchanges, and transportation networks were well enough developed to handle the growing output of cotton textiles. Spinning became localized in South Lancashire towns such as Oldham and Bolton, which, in turn, specialized in different types of yarns. Weaving became specialized in northwest Lancashire towns such as Blackburn and Burnley. The spinning and weaving companies were linked by merchants in the well-developed Manchester Exchange and by their geographical closeness to each other. Few textile makers had their own marketing outlets. Great Britain had a well-established system of marketers fully able to sell the finished products of their mills. As late as 1930 only 26 of Britain's 2,000 yarn and cloth producers possessed their own marketing facilities.

In a somewhat different scenario, small firms acted as subcontractors for larger companies. In the eighteenth century coal mines subcontracted work to gangs of men, a practice that spread to some iron foundries and textile mills. In the nineteenth century subcontracting sometimes extended beyond labor. The building and operation of canals was often managed on a subcontracted basis, as was that of some early railroads. Chartered in 1821, the Stockton & Darlington Railroad was constructed by subcontractors. Moreover, through the 1840s subcontractors maintained the railroad's right-of-way, repaired its locomotives, and even wound its clocks. However, as their lines grew longer and became more complex in their operations, railroads found it necessary to take over functions previously done by their subcontractors, thus internalizing actions earlier undertaken by independent small businesses.

BIG BUSINESS BEGINS

When compared to the situations in America and Japan during industrialization, big businesses were slower to develop in Great Britain. Still, some firms grew large by the international standards of their day. As early as the mid-1700s the ironworks of Ambrose Crowley consisted of rolling, plating, and slitting mills, four steel furnaces, and two large forges. The company also owned ten warehouses and four ships. The ironworks employed about 800 men, with another 150 engaged in transport, and an additional 150 handling the company's affairs in London. As one of Great Britain's largest business

British coal mine of the nineteenth century. The running of large coal mines helped introduce new management methods into Great Britain. (*Illustrated London News*, 1 March 1873)

enterprises, the ironworks began replacing personal with bureaucratic management methods. Frustrated in his attempts to run his large enterprise by himself, Crowley drew up a constitution, a set of written orders, to govern the work of his laborers, foremen, and middle managers.

The Companies and Industries

Crowley's ironworks was not alone as a good-sized industrial enterprise. By 1813 one coal mine employed 600 people and possessed twenty miles of underground railroads upon which 1,000 horses pulled carts. Sixteen years later forty-one Tyneside coal mines employed an average of 300 people apiece. By 1790 the four largest copper and tin mines employed over 1,000 people each and were using a total of seventeen steam engines. Forty-six years later thirty-six mines had an average employment of about 200. By the 1790s most British ironworks were giving work to about 300 hands, while those in Shropshire employed an average of 700. By 1830 some employed over 5,000 workers. Even the cotton textile industry, which was a stronghold of small

businesses, saw the development of some large firms. As early as 1795 Peels had twenty-three mills, William Douglas and Partners nine, and Robinsons five. By 1815 New Lanark employed 1,600 workers, James Finlay & Company 1,500, and Strutts 1,500. In the early 1830s the Manchester mills were employing an average of 300 to 400 workers, while seven firms employed over 1,000 apiece.

Great Britain experienced a wave of mergers in the late nineteenth century, and this merger movement led to the further development of big business. In 1902, for example, Dudley Docker, a Birmingham industrialist, linked five of England's largest rolling stock companies in a merger creating the Metropolitan Amalgamated Carriage and Wagon Company. Between 1888 and 1914 an average of 67 companies disappeared via mergers every year, and in 1898 through 1900 the average soared to 650. Many of these mergers were designed simply to limit competition and to preserve the status quo rather than to reduce costs of production in the interests of increasing the international competitiveness of the companies involved.

With these mergers, big businesses developed in many of the same fields in which they were also arising in the United States. In 1919, 177 of Britain's 200 largest industrial ventures operated in just a few fields: food processing, textiles, chemicals, metals, and machinery. In these fields, more than in others, there were advantages to be gained by combining all or most of the stages of production and sales in single firms, and there existed markets large enough to support such linkages. There were, then, economies of scale. That is, by building larger factories business leaders were able to reduce the cost of production per unit of their goods, and these cost reductions (passed on to consumers in the form of lower prices) broadened the markets for those goods. Then, too, there existed economies of scope. That is, business owners could often use factories to produce a range of related goods and, more importantly, could use marketing networks set up for one product to push additional products.

In the fields mentioned above it often made sense to handle all of the production and marketing functions in individual firms, what is called "vertical integration." To insure stability in their operations and to keep all of the profits for themselves executives sought to control all of the steps of making and selling their goods. When their output in a given period of time—their throughput—reached a high level, manufacturers found it valuable to own their own supplies of raw materials and their own sales outlets. In this way

they could be sure of protecting their firms from shortages of raw materials in times of peak demand, and they could also be reasonably certain of selling the growing throughput of their factories.

Still, when compared to what was taking place in the United States, British industrialists were less likely to integrate fully their operations. Britain's smaller, more compact, and more segmented markets, along with existence of a well-established network of wholesalers and retailers militated against total vertical integration. Even the largest British firms tended to be smaller than their American counterparts. In 1930 only the largest fifty British industrial companies would be big enough to make the list of the top 200 manufacturing ventures in the United States.

Beer and Cigarettes

While large firms arose in many of the same industries in Britain as in America, there was a major difference: in almost every one of those industries British enterprises tended to produce consumer rather than industrial goods. British entrepreneurs proved most successful in making branded, packaged goods: cigarettes, soap, sugar, flour, jams, and the like. Most began—as did, for instance, Cadbury Brothers in chocolates—in producing for regional markets. They then expanded to serve the national market later by exploiting economies of scale and scope.

The British brewing industry, especially the part located in London, witnessed the beginnings of big business at an early date. The experiences of firms in it reveal a great deal about the development of Britain's early industrial ventures, their growth, and their limitations. The experiences also illustrate that industrialization was a broad-based development, extending beyond such well-known industries as cotton textiles and ironmaking.

Industrialization in brewing involved the use of machinery. By the early 1800s London breweries were using machinery to grind grain, mash the ground malt in vats, and pump and move liquids. An increasing number of the machines were steam-powered; by 1805 steam power had nearly replaced horse power. Steam power was more economical and more reliable than horse power. The growing use of machinery led to more efficient factory designs. The sizes of vats and utensils increased dramatically. Malt and water were lifted by steam-powered machinery to the top floors of the breweries; then

gravity carried them down through the various processes involved in brewing beer. Lying behind these alterations was the unquenchable London market. At a time when beer was a perishable good, for this was before refrigeration or preservatives, only a large local market could support big breweries.

As they came to use steam-powered machinery and to be housed in larger buildings, the breweries became capital-intensive (that is, they required growing amounts of money for their expansion and operations) and grew in size. By the late 1700s the largest London breweries were giving work to 100 men apiece and were capitalized at 200,000 pounds each. By the 1830s firm capitalization had risen fourfold.

More than most other early industrialists, London brewers began linking in single companies the different steps involved in making and selling beer. In the 1780s some sought to control their sources of raw materials by entering into long-term contracts with farmers for their grain; and in the next decade some began setting up their own retail outlets, pubs (public houses) serving exclusively their beer in London and nearby areas. As yet, the perishable nature of beer precluded the development of national chains of pubs. Some brewers also kept pigs and cattle to eat the waste materials resulting from the brewing process, selling their meat and milk on the London market. Few brewers, however, fully integrated the work of their enterprises.

Even as they expanded, most breweries remained partnerships, whose members continued to raise capital from family and friends. Many of the brewers also had personal friendships with leading London bankers and received loans from those institutions. The partners ran their breweries directly, with little in the way of managerial organizations. The brewers made all of the key decisions on buying the raw materials, setting up production processes, and selling the beer. They walked the brewery floors to engage in hands-on management. While considerably larger than their preindustrial antecedents, the London breweries were not so large or complex as to need intricate management staffs or managerial techniques. Indeed, many brewers found time to become involved in other forms of trade and in local politics.

A somewhat similar story unfolded in Britain's tobacco industry at a later date. When it was formed in 1901, the Imperial Tobacco Company was capitalized at nearly 12 million pounds (then about $60 million), making it the largest manufacturer in Great Britain. Imperial Tobacco was a combination of thirteen formerly independent British firms joined together to oppose the

entrance of James Duke's American Tobacco Company, the largest American tobacco firm, into the British market.

Of the companies coming together to form Imperial Tobacco, the largest was W. D. & H. O. Wills of Bristol, England's leading maker of cigarettes, which was capitalized at almost 7 million pounds. Wills began its history in a competitive business environment. The linking of different regions in Great Britain by the railroad began breaking down local monopolies in the 1840s, though regional tastes remained more important than in the United States. In 1846 Wills began giving special brand names to some of its smoking tobaccos as a way of differentiating them from their competitors, and in the 1860s Wills led other tobacco companies in setting up a national selling network. The use of packing machines for loose tobacco and the adoption of airtight tins in the 1880s also moved Wills ahead of other British companies.

However, it was Wills's movement into cigarette making that gave the company dominance in the British market. Wills brought out its first hand-made cigarette in 1871. In 1884 Wills purchased exclusive British rights to the American-designed cigarette-making machine called the Bonsack machine. The Bonsack machine replaced hand labor with machine work, thus greatly speeding up cigarette making. A team of ten cigarette makers working by hand could produce 20,000 cigarettes per day; one person supervising a single Bonsack machine could turn out at least 100,000. Beginning in 1888 the company began making cheap cigarettes for the mass market with the Bonsack machines. Within two years, Wills had captured 59 percent of the British cigarette market, and, despite the acquisition of the Bonsack machine by other British companies, still held 55 percent of the market in 1901. As in the United States, the control of technology essential in increasing the throughput of business allowed some British firms to move ahead of their competitors and become big businesses. The Bonsack machine helped Wills, as it did Duke's American Tobacco, defeat rivals in the cigarette industry.

Management

Even within the largest big businesses in Great Britain family ownership and management long remained more common than in the United States. As late as 1930, 70 percent of Great Britain's 200 largest companies still had family members sitting on their boards of directors. Nonetheless, some changes oc-

curred in the structure of the management of Britain's newly emerging big businesses. Departmentalized central offices developed in embryo form, as proprietors and partners began delegating responsibility in a few companies. That is, in some firms there was a division of authority between the different partners so that each became, in effect, a department head with several paid managers under him. In other cases there was a single managing director, financed by sleeping (inactive) partners, with a number of managers below him. However, even after the British merger movement most of the resulting big businesses were loosely organized. Typically, the central offices of the British firms consisted of a large number of the executives from the former partnerships who met only a few times each year to set prices, review the activities of the different parts of the company, and allocate funds for expansion.

Below the level of top management some alterations also took place. The nature of the manager of a large works—that person below the active proprietor or partners, but above the foremen or clerks—was changing. Managers became better educated, and their salaries and social status rose. The differences in income and status separating works managers from the managing partners, which had been considerable in the mid-1700s, nearly vanished by the 1830s. As their companies became larger and more complex, some proprietors and managers devised new accounting methods to help them run their enterprises. Building upon the efforts of estate keepers, merchants, and very early industrialists, the nineteenth-century manufacturers began developing financial, cost, and capital accounting. None, however, went as far in developing new accounting methods as did some executives in the United States.

As would happen in the United States and Japan, some British railroads became big businesses for their day. Not all relied on subcontracting to handle their operations. As they grew in size and complexity, they began developing new management methods. The London and North Western Railroad (LNWR), formed in 1846 and capitalized at 29 million pounds, was employing 12,000 workers on 800 miles of track by the early 1850s. The LNWR, as it expanded the scope of its operations, devised a new system of management. The LNWR was composed of three regional divisions, each of which had its own secretary, superintendent, locomotive manager, and goods manager (purchasing manager). Each of these people reported to a general manager who coordinated their work and oversaw all of the operations of the line. New accounting methods that allowed for depreciation (something very important

in capital-intensive businesses) and more precise record keeping of all sorts—with middle managers in charge of gathering and analyzing the statistics and figures—developed well beyond what was being done in other British businesses.

Unlike what was occurring in America at about the same time, there was little spillover of new managerial techniques from British railroads to British industrial firms. Few British railroad executives were involved in other types of business ventures. Moreover, the smaller size of most British industrial ventures meant that extensive changes were not required. In America—to get ahead of the story just a bit—Andrew Carnegie applied management methods he learned from the Pennsylvania Railroad in running a gigantic steel empire he built in the 1870s through the 1890s.

Industrial Leaders

Who were Great Britain's business leaders? The pioneer industrialists were a diverse lot coming from many backgrounds, but men with mercantile links predominated. Most early industrialists came from middle-class origins, not from working-class families. Most successful industrial entrepreneurs used networks of families and friends to get ahead. Access to local and regional family networks often proved a crucial determinant of business success.

By the late nineteenth century patterns of business success, while still quite varied, showed more commonality. Cultural homogeneity among members of Britain's middle class, including many business people, increased as regional identities lessened a bit. In the years 1870 through 1889, 57 percent of the British business leaders were the sons of businessmen, 19 percent were the sons of public officials, 13 percent were the sons of farmers, and 11 percent were the sons of clerical workers and laborers. A desire to enrich themselves and move up socially motivated British business leaders. As in earlier times, entrepreneurs often moved from one venture to another, prepared to save what could be salvaged from business disappointments, while moving on to new enterprises.

Management and Labor

Relationships between management and labor took several forms in Britain's industrial establishments. Much of the conflict and accommodation revolved around the question of who would control the work process. Laborers, especially skilled ones, often sought to remain in control by subcontracting their labor as a group to business owners and factory managers. Subcontracting relieved a firm's managers of the need to supervise directly all of their company's activities. It was this situation that gave skilled workers in many fields considerable control over their work processes. The workers decided how and at what speed they would labor in return for a set amount of pay for a certain amount of completed work—tons of coal mined, yards of cloth produced, and so forth. These practically minded workers proved to be one of the strengths of Britain's industrialization. Improvements they made on the job—usually of an incremental, not breakthrough, nature—helped Britain stay competitive for decades.

Nonetheless, as time passed, employers sometimes sought to erode this control in bargaining sessions with workers joined together in trade unions. Employers tried to impose new forms of industrial discipline by gaining control of the pace, price, and organization of work. New agreements between employers and workers often favored the former. An 1898 agreement between employers and machinery makers (engineers in British parlance), for example, gave employers the right to determine the manning and operation of machinery, including the employment of apprentices. Few agreements went this far in extending employer control over shopfloor activities. Even in the area of engineering, workers retained considerable control over the details of their shopfloor activities. In fact, before World War I national collective bargaining was really just beginning. Regional collective bargaining was important in such industries as steel, shipbuilding, and textiles; but even here it often collapsed because of disagreements among manufacturers. Most agreements were sliding-scale ones, in which wages fluctuated with the price of the product.

The introduction of what was called scientific management failed to give British industrialists much control over workers. Begun in America in the late nineteenth century, scientific management, or Taylorism (named after its founder Frederick Taylor), sought to make factory work more efficient by

taking control of work processes from workers and giving it to factory foremen. Workers were instructed in the most efficient ways of fulfilling their
tasks and were paid when they met factory norms or quotas for those tasks.
This approach met stiff opposition from both British trade unions and from
many factory owners. Less interested than their American counterparts in
long runs of homogeneous products, British industrialists were less concerned
with scientific management as a way to make their businesses more efficient
and profitable.

Instead, some British manufacturers turned to welfare capitalism or welfare work, especially in fields in which big businesses sought to stabilize their
operations. Industrial welfare work encompassed a broad range of company-
supplied benefits for workers: the provision of sick pay, old-age pensions, safer
working conditions, sports facilities, and (occasionally) housing. The goal
was to keep workers loyal to their companies without changing relations of
power. Industrial welfare work was most common in those industries that were
capital-intensive, in those fields in which the main costs of doing business lay
in the capital tied up in the plant and equipment, not in workers' salaries.
Managers wanted to avoid conflict that might interfere with the throughput
of their plants: railroads, gas works, iron and steel factories, breweries, and
chemical plants. Smaller, less capital-intensive firms tended to rely more on
informal arrangements than on systematic welfare plans.

BUSINESSES IN SALES AND SERVICES

Businesses in sales and services grew up along with those in manufacturing
and were essential to the development of industrial firms. Far from being
afterthoughts, retail and service businesses were important for the growth
of the British economy, both in their own right and in terms of the roles
they played in their nation's industrialization. Banks helped finance industrial concerns, and shopkeepers sold the new factory products. As in so much
of British business, small firms long predominated in sales and services; but
there was a trend, especially in banking, toward bigness.

Retailing

If the country was long the "workshop of the world," Great Britain was also often called "a nation of shopkeepers." Fixed-place shops coexisted with itinerant trading and open-air markets throughout the eighteenth century. From the mid-nineteenth century, however, small shops took over most retailing from peddlers and public markets, especially in the larger cities. Already rising in numbers in southern England in the late 1700s, the number of family shops increased dramatically throughout the Midlands and northern England in the 1800s.

In the nineteenth and early twentieth centuries new types of outlets arose to challenge family retailers. Department stores, which developed in the United States at about the same time, served urban customers. William Whitley opened what is often called the first department store in Great Britain in 1863, bringing under one roof departments selling many different goods, thus offering convenience to his customers. But more than convenience was involved. By around 1900, featuring tearooms, restaurants, club rooms, and hair-dressing salons, the department stores brought glamour into the lives of middle-class consumers. Being consumers—not just producers—became a major part of a growing number of people's lives. By emphasizing stock turn, the rapid, high-volume sale of goods at fixed prices, department stores made considerable sums on low profit margins.

Still other forms of retailing developed. Multiples (or chain stores) appeared in nearly all types of British retailing by World War I, but especially in areas dealing with mass-produced, standardized consumer goods—just as was occurring in the United States. Most were regional in scope, but some grew to become national federations: Lipton, Maypole (in groceries), Jesse Boot (pharmacy), and Marks and Spencer (variety goods), to name a few. Cooperative stores owned by consumers also came to sell commodities such as tea, margarine, and flour. They expanded to form, as early as 1863, the Co-operative Society, through which local cooperatives could make bulk purchases of consumer goods. The Society also came to own factories to manufacture and process household and branded goods. For those in the countryside, stores selling through mail-order catalogs grew up—as did Sears and Montgomery Ward in America.

The Development of Banking

The trend toward concentration was even more pronounced in some service industries, most notably banking, than in retailing. The rate of growth in the number of retail banks peaked in the third quarter of the nineteenth century and then slowed down. The deposits of commercial banks in England and Wales rose eightfold between 1848 and 1913, to 800 million pounds. As this expansion occurred, the nature of bank ownership changed dramatically. In 1850, 327 private banks with 518 offices (branches) greatly outnumbered the 99 joint-stock banks controlling 576 offices. By 1913, however, 41 joint-stock banks had 6,426 offices, while 29 private banks possessed just 147 offices. Banking had been transformed: a relatively small group of joint-stock banks, mainly with headquarters in London, dominated British banking nationwide by the time of World War I.

Corporate capitalism replaced personal capitalism in British banking; here was an area where larger firms flourished. Banking legislation passed by Parliament in 1825 and 1833, together with the more general measures allowing the formation of joint-stock companies in 1856 and 1862, encouraged the formation of joint-stock banks. By the time of World War I the "Big Five" banks—Barclay, Lloyds, the Midland, the National Provincial, and the Westminster—had about 80 percent of the domestic deposits in England and were among the largest banks in the world. It was banks like these that came to make up the City of London financial establishment.

The banking situation in Britain differed from that of the United States. Possessing more compact urban-industrial markets than the United States, Britain came to have a banking system dominated by a handful of large city banks. Into the 1980s America's banking system was much more atomized and decentralized than that of Britain. American laws, in contrast to those of many other nations, long made it difficult for banks to own branches across state lines (or, in many cases even within single states). The desire of Americans to have a federal system of government (and state government regulation of business) contributed to the spread of a decentralized banking system. As a consequence, tens of thousands of smaller institutions dominated commercial banking in the United States well into the twentieth century.

Banking and Industry

Britain's banking system proved responsive to the capital needs of nineteenth-century industry. Hundreds of smaller country banks developed in the late 1700s and early 1800s, and many of these institutions made loans (often called overdrafts) to nascent manufacturers. Local networks of family and friends were important in arranging these transactions. In Sheffield, for example, close ties of kinship and sometimes ownership linked bank directors to manufacturing firms, creating an effective regional network of information and credit.

While often involved in financing foreign trade and in making investments overseas, the large City banks also helped finance British industry. While small and medium-sized manufacturing ventures often continued to rely on local sources of capital, including local banks, larger manufacturers found in the City banks an important source of funding. Contrary to charges sometimes leveled against them, City banks did not simply invest in overseas projects. The extension of City bank branch networks throughout England may even have increased the availability of capital to industry. There was enough bank funding to meet the demand for it. If any weakness existed, it was on the part of the manufacturers. Eager to maintain family control over their enterprises, they may not have asked for all of the funding they might have been able to use. Rapid expansion was not, perhaps, a key priority for them.

SMALL FIRMS TRIUMPHANT

Big businesses like Imperial Tobacco were the exception, not the rule, in prewar Great Britain; small and medium-sized firms rather than large ones led Britain's industrial advance. Even Imperial Tobacco, Great Britain's largest industrial enterprise, was a pygmy when compared to America's biggest business, United States Steel, which was formed in the same year, 1901, and capitalized at $1.4 billion. Only in a handful of manufacturing and service fields did large companies dominate Britain's business scene. Instead, smaller firms employing practical, skilled workers ruled the day. The nature of Britain's markets, along with the nation's geography, laws, and other factors, militated against the extensive development of big business. Britain's thousands of independent firms, often woven together in various sorts of arrangements short

of their merger into large, vertically integrated firms, made the nation the world leader in manufacturing for most of the 1800s. Only during the closing decades of the nineteenth century did the United States overtake Britain as an industrial power.

SUGGESTED READINGS

The essays composing Geoffrey Jones and Mary Rose, eds., *Family Capitalism* (Brookfield, Mass.: Frank Cass, 1993), examine the importance of family firms in Great Britain and beyond from the eighteenth through the twentieth centuries. Mary Rose, *The Gregs of Quarry Bank Mill: The Rise and Decline of a Family Firm, 1750–1914* (New York: Cambridge University Press, 1986), is a valuable case study. See also Charles Dellheim, "The Creation of a Company Culture: Cadburys, 1861–1931," *American Historical Review* 92 (February 1987): 13–44. Sidney Pollard, *The Genesis of Modern Management* (Cambridge, Mass.: Harvard University Press, 1965), looks at the beginning of big business in Great Britain. Katrina Honeyman, *Origins of Enterprise: Business Leadership in the Industrial Revolution* (Manchester: Manchester University Press, 1983); P. L. Payne, *British Entrepreneurship in the Nineteenth Century* (London: Macmillan, 1974); and François Crouzet, *The First Industrialists: The Problem of Origins* (Cambridge: Cambridge University Press, 1985), investigate business leadership during industrialization. Julian Hoppit, *Risk and Failure in English Business, 1700–1800* (Cambridge: Cambridge University Press, 1987), examines bankruptcy and the growing risks in British business.

Much has been written about the British cotton textile industry. S. D. Chapman, *The Cotton Textile Industry in the Industrial Revolution* (London: Macmillan, 1972); D. A. Farnie, *The English Cotton Industry in the World Market, 1815–1896* (Oxford: Oxford University Press, 1979); Anthony Howe, *The Cotton Masters, 1830–1860* (Oxford: Oxford University Press, 1984); William Lazonick, "Industrial Organization and Technological Change: The Decline of the British Cotton Industry," *Business History Review* 57 (Summer 1983): 195–236; Lars Sandburg, *Lancashire in Decline* (Columbus: The Ohio State University Press, 1974); and Mary Rose, ed., *International Competition and Strategic Response in Textile Industries Since 1870* (London: Frank Cass, 1991), examine the industry from different viewpoints. The journal *Business History* 32 (October 1990) is devoted to the textile industry.

B. W. E. Alford, *W. D. & H. O. Wills and the Development of the U.K. Tobacco Industry, 1786–1965* (London: Methuen, 1973); Maurice Kirby, *The Origins of Railway Enterprise: The Stockton and Darlington Railway, 1821–1863* (New York: Cambridge University Press, 1993); and T. R. Gourvish and R. G. Wilson, *The British Brewing Industry, 1830–1980* (New York: Cambridge University Press, 1994), are solid company or industry histories. H. L. Malchow, *Gentlemen Capitalists: The Social and Political World of the Victorian Businessman* (Stanford: Stanford University Press, 1992), presents four finely drawn business biographies. R. P. T. Davenport-Hines, *Dudley Docker: The Life and Times of a Trade Warrior* (Cambridge: Cambridge University Press, 1984), is an excellent business biography of an industrialist who sought to rationalize British business in the early twentieth century.

Less has been written on marketing and services than on manufacturing. For an introduction to the development of marketing, see the essays, mainly about the British experience, in Richard Tedlow and Geoffrey Jones, eds., *The Rise and Fall of Mass Marketing* (London: Routledge, 1994). Stanley Chapman, "British Marketing Enterprise: The Changing Roles of Merchants, Manufacturers, and Financiers, 1700–1860," *Business History Review* 53 (Summer 1979): 205–34, and R. P. T. Davenport-Hines, ed., *Markets and Bagmen: Studies in the History of Marketing and British Industrial Performance, 1830–1939* (Brookfield, Mass.: Gower Publishers, 1986), are also valuable. Thomas Richards, *The Commodity Culture of Victorian England: Advertising and Spectacle, 1851–1914* (Stanford: Stanford University Press, 1990), provides a provocative look at the spread of a consumer society in Great Britain. Youssef Cassis, *City Bankers, 1890–1914* (Cambridge: Cambridge University Press, 1994), offers a close look at the banking community composing the City of London. Forrest Capie and Michael Collins, "Industrial Lending by English Commercial Banks, 1860s–1914: Why Did Banks Refuse Loans?" *Business History* 38 (January 1996): 26–44, concludes that City banks such as Lloyds and Midland met all reasonable requests for industrial loans. Lucy Newton, "Regional Bank-Industry Relations during the Mid-Nineteenth Century: Links Between Bankers and Manufacturing in Sheffield, c. 1850 to c. 1885," *Business History* 38 (July 1996): 64–83, is a valuable regional study of links between bank directors and local industrial firms. For a comparative study of the impact of antitrust laws on industry, see

Tony Freyer, *Regulating Big Business: Antitrust in Great Britain and America 1880–1990* (Cambridge: Cambridge University Press, 1992).

E. P. Thompson, *The Making of the English Working Class* (New York: Alfred Knopf, 1963), and E. J. Hobsbawm, *Labouring Men* (Garden City: Doubleday, 1967), are classic studies of the history of British labor. Robert Fitzgerald, *British Labour Management & Industrial Welfare* (London: Croom Helm, 1988), and Isaac Cohen, *American Management and British Labor* (Westport, Conn.: Greenwood Press, 1990), place British labor practices in the context of industry structures.

4 [Big and Small Businesses in America

After the Civil War American industrialists were the world leaders in achieving high-volume, low-cost production in manufacturing—in the processing of liquids, agricultural goods, metals, and some other products. This approach to mass production, encouraged by the existence of a large national market and made possible by technological breakthroughs, led to the rise of big business in the United States. Only later did big business develop in as major a way in Great Britain or Japan. Still, the growth of big business in America did not mean the demise of small and medium-size firms, even in manufacturing. Manufacturers of all sizes coexisted in a sometimes uneasy mix that changed over time and continues to change to the present day. Beyond manufacturing, most types of sales and services remained in the realm of smaller firms, where most Americans continued to work.

LARGE BUSINESS FIRMS

The new big businesses that developed in the United States differed from their smaller counterparts in fundamental ways. Many big businesses were organized as corporations, rather than as partnerships; and many developed managerial hierarchies as time progressed. Bureaucratic management began replacing personal management. Most fundamentally, many big businesses, especially large industrial firms, sought to internalize within their operations all the steps involved in making and selling goods. They did not want to rely on other firms, and so tried to do everything themselves. To some extent, large British companies were moving in the same directions—as we saw in Chapter 3—but large American firms went much farther.

Incorporation and Firm Size

As the nineteenth century progressed, more and more American industrial companies were corporations, as permitted by the general incorporation laws of most states. A shrinking proportion were single-owner proprietorships or partnerships. Many manufacturing concerns were capital-intensive and needed to raise vast sums of money to build factories. The corporate form of organization, with its promise of limited liability for investors (investors were not held personally responsible for the debts of the corporations in which they invested), proved especially attractive to would-be industrialists. Another advantage of the corporation was that, unlike a partnership, it did not have to be reorganized every time an investor left the business. More than in Great Britain, business leaders in America embraced incorporation; by 1904 corporations accounted for three-quarters of the United States' industrial output.

As executives formed corporations, big businesses arose in America. The size of business firms increased dramatically. In the 1850s the largest industrial enterprises were cotton textile mills. Only a handful, however, were capitalized at over $1 million or employed more than 500 workers. In 1860 no single American company was valued at as much as $10 million, but by 1904 over 300 were. In 1901 the newly formed United States Steel Corporation was capitalized at $1.4 billion to become America's and the world's first billion-dollar company, employing over 100,000 workers. By 1929 the corporation employed 440,000.

Firm Structure

The new big businesses developed structures different from those of earlier enterprises. These structures evolved in response to the opportunities of the national market and in response to the growing complexity of manufacturing processes. The national market offered pleasing possibilities to American businessmen, a market of continental size for their products. Larger, richer, and more homogeneous than that of any other nation, the United States' domestic market stimulated business executives to develop firms that could produce and sell long runs of standardized goods; thus economies of scale could be exploited well in the American context. So could economies of scope, by which industrial firms could use their factories to turn out a growing variety of

The Corliss Steam Engine at the Philadelphia Exposition of 1876. The center of attention at the exposition, this engine represented industrial progress to most Americans. (*Graphic*, 10 June 1876)

goods and by which they could employ their marketing networks to sell those goods. However, the national market also created virulent competition. The railroad and the telegraph brought businesses across the nation into competition with each other by destroying local monopolies that had been based upon the high cost of inland transportation. Technological breakthroughs in production were also a double-edged sword. The innovations increased production, but this vast increase proved difficult to sell by conventional means.

Vertical integration was *the* common American response to the challenges of market and technological change. Much more than was true in either Great Britain or Japan, vertically integrated companies came to dominate the industrial landscape of the United States. In vertical integration a company that initially engages in only one stage of the production and sale of a good may integrate backward to control its sources of raw materials and may integrate forward to control the making and selling of its finished goods. Through vertical integration, big businesses in America combined mass production with mass distribution. (See Figure 1.)

Vertical integration offered several advantages to executives operating on

Major Railroads in the United States, around 1910

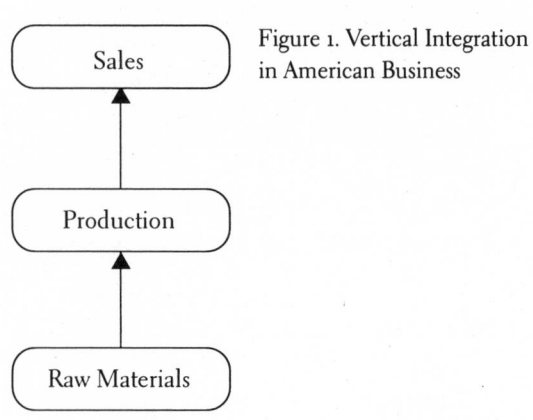

Figure 1. Vertical Integration in American Business

a large scale in the national market. Through vertical integration business leaders could partially insulate their firms from the buffets of the national market. By controlling raw materials, they could assure themselves of adequate supplies during times of peak demand, and by controlling all stages of manufacturing, they could keep all the profits within their own firms. There were also advantages in controlling marketing networks, and in some fields big businesses arose when industrialists set up marketing systems to handle their goods. Business executives using new types of machinery to turn out high volumes of matches, cigarettes, flour, and canned goods found America's wholesalers overwhelmed by the increased output—the throughput of their firms—and set up their own national marketing systems. Similarly, producers making or growing perishables such as beer, meat, and citrus fruits found marketers unable to guarantee the needed speed of delivery to market and also established their own national systems. Finally, manufacturers of technologically complex goods such as reapers, sewing machines, typewriters, and elevators set up their own systems, because established marketers could not adequately demonstrate such complex products to prospective customers, finance their purchase by customers, or service and repair the products after sales.

Horizontal integration provided a second mechanism by which American industrialists structured their big businesses. In horizontal integration a number of companies join together to control one step in the production and sale of goods. As in vertical integration, the aim was to decrease competition and control the vicissitudes of the national market. Thus, forty-one compa-

nies joined together in 1882 to form the Standard Oil Trust to control much of the refining of petroleum in America. To be successful, horizontal integration was usually accompanied by vertical integration, as businesses sought to control their raw materials and markets, as well as production. Standard Oil, for example, acquired its own crude oil fields, built its own long-distance pipelines, and set up its own sales outlets in the late nineteenth and early twentieth centuries.

Business integration, both vertical and horizontal, took place more through mergers of formerly independent companies than by internally generated growth. Mergers became increasingly common from the 1880s on, culminating in America's first major merger movement. Between 1894 and 1905 over 3,000 individual firms that were capitalized at over $6 billion merged in the United States.

Management Changes

In those industrial firms that grew in size and complexity, personal management gave way to bureaucratic management. Companies became too large and too complex to be run as one-man shows. With plants spread across the United States, industrial companies became multi-unit enterprises, and four interrelated managerial changes occurred.

Executives established strong central (corporate) offices for their companies. Staffed by the top management, these offices were in charge of making the big strategic decisions for the company, planning for the future, and coordinating the work of the different parts of the company. The central offices soon became functionally departmentalized, with different committees of executives in charge of different functions of the company—production, sales, transportation, and so on. By 1886 Standard Oil possessed a functionally departmentalized head office consisting of different committees for domestic commerce, foreign trade, manufacturing, and transportation. An executive committee of Standard's top officers was supposed to oversee and coordinate the work of these committees.

Middle management, which had not existed earlier, developed to run the many daily operations of the new big businesses and to staff the various production facilities and sales outlets. In the late nineteenth century the Burling-

ton, Chicago & Quincy Railroad had 191 middle-level managers, and in the early 1900s Singer Sewing Machine had 1,700 branch offices across America run by middle managers.

To control their growing industrial empires industrialists went beyond the preindustrial merchant's simple accounting methods based on double-entry bookkeeping. They developed new accounting methods to help plan for the future of their companies as well as to keep track of past and current operations. Big business leaders began developing financial accounting, including the use of operating ratios, as a way to judge the performances of their firms. They started using capital accounting, with its provisions for depreciation, as a way to plan for the future. True cost accounting was developed as a way to keep track of and to compare the internal workings of various parts of their plants.

There was also the beginning of the separation of ownership from management in big businesses. A growing proportion of corporate officers became men (rarely women in this time period) working on salary for their companies' stockholders. While far from disappearing, family firms became rarer in the realm of big business.

The replacement of personal by bureaucratic management took place first on America's largest railroads, some of which had become big businesses by the 1850s, and then spread to the mammoth industrial enterprises arising in the 1880s and later. Four railroads—the Pennsylvania, the Baltimore & Ohio, the New York Central, and the New York & Erie—controlled trackage from the East Coast to the Midwest by the mid-1850s. As they grew from small local carriers to interregional lines, these railroads faced unprecedented operating difficulties, such as how to schedule large numbers of trains and run them safely on time, and strategic problems, such as how to meet the moves of their competitors and how to raise the enormous amounts of capital needed for their expansion. All responded by establishing bureaucratic management systems.

Large industrial firms operating on a national scale encountered the same types of challenges and made a similar response—again, the adoption of bureaucratic management—a generation or two later. Andrew Carnegie, who served as the superintendent of the western division of the Pennsylvania Railroad, applied the lessons he learned on that line in running the steel company

he put together in the late nineteenth century. While always in control of strategic decision making, Carnegie delegated authority over operations to his steel mill managers, rarely interfering with their decisions. From his work on the railroad Carnegie also took an abiding concern for controlling costs and promoting high-volume production to his steel mills.

James Duke and the American Tobacco Company

The evolution of the American Tobacco Company presents a classic case study in the development of big business in American industry. James Buchanan Duke, known by most nineteenth-century Americans as "Buck Duke," transformed the American tobacco industry through the development of American Tobacco, the firm that brought the mass-production of cigarettes to the American public. Moreover, Duke's character was typical, in many important respects, of those of America's business leaders of the late nineteenth and early twentieth centuries.

By 1880 Duke had taken over a family business in pipe tobacco in North Carolina, and it was from this base that he soon built the largest tobacco-processing company in the world. Realizing that other well-established companies already controlled the plug (chewing) and pipe tobacco fields, Duke looked elsewhere for expansion possibilities. He found his chance in cigarettes, a relatively new field of tobacco processing whose market was rapidly increasing—1.8 million cigarettes were sold in America in 1869, but 500 million in 1880. As we saw in Chapter 3, in those days cigarettes were made by hand, with a supervisor and team of ten turning out about 20,000 cigarettes a day. In 1881 Duke hired a team of eleven men to begin his production. In this labor-intensive business there were no economies of scale, and Duke was, at first, simply one of many cigarette makers.

Duke surged ahead of the other cigarette producers with the purchase of rights to use automatic cigarette-rolling machines patented by James Bonsack of Virginia. Perfected in 1884, a Bonsack machine could turn out over 100,000 cigarettes a day. Use of the Bonsack machines gave Duke a cost advantage over his rivals, just as such machines helped W. D. & H. O. Wills move ahead of its competitors in Great Britain. By 1885 Duke controlled 10 percent of America's cigarette market. He then engaged in horizontal inte-

gration, taking over his competitors—Allen and Ginter of Richmond, Kinney Tobacco of New York, Goodwin and Company of Rochester, and others—to form one gigantic company, the American Tobacco Company, in 1890.

Duke next sought to move beyond cigarettes to acquire companies in chewing and pipe tobacco making both in and beyond the United States. By 1910 American Tobacco possessed 86 percent of the cigarette market, 85 percent of the plug market, 79 percent of the pipe tobacco market, and 14 percent of the cigar market in America. Duke went abroad by taking on British cigarette makers in 1901. After a fierce battle, American Tobacco and Imperial Tobacco agreed to a truce. American Tobacco agreed to get out of the British market, and Imperial Tobacco said it would leave the American market. Together they formed a new company, two-thirds owned by American Tobacco, to sell cigarettes to the rest of the world.

Some vertical integration followed American Tobacco's horizontal integration, as Duke acquired companies making licorice, cotton bags to hold tobacco, boxes, and tin foil. American Tobacco also purchased the United Cigar Stores, which had 392 retail outlets.

Eventually, American Tobacco's control over the American market led to its dissolution at the hands of the Justice Department of the federal government. In 1908 the department brought suit against the company under the terms of the Sherman Act of 1890, and three years later the United States Supreme Court ordered that the company be split up. From the dissolution of American Tobacco came new firms that long dominated the American tobacco market: the (new) American Tobacco Company, the Liggett and Myers Tobacco Company, the R. J. Reynolds Tobacco Company, and the P. Lorillard Company. Duke left American Tobacco a few months after its breakup and died in 1925.

Shortly before his death, Duke told a friend why he thought he had been successful in business. "I resolved from the time I was a mere boy to do a big business," Duke observed. "I loved business better than anything else. I worked from early morning until late at night. I was sorry to have to leave off at night and glad when morning came so I could get at it again." * Business was Duke's life. He loved the thrill of the game. He was an empire builder.

However, Duke was not a good administrator. He failed to establish a

---

* Robert Sobel, *The Entrepreneurs* (New York: Weybright and Talley, 1974), 194.

rational management system for his company. Nor did Duke really provide American Tobacco with a goal beyond growth for growth's sake. Perhaps not surprisingly, American Tobacco's earnings, as a percentage of sales, fell from 29 percent in 1891 to 22 percent in 1908. Duke left American Tobacco a few months after its dissolution. His later life was not a happy one. Disturbed by the death of his father, dismayed by marital difficulties, and upset by the breakup of his company, Duke tended to drift and turn to drink. However, he believed in the value of education and set up Duke University as his memorial.

The Visible Hand of Management

Big business was clearly established in America by the time of the First World War. By 1917 the United States possessed 278 companies capitalized at $20 million or more. Of these companies 236 were in manufacturing. Some 171 were in only six fields: food processing, chemicals, oil, metals, machine making, and transportation equipment. Even more than in Great Britain, it was in these capital-intensive industrial areas that there were the greatest opportunities for American executives to exploit economies of scale and scope through the formation of large vertically integrated firms. Parts of American industry came to be characterized by oligopoly; in these fields a handful of large companies dominated their markets. As early as 1904 just a few major companies controlled at least half of the output of 78 different industries in the United States.

As their companies became big businesses, the decisions of the corporate executives replaced market forces in determining the production and distribution of products in some industrial fields. Decisions made in earlier times by the free interplay of market forces, what the British economist Adam Smith called "the invisible hand" of the market in his famous book *The Wealth of Nations* in 1776, were now made by the visible hand of business management. Nearly all of the 236 big businesses in manufacturing were vertically integrated, and 85 percent of them were organized around some sort of centralized, functionally departmentalized management structure.

THE CONTINUING IMPORTANCE OF SMALL BUSINESS

With the development of big businesses like American Tobacco, smaller businesses found themselves in an ambiguous position. The proportion of America's industrial output coming from small businesses dropped as large manufacturing ventures rose to prominence. Still, opportunities in the nation's expanding industrial economy beckoned to small business owners, and small businesses increased in absolute numbers. Moreover, small firms remained mainstays in sales and services.

Small Business in Manufacturing

While not as important as in Great Britain, small businesses remained significant in American manufacturing. By 1914 nearly a third of America's industrial workers found employment in plants with 500 or more in their labor forces, and another third in those with 100 to 499. Even so, a third still were employed by firms with 100 or fewer workers. (And 54 percent worked in companies employing no more than 250 people.) Some 54,000 manufacturing businesses had six to twenty workers.

Most small businesses that succeeded in manufacturing did so as flexible firms producing specialty products for niche markets, either on their own or as members of regional business agglomerations. Rather than competing head-to-head with large mass-production industrialists, they coexisted with big businesses by differentiating their products from those of their larger competitors. Thus, the exploitation of economies of scale and scope were much less important for small businesses than for their larger counterparts. Small businesses used instead their flexibility to produce goods—often in small batches and short production runs—for rapidly changing regional and seasonal markets. Part of the ability to accomplish this task lay in the employment of intelligent, innovative work forces. Another part lay in the flexible use of the most advanced technologies of the day. This strategy remains at the core of much small business success in manufacturing to the present day.

Cotton Textiles and Iron and Steel

America's textile industry provides a good example of how large and small firms could coexist, and provides a real contrast to the situation in Great Britain, where the industry was composed mainly of smaller companies. As the nineteenth century progressed, America's textile industry divided into two segments. At Waltham and Lowell in New England large factories employed unskilled workers to turn out standardized goods for the mass market. By 1850, 12 corporations employed 12,000 textile workers in Lowell. However, a very different pattern unfolded at Philadelphia. There, in 1850 some 326 firms employed 12,400 textile workers. Two-thirds of these firms possessed 25 or fewer workers. Though employing as many workers in the aggregate as their counterparts in Lowell, the Philadelphia firms were capitalized at much less, $4.7 million, about a third of the amount invested in the Lowell companies.

The Philadelphia firms competed successfully throughout the nineteenth century by stressing specialization and flexibility in production and marketing. Like most of their British counterparts, few Philadelphia firms tried to master all aspects of textile production. Most specialized in one or two steps that they then did very well indeed, using the most up-to-date machinery and employing skilled workers, often men, at high wages. Productivity levels were high. With skilled work forces and modern machinery, the Philadelphia mills could rapidly switch to various types of cotton, wool, and other fabrics as needed. Small size and versatility continued to be hallmarks of Philadelphia textile firms into the mid-twentieth century. Only when national economic problems joined particular local problems of the Philadelphia mills during the Great Depression of the 1930s did the Philadelphia textile businesses decline.

A similar story developed in America's iron and steel industries. Pittsburgh's iron and steel industries took form as collections of relatively small specialized businesses. Not even the formation of United States Steel in 1901 radically altered this situation. Only a few of the small firms became part of United States Steel, and this development was more than offset by the formation of sixteen new iron and steel firms in Pittsburgh between 1898 and 1901. In 1901 the forty small independent producers in Pittsburgh had a production capacity of 3.8 million tons of iron and steel, compared to the 2.6-million-ton capacity of United States Steel. In 1920, 78 percent of the independents in existence two decades before were still doing business, and even after

America's second major merger movement, which occurred in the 1920s, about 50 percent were active. The Great Depression put many of these firms out of business, but on the eve of World War II, 28 percent of the original independents remained operative.

The success of small firms in the iron and steel industries was not limited to the Pittsburgh region or to firms that developed as part of regional groupings. The growth of the Buckeye Steel Castings Company of Columbus, Ohio, suggests the continuing importance of stand-alone small businesses in manufacturing.

Formed as a partnership in 1881, Buckeye Steel initially produced a variety of cast-iron goods for the local market. Buckeye lacked a specialty product or any other advantage over its competitors and came very close to failing during the mid-1880s. At that time a new president, Wilbur Goodspeed, changed the direction of the company. Coming to Columbus from Cleveland in 1886, Goodspeed had Buckeye Steel develop a specialty product for a niche market, an automatic railroad car coupler. This technologically sophisticated product gave Buckeye an edge over its competitors and allowed the company to break into the national market.

In entering this market, Buckeye Steel's executives relied heavily upon their personal connections with other business people. While in business in Cleveland, Goodspeed had come to know high-ranking executives at the Standard Oil Company, which was headquartered in that city. (Goodspeed and some of the Standard Oil executives set up the Cleveland Gatling Gun Regiment, a private paramilitary outfit, in the wake of nationwide railroad strike in 1877.) Soon after he took over at Buckeye Steel, Goodspeed negotiated an arrangement favorable to both parties. In return for receiving a large block of common stock in Buckeye Steel for free, the Standard Oil executives agreed to use their influence to persuade all of the railroads that shipped Standard's petroleum products to market (few long-distance pipelines existed then) to purchase their couplers solely from Buckeye Steel. Railroad orders soared, and Buckeye Steel emerged as a very successful business, becoming a medium-size firm by national standards at the time of World War I.

Open-hearth steelmaking in the United States at Buckeye Steel. (Courtesy of the Ohio Historical Association)

Small Business Success in Manufacturing

Common attitudes and circumstances run behind the success of the small companies that proved capable of coexisting with large manufacturing concerns. The smaller firms developed specialty products that they then sold in niche markets, thereby avoiding direct competition with their larger counterparts. To make this strategy work, small companies adopted (or developed themselves) the most advanced production technologies available. These small companies were not backward workshops using obsolete equipment but rather forward-looking companies run by managers deeply committed to their success. Most of the firms continued to be operated as family enterprises similar to their British counterparts, devoid, for the most part, of managerial hierarchies. A sense of personal satisfaction, almost a sense of craftsmanship, remained an important motivating factor for both executives and workers. Writing to his wife about business affairs in 1908, the president of Buckeye Steel captured this feeling when he observed, "We have had hard times to

bear, but surely we should not care to have our lives easy, for there would be no accomplishment, no development." *

Factors external to their companies also prepared the way to success. In some instances government aid helped, as was the case with Buckeye Steel. In 1893 Congress passed legislation requiring that all railroad cars be equipped with automatic couplers within five years. This act was a piece of safety legislation designed to protect trainmen who were often injured while joining cars together with the old-style manual couplers. This law helped create a national market for Buckeye Steel's main product. In other cases, especially where regional groupings developed, favorable local environments proved valuable. In Philadelphia, for example, the textile companies benefited from various sorts of local government aid and were also able to join together to support for many years a trade school to insure the availability of a steady supply of skilled workers.

Sales and Services: Realms of Small Firms

The rise of big business led to significant changes in distribution and sales. The growth of big businesses in marketing assumed several forms. As in Great Britain, department stores like Macy's, Bloomingdale's, and Lazarus grew up to serve large concentrated urban markets. Catalog stores such as Montgomery Ward and Sears, Roebuck served rural and small-town America. Chain stores also got their start. The Great Atlantic and Pacific Tea Company (A&P) began operations in 1859 and had about 200 stores selling tea, coffee, and groceries by 1900. Beginning in 1879 F. W. Woolworth set up Five and Ten Cent Stores, which had a sales volume of more than $15 million by 1905.

Most sales, however, especially at the retail level, continued to be made by small neighborhood stores in cities or by small general stores in the countryside. As late as 1929, 168,000 wholesalers employed 1.6 million people, for an average employment per establishment of just under ten people. Retailing remained even more the province of small businesses. In 1929, 1.5 million retail establishments employed 5.7 million people, for an average employment of just over three people per store. As late as 1890 just 10 chains (each composed

* Mansel Blackford, *A Portrait Cast in Steel: Buckeye International and Columbus, Ohio, 1881–1980* (Westport, Conn.: Greenwood Press, 1982), 67.

of at least two stores) existed in America, and even in 1915 there were only 515. Scale economies proved more elusive in selling than in making products and were often offset by a small marketer's knowledge of local conditions. As in Great Britain, the new market outlets such as department stores and chain stores (called "multiples" in Great Britain) cut into, but did not displace, the sales made by more traditional retail establishments.

In the service sector, commercial banking remained a home for small businesses in the United States. Unlike many industrialized or industrializing nations, the United States possessed no central bank. Nothing resembling the "Big Five" banks of Great Britain developed. Instead, Americans depended upon a mixture of thousands of nationally or state-chartered banks to meet their commercial needs. In 1896 there were about 11,500 commercial banks with assets of roughly $6.2 billion in the United States, by 1920 some 30,300 possessing assets of $47.5 billion.

Most of these institutions remained small and independently owned, a situation which possessed both positive and negative aspects. Bankers serving local areas could rely on their personal knowledge in making loans to farmers and business people. They could thereby serve their localities well. Still, there were weaknesses in this system. Banks operated almost in isolation from each other, which contributed to the development of financial panics and depressions of varying intensity in 1873, 1884, 1893, 1903, and 1907. Branch banking might have provided some stability, but federal and state laws resulting from Americans' fears about economic concentration severely limited branching.

BUSINESS, SOCIETY, AND POLITICS

America's business practices mirrored social and cultural norms in the United States. Thus, the fears that some Americans had of concentrated power stayed the development of a centralized banking system. Even so, the rise of big business led to innovations in social thought, law, and government activities. After a lag time, legal decisions and governmental actions caught up with changes occurring in the economic realm. In particular, the federal government began monitoring and regulating the actions of some big businesses through the creation of independent regulatory commissions. But taking this step required time. When compared to Great Britain, and in some ways Japan, the United States developed big businesses before it possessed big government.

A *Business Elite*

Large and small firms differed in the types of people they attracted as owners and managers. American business leaders formed something of an elite in the late 1800s and early 1900s. There was clearly social mobility in America. A penniless immigrant like Andrew Carnegie, the founder of Carnegie Steel, America's largest nineteenth-century industrial enterprise, could rise from rags to riches in a single generation; but Carnegie was the exception, not the rule. Most big businesses were run by well-educated men who came from middle-class or upper-class backgrounds and who were native born.

While an elite, America's business upper class was a relatively open one — at least for white males. (No women or minorities and very few immigrants rose to the top of large firms.) Money was the common denominator that provided the nation's newly rich railroad barons and industrialists access to the upper reaches of American society. Titles of nobility and the possession of a generations-old family name counted for less in the United States than in Europe. Through what the American economist Thorstein Veblen labeled "conspicuous consumption" — using their wealth to build mansions, acquire art, buy private railroad cars, and host lavish parties (at one, the tongues of peacocks were served) — America's business leaders could buy their way into society.

Business, *Public Attitudes, Politics, and Labor*

Americans loved the material abundance, the outpouring of goods, and the rising standard of living that they associated with big business. Yet, there was considerable ambivalence in the attitudes of Americans toward the rise of big business. In the late nineteenth century industrial development was so sudden, so new, and so disruptive of traditional ways of doing things that the general response to the rise of big business in America was to try to control it through regulation by the government.

Federal government regulation of business began during the Progressive period, the years 1900 through 1920. The Interstate Commerce Commission (ICC), a federal government agency set up by the Interstate Commerce Act of 1887, had its power to regulate railroads enhanced by new legislation. The Meat Inspection Act and the Pure Foods and Drug Act, both passed by Con-

gress in 1906, gave the federal government responsibility for the regulation of America's food and drug industries, and the Food and Drug Administration was set up in that year. In addition, the Federal Reserve Act of 1913 established the Federal Reserve System to regulate banking practices and the money supply in the United States.

Still, the federal government was far from the powerful organization that it would later become. In America's federal system much governmental authority, including the power to regulate many businesses, lay with state and local governments. In fact, much of the most effective regulation of business occurred at the state, not the federal, level. Then, too, there existed an anti-statism tinge to American thought that limited the power of the federal government. This strain of thought was sometimes expressed in Supreme Court decisions, including several that for some years limited the power of the ICC over railroads.

While the main thrust of American public policy at both the federal and state levels was to regulate rather than destroy big business, law makers did pass far-reaching antitrust measures. These measures grew out of America's common law tradition, which reflected a sense of distrust toward big business. Common law fell short of outlawing big business, but it did place restrictions upon how companies could act. The common law protected small firms from some, but not all, of the depredations of their larger competitors. A new level of action began when Congress passed the Sherman Act in 1890. The Sherman Act outlawed restraints of trade, but the law's sponsors intended that "reasonable" restraints—those not injurious to the public and not preventing new firms from entering business fields—be allowed to continue.

As interpreted by the United States Supreme Court from 1911, the Sherman Act permitted large firms to exist, as long as they grew big through reasonable means. The act was used to break up American Tobacco and Standard Oil in 1911, but only because these two companies were perceived as having become large by unreasonable methods. Ironically, the Supreme Court's "rule of reason" stimulated combination, not competition. The Sherman Act was used most commonly to break up loose combinations among businesses, especially cartels. Tight combinations, such as vertically integrated companies, were not attacked as often or as effectively, and as a consequence business leaders continued to form them. Of the 127 actions taken under the terms of the Sherman Act between 1905 and 1915, 72 were filed against loose combi-

nations of smaller firms, 32 against tight combinations, 12 each against labor unions and agricultural produce dealers, and 10 against miscellaneous others. Thus were laws, public attitudes, and economics reconciled, in a manner significantly different from that which prevailed elsewhere. In Great Britain cartels of smaller firms were tolerated, and in Germany they were encouraged by law, a situation that contributed to their greater significance, especially in manufacturing.

Labor in an Industrializing Society

Conflict between labor and management accompanied industrialization and the rise of big business in America. As large companies moved toward mass production in some fields, they produced goods in settings considerably larger than the plants in which British workers labored. This shift to large-scale factory production occurred so rapidly that it upset workers accustomed to traditional ways of making products. Industrial change was also often accompanied by dangerous working conditions, longer hours of work, and low wages. Throughout these years, managers and workers in America, as in Great Britain, vied with each other over the issue of who would control the work process—that is, how industrial work was performed, at what speed, and with what reward system.

In this struggle for control of the workplace, superintendents of large American factories increasingly employed the "drive" system of managing labor. In other words, they sought to extract as much work as possible in a given period of time, usually ten- or twelve-hour-long working days. Their goal was to operate their capital-intensive plants, in which the cost of labor was a relatively minor expense, at full bore. To do so, they wrested more and more power from foremen—men charged with hiring and firing workers and who had considerable say, along with skilled workers, in determining just how tasks were performed. By the turn of the century foremen found their authority circumscribed.

In the effort to seize control of the workfloor, managers were aided by the spread of scientific management—managerial practices that aimed at making tasks and the flow of work in factories more efficient. Scientific management stressed the need for better record keeping and accounting methods to keep track of work being done in manufacturing plants, but, above all, it empha-

sized the value of undermining labor's power in the workplace. Managers wanted to establish uniform and, presumably, more efficient work processes, allowing their plants to run at peak capacity, with no production bottle-necks hindering the transformation of raw materials into finished goods for America's voracious consumers. While no factory adopted all aspects of sci-entific management, many large ones put some of them into practice.

Workers, especially skilled ones, opposed efforts to reduce their control over the labor process. Workers wanted higher wages, shorter working hours, and better working conditions, not diminished power and privileges. In order to accomplish their goals, workers formed nationwide unions designed to bar-gain with the large industrial firms. The Knights of Labor, established in 1869, sought to group all workers, skilled and unskilled, into local "assemblies" across the United States. The Knights rejected the wage system, wanting, in-stead, for workers to own their own factories and to buy and sell goods through cooperatives. The Knights achieved some success in the 1870s, but they be-came less important in the mid-1880s, after losing a nationwide railroad strike. Longer-lived was the American Federation of Labor (AFL) formed in the 1880s as a group of trade unions composed mainly of skilled workers. The AFL accepted the wage system and sought to secure higher wages, shorter working hours, and better working conditions by bargaining collectively with management. Relatively unimportant in the nineteenth century, the AFL be-came America's leading labor organization in the early twentieth century.

The opposing interests of managers and workers led to a high degree of industrial conflict, and even violence. Between 1876 and 1896 the United States experienced more strikes—with more people killed and injured in them—than did any other industrial nation. The lists of conflicts was long. Nationwide railroad strikes in 1877 and 1885–86 featured pitched battles be-tween workers and private police in the pay of the railroads. So, too, did a strike against Carnegie Steel in 1892 in Homestead, Pennsylvania.

Over time, managers and workers partially reconciled their divergent inter-ests. By World War I some big businesses, like their British counterparts, had adopted welfare capitalism. To decrease labor turnover and to try to keep unions out of their plants, many large firms had improved working and living conditions for their employees. While significant, these efforts did not go as far as many workers wanted. Most worrisome to workers, welfare capitalism left control of the work process in the hands of the managers. When com-

pared to their counterparts in Great Britain, America's skilled workers had less control over shopfloor activities by the twentieth century. In the United States managers seized control of the work process in many industrial firms, especially large ones.

The control exerted by American managers helps explain the relative ease with which mass production techniques, especially those that de-skilled workers (that is, those which replaced craftsmanship with machine production), were introduced and diffused in the United States. In return for a higher material standard of living many American workers gradually yielded control over their working lives to others. In short, output soared in mass-production industries, but at the price of a loss of independence in the workplace.

In smaller manufacturing firms, the labor situation varied. Small businesses have a reputation for operating under sweatshop conditions, and many did—small firms in the garment trades, for example. But there is another side to the story. Operating less capital intensive plants and depending more on skilled workers, the heads of some smaller manufacturing plants were more likely to leave control of the shopfloor in the hands of their workers, approximating more closely the British practice.

Labor-management conflict was certainly less obvious in small manufacturing firms than in large ones. Particularly in textiles, the small Philadelphia industrialists relied heavily upon highly skilled workers who were—like the owner-managers of the companies—flexible in their approaches to their tasks. Willing and able to perform a wide variety of tasks, the workers were well paid and rarely went on strike. Perhaps because they were both close to their workers in relatively small plants and because they cared for the welfare of the city, Pittsburgh's independent iron and steel leaders tended toward a grudging acceptance of unions and a pragmatic willingness to try to work with them. More than the managers of the much larger Carnegie mills, the owner-operators of the small independent facilities sought to achieve a harmonious relationship with their workers, especially in the 1870s and 1880s. In the 1890s and later, however, following the lead of the larger firms, the independent mill owners became less tolerant of labor. As they adopted more capital-intensive equipment and were influenced by the examples of violence against labor at Carnegie Steel, they turned more of their attention to breaking unions. Nonetheless, small business, at least in these two cases, continued to be receptive to the needs of workers.

SMALL BUSINESS AND BIG BUSINESS
IN INDUSTRIALIZING AMERICA

As the United States industrialized, complex relationships developed between large and small firms. There was conflict between businesses as well as between workers and managers. The development of specialty products for niche markets did not shield all small manufacturers from the onslaughts of their larger counterparts. But the evolving situation was a mixed one. In some fields large and small firms grew up symbiotically. While many large industrial businesses became vertically integrated to some degree, few were totally integrated. Small firms frequently acted as subcontractors for their larger brethren. Buckeye Steel, for example, supplied the automatic couplers that large railroad car manufacturers used in their production efforts. A similar example of mutually beneficial arrangements lay in sales. As some manufacturers expanded their output to meet the demand of America's domestic market, they relied on franchised agents. Rather than own their sales outlets—a costly proposition—manufacturers depended upon agents closely tied to but still legally independent from their firms to make the sales. The Singer Sewing Machine Company and the McCormick Harvester Company, for example, employed primitive franchise sales systems in the nineteenth century, a practice that would be refined and become widespread in the twentieth century.

SUGGESTED READINGS

Alfred D. Chandler, Jr., *The Visible Hand: The Managerial Revolution in American Business* (Cambridge, Mass.: Harvard University Press, 1977) is a masterly survey of the rise of big business in America. See also Glenn Porter, *The Rise of Big Business, 1860–1910*, 2nd ed. (Arlington Heights, Ill.: Harlan Davidson, 1992); Glenn Porter and Harold Livesay, *Merchants and Manufacturers: Studies in the Changing Structure of Nineteenth-Century Marketing* (Baltimore: Johns Hopkins University Press, 1971); and David Whitten, *The Emergence of Giant Enterprise, 1860–1914* (Westport, Conn.: Greenwood Press, 1983). Harold Livesay, *American Made* (Boston: Little, Brown, 1979); and Robert Sobel, *The Entrepreneurs* (New York: Weybright and Talley, 1974), look at the contributions of individuals to the development of America's business system.

There is a growing literature on the history of small business. The essays in Stuart Bruchey, ed., *Small Business in American Life* (New York: Columbia University Press, 1980), examine the contributions small businesses have made to the economic and social development of the United States. See also Mansel Blackford, *A History of Small Business in America* (New York: Twayne Publishers, 1991); Philip Scranton, *Proprietary Capitalism: The Textile Manufacture at Philadelphia, 1800–1885* (Cambridge: Cambridge University Press, 1983); John Ingham, *Making Iron and Steel* (Columbus: Ohio State University Press, 1991); and Thomas Dicke, *Franchising in America* (Chapel Hill: University of North Carolina Press, 1992).

Thomas McCraw, *The Prophets of Regulation* (Cambridge, Mass.: Harvard University Press, 1984), examines government-business relations in modern America. Martin Sklar, *The Corporate Reconstruction of American Capitalism, 1890–1916* (Cambridge: Cambridge University Press, 1988), connects changes in America's corporate, legal, and business systems. Daniel Nelson, *Managers and Workers: Origins of the New Factory System in the United States, 1880–1920* (Madison: University of Wisconsin Press, 1975), is an excellent place to start in understanding changing shopfloor relationships in America.

5 [Zaibatsu and Non-Zaibatsu Businesses in Industrializing Japan

From a merchant house in Tokugawa times, Mitsui emerged in the late Meiji period as what is called a "zaibatsu." A large, diversified, nationwide company, Mitsui had extensive interests in banking, manufacturing, mining, and trading. As the transformation of Mitsui demonstrated, in Japan, no less than in the United States, industrialization changed business firms and business practices. New companies grew up, and as new firms and forms of business arose in Japan, the nature of business management, the status of business leaders, and the nature of labor relations underwent alterations. Yet, as in the United States and Great Britain, there was continuity as well as change in Japan's business system. Not all of Japan's businesses, even in manufacturing, became zaibatsu. While important to Japan's business system, zaibatsu did not totally dominate it. Smaller companies in manufacturing, sales, and services played significant roles in Japan's development.

THE RISE OF THE ZAIBATSU

Few of the large merchant houses of the Tokugawa period made successful transitions into the new industrial times of Meiji Japan. As we have seen, there was lots of economic activity in the late Tokugawa and early Meiji periods. However, much of this action took place outside of the realms of the large merchant houses. Mitsui and Sumitomo did adjust to new economic circumstances and, indeed, flourished in them, but those companies were exceptional. More commonly, new types of companies and company groupings developed, as Japanese business people sought to deal with rapid economic change.

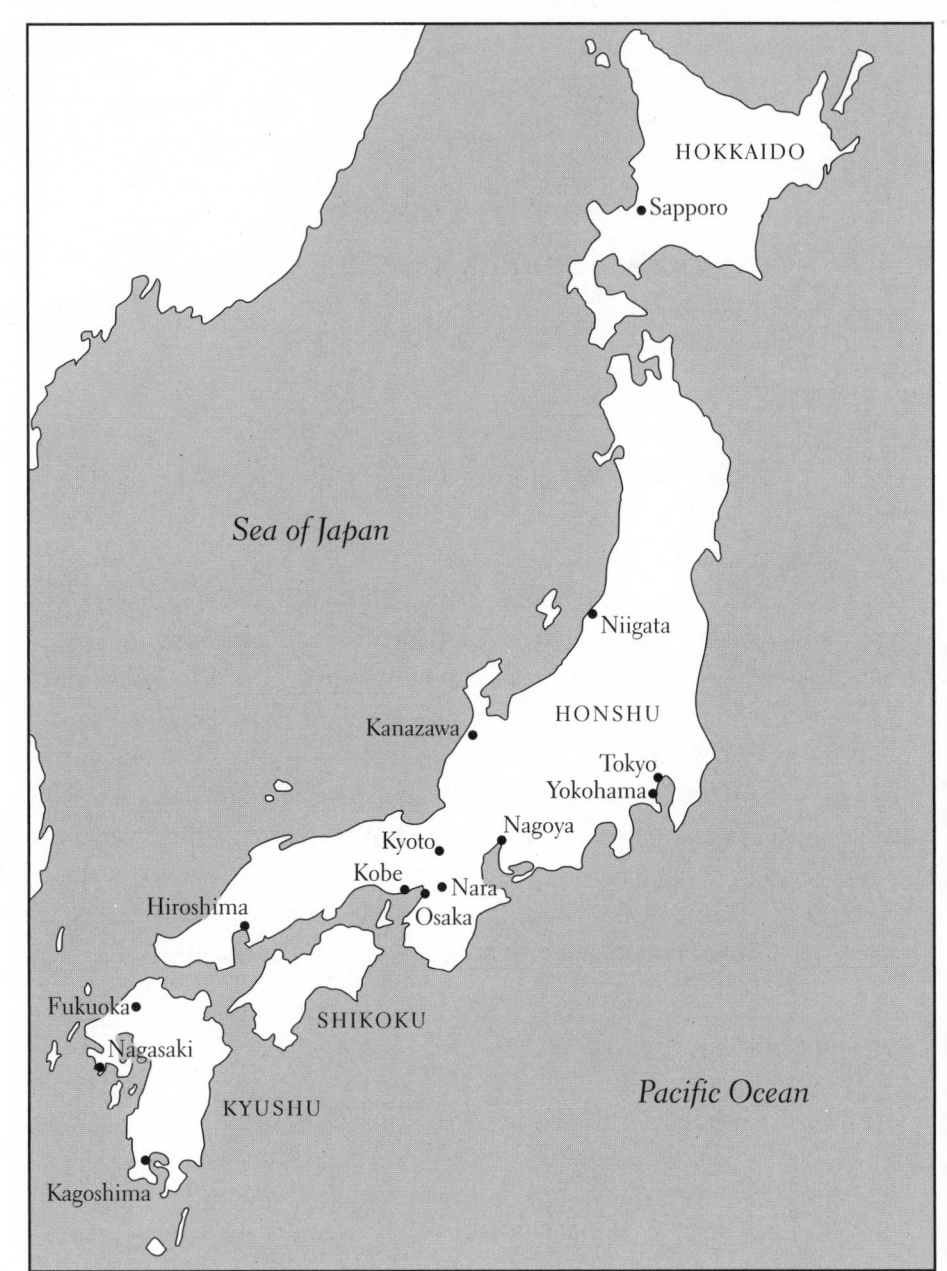

Modern Japan

The Merchant House and Industrialization

The political changes that accompanied the Meiji Restoration hurt many of the large merchant houses, and they declined in significance. They lost their ability to make loans to the daimyo and samurai, a major source of their income. Currency reforms, especially the adoption of a national currency based on the yen, decreased their importance as money changers. Then, too, many Japanese merchants had become more conservative than their British or American counterparts because of the restrictions placed on their activities in the Tokugawa period. Most lacked the daring to enter industrial enterprises.

Business leaders taking advantage of new opportunities to go into shipbuilding, railroads, manufacturing, and banking did so increasingly through the formation of joint-stock companies. Some joint-stock companies existed in an informal way as early as the 1870s and 1880s. Legal recognition through a General Incorporation Act of 1893 and a Commercial Code that went into effect six years later spurred their development. The code, especially, inspired budding businesspeople to think about businesses in new ways. Japan possessed 3,336 joint-stock companies in 1882 and 8,612 twenty years later. Several factors accounted for the popularity of joint-stock companies: the ease with which they could mobilize capital, their association with the greatly admired technology of the West, and the fact that ex-samurai preferred not to work in more traditional family businesses.

While few merchant houses made the transition into the industrial era, they may have helped pave the way for the spread of the joint-stock companies. Both the merchant houses and the joint-stock companies emphasized the perpetual existence of business enterprises and stressed the amassing of assets. However, in other ways merchant houses may have hampered the development of joint-stock companies. The stress the merchant houses placed on the family made it psychologically difficult for members of different merchant houses to cooperate in the formation of new business ventures.

Zaibatsu Development

While large, vertically integrated, single-industry corporations were particularly important in America's industrial advance, in Japan big diversified companies called zaibatsu became powerful in industry and other business fields

Opening day at the Bank of Japan, 1882. Banks provided some of the capital needed for economic modernization in Japan. (Courtesy of the Bank of Japan)

in the opening decades of the twentieth century. The zaibatsu provided a way for Japan to compete effectively with other nations. The zaibatsu were more diversified than big businesses in Great Britain or the United States. Zaibatsu were composed of manufacturing ventures (typically in both light industries such as silk reeling and cotton spinning and heavy industries such as ship-building, chemicals, and iron and steelmaking), mining ventures, a bank to finance these concerns, and a trading company to sell the products overseas.

Japan's zaibatsu developed in several ways. A few, such as Mitsui, evolved from Tokugawa merchant houses. More, such as Mitsubishi, grew out of enterprises closely connected to the fortunes of the new Japanese government and, like the government itself, were organizations founded in the Meiji period. Still other zaibatsu, such as Nissan, so-called "new zaibatsu," were formed in the 1920s and 1930s and were closely associated with the Japanese government's efforts to build up heavy industry for military purposes. In the years before the First World War eight major zaibatsu emerged—Mitsui, Mitsubishi, Sumitomo, Yasuda, Asano, Okura, Furukawa, and Kawasaki—the first four of which were known as the Big Four. By the early 1920s zaibatsu controlled much of the mining, shipbuilding, banking, foreign trade, and industry of Japan. Altogether, zaibatsu accounted for about one-quarter to one-third of Japan's GNP by the close of the 1920s.

The Growth of Trading Companies: The Sogo Shosha

Of special importance in the rise of the zaibatsu and the growth of the Japanese economy was the development of trading companies called sogo shosha. The trading companies often evolved to handle the foreign trade of the zaibatsu. Thus, Mitsui Bussan and Mitsubishi Shoji took care of the exports and imports of their zaibatsu. The trading companies were important not just to their zaibatsu but to the overall development of the Japanese economy, especially its industrial sector. The trading companies did more than trade. Possessing overseas offices, they provided much of the knowledge of foreign technologies and business practices, managerial expertise, and some of the capital needed by Japanese firms. Between 1868 and 1913 the sogo shosha were formed to compete with Western merchant houses that initially handled Japan's foreign trade, and by the end of this period they were operating throughout Asia, Europe, and the United States. Some were even beginning to handle transactions that did not involve Japan. Between 1914 and 1930 the sogo shosha greatly expanded the scope of their activities to become fully developed general trading companies.

Mitsui Bussan and Mitsubishi Shoji were the largest and most important trading companies. Mitsui Bussan was particularly significant in spurring the growth of Japan's cotton textile industry. Mitsui Bussan imported textile-making machinery and raw cotton for the cotton textile companies, which lacked the knowledge to do so. It also opened up foreign markets, especially in Asia, for the finished cotton cloth and in the years 1907 through 1910 handled about one-half of Japan's fabric exports. Mitsui Bussan also invested in new industrial companies; by 1940 it held investments totaling 275 million yen in 253 companies in 14 industries ranging from rayon to sugar refining to the making of elevators. Set up in 1918, Mitsubishi Shoji began with 900 employees and a capitalization of 15 million yen. By the 1930s Mitsubishi Shoji had grown to include six commodity divisions trading in metals, machinery, fuel (mainly petroleum), agricultural products, fishery products, and fertilizers. By the time of World War II Mitsubishi Shoji had 6,500 employees, possessed 100 million yen in capital, and had offices around the world.

Mitsui and Mitsubishi

The development of Mitsui and Mitsubishi typified common trends in the evolution of zaibatsu in Japan. As we have seen, Mitsui began as a merchant house in the Tokugawa period. Mitsubishi, on the other hand, was one of the many new companies of the Meiji years. However, despite the differences in their origins, both companies became zaibatsu in the Meiji period and, in altered form, both continue as leading businesses in Japan today.

Mitsui. As we observed in Chapter 1, the House of Mitsui had the foresight to back the new Japanese government during the Meiji Restoration and for its support was rewarded with the handling of government funds in the 1870s and 1880s. This major source of revenue lasted until 1887 and helped Mitsui make the transition into the new period of industrialization. New business leadership was also important in Mitsui's success.

Hikojiro Nakamigawa, an entrepreneur who had been involved in newspapers and railroads in the 1880s, was brought in from outside of the Mitsui family as the vice-president of Mitsui Bank in 1891. Nakamigawa soon became the head of the bank and then the head of the entire Mitsui combine. Nakamigawa imposed centralized management over the Mitsui enterprises. He reorganized Mitsui Bank, Mitsui Bussan, Mitsui Mining, and Mitsui Wearing Apparel as partnership companies, all of which were owned by the Mitsui family. At about the same time, what had previously been a temporary council of the Mitsui family emerged as a powerful board of directors that made all of the important decisions for the different partnerships.

Nakamigawa followed two other policies designed to bring Mitsui to a new stage of development. He purchased industrial and mining companies, especially those in silk reeling, cotton spinning, engineering, papermaking, and coal mining. He also brought in new men, particularly from Keio University, where he had studied and taught, to run the Mitsui enterprises.

Nakamigawa died in 1901, and after his death Mitsui underwent further alterations in the opening years of the twentieth century. In 1909 the central managing organ, the board of directors, was reorganized as the Mitsui Gomei Company, a general partnership owned by the Mitsui family, and some authority was delegated to the various Mitsui enterprises. Nonetheless, Mit-

sui's management remained centralized. For example, as late as 1922 Mitsui Bussan had to secure permission from Mitsui Gomei to lend money or make certain types of contracts. This centralization of authority may have stifled innovation and growth at Mitsui. Mitsui Gomei was composed of the heads of the different Mitsui operating companies, and as a result, no one took a long-range attitude toward the future of the entire Mitsui enterprise. Planning and strategic decision making suffered as a consequence. Mitsui proved slower than many of its rivals to enter the new fields of heavy industry that developed in Japan in the 1920s and 1930s.

In the interests of economic democracy, the United States, as the major power occupying Japan after World War II, broke up the zaibatsu in the years 1946 through 1949. This move was short-lived, however, for Cold War concerns soon overcame American desires for industrial democracy in Japan. In an attempt to rebuild Japan as a pro-Western bastion in Asia (especially after China became a communist nation in 1949), the United States encouraged economic growth in the nation. As part of this policy, the zaibatsu were allowed to reorganize.

Mitsui was among those zaibatsu dismantled, only to reorganize in a new form called a "keiretsu" in the 1950s and 1960s. By 1971 Mitsui consisted of Mitsui Bank, Mitsui Bussan, and 71 other major enterprises. The postwar Mitsui differed from the prewar Mitsui in that it was no longer held together by a head office that operated as a holding company owning stock in other companies. No such head office existed. Nor was Mitsui dominated by a single family. Instead, Mitsui came to consist of many companies loosely held together by meetings of the companies' executives every Monday, what became known as the Monday Club. Stock interchanges among the Mitsui companies and borrowing from the Mitsui Bank also provided some sense of unity.

Mitsubishi. Yataro Iwasaki founded Mitsubishi. Born the son of a peasant, he purchased samurai status in the Tosa domain and rose in the domain's bureaucracy as a procurer of arms and ships. (Some scholars argue that Iwasaki captured control of his domain government.) After the Meiji Restoration, the domain was abolished and its ships became the basis for an independent shipping company with Iwasaki as its manager. In 1873 Iwasaki took over this company as his own and renamed it Mitsubishi. He rallied support for his na-

scent venture by cloaking it in nationalism, saying that the firm would help make Japan strong in shipping. Iwasaki's approach appealed to his employees, many of whom were former samurai from Tosa.

Mitsubishi began business with ten ships. With them the company entered the coastal trade, edging out competitors by cutting rates. Mitsubishi bene-fited from government contracts, carrying troops and supplies for several military expeditions in the 1870s, and by the late 1870s controlled 73 per-cent of Japanese shipping. Mitsubishi's rapid rise attracted the attention of other Japanese business leaders who formed the Kyodo Unyu Shipping Com-pany to compete with Mitsubishi in the early 1880s. Out of this competition came the formation of a new shipping company in 1885, the Nippon Yusen Company (NYK), with Mitsubishi as the largest single stockholder. However, Mitsubishi's owners sold most of their holdings in NYK between 1887 and 1892 to enter fields that promised larger profits than did shipping.

Mitsubishi's diversification began even before the shipping competition of the 1880s. Yataro Iwasaki led Mitsubishi into warehousing, insurance, coal mining, and the ownership of a shipyard in Nagasaki. Under his guidance, Mitsubishi also entered banking in a tentative way with the formation of a for-eign exchange and discount bank to serve merchants using its ships. Yataro ran Mitsubishi with force and determination. There was little separation of owner-ship from management and almost no delegation of authority under his rule.

Yataro Iwasaki died in 1885, and Mitsubishi's management structure changed under the leadership of his successors. After making some prelimi-nary alterations in the late 1880s, Yanosuke Iwasaki, Yataro's younger brother, and Hisaya Iwasaki, Yataro's eldest son, took advantage of Japan's new Gen-eral Incorporation Law to reorganize Mitsubishi in 1893. Mitsubishi became a company with limited liability, consisting of a head office and departments in banking, mining, coal sales, and general affairs. The head office continued to run the company with an iron hand. As president, Hisaya Iwasaki dele-gated little in the way of responsibilities to the departments.

Major alterations occurred about a decade later. In 1906 Koyata Iwasaki, Yanosuke's eldest son, who had been receiving an education at Cambridge University, returned home and became a vice-president in Mitsubishi. When Yanosuke died in 1908, Koyata assumed his father's share in Mitsubishi and used his power to reorganize the company. The mining, shipbuilding, and

banking departments became divisions in the company, and by 1913 the company had grown to include six divisions: banking, metal mining, coal mining, trading (a forerunner of Mitsubishi Shoji), shipbuilding, and real estate. Each division possessed a considerable degree of autonomy. The divisions could determine their own investments, manage their own personnel affairs, establish their own business procedures, and maintain communications with other operating units. The head office concerned itself with coordinating the work of the divisions and planning for the future of the zaibatsu as a whole. Control was exercised by having thrice-weekly meetings of all the division managers (who were hired from outside the Iwasaki family) presided over by the vice-president of the head office.

In this manner, decentralized management replaced centralized management at Mitsubishi to some extent, as the functions of the head office and the divisions were differentiated and as the divisions assumed considerable authority over their own affairs. The changes also marked the spread of bureaucratic management in general at Mitsubishi, as rules and regulations became increasingly important in running the firm.

Further changes occurred when Koyata Iwasaki took over as president of Mitsubishi in 1916. Over the next three years, he reorganized the six divisions as joint-stock companies. The head office became a holding company owning a controlling share of the stock in each of the joint-stock companies. By selling some of the stock of the new joint-stock companies to the public, Koyata was able to raise funds for Mitsubishi's continuing diversification drive. Finally, in 1919 and 1920 a board of directors was set up as the top authority within Mitsubishi's management. With this reorganization, Mitsubishi moved away from decentralized management, and the joint-stock companies lost some of the power they had possessed over their affairs when they had been divisions.

With new management structures in place, Mitsubishi continued to diversify during the first four decades of the twentieth century. Koyata Iwasaki proved to be aggressive, much like his uncle Yataro, and his personality dominated Mitsubishi until his death in 1945. Mitsubishi's interests in shipbuilding at its yards in Nagasaki and, from 1905 on, in Kobe led the company into a broad range of heavy industries in the 1920s and 1930s: iron and steel, chemicals, mining, aircraft (including the famous Japanese "Zero" of the Second World War), and electrical equipment. Heavy industry became much more

important for Mitsubishi than it did for Mitsui. Mitsubishi eventually established a major bank to finance its concerns and the trading company Mitsubishi Shoji, which, as we have seen, had branches around the world.

While the Iwasaki family, especially Koyata, remained important in running Mitsubishi, nonfamily, bureaucratic management rose in significance. People from outside the Iwasaki family headed the joint-stock companies that evolved from the divisions, and standard procedures were developed to coordinate the work of the various components of the Mitsubishi empire. Yet, family ownership and management remained more important than it did in the United States. The Iwasaki family maintained their overall control of Mitsubishi through their grip on the head office, which, in turn, owned a controlling share in each of the joint-stock companies until after World War II.

The same American efforts that broke up Mitsui right after World War II led to a dissolution of the Mitsubishi holding company and some of Mitsubishi's joint-stock companies. Mitsubishi Shoji, for example, was split into 123 independent firms. But, again, this American antitrust work was short-lived. In 1954 Mitsubishi Shoji was reunited, and in the 1950s and 1960s the component companies of the Mitsubishi zaibatsu began working together again—eventually forming, like Mitsui, a keiretsu. Mitsubishi Bank provided some leadership for the group and gave it some cohesion by loaning money mainly to the Mitsubishi members; and, as at Mitsui, stock ownership among member companies lent some unity to the Mitsubishi group of companies. Finally, Mitsubishi executives met every Friday, in what became known as the Friday Club—informal get-togethers similar to Mitsui's Monday Club—to coordinate activities. By 1971 Mitsubishi consisted of Mitsubishi Bank, Mitsubishi Shoji, and eighty-six major companies in manufacturing and many other fields.

Managing Zaibatsu

The zaibatsu operated as loose confederations of companies owned by family groups in the 1890s and early 1900s. Then, in the 1910s and 1920s a considerable degree of centralization of managerial control over the different enterprises composing a zaibatsu occurred. Most zaibatsu came to consist of a center company organized as a family partnership and other companies, sometimes called "core companies"—the bank, trading company, mining

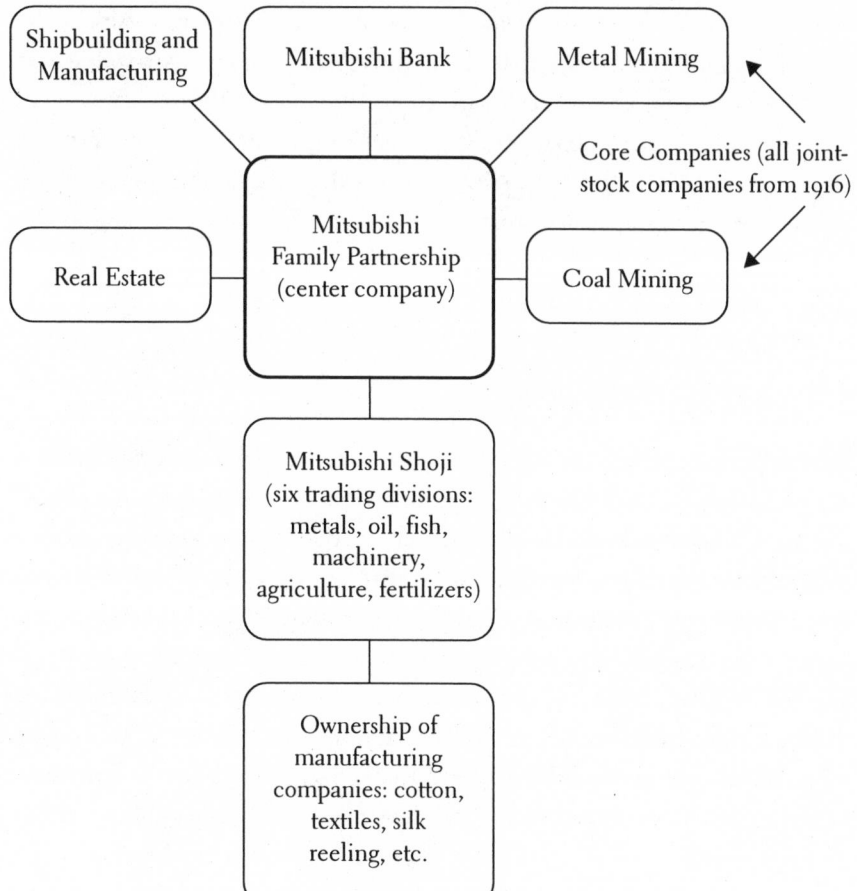

ventures, and manufacturing enterprises—that were often joint-stock companies, a majority of whose shares were owned by the center company. The core
companies, in turn, often owned many smaller companies as their subsidiaries. (See Figure 2.) Thus, as we have seen, Mitsui Bussan controlled wholly
or partly over 200 manufacturing businesses.

In a typical zaibatsu, officers in the center company, who were usually
family members, also held presidencies and directorships in the core companies and helped coordinate the activities of the zaibatsu as a whole. Despite this tendency toward centralization of authority, into the 1940s tension
existed between decentralizing and centralizing forces in the management of
zaibatsu, as the center companies often sought to increase their power and
the core companies tried to retain or increase their autonomy.

In many of the zaibatsu, professional managers selected from outside of the founding families came to hold much of the real power as managing directors of the various core companies. With the employment of these outsiders as managing directors, ownership and management began to become divorced in Japanese business, though not to nearly the degree as in the United States. As in Great Britain, personal management, despite some bureaucratization of business, remained strong. Families continued to control the center companies of most zaibatsu until after the Second World War.

The Significance of the Zaibatsu

Japan's zaibatsu offered a viable alternative to the congeries of small firms in Great Britain and the large, vertically integrated manufacturers in the United States. With their sogo shosha and their banks, the zaibatsu were able to compete effectively with leading Western companies. Especially up to about 1920, the zaibatsu succeeded more through the exercise of economies of scope rather than those of scale. Most of their individual manufacturing plants remained relatively small, often more labor-intensive than capital-intensive. It was by bringing together in family-controlled enterprises a wide range of financial, insurance, shipping, and marketing services that the zaibatsu moved ahead. Economies of scale in finance were especially significant.

THE CONTINUING IMPORTANCE OF NON-ZAIBATSU FIRMS

Not all of Japan's largest businesses were zaibatsu. Many, especially in the early and mid-Meiji years were single-industry businesses. Relatively large independent firms existed, for instance, in cotton textiles (these Japanese cotton textile makers were, however, generally smaller than their American counterparts in Lowell and Waltham). Then, too, small firms were significant in many types of manufacturing, much as they were in Great Britain. In sales and services a range of large and small non-zaibatsu companies jockeyed for position.

Cotton Textile Companies

Of Japan's fifty largest manufacturing and mining companies in 1896, twenty-eight were cotton textile companies. These firms became even larger as a re-

sult of a merger movement, influenced by the model of mergers in the United States. Between 1900 and 1903 the number of companies engaged in cotton spinning decreased from seventy-eight to forty-six. These and most other Japanese industrial companies were not as highly integrated as large American manufacturers. The Japanese firms were more like the British ones—or like smaller firms in American manufacturing, such as the Philadelphia textile companies. While many Japanese cotton textile companies had integrated spinning and weaving by World War I, the firms depended on other companies—often the trading companies—to buy their raw cotton and sell their finished cloth.

Several reasons account for this relative lack of vertical integration, factors similar to those explaining its rareness in Great Britain. Japan had a well-developed marketing system from the Tokugawa years, elaborated still farther by the sogo shosha in the Meiji period; and so manufacturers did not have to set up their own marketing networks. Then, too, Japan's national market was smaller than America's, allowing established marketers to handle the goods bound for that market adequately. For ideological reasons as well, manufacturers did not want to enter marketing, which they viewed as less virtuous than manufacturing. As a result of these various factors, fully vertically integrated companies were not the norm in Japanese manufacturing.

Trading Companies

Large non-zaibatsu companies arose outside of manufacturing. Not all sogo shosha, for example, were parts of zaibatsu. Marubeni, for example, was an independent trading company that became a major force in Japan's woolen and rayon cloth industries. Marubeni, and other trading companies such as C. Itoh, bought woolen yarn and rayon from spinning companies, sold them to weavers, and bought the output of the weavers for sale inside Japan or for export.

Ataka and Company's history illustrates another way trading companies were important to Japan's industrial growth. Formed in 1904, Ataka and Company was soon trading in steel, machinery, textiles, fertilizers, chemicals, and wood products around the globe. The company acquired agency rights from Western machinery makers such as the Gleason Company in the United States and was an important source of new technologies for Japan.

Smaller Businesses in Manufacturing

While zaibatsu and some other large businesses, such as those in cotton textiles, were very important in Japan's industrial development, smaller firms were also significant. Most of Japan's growing number of industrial workers labored in small or medium-sized enterprises. In 1909 businesses employing 5–49 workers accounted for 46 percent of Japan's manufacturing employment, those with 50–499 workers 37 percent, and establishments employing 500 or more workers 21 percent. Ten years later the corresponding proportions were 34 percent, 35 percent, and 32 percent. (In the United States about one-third of all industrial workers labored in companies with fewer than 100 employees in 1914.)

Thus, the proportion of Japanese workers laboring in large establishments grew, but even in what were boom years during World War I large establishments accounted for less than one-third of the nation's industrial workforce. Some of the smaller manufacturers were subcontractors for larger firms; they made semi-finished goods, for instance, for core companies of zaibatsu. But most were not: the importance of subcontracting to small firms really developed only in the 1920s, the 1930s, and later.

Up to World War I most of the small manufacturers were independent of their larger counterparts, with most operating as family enterprises or small workshops. These businesses were often composed of a factory owner employing family members and a few hired workers. Smaller industrialists processed food products or worked in traditional fields such as silk reeling and ceramics. Others ran small textile mills (not all textile mills were large-scale affairs). Only Japan's nascent heavy industry sector—chemicals, metals, machinery, and equipment—was dominated by big businesses. Indeed, heavy industry did not lead Japan's industrial development. It was only in the 1930s (and later) that heavy industries became more important than light industries, such as cotton textiles and silk reeling, as the engine of Japan's economic advance.

Many of the small-scale industrial facilities were located in the countryside rather than in urban areas, a continuation of a trend from the Tokugawa years. Farmers had long depended on by-employment in making tatami mats and similar items to supplement their incomes from the sale of crops, a situation which continued into the twentieth century. However, by the early 1900s some Western-inspired goods, as well as traditional items, were being

made, including new types of farming implements, wire brushes, and kerosene lamps, for example.

Businesses in Sales

In selling their products, nascent manufacturers sometimes set up their own sales outlets, a form of vertical integration similar to that which became increasingly common in America in the late nineteenth and early twentieth centuries. Some manufacturers of nontraditional goods—makers of beer, confectionaries, cosmetics, chemical seasonings, electrical appliances, Western-style paper, wheat flour, and sugar, for example—found distribution systems inherited from Tokugawa times inadequate and created their own marketing channels. A few, some makers of confectionaries and cosmetics, for example, went even farther, setting up retail outlets as well.

However, vertical integration into sales was not common in Japan until after World War II, and even then, less so than in America. Japan resembled Great Britain more than the United States in terms of marketing. Japan's major urban markets were relatively close together on one island, Honshu, and were well linked by traditional marketers. Small retailers, who bought their goods from larger wholesalers—often, in fact, from several levels of wholesalers—were the channels through which manufacturers reached the vast majority of Japanese consumers. In 1885 there were over 1 million retailers in Japan, which then had a population of about 38 million people. From the 1880s on Japan's retailers became increasingly specialized, particularly those serving the nation's growing urban markets. General stores came to deal in just a single line of goods. These specialty stores sometimes grouped together in planned shopping streets, such as the famous Ginza in Tokyo, which opened in 1878.

Large-scale retailing in the form of department stores represented something of a new departure in marketing. In the first two decades of the twentieth century old-line dry goods stores converted themselves into department stores, which, like their counterparts in America and Great Britain, served urban markets. By 1898, 18 percent of the Japanese lived in cities of at least 10,000 people, and by 1918, 32 percent did. Thus, Mitsui's Echigoya of Edo became the Mitsukoshi Department Store in Tokyo. Created by Osuke Hibi—a graduate of the new Keio University and one of the college graduates

recruited by Hikijiro Nakamigawa for Mitsui—Mitsukoshi was modeled on Harrods of London. By the time of World War I Mitsukoshi's five-story building sold a wide range of consumer goods, ranging from Western umbrellas to children's clothing. The store also contained a restaurant, a tailor's shop, and a photographic studio.

Department stores grew in importance as the twentieth century unfolded. Small businesses composed 98 percent of the retail outlets in Tokyo in 1931 but accounted for only slightly more than one-half of all sales. By way of contrast, the city's eight department stores made one-third of the sales. Still, Tokyo was not typical of all of Japan. In smaller towns and cities department stores were less significant. Moreover, even in Tokyo, an important variant in the retail store held sway for several decades in the Meiji period. Called "kan koba," this type of retail outlet consisted of a department store leased by the building's owner to various independent retailers. Originating in Tokyo in the late 1870s, kan koba spread to many Japanese cities in the 1880s, only to decline in significance during the 1890s due to poor managerial practices and fierce retail competition.

Japan, then, by around 1900 or 1910, possessed a complex marketing system composed of several tiers and types of wholesalers and retailers. To this day, foreign businesses often have a difficult time breaking into this complex, many-layered marketing network, and this difficulty helps explain why foreign firms often have had trouble getting started in Japan. As a result, many foreign companies, such as Starbuck's Coffee in the mid-1990s, have entered Japan with the help of a Japanese company in a joint-venture project. The Japanese partners have aided in opening markets, arranging financing, and smoothing the way with government officials for the non-Japanese firms.

Banking

Like sales, banking developed along several lines. The new government promulgated laws enabling the establishment of joint-stock banks in 1872 and ten years later set up the Bank of Japan as a national bank headquartered in Tokyo. With government promotion, Japan's banking system grew rapidly, especially after 1876, when the government stopped requiring the convertibility of bank notes into gold. Through World War I local traditional industries were the

most important customers of Japan's financial institutions. Much as had occurred earlier in Great Britain and America, local banks, often operating as parts of kinship networks, provided some of the financing for business development. Compared with what would develop later in Japan, this was a decentralized banking system. Large city banks and the Bank of Japan were important, as were banks that were parts of zaibatsu; but so, too, were many other banks in smaller urban centers. Of Japan's 1,345 commercial banks in 1919, some 1,155 had authorized capital of under 1 million yen apiece.

Only with financial crises of the 1920s and the resulting failures of many small and medium-sized banks did banking really begin to become concentrated. The passage of a new bank law in 1927 further promoted the concentration of banking. By 1931 only 310 of Japan's 683 commercial banks had an authorized capital of less than 1 million yen each. Concentration developed still more during the worldwide depression of the 1930s, as smaller banks continued to fail and be taken over by their larger brethren. By 1941 Japan possessed only 186 banks, of which just 78 had authorized capital of less than 1 million yen.

The increasing concentration of the banking business in Japan reflects a common trend in capitalistic economies. As we have seen, the Big Five city banks in Great Britain came to dominate that nation's financial activities in the early 1900s. In Germany, too, a handful of large universal banks were of most importance. Only in the United States, where a fear of concentrated economic power led to the passage of laws making branch banking difficult, was the banking system truly decentralized.

BUSINESS LEADERS, SOCIETY, AND LABOR

As Japan's business system changed, so did the nature of its business leaders, attitudes toward business, and the nature of labor relations. The management of big businesses in general (not just zaibatsu) became more bureaucratic; and managers became something of a business elite. Many Japanese adopted a more favorable attitude toward business leaders than they had held in Tokugawa times. With industrialization there also occurred changes in labor-management relations. Even so, important elements of continuity characterized relationships between business and society. It proved especially difficult

for many Japanese to change their ideas about the social status of business leaders, who had ranked behind all other groups in social standing during Tokugawa times.

A Business Elite

By 1903 Japan had 388 nonbanking businesses with capital assets of 10,000 yen or more, mostly joint-stock companies, that could be considered big businesses. These companies—like the zaibatsu—began developing bureaucratic management. Of these companies, 141 possessed managerial structures consisting of only a president and directors, but 152 had structures made up of a president, senior executive director (or managing director), and some other directors. Only 90 companies had neither a president nor a senior executive director. By the early 1920s company management had expanded to include typically a president, senior executive director, several other executive directors, and a junior executive director—each with fairly distinct responsibilities within their companies.

As in Great Britain and the United States, Japan's big business leaders formed something of an elite. In the 1880s about 19 percent of Japan's business leaders were the sons of merchants, 31 percent were the sons of small businessmen, another 23 percent were the sons of samurai, and 22 percent were the sons of farmers. By the 1920s some 35 percent were the sons of businessmen, 37 percent the sons of samurai, and 21 percent the sons of farmers. (No women made it to the top ranks of Japanese business.) Few farmers or laborers rose from rags to riches by going into business. Education played a greater role in helping define Japan's business elite than it did in most other nations. More and more top managers of large companies were college graduates. In 1924 some 244 of the top 384 business managers in the nation had earned the equivalent of a college degree. Most of these managers graduated from just three institutions of higher learning: 103 from Tokyo University, 49 from the Tokyo Higher Commercial School, and 48 from Keio Academy (later Keio University).

Changing Attitudes toward Business

Merchants in Tokugawa Japan ranked behind samurai, peasants, and artisans in the nation's social order. But this situation changed in Meiji Japan. The public image of business leaders rose, and their new heightened image was partially reconciled to the older Confucian ideals. However, this shift in how business leaders were viewed was neither easy nor complete by the 1920s and 1930s. The creation of new industries came to be seen by some Japanese as a service to the state because they would, it was hoped, make Japan strong. Some Japanese political and economic leaders came to view businesspeople as the new samurai of their nation. When conducted for the right reasons, for public as well as private gains, business enterprise could, they reasoned, be virtuous.

Eiichi Shibusawa did much to propagate this new attitude. Fourteen years old when Perry opened Japan to the West, Shibusawa was a member of the group seeking to overthrow the Tokugawa government. After the Meiji Restoration, Shibusawa spent the years 1869 through 1873 in the Ministry of Finance, rising to the position of assistant to the vice-minister. Shibusawa resigned from the government to go into business and founded the First Bank of Japan, the Oji Paper Company, the Tokyo Gas Company, the Osaka Spinning Company, and a wide variety of other concerns. Altogether, he was involved in starting over 200 business enterprises. Shibusawa also helped form business organizations, including the Tokyo Bankers' Association and chambers of commerce in Tokyo and Osaka. Shibusawa sought to place the mantle of the public-spirited samurai on the shoulders of Japan's new business leaders. By helping Japan modernize, business leaders were, he argued, worthy of public respect.

But how typical was Shibusawa? There can be no doubt that he and some other business leaders viewed their actions as building up Japan, or that some of the Japanese public also adopted this point of view. But, not all changed their attitudes overnight. Moreover, many business leaders were less public-spirited than Shibusawa. A desire for private profits and individual glory motivated them. For example, Hikojiro Nakamigawa, the head of Mitsui in the 1890s, ordered his subordinate Satoshi Hiraga to collect debts the government owed Mitsui, even though doing so went against the government's interests.

To starkly characterize Japanese business leaders as community-centered

and American executives as profit-centered oversimplifies the situation. Business leaders in both nations, and Great Britain as well, were motivated by a wide variety of factors. Classic Anglo-American works on self-advancement, such as *Self Help* by Samuel Smiles and *Pushing to the Front* by Orison Swett Marden, were best-sellers in Meiji Japan. These books emphasized individualism, not group cooperation, as the key to success. Letters written by young men to the *Eisai Shinshi*, a Tokyo magazine of the 1870s, also revealed a widespread desire for individual prosperity.

Labor Relations in Industrializing Japan

There has been much interest recently in Japan's system of labor relations, but confusion often exists about its historical origins. It is sometimes incorrectly assumed that the system, with its emphasis on cooperation between managers and workers (with workers having lifetime employment and wages and promotions based mainly on seniority and, in return, giving loyal service to their companies), is simply a holdover from the family-oriented business that existed in Tokugawa times, or that there is something unique to the culture of Japan that encourages such close cooperation.

At the outset three points need to be stressed. First, even in its heyday of the 1950s and 1960s, the system applied to only about one-third of Japan's industrial workers: mainly to men employed full time by large corporations, even though some smaller firms tried to move in this direction. Second, modern labor relations in Japan developed in response to specific challenges in the late nineteenth and twentieth centuries. The system did not grow out of innate characteristics of Japanese society or culture; there was nothing inherently familylike that predetermined the development of Japan's system of industrial relations. Finally, it is important to realize that there has never been a single model for labor relations in Japan, even among large firms.

Labor relations in Japan have, in fact, long been complex. While merchant houses operated as family enterprises, with clerks and other employees usually treated almost as family members, not all Tokugawa businesses were run this way. Artisans often labored on a contractual basis, frequently moving from firm to firm looking for higher pay and better opportunities. Unskilled laborers might be hired on contracts for seasonal projects or for specific tasks.

For most of these workers, lifetime employment and seniority-based wages were unheard of.

Cotton textile mills and silk reeling filatures led in the creation of the factory system in Japan. As late as 1919 textile mills employed 794,000 of Japan's 1,391,000 industrial workers. Women composed 62 percent of Japan's industrial workforce in 1909, and most textile workers were women. Neither lifetime employment nor seniority-based wages were in effect for them. Management regulated nearly all aspects of the textile workers' lives; women lived in company housing and needed passes to leave company property, a situation leading some observers to label their lives slavelike. In many other industries, nascent factories subcontracted the recruitment and supervision of workers to outside labor bosses, much as had been done in the United States into the 1880s. As late as 1890, for example, large shipyards and iron foundries relied on this system to provide gangs of 60 to 300 men at a time. Few permanent ties held these workers to their firms.

Dissatisfied workers responded to their situation in several ways. Some women ran away from the textile mills, leading to high turnover rates. Other workers continued to move from company to company in quest of better jobs; still others rioted and went on strike. As early as the 1880s isolated strikes occurred among workers in silk reeling and cotton textile mills. In the 1890s workers in a few industries, influenced by union development in the United States and sometimes aided by the American Federation of Labor, began establishing Western-style craft unions. By 1919 Japanese workers had formed 187 unions, and by 1923 the number had grown to 432. In 1921 Japanese workers organized the Sodomei (Japan General Federation of Labor), and within four years its member unions represented about 250,000 workers.

Members of these unions participated in strikes during the twentieth century. Labor unrest spread through many industries in 1906–7, as companies sought to rationalize (that is, make more efficient) their factory operations in the aftermath of the Russo-Japanese War of 1904–5, a time of rising inflation and industrial instability. Amid renewed inflation and a growing demand for skilled workers during World War I, more industrial laborers went on strike.

To dampen labor unrest, and especially to avoid strikes and to lower turnover rates, some industrialists resorted to strategies similar to those used in Great Britain and the United States. A few sought to institute aspects of sci-

entific management, for by the time of World War I Frederick Taylor's ideas about increasing labor efficiency were fairly well known in Japan. Industrialists achieved only limited success in this effort, for Japanese workers—like their British and American counterparts—resisted scientific management as a speed-up ploy and as an infringement on workers' prerogatives. Control of the shopfloor, while contested, remained mainly in the hands of skilled workers.

A few firms belonging to the Japan Industrial Club, which was dominated by zaibatsu and companies in heavy industry, began offering seniority bonuses during World War I, and some started forming company unions and engaging in aspects of corporate welfare work. Some employer associations, most notably the Osaka Industrial Association, called on the government to pass a law recognizing the right of craft unions to exist and to bargain collectively with management, reasoning that it would be easier to bargain with disciplined unions than with undisciplined, unorganized workers. (The Japanese government had generally been hostile to the formation of unions. The Diet passed a Factory Law designed to improve working conditions in 1911, but in doing so was motivated more by a desire to bolster the health of workers needed for the armed forces than to help workers deal with difficult working conditions.) In these business efforts around the time of World War I, then, one might see the bare beginnings of a labor relations system that would evolve throughout the twentieth century.

A BRIEF COMPARISON TO INDUSTRIALIZING GERMANY

Like Japan, Germany was a latecomer to industrialization, coming to the process after Great Britain and the United States; and a brief comparison of the how industrialization affected business development in Germany and Japan and, in turn, a comparison of the roles that different types of businesses played in industrialization and economic growth is revealing. While there were certainly similarities in the German and Japanese experiences, there was no single common path of development.

Big Business and Industrial Development

Germany became a politically unified nation in 1871, paving the way for the development of a national market. Even earlier, a customs union formed

among German states in 1834, and railroad growth from the 1850s spurred economic development. Much of Germany's industrial strength of the late nineteenth and early twentieth centuries lay in heavy industries—older ones, such as coal and iron and steel, and newer ones, such as chemicals, electrical equipment, and heavy industrial equipment. It was in these fields that Germany's largest and most vertically integrated firms arose; at the outbreak of World War I all of Germany's twenty largest companies were in these realms. In comparison to Japan, then, German industrialization stressed heavy industries rather than light industries (such as cotton textiles and silk reeling) and emphasized producer rather than consumer goods.

If zaibatsu were especially important for Japan's business development, banks and cartels were of particular significance for Germany. While their roles should not be overstressed, large universal banks, such as the Deutsche Bank (formed in 1870) and the Dresdner Bank (started in 1872), were of importance for some businesses in some industries. Combining the functions of investment, commercial, and savings banks, these institutions provided both capital and managerial advice—after changes in Germany's Company Law in 1884 bankers often sat on the supervisory boards of companies in heavy industry—for some of Germany's big businesses, especially in the years before World War I. The universal banks were deeply engaged in the affairs of businesses in the coal and the iron and steel industries but were much less involved in the work of chemical or mechanical engineering companies. Cartels were also especially important in Germany, probably even more important than they were in Japan. The German government allowed, and at times promoted, the development of cartels as a way of allowing the nation's newly industrializing firms to cooperate in their competition with better-established companies abroad. Cartels numbered 500–600 by 1911, with further cartelization occurring in the 1920s and 1930s.

While banks were important parts of zaibatsu in Japan, they did not assume the same significance that universal banks did in some industrial fields in Germany. In Japan ultimate managerial decision making rested with the families controlling the central organs of zaibatsu. Similarly, cartels were less important in Japan than in Germany. Cartels certainly existed in Japan, and would grow in significance (just as they would in Germany) in the 1920s and 1930s, but they never became as important a form of business organization in Japan as in Germany. In Japan there were always many small and medium-

size companies that either refused to participate in cartel activities or that found ways to evade cartel mandates.

Smaller Firms in German Industrialization

The picture of German industrialization and business development is more complex, however, than simply a story of big businesses, universal banks, and cartels. As in all of the other nations we have examined, smaller firms were of considerable significance. Small and medium-sized companies in Germany were a mix of handicraft trades, small craft shops, industrial firms, businesses associated with agriculture, and retailers and wholesalers. They often identified closely with their regions. Many were linked through local and regional chambers of commerce and were integrated only slowly and unevenly into Germany's national economy in the twentieth century. The adoption of electricity, which was a more flexible power source than steam power, encouraged the decentralization of some industrialization, allowing, for example, the development of Wuerttemberg as an industrial region. And, beyond manufacturing, small firms were the norm in sales. Between 1895 and 1907 the number of retail outlets with fewer than five employees rose from 560,000 to 800,000.

The small and medium-size firms in manufacturing were usually strongly controlled by families (with no input from universal banks, which concentrated on the larger national manufacturers). Municipal savings banks and cooperative credit unions, in addition to the families, provided the financing for the small and medium-size firms. The companies employed skilled craftsmen to produce manufactured products for niche markets—watches and clocks, cameras, optical and musical instruments, and engines of various sorts, to list a few.

Labor and Industrialization

A craft tradition, combined with the availability of an excellent polytechnic education, served well German industrial companies, large and small. Skilled, well-educated workers took considerable pride in their labors and were generally more receptive to the introduction of new technologies than were their counterparts in other industrializing economies, making technological transfers reasonably easy. Perhaps German workers were more open

to technological change because they did not have to fear that management would deploy technology in ways that undermined their control of work processes, as management often tried to do in Great Britain and America. At any rate, skilled workers in Germany seldom used their collective power to thwart the introduction of new ways of doing things.

BUSINESS AND INDUSTRIALIZATION IN JAPAN

With the development of zaibatsu such as Mitsui and Mitsubishi, big business arrived in Japan. As in the United States, the rise of big business changed Japanese business firms. Large businesses began adopting bureaucratic management systems. Nonetheless, as the examples of Mitsui and Mitsubishi also demonstrate, family control remained strong longer in Japan than in the United States, and in this respect Japanese big businesses resembled their counterparts in Great Britain and Germany more than those in America. The continued importance of smaller firms in industry, as well as in sales and services (such as banking), illustrates the complexity of Japan's business situation during industrialization. Companies of many sizes and sorts contributed to the development of Japan's economy.

While recognizing that complexities existed in all the nations we have examined—and especially that small and medium-size companies, as well as their larger brethren, played important roles—several generalizations are in order as we conclude our look at the relationships between business development and industrialization. As a very rough generalization, one may say that just as zaibatsu allowed Japan to compete with other industrializing countries, universal banks and cartels helped Germany in that competition. Moreover, as a gross generalization, one can say that large vertically integrated manufacturing companies, while not uniquely American, were most pronounced in the United States. Similarly, smaller firms, often linked in regional groupings, while existing in all the countries in this discussion, were probably most important in Great Britain. As we have seen, geography and political and legal systems, along with historical circumstances unique to each nation, influenced these business developments. Many complex factors converged to create the similarities and differences among the business firms of the world's industrializing nations.

SUGGESTED READINGS

Yasuo Mishima, *The Mitsubishi: Its Challenge and Strategy* (Greenwich: JAI Press, 1989); Hidemasa Morikawa, "The Organizational Structure of Mitsubishi and Mitsui Zaibatsu, 1868–1922: A Comparative Study," *Business History Review* 44 (Spring 1970): 62–83; William Wray, *Mitsubishi and the N. Y. K., 1870–1914* (Cambridge, Mass.: Harvard University Press, 1984); and Tsunehiko Yui, "The Personality and Career of Hikojiro Nakamigawa, 1887–1901," *Business History Review* 44 (Spring 1970): 39–61, analyze the development of Mitsubishi and Mitsui. William Wray, ed., *Managing Industrial Enterprise: Cases from Japan's Prewar Experience* (Cambridge, Mass.: Harvard University Press, 1989), is an important collection of case studies. Penelope Francks, *Japanese Economic Development: Theory and Practice* (London: Routledge, 1992), ch. 13, offers a valuable look at small business in industrializing Japan. On smaller firms, see also Johzen Takeuchi, *The Role of Labour-Intensive Sectors in Japanese Industrialization* (Tokyo: The United Nations University Press, 1991). Kunio Yoshihara, *Sogo Shosha: The Vanguard of the Japanese Economy* (New York: Oxford University Press, 1982), and M. Y. Yoshino and Thomas Lifson, *The Invisible Link: Japan's Sogo Shosha and the Organization of Trade* (Cambridge, Mass.: MIT Press, 1986), are useful studies.

Earl Kinmouth, *The Self-Made Man in Meiji Japanese Thought: From Samurai to Salary Man* (Berkeley: University of California Press, 1981), looks at business ideology in the Meiji period. Sheldon Garon, *The State and Labor in Modern Japan* (Berkeley: University of California Press, 1988); Andrew Gordon, *The Evolution of Labor Relations in Japan: Heavy Industry, 1853–1955* (Cambridge, Mass.: Harvard University Press, 1985); and Stephen Marsland, *The Birth of the Japanese Labor Movement* (Honolulu: University of Hawaii Press, 1989), provide insights into the development of labor relations. E. Patricia Tsurumi, *Factory Girls: Women in the Thread Mills of Meiji Japan* (Princeton: Princeton University Press, 1990), is revealing on the role of women in Japan's industrial development.

Wilfried Feldenkirchen, "Concentration in Germany Industry, 1870–1939," in *The Concentration Process in the Entrepreneurial Economy Since the late 19th Century*, ed. Hans Pohl (Wiesbaden, Germany: Steiner, 1978);

and Jeffrey Fear, "German Capitalism," Harvard Business School Case N1-796-004 (14 December 1995), provide valuable introductions to German business during industrialization. For an excellent history of one important firm, see Wilfried Feldenkirchen, *Werner Von Siemens: Inventor and International Entrepreneur* (Columbus: The Ohio State University Press, 1994).

6 [Business during the Interwar Period

In 1921 Japan's largest trading company, Suzuki Shoten, found itself in deep financial difficulties. Like many Japanese firms, Suzuki had expanded rapidly during World War I, only to face hard times in a worldwide economic contraction following the conflict. Suzuki failed in 1927, and only later did forty former employees of Suzuki establish a new and successful firm, Nissho, on its ashes. As the example of Suzuki Shoten suggests, the interwar years—the 1920s and 1930s—were unstable economic times. A recession of varying intensity and duration in different nations followed World War I. Business recovery in the mid-1920s was cut short by a global depression in the 1930s. The deepest and most widespread depression in world history, these hard times ended only as nations prepared for World War II.

As business executives faced new challenges during the interwar years, they continued to alter the nature of their companies and their nations' business systems. Still, as in earlier periods, continuity as well as change characterized the development of business practices. And, also as in the past, the differing cultures, social systems, and political situations of Great Britain, the United States, and Japan decreed that, while there would be many similarities in the responses of business leaders to their difficulties and opportunities, there would be marked differences as well.

AMERICAN BUSINESS

The same postwar recession that hurt Suzuki Shoten hit American companies hard. The sharp downturn revealed basic deficiencies in the management of

large manufacturing businesses in the United States. None had anticipated the onset of the recession, and most responded sluggishly to it. The recession thus exposed serious management problems previously hidden during a period of prosperity. However, over time some large manufacturers developed a new management system, called "decentralized management," designed to allow their companies to react quickly to market changes. Adopted sparingly in the interwar years, decentralized management would characterize large American industrial firms after World War II. Smaller firms experienced fewer changes in how they operated during the interwar years, though some alterations did occur, particularly in sales.

Diversification and Decentralization

During the opening decades of the twentieth century many large manufacturing companies produced a widening range of consumer goods—automobiles, electric stoves, refrigerators, radios, and the like—for more and more markets. As early as 1914 Henry Ford began using conveyor belt mass-production techniques to turn out his Model T, producing 15 million of the cars by 1928. In the 1920s the United States was rapidly becoming a consumer society, with consumer durables (items purchased for use over several years) bought on time through installment payments becoming central to the nation's economy.

As manufacturing businesses became more diversified in terms of their products and markets, and more directly affected by the ups and downs of consumer buying, centralized management could no longer adequately run the companies, a point driven home by the postwar slump. The executives of big businesses were so tied up in the daily affairs of their companies that they were not planning for the future. Companies as diverse in their operations as Goodyear Rubber, Ford, General Motors, Armour Meats, DuPont, and Sears Roebuck encountered severe problems. When new car sales collapsed, General Motors was forced to borrow $83 million in short-term notes to survive and Ford Motors sold all nonessential equipment, including 600 telephones, to raise ready cash.

In coping with their difficulties, some businesses developed decentralized management systems, wherein the head office came to concentrate upon

This Coca-Cola advertisement of 1929 epitomized the growth of a consumer society in America. (Courtesy of the Archives, Coca-Cola Company)

planning for the entire company and on coordinating the operations of its different parts. The daily operations of the company were delegated to managers of divisions, with the divisions usually organized around product lines or regions. As part of their reorganization, these diversified big businesses improved greatly their accounting systems, financial controls, and market forecasting. In short, no longer did a few people or a few committees in the head office run all aspects of their firm's business.

General Motors: A Pioneer in Decentralized Management

General Motors pioneered in decentralized management. William Durant, who was the father of General Motors, first became interested in automobiles in 1904, when he took over the Buick Company in Flint, Michigan. Durant used Buick as his base to found General Motors, and between 1908 and 1910 he brought together over twenty-five previously independent companies—including Olds, Oakland, and Cadillac—as the General Motors Corporation. A second period of growth occurred in 1918–20, as Durant added Chevrolet, Fisher Body, a tractor company, an electric refrigerator company, and a number of smaller concerns to General Motors. While an energetic empire builder, Durant failed to provide his company with adequate management. He tried to run the company as a one-man show, making both grand policy and daily operating decisions by himself; but, as the firm grew in size and complexity, major decisions on investment, expansion, marketing, and the like often simply were not made.

The postwar recession disclosed the managerial weaknesses that had developed at General Motors. Lacking any form of market forecasting, each division invested large sums in new plants to build more cars, even as sales dropped 20 percent in one year. Moreover, each division continued to buy large inventories of raw materials with which to produce its cars. Cash flow difficulties compounded the company's problems. Each division maintained its own bank accounts, making it hard for the head office to move funds internally within the company. Buick, in particular, was reluctant to give up its cash to the head office, even when the cash was desperately needed to keep the company afloat. Underlying these various difficulties was the basic problem of control: the head office was unable to either plan for the future of the company or coordinate the work of its different parts.

Management changes ensued. In late 1920 Durant resigned as president of General Motors, and Pierre S. DuPont, recently retired from the DuPont Company, became the new president of General Motors. (Looking for investment opportunities for substantial wartime profits, the DuPont Company had by 1919 purchased 29 percent of General Motors's stock.) In rebuilding General Motors, DuPont was greatly assisted by Alfred P. Sloan, Jr., a graduate of the Massachusetts Institute of Technology and a vice-president and major stockholder in General Motors.

Frustrated by Durant's chaotic way of doing business, Sloan prepared an "organization study" that contained a plan to revamp the management of General Motors even before the crisis of 1920. DuPont and others in top management adopted it in late 1920. This plan introduced decentralized management to General Motors by clearly delineating the duties and responsibilities of the head office and the divisions and by providing for effective communications among the different parts of the company. The plan's goal was to combine divisional autonomy with supervision by a strong central office.

Sloan and DuPont made significant changes at the operational level. Each division was now clearly defined by a distinct product line. Market segmentation in modern industrial firms began at General Motors. As the automobile market matured, Sloan and DuPont recognized the need to differentiate their cars from each other and from those of their competitors. They eliminated overlap in the prices, products, and markets of the divisions. Advertising and annual model changes identified each make of car. Run by a general manager, each division controlled its own engineering, production, and sales organizations, and each enjoyed a considerable degree of freedom in its daily operations.

To ensure coordination in the work of the divisions, DuPont and Sloan created the office of group vice-president. Freed from specific daily operating responsibilities, the group vice-presidents supervised the work of related divisions and helped set policies for the entire company. Four groups were established: accessories, affiliated companies, export, and car and truck. The officers in these divisions and groups were line officers.

Sloan and DuPont also created a strong central or head office (also called the corporate office) for General Motors. General officers, working through executive and finance committees, coordinated the work of the four groups, made policy decisions for the company, and planned for its future. In doing so, they were assisted by a vastly enlarged staff made up of financial and legal experts. Neither the general officers nor the staff officers concerned themselves with daily operating matters.

To arrive at cooperation and understanding between management in the divisional and the central offices, Sloan and DuPont established a number of interdivisional relations committees. Officers from all levels belonged to these committees that met at regular intervals to discuss common problems. Both staff and divisional engineers, for instance, composed the general tech-

nical committee that sought solutions for common engineering problems the different divisions encountered in designing and producing cars.

Finally, Sloan and DuPont improved greatly financial reporting and statistical controls, creating a model long followed by other diversified corporations. Three innovations were of special importance. First, the central office received weekly and monthly production reports from each group and division. Under Durant, no such data had been available. Second, the central office received reports every ten days from dealers on how many cars were actually being sold, and this information made market forecasting possible (the ten-day period of reporting sales is still the standard period in the automobile industry). Finally, the work of each division was assessed by the central office, using new accounting techniques that measured its rate of return on investment, making it easier for those on top to decide where to expand or contract the company's operations. (Figure 3 outlines decentralized management at General Motors.)

The decentralized management system instituted at General Motors in the 1920s worked well for decades. The company's share of the American automobile market rose from 19 percent in 1924 to 43 percent three years later, by which time its annual net profit amounted to an impressive $276 million. The Great Depression provided the acid test for the new organization. Although its sales fell by two-thirds between 1929 and 1932, General Motors continued to show a profit and to pay dividends every year throughout the 1930s. With only minor changes, the decentralized management structure pioneered in the 1920s remained the basic administrative framework of General Motors into the 1970s.

The Spread of Decentralized Management: Strategy and Structure

Over time, many big businesses in the United States and abroad followed the route pioneered by General Motors. Structure followed strategy in American business. The more diversified a company was in terms of its products and markets, the more likely it was to establish some form of decentralized management. International Harvester adopted decentralized management in 1943, and both Chrysler and Ford did so right after World War II. In the chemicals industry DuPont led the way in the 1920s, as it began making a broad range of consumer goods such as rayon, with Hercules and Monsanto

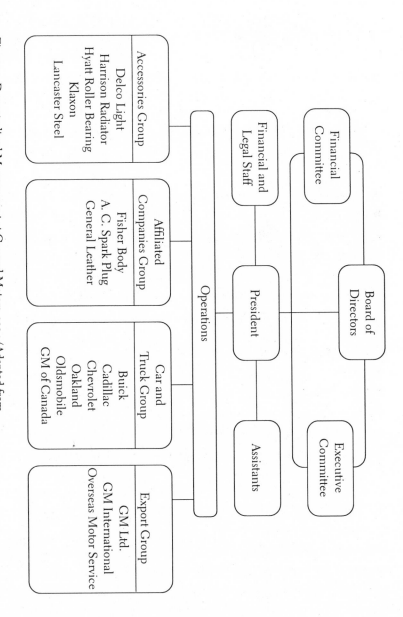

Figure 3. Decentralized Management at General Motors, 1924 (Adapted from *Management and Administration* 7 [May 1924]: 525. Courtesy of Houghton Mifflin)

following in the 1930s. As they moved into the production of many new household electrical appliances, Westinghouse adopted decentralized management in 1934, and General Electric did so in the 1950s.

While needed and appropriate for many firms in the mid-twentieth century, decentralized management eventually created problems for American companies. Over several decades, too many layers of management were created in many of the companies using this system. Companies ossified and reacted only sluggishly to market changes; and this hurt, as those changes came with increasing rapidity in the global market, especially in the 1970s and 1980s. Then, too, the use of decentralized management, with its tremendous dependence on reports, placed a premium on having top managers in the corporate office well versed in financial management methods—a situation that could lead companies to place too much emphasis on short-term financial objectives at the expense of longer-term goals. Too often managers in the corporate office lost touch with what was going on in their companies' factories, as too few of them understood operational management.

Small Business in Manufacturing

Small businesses experienced a long-term decline in their relative importance in American manufacturing between about 1880 and 1970. With the rise of large manufacturing companies, the shares of small firms in both industrial employment and output dropped. But not all small manufacturers suffered. Small businesses continued to thrive in areas in which they could carve out market niches—fields in which flexibility, especially the capability to turn out rapidly small batches of goods in short production runs, was of utmost significance.

The metal-fabricating and machinery-making industry of New England between 1890 and 1957 was one such field. Of the 80 firms composing the industry, all but 18 employed fewer than 100 workers, only 15 possessed tangible assets exceeding $500,000, and only 10 had a net worth of more than $500,000. Success came through the development of specialty products for niche markets. Some entrepreneurs specialized in products with only a limited demand, thus avoiding competition with big businesses disdaining to enter such unappealing fields. Others engaged in just one process: metal-stamping, heat-treating, or electroplating. By performing custom work, they

secured nonstandardized orders overlooked by larger mass-production firms. Still others differentiated their products by providing extraordinary service and by building up reputations for dependability.

Personal ties held these small New England businesses together. Most of the founders, like those in small businesses in other industries and in other times, began their enterprises as partnerships or single-owner proprietorships, though all except six eventually reorganized their businesses as corporations. Whatever legal forms they assumed, nearly all of the businesses were directly run by their owner-founders. Family enterprises in which fathers and sons or brothers jointly handled affairs frequently existed (sometimes wives participated, usually looking after the finances of the operations).

This personal approach to business carried over into financing and labor relations. Personal savings, supplemented by family funds, funds from local business acquaintances, and, to a much lesser extent, bank borrowing, provided most of the initial capital. Very few companies borrowed from federal government agencies. Capital used to finance expansion came mainly from retained earnings and debt-financing. Few of the entrepreneurs had access to equity markets, and even if they had had such access, few would have made use of it, for they were not willing to dilute their ownership and managerial control over their companies. Over one-half of the companies began with five or fewer employees. As the firms developed, they were able to acquire and keep their growing number of employees through a combination of monetary and nonmonetary incentives. Some offered more than the prevailing wage rate. Others provided chances for rapid advancement and opportunities to learn new skills, and, in all firms, the owner-managers continued to know their workers individually.

Big Business and Small Business in Industry

The continued development of big business in industry dramatically changed the world of the small manufacturer. Before the Civil War, nearly all American businesses had been small firms, single-unit enterprises without managerial hierarchies. With the acceleration in industrialization that occurred after the Civil War, this situation changed. Large companies benefiting from economies of scale supplanted small firms in mass-production fields. While continuing to grow in absolute numbers and while remaining important in

niche markets, small manufacturers became proportionally less important to America's overall economy.

The spread of large companies with decentralized management systems accelerated the trend toward concentration and the growth of oligopoly in the United States. America experienced its second major merger movement in the 1920s, as 5,846 mergers occurred in 1925–31. In some manufacturing fields there was a decrease in price competition, as prices in oligopolistic industries became less responsive to market forces. In those fields the decisions of the managers of big businesses rather than market forces determined the prices and quantities of goods produced. The visible hand of management became increasingly important in determining how part of America's business system functioned. It was in the interwar years, for instance, that the American automobile industry, once composed of dozens of companies, came to be dominated by the Big Three—General Motors, Ford, and Chrysler.

Businesses in Sales and Services

Small businesses remained dominant longer in sales and services than in manufacturing. However, the interwar years brought changes in business organization to these fields, especially to sales—as the continued development of chain stores and the rise of supermarkets eroded the importance of independent retailers. The most notable change lay in the rapid increase in the importance of chain stores in retailing, such as the Great Atlantic and Pacific Tea Company (A&P), Woolworth, and J. C. Penny. The spread of chain stores was part of a more general trend in retailing, the growth in importance of large-scale stores. By 1949, in addition to the 20 percent of the nation's retail sales made by chain stores, department stores accounted for 8 percent, supermarkets 7 percent, and mail-order houses 1 percent. Independent retailers, who had handled nearly all of the sales as late as 1890, accounted for less than two-thirds of the sales.

What accounted for this dramatic rise in the chains? Probably most important, chain stores gave lower prices to consumers, while still earning substantial profits. They did so by providing fewer personal services to customers than did independents, by making no deliveries, by dealing strictly in cash, and by dispensing fewer premiums and trading stamps. Chains engaged in the most up-to-date business practices: the use of new accounting methods

to keep track of inventories, new store layouts, and new forms of advertising. The scale of operations allowed the chains to pass on savings in costs to their customers. Many chains cut out middlemen in distribution, dealing instead directly with the growers and producers of goods. Chains also engaged in extensive backward vertical integration. A&P possessed subsidiaries that controlled many of its sources of milk, cheese, coffee, canned salmon, and bread.

Small service businesses also came under increasing pressure from large firms in some fields, though not to as great an extent as did small retailers. Possessing fewer economies of scale than stores selling goods, service industries were less conducive to the spread of large firms. Banking, for example, remained dominated by small businesses, though the trend was toward consolidation. The number of commercial banks in the United States fell by half during the 1930s and then stabilized at around 15,000 through the 1980s. (The coming of federal deposit insurance in 1933 enhanced the safety of small banks and gave them a new lease on life.) In the interwar years branch banking came to the United States in a major way. In 1920 less than 5 percent of banking offices were branches. Only twenty-one states permitted branch banking at that date, and until the passage of the McFadden Act by Congress in 1927, branch banking was forbidden at the national level. With the liberalization of the laws by the McFadden Act and later legislation, banks with branches came to compose one-fifth of the total by 1935, and in 1957 over one-half of the 13,617 commercial banks had branches.

From Associationalism to the Welfare State

One reason for the merger movement of the 1920s and a more general business rationalization movement, an attempt to make businesses more efficient and productive, in the 1920s and 1930s was that the federal government favored them. To be sure, the federal government continued to regulate business as it had begun to in the Progressive Era. However, there was more cooperation between government and business, to the extent that historians often label the nature of government-business relations in the United States "associationalism."

During World War I government officials and business executives worked together through government agencies, the most important of which was the War Industries Board, to mobilize industry for the war effort. After the

war, Herbert Hoover, first as secretary of commerce, and then as president between 1928 and 1932, sought to extend government-business cooperation. Hoover tried to set up an associative state as an alternative to either government control of the economy (what he called statism) or cutthroat competition and individualism. Hoover wanted government and business leaders to work together voluntarily to make the nation's economy strong. In Hoover's conception the federal government, aided by private research foundations, would be the source of up-to-date, scientifically derived economic information. The government would pass that information along to business leaders who, in turn, would make rational business decisions in their own and the national interest. Hoover's actions took several major forms. He worked with business leaders to try to reduce waste in their industries. For example, under Hoover's guidance, the lumber industry adopted standard sizes, terms, and grades in 1923. Hoover also labored with executives to try to smooth out the ups and downs of the business cycle.

The onset of the Great Depression of the 1930s, however, revealed the inadequacy of Hoover's ideas and added important new dimensions to economic rationalization. Between 1929 and 1932 there were a record 110,000 business failures in America. By 1932 industrial production had fallen to half of what it had been just four years earlier, and unemployment stood at about 25 percent. In this situation of widespread economic distress business rationalization came to mean much more than simply making individual firms more efficient or smoothing out small variations in the business cycle. Rationalization came to include economic recovery, with the recovery efforts led by the federal government.

In trying to solve the problems of the Great Depression, Franklin D. Roosevelt, who took office as president in 1933, built in part upon the foundations of government-business cooperation laid by Hoover. Roosevelt's key solution for the problems of the industrial sector of the economy was a piece of legislation passed by Congress during the spring of his first year in office, the National Industrial Recovery Act (NIRA). This act set up a new federal government agency, the National Recovery Administration, modeled upon the War Industries Board of fifteen years before. In the National Recovery Administration business leaders and government officials voluntarily cooperated to try to bring about economic recovery. Antitrust laws were suspended, and prices and production quotas were set in an attempt to help businesses get

back on their feet. However, because its economic principles were faulty (the higher prices resulting from price-fixing among manufacturers made it difficult for consumers to buy industrial goods), the NIRA did not work, and Roosevelt allowed it to die after the United States Supreme Court declared the law unconstitutional in 1935.

Roosevelt soon moved beyond Hoover's ideas to create with Congress the beginning of a welfare state in America, wherein the federal government assumed responsibility for the general welfare of Americans. A wide variety of federal government programs gave jobs or assistance to those out of work, something not done during the Hoover years. None of these actions, however, ended the Great Depression. While now helped by the federal government, some 10 million Americans remained jobless in 1939.

As long as Roosevelt's efforts at recovery aided them, business leaders supported New Deal measures. The NIRA initially had considerable business support. Nonetheless, much of the business backing faded by the mid-1930s. Economic leadership by government officials was something many business leaders were unwilling to accept, especially since, as we shall see, the New Dealers supported legislation promoting unionization. Then, too, the business community split over many of the New Deal's welfare measures, with few executives supporting the full range of Roosevelt's legislation. When rationalization moved beyond efforts to make companies more efficient and productive and threatened to impinge on management prerogatives, business leaders backed off from the movement.

Many government-business splits were healed during World War II, which brought renewed profits to businesses. In fact, government-business cooperation reached new heights during the conflict, as business executives and government officials worked together in a myriad of federal government agencies, most importantly the Office of War Mobilization and the Office of Price Administration, to ensure the successful mobilization of industry for the war effort. Federal government spending on the war ended the Great Depression, as unemployment finally dried up in 1942.

Labor Relations

As we have seen, adversarial relations characterized industrial labor relations in America, as employers sought to wrest control of the workplace away from

their employees, especially skilled workers. With United States' entrance into World War I in 1917, many labor leaders hoped that their unions might become more powerful. They proved correct, for the federal government struck a new arrangement with trade unions: in return for a pledge to refrain from strikes and to cooperate in achieving full industrial production, the unions were given the right to organize factory workers. During the war the National War Labor Board, a new federal government agency, mediated disputes in 1,100 plants affecting 711,500 employees and established work councils made up of representatives of management and labor in an attempt to prevent disputes from disrupting production.

Many labor officials, joined by a few business leaders, hoped that this type of cooperation—in which the federal government would continue to be involved—would expand after the war. They hoped that a contract of sorts could be reached between labor and management to protect, if not improve, workers' wages and working conditions and thus avoid conflicts in the future. Such was not to be, at least not in the 1920s. When labor leaders sought to unionize the steel industry, then central to America's industrial economy, they were sharply rebuffed and defeated, an outcome that ensured that labor-management relations in mass-production industries would remain much as before the war, with management dictating the terms of employment to workers and with conflict continuing between them.

With the crisis of World War I behind them, most business leaders rejected the idea of bargaining with labor unions. Instead, they tried to destroy them. Union membership peaked in 1920 at over 5 million workers, but then declined to 3.4 million in 1930, only 6.8 percent of America's nonagricultural workforce. Rather than accept independent labor unions, business leaders promoted welfare capitalism, which was based on the premise that the businesses, not independent trade unions, should look after the interests of workers. By the 1920s welfare capitalism encompassed housing, educational, medical, religious, and recreational facilities for employees, profit-sharing plans, and retirement pensions. It often also involved the establishment of company unions. Although company unions were of some help in improving working conditions, they did not bargain collectively with management on behalf of workers on such fundamental issues as wages and hours of work. Company unions were almost always controlled by management, were limited to individual companies, and mainly provided avenues of communi-

cation between management and workers. In short, welfare capitalism and company unions were largely designed to protect the power and prerogatives of management.

Labor relations underwent a fundamental shift in the 1930s, a particularly stressful time in American business and labor history. Changes resulted, in part, from the willingness of New Deal political leaders to mitigate the harm of the Great Depression by fostering unionization. Because the Great Depression cut so deep, politicians sought to restore vigor to the business system by granting workers the means of increasing their share of the nation's wealth through unions and collective bargaining. In doing so, workers would, it was hoped, purchase products of their own industrial handiwork and thereby stimulate recovery. More was involved, however. Changes also resulted from growing militancy in the workforce, which produced larger and stronger unions. Politicians were almost forced to respond to the growth in union strength.

The result was the National Labor Relations Act of 1935, which granted workers the right to form unions of their own choice and required businesses to agree to collective bargaining. Partly as a result of the new law, labor struggles broke out in mass-production industries employing great numbers of unskilled and semiskilled men and women. Led by autoworkers, laborers developed a new, and very effective, strategy designed to improve their standards of living: they sat down on the job and refused to leave their factories, thus shutting down production. On the eve of World War II over 8.7 million American workers, or 16 percent of the nonagricultural workforce, belonged to unions.

As workers bargained with management through independent unions, welfare capitalism faded away. Mass-production unions—the United Auto Workers, the United Steelworkers, the United Rubber Workers, and the like—along with the federal government assumed responsibility for the welfare of labor. Labor power rose still more during World War II, until 1945, when the number of workers who were unionized had climbed to over 14 million, nearly 22 percent of the nonagricultural workforce.

BRITISH BUSINESS

In the interwar years the formation of large companies accelerated in Great Britain. Mergers and efforts to make manufacturing firms more efficient were commonplace, and through the mergers large companies developed in some fields of British manufacturing. With the rise of these big businesses, the nature of the business firm and its management began changing. A handful of companies adopted the decentralized type of management pioneered in America by General Motors. Even so, Great Britain remained primarily a land of smaller companies. In many fields of manufacturing and in much of retailing, small firms dominated the business landscape. The British business system, like that of the United States and, as we shall see, Japan, was complex. While some parts performed well during the interwar years, others lost ground relative to competitors abroad.

The Rationalization Movement

From the outset of the 1920s economic distress lay behind much of the rationalization movement in Britain, and economic recovery was one of the movement's goals. The same postwar recession that hit America hurt Great Britain even more. In 1921 unemployment rose to 10 percent and never fell below that mark in the interwar years. In this new situation some of Britain's business leaders looked to rationalization—and to mergers, which they often equated with rationalization and efficiencies—for their salvation. Business leaders sponsored rationalization, in part, as an alternative to socialism favored by some labor groups. British executives were also influenced by the example of American companies. They observed American subsidiaries—Ford Motors, for instance—using mass-production methods to make their English plants more efficient. Moreover, they saw American firms leading mergers in Great Britain. General Electric brought together four electrical manufacturers to form Associated Electrical Industries, and General Motors took over Vauxhall Motors to become a large-scale automaker in Britain.

Some government leaders also favored business rationalization. As we have seen, the British government had been less directly involved than either the American or Japanese governments in industrialization and economic development in the nineteenth century. During World War I, however, British

government officials and business leaders cooperated closely in the crisis situation. The government encouraged businesses to adopt mass-production methods, a situation that stimulated merger activity, as firms sought to expand their production capacities. Private profits and national economic growth would, it was hoped, advance together.

In the 1920s mergers blossomed in Great Britain. Prodded by the Federation of British Industries, an organization of manufacturers, the government allowed mergers to take place. Rising real incomes enjoyed by many in interwar Great Britain, despite the persistent unemployment of some, led to increased consumer demand for goods. Between 1927 and 1939 the number of people owning radios soared from 2.2 million to 9 million and the annual output of cars rose from 239,000 to 507,000. Although not going nearly as far as in America, increased consumer demand created the possibility of economies of scale in some British industries, encouraging the growth of larger factories and firms. About 4,000 British companies merged during the 1920s and 1930s, especially in the foodstuffs, chemicals, metal manufacturing, shipbuilding, electrical engineering, and building materials industries.

With these mergers big businesses became more common. In 1919 only one British company, Coats Sewing, was capitalized at as much as 32 million pounds. By 1930 an additional six firms were: Unilever, Imperial Tobacco, Imperial Chemical Industries, Distillers, Courtaulds, and Guiness. By 1930, as well, at least ten British firms employed more than 30,000 workers. Industry became more concentrated. In 1909 the largest 100 companies accounted for 16 percent of Britain's industrial output, but they accounted for 24 percent by 1935, about the same proportion as in America. But even so, most British manufacturers remained considerably smaller than their American counterparts. In 1930 only the 50 largest British industrial companies would have made the list of the top 200 such firms in America.

Changing Business Management

As time progressed, more and more of the large British companies established centralized bureaucratic management systems. Within their head offices a division in management occurred. Entrepreneurial peak coordinators, business leaders roughly equivalent to senior vice-presidents in the United States, took charge of making grand policy and coordinating the different activities

of their companies. They were assisted by specialists in personnel, finance, accounting, and technical matters who took responsibility for the routine functions of the firms. As in America, however, centralized management could not adequately handle the growing complexity of the affairs of the largest of the big businesses in Great Britain. Two British companies, Imperial Chemical Industries and Unilever, influenced by what General Motors and other American firms were doing, turned to decentralized management. Activities were organized on a divisional basis, with the divisions set up by region or product. The division chiefs reported to peak coordinators in the head office who controlled financial matters and grand strategy for their companies. Increasingly sophisticated accounting and record keeping bound together the different parts of these companies.

Where did the managers come from to staff Great Britain's growing number of big businesses? At the highest level, that of peak executives, many came from business families, much more so than was the case in America. Some companies also recruited their top managers from government ministries — Imperial Chemical Industries recruited from Inland Revenue — or from the military, as did Vickers, Britain's leading armaments maker. Technicians, the functional specialists, usually received on-the-job training within their firms. Accountancy was one common avenue of advancement for such middle-level managers. As in times past, British business leadership tended to be self-replicating. In the years 1930 through 1949 about 45 percent of the nation's business leaders were the sons of businessmen, 10 percent were the sons of farmers, 28 percent were the sons of public officials, and only 17 percent were the sons of clerical workers or laborers.

Imperial Chemical Industries

Imperial Chemical Industries presents a glimpse of how a few large British businesses diversified their operations and adopted decentralized management during the interwar years. Formed as part of the business rationalization movement, the firm expanded its operations in the 1920s and 1930s to become one of Great Britain's largest and most complex companies. As their firm grew, Imperial Chemical's executives found it necessary to alter its management system, and centralized management gave way to decentralized management.

The formation of Imperial Chemical in 1926 can be traced to a lunchtime discussion between Harry McGowan, the chairman and managing director of Nobel Industries Ltd., and Reginald McKenna, a high-ranking government official. Both wanted to strengthen the British chemical industry in its growing competition with American companies like DuPont and German companies like I. G. Farben. From this conversation and lengthy negotiations came Imperial Chemical as a merger of the four largest British chemical companies: Nobel Industries, the United Alkali Company, British Dyestuffs, and Brunner, Mond. In the 1920s and 1930s Imperial Chemical was the largest manufacturing company in Great Britain and one of the largest chemical companies in the world. Imperial Chemical employed 47,000 people in Great Britain alone and possessed plants in Canada, South Africa, Australia, and South America, producing heavy chemicals, explosives, dyes, and fertilizers.

Imperial Chemical expanded its activities as time progressed, with two related projects receiving special attention. It moved into the synthetic production of ammonia, which could be used as a source of nitrogen, and nitrogen was used in making fertilizers and explosives. Employing a related chemical process, Imperial Chemical also started producing synthetic gasoline out of coal. In 1931 Imperial Chemical entered into an agreement with I. G. Farben to obtain the technical process of hydrogenation, and with government support began making synthetic gasoline in 1936. World War II brought further expansion to these and other projects, and between 1937 and 1943 Imperial Chemical invested the large sum of 58 million pounds in twenty-five new factories.

Of the four companies merging to form Imperial Chemical, Nobel Industries had the greatest influence on its management practices. Nobel had itself been created as a result of a merger of more than thirty companies in 1920. To rationalize this originally loose collection of firms, Nobel executives established a centralized management system. They set up a central research laboratory, centralized production in the most efficient factories, and established a strong central office to run the entire company as one entity. Within Nobel's head office functional departments handled publicity, personnel, purchasing, legal issues, and taxation matters for the entire company. By the mid-1920s, however, Nobel was beginning to move in the direction of decentralized management by having the head office shift some responsibilities for the company's daily operations to product divisions. What had

occurred at Nobel was repeated at Imperial Chemical, which is not surprising since Nobel men occupied many of the key managerial positions at Imperial Chemical.

Imperial Chemical began with a strong central management system in 1926. A Finance Committee and an Executive Committee controlled capital expenditures and made all policy decisions. Banking, purchasing, and commercial and statistical control policies were all standardized and centralized in the head office. In the field, operations were centralized in the most efficient factories. While this system of management succeeded in lowering production costs, it had flaws. Imperial Chemical was simply too complex in terms of its products and markets to be run well by a centralized management system.

In the late 1920s and early 1930s Imperial Chemical's executives replaced centralized management with decentralized management. They established eight groups based upon products, very similar to the product divisions set up at General Motors. These groups were given responsibility for daily operations. A General Administration Committee composed of those officers in charge of the groups plus officers from the head office coordinated the work of the eight groups. Two committees in the central office, the General Purposes Committee and the Finance Committee, composed of the president and directors, made the large strategic decisions for Imperial Chemical.

The Limits of Rationalization

Even with the merger movement, the growth in size of some industrial firms, and the adoption by some firms of new management methods and structures, neither business nor political proponents of rationalization achieved as much as they desired. Old habits died hard. The continued atomization of most industries into dozens, even hundreds, of small firms, proved difficult to change. So did the predominant attitude that the government should not be directly involved in business development. Moreover, it soon turned out that those big firms that did result from mergers were not necessarily as efficient as they might be. And, as in the United States, many business executives, while eager to support rationalization aimed at increasing the profitability of their individual firms, were often unwilling to support rationalization measures that might impinge on their prerogatives.

The Failure of Rationalization in the Steel Industry

What occurred in Great Britain's steel industry illustrates the limitations of industrial rationalization. Most business and political leaders agreed that this industry needed to be reshaped if it were to remain competitive internationally, but disagreements among steelmakers, bankers, and government officials meant that while some new approaches were tried little was ultimately accomplished during the interwar years.

There were aspects of both stagnation and growth in Britain's steel industry. The output of Britain's steel industry rose by 62 percent between 1913 and 1936–37, a growth spurt greater than the 37 percent increase of steel production in Europe as a whole or the 36 percent rise in German steel output. Nonetheless, the British steel industry experienced tremendous fluctuations in output from year to year, suffered from stagnation in exports, and came to possess a great deal of excess capacity (which translated into high unemployment for its workers).

Like so much of British manufacturing, the British steel industry had developed in the nineteenth century mainly as a disparate collection of small, unintegrated firms; and so the industry remained in the early 1920s. Despite the continuing growth of their industry, British steelmakers felt intensifying pressure from large vertically integrated American and German competitors in many markets (an increasing share of Britain's production went to Commonwealth markets, made up of countries associated with the British Empire).

Even under the gun of rising foreign competition, attempts by British steelmakers to rationalize their firms were disappointing. There were places where the merger of companies with overlapping capabilities might have led to the implementation of more efficient production methods and the elimination of excess capacity—among steelmakers of Britain's northeast coast, for example. Such did not occur. Well-entrenched family interests in the many small companies made mergers difficult, as did conflicts among various groups of creditors, shareholders, and customers about how to proceed. Even when mergers were possible, they did not necessarily result in efficiently run firms, as was true for Britain's largest steel company, United Steel. Formed through the merger of four iron and steel firms between 1917 and 1920, this company was unified in name only. Throughout the 1920s the four steelmakers composing it operated almost as independent entities, with little managerial coordination

of their work and few economies of scale. Only in 1928, faced with mounting financial losses, did United Steel begin centralizing its management and making its plants more efficient.

During the interwar years banks became more involved in the management of manufacturing concerns than they had previously been, and they might have provided leadership in rationalizing steelmaking. City of London, regional, and local banks had long invested in industry. British banks had not, however, taken much of a role in managerial decision making in those companies—especially when compared to the more active roles taken by German universal banks and the banks of Japanese zaibatsu. This began to change during the interwar years. In the early 1930s the Bank of England mapped out plans by which British steelmakers might form large vertically integrated regional amalgamations in the interests of production efficiencies, but the bank ultimately drew back from involvement in any such scheme. The bank not only did not want to invest in an unprofitable industry, it also lacked the management know-how to bring about rationalization, and it did not want to engage in activities that might make it more accountable to the British government.

Finally, the British government might have promoted rationalization schemes for the steel industry, abandoning its traditional stance of avoiding direct involvement in industrial matters. Like the Bank of England, the British government did, in fact, become more engaged than before; but, like the bank, the government did not go far enough to bring about effective rationalization. The government wanted the elimination of excessive competition in the steel industry, yet it also feared the development of regional steel monopolies. As a result, for years the government tried to foster mergers that would result in a more efficient industry, but it long refused to pass a protective tariff for steel. Only in 1932, at the nadir of the Great Depression and in response to similar actions by many other industrial nations, did the British government enact a protective tariff. In the 1930s the government sought also to form cartels in the steel industry; these efforts, however, accomplished little in the way of rationalization and increased efficiencies.

Problems in Cotton Textiles

A scenario similar in some respects to that which developed in steel unfolded in cotton textiles. The smallness of most of Great Britain's cotton textile companies had not hurt them in the nineteenth century—just as had been the case in the steel industry, and for similar reasons. British firms were the first on the scene with the most modern machinery, and they enjoyed an expanding world market for their cottons. However, as market growth slowed in the early twentieth century and then slumped precipitously in the 1920s and 1930s international competition increased. The specialized, unintegrated British firms faced difficult times.

The continuing failure of British firms to integrate spinning with weaving was particularly harmful, for it militated against long, efficient production runs and hindered the introduction of efficient automatic machinery. The lack of marketing coordination—most producers continued to rely on independent marketers—also hurt the British cotton textile industry. As a result, exports fell and imports rose. (Coincidentally, it was in the interwar years that the small, unintegrated firms composing Philadelphia's textile industry first ran into serious difficulties.) Efforts were made to rationalize Britain's cotton textile industry by private and government actions in the interwar years. These efforts reduced excess capacity, but they failed to integrate spinning and weaving or marketing and production. As late as 1964 the British cotton textile industry was dominated by relatively small specialized firms, which controlled a shrinking share of the global market.

Only the entrance of large companies making synthetic fibers into the cotton textile business saved some of the industry. A contest between Courtaulds, which had a monopoly on the production of rayon in Great Britain, and Imperial Chemical Industries was particularly important. In 1962 Imperial Chemical tried unsuccessfully to take over Courtaulds. This move prompted Courtaulds to revitalize its production of synthetic fibers through the acquisition of other companies and the construction of new facilities. Imperial Chemical meanwhile entered the Lancashire fibers industry by purchasing and combining many companies. The results of this contest were dramatic. For the first time, Great Britain's spinning and weaving industries were closely linked. By 1968 the five largest firms, led by Courtaulds, were fully integrated. Moreover, between 1963 and 1974 employment in the British cotton textile

industry was halved, while production stayed about the same. Productivity gains amounted to an average of 8 percent per year in that period.

Labor Relations

As we have seen, trade unions developed rapidly in some fields in Great Britain, becoming considerably more powerful than they were in the United States. Craft unions in such trades as iron- and steelmaking, cotton textiles, coal mining, shipbuilding, and construction, established in the 1880s or earlier, were joined by so-called new unions first set up in the 1890s. Made up of less-skilled workers, the new unions were less craft-based and more industry-based—leading to the formation of broad industrial unions such as the Miners' Federation in 1908, the Transport Workers' Federation in 1910, and the National Union of Railwaymen in 1913. Trade union membership rose from 750,000 in 1888, 6 percent of the industrial workforce, to 2.6 million in 1910, perhaps 30 percent of the industrial workforce.

Unlike the situation in the United States—where until the 1930s the government often opposed the formation of unions—the British government accepted and, indirectly at least, promoted the establishment of trade unions. Especially important was Parliament's passage of the Conciliation Act of 1896. Through this act the government could appoint an official to work as an arbitrator between labor unions and management. While neither management nor labor had to use the services of an arbitrator and while the findings of an arbitrator (when used) were not binding, the act encouraged the development of collective bargaining. In the years before World War I, most bargaining was regional in nature. During the conflict the British government became increasingly involved in labor disputes, and arbitration became compulsory. Bargaining shifted to the national level during the war and remained there in the interwar years, with national trade unions bargaining collectively with national employers associations.

The growth of trade unions may have hurt productivity in some fields of British industry. In the automobile industry, for example, British manufacturers rejected the American example of high throughput and capital-intensive technology, accompanied by the payment of relatively high wages. Fearing the resistance of workers to the introduction of labor-saving machinery, British automakers used more labor-intensive production methods that en-

abled workers to retain considerable control of work processes. Auto manufacturers in Britain balanced the relatively low productivity of their workers by paying lower wages than automakers in America. British cotton textile manufacturers adopted similar strategies.

There was more to industrial relations, however, than simply adjusting pay scales. Associated with labor relations was a failure on the part of both business and government to invest in advancing labor skills. Practical skills rather than academic training were seen as the proper basis for business success for both workers and managers. A much smaller proportion of British workers and managers received an education in engineering or the sciences — or, for that matter, any education beyond elementary education — than did their counterparts in Germany or the United States. The gap was greatest for workers. Only 230 junior technical schools, in which children leaving grammar (elementary) school might learn basic sciences before entering factory occupations, had been established in Great Britain by 1937–38. As industrialization became more technologically complex with the development of such fields as chemicals, synthetic fibers, automobiles, and electrical equipment, this shortcoming hurt Great Britain.

Retailing in Great Britain

As we have seen, new forms of retailing developed in Great Britain from the mid-nineteenth century—department stores, chain stores (multiples), and cooperatives. Yet, even as these types of retail outlets grew during the interwar years, small retailers continued to predominate in sales. As late as the 1930s independent retailers accounted for 80 percent of the sales of such new consumer durables as automobiles and electrical goods, along with a similar percentage of the sales of fruit and vegetables, fish, chocolates, and tobacco products. Altogether, over two-thirds of Britain's retail sales were made by single-outlet retailers, more than the proportion in the United States.

Several factors limited the rise of big business in retailing. Families often did not want to expand their enterprises to a size larger than they could easily oversee, which often limited department stores and multiples to growth in single regions. Rather than extending their stores into new areas, families invested in other types of local enterprises such as housing and factories. In addition, the ability of organizations of independent retailers to enforce resale

price maintenance agreements, agreements by which manufacturers refused to allow their products to be sold below certain prices, undercut advantages larger retailers might try to obtain by purchasing and selling in bulk. Unlike the situation in the United States, where such agreements could not usually be enforced, in Britain resale price maintenance agreements meant that large retailers could not lower prices to compete with mom-and-pop stores. Competition had to take place in terms of service, where small retailers close to their customers often had the advantage. Finally, the regionally fragmented nature of the British market slowed the growth of large national retailers, so that only after World War II did many develop.

The Question of International Competitiveness

Only a handful of Britain's industrial firms rationalized their operations and management systems as dramatically as Imperial Chemical. Most big British manufacturers were loosely run confederations of formerly independent companies with lax central direction over their operations. United Steel epitomized this approach to management for about a decade. Family connections and influence remained pronounced in Britain's large manufacturing firms, considerably stronger than in their American counterparts. Beyond the world of large companies lay the realm of small business. Despite the merger movement, small firms remained the norm in Great Britain, even in manufacturing.

Did the continuing family nature of British business and the smallness of many of its industrial companies hurt Great Britain in international competition with nations like the United States and Germany? Did larger, better managed, better organized, more efficient companies in other nations destroy Great Britain's industrial dominance? These questions, first voiced in the late nineteenth century, were more commonly asked during the interwar years, and they swelled to become a loud refrain after World War II. In some industries during the interwar years, such as cotton textiles, the answers were probably "yes." However, Great Britain's overall industrial picture was ambiguous, as the steel story suggests. Steel's inability to rationalize fully was due, in part, to the continued dominance of relatively small, family-owned companies — but only in part. Banks and the government must also bear some of the blame for the failure to form a truly efficient industry. Moreover, it is worth remem-

bering that, for all of its problems, Britain's steel industry expanded faster than that of any of its major European competitors in the 1920s and 1930s.

The issue of national economic decline, in Great Britain or in any nation, is complex. There is, first of all, the question of what is meant by decline. Britain lost ground *relative* to some other nations in heavy industries in the interwar years, especially in the more technologically advanced fields of the Second Industrial Revolution, such as chemicals. But, even in these fields British production generally increased, although at a slower rate than in some other countries. Overall, the British economy continued to grow in the interwar years, and would do so after World War II. Up to World War II Britain's Gross Domestic Product, a measure of a nation's economic output, remained substantially larger than that of Germany or France.

In some fields of business, especially those beyond heavy industry, the British excelled. City of London institutions continued to lead the world in financial services during the interwar years. Then, too, Great Britain remained, as it had been in the nineteenth century, the world leader in foreign direct investment (FDI)—that is, investments in overseas mining, service, and manufacturing establishments—with FDI totalling $10.5 billion in 1938. British investment groups, such as Matheson and Butterfield & Swire, diversified into international trade and manufacturing with sophisticated management practices. The number of British multinational manufacturers (British companies having at least some of their factories overseas) rose from just over 200 in 1914 to 448 in 1939.

In the areas in which Great Britain lost ground relative to some other nations there was generally more than one cause. Certainly more was involved than shortcomings in the personal nature of family management during the interwar years; there is no convincing proof that managerial failures were widespread in family-run firms. Both financial institutions and multinationals did well with family-style management. Just which factors contributed to Great Britain's relative decline in some areas of heavy industry is a hotly debated topic. Often it is attributed to management failing to adopt the most up-to-date production methods. For example, in cotton textiles, for reasons that seemed to make sense at the time, British manufacturers stayed with older spinning and weaving methods longer than their counterparts in some other nations. The failure of the British government to provide adequate

education in the sciences and technologies, often reinforced by a failure of businesses to invest in human skills, was probably even more important in causing problems in heavy industries—in steelmaking and automaking, for example. And, as we have seen in steelmaking, the inability of British industrial, banking, and government leaders to agree on courses of actions could thwart efforts to make industries more competitive.

JAPANESE BUSINESS

Like other industrial nations, Japan experienced marked economic ups and downs during the interwar years. World War I brought an economic boom to Japan, as Asian markets were thrown open by the inability of Western nations like Great Britain to supply them with goods. However, this boom collapsed in 1920, and Japan was caught up in the worldwide recession. The 1920s were perilous times for Japanese businesses, for a series of financial panics interrupted economic recovery. The 1930s initially brought little relief; for, as world trade stagnated, Japan found demand for her chief exports—silk, cotton, and tea—drying up. Economic recovery in the mid- and late 1930s revolved around two developments: there was a revival of Japanese exports when the country left the gold standard and devalued the yen in 1931; and government spending on military goods rose dramatically. In 1931 the Japanese army occupied southern Manchuria in northern China, a full-scale war broke out between Japan and China in 1937, and Japan's attack upon the United States in 1941 signaled the beginning of World War II in the Pacific. By 1934 Japan's GNP had recovered from its nadir in 1931 to surpass its previous high point of 1929.

Japanese business and political leaders responded to the economic swings, especially the downturns, in ways roughly similar to their Western counterparts. They tried to rationalize their firms and industries—but, again, with only partial success. Business leaders established new zaibatsu based on heavy industries and experimented with new types of labor relations. Small manufacturers became increasingly important as subcontractors to their larger brethren. Yet, as in Great Britain and America, there was also continuity in Japanese business. Many small manufacturers continued operations as independents, and small firms remained dominant in sales.

The Business Rationalization Movement

As in Great Britain and the United States, a business rationalization movement took place in Japan during the interwar years, as political and business
leaders tried to deal with economic shocks. At the level of the individual firm,
many companies redesigned their factory layouts, imported new technologies, and standardized production methods. At the industry level, companies
joined cartels to fix prices and limit production. The Japanese government
backed the formation of cartels as a way to make Japanese business strong in
world trade. A Major Industries Control Law of 1931 sought to create a cartel
for every large-scale industry, and by 1932 Japan possessed thirty-three cartels
in heavy industry, thirty-one in chemicals, eleven in textiles, eight in food
processing, and eighteen in finance.

The cartels varied tremendously in their effectiveness, however. Generally,
the efforts of the Japanese government to bring about recovery through cartelization were only partly successful. As in Great Britain and the United States,
companies tended to support their government's rationalization efforts only
when they perceived direct benefits from doing so. When cartelization did
not fit in with their plans, companies found ways to avoid it. It was more government spending on war industries, as in the United States, than the success
of cartelization and rationalization that brought revival to Japan's economy—
as may be seen in looking at what happened in the steel industry.

For all intents and purposes, Japan's modern steel industry began with the
operations of Yawata Iron and Steel, a government works, in 1901. World
War I, with its great demand for steel, led to a major expansion of Japanese
steel production. When Yawata failed to keep up with the soaring demand,
private companies entered the steel business. By the end of the war 200 private companies were turning out 60 percent of Japan's raw steel. However,
the wartime boom in steelmaking became a bust in the 1920s, as the Japanese companies faced renewed imports of pig iron from India and steel from
Western nations.

Japanese steelmakers tried to counter international competition with a
rationalization movement. They introduced new, more efficient ways of producing iron and steel; and companies merged, until there were only about
ten major steelmakers in Japan by 1926. Between 1926 and 1930 these companies formed various cartels, but the cartels proved unable to deal with the

slump in demand for steel that accompanied the depression of the 1930s. Finally, in 1933 the Japanese Diet passed the Nihon Iron and Steel Company Act, which aimed at consolidating all Japanese steelmakers into one company. However, despite this legislation, enough companies remained outside of the consolidated enterprise to limit its effectiveness. It was only military orders for steel products from the mid-1930s on that lifted Japan's steel industry out of its depression.

The New Zaibatsu: Nissan and the Riken Group

The growth of heavy industry was a particularly noticeable aspect of economic recovery and military spending in Japan during the 1930s. The collapse of foreign markets for silk, cotton, and other products of light industry combined with military purchases of steel, chemicals, machinery, and the like to build up heavy industry. As late as 1928 light industry accounted for more than twice as much of Japan's total industrial output as did heavy industry, but by 1935 heavy industry had become more important than light industry.

As Japan's economy changed, alterations occurred in the nature of its business firms, especially big businesses. A major development during the interwar years was the establishment of so-called new zaibatsu, business complexes firmly based upon heavy industries—steel, chemicals, engineering, electrical machinery, and automobiles. Japan Nitrogen, Nissan, Nakajima Aircraft, and Toyota were among the most important. The new zaibatsu were less diversified than the older zaibatsu such as Mitsui and Mitsubishi, often lacking their own banks or trading companies.

Nissan, the largest of the new zaibatsu, originated in mining. Nissan can be traced to the Hitachi Copper Mine, which was modernized and incorporated as the Kuhara Mining Company a few years before World War I. During the war boom Kuhara Mining became one of Japan's leading industrial firms. When the war ended, the company diversified by entering new fields, including shipping and trading. However, a fall in the price of copper and problems encountered in diversification brought Kuhara close to bankruptcy in the mid-1920s. In 1926 Yoshisuke Ayukawa, who was in the cast-steel business, bought Kuhara, reorganized it, and renamed it Nihon Sangyo, soon shortened to Nissan. By selling some stock in Nissan to the public Ayukawa raised funds for expansion, and by concentrating the company's efforts on

Mitsubishi shipyard in 1935. In the 1930s Japan made the transition from light to heavy industry. (Courtesy of the General Affairs Department, Mitsubishi Heavy Industries, Ltd., Kobe)

heavy industry he was able to secure still more from retained earnings. By the mid-1930s the Nissan zaibatsu had grown to consist of over eighty companies, mainly in heavy industry.

Like Nissan, the Riken Group was a new zaibatsu that came into being in the 1920s, and its development illustrates well the close ties that often existed between the Japanese government and heavy industry. The Riken Group originated in discussions between Jokichi Takamine, a well-known Japanese chemist, and Eiichi Shibusawa, both of whom lamented the fact that Japan lagged behind in the development of a chemical industry necessary for the expansion of heavy industry and the growth of national power. World War I cut off the importation of many drugs and industrial products from Western nations, leading the Japanese government to look favorably upon the estab-lishment of a chemical research program. Out of these concerns came the formation of the Institute (Riken) of Physical and Chemical Research in 1917. The government provided three-fifths of the funding for the Institute, with the rest coming from private businesses. The Institute's goal was to make Japan self-sufficient in the development of military supplies and industrial materials.

The Institute developed a number of drugs, vitamins, and chemicals in the 1920s and was soon searching for a way to produce them commercially and expand their use in the Japanese economy. The result was the formation in 1927 of the Rikagaku Industrial Company, funded mainly by leading zaibatsu—Mitsui, Mitsubishi, Sumitomo, Yasuda, and Okura. The Institute and its director also bought shares in Rikagaku. By 1936 the Institute had developed 167 major products, including drugs, synthetic sake, photographic printing paper, and corundum. Particularly important for the military was the development of new ways of making magnesium and piston rings for internal combustion engines.

The Riken Industrial Group, as it came to be called, took form in the late 1930s with Rikagaku as its nucleus. Rikagaku acted as a holding company owning stock in subsidiary companies and providing some coordination of their activities. By 1940 the Riken Group consisted of fifty-eight major companies, including Riken Magnesium, Riken Piston Ring, Riken Special Steel, Riken Electric Wire, and Riken Corundum, some of which also controlled subsidiary companies. Very important to Japan's war efforts in the late 1930s and early 1940s, the Riken Group filled its role in helping build up heavy industry so necessary for military expansion. Broken up by American authorities after World War II, the Riken Group later partially reformed with new goals.

Continuity in Big Business: Kikkoman

Not all of the large firms that formed or expanded in interwar Japan were new zaibatsu associated with the government's push to develop heavy industry and the military. Kikkoman's history illustrates a different path.

Kikkoman traces its origins to the Tokugawa period. As cities like Edo became major consumption centers, the demand for shoyu (soy sauce) increased greatly, and new shoyu producers set up rural plants in the countryside in response to this demand. One such place was the area around Noda in central Honshu. Noda possessed a good river link to Edo, which practically assured Kikkoman's rise, as Edo continued to grow. In the Tokugawa and Meiji periods, the technology of brewing shoyu remained traditional. It involved the mixing of roasted wheat and steamed soybeans, setting aside this mixture to mold, adding salt water to the mixture as it was molding, allowing this mixture to ferment for one or two years, and then extracting the liquid

shoyu from the fermented result. There were about 14,000 makers of shoyu in Japan in 1910, mostly small-scale.

Among those going into shoyu production in Noda were the Takanashi and Mogi families, who began operations in the early 1660s and who became interrelated by marriages. The Mogi and Takanashi families soon dominated shoyu production in Noda. They did so by setting up branch households to run more and more new shoyu-making plants, not by setting up larger plants; for, given the technologies of the day, there were few economies of scale. There was a division of responsibilities among the households, including a separation of ownership from management. Some families provided the capital for the shoyu factories but did not play an active role in running the operations. Other households bought the raw materials and sold the shoyu. Still other households were in charge of the actual production processes. In these circumstances there was a lack of coordination—a situation that could be endured when traditional, small-scale production was the norm, but that could not be permitted as the Mogis and Takanashis began moving into large-batch production.

Technological improvements began in the late Meiji period and continued in the Taisho and early Showa periods—that is, during the 1920s and 1930s. Machinery and heat were applied wherever possible to speed up the production process. Large-batch production in new factories dwarfed earlier traditional production efforts. In 1926 the company opened the biggest factory of any type in Japan, and three years later it opened a still larger one. As production facilities became larger and more complicated, better coordination between them and their sales outlets were needed. In 1917 the heads of the Mogi and Takanashi families met to discuss amalgamation. After a year of negotiations the result was a merger of many of the separate family production facilities into one new company, the Noda Shoyu Company (the immediate predecessor of Kikkoman).

Noda Shoyu was set up as a joint-stock company in 1918, embracing 1,000 workers, 50 managers, scores of plants, research facilities, sales offices, and transportation and storage sites. Still owned exclusively by the Mogi and Takanashi families, Noda Shoyu centralized its management. Functional committees within the company's head office sought to centralize planning, coordinate all business operations, and standardize production methods. The three most important committees were those of managerial coordination, sales, and

research. Business methods were standardized; in 1922 the first codification of company rules and regulations was issued. As part of its efforts to become more efficient, Noda Shoyu reduced the number of its brands of shoyu from thirty-four to just sixteen.

In 1925 a very important legal change was made; and from this alteration Noda Shoyu emerged as a zaibatsu—though, unlike Nissan or the Riken Group, one not closely associated with the Japanese government. An un-limited partnership called Senshusha, owned by the Mogi and Takanashi families, was set up. Senshusha owned 60 percent of the shares in Noda Shoyu and six other concerns. Some of these other enterprises were food-production companies, but they also included a bank and trading company. By the early 1930s Senshusha was only slightly smaller than Furukawa, the smallest of Japan's so-called Big Eight zaibatsu. Noda Shoyu remained the most important manufacturing company in the Senshusha group. By 1930 it was one of the fifty largest manufacturing companies in Japan. More and more salaried professional managers were introduced into the management of Senshusha and Noda Shoyu, and the involvement of Mogi and Takanashi family members in daily management operations lessened.

Kikkoman—the name Noda Shoyu assumed in 1964—survived and, after solving critical problems, prospered in the postwar years. In 1946 the old hold-ing company Senshusha was dissolved, much as Mitsui and Mitsubishi were, in the interests of economic democracy. Kikkoman officially became an in-dependent company, no longer having any official connection to the bank or trading company that had been owned by Senshusha. However, democratiza-tion existed, perhaps, more in name than in reality. The Mogis and Takana-shis still owned 20 percent of the stock in Kikkoman, and companies in which they had interests held an additional 20 percent. After World War II Kikko-man first focused on making soy sauce. It further mechanized operations in the 1950s and 1960s, and in doing so moved from large-batch to continuous-process production. By 1973 it made nearly one-third of the shoyu produced in Japan. Then, Kikkoman diversified its efforts, as per capita Japanese con-sumption of soy sauce declined due to dietary changes. By 1980 Kikkoman sold three dozen different food and food-related products in Japan and abroad, and a year later shoyu accounted for only 62 percent of Kikkoman's total sales.

Despite the growth of many new industrial businesses in the postwar period, Kikkoman was still one of Japan's 200 largest industrial firms in

1980, with sales of $600 million and an employment of 4,000. Kikkoman's history shows the continuing importance of successful family businesses to Japan's business system, especially when compared to business in America. Yet, Kikkoman's history also illustrates that changes did take place. The demands of technology and market—as Kikkoman moved from small-scale to large-batch and then to continuous-process production—led to the development of new legal and managerial forms and forced the employment of more professional managers, sorely needed to coordinate the work of the company's different parts.

Small Businesses in Manufacturing

Even with the development of zaibatsu such as Nissan, the Riken Group, and Senshusha, small and medium-size firms were important to Japan's industrial growth in the interwar years. Despite the rationalization and concentration that occurred, small businesses remained significant industrial employers. In 1930, 58 percent of Japan's industrial workforce labored in factories with four or fewer employees, and in 1934 companies with no more than 500 workers accounted for 62 percent of Japan's industrial output.

More than in earlier times, small manufacturers acted as subcontractors for larger industrial companies. The heavy industry companies of older zaibatsu such as Mitsui and Mitsubishi controlled scores of small subcontractors, as did many of the new zaibatsu. Large firms used smaller enterprises as subcontractors to take advantage of their lower wages, technical strengths, and underemployed workers. They increasingly relied on networks of suppliers for raw materials, semifinished goods, and components—a strategy very different from the one of vertical integration followed by large American manufacturers. In the mid-1930s, at least 20 percent of the manufacturing value of products in Japan's automobile, textile-weaving, and electrical equipment industries came from subcontractors.

The use of subcontractors helped Japanese industrialists compete with their Western counterparts, for through the establishment of networks of suppliers large firms could avoid the tremendous capital outlays involved in doing all of the manufacturing and marketing by themselves. By working through networks, large firms could also avoid, to some extent, the need to establish complex managerial systems. As they did in zaibatsu, these business networks ex-

tended beyond relationships between mother companies and subcontractors. Many types of financial and marketing networks developed, leading one commentator to note that by the close of the interwar years, it was the existence of constellations of firms that most characterized Japanese manufacturing.

Still, many small industrialists operated as independent firms not tied to any one large manufacturer. While growing in importance during the interwar years, subcontracting would become still more significant for the Japanese economy after World War II. Throughout the 1920s and 1930s independent small industrialists were important in heavy industries as well as light industries, and small firms got ahead with little government aid. Indeed, some small firms prospered despite government efforts to force them to join cartels and merge with their larger brethren in the interests of business rationalization and productivity. What occurred in the machine tool industry provides a look at independent small business manufacturing in interwar Japan. Zaibatsu and their affiliated subsidiaries were not important.

Many small entrepreneurial firms composed the machine tool industry. Of the machine tool industry's 1,978 companies in 1938 (up from 397 firms in 1932), only 93 had more than 100 workers and 1,531 had no more than 30. These firms resisted government efforts to merge them or organize them into cartels. As occurred in the iron and steel industry, firms in the machine tool industry found ways to avoid joining cartels decreed by the Major Industries Control Law of 1931. And a licensing scheme embedded in a Machine Tool Industry Law of 1938 did not make the industry more efficient and productive, either.

Resistance to government rationalization work continued even during World War II. In 1941 the Japanese government sought to consolidate strategic military industries into control councils. It was hoped that small firms could be forced to merge with larger ones and that resulting economies of scale would make the production of war goods more efficient. Such did not occur, at least in the machine tool industry. Instead, many of the smaller producers formed regional groupings that then successfully brought pressure on the control councils to keep supplying them with raw materials needed to make military goods.

Businesses in Marketing

Marketing continued to develop along lines established before World War I. Older zaibatsu used their sogo shosha (trading companies) to sell their goods abroad, and also sometimes inside Japan; and independent sogo shosha handled foreign sales for non-zaibatsu manufacturers. With regard to marketing in Japan, differences in how the makers of traditional and nontraditional products sold their goods, already apparent before World War I, widened during the interwar years.

Most makers of traditional products, such as sake and soy sauce (including even Noda Shoyu), sold their goods through Japan's elaborate system of wholesalers and retailers. While department stores expanded and some chain stores began operations, the most typical retail outlet remained the mom-and-pop store. In 1937 the Diet—responding to pressures small retailers were feeling from encroachments of department stores and other large-scale retailers—passed a Department Store Law limiting the size of stores. Legislation of this sort restricted store sizes into the 1980s.

Most producers of traditional goods made items for local or regional markets. Only a few went farther before World War II. Fukusuke Tabi, a maker of footwear, was one of those few. Established in 1885, the company had within a decade started making footwear with sewing machines imported from Germany; and three years later it established the factory system of production, to which the moving assembly line was added in 1923. After encountering problems in trying to sell its footwear through established marketers—competition between sales agents, the giving of profit-destroying discounts—Fukusuke set up its own national distribution system in the late 1920s and the 1930s. All of its wholesalers and many of its retailers were integrated into the Fukusuke organization.

For companies manufacturing Western-style goods, Japan's established distribution system often proved unworkable, and an increasing number of them set up their own distribution channels. Established in 1898, Morinaga and Company manufactured marshmallows, caramels, and chocolates by Western methods, at first selling the candies through 250 wholesalers in Tokyo and Osaka. However, when those wholesalers competed by invading each others' territories, the resulting chaotic sales situation bit into Morinaga's profits. The situation worsened when Morinaga set up a factory using continuous-

production methods in 1925, leading to an outpouring of candies. Morinaga's solution was twofold. The firm worked with wholesalers across Japan to set up candy retail outlets as joint ventures, with the wholesalers putting up 90 percent of the capital for the stores. And, in 1928 Morinaga organized a group of existing independent retailers, who were beginning to feel the pinch of competition from department stores and chain stores, into its marketing network.

As manufacturers of many new products in the United States had already discovered, producers of nontraditional goods in Japan found that wholesalers and retailers dealing with many different items could not provide the specialized services—demonstrations, sales, and, in the case of big-ticket items such as sewing machines, financing and after-sales repairs—needed to introduce new products to the emerging national market. Increasingly, therefore, they organized their own sales networks. Still, Japanese manufacturers rarely exercised as high a degree of control over sales as Morinaga. Most reorganized existing wholesalers into sales companies, with the wholesalers putting up most of the capital, for manufacturers were simply hard-pressed to build their factories. Usually, the sales companies remained legally and financially independent of the manufacturers. Few manufacturers set up their own retail outlets; Morinaga was exceptional in this respect.

Business, Government, Society, and Labor

Despite business leaders' growing association with the Japanese government's military efforts, they dropped in public esteem in the interwar years. The heads of the zaibatsu, in particular, came under intense criticism for supposedly following their own interests to the detriment of those of the Japanese nation. The zaibatsu and big businesses in general were accused of corrupting politics. It was a common saying, if an exaggeration, that whenever Mitsui or Mitsubishi caught a cold, the Diet came down with pneumonia. Antagonism came to a climax with the assassination of the head of Mitsui by a group of young army officers in 1932. This anti-zaibatsu sentiment had some influence on business. The zaibatsu began to make voluntary donations, actually forced gifts, of funds to the Japanese government; and, at the request of the government, some accelerated their movement into heavy industry.

Under pressure, large firms also extended labor practices incorporating long-term employment and seniority-based promotions and wages to a grow-

ing number of managers and employees. Managers and workers were increasingly recruited right out of school and then given additional training in their companies, as firms sought to heighten bonds of company loyalty. Companies provided more benefits for their workers—dining rooms, assembly halls, clubhouses, and housing—much as those American and British companies embracing welfare capitalism were doing.

The pressures on the companies came from several sources. There was a continuing scarcity of skilled workers in some fields, especially in heavy industry, and a corresponding desire by employers to keep workers loyal to their firms. In addition, the power of organized labor increased into the mid-1920s. By 1925 the Sodomei, the Japan General Federation of Labor, had 250,000 members. For a while there were prospects for the passage by the Diet of a law recognizing the rights of workers to form independent unions to bargain collectively with management. Even some employer associations supported the establishment of such unions around the time of World War I as a way of stabilizing their nation's chaotic labor situation. This possibility faded in the late 1920s, however, and disappeared in the early 1930s. A revival of traditional values in Japan, combined with the increasing power of the army and accompanying crackdowns on leftist leaders, eroded the strength of Japan's labor movement.

Large companies came to resist bargaining collectively with their workers. During the interwar years Japanese executives instead turned to scientific management to rationalize labor practices, with somewhat more success than they had before World War I. Most common were the adoption of time/motion studies and the rearrangement of production facilities, both of which sought to take shopfloor power away from skilled workers and placed it in the hands of managers.

In addition, influenced by the formation of work councils in Great Britain and company unions in the United States, Japanese business leaders set up work councils for the sake of mediating differences between management and labor. By 1929, 112 work councils composed of managers and workers existed. The work councils were forerunners of enterprise unions, which became common in Japan after World War II. These were (and are) unions organized around companies, not industries. The enterprise unions tend to reinforce company loyalty and do not really bargain collectively with man-

agement on the part of workers. They resemble in many ways the company unions common in America in the 1920s.

The extension of the new system of labor relations was achieved only painfully, as can be seen in the case of Noda Shoyu. At Noda Shoyu a short strike in 1923 was followed by a much longer and more serious one in 1927–28. The major issue was who would control the pace and nature of work as production processes were modernized and standardized: workers or managers. The 1927–28 strike lasted seven months and resulted in the firing of 1,100 workers. It was the most celebrated (or notorious) of all of the many strikes in Japan in the interwar years. Management won; but to improve its public image, to keep skilled workers loyal to the company, and to avoid labor unrest in the future, Noda Shoyu began putting in place seniority-based wages and promotions, a wide range of benefits, and work councils.

Toward a Dual Economy

Neither long-term employment nor seniority-based promotions and wages were usually extended to workers in small firms. The lives of workers in small firms were often tenuous and unstable. In the interwar years relationships between large and small manufacturers were one-sided. During recessions it was the small subcontractors, not the larger manufacturers, that laid off workers. Most small companies paid wages lower than those offered by their larger counterparts, and that gap widened through the interwar years. By 1932–33 workers in firms with 5–9 employees earned wages equal to only 61 percent of the wages of employees in companies with at least 100 workers, workers in companies with 10–29 employees earned 74 percent, those in firms with 30–49 employees earned 81 percent, and workers in companies with 50–99 employees earned 89 percent.

The spread of wage differentials signaled a larger trend, the development of what has often been called a dual economy in Japan. While small firms remained important in some fields as independent manufacturers, as in the machine tool industry, the overall significance of small independent industrialists lessened in the interwar years. Japan's industrial economy tended to divide. Large, efficient firms geared to the export market and to Japan's military needs came to dominate smaller subcontractors serving them and Japan's

home market. This trend began in the early 1900s and accelerated during the interwar years. It would remain a characteristic of the Japanese economy into the years after World War II, but without the military aspect.

Japanese Business during World War II

The Japanese government used public dissatisfaction with big business and the needs of war to increase its powers over the economy. A government planning office was set up in 1937 to begin coordinating the work of the different parts of Japan's wartime economy. The Diet passed a General Mobilization Law in 1938, giving the government broad powers to control wages, prices, and the allocation of raw materials in the economy. In addition, many detailed laws determined what businesses could and could not do in specific industries, but these laws did not always work as well as was intended. Just as firms in some industries evaded the Major Industries Control Law of 1931, they also thwarted government efforts to control them during World War II, as took place in the machine tool industry.

Nonetheless, the laws were important, not only for what they did accomplish during the war years, but also for the precedents they set. To some extent, the laws served as models for legislation passed by the Diet after World War II. That legislation sought to provide government guidance of the postwar Japanese economy (although, as we shall see, much of the postwar legislation met with the same sort of mixed response from businesses as did the legislation of the interwar years).

A Comparison to Germany

What occurred in Germany during the interwar period offers a valuable comparison to the course of events in the other nations examined in this chapter, especially Great Britain and Japan. Despite the devastation of World War I, many German businesses recovered in the mid- and late 1920s to regain leading places in the world economy. During the interwar years, too, the German state increased its involvement in economic affairs, until under the Nazis, businesses, especially those in heavy industry, became almost simply part of the state apparatus.

World War I left many German industrial firms in ruins. Runaway infla-

tion and high interest rates (20 percent per day in 1923!) added to problems in the early 1920s, making it impossible for German business leaders to plan for the future. In this chaotic situation German manufacturers found the loose cartels and the universal banks that had earlier been of great help to be less useful, and they turned to tighter business associations and their own internal resources to rebuild and expand. With general economic stability returning to Germany from 1924, industrial firms were able to regroup quickly and then move ahead. Generally speaking, the German companies that had built strong foundations before the war—large, efficient manufacturing plants, extensive marketing systems, and competent management teams—recovered most rapidly and fully. In the industries of the Second Industrial Revolution—such as alloyed metals, chemicals, and machinery—German firms were soon driving their British counterparts from world markets. The same was true of some German companies in light industries—those making rayon, for example.

World War I brought changes to government-business relations in Germany. As in the United States and Great Britain, the government became increasingly involved in business affairs. After the war a new government, the Weimar Republic, was formed; and under its aegis a compromise was reached between employer and employee associations, giving Germany the most complete system of social welfare programs and industrial relations in the world. Basically, German manufacturers agreed to some of labor's demands to avoid even more radical changes. Backed by labor more than by business, efforts were made to rationalize German industry; large nationwide business organizations appeared, and many smaller regional cartels developed. Even so, the continued importance of smaller firms in industry limited the effectiveness of German rationalization attempts; and, as in other nations, rationalization was only partially fulfilled. Business and government actions brought prosperity to Germany in the mid- and late 1920s.

That prosperity vanished with the coming of the Great Depression: unemployment rose to 10 percent in 1929 and to 33 percent in the winter of 1932–33. It was in these hard times that Adolph Hitler's National Socialists (Nazis) came to power, with Hitler appointed chancellor in early 1933. The roles played by big business leaders in facilitating Hitler's rise to power are controversial. Some business leaders may have thought they could use Hitler to achieve ends of their own; other executives may have backed Hitler as they turned away from Weimar democracy. Business support for Hitler was,

however, far from unanimous; and more was involved in Hitler's ascent than business backing. In the chaotic economic times of the early 1930s Hitler garnered substantial popular support. The Nazis won less than 3 percent of the national vote in 1928, but they increased their share to 18 percent in 1930 and then to 37 percent in April 1932.

Under Hitler the Weimar constitution was abandoned, and the government became a dictatorship. The Nazi government forced all major industries to form cartels, with the cartels becoming, not independent business associations, but arms of the state (as did labor unions). Government control of business, especially heavy industry, tightened as Hitler prepared for war. During World War II—especially from 1942, when Albert Speer became Minister of Armaments—efforts were made to rationalize industry more fully. Product "rings" composed of business and government leaders were formed to design and produce simplified weapons with long production runs.

Even so, smaller firms remained important in Germany's economic mobilization. As in Japan, medium-sized and small manufacturers were joined into networks of subcontractors for big businesses. In fact, about one-half of Germany's armament companies had no more than 100 employees. And, the Nazi government sought to aid small retailers, one of its sources of support. In 1933 it placed a temporary ban on the opening of additional retail outlets and controlled their establishment-opening thereafter. Enforceable retail price maintenance laws, as in Britain, also favored small retailers. In 1933 German retail shops had an average of 2.6 employees.

CHANGING BUSINESS SYSTEMS

The wide swings in national economies together with market changes, especially the growth of consumer markets, altered business firms and their management in the United States, Great Britain, Japan, and Germany in the interwar years. As big businesses became more diversified in terms of their products and markets—particularly in the United States, but to some degree in Great Britain as well—some adopted new management systems. In Japan, special circumstances spurred the growth of zaibatsu, but here, too, changes occurred, as new zaibatsu based upon heavy industry grew in importance. Large and small firms increasingly came to occupy different spheres

in manufacturing, with smaller companies either acting as subcontractors for larger ones or producing as independents for niche markets, not mass markets. Still, the business systems of all four nations remained complex, with smaller firms continuing to play significant roles in sales. In smaller firms managerial changes were less pronounced, with families often in control.

More than individual companies changed during the interwar years; so did the business systems of each nation. As they sought to mitigate the impacts of recessions and depressions and as they prepared for World War II, governments became more involved in the workings of their national economies and in the operations of specific industries than they had before. Government-sponsored or -permitted rationalization movements sought, though with limited success, to make individual firms, industries, and entire economies more efficient and productive. Spending during depressions, and even more during World War II, led governments to become more deeply involved in economic matters than they had earlier been. That involvement would continue and grow after World War II.

SUGGESTED READINGS

Alfred D. Chandler, Jr., has written extensively about the development of decentralized management in the United States in his *Strategy and Structure* (Cambridge, Mass.: MIT Press, 1962), and, with Stephen Salsbury, *Pierre S. DuPont and the Making of the Modern Corporation* (New York: Harper & Row, 1971). Alfred P. Sloan, Jr., *My Years With General Motors* (New York: Macfadden-Bartell, 1965), provides an inside look at managerial change. James Soltow, "Origins of Small Business: Metal Fabricators and Machinery Makers in New England, 1890–1957," *Transactions of the American Philosophical Society* 55 (December 1965): 1–58, is the seminal study on the history of small business in industry in the United States. Martha Olney, *Buy Now, Pay Later: Advertising, Credit, and Consumer Durables in the 1920s* (Chapel Hill: University of North Carolina Press, 1991), examines the relationship between the development of a consumer society and business change. Guy Alchon, *The Invisible Hand of Planning: Capitalism, Social Science and State in the 1920s* (Princeton: Princeton University Press, 1985); Ellis Hawley, *The New Deal and the Problem of Monopoly* (Princeton: Princeton University

Press, 1966); and Collin Gordon, *New Deals: Business, Labor, and Politics in America, 1920–1935* (Cambridge: Cambridge University Press, 1994), examine government-business relations.

Leslie Hannah, *The Rise of the Corporate Economy*, 2nd ed. (Baltimore: Johns Hopkins University Press, 1984), is an essential account on British business. Derek H. Aldcroft, *The Inter-War Economy: Britain, 1919–1939* (New York: Columbia University Press, 1970), surveys economic changes. W. J. Reader, *Imperial Chemical Industries: A History*, 2 vols. (Oxford: Oxford University Press, 1970 and 1975), is a solid examination of a leading British firm. Michael Dintenfass, *Managing Industrial Decline: Entrepreneurship in the British Coal Industry between the Wars* (Columbus: The Ohio State University Press, 1992), and Steven Tolliday, *Business, Banking and Politics: The Case of British Steel, 1918–1939* (Cambridge, Mass.: Harvard University Press, 1987), are valuable case studies. Aaron L. Friedberg, *The Weary Titan: Britain and the Experience of Relative Decline, 1895–1905* (Princeton: Princeton University Press, 1988), is provocative. Larry Gerber, "Corporatism in Comparative Perspective: The Impact of the First World War on American and British Labor Relations," *Business History Review* 62 (Spring 1988): 93–127, and David Mowery, "Firm Structure, Government Policy and the Organization of Industrial Research, Great Britain and the United States, 1900–1950," *Business History Review* 58 (Winter 1984): 504–31, are comparative.

Takafusa Nakamura, *Economic Growth in Prewar Japan* (New Haven: Yale University Press, 1983), provides an overview of economic changes before World War II. Mark Fruin, *Kikkoman: Company, Clan and Community* (Cambridge, Mass.: Harvard University Press, 1983), stresses continuity in the development of zaibatsu. David Friedman, *The Misunderstood Miracle: Industrial Development and Political Change in Japan* (Ithaca: Cornell University Press, 1988), looks at small firms in Japan's machine tool industry. Nobuo Kawabe, "The Development of Distribution Systems in Japan Before World War II," in *Business and Economic History*, ed. William Hausman (Williamsburg: College of William and Mary, 1989), is an excellent survey.

The development of business and its relationship to government in Germany may be examined in R. J. Overy, *War and Economy in the Third Reich* (New York: Oxford University Press, 1994). Valuable case studies include John Gillingham, *Industry and Politics in the Third Reich: Ruhr Coal, Hitler, and Europe* (New York: Columbia University Press, 1985); Peter Hayes, *Industry*

and Ideology: IG Farben in the Nazi Era (New York: Cambridge University Press, 1987); and Ray Stokes, "The Oil Industry in Nazi Germany, 1936–1945," *Business History Review* 59 (Summer 1985): 254–78. Henry Ashby Turner, Jr., *German Big Business and the Rise of Hitler* (New York: Oxford University Press, 1985), is controversial.

7 [Business in an Expanding International Economy, 1945–1973

Even as the final phase of World War II began, allied leaders met at Bretton Woods, a resort in the White Mountains of New Hampshire, to plan what they hoped would be a financial system that would facilitate the development of a prosperous international economy after the war. In the summer of 1944 the Bretton Woods Agreement was completed by representatives of the forty-four nations present. Shortly thereafter, United Nations governments, without the participation of the communist bloc, sought to reduce trade barriers among themselves, an effort culminating in 1947 with the General Agreement on Tariffs and Trade (GATT), which Japan joined in 1955. The goals of the Bretton Woods Agreement and the GATT were similar: to stimulate the growth of the national economies around the globe and through this stimulation to remove what was believed to be one of the major causes of war: economic recession.

The goal was a more prosperous international economy of nations trading freely with each other, for it was believed that only in a situation of world prosperity could democracies endure and world peace prevail. While these goals were certainly not brand-new in the 1940s, more was done to make them a reality in the 1950s and 1960s than in previous decades. With the Bretton Woods Agreement came two institutions, the International Monetary Fund and the International Bank for Reconstruction and Development. These organizations labored to stabilize currency exchange rates between nations and sought to promote economic development in war-ravaged and underdeveloped nations. The nations adhering to the GATT took part in a series of negotiations called "rounds" that lowered tariff barriers on a wide variety of products around the world in an effort to expand trade. An agree-

ment in 1967 resulting from the Kennedy Round lowered tariff duties an average of 35 percent on 60,000 items, for example.

The Bretton Woods Agreement and the GATT helped to link national economies as never before. World trade rose at an average annual rate of about 4 percent in the century before 1945, but at a much higher 7 percent over the next twenty-five years. The value of world trade increased fivefold between 1950 and 1970! Foreign trade became more and more important for the economies of nations around the world. In 1950 the United States sold 9 percent of its production abroad, but by 1970 about 13 percent. For Great Britain the comparable figures were 43 percent and 48 percent, for Japan 18 percent and 30 percent.

The more open international framework set up by Bretton Woods and the GATT helped fuel economic growth. However, in relative terms nations fared differently. In 1950 the United States accounted for 39 percent of the world's GNP, twenty years later only 30 percent. The comparable statistics for Great Britain were 5 percent and 3.6 percent. By way of contrast, the European community (including West Germany) and Japan produced 12.6 percent of the world's GNP in 1950, but 21 percent by 1970. International economic growth reshaped business firms and policies in the 1950s and 1960s, and it is to those business changes that this chapter is devoted.

AMERICAN BUSINESS

New market opportunities led large American industrialists to diversify in terms of their products and markets; and, as the companies diversified, they adopted decentralized management systems, extending a trend from the 1920s. The federal government was important in continuing business growth at home and abroad, as it both promoted and regulated businesses. As in earlier times, the development of large firms did not mean the extinction of smaller ones. Small industrialists persisted when they could develop specialty products for niche markets. However, when compared to what had occurred in most earlier time periods, small businesses in manufacturing and sales declined rapidly relative to larger companies.

Government-Business Relations

Government actions continued to influence greatly American business developments in the postwar years. The federal government actively promoted business development. Most of the financing for airports and interstate highways came from the federal government, for example. At the same time, the federal government continued to regulate businesses through a host of independent regulatory commissions, such as the Securities and Exchange Commission set up in 1934. Government-business cooperation, with business executives joined together in groups such as the Business Round Table, also continued, in a manner similar to associationalism under Herbert Hoover in the 1920s. Business leaders, for instance, played a major role in the writing of the Employment and Production Act of 1946, by which the federal government for the first time assumed responsibility for trying to manage the overall level of economic prosperity in the United States.

American governmental actions at the international level also greatly affected business in the postwar period. The Bretton Woods Agreement and the GATT, both strongly promoted by the United States government, sought to create a prosperous international economy open to American trade. America's Marshall Plan of 1948 had similar goals. The Marshall Plan used a blend of public aid from the federal government and private technical assistance from American businesses to promote the economic recovery of Europe. The objective, largely successful, was to ensure the creation of prosperous democracies in Western Europe. Through various programs, including massive purchases of supplies for the Korean War of the early 1950s, the federal government also helped revive the Japanese economy, which lay prostrate after World War II. These governmental actions all contributed to the economic revival of much of the world in the postwar years, and this revival, in turn, opened new markets for American business.

As a result of both favorable governmental policies and business actions, the economy of the United States experienced rapid expansion during the first twenty-five years after World War II. Between 1945 and 1960 America's GNP increased by 52 percent, and the nation's per capita GNP rose by 19 percent. Then, in the 1960s the GNP of the United States climbed 46 percent, and the per capita GNP grew by 29 percent. Part of this economic growth came from the continuing development of a consumer society in America,

with its seemingly insatiable demand for consumer goods—television sets, cars, and household appliances—and (increasingly) for services. Part of the economic growth also came from the growing involvement of American business in the world market. An ever-higher proportion of America's industrial output found overseas markets in the 1950s and 1960s.

Labor in the Immediate Postwar Decades

The immediate postwar decades saw changes in America's labor situation, as large businesses sought to roll back gains made by workers in the New Deal of the 1930s. The National Association of Manufacturers, joined by the Business Council, the Chamber of Commerce, and other business associations, led an effort to revise the National Labor Relations Act of 1935. The business groups sought to reshape the law to restrict union activities and to retard future union growth.

When Congress passed the Taft-Hartley Act in 1947, it was responding to the desires of business leaders. This law required union leaders to swear that they were not members of the Communist Party, to account for their organization's finances, and to refrain from making political contributions. It prohibited the closed shop but allowed the open shop, thereby preserving management's right to hire whomever it chose. Unions had to provide a sixty-day notice before launching a strike; and the federal government, when it deemed that disputes hurt the public interest, could order striking workers to return to their jobs for eighty days while bargaining continued. To slow the growth of unions, the new law allowed states to require the open shop by enacting so-called right-to-work laws. That is, workers could not be forced to join unions.

The passage of the Taft-Hartley Act had important consequences. Union membership began a period of long-term decline, falling from a peak of almost 36 percent of the nonagricultural workforce in 1945 to slightly more than 25 percent in 1980. In manufacturing fields that had arisen with the Industrial Revolution there was still occasional labor-management conflict, but the common pattern of management behavior in dealing with labor was one of aggressive realism. In effect, a social contract was struck. As long as the economy was experiencing long-term growth, management was generally willing to grant higher wages (which could be accommodated by automation, productivity growth, and higher prices for consumers)—but only if

unions gave up any aspirations to affect how executives ran their companies and worked to discipline local leaders and rank-and-file members who supported disruptions of production processes. The relinquishment of authority by unions was not usually voluntary. Most often management dictated the terms of the bargains, continuing an effort to dominate labor-management relations dating back to at least the 1920s and 1930s.

Business Diversification: Multinationals and Conglomerates

The expansion of the international economy combined with the continued development of America's domestic market to open new opportunities for business. Accordingly, a growing proportion of businesses chose diversification as its growth strategy. An increasing number entered foreign markets for the first time, and more and more set up overseas manufacturing operations to become multinational corporations. Those emphasizing the domestic scene also diversified, often by both product and market. As they diversified, American companies often adopted decentralized, multidivisional management systems similar to the one pioneered by General Motors in the 1920s. By 1970 some 86 percent of the 500 largest industrial companies in the United States were diversified to the extent that they possessed at least three major divisions, and most of these firms had adopted some form of decentralized management.

Multinational corporations (MNCs), usually defined as companies with production facilities in more than one country, were a major response of American business leaders to expanding business opportunities around the world. MNCs had long existed, but they increased in numbers and in the scope of their activities in the immediate postwar period. By 1970 over 3,500 American companies possessed direct foreign investments in some 15,000 overseas enterprises, and in that year the direct foreign investments of American companies amounted to about $78 billion, a sum equal to roughly 8 percent of the nation's GNP.

International Telephone & Telegraph (ITT) was one of the most far-flung of American MNCs. The company's president, Harold Geneen, and forty members of his New York headquarters staff jetted to Europe each month to go over reports with the company officers there. Some joked that the initials ITT stood for International Travel and Talk. Geneen believed that only

McDonald's franchise, Fukuoka, Japan. American multinationals experienced a tremendous expansion during the 1950s and 1960s. (Author's collection)

through detailed face-to-face meetings could he achieve one of his prime goals in running his company: "no surprises." With 200,000 employees in Europe by 1970, ITT Europe had become the seventeenth largest company on the continent. Not surprisingly, Europeans complained of the American "invasion" of Europe. ITT had by the late 1960s also become a conglomer-

ate, for by the close of that decade it was an extremely diversified company with interests in car rentals, house building, hotels, and glassmaking, in addition to its businesses in communications.

Conglomerates were an extreme form of business diversification that appeared in the United States in the postwar years. Conglomerates were companies with many different divisions, at least eight, producing and selling unrelated goods and services. Thus, conglomerate businesses resembled the geologic formations from which they took their name. (A conglomerate rock is composed of fragments varying in size from small pebbles to large boulders in a cement mixture such as hardened clay.) Conglomerates became a major part of the American business scene in the 1960s. In 1966 about 60 percent of all mergers in America were conglomerate-type mergers, and by the close of that year 46 of the nation's largest 500 industrial companies were conglomerates.

The officers of conglomerates claimed that a new type of business executive was developing in the United States. This new breed consisted of young, ambitious managers with generalized management talents and skills, people versatile and adaptable enough to solve any problem in business. Trained especially in financial management, these new business leaders could, it was said, run a company well without knowing much about its products or production methods. Yet, in fact, conglomerates often experienced problems due to faulty management. In 1960 through 1962, for example, General Dynamics lost $425 million because the corporate office located in New York failed adequately to understand and supervise sloppy work being done by its Convair Division across the continent in Los Angeles. Problems of this type would multiply in the 1970s and 1980s.

Small Businesses in Manufacturing

The relative decline of small businesses in manufacturing continued in the 1950s and 1960s. Small firms continued to succeed as producers of specialty goods for niche markets, much like the Philadelphia textile makers of the nineteenth century and the New England metal fabricators and machinery makers of the early twentieth century. However, the relatively stable economic situation of the day together with the filling of American needs and desires for consumer goods—automobiles, color televisions, and household

appliances—were conducive to the development of large firms using big factories to make a range of fairly standardized goods in long production runs. As a result, small manufacturers declined in importance relative to large ones into the early 1970s.

Sales and Services

Hit hard by the entrance of large chain stores and large grocery stores into their fields, small retailers mounted spirited, but only partially successful, responses. Mom-and-pop grocery stores continued to attract patronage by offering services, such as home delivery, which were no longer provided by the chains and supermarkets. Or, they specialized in the types of goods they carried. In field after field, many small retailers also banded together in associations to secure some of the benefits, especially the discounts won through high-volume purchases, obtained by large-scale enterprises. In the grocery industry, for example, independent retailers formed voluntary groups, such as the Independent Grocers' Association (IGA), and retailer-owned cooperative warehouses. By the 1940s over one-third of all grocery wholesale sales passed through these institutions.

Changes taking place in hardware sales demonstrate well the alterations occurring in retailing. Some hardware retailers specialized in the goods they handled, and in the postwar years still more joined retailer-owned cooperatives. John Cotter put together one such cooperative as True Value hardware stores. Brought up in the hardware business, Cotter founded True Value in 1948, by which time independent hardware retailers were facing severe competition from chain stores and discount outlets. In this system hundreds of independent retailers came to own Cotter & Company, which, in turn, acted as their wholesaler. Profits earned at the middleman's sales level were rebated every year to the retailers, which remained independently owned. By the mid-1980s True Value had 7,000 member stores and 14 major distribution centers, making it the largest hardware distributor in the United States.

The effectiveness of the economic responses of small retailers varied considerably by field. Many small independent retailers failed to adjust to the new way of selling groceries. In this field, in which low prices were of utmost significance, the chains and supermarkets ruled supreme. By 1971 five large supermarket chains dominated food retailing in the United States by empha-

sizing rapid turnover of stock, high sales per employee, and large store size. In hardware, a field in which individual customer service remained more important, independents working through groups like True Value did better. The number of retail hardware outlets in the United States declined from 35,000 in 1954 to 26,000 in 1972 but stabilized and even rose a bit in the mid- and late 1970s.

A new phenomenon in the postwar years was the development of discount stores as a challenge to established retailers, large and small. The number of discount outlets in the United States soared from 1,329 in 1960 to 3,503 just six years later. By the mid-1960s discounting was well established in the East and Midwest and was beginning in other parts of the nation. Discount stores were particularly important in sales of toys, infants' clothing, sporting goods, automobile accessories, and housewares. E. J. Korvette, with 40 stores, was the largest discounter, with sales of $594 million, followed by S. S. Kresege (K-Mart, Jupiter), with 233 stores selling $490 million worth of goods. The top ten retailers each had sales of at least $173 million in 1965. Wal-Mart, just getting underway in the 1960s, would take discounting to new heights in later decades to become the world's largest retailer in the 1990s.

The service industry more than retailing remained the home of small businesses. Possessing fewer economies of scale than stores selling goods, service enterprises were less conducive to the spread of large firms. Most real estate companies were small and closely tied to their local communities. Only with the development of new communications and computer technologies in the late 1970s and 1980s would local and regional companies like Century 21 and Coldwell Banker grow to become national giants. Small local businesses also dominated the field of law. As in real estate, it required the development of new media and communications techniques for some law firms to grow large, as did Hyatt Legal Services in the 1980s. However, the power of small companies was eroded in some service industries. For example, national insurance and banking companies expanded their reach. Although small firms continued to thrive in both of these fields, their status was less secure than in earlier times.

America's Corporate Business System

The spread of conglomerates and MNCs, together with development of more traditional big businesses, continued a trend begun in the mid-nineteenth century: a relatively few big businesses dominated key segments of the American business system, especially in manufacturing. The distinction between center and peripheral firms widened; by 1962 the 50 largest companies possessed over one-third of America's manufacturing assets, and the top 500 had over two-thirds.

As in the past, the business leaders who managed America's big businesses remained something of an elite. A detailed study of the backgrounds of the leaders of the nation's largest 500 companies in 1976 revealed that all except one were men, all were white, 85 percent were from middle-class families, and 71 percent were Protestant. Most were also well educated: 86 percent had graduated from college, 24 percent had earned masters degrees, and 16 percent had received doctorates. Moving from rags to riches remained as difficult and unusual as it had been a century earlier.

BRITISH BUSINESS

In the immediate postwar decades British business continued to develop along many of the lines laid down during the interwar years. A renewed rationalization and merger movement led to the development of larger firms (and a corresponding decline in the significance of smaller companies), most of which came to be run by decentralized management systems similar to that developed earlier at Imperial Chemical Industries. The national government continued, and indeed increased, its involvement in economic and business affairs, especially when the Labour Party was in power.

Backed by trade unions, the Labour Party engaged the government more deeply in general economic planning and ownership through the nationalization of some basic industries, such as coal mining and steelmaking. The government also further developed the welfare state. Three pieces of legislation passed right after World War II were of most importance: the National Insurance Act (1946) provided unemployment benefits and retirement pensions; the National Health Service Act (1946) provided free medical and

dental care; and the National Housing Act (1947) endorsed the principle of public housing.

Despite the growth of big business and big government—some would say *because* of their continued development—Great Britain's economy did not advance as rapidly as did that of the United States or Japan. In some fields of heavy industry, especially, Britain continued the relative downward slide that had started during the interwar years, a slide that would become a drop during the 1970s.

Government, Business, and the International Economy

During the late 1930s and the 1940s the main thrust of British business was to avoid competition through collective action, a stance that left companies poorly prepared for the intense international competition of the postwar years. The merger movement of the 1920s and early 1930s, which had led to some rationalization in British business, slowed in later years. Instead of combining via mergers, businesses stifled competition by setting up a growing number of cartels and trade associations. Government actions encouraged this shift. In 1935 the government granted tax concessions to businesses working with each other to limit output, and during World War II the government worked with trade associations to plan the economy.

The major change in the business environment faced by British firms in the postwar years was a tremendous increase in competition, both at home and in the world marketplace. British firms faced increasing challenges from multinationals making and selling goods inside their nation's boundaries. The number of American firms having manufacturing subsidiaries in Great Britain rose from 43 in 1907 to 222 in 1935 and to 493 in 1962. By 1962 American MNCs in Britain accounted for over 50 percent of the British market for automobiles, vacuum cleaners, electric shavers, razor blades, sewing machines, typewriters, breakfast cereals, and potato chips, and for 30 to 50 percent of the market for computers, rubber tires, refrigerators, and washing machines. Actions taken by the British government also increased competition. Reversing its earlier position, the government sought to encourage business competition through new laws: the Monopolies and Restrictive Practices Act of 1948, the Restrictive Trade Practices Act of 1956, and the Restrictive Trade Practices Act of 1968.

British businesses faced growing competition in world trade as well. With the maturation of national independence movements in former colonies such as India, British business lost most of its heavily protected Empire market, which had been a major outlet for British goods before World War II. At the same time, Great Britain's adherence to the Bretton Woods Agreement and the GATT opened the nation to growing imports. In 1952 Great Britain had 22 percent by value of world trade in manufactures, but by 1969 only 11 percent.

The Spread of Diversified, Decentralized Big Businesses

British business leaders responded to the increase in competition by renewed rationalization. A major merger movement began in the 1950s and, like America's conglomerate movement, peaked in 1968. Between 1957 and 1967 about 38 percent of the companies traded on the London Stock Exchange were acquired by other quoted companies. The British government encouraged some of these mergers in hopes of making British companies more competitive in world trade. Thus, the government backed the formation of the British Aircraft Corporation in 1960 as a merger of Vickers-Armstrong, English Electric, and Bristol Aeroplane and supported the creation of the British Steel Corporation seven years later as a merger of fourteen previously independent firms.

While often not bringing about the increases in economic efficiency hoped for (just as the rationalization movement of the 1920s had failed to), the mergers did increase the power of big business in Great Britain in the post-war years. British companies became large by international standards. In 1972 thirty British manufacturing enterprises employed at least 40,000 people apiece. This figure was nearly as great as the number of such companies in all of the six original nations of the European Common Market, but less than the eighty-nine such companies in the United States. Of the largest 200 companies in the world outside of America in 1969, over one-fifth were British. Of the largest 300 manufacturers in Western Europe in 1969, about one-third were British. British big businesses clustered in many of the same fields as in the United States: food processing, chemicals, metals, electrical machinery, and transportation equipment.

Pushed by competition and pulled by new market opportunities, British

companies diversified their product ranges and decentralized their management structures. By 1970, 94 of Great Britain's largest 100 companies had diversified to some degree. Diversification came later to Great Britain than to the United States and, at first, was slower to spread in Great Britain. But when diversification did occur, it took place rapidly, in the single decade of the 1960s. The rapidity of diversification was due, in part, to the work of McKinsey & Company, an American management consultant firm. Hired by many British companies to give advice on what growth strategies to follow, the American consultants usually suggested diversification by products or markets. As in the United States, diversified companies in Great Britain adopted decentralized management structures to handle the growing complexity of their operations. By 1970, 72 of the 100 largest British companies were being run by some form of multidivisional, decentralized management—just as Imperial Chemical Industries had been by the 1930s. However, few British firms, only 6 of the top 100, went so far as to become conglomerates.

Great Britain's diversified, decentralized companies possessed structures like those of similar companies in America. General managers in the corporate office, advised by staff officers, made the grand policy decisions. Divisional officers ran the daily operations. However, there were some differences. Divisional managers often took part in policy-making in British companies, not just operations. This situation raised some doubts about their objectivity in measuring the performance of the various divisions of companies. Secondly, financial controls were not as well developed in Great Britain. Annual budgets were not the control devices they had earlier become at American companies like General Motors. Then, too, managerial hierarchies were less fully developed in Great Britain. As late as 1968 two-thirds of Great Britain's largest 120 companies possessed no hierarchy beyond that of chairman and managing director.

Ironically, as leading British companies adopted American management practices and structure, if at times only incompletely, they fell prey to some of the same problems afflicting United States firms. By the late 1960s, and especially during the 1970s and 1980s, some large multidivisional, decentralized British companies became hidebound. With their many layers of management and with executives trained increasingly in finance, the British firms, like their American cousins, had difficulty dealing with the rapid economic changes taking place in the global marketplace. For the moment, however,

most managerial weaknesses were papered over by the worldwide economic expansion of the immediate postwar decades.

Paths to Diversification

Two main paths pointed the way to diversification and decentralization in Great Britain. Some companies—especially those in electrical and electronics engineering, chemicals and drugs, and mechanical engineering—diversified as their technologies led them into new areas. The second route lay through acquisition and mergers and was often a defensive strategy pursued by companies seeking escape from declining fields or from fields in which competition was rapidly rising.

The British Oxygen Company was a good example of technology-driven diversification. Before World War II British Oxygen had built up a near monopoly in Great Britain and had extensive overseas interests in the supply of oxygen and industrial gasses. After the war the company faced increased competition from MNCs, most notably the American Air Products Company. British Oxygen's response was to enter new fields—resins, engineering equipment, cryogenics, vacuum equipment, and food processing—and as the firm diversified it also switched from centralized to decentralized management.

Unilever grew by acquisitions. Unilever resulted from a merger of the Dutch Margarine Union and the British soapmaker, Lever Brothers, in 1929 (the main products of each company used natural oils as raw materials). Unilever's interests in soap led the company to expand in the direction of detergents and toilet preparations, while its interests in margarine led it to form a diversified food group composed of companies in frozen foods, soup mixes, canned and dehydrated foods, jams, tea, coffee, and dairy products. An interest in animal feeds led Unilever into packaging and chemical companies. Purchases of other companies permitted Unilever's expansion. Initially, Unilever set up a multidivisional structure with its divisions based on regions, but in 1949 the company began establishing product divisions. By 1970 Unilever had become a decentralized company with twelve product coordinators and four regional coordinators.

British Multinationals

Like their American counterparts, British executives expanded or established MNCs in the postwar years. The world's leader in foreign direct investment (FDI) before World War II, Britain fell to second place after the conflict, trailing the United States. Perhaps 40 percent of British FDI was lost between 1938 and 1956 as a result of wartime destruction, sequestrations, and forced sales. Even so, in 1971 Britain accounted for 14 percent of the world's accumulated FDI—behind the 48 percent share of the United States, but ahead of Germany's 4 percent and Japan's 3 percent. During the first fifteen years after World War II the lion's share of British FDI went to Commonwealth countries, but from the 1960s on, more and more went into Western Europe and the United States.

As in the case of other nations, the existence of MNCs headquartered in Great Britain raised basic questions about their control. Could a national government adequately regulate the affairs of international companies? To whom, if anyone, were MNCs responsible? These issues were placed in the spotlight in 1965, when Prime Minister Harold Wilson sought to impose economic sanctions, including an oil embargo, on white rebels in Rhodesia. Working against the wishes of the British government, Royal Dutch Shell and British Petroleum, Great Britain's two leading MNCs, found ways to ship oil into Rhodesia, and a bit later, the oil companies worked against the intentions of the British government by supplying oil to the Union of South Africa.

Smaller Industrial Firms

As large firms grew in importance in British manufacturing, smaller companies declined in significance, even more rapidly than was occurring in either the United States or Japan. Small manufacturing establishments (those with 200 or fewer employees) dropped in number from 103,000 in 1948 to just 75,000 in 1971. During the same years the proportion of industrial workers employed in Britain by smaller manufacturing firms fell from 37 percent to just 28 percent. By the mid-1970s small industrialists accounted for only about a quarter of Great Britain's output of manufactured goods.

Several reasons accounted for the decline of small manufacturers. Few government policies aided small firms in the immediate postwar decades; only

in 1971 did the British government mount a concerted effort to foster small business growth. In fact, most government policies in the 1950s and 1960s probably worked to the disadvantage of smaller companies, as the government favored mergers and rationalization in pursuit of imagined production efficiencies. Moreover, as in America, consumer demand for standardized goods favored large-scale production in big factories operated by big businesses. Smaller firms were generally at a disadvantage in this situation.

Sales and Services

Small retailers also lost ground to their larger brethren after World War II. Changes in British laws may have contributed to their loss. Legislation passed by Parliament in 1956 and 1964 outlawed retail price maintenance schemes, greatly enhancing competition in retailing. While important, these legal changes probably simply hastened trends already under way. Owning small retail businesses was becoming less attractive than it had been in the interwar years. As Great Britain became more of a welfare state, with considerable aid given to citizens out of work, going into retailing as an alternative to unemployment was less appealing. Then, too, technological and social changes — the growing use of refrigeration in the distribution of foodstuffs, an increased acceptance of self-service and prepackaging, and the development of a better national road system — bit into sales made by small retailers.

By the mid-1980s small shops accounted for only about one-third of Britain's retail sales (and only 13 percent of grocery sales). Multiples (chain stores) were big gainers, especially in such fields as consumer durables, clothing, and alcohol. By the close of the 1980s the four largest grocery chains accounted for 80 percent of all sales in that field. Much the same trend was apparent in services. The Big Five banks that dominated Britain as early as 1914 became the Big Four in 1968, and the four banks accounted for 92 percent of Britain's bank deposits by the mid-1970s.

British Business Leaders and the Labor Situation

What of Britain's business leaders, those who headed the new diversified companies and MNCs? Family businesses became less important than before. As late as 1950 one-half of Great Britain's largest 100 businesses were controlled

by families, but twenty years later only one-third were. By the late 1960s and early 1970s the average company director in big business was fifty-six years old and not very mobile. He (very few were women) had an average salary of 11,000 pounds (about $26,000) in 1970, much less than the average $210,000 earned by the heads of the largest 500 American companies just a few years later in 1976.

In terms of background, business leaders had most likely attended a public school (that is, a private school; in Britain private schools were and are called public schools). Only about one-half possessed a university education, most commonly from Oxford or Cambridge (this proportion of top executives going to a university was much less than the 89 percent in France, the 83 percent in the United States, or the 78 percent in West Germany and Italy). Perhaps most startling, as late as 1970 only 9 percent had received any professional education in business management. Although a bit more open than in the past, Great Britain's business leadership remained an elite in the postwar years. In the 1950s some 36 percent of the nation's business leaders were the sons of businessmen, another 36 percent the sons of clerical workers or laborers, 21 percent the sons of public officials, and 7 percent the sons of farmers.

Poorly educated themselves, Britain's business leaders failed—as they had during the interwar years—to invest in the education of the workforce. In stark contrast to what was occurring in Japan, executives did little to upgrade the training of their workers. The idea that the practical man, a person untrained in theory, could adequately design and make products continued to hold sway in Britain's manufacturing enterprises. And improvements in public education did not compensate for the lack of on-the-job training. The British government increased funding for education (at least before 1979), but the educational improvements that occurred benefited industry little. For instance, technical schools, which might have imparted skills valuable for industrial work, dropped in number from 321 in 1947 to just 225 in 1962. In many industries, workers, lacking skills and knowledge that might have allowed them to adjust to new ways of doing things, resisted automation and other innovations in factory operations. This deficiency, already apparent in the interwar years, and growing in the immediate postwar decades, became pronounced in the 1970s and 1980s. Already by the mid-1970s the productivity of British indus-

trial workers lagged behind that of their West German counterparts by about 50 percent, with an even wider gap separating British from Japanese workers.

JAPANESE BUSINESS

Even more than in the United States, and in sharp contrast to Great Britain, high-speed growth characterized the Japanese economy in the 1950s and 1960s. That this would be so was not apparent in the immediate postwar years. Japan was a defeated nation with widespread unemployment, rampant inflation, and shortages of food and fuel. It was feared that thousands might starve. Japan's recovery from this low point was remarkable, aptly labeled by many as an economic "miracle." In the 1950s and 1960s investment in plants and equipment rose 22 percent per year, and Japan's GNP soared by an average of 10 percent annually! The development of consumerism in Japan—similar to what had been occurring in the United States since the 1920s—fueled much of this economic growth. A surge in demand for what the Japanese called the Three Cs—cars, color televisions, and air conditioners—was especially important. By 1970 Japan's real national income was six times greater than it had been in the mid-1930s, and industrial output was ten times larger. Unemployment had dried up, and inflation disappeared. Despite a 42 percent increase in Japan's population, the nation's standard of living was far above that of the prewar years.

Japan's economic expansion opened new opportunities for business. Older zaibatsu—Mitsui, Mitsubishi, Kikkoman, Nissan, among others—were broken up in the interests of economic democracy by American authorities in the 1940s but reorganized in new ways in the 1950s and 1960s. In addition, there was more room in the Japanese economy than in earlier times for entrepreneurial firms to grow in size. Then, too, smaller companies, whether operating on their own or as subcontractors, remained an important part of Japan's mix of businesses. In general, companies in heavy industry—automaking, chemicals, steel, and the like—expanded more rapidly than those in light industries such as cotton textiles, continuing a trend begun in the late 1920s. The availability of relatively cheap raw materials and oil encouraged this trend.

With business expansion Japan possessed the world's third largest economy by 1968, trailing only the United States and the Soviet Union. No single

factor explains Japan's dramatic rise from the ashes of defeat to the status of economic superpower. Rather, a coincidence of many elements led to the nation's economic recovery and expansion.

The External Environment

Factors external to Japan's economy were important. The same worldwide movement toward free trade that helped American companies and that increased business competition in Great Britain aided Japanese firms. Only with large parts of the world available as sources of raw materials and as markets for her finished products could Japan, now stripped of her colonial possessions, survive and prosper. The GATT was of particular importance. While reaping the benefits of markets open to her goods, Japan was able by special arrangements to restrict foreign investments in her companies and limit the entrance of unwanted goods into the Japanese market until the 1970s and 1980s. Legislation enacted in 1949 and 1950, and liberalized only in the late 1960s and 1970s, limited imports into Japan and restricted foreign investments in the nation.

American policies also helped rebuild Japan. Immediately after World War II, the United States government, which dictated economic policy to Japan between 1945 and 1952, sought to democratize Japan's business system: some business leaders lost their jobs, some zaibatsu were dissolved, and an antimonopoly law was passed. However, as the Cold War began, American leaders revised their attitudes toward Japan. Americans sought to revitalize Japan as a bastion of democracy and capitalism in the Far East, especially after communists won control of China in 1949. Americans also desired an economically strong Japan so that Japan would be able to import goods made in America (until 1968 the United States enjoyed a trade surplus with Japan). The zaibatsu were allowed to reorganize in the 1950s, the antimonopoly law was ignored, and most American leaders favored an extension of Japanese exports throughout the world. Even more specifically, American military expenditures in Japan, especially for the Korean War, allowed the Japanese to finance a major increase in their imports. Key Japanese industries that depended on imports for their raw materials doubled their scale of production.

Government-Business Relations

Changes occurring within Japan spurred economic growth as well. Often remarked upon was the nature of government-business relations. Observers thought they discerned a particularly cooperative relationship between government and business, in which the government provided valuable guidance for the expansion of Japan's economy. In fact, there was often considerable cooperation between government and business in the postwar period, and this cooperation did in some cases spur business growth.

The Japanese government, working especially through the Ministry of Finance and the Ministry of International Trade and Industry (MITI), sought to guide the development of the nation's economy. The MITI, in particular, tried to provide planning for economic development, most often in the realm of heavy industry. This planning was attempted not by government order or fiat but by government guidance of the economy—by providing incentives for business development. Thus, the Japanese government sought a middle way between the heavy-handed government ownership of industry and centralized government economic planning by fiat that characterized the Soviet Union, on the one hand, and the open, free-market economy of the United States, on the other hand.

The attempt to guide economic growth was not brand-new in the postwar years, nor were the institutions devised to do so. The MITI's origins date to 1881, when the Ministry of Agriculture and Commerce was formed to stimulate and guide Japan's economic growth by indirect methods as part of the shift away from direct controls begun by the new minister of finance, Masayoshi Matsukata, in 1880. The Ministry of Agriculture and Commerce split into two parts in 1925, with one of the new parts becoming the Ministry of Commerce and Industry. The Ministry of Commerce and Industry led much of the rationalization program of the interwar years and was significant in encouraging the switch from light to heavy industry. Reorganized in 1939, the Ministry of Commerce and Industry helped mobilize the Japanese economy for war and was converted into the Ministry of Munitions in 1943. With the defeat of Japan, the Ministry of Munitions went through several changes that resulted finally in the establishment of the MITI in 1949.

After World War II the Japanese government took numerous actions to encourage and guide business development. The national and prefectural

governments improved Japan's economic infrastructure: harbors, highways, railroads, electric power grids, and so forth. Government banks, backed ultimately by the Bank of Japan, loaned funds to large private city banks, which, in turn, loaned to business. Japanese business came to depend on bank borrowing for about three-quarters of its funds. Laws passed by the Diet also helped business. A 1952 law gave subsidies and quick tax write-offs to companies investing in new equipment and research, and a 1956 income tax reduction stimulated consumer spending.

The MITI's work was of most importance. It labored to rationalize inefficient companies and industries and could be forceful in doing so. In 1952 the MITI advised ten large cotton spinners to reduce their output by 40 percent and informed them that a failure to lower production would lead to a cutoff in the foreign exchange allocation needed for their importation of raw cotton. MITI's guidance also meant targeting companies for growth, helping them secure technology, capital, and markets. Many of the specific laws by which the MITI sought to guide Japan's economic growth in the 1950s and 1960s had important predecessors in the interwar years. A 1937 trade law served as the precedent for legislation in 1949 giving the MITI power over Japan's foreign exchange. The Petroleum Industry Law of 1934 served as a direct model for legislation with exactly the same title in 1962. Laws encouraging industry-wide rationalization and stabilization efforts in the 1920s and 1930s paved the way for similar legislation in the 1950s and 1960s.

Taken together, governmental actions encouraged economic growth and business development. However, it is difficult to judge precisely how important government aid was in Japan's postwar economic recovery and expansion. The MITI's actions, while significant, should not be overstressed. Many other factors were involved, for the business situation in Japan was complex. The coal industry, targeted for nurturing by the MITI, never fully developed. Then, too, some companies, such as Honda, prospered despite their opposition to MITI's desires and actions. Japan recovered economically from its wartime devastation and then surged ahead at least as much through the actions of its business leaders and industrial workers as through steps taken by its government officials.

The Variety of Businesses in Manufacturing

As in the United States, economic growth in the 1950s and 1960s opened new opportunities for business leaders in Japan, opportunities of which they were quick to take advantage. Their actions, in turn, caused additional growth. Japan's business situation was fluid after World War II, a situation that encouraged business experimentation and entrepreneurship. As they sought out new opportunities, Japanese executives shaped new types of companies, making the business picture in their nation diverse.

Typical of the rebirth of entrepreneurship was Soichiro Honda and Honda Motors. Notorious as something of a playboy in his youth—he was a lover of fast driving, geisha houses, sake, and traditional epic poetry—Honda rebuilt his destroyed factory in a new mode after World War II. He was one of the first to recognize the need for cheap, reliable transportation in Japan at a time when gasoline was scarce and streets congested. He began by attaching war surplus engines to bicycles. In 1949 Honda produced his first motorcycle, and by the late 1950s his company was mass producing small motorcycles for Japan's urban market. Honda invaded the American market in 1959 and a decade later boasted 1,600 dealers in the United States. Automobiles, the Honda Civic and Accord, came in the 1970s.

Honda built his company as an independent entrepreneur. He avoided tie-ups with other firms, breaking a prewar arrangement with Toyota and avoiding bank loans wherever possible. He prospered despite conflicts with the Japanese government. In 1951 Honda refused to take part in an attempt at government-business cooperation designed to boost Japanese exports, and in the early 1960s Honda successfully opposed a MITI initiative to merge Japanese automakers into just a few large companies.

Japan's more traditional big businesses also reorganized in the postwar years, after some efforts to break them up. Between 1946 and 1948 some twenty-eight holding companies with family control were dissolved. However, with the advent of the Cold War this American effort ended, and by 1971 six major business groups had reorganized: Mitsubishi with eighty-six major firms, Sumitomo with eighty, Mitsui with seventy-one, Fuji with seventy-one, Sanwa with fifty-two, and Dai Ichi with twenty-seven. As in the prewar zaibatsu, these groupings usually consisted of a bank, a trading company, and many manufacturing companies. However, there were important differences.

These new groupings lacked any central headquarters or holding company owning stock in subsidiary companies. Instead, the groupings—often called "keiretsu"—were much looser, held together by informal meetings of the heads of the various companies and by some stock interchanges among constituent firms.

The formation and expansion of MNCs, as in Great Britain and America, was yet another response of business leaders in Japan to the economically open postwar world. Even before World War II, Japanese businesses had set up some overseas production facilities. However, most were located in Japanese colonies and were limited to mining, communications, and some types of heavy industry. True overseas production facilities were first established during the 1950s and 1960s. The direct foreign investment of Japanese firms climbed from $447 million in 1961 to $1.45 billion just six years later and then soared to $3.5 billion by 1973. The average annual growth rate of Japan's direct investment in overseas ventures came to 31 percent between 1967 and 1974—much more than West Germany's 26 percent, America's 10 percent, or Great Britain's 9 percent. The sudden increase in Japan's overseas investments in the late 1960s and early 1970s came mainly from investments in the United States, especially in the commercial and service sectors of the American economy.

One reason Japan's large manufacturers were able to expand rapidly at home and abroad was their increased use of subcontractors. Subcontracting became increasingly common after World War II. By 1971, 59 percent of all of the small industrial companies in Japan were acting as subcontractors for larger concerns, and ten years later the proportion had risen to 66 percent. By the late 1970s and the 1980s, 82 percent of Japan's manufacturing firms with more than 300 employees used subcontractors, employing an average of 68 subcontractors apiece. The importance of subcontracting differentiated the Japanese system of manufacturing from the American one. In the United States, as in the past, large manufacturing companies were more likely to be vertically integrated and less likely to depend on subcontracting.

Subcontracting was particularly well developed in Japan's automobile industry. Toyota and Nissan, for example, turned to subcontracting as a way to meet the growing demand for their cars from the mid-1950s on. In the 1950s Toyota and Nissan accounted for about 50 percent of the manufacturing costs for each car sold under their names, the other 50 percent coming

from their subcontractors. By the late 1970s and early 1980s the contribution of Toyota and Nissan had dropped to about 30 percent, with subcontractors accounting for 70 percent. In 1977 Toyota had 168 first-level subcontractors; these companies, in turn, controlled 5,437 second-level subcontractors; and the second-level subcontractors had 41,703 third-level subcontractors.

By using subcontractors, Toyota and other companies were able to expand greatly production at little cost. The use of subcontractors allowed them to keep their capital investments and labor costs lower than they would otherwise have been. In 1989 Toyota produced 4.5 million cars with 65,000 employees; by way of contrast, in the same year General Motors used 750,000 employees to make 7.9 million cars. Toyota made its system work by cooperating very closely with its subcontractors, especially the first-level ones — providing them with technical help, financing, and other skills. In turn, the subcontractors provided high-quality parts and subassemblies to Toyota on time, as needed. The growing importance of subcontracting was often a mixed blessing for smaller firms, however. Increasingly, the larger companies dictated the terms of doing business to the smaller firms. In recessions it was the subcontractors that suffered most, accepting price cuts for their products and laying off employees. As a consequence, wages and productivity were usually lower at subcontractors than at the mother companies, especially in the immediate postwar years.

Businesses in Sales

In retailing, mom-and-pop enterprises continued to grow in absolute numbers in Japan but, as in America and Britain, lost ground relative to larger retail outlets. Pressures on small retailers, apparent before World War II, increased after the conflict. More and more manufacturers, including Nissan and Toyota, set up their own nationwide distribution and sales channels to bypass Japan's cumbersome, many-layered system of wholesalers and retailers. In 1983 Toyota possessed 318 dealerships that had 3,665 sales outlets employing 116,000 people, and Nissan had 258 dealerships with 3,265 outlets employing 82,000. In general, companies making technologically advanced products found, like many American firms at an earlier date, that general wholesalers and retailers could not adequately demonstrate, sell, finance, and service their goods, leading them to enter sales.

Fish-seller's stall in a superstore in Hiroshima. Small business declined in importance relative to big business in Japan in the 1950s and 1960s. (Courtesy of Rand Blackford)

Then, too, large department store and superstore chains grew in importance. As part of Japan's postwar consumer revolution, department stores increased their share of Japan's retail sales from less than 1 percent in 1945 to nearly 10 percent fifteen years later. Superstores combined general-merchandise and supermarket sales under one roof. Borrowing directly from American supermarkets, superstores stressed chain operations, self-service, checkout lanes using cash registers, heavy advertising, and high-volume sales with low profit margins. In 1972 there were over 2,000 superstores in Japan, and five years later there were 3,100. Having negligible sales in 1960, superstores surpassed department stores in total sales by 1973.

Responding to the cries of small retailers, in 1956 the Diet passed the Department Store Law, modeled on a 1937 law with the identical title. The 1956 law required permission from the MITI for the opening or expansion of any retail store with more than 1,500 square meters of floor space (or 3,000 square meters in some large cities), and such permission was rarely given. There were, however, ways to get around this law. Some entrepreneurs—Isao Nakauchi of Daiei, for example—created their department stores and superstores by

limiting each floor to 1,500 square meters and setting up each floor as a legally separate company. By 1972 Daiei was the leading retailer in Japan. Even so, as late as 1976, 1.6 million retail outlets employing 5.6 million workers served Japan's population of 112 million. Despite the inroads of large department stores, superstores, and the like, Japan had many more retailers per capita than most other industrial nations. As a result, the Japanese paid higher prices for their consumer goods. Service by small-scale retail outlets was expensive.

The Tsutsumi Family and the Seibu-Saison Enterprises

Members of the Tsutsumi family were among the first business people to see clearly new opportunities in retailing and leisure activities in Japan. They rode and, to some degree, directed their nation's postwar consumer revolution. Yasujiro Tsutsumi founded the family businesses during the interwar and immediate postwar years, basing them mainly on the development of resorts for Japan's emerging middle class, Tokyo's Seibu Railroad, which possessed valuable landholdings, and a fledgling department store. Like Honda, Yasujiro built his business empire with little government help and by operating outside of zaibatsu groups. Yasujiro died in 1964, and two of his sons greatly expanded the businesses he had started.

Yoshiaki Tsutsumi took charge of what became the Seibu Railway Group. By the early 1990s the railroad carried about 2 million passengers daily, along with thousands of tons of freight. By then the railroad group had also parlayed its landholdings into Japan's largest group of luxury hotels (the forty-one Prince Hotels in Japan, along with six Princes overseas), and was developing the nation's most extensive chain of ski, golf, and vacation resorts. In the mid-1990s the Seibu Group employed about 45,000 people and had annual revenues of about $7.2 billion. Yoshiaki was by some estimates the world's richest private person, worth $280 billion in 1990, mainly because of the value of the landholdings of his companies.

His brother, Seiji Tsutsumi, controlled a second complex of enterprises that became known as the Saison Group. This group evolved from a Tokyo dry goods store purchased in 1940, from which became one of Japan's leading department store chains, Seibu Department Stores. In the 1960s Seibu became the first department store group to move successfully into superstores — with the Seiyu stores, which trailed only Daiei in superstore sales by 1972. In

the 1970s and 1980s Seibu (now called Saison) diversified into a broad range of consumer services—insurance, credit, information networking, consulting, and so on. By the mid-1990s the Saison Group employed nearly 150,000 workers and had annual net sales of $35 billion, compared to Nissan's $43 billion and Toshiba's $33 billion.

Seiji and Yoshiaki took important leaves from their father's book. Both expanded their businesses outside of the work of keiretsu and with little government aid. And neither played much of a role in business associations in Japan.

The Management and Organization of Businesses

Like the companies themselves, Japanese business management methods were diverse. In the entrepreneurial firms the word of the owner-founder was law. Yasujiro Tsutsumi ruled his railroad and resort empire as an autocrat. Under him there was no president's office in any Seibu company, no director's offices, nor even any rooms set aside for department or section chiefs. Known within the company simply as the boss, Yasujiro held board meetings at his private residence in Tokyo. His sons delegated some responsibilities to others as their enterprises grew in the 1970s and 1980s, but not many. Yoshiaki, in particular, continued to rule by himself, visiting his enterprises by helicopter.

In many of Japan's large business groups, however, consensus decision making was more the norm. An important aspect of this type of management was the *ringi* system (meaning circular discussion system). A *ringi* was a proposal put forward by a manager of one department that was passed on to managers of related departments and finally to the president. As the proposal was passed around, all those who saw it could make comments on an attached form. When it finally reached the president, he made his decision on how to proceed on the basis of what his subordinates had written. Closely related to the *ringi* system was *nemawashi*. Roughly translated as "rootbinding," *nemawashi* was a term taken from horticulture; it referred to the informal discussion and consultation that occurred in a Japanese company before a formal proposal was presented, much as the roots of a bush must be carefully bound up before a bush is transplanted.

In the immediate postwar decades changes occurred in the management structures of many large Japanese companies. Staff offices—personnel, long-

range planning, public relations, and so forth—were added to Japanese firms, largely as a result of American influences. Many Japanese companies also added an operating committee called the *jomukai* to their administrative hierarchies. This body consisted of the president, vice-president, and several senior managing directors; and, as the importance of *jomukai* rose, the significance of boards of directors was correspondingly reduced, as was also taking place in Great Britain and the United States.

So, regardless of precise structure, big businesses in Japan, the United States, and Great Britain became more and more similar in that they were multi-unit enterprises run by bureaucratic management. Nonetheless, significant differences remained. Japanese managerial hierarchies remained much flatter than those in the United States—that is, large Japanese companies had far fewer layers of management than their American counterparts.

Then, too, few of Japan's big businesses adopted fully developed decentralized management systems, in contrast to what occurred in the United States or Great Britain. Japanese firms were more focused, less diverse in their product offerings and in the markets they served (Seibu and Saison were exceptions). At a time when most large American manufacturers produced a wide range of goods, most large Japanese manufacturers made only one or two major products. As a consequence, decentralized management was less necessary in Japan. Most Japanese firms did well with centralized management systems or with moving partway into decentralized management. Matsushita Electric Industrial, for example, organized product groups with divisions for product design, engineering, production, and sales, but it kept the actual selling of the goods at the corporate level. Corporate management also took care of the finances, labor relations, and legal matters for all of the company.

In short, less responsibility was delegated to the divisional level in Japan than in Great Britain or the United States. Instead of becoming large, multidivisional, decentralized firms, Japanese big businesses operated more as parts of constellations of firms joined together in various types of business networks, just as they had in times past. Networks linking banks, trading companies, and manufacturers in keiretsu were one type of such an arrangement. The linkage between industrial firms and their subcontractors was another. These types of linkages combined with their flatter managerial hierarchies to give Japanese firms advantages over many of their foreign competitors. Japanese companies

could respond quickly to economic changes and market alterations. Only in the 1980s and 1990s did some big Japanese businesses become rigid in their management setups.

Whether the heads of entrepreneurial firms or companies within the keiretsu groups, several characteristics stood out about Japanese business leaders of the 1950s and 1960s. They were somewhat younger and more vigorous than those of the interwar years, for as a result of American actions about 3,600 business leaders were forced to retire in the years 1946 through 1948. Even more than in the interwar period, the top management of big business was college-educated, some 90 percent by the early 1960s. With big businesses hiring from only a handful of prestigious universities, a new business elite based on education came into being. These business leaders often came to view themselves as the true saviors of Japan, in a manner reminiscent of early Meiji times. Indeed, their wholehearted pursuit of profits and economic growth helped spur Japan's economic recovery.

Labor Relations

Changes occurring in labor relations both reflected the concern for economic growth and were one reason for that growth. As we have seen, the origins of what became known as the Japanese system of labor relations date back to at least the interwar period. Faced with shortages of skilled workers and worried by labor disruptions, some big businesses offered wages and promotions based on seniority, along with extensive benefits, even before World War II. Following the conflict, Japan's labor situation was chaotic, as workers in many industries rushed to form nationwide unions and go on strike. Unions, which had been illegal during the interwar years, were legalized after World War II; efforts by workers desiring unionization combined with the wishes of American authorities helped to bring that about.

To dampen labor unrest, keep workers loyal to their companies, and break nascent national unions, business leaders greatly extended the system of labor relations begun earlier. Increasingly, big businesses hired men graduating from high schools and colleges for lifetime employment that would end only with retirement. (And, that retirement often came early, at age fifty-five to sixty, with the men often going on to a second career.) Companies provided

promotions and wage increases based mainly on seniority, and a broad range of welfare services such as subsidized housing and recreational facilities. In return, employees generally remained loyal to their companies. Workers belonged only to enterprise unions, organizations based on a single company rather than a nationwide industry or trade.

A compromise was reached between labor and management. By the mid-1950s labor challenged companies' managerial hierarchies less and less. Labor disturbances and strikes became rarer, usually limited to the wearing of symbolic red armbands during the spring offensive when new annual contracts were negotiated. In return, in addition to providing lifetime employment and seniority-based promotions and wages, companies gave more control over the workfloor to their employees: control over such matters as the layout of production, personnel transfers, and how tasks would be performed. Management and labor saw this as helping them both. Business leaders obtained the labor stability that they needed for high-speed economic growth, and labor received increased security, wages, benefits, and authority over work processes.

One of the major advantages to emerge from the Japanese system of labor relations was the flexibility that businesses had in using their workforces. Committed to their workers, the companies provided extensive and ongoing training and education for employees, from shopfloor workers to top-level managers. In return, businesses came to possess well-educated employees able to adjust to changing situations. More than that, workers often contributed ideas about how work processes could be made more efficient and how products might be improved. Then, too, because of their commitment to their companies, workers were unlikely to move to another firm, justifying the educational investments made in them. There was, as well, a willingness on the part of Japanese workers—much more than was the case with either their American or British counterparts—to undertake whatever job was needed in their firm. Unlike the situation in the United States, union-based work rules did not restrict what Japanese employees would do on the shopfloor.

It is important to realize, however, that in the 1950s and 1960s, just as in the interwar years, the Japanese system was limited to only a minority of workers and managers, namely, to male employees working on a permanent basis for big businesses, perhaps one-third of Japan's industrial workforce. Smaller companies, men working on temporary assignments, and most women em-

ployees were not part of this employment system. Even in some large firms there were occasionally mutterings of dissent. For instance, a journalist disguised as a shopfloor worker at Toyota found that far from all factory workers were satisfied. Some workers, he discovered, thought that management benefited most from the company's system of labor relations and complained about company tyranny in controlling the work process and in speeding up work on the assembly line.

Germany: A Comparison to Japan

German businesses underwent postwar experiences similar in important ways to those in Japan. The first impulse of the Western occupying powers—the United States, Great Britain, and France—was to democratize Germany economically. In the western zones of occupation (the Soviet Union controlled an eastern zone, later East Germany) cartels were broken up and wartime business leaders were removed from office. German companies closely associated with the nation's war effort—I. G. Farben, Krupp, and others—found their assets confiscated. As in the case of Japan, however, these efforts were short-lived. As the Cold War intensified, the Western powers decided that West Germany, formed as a nation from the western occupation zones in 1949, would be rebuilt as an industrial nation and bastion of democracy against the Soviet Union. The Marshall Plan was put forward, in part, to aid in West Germany's recovery.

During the 1950s and 1960s West German businesses, building on foundations laid in the interwar years and earlier, reorganized to lead their nation into a period of high-speed economic growth similar to Japan's. Government actions were significant in aiding this business redevelopment. The Law for Promoting Stability and Growth of the Economy, passed in 1967, brought to culmination earlier efforts; the law made currency stability, economic growth, full employment, and a positive trade balance official governmental goals. Nonetheless, as in the case of Japan, private initiatives were at least equally important. From the mid-1950s into the 1960s universal banks once again played important roles in providing industrial financing. Various business associations reemerged or were developed anew; perhaps most important was the new Federation of German Industry, which helped coordinate

national economic legislation. And, of course, individual companies rebuilt their capabilities. As they did so, they were less likely than their British or American counterparts to adopt decentralized management or to be involved in mergers. Instead, they resembled Japanese firms more in their growth strategies and structures. By the 1960s German firms were taking parts of international markets away from their British competitors.

As in Japan, cooperation typically characterized relations between management and labor in Germany. The Codetermination Law of 1976 required that large firms (those with 2,000 or more employees) have supervisory boards consisting of equal number of representatives of labor and management to set grand policies for the firms. Codetermination grew out of earlier precedents—experiments with works councils in the 1920s and a 1951 codetermination law for companies in the coal and steel industries. However, codetermination did not extend to medium-size and small firms, thus excluding 80 percent of Germany's workers from its coverage.

THE POSTWAR BUSINESS WORLD

By the close of the 1950s and 1960s big businesses were firmly entrenched in the United States, Great Britain, Japan, and Germany. Large companies existed in many of the same basic fields worldwide: transportation equipment, metals, electrical machinery, chemicals, textiles, petroleum, tobacco processing, and stone, clay, and glass. To some degree, companies in these fields became similar in their management schemes, as large manufacturers moved toward bureaucratic management. The growing similarity was most pronounced in the United States and Great Britain, as large, diversified British companies adopted decentralized management directly from America.

Convergence also typified some aspects of the business systems of the nations discussed in this study. The first twenty-five years after World War II were ones of tremendous economic expansion, and businesses in many industrial nations, though less so in Great Britain, benefited from the expansion of international trade. Big businesses usually profited more than smaller concerns. Consumer demand for large numbers of standardized goods spurred the development of big, efficient factories devoted to long production runs; and big businesses usually owned and operated those factories. As a result, in

the United States the distinction between center and peripheral firms broadened; in Japan the dual economy developed apace; and in Great Britain a meaningful difference between large and small firms grew up.

However, marked differences continued to separate businesses in the different lands. As in the past, many Japanese firms (and, to some extent, German companies as well) operated as parts of constellations of businesses and did not adopt decentralized management. In general, large American companies, run by executives increasingly trained in finance and marketing rather than in operations, had more levels of management than their counterparts elsewhere. In the immediate postwar decades these characteristics of American management did not hurt the companies. However, as Japan and West Germany recovered from the devastation of World War II and as global competition heated up in the 1970s and 1980s, those layers of management and the lack of knowledge about what was taking place on the factory floor acted as drags on American firms, as they too often failed to respond quickly enough to changes in the international business situation.

SUGGESTED READINGS

Much has been written about global postwar reconstruction. Important aspects of it may be examined in William Borden, *The Pacific Alliance: United States Foreign Economic Policy and Japanese Trade Recovery, 1947–1955* (Madison: University of Wisconsin Press, 1984); Alfred E. Eckes, Jr., *A Search for Solvency: Bretton Woods and the International Monetary System, 1941–1971* (Austin: University of Texas Press, 1975); and Michael Hogan, *The Marshall Plan: America, Britain, and the Reconstruction of Western Europe, 1947–1952* (Cambridge: Cambridge University Press, 1987).

Harold Vatter and John Walker, eds., *History of the U.S. Economy since World War II* (Armonk: M. E. Sharpe, 1996), and Alfred D. Chandler, Jr., "The Competitive Performance of U.S. Industrial Enterprises since the Second World War," *Business History Review* 68 (Spring 1994): 1–72, offer overviews of American economic and business development since 1945. Charles Gilbert, ed., *The Making of a Conglomerate* (Hempstead, New York: Hofstra University Press, 1972), investigates the growth of conglomerates. Harold Geneen, *Managing* (New York: Doubleday, 1984), provides insights into the operations of a large, diversified American multinational. Mira Wilkins, *The*

Maturing of Multinational Enterprise: American Business Abroad from 1914 to 1970 (Cambridge, Mass.: Harvard University Press, 1974), is the standard work on the modern development of American multinationals. Robert M. Collins, *The Business Response to Keynes, 1929–1964* (New York: Columbia University Press, 1981), examines postwar government-business relations. Sandra S. Vance and Roy V. Scott, *Wal-Mart: A History of Sam Walton's Retail Phenomenon* (New York: Twayne Publishers, 1994), provides a valuable look at changes in retailing. David Stebenne, *Arthur Goldberg* (New Haven: Yale University Press, 1996), contains a valuable analysis of the changing nature of labor relations in modern America.

Derek Channon, *The Strategy and Structure of British Enterprise* (Cambridge, Mass.: Harvard University Press, 1973), and S. J. Prais, *The Evolution of Giant Firms in Britain* (Cambridge: Cambridge University Press, 1976), are important overviews of British businesses after World War II. Ronald Dore, *British Factory-Japanese Factory: The Origins of National Diversity in Industrial Relations* (Berkeley: University of California Press, 1973), examines factory management and labor relations. David Vogel, *National Styles of Regulation: Environmental Policy in Great Britain and the United States* (Ithaca: Cornell University Press, 1986), is comparative. Geoffrey Jones and Frances Bostock, "U.S. Multinationals in British Manufacturing before 1962," *Business History Review* 70 (Summer 1996): 207–56, is valuable.

Takafusa Nakamura, *The Postwar Japanese Economy: Its Development and Structure* (Tokyo: University of Tokyo Press, 1980), surveys economic changes occurring in postwar Japan. Chalmers Johnson, *MITI and the Japanese Miracle: The Growth of Economic Policy, 1925–1975* (Stanford: Stanford University Press, 1982), focuses on the roles government played in Japan's economic advance. On the business firm and its management, see Hiroshi Mannari, *The Japanese Business Leaders* (Tokyo: University of Tokyo Press, 1974); Michael Cusumano, *The Japanese Automobile Industry: Technology & Management at Nissan and Toyota* (Cambridge, Mass.: Harvard University Press, 1985); Thomas R. H. Havens, *Architects of Affluence: The Tsutsumi Family and the Seibu-Saison Enterprises in Twentieth-Century Japan* (Cambridge, Mass.: Harvard University Press, 1994); Sol Sanders, *Honda: The Man and His Machines* (Tokyo: Charles E. Tuttle, 1975); Akira Sueno, *Entrepreneur & Gentleman: A Case History of a Japanese Company* (Tokyo: Charles E. Tuttle, 1977), an autobiography; and Terutomo Ozawa, *Multinationalism, Japanese Style*

(Princeton: Princeton University Press, 1979). Koji Taira, *Economic Development & the Labor Market in Japan* (New York: Columbia University Press, 1970), remains useful on labor developments. Satoshi Kamata, *Japan in the Passing Lane* (New York: Pantheon, 1982), examines the lives of assembly-line workers at Toyota.

8 [Toward the Twenty-First Century

The stable international economic system created by the Bretton Woods Agreement and the GATT eroded from the early 1970s. In 1971 President Richard Nixon, responding to pressures on the American economy and the American dollar, suspended the convertibility of the dollar into gold and other reserve requirements (this convertibility had been one of the main underpinnings of the Bretton Woods Agreement). Currency exchange rates were (and are) no longer tied to any fixed standard. The rates "float" with regard to each other according to the values placed upon them by market forces. Two years later the Organization of Petroleum Exporting Countries began rapidly increasing oil prices, an action that further disrupted the international economic situation, as did a similar move in 1979. Major recessions in the early 1970s, early 1980s, and early 1990s further upset longstanding ways of doing business, challenging executives to alter their practices. So did increased international competition, made possible in part by transportation and communication advances—from jumbo jet airliners to computers. For businesses across the world the 1970s, 1980s, and 1990s were very unstable decades.

Restructuring, of both individual firms and national economies, became the watchword, as business and political leaders responded to the challenges of change. The British business system, which had shown signs of weakness in earlier years, slumped in the 1970s and 1980s, but showed some signs of recovery in the 1990s. The American business system no longer grew at the rapid rates of earlier times and presented a spectacle of mixed strengths and weaknesses to observers. Parts of the Japanese business system were caught up in the development of what became known as a bubble economy in the 1980s,

a speculative boom that crashed in the early 1990s. Clearly, as businesses in different nations moved toward the twenty-first century, global economic relocations were occurring and could be expected to continue into the future.

CHANGES IN AMERICAN BUSINESS

By the late 1970s most Americans recognized that their nation faced economic problems and, more specifically, that many American businesses were not faring well in international competition. Events in the 1980s reinforced doubts Americans had about their nation's economy. A sharp recession in the early 1980s — a high rate of unemployment coupled with inflation — troubled Americans. Trade imbalances clouded America's economic horizon. The most basic problem Americans faced was a decline in the competitiveness of their nation's businesses, especially manufacturing firms, in the international marketplace. After boasting trade surpluses through 1968, the United States developed an unfavorable balance of trade, a trade deficit amounting to $69 billion in 1983 and over $150 billion by 1985. These developments, along with the general uncertainty of the international economic situation, led to a restructuring of American business.

Problems in Management and Industrial Relations

As we have seen, many foreigners greatly admired American business management in the 1950s and 1960s. The British imported the American concept of decentralized management, and the Japanese imported American ideas about quality controls. Yet, this admiration was partly misplaced. Problems in managerial decision making lay at the heart of the decline in the competitiveness of American business. A basic difficulty was that too much of American industry was obsolete, for businesses failed to reinvest enough of their earnings in capital improvements. Moreover, when capital improvements were made, they were too often made in a hasty, add-on manner that failed to increase the overall production efficiency of the plants. Rather than building new, efficient factories from the ground up, business leaders added onto existing, often inefficient installations.

The shortsightedness of American executives was a major factor in the lack of effective capital investments. Several reasons accounted for their

short-run point of view. One was their education. More and more business leaders were graduates of university schools of business administration, and the case method of instruction employed by most of the schools emphasized short-term solutions to business problems. The nature of the management of American corporations reinforced the short-term approach to decision making. With the divorce of ownership from management in most large American companies, most executives came to have less of a personal stake in the long-term success of their companies than in earlier times. Since advancement within their companies often depended upon tangible evidence that their firms were performing well in the immediate present, executives stressed maintaining or raising profits, dividends, and stock prices every quarter. They focused increasingly on short-term financial gain rather than sustained economic growth.

Reinforcing this outlook was the proliferation of levels of management in America's large multidivisional firms. Companies developed too many layers of management, making it difficult for them to respond quickly to changes occurring in their markets and their general economic environments. In the early 1970s General Motors had twenty major levels of management, compared to nine at Toyota. The growth in management levels divorced managers from the factory floor and placed a premium on managing by the numbers— that is, using financial reports as the way to run companies. Managers trained in finance, not operations, came to the fore.

The vulnerability of most large American corporations to hostile takeovers by other firms also led corporate managers to take shortsighted actions. Officers were forced to spend much of their time and effort fending off unwanted takeover bids. Some 143 of the largest 500 industrial firms in the United States were acquired by other companies in the 1980s, and the total value of business assets changing hands in America during the decade came to $1.3 trillion. In addition to consuming the time of executives, this situation led to the deferring of needed expenditures for capital improvements and research and development. The funds too often went instead to higher dividend payments to keep stockholders happy so that they would not sell out to corporate raiders.

Conflict between management and labor added to the problems American business faced. Management worried that a lack of dedication of workers to their companies and jobs was eroding labor productivity and thus business profits. There were grounds for concern. After rising at an average annual

rate of 3.4 percent between 1947 and 1964, the productivity of workers in American manufacturing increased only 2 percent per year between 1965 and 1975, and just 1 percent annually during the years 1976 through 1978. In 1979 labor productivity fell by 0.9 percent, and it dipped another 0.3 percent in the following year. (By way of contrast, the productivity of industrial workers in Japan climbed an average 7.4 percent annually between 1947 and 1980.) However, to assert, as some observers of the American scene did, that the cause for the decline in American labor productivity was simply that workers lacked pride in their jobs and so did not work hard enough missed a crucial point: the failure of management to modernize factories meant that workers often had inefficient equipment with which to work. By 1980, for example, Japanese factories used 10,000 robots to speed their work processes, but American plants employed only 3,000.

Nowhere were the differences in the productivity between American and Japanese workers more pronounced than in basic heavy industry. In the early 1980s, for instance, Japanese companies could produce a subcompact car for about $2,000 less than their American rivals. Part of this difference was due to lower wages in Japan, but most of it resulted from the greater productivity of Japanese workers. A Japanese subcompact car could be assembled in fourteen worker-hours, while a similar American car required thirty-three.

The Restructuring of American Business: BFGoodrich

In response to the challenges they faced, American firms, especially those in manufacturing, restructured their operations. Restructuring involved a search for profits, which, in turn, led to an increased focus on what business executives considered the core capabilities of their corporations. But it involved still more. Business leaders often sought to make their firms more entrepreneurial in their management and more flexible in their production methods, allowing them to move away from long, standardized production runs of homogeneous products in favor of making smaller batches of specialty products for niche markets.

BFGoodrich—for decades one of America's leading tiremakers and a leading producer, as well, of industrial rubber products and goods made of polyvinyl chloride (PVC)—was one of the many industrial companies to restructure its operations. By the late 1960s and early 1970s Goodrich faced greatly

increased domestic and foreign competition in its two major product lines, commodity PVC goods (PVC is a type of plastic used to make goods ranging from house siding to water pipes) and car tires, setting the stage for its transformation. Between 1971 and 1995 BFGoodrich sold over $2 billion worth of its assets, while making about $1 billion worth of acquisitions (the difference went mainly to pay off huge debts incurred primarily in the 1980s).

The restructuring of BFGoodrich entailed basic changes in the firm's product lines. Goodrich found itself unable to compete in tires and rubber products, for its plants were obsolete compared to those of other firms, a legacy going back to the 1920s. Goodrich left the making of original equipment tires in 1982 and the making of replacement tires (through a joint-venture with Uniroyal) in 1987. Michelin later bought what was left of this venture. For decades Goodrich's industrial rubber operations, located in an out-of-date hodgepodge of buildings in Akron, Ohio, had also been a major problem, often losing tens of millions of dollars a year. In the mid-1980s Goodrich either sold or closed most of them. In the 1970s and early 1980s Goodrich was America's leading producer of PVC, but in the early 1980s Goodrich ran into major problems in trying to control the raw materials and intermediates that go into the manufacture of PVC. Faced with financial problems and growing foreign competition in the making of commodity PVC, Goodrich sought in the late 1980s and early 1990s to move into specialty, higher-margin PVC products, but this attempt only partly succeeded. In 1993 Goodrich sold nearly all of its PVC operations.

What did BFGoodrich become? By the mid-1990s Goodrich consisted of two loosely related divisions, specialty chemicals and aerospace. Both had histories at Goodrich dating back to the 1910s and 1920s but neither became really important until the 1980s. Beginning in the mid-1980s Goodrich's executives poured hundreds of millions of dollars into acquisitions to expand aerospace operations. They tended, by contrast, to develop specialty chemicals more by internal growth. Goodrich, thus, eschewed the making of commodity products for large homogeneous markets. Instead, the company came to make specialty products for niche markets, from carbon brakes for America's space shuttle to a wide range of chemical adhesives (and in the case of aerospace, Goodrich provided repair and maintenance services as well).

BFGoodrich also changed its management. From centralized management it moved to decentralized management. Corporate executives pushed

extensive authority over operations far down the managerial line. Layers of management were shed. By 1996 BFGoodrich consisted of several dozen almost independent business units (or profit centers) set up around products only loosely controlled by the corporate office. John Ong, the CEO from 1979 through 1995, explained how management worked. "No one is in control of you [the manager of a business unit], or can interfere with you. You can do the r & d the way you want, operate your plants the way you want, do marketing the way you want, do your own management hiring and firing, do your own capital spending (within generous limits). You are operating your business almost as if you owned it." * These actions worked. While reporting mainly losses or only small profits in the 1980s, Goodrich emerged as quite a profitable concern in the mid-1990s.

Restructuring, such as that conducted at BFGoodrich, appears to have worked. Large industrial companies, which had been losing ground to their smaller counterparts, grew in relative importance after 1991. Corporate restructuring made American manufacturers more efficient. Manufacturing productivity, as measured by output per worker-hour, rose 30 percent in the United States between 1983 and 1990—far ahead of the 13 percent gain in Canada or the 19 percent increase in Germany, and not far behind the 35 percent rise in Japan.

Restructuring affected America's workers. Between 1979 and 1996 the United States witnessed a net increase of 27 million jobs, enough to provide work for all of those laid off as a result of corporate restructuring and downsizing and all new job-seekers. However, the availability of jobs hid a growing lack of job security. One-third of all households had a family member who was laid off, and 40 percent more knew of a relative, friend, or neighbor who lost a job. Moreover, while most found another job, only about one-third found a new job that paid as well as the one lost. Between 1973 and 1990 real hourly wages for nonsupervisory workers (about two-thirds of the nation's workforce) dropped 12 percent, before recovering a bit in the 1990s.

Company executives, like their workers, found restructuring unsettling. It became harder to motivate workers in such activities as quality control, when those workers feared they might soon be downsized out of their jobs. More-

* Mansel Blackford, "Small Business in America: An Historical Overview," paper presented at the International Conference on Business History (the Fuji Conference), Hakone, Japan, 5–8 January 1997, 28.

over, as companies let middle managers go, essential work, such as accounting, sometimes did not get done. Clearly, there were limits to how far corporate downsizing and restructuring could go without injuring a company's
capabilities.

Small Businesses in a Restructured Economy

Despite an apparent loss in importance relative to that of big business in
the 1990s, small business remained a significant segment of America's industrial economy. As in earlier decades, small firms proved adept at exploiting
niche markets with specialized products based on short production runs. By
the 1970s and 1980s, however, perhaps more was involved. Some observers
have suggested that the ability of small businesses to react quickly to alterations in markets and fluctuating exchange rates in an increasingly complex
international economy helped explain their continuing significance. Then,
too, the use of computers in computer-aided design, engineering, and manufacturing allowed small, independent firms to perform tasks that only larger
businesses could earlier accomplish, thus allowing more direct competition
with their larger counterparts. What developed in some fields in the 1970s
through the 1990s were congeries of small industrial firms, similar perhaps
to the nineteenth-century textile makers in Philadelphia or the independent
steel mills in Pittsburgh in the same period. Often located near each other
in specific locales, the small firms supported each other and in some fields
offered a viable alternative to mass production by big businesses.

High technology firms in California's Silicon Valley just south of San
Francisco provided a case in point. Here few large vertically integrated companies existed. Instead, most of the area's makers of computer hardware and
software, producers of communications equipment, and manufacturers of
defense products were smaller firms that consciously avoided vertical integration. Instead of trying to internalize all facets of their companies' work in
single firms, Silicon Valley entrepreneurs got ahead by forming a large, informal, and very flexible network of linked—but independent—companies.
Companies worked very closely with suppliers of components, with venture
capitalists, and with specialized legal and marketing consultants. Workers
moving from job to job and company to company transferred information
across firm boundaries. Located in one area, this agglomeration of many

mainly small companies allowed producers to reap economies of scale without forming big businesses.

The system established in the Silicon Valley was a formula for business success. By the close of the 1970s the Silicon Valley possessed nearly 3,000 electronics firms, 70 percent of which had fewer than 10 employees and 85 percent of which had fewer than 100. These firms faced a crisis in the mid-1980s, as they lost most of the market for semiconductor memories to Japanese companies. However, as a mark of their flexibility and resilience, most Silicon Valley firms recovered later in the decade as producers of specialized, high-value-added, complex electronics goods. As in the 1970s, most of these companies were smaller firms, which avoided vertical integration.

A hotly debated topic rife with consequences for policy-makers was the issue of the roles small businesses played in job creation in modern America. While the Silicon Valley firms certainly created jobs—they employed 270,000 by 1990—not all small businesses were as important in this respect. The best evidence on this controversial topic does not support the notion that small firms were outstanding as engines of growth, at least in manufacturing. Between 1972 and 1988 plants with at least 100 employees accounted for two-thirds of job creation in America. Small manufacturers were no better than their larger counterparts in *net* job creation. Small firms were better at *gross* job creation, but small firms also went out of existence more frequently than large companies, thus destroying more jobs.

Small businesses did not do particularly well in sales or services in the 1990s, either. Larger companies such as Wal-Mart, K-Mart, Sears, Metro International, and Daiei increased their market shares in the United States and elsewhere. Between 1987 and 1993 the market share of America's top ten supermarkets rose from about 23 percent to nearly 30 percent, the market share of the top ten specialized clothing chains rose from about 24 percent to 30 percent, the share of the top ten home improvement chains rose from about 17 percent to about 27 percent, and the top ten department store groups increased their market share from about 42 percent to about 53 percent. In services, nationwide chains and groupings of banks, insurance companies, and real estate firms, often using computers to link themselves together, grew in importance.

Whether in manufacturing or in sales and services, the trend in America's capitalistic economic system seemed to be toward concentration and the

Banc One Service Center, Columbus, Ohio, in 1987. Service industries became increasingly important to the American economy in the 1970s and 1980s. (Courtesy of Johanna White, Bank One Corporation)

growth of oligopolies. True, small firms remained significant, but mainly as niche players. Larger companies, using capabilities in management, production, and sales, continued—especially in the 1990s—to move ahead in importance.

Government: Deregulation

Restructuring reached into the realm of government-business relations. Some observers of American business believed that the deregulation of business by the federal government would spur economic growth and business development. Begun by President Jimmy Carter and continued by President Ronald Reagan, deregulation aimed at removing what many viewed as excessive federal government regulations from a wide variety of industries, ranging from electric utilities to communications. What occurred in transportation and banking illustrates well the many twists and turns to deregulation.

Transportation industries were the first to experience the full force of deregulation. The federal government, through the Civil Aeronautics Board

(CAB), had regulated the airline industry since the 1930s, controlling both the fares that carriers could charge and the routes the airlines could fly. The reform of the airline industry began in 1976, when the CAB started to ease restrictions on routes and fares. Then the Airline Deregulation Act of 1978 called for the dissolution of the CAB over a six-year period, with free entry of airline companies into routes of their choosing at fares determined by competition. After deregulating the airlines, Congress turned to trucks and railroads in 1980. Economists had complained that the regulation of the trucking industry since 1935 by the Interstate Commerce Commission had resulted in gross inefficiencies. In 1980 Congress made it easier to enter the trucking business and allowed competitive forces to determine rates. Similarly, the Rail Act of 1980 allowed rail executives much greater flexibility in charting the course of their firms.

Deregulation profoundly affected banking. Deregulation combined with economic circumstances to bring about unexpected and unwanted changes in the nation's savings and loan industry. The Depository Institutions Deregulation and Monetary Control Act of 1980 allowed various types of financial institutions to compete with one another for deposits and loans. Savings and loan institutions, which had traditionally made long-term loans to homeowners, entered new fields. Seeking higher returns on their loans than could be obtained in the residential housing field, they made loans for real estate development and construction, which carried a high degree of risk. Inexperienced in these fields, and sometimes engaging in fraudulent activities, savings and loan executives often found themselves overextended. The failure of federal agencies to monitor the activities of the thrift institutions adequately made the problem worse. As a result, by 1989 some 500 of the nation's 3,000 savings and loan banks were insolvent, and Americans faced a bill of over $500 billion to protect depositors. That year Congress passed the Financial Institutions Reform, Recovery and Enforcement Act to bail out the failed thrift banks and, in effect, to reregulate the industry.

As the 1990s come to a close, it is too early to discern clearly all of the effects of deregulation on the United States, but it is clear that some of those effects will be unexpected, as in the failure of the many savings and loan institutions. While supporters of deregulation touted it for increasing the efficiency of the American economy and for generating economic growth and

jobs, critics of deregulation viewed it as a government retreat from responsibility for the public welfare.

BRITISH BUSINESS: DECLINE AND REVIVAL

The decline of British business was much in the news during the 1970s and 1980s, as Americans, worried about their own nation's economic troubles, feared that the United States might catch what they called the British disease. British industry did decline relative to that of other nations. Great Britain accounted for 22 percent of the world's exports of manufactured goods in 1952, but only 11 percent by 1969, and a scant 6.8 percent in 1980. In 1983, for the first time since the start of the Industrial Revolution, Great Britain imported industrial goods greater in value than those she exported.

Still, several points need to be observed. First, this decline was only *relative* to what was occurring in other nations; the British economy continued to grow in the 1970s and 1980s. In fact, Great Britain's real Gross Domestic Product (GDP) per capita more than tripled between 1900 and 1984, and real disposable income per capita rose 46 percent between 1971 and 1992. By the 1980s nearly all households had refrigerators, washing machines, and color televisions. Car ownership stood at 224 per 1,000 people in 1971, but had risen to 380 in 1995. By way of contrast, even bicycles had been luxury items in the late nineteenth century. Second, some parts of Britain's business system continued to do very well during these decades, showing no signs of decline. Moreover, by the 1990s some segments of the British economy that had earlier slumped, including some areas of heavy industry, were rebounding.

Business Problems

Business and economic problems were, perhaps, most apparent in the 1970s. British management remained parochial, with a lack of breadth and an unwillingness to take risks. This situation was not due to the more personal nature of British management than what prevailed in the United states (at any rate, by the 1980s families were no longer very important in the management of the largest British companies). Ironically, the adoption of decentralized management methods from the United States, with their many layers of

managers and emphasis on financial reporting, contributed to the rigidity of some British firms.

Rigidities showed up in both marketing and manufacturing. Their conservatism led British executives to place too much emphasis upon trying to sell in Britain's former colonial markets, while not paying enough attention to potentially richer markets elsewhere. Some British businesses scored marketing successes—Lipton, Boots (in pharmaceutical products), and W. H. Smiths (also in drugs)—and performed well. By and large, however, effective marketing was limited to those sectors of the British economy already immune to foreign competition or was confined to industries that contributed little to employment or foreign trade. Thus, woolens and bicycles were marketed more effectively than cotton goods or automobiles. In making goods British business leaders tolerated poor production efficiencies, never fully adjusting their methods to the needs of large national and international markets as well as did their American and Japanese competitors.

Germany and France caught up with and then surpassed Great Britain in manufacturing output per person hour between 1951 and 1979, and throughout these years the United States led the Western European nations. By 1988 Great Britain still lagged the other nations but had begun to lessen the gap.

Britain's system of education continued to be a drag on business. As in the past, the British tended to elevate the practical man, who could learn on the job, at a time when the development of new science-based industries made this approach even less realistic than it had been earlier. Great Britain had a far lower proportion of her population enrolled in places of higher learning than did the United States. Engineering education, stressed at many of America's state-supported land grant universities, too often received scant attention in Great Britain. Lying behind the conservatism of many British businesses—their reluctance to adopt new production processes and to move into new products—was the poor education of their workers and managers. In the mid- and late 1970s, 60 percent of German workers, but a scant 30 percent of British workers, possessed intermediate or vocational qualifications (that is, the equivalent of an apprenticeship or full secretarial training). In the 1980s, 85 percent of the senior managers in America and Japan held college degrees, but only 25 percent did in Britain. Few of those British managers holding degrees did so in engineering. One leading scholar of Britain's decline has re-

cently concluded that "the enduring failure of the British educational system to supply an adequate number of trained people to each occupational level produced and then sustained a vicious cycle of uncompetitive products, processes, and personnel. Lacking higher education, top officials have been less attuned to innovations in products and production methods than executives abroad and less appreciative of their potential." *

Some Continuing Successes

Of course, not all British industrial businesses were in trouble, even in the 1970s. Pharmaceutical companies and makers of food and drink remained world leaders. Through its invention and development of Zantac, an anti-ulcer drug, Glaxo emerged as Great Britain's largest company in terms of market capitalization by 1992. Glaxo found ways to reduce the time needed to bring drugs to market and succeeded in marketing them well. Nor was Glaxo alone; SmithKline, Wellcome, and other pharmaceutical companies performed ably on the world stage. In Glaxo's case the entrepreneurial orientation of its CEO, Paul Girolami, the competitive environment resulting from American drug companies operating in Britain, and a market provided by Britain's National Health Service contributed to the success of the firm.

Beyond manufacturing, some businesses in service industries did well. Great Britain lost ground relative to other nations in the provision of private services—freight, insurance, and transportation—in which the nation had once excelled. Between 1955 and 1976 Britain's share of international trade in private services dropped from 40 percent to just 15 percent. Nonetheless, even amidst this gloomy picture there were bright spots. City of London financial enterprises, long preeminent in the international equity, bond, and foreign exchange markets, expanded their roles worldwide. The deregulation of Britain's financial sector in what was dubbed the Big Bang of 1986 stimulated competition. For the first time in decades, merchant bankers, stockbrokers, and insurance companies could cross over financial lines to compete with one another.

---

* Michael Dintenfass, *The Decline of Industrial Britain* (London: Routledge, 1992), 37–38.

Governmental Actions: The Thatcher Revolution

Despite some rays of success and hope, Great Britain's general economic position was not promising in the 1970s. In 1976 the nation had to borrow a large sum from the International Monetary Fund to stay solvent, a step usually taken only by third-world nations. In addition to business problems, there were difficulties emanating from government actions. Most basically, the expansion of the welfare state after World War II was more than Great Britain could afford, given the nation's existing structure of property relations, class, and race. According to the Treasury, public spending took 60 percent of Britain's GDP in 1976 (these figures were later shown to be 10 percent too high, but even 50 percent of GDP was a large proportion).

Yet, it long remained impossible politically to alter the welfare state much. Edward Heath, the leader of the Conservatives during the 1960s and early 1970s, was one of the relatively few British politicians who clearly saw the need for alterations. His party won a surprise victory in 1970, and as prime minister Heath tried to limit welfare growth, even at the expense of cutting aid to many less fortunate members of British society. He failed. Soon viewed as a divisive figure, Heath quickly found most of his program in tatters, even before the Conservatives were swept out of office by the Labour Party in 1973–74. Harold Wilson and James Callaghan, the Labour Party leaders, promoted social harmony and economic stabilization more than limiting the state's role in providing welfare.

A sustained new approach began when the Conservatives, led by Margaret Thatcher, returned to power in the late 1970s. Thatcher was an outsider to the inner circles of political and economic power in Great Britain, just the sort of person to shake things up. Thatcher grew up in the small town of Grantham located in Lincolnshire in the Midlands, not in London; she was the daughter of a grocer, not a political or business leader; and she was a Methodist rather than an Anglican. She attended grammar school on a county scholarship and went on to Oxford where she studied chemistry, which was unusual for women then. After graduation, she worked as a research chemist and entered the bar. Drawn to politics, Thatcher became the leader of the Conservatives in 1975 and prime minister with a Conservative victory in 1979, the post she held until stepping down in favor of John Major, another Conservative, in 1990.

Thatcher wanted, above all, to make the British economy and British business more competitive in the capitalistic international marketplace. During the decade she was in power, Thatcher sought to attain this end through three interrelated steps. She reduced taxes while at the same time limiting inflation. Her preoccupation with lowering taxes and inflation marked a real shift in public policy, which earlier had stressed ending unemployment. Hit by problems beyond her immediate control in the early 1980s, Thatcher hung on grimly to her policies; and by 1983 they had borne fruit, with both inflation and unemployment down.

Thatcher also sought to check the power of Britain's trade unions, arguing that the demands of their members for hefty wage hikes contributed to inflation and priced British goods out of international markets. Added to these difficulties was the problem of work stoppages. Some 2.3 million workdays were lost to stoppages in 1964–67, and a whopping 6.8 million days in 1969 alone. Since many of the strikes and stoppages took place in nationalized businesses, they directly involved the government. Legislation passed by Parliament in 1980 and 1982 placed limits on union activities, including limits of their right to strike. Even more significant in signaling a new direction was the settlement of a nationwide coal strike in 1985 (coal was a nationalized industry at the time) on terms more favorable to the government than the unions. Most important in the long term, and very troubling to trade union leaders, was that a shrinking proportion of Britain's industrial workers were covered by collective-bargaining agreements: over 70 percent in the early 1980s, but just over 50 percent by 1990. (Of course, Thatcher's policies were not the only reasons for the decline of trade unions. As industrial businesses, in which unions were heavily entrenched, became less important to Britain's economy, and service businesses, which were much less unionized, grew in significance, unions declined in importance.)

Finally, Thatcher moved to end government ownership of Britain's many nationalized industries, or, as they were often called, public industries. In the late 1970s nationalized industries accounted for 10 percent of Britain's industrial output and employed 1.75 million workers. Many were privatized by their sale via stock market flotations: British Aerospace and Cable and Wireless in 1981, National Freight in 1983, Jaguar and British Telecom in 1984. Then came a host of others in the mid- and late 1980s: British Gas, British Airways, Rolls-Royce, British Airports Authority, the British Steel Corpora-

tion, and British Coal. While spurring competition and often contributing to economic revival, privatization came at a price. Often the government sold its businesses for a pittance of their actual value. For instance, British Gas was sold for 6 billion pounds, when, according to one estimate, it was worth 16 billion pounds. In addition, privatization often hurt workers. Some lost their jobs as the new private businesses downsized their workforces, and others found their unions under attack by the new private managers of the companies.

Big Business and Small Business in British Industry

What occurred in the British steel industry typified some of the changes going on in that nation's heavy industry. As we saw in Chapter 6, the British steel industry faced major problems in the interwar years. Postwar difficulties made a bad situation worse. There can be no doubt that the British steel industry—and specifically the British Steel Corporation (BSC), which was formed as a nationalized company in 1967 by the merger of fourteen companies—suffered from major deficiencies. The BSC lost money every year between 1975 and 1981, some $3.6 billion in 1980 alone. In the same years, the number of employees fell from 250,000 to 110,000, 40,000 of whom were in nonsteel activities. The BSC's share of the British steel market dropped to only 50 percent, due to the inroads of both foreign importers and small, private British mini-mills.

The conservatism of the steelmakers continued, ensuring that most plants and companies would fall behind their foreign competitors. Even after the BSC was formed in 1967, few steps were taken to upgrade facilities. Only in 1977 were twelve hopelessly antiquated plants finally closed. At a time when the world steel industry was becoming more competitive as a result of the entrance of Japan and third-world nations, this was not an adequate response.

The future of the BSC became brighter when Ian MacGregor, an American (the former president of Amax of Connecticut), became chairman in 1980. MacGregor took several actions to revive the BSC. With the advice of McKinsey & Co., MacGregor put in place decentralized management. The BSC was broken up into units based on product lines—much as was being done at BFGoodrich at about the same time—and managers were given substantial responsibilities in producing and marketing their products, a step that restored management morale. MacGregor also slimmed down the BSC, cost-

ing thousands of workers their jobs and earning MacGregor the nickname Mac the Knife. At the same time, MacGregor sought, with some success, to increase labor productivity. He was aided by the British government, which poured a massive amount of funds into the BSC to improve its operations. MacGregor also worked out a fairly effective bonus system with the sixteen unions at the BSC. MacGregor even became a salesman for the BSC's products. Among other things, he persuaded Japanese companies to limit their imports into Great Britain. And, at home he took on the mini-mills. Although not a fully successful company even in the 1990s, the BSC—now privately owned—was in much better shape than it was a decade earlier, reporting profits in 1993 and 1994.

Into the 1970s British industry continued its march toward concentration. Large firms like the BSC reigned supreme. The share of manufacturing output produced by Britain's 100 largest enterprises was 43 percent, almost one-third greater than the share of the 100 largest firms in the United States. British industry's movement toward centralization ended in the 1980s and 1990s. Interestingly, the improvement in Britain's industrial productivity relative to other nations during the 1980s coincided with the decline in industrial concentration.

In the 1980s and 1990s smaller firms, in manufacturing and in other fields, became increasingly important to Great Britain's economic health. The restructuring of large companies like the BSC was only part of the story of Britain's partial economic revival. The growth in number of small manufacturers, those with no more than 200 employees, was remarkable: from 71,000 (of a total 75,000 manufacturers in Britain) in 1971 to 133,000 (of a total 135,000) by 1988. In 1971 small manufacturers gave jobs to just 21 percent of Britain's industrial workers, but by 1988 they provided work for 31 percent.

To some extent, the growing importance of small business in manufacturing was replicated in other business fields. In 1979 enterprises with fewer than 500 employees accounted for 57 percent of Britain's private-sector employment; by 1986 their share had risen to 71 percent. Government policies favoring small firms, the spread of public attitudes favoring entrepreneurship, the development of the same flexible manufacturing techniques that helped small industrialists in the United States, the embrace of subcontracting and outsourcing by large manufacturers (similar to what had been occurring in Japan for decades), and the search for employment opportunities by people

out of work in Great Britain contributed to the resurgence of small business. Even so, the overall contribution of small firms to Great Britain's economy remained less than elsewhere. By one estimate, small companies—generally those with no more than 300 employees—accounted for 32 percent of Great Britain's private-sector GDP in the 1980s, compared to 46 percent of West Germany's, 50 percent of the United States', and 60 percent of Japan's.

Even with partial business revival in the 1980s and 1990s, problems continued for the British. While average income rose in the 1970s and 1980s, it was—as in the United States—unevenly distributed. There were winners and losers in Britain's uneven economic growth. The poorest 10 percent of British households suffered from a fall in real income. Those in London and southern England benefited more than those in the industrial North, exacerbating a longstanding socio-economic rift in Great Britain. Job insecurity increased, again as in the United States. In 1970 unemployment stood at about 500,000; by 1994 it was five times as great. In 1966, 84 percent of British men were economically active, by 1993 only 72 percent were. One economic journalist was probably correct when he noted in 1995 that Britain had become a 40:30:30 society. That is, a privileged 40 percent of the population was secure and well-off, another 30 percent was marginalized and insecure, and a final 30 percent hovered between the two extremes.

JAPANESE BUSINESS: ADJUSTMENT TO NEW REALITIES

Japan's businesses, no less than those of Western nations, faced challenges resulting from the uncertainties of the international economy. As we have seen, Japan experienced explosive economic expansion in the 1950s and 1960s. That growth slowed dramatically during the 1970s, impeded especially by the oil shocks of 1973 and 1979, which hit Japan even harder than America and Britain, by the collapse of the Bretton Woods Agreement, in whose wake the prices of Japan's export products soared, and by the opening of Japanese markets to foreign firms. Considerable recovery occurred in the 1980s, leading, in fact, to an overheated boom in several fields, particularly real estate and stocks and bonds—what the Japanese labeled a bubble economy. The bubble economy burst in the early 1990s, and its collapse sent shock waves through Japan's business system, especially through the nation's financial institutions,

many of which had invested heavily in securities and land. Some recovery had occurred by the mid-1990s, but it was spotty and incomplete.

The Role of Government

In the 1970s and 1980s government agencies such as the Ministry of International Trade and Industry (MITI) sought to work closely with business to try to move the Japanese economy into a variety of high-technology fields—biotechnology, computers with artificial intelligence, and so forth—with only limited success. In fact, the Japanese government had difficulty picking industries to target for growth through government nurturing. Japan's industrial policy did not, in many cases, pick winners—with support, on the whole, going to industrial segments that grew the slowest.

However, even as the government tried to continue providing some guidance to the Japanese economy, a countertrend began in the 1970s and 1980s and accelerated in the 1990s. As in the United States and Great Britain, an effort to deregulate the economy started. In the 1980s the government's tobacco monopoly was ended, and Nippon Telegraph and Telephone, Japan's leading communications company, was privatized. In the late 1980s and early 1990s Japan National Railways was broken up into regional railway systems and privatized. In the mid-1990s the Japanese government began deregulating the nation's banking system, allowing different types of banks to compete with one another. More generally, in 1997 Japan's prime minister vowed to remove barriers to competition throughout his nation's economy; and, as one sign that he was serious, he rejected government intervention when the Tokyo stock market slumped precipitously early that year.

Changes in Business Management and Industrial Relations

From the late nineteenth century to the present, many large Japanese businesses, like their American counterparts, developed bureaucratic management. However, there was always also a strong streak of entrepreneurialism in Japanese business, even in big business. In the nineteenth century Yataro Iwasaki was a very strong individual instrumental in the founding and growth of Mitsubishi. Individuals were important in the 1950s and 1960s. Soichiro

Honda, Masaru Ibuka of Sony, and Takashi Mitarai of Canon were a few of the innovative, entrepreneurial business leaders active after World War II. In other words, there were always elements of both individualism and groupism in Japanese business management.

In the mid-1980s the emphasis shifted in the direction of entrepreneurialism. Hit by the same global economic uncertainties that affected their Western counterparts, Japanese companies found that they could not always afford the long time periods required for making decisions by consensus. Too often, fast-moving events overtook slow-moving decisions. In the summer of 1985 the Keizai Doyukai (the Japan Committee for Economic Development), whose 1,030 members were top managers in major Japanese firms, issued a report calling for the adoption of less bureaucratic, more flexible types of management styles and structures. The Japanese even coined a term to describe the problems they saw their companies as facing: *daikigyo-byo*, or large enterprise disease.

Some managers took steps to change the ways in which they ran their firms by stressing the use of small management and work groups that could respond quickly to alterations in a company's environment. They simplified their management structures, eliminating a multiplicity of divisions and sections, much as was happening at BFGoodrich and the BSC. The Recruit Company (a firm in publishing, leisure businesses, and hotel management), the Osaka Gas Company, Honda Motors, and Nippon Steel were among those experimenting with new management methods. As they altered their management methods, companies slimmed down by shedding surplus middle managers, in a manner similar to what was occurring in American and British firms. Lifetime employment was no longer a certainty for managers, not even for those in big businesses. Increasingly, large companies forced white-collar workers who had been passed over for promotion to take early retirement or to accept positions found for them with smaller firms, often with a large reduction in pay.

Relationships between companies, especially those composing keiretsu groupings, also changed. The tight linkages so characteristic of big businesses in the 1950s and 1960s became attenuated in the face of growing competition and instability. Interlocking stock ownership between companies belonging to the same keiretsu became less common. By the same token, keiretsu banks loaned a higher and higher proportion of their funds to firms outside of the keiretsu; and firms seeking the lowest interest rates on loans went far afield to

Small businesses, even handicraft businesses such as basketmaking, were important in Japan in the 1980s. (Author's collection)

secure those loans. Stockholder loyalty to companies lessened, and corporate takeovers — even unfriendly ones — began.

Small businesses remained, as in earlier times, a significant part of Japan's business system and, as in Great Britain, may have increased somewhat in importance. Small-scale firms (those with no more than twenty employees) composed 78 percent of Japan's companies in 1987 and gave work to about 31 percent of the nation's employees. Small-scale businesses accounted for 86 percent of Japan's industrial companies in 1972 and 87 percent in 1986. Squeezed by larger companies anxious to cut costs, many smaller manufacturers sought to escape from unremunerative subcontracting arrangements by striking out on their own as truly independent firms. Small firms were also important in nonmanufacturing fields. They rose from 79 percent of Japan's retail outlets in 1972 to 84 percent in 1986, but during the same years they dropped from 78 percent of the nation's service businesses to just 73 percent. (Unfortunately, it is difficult to get reliable figures on the market shares of small firms. However, it would appear that small firms saw their market shares decline.)

Many of the same factors that changed business management altered indus-

trial relations. The economic slowdowns, combined with an aging of their workforces, led many company managers to rethink their systems of labor relations. Many large industrial companies switched to what the Japanese called a modified seniority wage system. In this arrangement, wages were determined by the function a person performed on the job as well as by seniority. By the mid-1980s over half of Japan's large manufacturing companies had adopted such a wage system. Companies also hired more and more temporary workers, especially women, who were not part of the same systems of industrial relations as permanent workers. As much as 10 percent, and sometimes even more, of a big business's workforce became composed of these temporaries. In addition, companies offered early retirement plans and transfers to other firms, often their subcontractors. Japanese managers feared that the aging of their workers would increase the wages their companies would have to pay and would prevent the movement of young people with fresh ideas into positions of authority.

Continuities in Japanese Business

However, for all of these changes in Japanese business management, there were many elements of continuity. Most basic was the outlook of Japanese executives. As has often been noted by foreign observers, Japanese business leaders have taken a long-run point of view toward their business affairs. Whether working for entrepreneurial or bureaucratic companies, the managers were interested in more than short-term profitability.

This attitude manifested itself in the sense of mission that many Japanese companies still possessed in the 1980s and 1990s. Most large companies had published statements of mission, and their managers were well versed in what their goals were. The statements of mission often stressed the importance of service. Mazda's stated mission, for example, was to work for improvements in the lives of its shareholders, employees, customers, suppliers, and sales personnel. It would be tempting, but incorrect, to view such statements as simply hot air. They were not. Japanese companies did emphasize service and high quality in their products, as in the zero defects movement. It was not that Japanese executives ignored profits. Of course they wanted their companies to be profitable. However, they tended to view profits as a natural result of

their long-term approach to business, rather than as something to be sought on a quarterly basis for their own sake.

As in the case of business management, continuity as well as change characterized industrial relations. Hard work and company loyalty did not vanish. Small things indicated their continuance. Work places remained clean—immaculate, in fact—for it was the responsibility of each worker to clean up his or her work area. Workers also usually maintained their own tools and machinery. Factories bristled with banners urging workers on to new, ever-higher levels of productivity and quality. Both workers and management were still proud of the levels of productivity and quality their companies achieved, in stark contrast to the situation in some American manufacturing companies.

The continued dedication of many workers to their jobs and their companies was apparent in their participation in small group activities associated with their firms. Introduced from America after World War II, quality control circles continued to thrive in Japan. In the 1980s and 1990s many companies moved beyond quality control circles to sponsor a much broader range of small group activities designed to involve their workers in nearly every aspect of corporate life. One example of this engagement was readily manifest at Bridgestone's large tiremaking factory just outside of Tokyo (Bridgestone was the world's fourth-largest tiremaker in the mid-1980s, and in the late 1980s it purchased Firestone). Inside one of Bridgestones's huge factory buildings was a beautiful Japanese garden, complete with a placid pond containing multihued carp. The garden was a place of rest and repose surrounded on all sides by massive machinery, an oasis suggested by one of the firm's groups of workers and constructed at company expense.

As this example suggests, corporate concern in Japan for the welfare of workers, the reciprocal worker loyalty to the company, also continued. Most big businesses in manufacturing still maintained a full range of benefits for their permanent employees: housing, medical care, recreational facilities, vacation lodges, clubs of all sorts, and discounts on purchases of company-made products.

INTO THE FUTURE

Several tentative conclusions may be drawn about the future of business in Japan, the United States, and Great Britain. The economic shocks and instabilities of the 1970s, 1980s, and 1990s spurred business restructuring in all three nations, though the pace of change was perhaps slowest in Japan. Executives adjusted their management methods to meet new socio-economic situations developing within their nations and abroad with varying degrees of success. Restructuring involved more than the business firm, for it meant alterations in government-business relations as well. Government regulation of business—and in Great Britain and Japan, government ownership of business—lessened as governments tried to spur business development through the creation of more competitive environments. As is so often the case, far from all of the results of restructuring were predictable, as the international marketplace remained complex and ever changing.

In fact, one of the few things that was predictable was precisely the continued complexity of the global economy. Anyone searching for easy answers to questions about international business was bound to be disappointed. The business systems of Great Britain, the United States, and Japan are not monolithic; nor are their interactions with each other and with the business systems of other nations simple. Moreover, as in the past, businesses have been evolving as their economic, political, and cultural environments have changed and will continue to do so in the twenty-first century—making it necessary to look beyond the individual business firm to understand fully business successes and failures.

SUGGESTED READINGS

Ira Magaziner and Robert Reich, *Minding America's Business* (New York: Vintage, 1982); Thomas Peters and Robert Waterman, Jr., *In Search of Excellence* (New York: Harper & Row, 1982); Michael T. Jacobs, *Short-Term America: The Causes and Cures of Our Business Myopia* (Cambridge, Mass.: Harvard Business School Press, 1991); and Robert L. Locke, *The Collapse of the American Management Mystique* (New York: Oxford University Press, 1996), examine American business from different perspectives. Annalee Sax-

enian, *Regional Competitive Advantage: Culture and Competition in the Silicon Valley and Route 128* (Cambridge, Mass.: Harvard University Press, 1994), and Mansel G. Blackford and K. Austin Kerr, *BFGoodrich: Tradition and Transformation, 1870–1995* (Columbus: The Ohio State University Press, 1996), are useful. Richard H. K. Vietor, *Contrived Competition: Regulation and Deregulation in America* (Cambridge, Mass.: Harvard University Press, 1994), looks at the deregulation of American business through a series of case studies.

Michael Dintenfass, *The Decline of Industrial Britain, 1870–1980* (London: Routledge, 1992), provides a provocative introduction to the many problems afflicting the British business system. Geoffrey Jones, "Great Britain: Big Business, Management, and Competitiveness in Twentieth Century Britain," in *Big Business and the Wealth of Nations*, ed. Alfred D. Chandler, Jr., Franco Amatori, and Takahi Hikino (Cambridge: Cambridge University Press, 1997), is illuminating. Ray Oakey, Roy Rothwell, and Sarah Cooper, *Management of Innovation in High Technology Firms* (New York: Quorum Books, 1988), compares the development of high-technology firms in parts of the United States, Scotland, and England. Charles Dellheim, *The Disenchanted Isles: Mrs. Thatcher's Capitalistic Revolution* (New York: W. W. Norton, 1995), is a balanced examination of the relationships between political and economic changes in postwar Britain. On the role of education, see S. J. Prais, *Productivity, Education, and Training: An International Perspective* (Cambridge: Cambridge University Press, 1995). John Stanworth and Colin Gray, eds., *Bolton 20 Years On: The Small Firm in the 1990s* (London: Paul Chapman Publishing, 1991), surveys the development of small business in Great Britain during the 1970s and 1980s. D. J. Storey, ed., *The Small Firm: An International Survey* (New York: St. Martin's Press, 1983), is a collection of essays on the status of small business and its relation to big business around the world.

Rodney Clark, *The Japanese Company* (New Haven: Yale University Press, 1979); James C. Abegglen and George Stalk, Jr., *Kaisha: The Japanese Corporation* (New York: Basic Books, 1985); and W. Carl Kester, *Japanese Takeovers: The Global Contest for Corporate Control* (Cambridge, Mass.: Harvard Business School Press, 1991), look at Japanese business in the 1970s and 1980s. MITI, Small and Medium Enterprise Agency, *Small Business in Japan, 1988* (Tokyo: MITI, 1988) is an overview. For an excellent case study of small busi-

ness development, see D. H. Whittaker, *Small Firms in the Japanese Economy* (New York: Cambridge University Press, 1997). Sheridan Tatsuno, *The Technopolis Strategy: Japan, High Technology, and the Control of the 21st Century* (New York: Prentice Hall, 1986), offers insights into Japan's high-technology businesses.

Conclusion: Convergence and Divergence in World Business

In the mid-1990s an American firm sought to introduce the drink Snapple, which is very popular in the United States, into the Japanese market. The attempt failed. Part of the problem lay in the outlets through which Snapple was marketed, Seven-Eleven stores. The stores had limited shelf space, and, when Snapple did not immediately catch on with the Japanese public, they took it off their shelves. An even more basic difficulty, however, was cultural. Many Japanese prefer to drink clear liquids and so passed by the opaque Snapple.

And so we conclude this study with a realization that business both shapes its external environment and is shaped by that environment. At no time was that realization clearer than at the close of the twentieth century. Businesses, especially multinational enterprises, affected the lives of people worldwide; but those same businesses were, in turn, affected by the many social, economic, and political environments in which they operated. Among those new environments, growing in importance into the mid-1990s, were regional trading blocs that were coming to influence greatly how business was conducted in some parts of the globe.

THE SPREAD OF MULTINATIONAL ENTERPRISES

During the 1990s multinational enterprises remained, as they had been for a century, agents of change in world business. They spread forms of business organization and business methods from nation to nation. In the 1980s Ford Motors flew some of the foremen and workers from its Mexican plants to Hiroshima. There they were trained in new production methods on Mazda's assembly lines (Ford owned a large share of Mazda), preparatory to introduc-

ing them to Ford's Mexican factories. Yet, even multinationals had to adjust to local environments and cultures to operate effectively. Multinationals were important for all the nations examined in this study, at no time more so than in the 1990s.

Great Britain was still a leading nation in terms of direct foreign investment overseas. In 1990 Britain held 15 percent of the world's outward direct foreign investment (mainly sums invested in overseas industrial plants), second only to the United States, which held 26 percent, and ahead of Japan, with 12 percent, and Germany, which had 9 percent. This continued importance of British businesses in direct foreign investment offered a leading example of British business success. As one business historian has noted, "The British multinational investment must have involved considerable organizational and management skills, or else it could not have been sustained."* Conversely, foreign multinationals operating within Great Britain were important sources of that nation's industrial revival. Japanese makers of cars and electronic goods, along with many American, German, French, and Swedish firms, found it profitable to manufacture a wide variety of goods in British factories for sale in Great Britain and in markets beyond that nation. These MNCs were generally more efficient than their British counterparts — in 1987 they accounted for about 18 percent of the gross value added in British manufacturing, but only about 13 percent of manufacturing employment in Britain.

Similarly, Japanese businesses generally succeeded in transferring their production methods to America, illustrating persuasively that those techniques were not embedded in Japanese culture and society. Japanese firms in the automobile, automotive supply, steel, rubber, and consumer electronics industries transferred their production methods to American transplants. In 1990 companies in these industries owned about half of the 1,275 Japanese plants in America, and those factories employed nearly three-quarters of 300,000 Americans working for Japanese firms in the United States. In the 1980s and 1990s Japanese companies ranging from Honda Motors to Nisshin Steel to Bridgestone Tires built an integrated, self-reinforcing industrial complex in the American Midwest, increasingly including transplanted Japanese subcontractors.

---

*Maurice Kirby and Mary Rose, eds., *Business Enterprise in Modern Britain* (London: Routledge, 1994), 202.

Making cars at Honda of America, Marysville, Ohio. Japanese multinationals stepped up their overseas production in the 1970s and 1980s. (Courtesy of Honda of America Manufacturing, Inc.)

These Japanese transplants succeeded in some of the very industries American businesses exited by putting in place business methods markedly different from those of their less successful American competitors: labor recruitment and payment systems that bound workers to their companies, the use of production teams, the rotation of jobs among workers, the adoption of worker ideas in process and product advances, reliance on just-in-time production systems, and other matters. Even so, as two investigators found in the late 1980s, "the transplant factories are not paradises." * Overwork, repetitive-motion injuries, poor race relations, and other problems plagued the start-up of transplants.

Just as foreigners have invested in the United States, so have Americans invested abroad as part of the development of the post–World War II global economy. A growing American presence in Japan has been part of this over-

---

* Martin Kenney and Richard Florida, *Beyond Mass Production: The Japanese System and Its Transfer to the U.S.* (New York: Oxford University Press, 1993), 263.

seas expansion of American business. Americans who visit Japan are struck by the pervasiveness of familiar corporate names: IBM, Coca-Cola, McDonald's, Kentucky Fried Chicken, to name a few. By 1984 there were 1,000 firms that were either wholly or substantially owned by Americans doing business in Japan, and in that year the largest 200 had gross sales of $44 billion. Even so, much remained undone. In 1984, 80 of the 200 largest American manufacturing and mining companies had no major operations in Japan.

American companies operating with success in Japan in the 1980s were in a wide range of industries. For example, the Japanese drank more Coca-Cola than anyone else in the world, except Americans and Mexicans. Yet, this was only part of Coca-Cola's Japanese business. Altogether, Coca-Cola Japan produced 60 percent of Japan's carbonated beverages. IBM Japan was the number three computer maker in Japan (after Fujitsu and Nippon Electric Company), it employed 16,000 people, and it had annual sales in Japan of $2 billion. McDonald's Japan had sales of over $400 million annually. By the mid-1990s it had over 2,000 outlets in Japan. The Ministry of Education complained that, because of the influence of fast foods, Japanese school children were forgetting how to use chopsticks! Like IBM Japan, some successful United States ventures in Japan are high-technology firms—Yamatake-Honeywell, Yokogawa-Hewlett-Packard, and Texas Instruments, but many are not—Johnson Wax, Yamazaki-Nabisco, and Japan Tupperware.

No single factor led to success for the American companies operating in Japan. Most American companies that ultimately succeeded in Japan were persistent and patient, willing to forgo short-term gains in favor of profits over the long haul. It typically required five to ten years before a profit was earned. Even McDonald's, which took off very quickly, needed three years to break out of the red. Japan Tupperware required three changes in its top management and nine years of experimentation before setting up a successful distribution system. (By the same token, Japanese companies setting up manufacturing operations in America were willing to wait ten years or more before earning profits.) In addition, successful American companies were willing to take risks. Coca-Cola entered Japan in 1946 as a yen company (it was not allowed to convert yen earned in Japan into dollars for repatriation home to America), gambling that it would be allowed to convert its yen to dollars at a later date.

Successful American firms adjusted to the Japanese culture and the Japa-

nese way of doing business. This adjustment sometimes entailed entering Japan as a joint venture with a Japanese company and only later setting up a wholly owned subsidiary. The Japanese partner could smooth the way with banks, government officials, and product distributors. It often meant placing Japanese in positions of power and having just a few Americans on the scene, adopting Japanese as the official company language, using open offices preferred by the Japanese (because they can confer with each other more easily than in work spaces made up of private offices; Texas Instruments and Warner Lambert tore out partitions separating private offices to create open work spaces), and adopting in part the Japanese systems of hiring and keeping employees. However, being Western could help in some situations: college-educated women overlooked by Japanese companies except as temporaries went to work for United States firms in Japan.

THE DEVELOPMENT OF GLOBAL TRADING BLOCS

Even as multinationals seemed to bring businesses and people in different lands closer together, the development of regional trading blocs seemed to put up barriers. While flows of trade, people, and funds across national boundaries within regional blocs were eased, flows across boundaries separating the blocs were restricted. As the 1990s came to a close, the results of the formation of the trading blocs remained uncertain. Would they eventually stimulate free trade worldwide, leading, perhaps, to prosperity for many nations? Or, conversely, would they restrict trade—except for trade among their members—and, perhaps, contribute to growing disparities of national income and wealth? Three trading blocs were of most importance: North America, Europe, and Japan-Asia.

Following World War II, American policy encouraged the economic integration of Western European economies as a way of strengthening the region during the Cold War. Many European leaders began to dream of integration, first in coal and iron production and later in other fields, as a way of ensuring that no Western European nation would ever again have the capability of waging industrialized combat against its neighbors. With the revival by the 1960s of the West German economy and a generally high level of prosperity across the continent, leaders began to consider more ways of effecting economic union, even with a view toward political integration.

The European Community, later renamed the European Union, originally composed of twelve nations, was the result. Members of the Union integrated their markets by ending most tariff barriers in 1992–93, creating the world's largest single unified market, one of 380 million people. Member nations allowed the free movement of goods, people, and capital across national boundaries. Once a product adhered to the rules and regulations of one member nation, it could be sold to all. A major purpose of the formation of the European Union was to protect European nations from foreign competition, whether from America, Japan, or elsewhere; and many American business leaders viewed the European Union as Fortress Europe. By the late 1990s European nations were also moving, though with considerable difficulty, toward the adoption of a single currency.

Meanwhile, the United States set about developing a trading bloc for North America. The North American Free Trade Agreement (NAFTA) began to take shape in 1989, when the United States and Canada signed a Comprehensive Free Trade Agreement and started to lower trade barriers, a process scheduled for completion in 1998. Almost immediately economic benefits appeared to flow as a result of the agreement. Merchandise shipments between the United States and Canada rose 35 percent between 1987 and 1991, and each nation gained jobs as a result. In 1992 the United States and Canada expanded their trade agreement to include Mexico (and other nations were under consideration for membership by the mid-1990s). As trade restrictions eased over time, the three nations—with a total population of about 360 million in the early 1990s—began to form a large unified market for goods and services. By 1992 Mexico was already America's third largest market, after Canada and Japan.

The creation of the NAFTA did not occur without adding to uncertainty in the economies involved, however. American banks and insurance companies, long frozen out of Mexico, looked forward to benefiting from the arrangement. American manufacturing was relocating into Mexico well before the NAFTA to take advantage of the lower wage scales south of the border, and the NAFTA appeared to accelerate that trend. Some American industrial workers saw the NAFTA as a political decision that threatened to erode their job security and standard of living. It was not surprising, then, that organized labor in the United States generally opposed the NAFTA.

Reacting to the formation of the NAFTA and the European Union, Japan

stepped up its backing for the creation of an Asian trading bloc. First proposed by Australia, this bloc, tentatively called the Asian Pacific Economic Co-operation, would be composed of Japan, Australia, and the nations making up the Association of Southeast Asian Nations (ASEAN)—Thailand, Singapore, Malaysia, Indonesia, Brunei, and the Philippines. Great uncertainties surrounded the possible formation of this trading bloc. In the early 1990s Japan, while boosting its support for the group, proved unwilling to provide whole-hearted backing. Then, too, some of the ASEAN nations had closer economic ties to the United States than to each other and did not want to endanger those connections. Leftover enmities from World War II also separated the nations. In the mid-1990s no such effective trading bloc had been formed.

SIMILARITIES AND DIFFERENCES IN WORLD BUSINESS

This book has stressed the importance of the interaction between business and its political environment as partially explaining the ways in which business developed in Great Britain, Germany, the United States, and Japan from preindustrial times to the present. While, as we have repeatedly seen, certain economic and technological factors led to changes in the world of business, the differing environments of business in the nations we have studied ensured that those changes would not be uniform.

In preindustrial times, Great Britain, Germany, America, and Japan all possessed expanding commercial economies, not stagnant economies. In part, the growth of these economies resulted from the fact that their political frameworks were conducive to economic integration and development. Nonetheless, when compared to the economies that would develop with industrialization, these preindustrial economies were primitive. The low volume and slow pace of business allowed merchants to carry on their businesses in traditional ways. Personal trust based on family ties and friendships was the key to preindustrial business. Business was a personal affair practically devoid of managerial hierarchies. Few big businesses existed.

Industrialization quickened the pace of economic life. The Industrial Revolution both dramatically speeded up the production of goods and increased their output exponentially. As we have seen, the throughput of business rose tremendously. As companies sought to cope with this increased throughput, big business began developing. In time, large companies with managerial

hierarchies replaced the simpler merchant houses of earlier days, and the personal business world of the merchant gave way to the more impersonal business world of the industrialist. However, because of differences in the politics, cultures, and social systems of the nations, as well as some economic differences, big businesses developed at different paces and took significantly different forms in different nations. And, in all nations small business persisted as an important economic force. Even though Great Britain was the first nation to industrialize, it was the last of the nations dealt within this study to possess a significant number of big businesses. Vertically integrated companies, the norm among large manufacturing firms in the United States, were and remain much less common in Great Britain or Japan.

Similarities and differences also became apparent in the business systems, as well as in the individual firms, of the nations as industrialization proceeded. Great Britain, the United States, Germany, and Japan all developed major differences between large and small businesses. However, this difference was (and is) most pronounced in Japan. Subcontracting by small firms for larger companies, with the smaller concerns in decidedly subordinate positions, became most common in Japan.

As their economies developed after 1920, both similarities and differences continued to appear in individual companies and in the business systems of the various nations. Big businesses, already entrenched in America and Japan, continued their development, and they grew up in Great Britain for the first time in large numbers. However, despite some convergence in world business, differences remained marked. No one would mistake the decentralized companies of the United States and Great Britain for big businesses in Japan and Germany. Indeed, differences in managerial styles and structures continued to impede business negotiations and the formation of joint ventures throughout the world.

SUGGESTED READINGS

George Fields, *From Bonsai to Levi's* (New York: Macmillan Publishing, 1983), stresses the importance of understanding cultural differences between nations for business executives hoping to succeed in international operations. Mamoru Yoshida, *Japanese Direct Manufacturing Investment in the United States* (New York: Praeger, 1987); Duane Kujawa, *Japanese Multinationals*

in the United States: Case Studies (New York: Praeger, 1986); Martin Kenney and Richard Florida, *Beyond Mass Production: The Japanese System and Its Transfer to the U.S.* (New York: Oxford University Press, 1993); and Tetsuo Abe, ed., *Hybrid Factory: The Japanese Production System in the United States* (New York: Oxford University Press, 1994), examine the operations of Japanese industrial multinationals in the United States. For the reverse story, that of American companies with manufacturing operations in Japan, see Mark Mason, *American Multinationals and Japan: The Political Economy of Japanese Capital Controls, 1899–1980* (Cambridge, Mass.: Harvard University Press, 1992), and Robert Christopher, *Second to None: American Companies in Japan* (New York: Crown Publishers, 1986).

Index

Contents

For Al and Mo, with love

© 1998 The University of North Carolina Press

Manufactured in the United States of America

The paper in this book meets the guidelines for permanence and durability
of the Committee on Production Guidelines for Book Longevity of the
Council on Library Resources.

Library of Congress Cataloging-in-Publication Data

Blackford, Mansel G. 1944–

The rise of modern business in Great Britain, the United States, and Japan /
by Mansel G. Blackford. — 2nd ed., revised and updated

p.   cm.

Includes bibliographical references and index.

ISBN 0-8078-2426-7 (cloth: alk. paper)

ISBN 0-8078-4732-1 (pbk.: alk. paper)

1. Industries—Great Britain—History.   2. Industries—United States—
History.   3. Industries—Japan—History.   I. Title.

HC255.B59   1998

338.09—dc21   97-32867

CIP

02   01   00   99   98   5   4   3   2   1

MANSEL G. BLACKFORD

The Rise of Modern Business

in Great Britain,

the United States,

and Japan

Second Edition,

Revised and Updated

The University of North Carolina Press / Chapel Hill and London

The Rise of Modern Business
in Great Britain,
the United States,
and Japan

OF PRUDERY

Doubleday & Company, Inc., Garden City, New York, 1950

CONTENTS

54315

ILLUSTRATIONS

A DEGREE OF PRUDERY

1. THE ELEGANT CIRCLES

THE GENERALITY of women who have excelled in wit have failed in chastity," declared the icily correct Mrs. Montagu. In the eyes of her followers the failure outweighed the excellence, though Mrs. Montagu and the other Blues liked wit well enough. Fortunately for Frances Burney, who thoroughly enjoyed her unexpected success as a writer, she was born into the middle of the eighteenth century, and in England instead of France. She produced her first and best book at just the time when her extraordinary combination of decorum and literary talent exactly suited the taste of the English. Fanny possessed the dangerous quality of wit, but Fanny was also, indeed above all, chaste.

In 1752 chastity, having risen in favor (though in an unsteady curve) since the death of Charles II, was definitely the fashion. Not that the current King, George II, set this pace, but, unlike good King Charles, the Hanoverian monarch had failed to make vice glamorous. One of his mistresses was an unattractive, unpopular German; another was stone deaf, though placidly pleasant. The leaders of society avoided the court whenever possible, because it was so dull. George's England was not Charles's, a country of distant detached settlements poorly represented at Whitehall. There was room for more than one center of interest in the London of 1752; no court, even one as gay and dazzling as that of the Restoration, would have been able to lead society as Charles's had done. There was nothing dazzling about Leicester House in any case.

The usual politicians whose duty demanded attendance, and the usual favor-seekers whose nature led them to it, still hung about the King. Fashion went elsewhere in search of inspiration—to France and Italy, to the classics, to the theater. Men and women of good breeding were eager for the art and literature of foreign countries; xenophobia had not as yet afflicted the English upper classes, for xenophobia is the result of fear and of a feeling of inferiority, and the English had no reason to entertain either. There was still much to find out about the countries of the Continent. Nor was it considered shameful, in the eighteenth century, to show a liking for music. No gentleman would have felt impelled to announce, as soon as the subject of harmony was broached, that he had no ear whatever for music. In our century such a claim is commonly and complacently made. Fortunately for the Burneys, the times were different then.

The world had long been finding its way over the sea to England, in ships which carried tea and coffee, silks and muslins, paintings and marbles into the homes of noblemen and rich merchants. The English were making money, and they wanted to enjoy their gains in the capital. Travel overland, by road or canal, was more comfortable and safer than it had ever been. Better roads must have opened the world to the English much in the same way as air travel pushes back our own horizons. London in 1752 had a population of more than six hundred thousand, and was growing larger with every month.

The stability of a long reign—George had been on the throne twenty-five years—was a thing which the people felt in inverse ratio to their propinquity to Leicester House. In an age when ministers staked their futures on the likelihood of the King's death or survival, less exalted personages went their placid ways trying to stir up other excitements. The King had been the King for ages, and so he would continue as King for ages more. Gambling was a favorite time killer, but there were other pleasant pursuits, too, for lords and ladies and such wealthy commoners as need not earn their bread. Upon this group of people, leisured and eager for the best of civilization, depended Fanny Burney's father Charles, the music master.

We cannot assess Burney's position by any comparison with music teachers of the present day. The importance in our daily life of music qua music may not have diminished, but we no longer feel the urgency to produce it for ourselves when there are so many mechanical devices to save us the trouble and the training. In the eighteenth century Charles had no difficulty in finding pupils: his difficulty lay rather in the enthusiasm with which London demanded his attention. His day was always overcrowded.

In a period like that of the mid-century, when it was every middle-class man's boast that he had a fortune, or hope that he might make one, Burney was a cheerful adventurer. He had no fortune, he was a younger son of a father without money, but he seems never to have fallen victim to any neurosis of insecurity. Considering his story, this is remarkable testimony to his emotional strength and clarity of purpose. Charles Burney came to London as apprentice to Dr. Thomas Augustine Arne, nowadays best known as the composer of "Rule Britannia." His apprenticeship ceased in an unusual manner: a well-to-do gentleman, Fulke Greville, took a fancy to the young musician and bought his exclusive attention from Dr. Arne for three hundred pounds. Burney didn't like Arne, and was pleased by his new job as private tutor and companion. He initiated Fulke Greville into the mysteries of the harpsichord and the newly invented pianoforte, and Greville, in turn, introduced his protégé to the gentlemanly pastimes of "Hunting . . . shooting, riding . . . drawing, dancing, fencing, tennis, horse-racing, the joys of Bacchus . . ." and gambling, added, one supposes, to other dissipations which Fanny in her prim old age lumped together in the phrase "nocturnal orgies."

It was a glamorous life, and perhaps another man in Burney's place might have developed the bitterness of the social parasite. But Burney was no parasite. He proved it by giving up his patron and making an imprudent marriage in full consciousness of what he was doing. Esther Sleepe, who was portionless like himself, was unhappy at home. Charles had either to marry and sever his connection with the Grevilles or leave his Esther unwedded and miserable while he trotted after his patrons on a continental tour. He chose marriage. Greville readily gave him his freedom, and Charles Burney was left to face the world as a free lance.

Burney was an optimistic man, with the constant cheerfulness of those who have tough constitutions and plenty of energy. His portraits show him as slender, smallish, and wiry—Fanny bears this out in her Journal—with a pleasant yet keen expression. His was a restless, curious mind, forever peering and speculating on the new current ideas, what we would call a "well-rounded" mind. He was vital, gregarious, facile at writing as was his daughter, humorous, and always incredibly busy.

Mrs. Thrale, in one of her frequent and perhaps comprehensible bursts of cattiness, describes him: "He was a man of uncommon attainments: wit born with him, I suppose; learning, he had helped himself to, and was proud of the possession; elegance of manners he had so cultivated, that those who knew but little of the man, fancied he had great flexibility of mind. It was mere pliancy of body, however, and a perpetual show of obsequiousness by bowing incessantly as if acknowledging an inferiority, which nothing would have forced him to confess."

Ah, well. Mrs. Thrale was hurt and angry when she wrote that. Fanny had certainly let her down, and it had been reported to her by the mischief-making Lord Fife that all the Burneys were leagued with her enemy Baretti against her. Charles Burney was one of those men with charm. When one says a man has charm one means that he is to some extent an actor in everyday life, a person who scatters his sweetness broadcast. No misanthrope can believe that a man who seems to like everyone can be anything but insincere, and many of us are misanthropic at times. Certainly Mrs.

Thrale was. But in all his long life, until the very end when he became querulous with old age, Charles Burney showed no signs of a bad character or of spitefulness hidden beneath his vigorous optimism. He was simply one of your outgiving, outgoing persons. It is strange that he should have produced such a daughter as Fanny, who, though she inherited his wiry toughness concealed behind the elegant vapors and ladylike faintnesses of the period, was woefully lacking in his hardihood of temperament. Burney was not brash, but he was quietly sure of himself. Fanny was unsure, to say the least; unsure and sensitive.

Perhaps the moods of the father who begets a child have as much effect on that child as does the condition of the mother who bears it. Fanny was the fruit of some connubial night during the period when Charles Burney, most uncharacteristically, was suffering from a nervous and physical breakdown.

Until then the free-lance venture had succeeded to a surprising extent. Charles Burney with his knowledge of such drawing-room instruments as the spinet and harpsichord, and his dexterity on the organ, was in demand everywhere there was a child to be educated in music or a church congregation to be uplifted with sweet strains. In a typical day of "the season" he gave lessons from 8 A.M. to 11 P.M., wrote at home until 4 A.M., and rose at 7 A.M. He lunched on sandwiches as he ran, and when his duties did not fill the day completely, he was absorbed in his many friendships. For of course he had friendships: before his marriage he had been admitted to the cheerful circle of artists which made London a center for art and drama. The Burney marriage made no difference to his habits unless it curtailed his time a bit. Charles kept on with his old friends, through a mingling of natural gregariousness and a shrewd knowledge that these were the people through whom he could make good "contacts."

Garrick was the most popular of them, but there were others, too, whose names have come down to us: Benjamin West, Mrs. Cibber who was Dr. Arne's sister, Hogarth, Reynolds the portrait painter whose success overshadowed his great contemporary Gainsborough. There was the poet Kit Smart, poor crazy Kit, who loved to pray and who spent a great part of his time in prison, or, worse, in Bedlam. Charles Burney adored the theater, even non-musical drama, and those were the days which produced *The Beggar's Opera*. Like his friends in those good times he enjoyed paintings, and thought his own opinions on them as good as another man's. Like many others, he dabbled in writing, in versifying and journalizing. He was a clever dog, as Dr. Johnson called him.

Esther Burney made no great splash on the London scene, and it is small wonder that she did not. One live wire like Charles was enough for any family. She was preoccupied with the business of keeping house and of bearing her children: first Esther, or Hester—the names were interchangeable in those days before English spelling became cut and dried—and then James. The pages of Fanny's Journal, though they express the proper encomiums, do not afford us any sort of mental picture of her mother beyond these. As she died when Fanny was very young, she probably remained in her daughter's memory more as a universal loving mother-pattern than as an individual woman. We must reconstruct her in outline from the general facts of the period. No doubt she provided her family with as comfortable a home as any professor's wife could nowadays afford. Perhaps the house was less convenient to keep clean, and the cooking was done under more difficulties, but the eighteenth century maintained its elegance and luxury on a foundation of plenty of unskilled labor. Servants were cheap in London and easy to come by. The wife of Charles Burney may have worried about household expenditure, and certainly she intended to bring up her daughters to understand the fundamentals of cookery and needlework; every lady in the land knew that much of housekeeping. (Dr. Johnson wrote to Queeney Thrale in 1783, "If ever therefore you catch yourself contentedly and placidly doing nothing . . . break away from the snare, find your book or your needle, or snatch the broom from the maid.") But for scrubbing floors, emptying chamber pots, cleaning out fireplaces, there was always some representative of "the poor" to do the dirty work. Mrs.

Burney as housekeeper was executive and accountant, not laborer. The Burneys had no fortune, but they were not "the poor." An immense abyss yawned between their class and that one.

In all Fanny's varied life she was never to trouble herself with any real indignation on the subject of social injustice. Such a conception would have been impossible in her time, given her training. She believed, of course, in kindness to the poor, and sometimes spoke jokingly about her "republican feelings" when she felt cross with her employer, the Queen, but that was as far as it went. Any true republican feelings she may have entertained tentatively were completely put to rout by her horror at the French Revolution.

The house was probably as comfortable as are most houses in London today; perhaps because of the cheap labor it was more comfortable in everything but bathroom facilities. Well-to-do people ate well. Even many of "the poor" ate well, though they lacked other necessities such as fuel, clothing, and room to live in, for meat was becoming plentiful, though then as now strong tea, much sweetened, often took the place of necessary solids. The cookery was uninspired, boiled and roasted meat and fowl, and simple pastries, but it was filling food, and people ate more of it. They drank beer and wine; hard-bitten gentlemen drank brandy, and "the poor," gin.

In essentials Mrs. Burney and her daughters dressed alike, for the practice of designing special costumes for children had not yet found favor. Little girls were almost replicas of their mothers. One wonders, seeing them in the contemporary prints in their little bonnets and long skirts, how they were able to romp and play, though their mammas did not go to the lengths of the fond mothers of France. Hetty Burney when a schoolgirl wrote Fanny from Paris in 1764: "The Girls at nine and ten years old weare sacks and Coats here, and have seen severall about my size in Hoops, and if little Charley [Charley was seven] was here he might wear a Bag and Sword, for he wou'd be thought big enough." Esther Burney as a bride must have worn a hooped ankle-length petticoat, three-quarter sleeves with falling lace cuffs, and a sacque. The sacque was a garment somewhat like our peignoir, loosely gathered in the back and left open, or closed only at the bodice in front. Her shoes were pointed and high-heeled. Her hair was her own, since wigs for ladies had not yet come into their eighteenth-century glory, but it was puffed and powdered, and to be in style she would have discarded her cap on dress-up occasions and worn a veil over the back of her head. At home she wore a small cap tied under the chin and an apron, probably a long one, though more dressy ladies favored the short frilly article.

If Esther did not wear a wig, her husband most certainly did. Like all husbands of his time, Charles, though he dressed plainly, was more elaborately costumed than was his wife, with his full-skirted coat, his waistcoat and cravat, his lace ruffles, and his buckled shoes.

James had just been born and little Esther was a toddler when the young paterfamilias fell ill from overwork. Fanny describes the ailment as a severe eight weeks' fever which left him with signs of consumption. The doctors of the day blamed it on the air of London, reminding their patient that he was a country boy, accustomed to the atmospheres of Shrewsbury and Chester rather than to London's damp fogs, and they were probably right. London air was filthy. Trevelyan says, "since coal was burnt on almost every hearth, the air was so infected that a foreign scholar complained 'whenever I examine London books I make my ruffles as black as coal.'" The medicos took a grave view of Burney's tendency to cough and his slowness in regaining strength; they advised him to get out of his beloved town as soon as possible and not to think of coming back for a good long time. Poor Charles Burney! He loved the great Wen. But since it was a matter of life and death, as Dr. Armstrong assured him, there could be no hesitation, and he hastily accepted a good offer from the city then called Lynn Regis and now known as King's Lynn, in Norfolk, to become their organist at St. Margaret's Church, with the privilege of taking "the most respectable pupils from all the best families in the town and its neighbourhood."

The seaport Lynn is in flat country, and had a name which it carries until today for healthy, bracing air. Its chief industries were importing wine from abroad for distribution in England, and brewing, also exporting, beer. In those days of difficult land travel English seaports held an importance of which many were later to be bereft. The community of Lynn felt itself becoming large enough to afford the less common amenities of civilization. The leading citizens were so anxious to procure the services of this distinguished musician that they increased the customary salary for organists from twenty pounds a year to one hundred. Though Lynn sounded dreadfully provincial to a true Londoner, it was a good job, with prospects.

Buoyed up by the enthusiasm of his new patrons, with a light heart Charles Burney set out to look the land over and select a house for his family. He met all the leading citizens, "the mayor, aldermen, recorder, clergy, physicians, lawyers, and principal merchants. . . ." A glittering array from Lynn Regis's point of view, no doubt, but desperately dull to the man from London. "In looking, he said, around him, he seemed to see but a void." He wrote sorrowfully to his wife, ". . . it shames me to think how little I knew myself, when I fancied I should be happy in this place. Oh God! I find it impossible I should ever be so." And the organ was execrable.

Still, he couldn't live in London. Soothed by Esther and comforted by the hope of someday being able to get back to the splendid, elegant, classical, amusing circles from which he had been exiled, Charles resigned himself. He brought his family to Lynn, to the house he had chosen, and set to work on the execrable organ and on teaching his worthy, respectable, best-family pupils.

Fanny was born in Lynn Regis in 1752, on June 13.

2. I CANNOT HELP IT!

BURNEY's private writings, at least the specimens which his daughter Fanny has left to us—for she was, alas, a vigorous censor when she compiled his Memoirs—indicate that he managed to find some fun in life, even in Lynn Regis. He had the most exemplary plans for his home program and set them forth in a long rhyming piece which Fanny permits us to see, though "they must not, in these fastidious days," said she, "be called verses." The connotations of words change with the years, and today we would be perfectly willing to give Charles's rhymes the name of verses. But poetry? Well, no. Still, he was a goodhearted, good-natured, clever dog of a fellow; one likes him immensely.

> If unadulterate wine be good
> To glad the heart, and mend the blood,
> We that in plenty boast at Lynn,
> Would make with pleasure Bacchus grin.
> Should nerves auricular demand
> A head profound, and cunning hand,
> The charms of music to display,
> Pray,—cannot I compose and play?
> And strains to your each humour suit
> On organ, violin, or flute?

If Homer's bold, inventive fire,
Or Virgil's art, you most admire;
If Pliny's eloquence and ease,
Or Ovid's flowery fancy please;
In fair array they marshall'd stand,
Most humbly waiting your command.
    To humanize and mend the heart,
Our serious hours we'll set apart.

We'll learn to separate right from wrong
Through Pope's mellifluous moral song.
    If wit and humour be our drift,
We'll laugh at knaves and fools with Swift.

Going on thus for a good long time, Charles promised his Esther
happy hours with Addison, Bacon, Congreve, Dryden, Milton,
Cervantes, Butler, Locke, and Shakespeare. We must hope Mrs.
Burney did not place too much stock in these glowing prophecies,
since if she did she was bound to be disappointed. Actually the
London pattern was repeated, with Charles abroad all day giving
lessons or concerts and Esther at home taking care of the babies.

Mrs. Burney could have had a full social life in Lynn Regis, but
she didn't very much care to go out. Her husband, on the
contrary, "immediately visited every house in the county," including as one of first importance Haughton Hall, the seat of Lord
Orford, nephew of the acidulous Horace, who later inherited the
title. Mrs. Burney would not have cared to visit Haughton Hall,
in spite of all its treasures of library and gallery, for Lord Orford—
"the reckless Lord Orford," as the Encyclopaedia Britannica calls
him—openly, brazenly kept a mistress there. Patty, "the fond,
faulty Patty,"—not the E. B. this time, but Fanny—sat at the head
of his table. It was all very sad. Lord Orford, said Madame
d'Arblay, ought to have been the guide and protector of his neighborhood instead of setting it such a bad example. Yet the picture
was not wholly bad. "In all, save that blot, which, on earth, must to
a female be ever indelible, Patty was good, faithful, kind, friendly,

and praise-worthy." Anyway, Patty suited Lord Orford, and he an earl. . . . Nevertheless it was all very sad and Mrs. Burney wouldn't have dreamed of visiting Haughton Hall. Charles Burney went there often. It was different for a man; besides, the dinners and conversation were excellent.

Burney traveled from lesson to lesson on horseback, as there was no other means of getting around the country in that age of few roads. His mare was a quietly intelligent beast who after a few journeys could find the way for herself, which was a good thing, since her master had an unorthodox taste for studying Italian en route. He made a compact little dictionary of the language, "and from this in one pocket, and a volume of Dante, Petrarch, Tasso, Ariosto, or Metastasio, in another, he made himself completely at home in that language of elegance and poetry."

Meanwhile, at home, Mrs. Burney hadn't much similar enjoyment. She, too, liked books and foreign languages, but she found the ladies of Lynn Regis very small-town in their ideas, most uncongenial. Of course, said the tactful Madame d'Arblay about eighty years later, it is all different now, but in those benighted days most of the ladies of Lynn could talk nothing but London fashions and kitchen gossip. It wasn't only Lynn Regis, said Fanny solemnly. All the small towns were alike: the women very dull, the men somewhat better. It must be, she decided, that men, in getting out of the house as they did, were able to develop more "vigour of mind"—but the bad old days are over now. Fanny said that in 1832.

Two Lynn women escaped her mother's condemnation. Miss Dorothy Young was deformed in face and body, but she had an excellent heart and a quick intelligence. She became a beloved intimate of the Burney household. Mrs. Stephen Allen was beautiful, elegant, and intellectual; as the wife of a wealthy wine merchant she was a power in the community.

When Esther Burney lay dying in '61 she counseled her sorrowing husband to marry again, and her dear old friend Dolly Young was the woman she chose as stepmother for the children. But

Charles couldn't bring himself to follow his dear wife's wishes to that extent. He compromised. As Esther had suggested, he married her old friend, but it was the other one, the beautiful widow, Mrs. Allen.

But we are speaking now of Fanny's birth, when Esther was still very much in the land of the living. After Fanny came Charles and Susanna, who with the older children, Hetty and James, kept their mother busy enough. People had plenty of children in the eighteenth century. No doubt the clean bracing air of the Norfolk broads was good for babies as well as for Charles. At any rate, they lived to grow up, little James and little Esther, or Hetty, and Frances and Charles and Susanna, and, later, Charlotte.

Fanny's education was neglected. It is a point of which much has been made, and by force of repetition it has attained more significance than it should possess. Most girls of the time received less education than their brothers. This happens even today to some extent, and in 1760 the exception was not so much in Fanny as in her sisters, especially her elder sister Hetty, with whose training Mrs. Burney went to unusual trouble. Together mother and eldest daughter read all of Pope and *The Aeneid*, fairly solid literary sustenance for even an older person than Hetty. Young Fanny, though she didn't learn to read until she was nine or ten, listened to the lessons and memorized a portion of Pope's works. But a retentive memory for poetry was not enough to save her from the other children's teasing. Nine years is indisputably an advanced age at which to learn reading and writing. Her sisters and brothers called Fanny "the little dunce." This hearty family joking no doubt had its share in producing the shyness which was to plague her in later years. Her elders were not so brutal as the children in making fun of her, but they agreed among themselves, in the careless, audible way elders have, that she was a sadly backward child. Only Fanny's mother defended her.

For some time Charles Burney, who had been in Norfolk nearly a decade, had been asking himself and his friends if he was not well enough now to brave the smoky atmosphere of London once again. Everyone seems to have agreed that he was, but however reluctantly he first made the move from London, he hesitated now to make the opposite, equally radical change. In her old age Fanny found a letter among his papers which may well have spoken the decisive word. It was written, long before she knew him, by her beloved Mr. Crisp. Samuel Crisp bears a rather specialized distinction: he brought into England what was probably the first pianoforte ever to arrive in Albion. It was called a harpsichord, but it was equipped with hammers which struck the strings rather than with quills which plucked them. Perhaps this is too special a claim to fame. Crisp has another: for many years he was to be Fanny's best friend and wisest guide. All his life, or what remained of it after the mid-century, this charming, crotchety man was to wield an important influence on Burney destinies. He wrote:

> . . . I have no more to say, my dear Burney, about harpsichords; and if you remain amongst your foggy aldermen, I shall be more indifferent whether I have one or not. But really, among friends, is not settling at Lynn, planting your youth, genius, hopes, fortune, etc., against a north wall? Can you ever expect ripe, high-flavoured fruit, from such an aspect? Your underrate prices in the town, and galloping about the country for higher, especially in the winter—are they worthy of your talents? . . . Take, then, your spare person, your pretty mate, and your brats, to that propitious mart, and
>
> "Seize the glorious, golden opportunity,"
>
> while yet you have youth, spirits, and vigour to give fair play to your abilities. . . .

The Burneys obediently said good-by to Lynn Regis and moved back to London in 1760, to a house in Poland Street, Soho. It was the beginning of a new era in more ways than one: 1760 was the year of the old King's death, when George III mounted the throne.

Madame d'Arblay, sorting out her father's effects, remembered

Poland Street and described it as it was when she was brought to live there, at the age of eight. Oxford Street was Oxford Road then, and marked the edge of the urban area; on the far side there was little but "fields, gardeners' grounds, or uncultivated suburbs . . . Portman, Manchester, Russel, Belgrave Squares, Portland Place, etc. etc., had not yet a single stone or brick laid. . . ."

The Burneys had lived a year in Poland Street; Charlotte, the last of Esther's children, was still a baby when her mother fell victim to "a cough, with alarming symptoms," and died of what her husband in a letter to Dolly Young called "an inflammation of the stomach." According to his account of her deathbed scene, it was most edifying, but for a lady dying, as he describes it, of a "mortification," Esther was remarkably calm and piously talkative: more like a literary creation of Madame d'Arblay's than a human female. At any rate, the writing of such letters seems to have given the sorrowing husband an exhaust which he needed. He wrote lengthily to Dolly Young of his bereavement; he also wrote to Mrs. Allen. To neither lady, however, did he at that time mention Esther's nomination of her successor.

There now arose the sad necessity of dealing somehow with all those motherless children. Charlotte was so young she was hardly a difficulty as yet; Charles left her to the nurse. The boys were easy to dispose of, for James was already settled in as midshipman in the Navy and Charles Junior was at Charterhouse. Motherless boys were not considered such a problem as were girls, but Charles Burney had a plan for his daughters too. Hetty and Susanna, the bright ones, must be educated: their father decided they should go to France and live there en pension in order to perfect their French. Esther Sleepe was descended from French Huguenots, so in sending his daughters to France, Charles was only renewing old bonds.

As for Fanny, well, in every large family there was usually one girl left at home to keep things going, and Fanny had never been a promising scholar: it might as well be Fanny. That is probably why her father did not include her in the pension scheme, though the reason he gave was different and more tactful. Esther Sleepe had been brought up in the Church of England, but her mother, a great favorite of Fanny's, was a Roman Catholic. Charles Burney said he was afraid the child might be influenced to join the Catholic Church if she lived in France. It is far more likely that he weighed the cost of educating a little dunce who might never profit from such a move, and found it too heavy.

Nobody criticized Burney for his decision until years later when the little ugly duckling made her swanlike appearance in London literary circles as author of a best seller. Dr. Johnson then pounced on the facts and broadcast them, marveling that such a talent could have flourished without training or encouragement. Speaking generally, the world of manners and wealth was not unkind to women who wanted to think for themselves, as long as their thoughts were confined to scholarship and did not stray to the forbidden fields of politics or sexual freedom. The Duchess of Portland considered herself an intellectual, and she encouraged her lady friends to join her in her rare delights, making collections of "curiosities," for example. Mrs. Montagu's name was famous, and to a lesser degree so were those of her circle. Cornelia Knight made translations from the Italian and wrote poetry, yet maintained her social position. Sophy Streatfeild, who was ravishingly beautiful, actually knew Greek; she was acknowledged a freak, but a harmless one. But all these were ladies well known for their independent minds, ladies who had been recognized as clever girls as soon as they emerged from the nursery. Not one of them was in Fanny's position. She had grown up without any signs to distinguish her from the riotous crowd of Burney children. Hetty was the musical one, Susanna was her father's favorite because of her sweet nature, Charles the younger was clever and a scholar, James was for the Navy, and Charlotte was an adorable little flirt; Charlotte was the family beauty. Fanny was just the good, quiet one, obviously formed by Nature to be a spinster aunt. In the meantime she did such secretarial work as was needed on her father's behalf; Charles Burney was busier than ever, but the habit of scribbling was growing on him.

It occurs to us, looking at the situation from this distance in time, that Dr. Johnson may have wasted his indignation on Fanny's behalf. It was a mild indignation at best, for the doctor was very fond of Charles Burney and never went to the length of scolding him for neglecting his second daughter. (It remained for Macaulay to do that, with all the ferocity, vigor, and inaccuracy of his tempestuous style.) But even if she had received the encouragement and the education her sisters did, Fanny would probably not have written a better book than her first, the astonishing *Evelina*. Learning French well at a tender age might not have been an unalloyed blessing to an English girl. It often happens that too thorough a knowledge of several languages vitiates one's literary style. A few letters of Fanny's sister Susan, written when she was a schoolgirl, support this thesis. Susan was uncertain which language she was using, and her style is sometimes a sad hodgepodge of French idiom where English would do as well, or of English grammar where the French turn of phrase would have been better. In maturity these difficulties persisted: her letters are spirited and full of charm, but she did not have her sister's clarity or stamina in writing. Fanny's development is another case in point, even more pertinent. As a child she did not use much French, but later, because of her marriage and removal to France, she did. It is notorious that she wrote a dreadful English as she grew old; turgid, inverted, exaggerated sentences cluttered her pages, and it is very likely that her long residence in France during the Napoleonic Wars, when she had to speak and write French almost constantly, contributed to this deterioration if it was not solely responsible. (Macaulay's theory, that Johnson's example spoiled Fanny's style, seems oversimplified. Why such a delayed reaction?) English in Fanny Burney's time was not the sturdy, self-assured language it has since become. She had to work with delicate tools, and in time, leaving them untended, she blunted and twisted them, and they had no more balance.

At the beginning of her career Fanny's written English was simple, flowing, and conversational. In fact, it was conversation rather than what was then accepted as written English. That was its chief charm and virtue. Long before Fanny thought of her private pastime as anything more than that, she was making up stories and poetry, scribbling in imitation of her father, writing doggerel letters and showing the results to Susan, as he had shown his versifications to his Esther, in a sort of family game.

The right true business of life for Fanny as the world saw it was to be an adequate little housekeeper for her beloved father as long as the more efficient Hetty was not home. It was not so dull a career as one might think. There were always amusing people dropping in on Charles Burney. Quiet, demure, and painfully shy, Fanny kept her place and watched the world as it passed in procession through the hospitable doors of the house in Poland Street. It was not Bohemia, because it wasn't raffish: one preserved propriety at the Burneys', but one could be lively all the same. Theirs was a gay world though a thinking one, sensual but not brutish, mannered yet not completely artificial. In spite of Dr. Johnson's flattering amazement after the event, Fanny was better off in Poland Street than she could ever have been with Hetty and Susan, walled up in a foreign *pension*, acquiring culture the hard way.

In another century, Poland Street might even have given a Fanny Burney enough understanding of human nature to counteract her priggishness. But life didn't. The eighteenth century, the Age of Reason, of prunes and prisms, saw to that. It was impossible for a woman of her class to avoid being segregated from most of the harshness of life, and ladies made a virtue of this necessity. Childbirth, illness, heartache, these were trials which even a lady could not be spared, but all the rest of human pain and trouble was outside her sphere.

Compare the writings of a lady and a gentleman of the times. Mrs. Delany, who was Fanny Burney's friend in later days, writing her sister in 1759, said of the recently published *Tristram Shandy*: "D.D. [the Dean, her husband] is not a little offended with Mr. Sterne: his book is read here as in London, and seems to divert more than it offends; but as neither I nor any of my particular set have read it, or *shall* read it, I know nothing of it more than what you have said. Mrs. Clayton and I had a furious argument about reading books of a bad tendency; I stood up for preserving a purity of mind and discouraging works of that kind; *she*, for trusting to her own strength and reason . . . but as I cannot presume to depend upon my own strength of mind I think it safest to avoid whatever may prejudice it."

William Hickey, then a young man in a London law office, describes an evening at a Drury Lane dive in 1768: "At this time the whole room was in an uproar, men and women promiscuously mounted upon chairs, tables, and benches, in order to see a sort of general conflict carried on upon the floor. Two she devils, for they scarce had a human appearance, were engaged in a scratching and boxing match, their faces entirely covered with blood, bosoms bare, and the clothes nearly torn from their bodies. For several minutes not a creature interfered between them, or seemed to care a straw what mischief they might do each other, and the contest went on with unabated fury.

"In another corner of the same room, an uncommonly athletic young man of about twenty-five seemed to be the object of universal attack. No less than three Amazonian tigresses were pummelling him with all their might, and it appeared to me that some of the males at times dealt him blows with their sticks. He however made a capital defence, not sparing the women a bit more than the men, but knocking each down as opportunity occurred."

William Hickey was certainly no member of Mrs. Delany's "particular set," nor she of his. Yet the contrast is not one of the most extreme. Ladies like Mrs. Delany habitually created their little inviolable world and willingly stayed within it.

Though the Restoration was a century past, there still remained in the air of that world a light glitter, a golden dust from the wings of vanished butterflies. Some of this rare gilt sparkles on the pages of *Evelina*, but as the years went by the air no longer glittered; Fanny was to capture no more of it. Her blithe step slowed with the tempo of her "set" and Mrs. Delany's. She always kept in step with the world, though she must have regretted growing old along with it. Fanny did not want to grow up.

What remains of her earlier diary begins in 1768. At the same time William Hickey was experiencing the delights of low life in London, and observing with horror—though he was a hard-bitten youth—those bloodstained, naked, drunken Amazons, a dreamy little creature of sixteen started her Journal, writing gushily (Poland Street was not far from Drury Lane.) "A Journal in which I must confess my every thought, must open my whole heart!"

There was nothing at all out of the way in this idea. Most sixteen-year-olds kept journals then—for that matter they do so now—so Fanny need have no guilt complex about it. She did, though. She was abnormally shy to begin with. Also she felt those agonizing reserves of adolescence, those inhibitions which alternate so confusingly with equally agonizing impulses to confide in somebody. Moreover, she had already come to grief about her writing habits. Fanny had stepmother trouble.

From the beginning to the end little Burney never lived up to her avowed intentions of confessing every thought, or of opening her whole heart. Few people can do it even when they want to, and Fanny didn't want to. Being a human female in the eighteenth century, she had a host of feelings of which she was ashamed and which she hastily quashed long before she found words to clothe them. Her father married Mrs. Stephen Allen a year before the Journal opens. The custom of making social occasions out of weddings had not yet been generally adopted. ("Well of all things in the world I don't suppose anything can be so dreadful as a publick wedding—my stars! I should never be able to support it!" wrote Fanny in the Journal.) Marriages were usually quiet, private affairs, but the Burney-Allen alliance was more than quiet: it was secret. Mrs. Allen's people at Lynn were opposed to it. There is no written evidence as to their reasons, but families can usually find plenty of reasons for objecting to marriages. Mrs. Allen's mother may well have argued that a widower with six children and no capital but his talents was not a good match for a widow with three children who had recently lost her fortune. In spite of this they married, and by the time the secret came out it was too late for their in-laws to spoil the Burneys' plans. The combined groups make a list which in length is fairly staggering: of the Burneys, there were James, about twenty, Hetty eighteen, Fanny sixteen, Susan thirteen, Charles ten, and Charlotte seven. On the Allen side we cannot be sure of the respective ages of the children, but Maria was probably about seventeen and her sister Bessy and brother Stephen not much younger or older.

Maria Allen and the Burney girls were good friends on the whole; one can see this in their letters and in Maria's love story, in which her stepsisters aided and abetted her. Nothing has been found in the family correspondence to indicate that the Allen children objected to their new father, but the relations between the second Mrs. Burney and her stepdaughters cannot be so summarily dismissed. Some friction there was, undoubtedly. In Charlotte's published scraps of journal are a few references to Mrs. Burney (whom she called "the Lady") which do not emit sweetness and light exactly. Maria often called her mother "the Governor." Twice in Fanny's Journal, though she tried to delete from her writings everything which might indicate trouble between them, she mentioned feeling vexed at her stepmother, and a surviving letter of hers talks outright of Mrs. Burney's dreadful temper.

On the whole, though, they all must have managed to rub along cheerfully, with a restraint all the more commendable considering what hell life could have been for them under the circumstances. Fanny must have suffered from jealousy when her darling father married again. Hetty, too, could not have relished being robbed of her dignity as official housekeeper just as she returned from school to take up her duties, but she married and got away fairly soon. The younger girls had to stay home.

Maria Allen quarreled openly with her mother, but then that was Maria's special right: she was a true daughter and the Burney girls were not. As nice girls they couldn't quarrel with the newcomer, the stranger within the gates. As far as we know, they didn't. They settled down to it, and Mrs. Burney settled down to it too.

We must remember that in Lynn, if not in London, she was the leader of the intelligentsia, or anyway she was half of it, with Dolly Young the other half. She liked company, preferably of the sort Charles Burney naturally collected around himself—painters, musicians, actors, opera singers and their patrons, men of letters, and all the attendant satellites; then there were the scientists and explorers, and the mere people of fashion, and the others. Come to think of it, what sort of person did not Charles Burney attract? Mrs. Burney aptly filled her place as hostess of this variegated company. She was not diffident. She liked to hold forth; she liked discussion, and chiefly she liked to lead it. She was not a type to suffer from uncertainties, and there was no uncertainty on her part as to her duty in bringing up children, either her own or her second husband's.

"I make a kind of rule," wrote Fanny at Lynn, during one of her frequent visits to her birthplace, "never to indulge myself in my two *most* favourite pursuits, reading and writing, in the morning—no, like a very good girl I give that up wholly, accidental occasions and preventions excepted, to needle work, by which means my reading and writing in the afternoon is a pleasure I cannot be blamed for by my mother, as it does not take up the time I ought to spend otherwise."

The bonfire story, like Fanny's lack of schooling, is well known. Mrs. Burney didn't approve of her scribbling, and Mrs. Burney was not unique in this. The prejudice against that singular anomaly, the lady novelist, was general. It may be, as some writers have suggested, that this disapproval dated from the days of the Restoration writer Aphra Behn, whose plays were so successful that her male colleagues became righteously shocked and created an outcry against her morals, not wishing, naturally, to place the onus on her talent, because that would have looked like jealousy, which it was. It may be that Mrs. Burney's condemnation of writing as a pastime for young girls was thus derived from the seventeenth century. It is more likely, though, that it stemmed directly from the trashy novels which her contemporaries were producing. No proper mother of Mrs. Burney's circle liked the idea of her daughters wasting time reading such poor stuff, though most girls did nevertheless, the Burneys included. Perhaps Fanny's stepmother assumed that Fanny was not only reading but imitating that sort of thing. It would not have been an objection made merely for aesthetic reasons. The Mrs. Burneys of England were first and foremost guardians of virtue in their daughters. Romance as it was set forth in novels was a dangerous lure, perhaps a stimulation: Romance must be held at bay.

No, the unusual thing is not so much Mrs. Burney's attitude as Fanny's. When her stepmother lectured her for her wicked habit of writing, the good little girl did not put up any struggle whatever. Owning her weakness, her evil behavior, she went straight away and burned the lot—tragedies, epic poems, novels, and everything. Perhaps it is not remarkable, after all, that a sixteen-year-old girl should so easily be shamed. Most novitiate writers are not hardy enough to set themselves up against ruthless criticism. But the pattern set by the child was followed through life by the woman. We shall see in time how readily Fanny always gave way to adverse criticism. Even when she could have felt backed up by success and by acclaim so general that today it looks ridiculous, Fanny was not sure of herself. In regard to her work, an element which usually stiffens one's backbone when all else fails, Fanny through her long life remained the good little girl.

The bonfire, thought Mrs. Burney, would mark the end of Fanny's writing days, but we learn from the early Journal that the gentle child continued to offend her elders. True, she was not exactly forbidden to keep that Journal. But journals were supposed to be truly secret. They were to be written in a lady's private boudoir and locked within heavy covers or at least kept inside locked bureau drawers. They were intimate things, like underwear but more so.

"You must know," wrote Fanny to her alter ego, the diary, "I always have the last sheet of my Journal in my pocket, and when I have wrote it half full I join it to the rest, and take another sheet —and so on. Now I happen'd unluckily to take the last sheet out of my pocket with my letter—and laid it on the piano forte, and there, negligent fool!—I left it. . . . Well, as ill fortune would have it, papa went into the room—took my poor Journal—read, and pocketted it. Mamma came up to me and told me of it. O dear! I was in a sad distress—I could not for the life of me ask for it —and *dawdled* and fretted the time away till Tuesday evening. Then, gathering courage 'Pray, papa,' I said, 'have you got—any *papers* of mine?'

" 'Papers of yours?' said he—'how should I come by papers of yours?'

" 'I'm sure—I don't know—but——'

" 'Why do you leave your papers about the house?' asked he, gravely.

"I could not say another word—he went on playing on the piano forte. Well, to be sure, thought I, these same dear Journals are most shocking plaguing things—I've a good mind to resolve never to write a word more. However, I stayed still in the room, walking, and looking wistfully at him for about an hour and half. At last, he rose to dress—Again I look'd wistfully at him—He laughed— 'What, Fanny,' said he, kindly, 'are you in sad distress?' I half laugh'd. 'Well,—I'll give it you, now I see you are in such distress —but take care, my dear, of leaving your writings about the house again—suppose anybody else had found it—I declare I was going to read it loud—Here, take it—but if ever I find any more of your Journals, I vow I'll stick them up in the market place.' "

She adds, "I was so frightened that I have not had the heart to write since, till now, I should not but that—in short, but that I cannot help it!"

The struggle between Fanny's wicked urge for self-expression and all her kindly mentors continued apace. Dolly Young in the nicest way, but very seriously and earnestly, told her that she really should give up her Journal. Keeping a diary, said Miss Young, was a most dangerous employment for young persons. Young persons put down things which should not be recorded at all, things best forgotten. Fanny replied that her Journal was kept only for herself and nobody else; indeed Fanny showed what, for her, amounted to a spark of spirit: she said that in such a case nobody could be angry or displeased at what she wrote. Ah, said Dolly Young, pouncing, but how could one be *sure*? Look at the way Fanny had left a page of Journal lying about so that her father found it! Didn't it all go to show? "Suppose now, for example, your favorite wish were granted, and you were *to fall in love*, and then the object of your passion were to get sight of some part which related to himself?"

It was a dreadful supposition, but Fanny turned it off with a laugh. Why, then, she said, she would simply have to commit suicide.

Yet the argument was won by Fanny in the end. She showed part of the suspect work in progress to Miss Young, and Miss Young scrutinized it very carefully, and Miss Young gave it back with her sanction, qualified, it is true: "*If it is equally harmless everywhere*," said Miss Young.

"The characteristics of Hetty," wrote Susan at this time, "seem to be wit, generosity, and openness of heart:—Fanny's,—sense, sensibility, and bashfulness, and even a degree of prudery."

The prudery is not unpleasantly evident in the early pages of the Journal. Fanny was living the ordinary life of a young girl—a young girl living at home with very busy parents, whose father kept her as much occupied as she could have been at finishing school. When she was not copying for him or paying and receiving calls with Hetty, she talked with her pen to the shadowy figure she apostrophized in the Journal as "Nobody" or "Miss Nobody." Every writer knows that figure, which in the end takes on the name of Dear Reader, or The Public. To Fanny it was from the first a very personal relationship she bore to that hypothetical reader. Sometimes she addressed it as "my dear creature"; later, as she outgrew the possibility of satisfying herself with a shadow she used her sister Susan and Mr. Crisp instead. But it was all the same impulse really.

She chattered to the Journal, sometimes of her friends, sometimes of the books she was reading, and occasionally of the anxieties which members of the family caused her. Susan was very ill of lung trouble, and nearly died; she talked in her delirium "in a manner *inconceivably* affecting—and how greatly I was shock'd, no words can express. My dear papa out of town too! . . . O my good God! what did poor Hetty and myself suffer! . . ."

"I seldom quit home considering my youth and opportunities. But why should I when I am so happy in it? following my own vagaries, which my papa never controls, I never can [want] employment, nor sigh for amusement."

Occasionally the Journal records a brief moment of rebellion. Even Fanny, the good little girl, had her moments of revolt. An outburst against conventional social duties which she recorded in '69 sounds like a first brave trumpeting which all but died away two decades later, when she was subjected to long desert periods of boredom at court but did scarcely more than murmur to the diary.

"Why may we not venture to love, and to dislike—and why, if we do, may we not give to those we love the richest jewel we own, our time?" she demands in '69 with all the tragedy airs of a teenage girl. "—What is it can stimulate us to bestow that on all alike? —'tis not affection—'tis not a desire of pleasing—or if it is, 'tis a very weak one;—no! 'tis indolence—'tis custom—custom—which is so woven around us—which so universally commands us—which we all blame—and all obey, without knowing why or wherefore."

In viewing her later career one likes to remember this little show of spirit, even though one knows that after writing it she probably went down and duly wasted more time, being polite to some old bore. In the last analysis, Fanny liked old bores.

Fanny had a good time those years when she was a young girl. There were plenty of dancing parties and dinners, amateur theatricals and concerts. Hetty and Fanny went to a masquerade; the Journal with a note of apology calls it "a very private one, and at the house of Mr. Laluze, a French dancing master." This explanation was almost necessary at the time, for George III discouraged the public masquerades which until his reign had been a joyous but rowdy form of entertainment. He "did not approve of an amusement," wrote Cornelia Knight, "which he thought might lead to much that was wrong."

In Fanny's case it led to one remarkable item: she was so carried away by frivolous gaiety that she described her masquerade costume: "a close pink Persian vest . . . covered with gauze, in loose pleats, and with flowers etc. etc. . . . a little garland or wreath of flowers on the left side of my head." Fanny hardly ever did descend to chitchat about her own dress. But the close pink Persian vest suited her so well that she was impressed, in spite of her austere little self. "To say the truth," she admitted, "those whimsical dresses are not unbecoming."

There was another party soon after that meeting: a ball, at the Reverend Mr. Pugh's, who had married Mrs. Allen and Dr. Burney; there Fanny was introduced to an attractive dancing partner named Captain Bloomfield. "Indeed he was very unfortunate—for he did not himself tire the whole evening, and poor little I was fatigued to death after the second dance."

When one becomes acquainted with Fanny's demure style of non-confession, there is evident in it a kind of code by which one can decry her genuine feelings. She never affirms; she sometimes denies, which amounts in the end to the same thing. It is usually done with a record of dialogue, so stark as to resemble a play with stage directions rather than a typical eighteenth-century narrative. It is found here in her account of the evening with Captain Bloomfield, much erased and changed around by the writer almost sixty years later. Fanny decided at supper that she simply could not dance another step. It is small wonder, for those dances were exceedingly vigorous, and she considered herself a delicate person. A certain Miss Kirk was not dancing, for some reason which Fanny has written and then rubbed out, but Captain Bloomfield "could assuredly be no sufferer by an exchange, for Miss Kirk was very pretty and agreeable." Fanny being "completely finished," the captain led her to a seat which happened to be next to that of the wallflower, poor Miss Kirk.

Fanny proposed an exchange to the captain.

"Do you want to get rid of me?" he cried.

Confused at this, for a moment she dropped the subject without affirming or denying, like the perfect lady she was. When again she suggested it, he said, "But I would rather *sit* with you, than *dance* with any other lady."

It was very embarrassing, she protested to her diary, especially as she had already asked Miss Kirk to take her place and Miss Kirk had accepted. . . . It was very embarrassing. Yet it might conceivably have been gratifying too. Was Fanny Burney gratified? One cannot say for certain; she neither affirmed nor denied it.

Little by little one learns the code.

Mr. Mackintosh, a very stupid young man with a large fortune, wrote an execrable acrostic upon his admired lady's name, on a fan-shaped piece of paper.

> *Fancy ne'er painted a more beauteous Mind,*
> *And a more pleasing Face you'll seldom find:*
> *None with her in Wit can vie,*
> *No, not even Pallas, may I die!*
> *You'll all know this to be Fanny!*
>
> *Beautiful, witty and young,*
> *Unskilled in all deceits of Tongue,*
> *Reflecting glory on her Sex,*
> *None can her in Compliments perplex*
> *Easy in her manners as in her Dress*
> *You'll that this is Fanny, all must guess.*

Fanny's girlhood prudery did not languish for want of encouragement. There was, for example, that matter of Mrs. Pringle, when Mrs. Burney and Mr. Crisp had to step in. It began when Mrs. Pringle, "a widow lady who lives in this street"—Poland Street—invited Hetty and Fanny to tea. In the course of the next half year or so the Misses Burney met many young people at Mrs. Pringle's, among them a Major Dundas (impertinent coxcomb!), Captain Pringle, who was Mrs. Pringle's son, and Mr. Alexander Seton. Mr. Seton ("he is a charming man") was a flirt. One afternoon he dropped in on the Burneys with a message from Mrs. Pringle. Finding Fanny alone, he sat with her for about three hours, talking, "for Hetty, unluckily, was out, and Susette kept upstairs." Hetty's absence was unlucky for Hetty, because she had already declared herself quite charmed with Mr. Seton, but it was lucky for Fanny, who solemnly wrote in her Journal as soon as he had gone,

"I have had today the first real conversation I ever had in my life, except with Mr. Crisp."

It was the highest praise Fanny could have given. At sixteen intelligent young ladies are very grateful to be taken seriously, and Mr. Crisp had thus already won Fanny's heart forever. But Mr. Crisp was an elderly man, whereas Mr. Seton, though not at all elderly, unwittingly used Mr. Crisp's line and bait. "He is very little, and far from handsome, but he has a sensible countenance, and appears quite an Adonis after half an hour's conversation. . . . I own to you that I am not a little flattered that a man of his superior sense and cleverness, should think me worth so much of his time." Fanny had good reason to feel flattered. Mr. Seton drew comparisons between Englishwomen and Scots ladies in which the English (with the exception of Hetty and Fanny) came off very badly indeed. Mr. Seton, it is scarcely necessary to add, was a Scot.

"The truth is, the young women here, are so mortally silly and insipid, that I cannot bear them—Upon my word, except you and your sister I have scarce met with one worthy of being spoke to. Their chat is all on caps—balls—cards—dress—nonsense."

Fanny, thrilling deliciously, protested that Mr. Seton was too severe. Mr. Seton repeated and added to his asseverations. With the exceptions of Hetty and Fanny, no girl he had ever met in England could keep up a conversation. "I vow, if I had gone into almost any other house, and talk'd at this rate to a young lady,—she would have been sound asleep by this time," said Mr. Seton.

Pleasant words for a sixteen-year-old girl who had always heretofore been called a little dunce. Fanny fluttered—"I said a great deal in *defence* of our poor sex," she wrote—but she loved it. We need not take too much to heart the remark made on this passage by her editor, that "Fanny does not appear to have seen that the wily Mr. Seton was trying to please her as well as her lovely sister." Fanny saw well enough.

Alas for Hetty, the next few months proved that Mr. Seton was hopelessly inconstant. The Burneys kept meeting girl friends of his. He paid court to Hetty, but he paid court to many others too. One was Fanny herself, though her Journal never admits that Mr. Seton was after anything of Fanny's but her influence with Hetty. After quoting a number of his compliments, she wrote, "I have no fixed opinion of him. I know he is agreeable to a superior degree: and I believe he is as artful as agreeable."

This conversation marked a turning point in the *affaire Seton*. In vain the artful Alexander devoted himself to Hetty in a most flattering way (after having given Fanny her due share of attention); his day was drawing to a close. "We took our leaves at about three in the morning, I mine with much concern, assured as I was of not seeing them again so long, if ever: for mama's not being acquainted with this family, may probably put an end to our intimacy when we are all in town again." And afterward, "Poor Hetty passed an uneasy night, racked with uncertainty about this Seton, this eternal destroyer of her peace!—Were he sincere, she owned she could be happier in a union with him than with any man breathing:—indeed, he deserves her not;—but the next morning when she had considered well of every thing, she declared were he to make her the most solemn offer of her hand, she would refuse him,—and half added—*accept of Charles!*"

Charles was their cousin Charles Rousseau Burney, and Hetty did marry him not long after, though in the meantime Mr. Seton continued to pay his tantalizing attentions.

"Papa has bought a house in Queen Square. It is settled by Mr. Crisp to my very great grief that we are quite to drop Mrs. Pringle, that we may see no more of Mr. Seton."

Mr. Crisp was more than an uncle to the children, more than a father. An uncle usually leads his own life; a father leaves certain matters regarding the children to his wife. Mr. Crisp was something special. There is no one word to explain Mr. Crisp. He had few interests aside from the Burneys, and his advice was evidently taken without demur by Fanny's father and Maria Allen's mother. For the moment, however, we shall leave the wise old gentleman to wait for a more detailed explanation; our immediate business is with Mrs. Pringle. Mr. Crisp was not so easily fooled as Fanny's editor was to be. Hetty was married and out of danger, but Mr. Crisp knew his little Fanny was no longer the family dunce; he knew that the fascinating Mr. Seton might still cause a flutter in the Burney dovecot.

"For this reason I shall be glad to quit Poland Street,—that I may no longer see Mrs. Pringle since I dare not visit or even speak to her, when it is not unavoidable, as it was a few days since, when Miss Allen and I were standing at the parlour window, and Mrs. Pringle passed, but seeing me turned back and made a motion for me to open the window, which I did, though I was terribly confused what to say to her, for it was not in my powers to explain the reasons of my absence from her; yet, after so much kindness and civility as we have met from her, I am sure excuses were very necessary."

Poor Fanny. A few years later such a meeting with a condemned acquaintance was to cause her much less pain. She was to continue fluttering and protesting embarrassment, but through the years, with every snub the little prude administered, she found snubbing come more easily to her nature. Yet this was the first time, and Fanny was still alive to the other side of such matters. Remorse, shamed gratitude, guilt or cruelty could still wring her heart.

Mrs. Pringle asked her why she had stopped coming to call. Fanny tried to get out of it gracefully by pleading the demands on her time of removing to another house, but the widow lady was not deceived. Young Fanny was left with the decidedly unpleasant sensation of having behaved shabbily.

"I have a very strong sense of the favours we have received from her, and were it in my power, would convince her that I have—but it is not."

She had evolved a formula, one she was often to use again.

3. CHESINGTON AND TINGMOUTH

W<small>HAT</small> did these young ladies wear when they went to parties? Fanny was "easy in her Dress," but she must have taken a long time getting ready for a ball. The first thing that strikes our modern eyes in any picture of a lady of the times is her enormous head. A huge white curled headdress towers over her, and as if this were not enough, she ties a huge cap like a bonnet over the structure. ". . . those masses of meal and stuffing, power and pomatum, the dressing of which took many hours. Those piles of decorated, perfumed, reeking mess, by which a lady could show her fancy for the navy by balancing a straw ship on her head, for sport by showing a coach, for gardening by a regular bed of flowers. Heads which were only dressed perhaps once in three weeks, and were then rescented because it was necessary. Monstrous germ-gatherers of horse-hair, hemp-wool, and powder, laid on in a paste, the cleaning of which is too awful to give in full detail. 'Three weeks,' says my lady's hairdresser, 'is as long as a head can well go in the summer without being opened.' "[1]

Stanzas to the Ladies
Have ye never seen a net
    Hanging at your kitchen door,
Stuff'd with dirty straw, beset
    With old skewers o'er and o'er?

[1]*English Costume*, Dion Calthrop, 1907, p. 437.

> *If ye have—it wonder breeds*
> > *Ye from thence should steal a fashion*
> *And should heap your lovely heads*
> > *Such a deal of filthy trash on.*
>
> *True, your tresses wreath'd with art*
> > *(Bards have said it ten times over)*
> *Form a net to catch the heart*
> > *Of the most unfeeling lover. . . .*
>
> *When he scents the mingled steam*
> > *Which your plaster'd heads are rich in,*
> *Lard and meal, and clouted cream,*
> > *Can he love a walking kitchen?*[2]

One cannot wonder that a quiet creature like Fanny Burney found details of the wardrobe somewhat of a bore. She couldn't live up to the high fashionable standards of the day in any case. Her pocket money and dress allowance were as nothing compared to the sums fine ladies lavished on their clothes—eighty pounds for a mantua with French brocade petticoat, for example, or thirty guineas a yard for choice paduasoys. When even moderately fashionable women spent two thousand pounds a year on dress, how could the Burneys compete?

Fortunately, Fanny's tastes were not for clothes, and there was no young man to give her desires for fine feathers which she couldn't satisfy. She wasn't susceptible to young men, though she mentioned one or two favorably in the Journal. Fanny's one true love was Mr. Crisp, who was forty-six years older than herself. It was characteristic of her determined innocence and immaturity that she should elect a father-figure to worship, instead of an ordinary young lover.

Crisp had known her father in the Greville period and renewed the friendship later. It was Charles Burney who nicknamed him "Daddy." He was a gentleman of some fortune, of the Queen

[2] *The Foundling Hospital of Wit.* Edited by Garrick.

Anne era, a dilettante; he liked music, painting, "marbles," literature, and conversation. The greatest of these for Sam Crisp was literature; in 1754 Garrick produced his tragedy *Virginia*. Madame d'Arblay, when she read it years later, was disappointed. But *Virginia*, though badly written, had a fair amount of success. It ran for eleven nights on first production, which for the times was fairly good, as nine days' survival was the crucial test. Garrick did his best with unpromising material, though Crisp, like most playwrights, was not satisfied.

Nowadays few of us would be able to read *Virginia* at all, and fewer still with pleasure. Yet Crisp, judging from his letters, was a first-rate writer in the vernacular. He was vigorous, intelligent, balanced, and immensely likable. He was a good-looking man even in old age—tall and well made, with strong features. Fanny spoke of his "Roman nose."

Most of the facts we have of his life we owe to her memoirs. He became alarmed by the swift reduction of his fortune, and after an attempt to draw in his horns, which was unsuccessful because he lived within easy reach of London's temptations, he cut himself off more drastically. He moved into Chesington Hall near Kingston, a long way from the city, and shared the expenses of the rambling old farmhouse with its heir and owner, Christopher Hamilton. The arrangement was suitable not only financially but for reasons of health, for Crisp was fast falling victim to the terrible gout (perhaps rheumatism?) which claimed so many of his contemporaries. As his health declined and gout crippled his hands he became more and more of a recluse. During the days when Fanny was beginning her Journal he sometimes visited London, but by the time she published her first book it was only on very special occasions that Daddy Crisp left home.

Chesington was an excellent place for a hermitage, as no road led to the door: it stood remote and lonely in the middle of the wild common. When Hamilton died his relatives, Mrs. Hamilton and Kitty Cooke, who had been keeping house for him, divided the building and let one half to a farmer. Of the other part Mr.

Crisp kept a large slice for his own convenience and was able to entertain his good friends the Burneys whenever they came to stay. Chesington Hall became a sort of private boarding house for the Crisp elect. The Burneys visited there as readily as they went to Lynn. Charles and his bride, the former Mrs. Allen, spent their honeymoon hidden away at a nearby farm. Maria Allen disclosed the secret of her elopement at Chesington, with Daddy Crisp representing the horrified older generation at the recital. Hetty and her Charles were often guests of Daddy Crisp, who always called her "Hettina," after the fashion, popular among the musical Burneys, of Italianizing names. Lovingly in her old age Madame d'Arblay described the house as she remembered it, detail by detail, one never-forgotten day when with her new friend Mrs. Thrale she went exploring the building "with gay curiosity. Not a nook or corner; nor a dark passage 'leading to nothing'; nor a hanging tapestry of prim demoiselles and grim cavaliers; nor a tall canopied bed tied up to the ceiling; nor japan cabinets of two or three hundred drawers of different dimensions; nor an oaken corner cupboard, carved with heads, thrown in every direction, save such as might let them fall on men's shoulders; nor a window stuck in some angle close to the ceiling of a lofty slip of a room; nor a quarter of a staircase, leading to some quaint unfrequented apartment; nor a wooden chimney-piece, cut in diamonds, squares, and round nobs, surmounting another of blue and white tiles, representing, vis a vis, a dog and a cat, symbols of married life and harmony— missed their scrutinizing eyes." The old house has survived until today, no longer in the middle of a lonely common but in a thriving part of Suburbia. Even in its modern shape, however, it is doomed. As these words are written a bulldozer is hard at work finally leveling to their foundations the walls of Chesington Hall.

The removal from Poland Street must have been because of congestion in the house. Charles, now Dr. Burney—he took both bachelor's and doctor's degrees at Oxford in 1769—was rid of some incumbents, for James was away on a voyage, and Hetty was

married, and young Charles was at school. But already the fecund
man had started his second family, and there was a new baby, little
Dick. While the doctor was on the Continent collecting material
for a projected History of Music, Mrs. Burney moved the family
into a house in Queen's Square, Bloomsbury, with what Fanny
called "a delightful prospect of Hamstead and Hygate." Queen's
Square was not yet built up, and Fanny must have seen Hamp-
stead and Highgate as villages on the heights, cut off from Bloomsbury by country fields. She spoke of the neighborhood as a rural
place, with good fresh air and tempting walks.

Dr. Burney liked his residences to have some connection with
people he admired. Poland Street had no historical connotation
of which he could boast, but the house in Queen's Square had once
been occupied by a friend of Swift, and Burney took pleasure in
thinking that the great man himself must often have called there.
The Burneys swore by Swift. In Fanny's letters she sometimes referred to a "flapper" as we might mention a "Babbitt," with the
same confidence of being understood.

Queen's Square was also the habitat of Sir Richard Bettenson,
Bart., whose family became mixed up with the Burneys through
Maria Allen. Prudent Fanny, when she blue-penciled her diary, cut
out many entries about Maria, but we can still make out what happened.

Maria was more of a Lynn girl than was Fanny. She was older
and her life was set in Norfolk ways, whereas Fanny early became
a confirmed Londoner. Maria, who spent a lot of time in Lynn
after her mother moved away, fell in love with a fellow townsman,
Martin Folkes Rishton, nephew and heir of Sir Richard Bettenson
of Queen's Square. Neither Mrs. Burney nor the baronet favored
the attachment. Martin's father had been an indigent bookkeeper,
Martin had been extravagant as an Oxford undergraduate, and
there was some vague hint of a scandal. Mrs. Burney set herself
against the match.

But Maria had her way. A letter to Fanny, written at Lynn,
sounds as though the girl were whispering it behind a fan.

"I was at the Assembly forced to go entirely against my own Inclination. But I have always sacrificed my own Inclinations to the will of other people—could not resist the pressing Importunity of —Bet Dickens—to go—tho it proved Horridly stupid. I drank tea at the—told old T[unner] I was determined not to dance—he would not believe me—a wager ensued—half a Crown provided I followed my own Inclinations—agreed—Mr. Audley asked me. I refused—sat still—yet followed my own Inclinations. But four couple began—Martin was there—yet stupid—nimporte—quite Indifferent—on both sides—Who had I—to converse with the whole Evening—not a female friend—none there—not an acquaintance— All Dancing—who then—I've forgot—nimporte—I broke my Earring—how—heaven knows—foolishly enough—one can't always keep on the Mask of Wisdom—well n'importe I danced a Minuet, a quatre the latter end of the Eve—with a stupid Wretch—need I name him——"

News of the party reached Sir Richard and he sent Martin away on the Grand Tour, with orders to remain abroad for two years. Five months later, however, Maria wrote in her customary agitated style to Susan and Fanny:

"If it does but astonish you equal to what it did me in hearing it you won't have recovered your surprise by the time I see you again—Rishton—my—yes the very identical Martin—Folkes—Lucious—etc.—Rishton—is come over—and now in England——"

The older generation decided to apply pressure from the other side. Maria wrote the girls, soon after Martin came back; she was now to go abroad in her turn, since Martin wouldn't stay put— to Geneva to finish her education. Yes, she had seen Martin. Yes, she had danced next to him a whole evening. But now it was over and she was going to Geneva, and would stay the night in Queen's Square en route.

"You, Mrs. Fanny, I desire to dress neatly and properly—without a hole in either Apron or Ruffles——"

From Geneva a few weeks later she demanded indignantly, why

no letters? Not a line from her mother, and she was penniless because everyone had advised her to buy her clothes in Paris and Lyons *en passant* and she had taken their advice. Were her uncles in Lynn holding back her money? If so, she would not be balked; she would borrow against her imminent coming of age, or sell her jewels. Would Fanny please forward her pianoforte and music, and Fordyce's sermons, all to be found at her landlord's house. Would Hetty please buy her "a very elegant tea cadet, very like that I bought my mother, and at the same shop, which is in Piccadilly—on the same side as the haymarket—7 or eight doors farther you will see all sorts of things of inlaid work stand out at the window, buy me a little black ebony inkstand with silver plaited tops to the bottles—and a handle like one to a basket of the same metal—— They were new last winter, and then cost 18s. and the cadet not more than 12s. These two things and a very pretty naked wax doll with blue eyes, the half crown sort—I fancy at the wax-work in fleet street will be the place . . . and do it up that it will not be broke with cotton all over it and 100 papers. I fancy they will all come in the piano forte case."

Sympathy for Maria, whose romantic yearnings were being crushed by Mrs. Burney and the other elders, made Fanny pensive. As she came home one day from an errand on Maria's behalf at the house of the Guiffardières, she walked through Poland Street. A host of sentimental thoughts assailed her. *Eheu fugaces!* No more, oh, nevermore! Oh, Fanny's lost youth of two years back! "I passed with great regret by Mrs. Pringle's windows"; there was a strange name on the door.

Two days later she heard that Mrs. Pringle had gone to the East Indies. "And thus I suppose will close for ever all acquaintance with the agreeable woman and our family. On my side how unwillingly! for I cannot join in the bad opinion mama and Mr. Crisp have so strangely, so causelessly conceived of her. . . . I must also own that since we have dropped her acquaintance, we have never made any half so lively and agreeable. . . . Dear, wise, and good Mr. Crisp has surely been too severe in his judgment. What a misfortune I should deem it to think so ill of mankind as he, the wisest of his race, tries to make me think!"

Owing to this timorous and hidden rebellion, Fanny did not do so much violence to her feelings as one would expect of a little prude when Maria confided a dangerous secret to her six months later. Fanny kept faith. Maria was actually corresponding with Rishton! She sent copies of the letters to Fanny and Susan, though she was acutely conscious that Martin and she were behaving badly in corresponding at all. "I only wish you would not be guided by prejudice—put yourselves a few minutes in my place—you know my heart has never once Ceased to *Beat* in his favor even when I *thought* him most unworthy——"

In stout if incoherent defense of her lover's honor she quoted his letter: "You tell me the remembrance of the first letter you sent me . . . has embitter'd many hours of your Life & Cost you many tears.—I grant you—such a step might have disagreeable Reflections —But pray! what reason had you for such Uneasiness? did my Character ever give you room to Imagine I should expose you because you Loved Me? Tis thoroughly unnatural—I defy the world to bring any Instance of my behaving unworthy the Character of a Gentleman—(unless you Accuse me) your letter was immediately destroyed—& had I vainly boasted of such honours who would have believed me."

"I think those the sentiments of a Man of honour and such I hope to find him," added Miss Allen.

Twentieth-century readers may be mystified by all this fuss and fuming over a mere declaration by a lady. Maria could not have made more of a squawk, speaking crudely, if she had been seduced outright instead of simply avowing her tender passion in writing, and from a good safe distance at that. But when she said she suffered, she meant it. She was properly brought up in the School of Prudery, and she meant it. They were easily compromised in the eighteenth century. They knew exactly what they must not do. It wasn't like the Victorian age, where propriety demanded a pretense of complete ignorance rather than innocence. Nobody was ignorant in Fanny's world: how could Pamela have played her careful game if she had not known the rules? and Clarissa, though a weak female, certainly knew what she was doing, and lamented it every step of the way, poor girl.

The Female Complaint[3]

Custom, alas! does partial prove
   Nor gives us even measure;
A pain it is to maids to love
   But 'tis to men a pleasure.

They freely can their thoughts disclose,
   But ours must burn within;
Tho' nature eyes and tongues bestows,
   Yet truth from us is sin.

Men to new joys and conquests fly,
   And yet no hazards run;
Poor are we left, if we deny;
   And, if we yield, undone.

Then equal laws let custom find,
   Nor thus the sex oppress;
More freedom grant to woman-kind,
   Or give to mankind less.

Maria gravely jeopardized her standing as an innocent maiden in writing to Martin at all. Certainly she trusted him, for by merely showing some companion a letter, any letter, addressed to him in her handwriting, Martin could have ruined her reputation.

"An inflexible law forbade correspondence between marriageable persons not engaged to be married. Elinor Dashwood was not satisfied that Willoughby and Marianne were engaged, though she knew that he had been permitted to cut off a lock of her hair; but

[3]*The Foundling Hospital,* Garrick.

when she saw her write him a brief note to inform him of their being in town, 'the conclusion which as instantly followed was, that . . . they must be engaged.' Darcy's letter to Elizabeth is clandestine: it receives no answer, and the possibility of an answer is not started. Even the sophisticated Mary Crawford could not write to Edmund Bertram to ask him to call on her before he left London; 'he had received a note from Lady Stornaway to beg him to call.' Captain Wentworth writes a letter to Anne (which is delivered by stratagem); but though her answer would constitute an engagement, Anne does not conceive the possibility of sending a note to his rooms; she has to trust to ambiguous messages and untrustworthy messengers."[4]

No wonder there was so much agonizing in the Rishton-Allen correspondence! For the same reason tired old roués prefer the long skirt and the stolen glimpse of feminine ankle to complete nudity, Maria Allen and Fanny Burney trembled with delicious terror when they thought of the threat that avowal afforded Maria's reputation. It was just like a novel, and Maria sometimes referred to novels they had read together when she wrote her tempestuous letters to Fanny.

Just as in most fiction of the sort, Maria's vessel of romance was conducted to a safe harbor. In spite of his sweetheart's madly indiscreet behavior in confessing she loved Rishton, they were quietly married in France. Back in England, Maria whispered the secret to Fanny and Susan, and for some days the three girls tiptoed about in a highly enjoyable state of romantic terror.

They decided to break the news first to Crisp, so Susan and Maria went to Chesington. Maria talked to Daddy Crisp of Rishton and her unalterable love; she showed his picture and declared her intention of marrying him no matter what. (This was the customary way of breaking bad news gently. Your husband is ill—is very ill—is dead. I love Rishton—I *will* marry Rishton—I *have* married Rishton.)

[4]*Manners of the Age*, Chapman.

But Daddy Crisp reacted too violently. He blew up when Maria mentioned her darling Martin: "If he had been a Mahoon he could not have merited what Crisp said," she wrote indignantly. (She must have meant "Mahound," i.e., Turk, or polygamist.)

Maria and Susan hastily retired to their bedroom and dispatched, via Kitty Cooke, a pert message to Crisp that Mrs. Rishton sent her compliments and hoped to see him at home that summer.

"He came into the room to us," wrote Susan. "Maria fell on her knees instantly and hid her face on the bed—Why what is all this? said he. Kate claw'd hold of her left hand, and shew'd him the Ring."

It was a most satisfying scene. Mr. Crisp called Maria all sorts of names, which the diary's editor carefully explains away and apologizes for. Crisp had Queen Anne habits, she reminds us, and to call a lady a little devil in Queen Anne's time was not exactly an *oath*. First Mr. Crisp ranted. Then Mr. Crisp laughed. Then Mr. Crisp took back what he had said about Martin and gave Mrs. Rishton a lot of worldly advice, something he was fond of doing at any time.

Fanny had to tell Mrs. Burney. There was another fearful scene, which Fanny probably thought she dreaded and abhorred, but she loved it really.

No, life in Queen's Square could not, in all justice, be called insipid.

We of this hurried age must respect young Fanny for having put so much work into her ordinary day. She toiled at a tremendous rate as unofficial secretary for the doctor, copying out his voluminous writing. Then she would repair to her hideaway, the children's playroom, to write page after page of her Journal and letters to Daddy Crisp, not to mention the secret manuscripts which were her mingled shame and delight. Yet her social life took precedence in her mind over any of these pursuits, or perhaps it would be more exact to say that her excursions and friendships were an inextricable part of the Journal, for like many born writers Fanny was always unconsciously observing and putting away little hints and incidents in order to repeat them later on paper. Without tutelage except for her reading, Fanny was training herself. It is strange that no one has credited her with the unusual detachment with which in her writing she treated even her own person. She has been accused of many faults, and some of the accusations are justified, but it is unfair to call Fanny unduly vain or egotistic. Considering the times she lived in, the training she received, and the horror she might have been, Fanny was remarkably honest. She had an instinct for clinging to the facts as she saw them. She was a true reporter, and achieved a high degree of happiness with that talent, as long as its first vigor lasted.

How had it happened? We have a flood of evidence—family letters, family memoirs, other people's letters and memoirs—but it is not easy to reconstruct the secrets of even the most articulate soul, and we will never be able to do more than guess at the reason for Fanny. Certainly her father bequeathed her many characteristics, through heredity, example, or friends. He had an easy capacity for hero worship as well. All his daughters and perhaps his sons held firmly to certain ideas which they got from Charles Burney. They scorned English music in general, favoring the Italian, and battled fiercely against any barbarian John Bull who tried to argue them down on those grounds. (Their spiritual heirs are still fighting the same war.) They revered Samuel Johnson, the Great Lexicographer, long before they met him. Why? One would have to know the eighteenth century well to understand why the author of a dreary tragedy and a long-deferred dictionary should have become so much the rage.

Then there were Charles's intimates. Fanny as a giggling girl probably paid only lip service to some of them, for she was preoccupied with her youthful interests. But many visitors to Queen's Square made as much impression on the children as they did on the father, and chief of them all was Garrick the inimitable.

David Garrick, like Esther Sleepe, was descended from French Huguenots. As a boy in Lichfield he went to school to Samuel

Johnson for a while, then set out with his schoolmaster, his senior by only a few years, to London in search of fortune. He made a brief gesture of reading for law, but it did not last. He was a wine merchant for a space of time, like so many other Englishmen— wine and brewing were both assuming an important place in industry—but Garrick as a businessman *tout simple* did not succeed. Anyhow, he was always so strongly attracted to the theater that it was no use trying to do anything else. As soon as he did go on the stage he was a tremendous success.

People who saw his performances said that it was his *natural* style which gave him so much merit. Before Garrick popularized this method actors declaimed instead of imitating everyday speech and behavior. This declaiming school has survived on the Continent until very recently, in the classical dramas of France and Germany; a few old actors cling to the style even now. But Garrick, with his wealth of vivacity and invention, brought naturalism to England's drama two hundred years ago. Today we might possibly argue that he was not so natural as all that: we would probably call him a ham, or a ranter of the worst order. But we must remember that most of the stuff he interpreted lent itself readily to melodramatic delivery.

"Garrick was sublimely horrible!" gasped Fanny after a performance of *Richard the Third*. "Good Heavens how he made me shudder whenever he appeared! It is inconceivable how terribly great he is in this character! I will never see him so disfigured again; he seemed so truly the monster he performed, that I felt myself glow with indignation every time I saw him. The applause he met with, exceeds all belief of the absent. I thought at the end they would have torn the house down: our seats shook under us."

Garrick's quickly changing facial expressions were not the least of his assets; people said his French blood gave him the vivacity and fire which always animated his small body, and Sam Johnson, remarking on his aging appearance, said with his own brand of humorous elephantine malice that David naturally would wear out his face long before most people did because he used it so much more. But he was remarkable as well for his variety of talents over and above that particular one. David Garrick was an excellent actor-manager. When we add to his record of "adapted" Shakespearean productions and his well-trained stock company the genuine flair he showed for literature in his epigrams, prologues, and epilogues, we may well wonder whether such a man will ever tread the boards again.

It was David Garrick who stormed the fortress of fashionable society on behalf of actors as a class. Until he became the rage of London, male actors were never accepted as companions to aristocracy except when aristocracy went slumming. Actresses sometimes made the grade, in time-honored style; actresses became mistresses and sometimes wives of the great men of England, but actors had not the same recourse. They were classed as rogues and vagabonds. If it was hard going for a socially ambitious actor in England, his brother Thespian in France occupied an even lower place.

Just why this attitude should have prevailed is not clear, though it seems to have come straight down the ages from the days of the Roman Empire, when, until Nero shocked the populace so badly, only slaves made public appearances as actors and musicians. The prejudice wasn't confined to western Europe. In Russia, noblemen drew on their ranks of serfs for actors and dancers. In China, actors, when children, were bought and sold, and brought up in slavery, a custom which persisted until very recently, within the span of Mei Lan-fang's life.

Garrick changed the actors' luck in England. He went everywhere, and everyone in London went to him. He often dropped in on the house in Queen's Square, delighting the children and scandalizing the servants. The child Fanny sometimes watched him on the stage from Mrs. Garrick's box, and when she came home she would mimic the actor's gestures and recite his speeches.

For the rest, aside from the adored Mr. Crisp, no one but her young friends seems to have made much impression on Fanny in the years before she began her career. But in May 1772 she wrote in her Journal, "My design upon the correspondence of Mr. Crisp has succeeded to my wish. He has sent me the kindest and most flattering answer, which encourages me to write again. He says more in three lines than I shall in a hundred, while I live." (There was a good deal of truth in that.) She appended to her report of a musical evening at home the declaration, "To this select party had Mr. Crisp and Miss Allen been added, we should scarce have wished another."

There were other parties enjoyable as that one. The doctor had just published a book, *The Present State of Music in France and Italy*. It was started merely as a collection of notes he kept while traveling in preparation for his *History of Music*. More and more inveterately a scribbler, he wrote the book almost without realizing it, and it had a success. Burney's circle was never a small one, but now it became larger.

Aside from parties which were framed chiefly for the older generation, Fanny depended for excitement and a youthful private life on that never-failing source of both, Stepsister Maria. Mama, "the Governor," had not yet surrendered gracefully, but Fanny and the bride corresponded nevertheless. Shortly before Fanny's coming of age Maria wrote from Teignmouth in South Devon, where she was sojourning on a prolonged holiday with her husband. Why should not her dear Fanny come to "Tingmouth" for the summer, instead of to Lynn where she always did go? It would be convenient as well as pleasant, for Fanny need spend nothing on dress, as she would have to for Lynn; Maria wore only a "common linnen gown" every day; nor need Fanny worry about her hair, for Maria had not had her hair dressed since arriving. Martin himself suggested the visit, as he would feel free to go fishing and shooting if Maria had another companion.

Fanny went to Teignmouth, and by so doing she became all at once almost a professional writer. Until she began the *Tingmouth Journal* her diary was kept like any girl's, for herself alone, though unconsciously she had her eye on a shadowy, undefined reader. She now carried on a formal exchange of letters with Mr. Crisp, and though Susan as well corresponded with their Daddy, and Maria sometimes favored him with one of her breathless epistles, it was understood that Fanny's letters were the best. Mr. Crisp took a lot of trouble with his answers to Fanny, as if he had suddenly realized her vigor and talent.

When she went to Teignmouth, Fanny promised Susan to keep her Journal faithfully, and Susan replied as faithfully from home. Susan acted as official clearinghouse between Fanny and Mr. Crisp. What Fanny wrote, she knew, would be forwarded to Mr. Crisp to read; she was now turning out a sort of serial story for her public; she took pains. The daily stint created a habit not only of writing, but of polishing afterward; polishing, in a way, for publication.

She found the Rishtons living in a "small, neat, thatched and whitewashed cottage, neither more nor less," and very close to the sea, where Maria bathed every morning. There was a lot of company at Tingmouth, but Martin Rishton did not care for the pleasures of society. Only two families in the whole place gained his approval, but he did go so far as to express praise for "a half name-sake of my dear Daddy Crisp—i.e. a Mr. Crispen. . . . It seems he has interested himself very much in my father's musical plan. He is on the wrong side of an elderly man, but seems to have good health and spirits."

Another acquaintance of the Rishtons who wasn't equally popular with Martin was Miss Bowdler, a sister of the man who "edited" Shakespeare. The word "bowdlerize" is probably a more lasting contribution to literature than was Bowdler's editing. His sister didn't share his ideas of propriety. She bore a rather singular character, said Martin. "She is very sensible and clever, and possesses a great share of wit and poignancy which spares, he says, neither friend or foe. She reckons herself superior, he also adds, to the opinion of the world and to all common forms and customs, and therefore lives exactly as she pleases, guarding herself from all real evil, but wholly regardless and indifferent to appearances. She is about six and twenty; a rather pretty little figure, but not at all handsome, though her countenance is very spirited and expressive. She has father, mother, and sisters alive; but yet is come to Tingmouth alone; though for the moment indeed, she is with a Miss Lockwood, a rich old maid; but she will very soon be entirely at liberty. She and her family are old acquaintances of Mrs. Rishton, and of mama; she is therefore frequently here; but Mr. Rishton, who gave me most of this account of her, cannot endure even the sight of her, a woman, he says, who despises the customs and manners of the country she lives in, must, consequently, conduct herself with impropriety. For my part I own myself of the same sentiment, but, nevertheless, we have not any one of us the most distant shadow of doubt of Miss Bowdler's being equally innocent with those who have more worldly prudence, at the same time, that her conduct appears to me highly improper; for she finds that the company of gentlemen is more entertaining than that of ladies, and therefore, without any scruples or punctilio, indulges her fancy. She is perpetually at Mr. Crispen's, notwithstanding a very young man, Mr. Green, lives in the same house; not contented with a call, she very frequently sups with them; and though she does this in the fair face of day, and speaks of it openly and commonly as I should of visiting my sister, yet I can by no means approve so great a contempt of public opinion."

Unfortunately, Miss Bowdler did not seem to care whether or not Fanny approved of her. She may have suspected the fact, and she must surely have known that Mr. Rishton almost *detested* her, since he had a way of bolting out and disappearing the minute she came to call. But Maria was an old friend, and Maria liked her, and though Maria, the adoring, submissive wife, offered to give Miss Bowdler up, her Rishton would not consent to it, "because he knows it would be much against her will, and because if it was not, he would not risque her character to the *lash* of Miss Bowdler's tongue."

With Miss Bowdler and more approved friends, the days went by. Fanny made some sage observations on the Rishton marriage, which seemed to be going well in spite of Mama's gloomy prophecies. She was happy with them and their four dogs. But nothing is static, and very shortly the peaceful surface of life was ruffled, by Mr. Crispen of all people. Though the wrong side of elderly, Mr. Crispen had some ideas which seemed to Fanny too youthful. "This Mr. Crispen," she wrote, "seems attached to the fair sex in the style of the old courtiers. I am told that he has Dulcineas without number, though I am the reigning sovereign at present." The Rishton party called on Mr. Crispen one Sunday evening and found Miss Bowdler sitting with him. "Miss Bowdler, who is on the list, and who I take for a very formidable rival. . . ." Mr. Crispen made oncoming speeches to Fanny right in front of everyone, and when his young housemate, Mr. Green, came in they vied with each other in gallantry.

" 'Miss Bowdler, do you allow of all this?' cried Mrs. Rishton. 'O, I am obliged to it,' replied she—'for I am but an old wife!' She made no scruple of being left with the two gentlemen, when we came away."

Obviously Fanny was set for a good summer, and it is safe to say that she had it. Mr. Crispen and Miss Bowdler would each alone have been sufficient to ensure that. Together they spelled what must have been perfect bliss. One day at Brixton the Rishtons encountered a gay party from Tingmouth, among them the daring Miss Bowdler. Fanny said, "I was sorry to see the latter in such company, for they behaved in a most ridiculous and improper manner dancing about the town and diverting themselves in a very unmannerly easy and careless style, and though Miss Bowdler herself behaved with propriety yet her party reflected some thing on her [sense?] and has much added to Mr. Rishton's aversion to her."

Then Fanny found herself the object of warm declarations of love from Mr. Crispen. "He protested . . . that where the *thoughts* were, there the *person* must wish itself!—&c.—all addressed to little me!"

Miss Bowdler grew angry. "I fancy she wishes to be more *unique* with him than she finds it is in her power to be."

National Portrait Gallery, London

FANNY BURNEY

A CONCERT

Dr. Burney is in right foreground.

But the reckless young woman was unable to manage Mr. Crispen: he was irrepressible. Once, calling at the Rishtons' with some of Mr. Green's drawings on cards, "Two of them were views of Tingmouth, and he made a great fuss about them, asking me how I would bribe him for a sight? I told him that I had nothing at all to offer.——

" 'Why, now,' said he, 'methinks two drawings deserve two kisses —and—if——'

" 'No, no, no,' cried I, 'not that!' much surprised at his modest request. But he only spoke in sport I am sure." . . .

"Miss Bowdler might have blushed to have heard the benevolence with which he spoke of her. He lamented in very affectionate terms that she had been unfortunately mixed with so giddy and imprudent a party, and recommended it very strongly to Mrs. Rishton to make it known as much as she could, that Miss Bowdler was an exception to the general set, when the company was named. . . . He spoke of her in very high terms and said he owed her so much regard and respect that he would himself be always with her, but that he knew the people here would only sneer about it. It seems, in a bad illness which Mr. Crispen had, she was his constant nurse.

"Mr. Rishton very openly blamed her for mixing with the Brixham party. Mr. Crispen could hardly justify her. 'I would not,' said he, 'have had a daughter of mine there—or my little Burney, for the whole world!'

". . . Now, to tell you my private opinion, my dear Susy, I am inclined to think that this gallantry is the effect of the man's taking me for a fool; . . ."

When Fanny talked of the Races, Mr. Crispen cried, "Ah! would that your heart was to be run for! What an effort would I make!"

"Yes," cried Miss Bowdler (not very delicately), "you would break your wind on the occasion, I doubt not."

One likes Miss Bowdler, somehow, better and better as the summer goes on.

"To day has been very so-so. . . . Mr. Gibbs came on my side pretending to screen me from the wind, and entered into small talk with a facility that would not have led me to supposing how high his character stood at the university. Mrs. Rishton was in one of her provoking humours. She came behind me every now and then and whispered 'Fie, child!' and then shaking her head and walking off 'Upon my word, the girls of this age! there is no more respect for a married woman than if—well, I'd rather be whip't than married, I declare! Really Mrs. Western, we matrons are no more regarded by these chits than so many pepper-corns!' Mr. Gibbs stared, but continued his talk. Then in a few minutes she returned to me again, 'Really, Miss Fanny Burney, I don't know what you mean by this behaviour! O girls! girls! girls!'

"We seem to have quite dropt Mr. Crispen. He cannot but have perceived Mr. Rishton's coldness, as he never calls. Mr. Rishton has an uncommon aversion to every thing that leads towards flirtation, and Mr. Crispen from being much regarded by him, as the first man here, is become almost odious. I fancy that this friendship for Miss Bowdler has much contributed to make Mr. Rishton dislike him. . . . It is not possible for a man to make a better husband than Mr. Rishton does. He spends almost every minute of his time with his wife, and is all attention and kindness to her. He is reading Spencer's *Faery Queen* to us, in which he is extremely delicate, omitting whatever, to the poet's great disgrace, has crept in that is improper for a woman's ear."

Without doubt, Miss Bowdler would have read Spenser in the original, and gloried in it. One wonders what she and her famous brother ever found to talk about. The weather, perhaps?

4. UNALTERABLY FIXED

M<small>R. CRISP</small> to Fanny: "Now, you are young, art-
less, open, sincere, unexperienced, *unhack-
ney'd* in the Ways of Men; consequently you
have high notions of Generosity, Fidelity, disinterestedness, Constancy and all the sublime train of Sentimental Visions, that get
into girls' heads, and are so apt to turn them inside out—— No
wonder therefore, that you rail at men, and pull the poor devils to
pieces at such a rate—— Now I must endeavour to set you right,
and persuade you to see things as they really are, in Truth and in
Nature; then you will be more favourable, and no longer think
them monsters, wretches, etc.—be assured, my Fanny, they are
just what they were design'd to be—Animals of Prey—all men are
cats, all young girls mice—morsels—dainty bits—Now to suppose
when the mouse comes from her hole, that the generous sentimental Grimalkin will not seize her, is contrary to all Nature and
Experience, and even to the design and Order of Providence—for
depend on it, whatever is, is right; . . ."

Armed with this excellent advice, the mouse went her ways,
visiting with Mama and being visited. There was young Mr. Twiss,
for example, whom the Burneys called the Spanish traveler, though
he aimed rather to be a traveler of the entire world and had already
rolled up twenty-seven thousand miles to his credit. Today his

book is an obscure, high-priced item on the Charing Cross Road bookstalls, but when Fanny met him in Queen's Square he was discussed in drawing rooms as an intrepid soul. There was a run on intrepid travelers that season, such as Captain Cook and Abyssinian Bruce.

Twiss started out on the wrong foot at the Burneys' by telling a tall story. Mama and her mother were quite angry with him for saying Spanish ladies wore glowworms for jewels, strung or sewed to their dresses and hair of an evening. A vigorous family argument took place after he had gone, relative to the staying power of glowworms.

Mr. Twiss's next call made even more of a flutter. He got on to the subject of *the ladies*, and there he stayed happily talking of awkward matters, nor would he be budged. Sometimes Dr. Burney tempted him to some safer topic, but Mr. Twiss kept bouncing back to *the ladies*. In Madrid, he said, these creatures were wildly enthusiastic about bullfights in a manner curious to observe. And from Naples he had been absolutely forced by them to flee. Scenting the boastful implication of a love affair, Fanny's father set out to "smoak" (tease) his guest. When starting for Naples, Burney said gravely, he was warned that *the ladies* were oncoming and that he would surely receive three or four billets-doux within a few moments of showing himself in the public square. "Accordingly, as soon as I got there, I dressed myself to the best advantage, and immediately went to the Piazza, but to no purpose! and though I walked there every morning I stayed, the devil of a billet-doux did I ever meet with!"

Ignoring the hint, Mr. Twiss continued his story; he had been dangerously involved, he insisted. Then why, asked a dull old man of the party, had he run away?

"Oh, sir, the *ladies* are concerned!" cried Mr. Twiss, "but another time, Dr. Burney, when we are alone——"

What might have been an awkward silence was filled with vivacious comment on harmless topics from the others. Dr. Burney was just going to ask Mr. Twiss some nice safe question about harpsi-

chords when the traveler got in ahead of him. "But Dr. Burney, was
you never accosted by *una bella ragazza*? You know what a *ragazza*
is, ma'am?" he added in the kindest way to Fanny.

"Sir?" said Fanny, trembling like a leaf. Really, in front of all
those people!

"A signorina?" asked the terrible Mr. Twiss.

He paid her preposterous compliments in Italian. Fanny blamed
herself that he took such a liberty: "I believe he had already drawn
his conclusions from my foolish *simpering* before, upon his first
visit," she said ruefully to the Journal.

She protested she couldn't talk Italian, so Mr. Twiss tried her
out with French. By this time she was so frightened that she did
not speak at all: she simply shook her head. Mr. Twiss spoke of
masquerades; Fanny managed to reply that she had been only to
a private one. Mr. Twiss said he loved to dance: "Don't you love
dancing, ma'am?"

"Me, sir? Oh, I seldom dance—I don't know."

"What assemblies do you frequent, ma'am?"

"Me, sir? I hardly ever dance; I go to none!"

"To none? Bless me! But—pray, ma'am—will you do me the
honor to accept any tickets for Mrs. Cornely's?"

"Sir, I am obliged to you; but I never——"

"No, sir," said Dr. Burney, coming to his daughter's rescue, "she
does nothing of that sort."

To add to poor Fanny's discomfort, Mrs. Allen made a personal
remark which was not in the best of taste: "Well! my dear, you
have it all! Poor Susy is nothing tonight." Fanny was in a perfect
tremor that Mr. Twiss would hear her. And Mrs. Young, Mama's
sister, fixed her eyes on the pair with curious observation. And
Father began to grow very grave. Everybody tried to turn the conversation, but in vain; the "florid traveler" would not regard their
efforts, and chattered on in his own peculiar way. It was such an
uncomfortable way, too—raving about Miss Aiken's *Poems*, and
recommending one in particular because it described the symp-

toms of love. To be sure, he recommended it to Dr. Burney rather than the ladies, but still . . .

The worst was yet to come. "But, Dr. Burney," cried the amazing man, "of all the books upon this subject, none was ever equal to Rousseau's *Eloise!* What feeling! What language! What fire! Have you read it, ma'am?"

"No, sir," said Fanny miserably. It was all very well to admire French philosophy and to have a cousin named after Rousseau, but even well brought-up girls knew there were things Rousseau, though a Frenchman, should not have written, and one of them was *La Nouvelle Héloïse.*

"Oh, it's a book that is alone!" cried Mr. Twiss.

"And *ought* to be *alone,*" said Dr. Burney with portentous gravity.

"Mr. Twiss perceived that he was now angry, and with great eagerness he cried, 'Why, I assure you I gave it to my sister, who is but seventeen, and just going to be married.'

" 'Well,' returned my father, 'I hope she read the Preface and then flung it away.' "

Not even that rebuke was capable of stopping Mr. Twiss. Heedless of his host's lowering brow, he galloped along. Had the doctor ever read a little book on the same subject called the *Dictionary of Love?* A most elegant work, difficult to find because it was out of print. But Twiss had a copy. ". . . I shall do myself the honor to show it to you, ma'am," he said to Fanny in a low voice. "Though you cannot want it—you have it all ready—it is only for such bunglers as me."

The mouse deemed it wiser to pretend she had not heard, and she hoped devoutly that nobody else had either. Still resilient, Mr. Twiss begged her to give the company some music. Fanny refused. He turned to Mama and asked her to use her influence.

"Sir," said Mama rather sharply, "I am not a duenna!"

"Duennia, ma'am," said he, "is the true pronunciation. . . ."

"I think this was the most extraordinary evening I ever passed," wrote Fanny. We cannot in justice accuse her of exaggeration.

"My father has bought a House in St. Martin's Street, Leicester Fields,—an odious street—but well situated, and nearly in the centre of the town; and the house is a large and good one. It was built by Sir Isaac Newton! and, when he constructed it, it stood in Leicester *Fields*,—not *Square*, that he might have his observatory unannoyed by neighbouring houses, and his observatory is my favourite sitting place, where I can retire to read or write any of my private fancies or vagaries."

Dr. Burney was so proud of his house's connection with Isaac Newton that it is to be hoped nobody ever told him the less romantic truth. Newton didn't build it; he moved in when he was seventy years old. Perhaps he used the little penthouse affair as an observatory and perhaps not, but the entire room, glass windows and all, after being blown away in a storm during the Burneys' tenancy, was lovingly rebuilt by the doctor. Nowadays a public library stands on the site. Nowadays St. Martin's Street is no more odious than any of its surroundings, which are all pretty bad; it is dangerously narrow, and, though short, does not give one a clear view from one end to the other. New house fronts stick out like elbows. Cinema doorways, cigar warehouses, shamefaced art galleries, and a Moo-Cow Milk Bar adorn Leicester Square where once there stood a king's town palace. But Leicester Fields has always smacked faintly of the sinister, what with its duels, its public executions, its robberies: today's dejected shoddiness has its atmosphere too.

The Burneys' house saw some remarkable gatherings. Garrick complained of its central position in the town. He regretted his long country walks to Queen's Square; besides, Leicester Square was full of theater fans who followed him about and plagued him whenever he appeared, and Garrick said he hated that. (Though he also claimed to be insulted when the Burneys' servant failed to recognize him.) But everyone else was ready and eager to attend the musical evenings which were a Burney specialty, and Fanny's Journal prattled of the new *Lyons* who were entertained under their roof. With still lively pleasure she harked back, six decades later, to a favorite lion of that season—Omai from Otaheite. (That name is now spelled, not so exactly, Tahiti.)

Omai, or Omy or Omiah, called "Jack" by the sailors, was by way of being a special ward of Fanny's brother "Jem"—Second Lieutenant James Burney, who had gone out with Captain Cook on the second of the famous voyages. He figures in Cook's works in his report on the fate in New Zealand of ten men from the *Adventure* who were massacred and eaten by natives. James commanded the search party which found a few of the human remains and identified them through a tattoo mark someone recognized on one of the fragments of flesh. He was often pressed to tell this story to his family, and he readily obliged, though his sisters invariably screamed before he came to the end, and said it was too horrible to talk about. A more acceptable souvenir of the voyage, more fascinating even than a cannibal story, was the puzzled Polynesian, Omai. In a genial, unconscious way, Omai served as unofficial ambassador to England for the South Sea Islands. He liked Jem Burney's company because Jem spoke his language fluently.

Captain Cook said in his book that he hadn't been too keen on bringing Omai back, but the Polynesian wanted to get away from Otaheite, where he was in financial difficulties. "Omai, in my opinion, was not a proper sample of the inhabitants of these happy islands, not having any advantage of birth, or acquired rank; nor being eminent in shape, figure, or complexion: for their people of first rank are much fairer, and usually better behaved, and more intelligent, than the middling class of people, among whom Omai is to be ranked. I have, however, since my arrival in England been convinced of my error: for excepting his complexion (which is undoubtedly of deeper hue than that of the *Earies*, or gentry, who, as in other countries, live a more luxurious life, and are less exposed to the sun), I much doubt whether any other of the natives would have given more general satisfaction by his behaviour among us. . . ."

Mr. Solander and Mr. Banks (afterward Sir Joseph Banks), who had gone on Cook's first expedition, brought Omai to dine in St.

Martin's Street: Fanny thought the Polynesian tall and very well made, much darker than she had expected, and, though by no means handsome, of a pleasing countenance. He had visited the House of Lords to be presented to the King on the morning of the Burney dinner, so he was all dressed up—velvet lined with white satin, a bag wig, lace ruffles, and a splendid sword which the King had given him. A Mr. Cradock waspishly recorded after a dinner party at the Admiralty that Omai kicked up a stink when he discovered his new clothes were only of English velvet, whereas all the fine gentlemen he met around town were partial to the Genoese variety. Omai did that, said Mr. Cradock. Omai, who until that time had never owned a coat at all!

Fanny was much impressed with Omai's beautiful manners. He made *remarkable* good bows. His manners were so polite, attentive, and easy that you would have thought he came from some foreign court. He showed perturbation only once at dinner, when a man-servant spilled a little beer on his velvet; he spread his handkerchief over his knee protectingly. When his coach arrived he went to Dr. Burney first, just as he should, in order to take his leave by making one of those fine bows. Burney was talking to somebody else for a moment, so Omai stood still and did not attempt to interrupt. He was altogether charming, one can see that. "Indeed," said Fanny in pleased surprise, "he appears to be a perfectly rational and intelligent man, with an understanding far superior to the common race of us *cultivated gentry*. He could not else have borne so well the way of Life into which he is thrown, without some practice."

This attitude, reflected as it was by many of London's cultivated gentry, must have thrown the Mr. Cradocks into high-blood-pressure fits of amused indignation. Why, they snorted, should a low-class fellow like that get so much attention? Even Sir Joshua Reynolds painted his portrait. But the knowledgeable gentlemen had their innings when Omai went back home. They later reported with satisfaction that his head had been completely turned by all that fuss; Omai was ruined. His sojourn in eighteenth-century London had given him outrageous notions of his own importance. Having seen the world and learned that any Polynesian has better manners than most noble English lords, Omai became confused and arrogant. He may even—who knows?—have read Rousseau, or had Rousseau read to him. Anyway, back on his South Sea island Omai became antisocial: he got into fights with people, and had to move to another island and set up on his own with the settlement his patrons made on him. He died young, still confused, probably wildly unpopular, and perhaps, even, still arrogant.

Another traveler visited St. Martin's Street who knew how to behave better than Mr. Twiss and was more loquacious than Omai. James "Abyssinian" Bruce looked an immense creature to Fanny: the largest man, she averred, that she had ever seen gratis. Bruce was actually six feet four, tall but not abnormal; however, as Fanny was very small, and as Bruce was broad as he was tall, and had a beard which made him seem truly gigantic, there was some excuse for his behavior to Miss Burney. On first acquaintance he was overpowering, with an irritating way of entering the room all grand and pompous, like a monarch, but he had a weakness: he unbent in the presence of little girls. Among these little girls, somehow, he included poor Fanny, who at twenty-one resented the misapprehension far more than she appreciated his flattering particularity. He would bend way down to whisper to her; he assumed, when addressing her, a playful majesty, and all but used baby talk.

"These immense-sized men speak to little women, as if they were children," wrote the Diarist resentfully.

She found some compensation in referring to Mr. Bruce, with a trace of spite, as the King of Abyssinia, but after a time the great man began to "mend on her hands." He was better either without other company or with a lot of it; a few visitors only were apt to plunge Bruce into a haughty, sulky fit. Living as he did in Leicester Square, he could easily drop in on the Burneys, and as he was genuinely fond of music, the Abyssinian king figures prominently in Fanny's Journal for 1773.

The significant name of Barlow also made its appearance in the Journal at this time. Mr. Barlow, take it word for word and page for page, cuts a poor figure beside Mr. Bruce's record, but Fanny as an old lady, editing herself, expurgated a quantity of Mr. Barlow. This she had a perfect right to do: Mr. Barlow was her own personal property rather than a mere public figure like Abyssinian Bruce. She didn't want Mr. Barlow one little bit, but for a distracted space of time she had him nevertheless.

It all began with an evening at Hetty's, to help entertain "a very stupid family, which she told me it would be charity to herself to give my time to." They were a Mrs. O'Connor and her deaf-and-dumb daughter. Fanny's grandmother was also included in the party, as were two maiden aunts. Lost among these worthy women sat Mr. Barlow, Mrs. O'Connor's lodger.

"Mr. Barlow is rather short, but handsome," reported the Diarist. "He is a very well bred . . . good-tempered and sensible young man. . . . And he is highly spoken of both for disposition and morals. He has read more than he has conversed, and seems to know but little of the world; his language therefore is stiff and uncommon, and seems laboured, if not affected——"

The determined detachment of the first few lines, you observe, is running out; very shortly it comes to an abrupt end.

". . . if not affected——" wrote the Diarist, perhaps with an increasingly rapid pen and a certain vicious jab when inscribing the dashes. "He has a great desire to please, but no elegance of manners; neither, though he may be very worthy, is he at all agreeable."

This eminently respectable young man fell hard for Fanny the first minute he saw her. After an evening of what would have been crushing boredom for any young lady, Mr. Barlow introduced a spice of novelty into the proceedings. It happened when everyone was saying good night, when Fanny kissed her grandmother "according to custom." "I would fain have eluded my aunts," she said, "as nothing can be so disagreeable as kissing before young men; however, they chose it should go round." The generation before Fanny's had seen nothing disagreeable or extraordinary in kissing. In King Charles's glorious days and Queen Anne's, when visitors to England commented on the custom, a kiss was as freely given between acquaintances, male and female, as a spoken greeting, just as it was about twenty years ago in our own time. But when Fanny was a girl the pendulum happened to be swinging the other way. ". . . and after them Mrs. O'Connor also saluted me," she wrote resignedly, "as did her daughter, desiring to be better acquainted with me. This disagreeable ceremony over, Mr. Barlow came up to me, and making an apology, which, not suspecting his intentions, I did not understand,—he gave me a most ardent salute! I have seldom been more surprised. I had no idea of his taking such a freedom. However, I have told my good friends that for the future I will not chuse to lead, or have led, so contagious an example."

Soon Fanny received a letter from Mr. Barlow, such a letter that she had to read it three or four times before she could credit her eyes. We might read it oftener than that before we could make sense out of it. The document survived all Fanny's bonfires. Though she never did bring herself to include it in the Journal, she kept it.

"Madm," wrote the impassioned Mr. Barlow, "—Uninterrupted happiness we are told is of a short duration, and is quickly succeeded by Anxiety which moral Axiom I really experienced on the Conclusion of May day at Mr. Charles Burney's, as the singular Pleasure of your Company was so soon Eclips'd by the rapidity of ever-flying Time; . . ."

There is much more of the same, and worse. Perhaps if Fanny had liked the writer from the beginning she would have made allowances for his literary style; after all, as Hetty kept telling her, he *had* read more than he had conversed, and studious habits can easily vitiate a man's epistolary talents. But Mr. Barlow was not agreeable. Just why, Fanny doesn't explain, or if she did she later erased the explanation. It is probable that she did not know and could not have told, even if she had wanted to, why she didn't like Mr. Barlow. The chemistry of attraction and repulsion isn't understood much better today than it was in the eighteenth century, but there is a large difference between our attitude toward it and that of Fanny's contemporaries. We assume that personal attraction is the most important part of marriage, whereas Fanny's relatives and friends tried to persuade her to ignore such a triviality.

For once the quiet, obedient little girl was obdurate, and she was to remain obdurate on that subject for many years to come. But a formidable lot of pressure was brought to bear on her. Hetty, the happily married elder sister, was an urgent champion of Mr. Barlow, who had got on the right side of her. Grandmother and the old-maid aunts added their support. "They all of them became most zealous advocates for Mr. Barlow. They spoke most highly of the character they had heard of him, and my aunt Anne humourously bid me beware of her and Beckey's fate!"

Charles Burney was not so precipitate as the others, who threw themselves into the fray on the most slender knowledge of the case, without even a second look at Fanny's suitor or a talk with his banker. He urged his daughter not to turn away her admirer immediately; in all his advice he played for time, but his reasoning was judicious. His first marriage had been for love, not gain, and perhaps he thought of that. Wait a bit, he said to Fanny; how do you really know you don't like him? Don't say No immediately. Give yourself a chance to be sure.

Fanny's reaction to all this sounds a trifle hysterical, but we must remember she was doing considerable outrage to her character in putting up any resistance at all. Like most weak people, when she was driven to make a stand she overdid defiance. Besides, nobody could tell her anything about her own feelings for Mr. Barlow. She just didn't like Mr. Barlow, very strongly indeed did she dislike him, and it naturally irritated her to be told she might be wrong on such a matter as that. It would irritate anyone; it always does.

"Further knowledge will little avail in connections of this sort; the *heart* ought to be heard. . . . I am too spoilt by such men as my father and Mr. Crisp to content myself with a character merely inoffensive. I should expire of fatigue with him. . . . [Mr. Crisp]

has written me such a letter! . . . Everybody is against me but my
beloved father. . . . They all of them are kindly interested in my
welfare; but they know not so well as myself what may make me
happy or miserable. . . . How [can] I see more of Mr. Barlow
without encouraging him to believe I am willing to think of him?
I detest all trifling. If ever I marry, my consent shall be prompt
and unaffected."

Poor Fanny. There was perhaps some gratification for her, hidden away in all this fuss; certainly she had never before been such
a central figure of the family group. Nevertheless the affair was, in
sum, distressing. Her adored Daddy Crisp in a long letter accused
her of recoiling from the young man merely because he had been
so indelicate as to hint at *Matrimony*. "What you take it into your
head to be displeas'd with, as too great a liberty, I mean, his pre-
suming to write to you, and in so tender and respectful a strain,
if you knew the world, and that villainous Yahoo called Man, as
well as I do, you would see in a very different light,—in its true
light,—fearfullness, a high opinion of you, a consciousness (an unjust one I will call it) of his own inferiority. . . ."

Good old Sam Crisp worked himself up into passionate parti-
sanship of a young man he had never seen and of whom he knew
nothing more than Hetty, herself almost ignorant of the subject,
had written him in a paragraph. Crisp precipitately promised
Fanny not only security but happiness with Barlow. "Such a man,
as this young Barlow if ever you are so lucky and so well-advis'd,
as to be united to him, will improve upon you every hour. You
will discover in him graces and charms which kindness will bring
to light, that at present you have no idea of;—I mean, if his character is truly given by Hetty." (This is what Hetty had written: "A
young man, whose circumstances I have heard, are easy; but am not
thoroughly inform'd of them; but he bears an extraordinary character for a young man now a-days,—I have it from some who have
known him long, that he is remarkably even-temper'd, sedate, and
sensible; he is twenty-four years of age; is greatly esteem'd for
qualities rarely found at his age—temperance and industry;—well

educated, understands books and words, better than the world, which gives him something of a stiffness and formality, which discovers him unus'd to company, but which might wear off.")

Poor, poor Fanny. Mr. Crisp's reasons were good, from his point of view and from that of Dr. Burney: "Look round you, Fan; look at your aunts! *Fanny Burney* won't always be what she is now! Mrs. Hamilton once had an offer of £3000 a-year, or near it; a parcel of young giggling girls laugh'd her out of it. The man forsooth, was not quite smart enough, though otherwise estimable. Oh, Fan, this is not a marrying age, without a handsome Fortune! . . . Suppose you to lose your father,—take in all chances. Consider the situation of an unprotected, unprovided woman! . . . Observe how far I go; I don't urge you, hand over head, to have this man at all events; but, for God's sake and your own sake, give him and yourself fair play. Don't decide so positively against it. If you do, you are ridiculous to a high degree."

It was a formidable argument, and one which led to many marriages of the day. What indeed could Fanny do but marry? If her father were to die, any money he happened to have—and with his enormous household he never was able to put anything by—would go to his wife, Fanny's stepmother. Fanny could only take the sort of job some lady of her acquaintance would offer in charity, as governess or companion. She was now twenty-three and not outstandingly attractive; pretty enough, though a more apt adjective might be piquant, or, in the American sense, "cute." But she was shy and mousy, and as far as one could see, she had no special gifts to tempt a man to forget her poverty and propose marriage. Mr. Barlow must have seemed to Mr. Crisp and Dr. Burney a gift straight from heaven. The two men sincerely loved Fanny: they were worried about her—at least Daddy Crisp was. Charles Burney was too busy to worry much about any one matter very long, but we must give him credit for an unusual depth of understanding and gentleness; he did not press Fanny, as Daddy Crisp did, to accept Mr. Barlow and take herself off his hands.

"I must assure you I am *fixed* in the answer I have given you—

unalterably fixed," she said to her suitor. When he asked why he should be thus refused, she spared his feelings and told a fib. At least she didn't tell the emphatic truth. She just didn't intend ever to marry, she said. Yes, she was probably singular, odd, queer, even whimsical, but there it was: at least, she said, she was not trifling. There it was.

Then what, asked Mr. Barlow forlornly, was he to do?

"Why—go and *ponder* upon this affair for about half an hour. Then say—what an odd, queer, strange creature she is—and then— think of something else."

"Oh no, no!—you cannot suppose all that? I shall think of nothing else; your refusal is more pleasing than any other lady's acceptance."

He was so serious when he said this that she dared not laugh.

But at the close of the affair her father badly frightened her by speaking out definitely in favor of the man. A word more, the slightest increase of pressure, and she knew she would give in; it was beyond her power to deny her malleable nature any further. She had only an emotional conviction, not a rational one. "I felt, too, that I had no argumentative objections to make to Mr. Barlow, his character—disposition—situation—I know nothing against; but, Oh! I felt he was no companion for my heart! I wept like an infant, when alone; eat nothing; seemed as if already married, and passed the whole day in more misery than, merely on my own account, I ever passed in my life. . . ."

No sense of self-preservation, Daddy Crisp would have sighed: the sublime train of Sentimental Visions that get into girls' heads! But Dr. Burney did not speak the final, fatal word. When Fanny went into his study, all tear-stained, to bid him good night, he affectionately embraced her, saying, "I wish I could do more for thee, Fanny!"

"Oh, sir, *I* wish for nothing! Only let me live with you."

"My life!" cried Charles Burney. "Thou shalt live with me forever, if thee wilt! Thou canst not think I meant to get rid of thee?"

Fanny triumphant to Mr. Crisp:

"Don't be uneasy about my welfare, my dear Daddy, I dare say I shall do very well, I cannot persuade myself to snap at a settlement. . . . After all, if I live to be of some comfort, (as I flatter myself I am,) to my father, I can have no motive to wish to sign myself other than his and your,

Ever obliged, affectionate,

and devoted,

FRANCES BURNEY, to

the end of the chapter,

Amen."

5. *THE SECRET SIN*

S^AD TO relate, Fanny's venture into the realms of romance did not soften her at all: she seemed now fairly to bristle with militant virtue. Meeting Mrs. Pringle in the park one evening did not again confuse her. Where before she would have been overcome with guilty embarrassment, she was now quite at her ease, fully able to parry the good woman's invitations. "I much wish it was in my power to accept them," she said smoothly, but one sees this remark for the empty politeness it is. The acquisition of Mr. Barlow's heart had given Fanny a new confidence, and perhaps it is not strange that this should be. Surely the maiden who has had a chance to marry, though she has spurned it, is entitled to some, at least, of the airs and graces of the matron.

Witness her merciless comment on Miss L., an acquaintance who tossed her cap over the windmill. On that same evening, after disposing of Mrs. Pringle, Fanny with her sisters encountered Miss L., also walking in the park. ". . . [Her] face immediately showed that she recollected my elder sister and me; however, we walked on wishing to avoid speaking to her; but when we were at Spring Garden gate, she just touched my shoulder as she came *suddenly* behind me, and said—'Miss Burney!—how do you do?' I answered her rather coldly, and Hetty turned from her abruptly. I was afterwards very sorry that I did not speak with more kindness to her, for Susette says that she looked greatly disappointed. It is, however, impossible, and improper to keep up acquaintance with a female who has lost her character, however sincerely she may be an object of pity. . . . Should she quit her way of life before she grows more abandoned, I shall have great pleasure in shewing her any civility in my circumscribed power, for the remembrance of her innocence when I first knew her."

Fanny's adherence to this philosophy remained admirably consistent, if consistency per se is admirable, throughout her life, with the one great exception of her attitude toward the musical world. It was Dr. Burney who here held her in check. Because of him she regarded musicians as a race apart from all the ordinary standards she so fiercely imposed. Some prudes allow this dispensation to artists in general, painters, actors, and writers as well as singers, but Fanny was no such weakling. Ruthlessly she carried on the battle for virtue, cutting herself off from any female who lost her character, save only singing females such as Agujari. Even Fanny could not set herself up as a judge or censor of Agujari's morality, and she was wise enough not to try. Agujari was too big to handle.

Like actors, the singers of another day live for us only in the words of their contemporaries. Who today can know why people went mad about certain voices of another time? Fanny's was an age when ladies were not ashamed to gush. The members of polite society affected to like music, whether they really did or not; many of them laid claim to being discerning critics as well. Agujari, cheerfully called "The Bastard," was the favorite of the Burney girls en masse, as well as most of London, for her lovely voice, which allegedly surpassed in range anything theretofore known. Neither her famous illegitimacy nor her ambiguous relations with her maestro Signor Colla shocked Fanny in the least.

There was also the charming young Rauzzini. All the ladies fell in love with Rauzzini, until he was supplemented in their affections by adorable, divine Pacchierotti. Then there was Gabrielli, whose performance was the chief topic of conversation at Dr.

Burney's concert in honor of Prince Orloff. Fanny had great fun writing about that concert. It was a splendid gathering, the *haut ton* of London being eager for a peep at the notorious Orloff. He was "supposed by some to be the very man, who seized the late Czar; but however that may have been, he was certainly the man, who was honoured with the Czarina's most unbounded favour."

"Enter the Dean of Winchester. . . .

Dr. Burney: Was you at the Opera last night, Mr. Dean?

Dean of Winchester. No, Sir; I made an attempt, but soon retreated; for I hate a crowd,—as much as the *ladies* love it,—I beg pardon! (bowing to *we* fair *Sex*).

Dr. Burney. The Gabrielli is a very fine singer; but she has not voice enough for the people of this country; she will never please *John!* . . .

Enter Lady Edgecumbe. . . .

Dr. Burney. Your Ladyship was doubtless at the Opera last night?

Lady Edgecumbe. Oh, yes! but I have not heard the Gabrielli! no; I will not allow that I have *heard* her yet.

Dr. Burney. Your Ladyship expected a more powerful voice?

Lady Edgecumbe. Why no; not that; the *shadow* tells me what the *substance* must be. She cannot have acquired this great name throughout Europe for *nothing*; but I repeat, I have not yet *heard* her; so I will not judge. She had certainly a bad cold. . . .

Enter The Honble. Mr. & Mrs. Brudenel. . . . *The Question of the Night* was immediately asked, of, *How did you like Gabrielli?*

Mrs. Brudenel. Oh, Lady Edgecumbe and I are exactly of the same opinion; we agree that we have not *heard* her yet.

Lady Edgecumbe. The ceremony of her quitting the house, after the Opera is over, is extremely curious; First, goes a man in a livery, to clear the way; then follows the sister; then, the Gabrielli herself; then a page to hold her train; and lastly, another man, who carries her *muff*, in which is her little lap-dog.

Mr. Brudenel. But where is *Lord March* all this time?

Lady Edgecumbe. Oh—he, you know, is Lord of the Bed-Chamber!"

Everyone must have laughed heartily at that bit of fashionable scandal, and Fanny didn't mind a bit. Yet later in the evening, when she was enjoying a very witty *confabulation* with Mr. Chamier, who had got himself into a *snug recess* behind the bookcase, her stepmother embarrassed her cruelly, saying, "So, Fanny, I see you have got Mr. Chamier into a corner!"

"You must know," wrote Fanny to Mr. Crisp, "I don't at all like these sort of jokes, which are by no means the *ton*, so I walked away."

It was about this time, toward 1776, that Fanny turned her serious attention to *Evelina*. The Journal, her letters to Crisp, and her secretarial work must have interfered vastly with her leisure, but fiction writing had become a pleasant habit by this time, and her father's parties gave her the idea of a comedy of manners. Little by little the book took shape, though family matters still claimed most of her attention.

"My brother James, to our great joy and satisfaction, is returned home safe from America," she wrote on December 30, 1775, "which he has left in most terrible disorder." The girls had been uneasy when Jem was sent to America, it being generally agreed in England that the colonies were getting out of hand. But there was not much talk of overseas affairs in Fanny's circle. America, the Indies, the South Sea Islands, were all very far away. Mr. Twiss, who traveled to Portugal, seemed to the ladies at home a daring soul enough.

There followed a year cluttered with family problems. Mrs. Burney was seriously ill for a time and went away to recuperate. Fanny was left in London for the summer, in charge of the house and of Sally, the latest little Burney. Writing to Daddy Crisp, she begged to be excused her long silence, as she had an inflammation of the eyes which almost kept her from using them at all: ". . . indeed they are still so weak, that any exertion of them gives me a good deal of pain." She was much troubled with her eyes, and often mentioned her nearsightedness. This disability and a tendency to bad colds make the total of such illnesses of Fanny's as she ever described. "Poor health," "languor," "gout"—those were the vague ailments of the eighteenth century.

Fanny in her way was an ascetic. Though she would not have admitted it, she had a tough constitution, like many other ascetics. Besides caring little or nothing for clothes or rest, she was indifferent to diet. Her stepsister Maria Allen took a keen interest in cookery; Dr. Burney was not above praising a good dinner; Mrs. Thrale, who had great influence over Fanny in later days, showed a normal housewifely concern in affairs of the table. Yet Fanny, though she often had to do the honors of her father's house, never mentioned cookery, the chief duty of housekeeping. No doubt she saw to it that adequate meals were served, but the subject evidently bored her, and when she took up her pen she dismissed all thoughts of the larder. Possibly, too, she preferred to play a *spirituelle* role, drifting through life like a little wraith, a woman of pure intellect who could live on air. The only nourishment of which she ever spoke with even moderate enthusiasm was tea.

Whether sustained by tea or mutton, she found enough energy during that year to make good headway on *Evelina*. In one of her journalistic roundups wherein she made up arrears in her accounts of family and personal affairs, she spoke of *Evelina* as if it were two thirds completed. "When with infinite toil and labour, I had transcribed (in a feigned hand) the second Volume (of my new Essay), I sent it by my brother Charles to Mr. Lowndes."

That, in skeleton, is the story. Her reason for making a copy in a feigned hand was this: she had done so much work for her father, copying out his *Tours* and *History*, that she was afraid the publisher or printers would recognize her handwriting, an eventuality by no means impossible in those days of limited printing. It was a formidable task, comprising "infinite toil and labour," especially as she wished to keep the matter a secret from everyone but her sisters.

"The fear of discovery, or of suspicion in the house, made the copying extremely laborious to me; for in the day time, I could only take odd moments, so that I was obliged to sit up the greatest part of many nights, in order to get it ready." Working so long by candlelight could not have been good for her eyes, either.

Evelina is composed of three volumes, not very long, but they must have seemed endless by the time Fanny had made them up, rewritten them, and then made fair copies in a strained false hand. Urged on by the faithful Susan, she was now ready to embark on her daring adventure. There was a large obstacle, however: how could she maintain secrecy and still arrange for publication? It would have been impossible for Fanny Burney to produce a novel in her own right. It would have meant publicity. All her training, all her nature was opposed to such an indelicate procedure. It simply could not be. Somehow she and Susan, all alone, must devise a way out of the difficulty—not an easy task for well-bred young ladies in the 1770s.

The Burneys were a close-knit clan. After considering the problem, the girls enlisted the help of young Charles, their brother, who was inducted into the secret. In solemn conclave the three conspirators fixed on Mr. Dodsley, a West End bookseller, as the man to publish *Evelina*, because they rather liked the books he carried in his stock. (Booksellers were publishers, too, in those days. There was no middleman, and no royalty system: the bookseller bought manuscripts outright.)

Fanny wrote and asked Mr. Dodsley if he would be interested in her manuscript. The letter itself must be signed with a pseudonym, while for a mailing address she gave that of the Orange Coffee House near by. As a male Charles could safely call for letters in a public coffeehouse, which the Misses Burney were powerless to do.

Mr. Dodsley, unfortunately for his pocket, chose to reject the notion of publishing *Evelina*; he scorned it sight unseen, saying he did not care to publish anything anonymously. Today Mr. Dodsley would take his place among those publishers, so right-

fully condemned by young writers, who will never take a chance,
preferring to bet on sure things, writers who have already arrived.
The young Burneys were somewhat dashed by "this lofty reply,"
but their spirits rose after a little and they resolved next to try
the bookseller Lowndes, whose shop was down in Fleet Street. Mr.
Lowndes, a more oncoming man than Dodsley, was at least
willing to look at the manuscript before closing every door to hope.
So Charles, muffled by his giggling sisters in an old greatcoat
and made up with grease paint to look older, took to Fleet Street
the two completed volumes which Fanny had carefully copied.
It must have been a thrilling afternoon.

"And, after all this *fagging*, Mr. Lowndes sent me word, that he
approved of the book; but could not think of printing it, till it was
finished; that it would be a great disadvantage to it, [i.e., to publish
it volume by volume at long intervals, as was then often done
with novels] and that he would wait my time, and hoped to see
it again, as soon as it was completed.

"Now, this man, knowing nothing of my situation, supposed, in
all probability, that I could seat myself quietly at my bureau, and
write on with all expedition and ease, till the work was finished.
But so different was the case, that I had hardly time to write half
a page in a day; and neither my health nor inclination would allow
me to continue my nocturnal scribbling for so long a time, as to
write first, and then copy, a whole volume. I was therefore obliged
to give the attempt and affair entirely over for the present."

In March she found a chance to get well ahead on the last
volume, when she was invited to Chesington to make one of the
visits which so pleased her adopted Daddy. There in the enforced
quiet and idleness of the country she made long strides toward
completing the work. She wrote to Susan: "We pass our time
here very serenely, and distant as you may think us from the great
world, I sometimes find myself in the midst of it, though nobody
suspects the brilliancy of the company I occasionally keep."

Looking back on those days, Madame d'Arblay recalled that the
composition of the book had given her no trouble at all; ideas

bubbled up in profusion, and she had only to make her choice among them. All the difficulty she encountered was the mechanical one of writing and then of copying such a lot of words. Plot, to be sure, was not likely to trouble any novelist of the eighteenth century; readers were not exacting, and the story Fanny Burney had to tell in *Evelina* was neither complicated nor fresh in design. What gives *Evelina* its quality is the zest the author felt for depicting her characters. She had a keen eye for the ridiculous, and for the shades of behavior, the forbidden emotions which manifested themselves in spite of the mannered elegancies of the day. Almost any plot would have done for Fanny, as long as she could work it out at her own pace, with her own special touch.

The country visit was cut short, much to Daddy Crisp's annoyance, by Fanny's uncle, Richard Burney of Worcester. Uncle Richard suddenly descended on St. Martin's Street with two of his children, who were more or less of Fanny's age, so she was hastily summoned from Chesington Hall to entertain them. It was decided by her parents that she should go back with these relatives to stay with them awhile. Though Fanny didn't particularly wish to go to Worcester, she never thought of disobeying.

Before she set out for what was to prove, after all, a most entertaining round of visits, she had time to write to Crisp about a particularly interesting concert party at home, which had been arranged between Dr. Burney and Mrs. Thrale, the wife of a wealthy brewer, who was becoming known among *littérateurs* and bluestockings as the friend of Dr. Johnson. The object of this gathering was to introduce Dr. Johnson to his ardent admirers, the Burneys.

Dr. Burney had made Mrs. Thrale's acquaintance when she engaged him to give music lessons to her eldest daughter Hester, commonly called "Queeney." As we get to know Mrs. Thrale better we will understand how inevitably it came about that the music lessons deteriorated into a series of conversations between herself and the popular musician. Sometimes the lesson had to fight for existence against the noise of a large tea party in the same room. Ultimately all pretense of Burney's teaching music to the twelve-year-old Queeney was abandoned, but by that time a family friendship had been established. Mrs. Thrale said that if Dr. Burney's family would give one of their concerts, she would bring to the house the special property of the Thrales, no less a lion than Lexiphanes, Dr. Johnson himself.

Mrs. Thrale arrived with a train of attendants. The chief guest, the captive lion, was not to come until later. Fanny's first impression of the lady was not favorable. Mrs. Thrale was much too aware, thought the little diarist, of her own importance, and entered the library with a self-conscious bustle as if to proclaim it. But her tremendous vivacity soon charmed Fanny out of this prejudice. "Mrs. Thrale is a very pretty woman still [she was in the middle thirties]; she is extremely lively and chatty; has no supercilious or pedantic airs, and is really gay and agreeable." Queeney seemed to Fanny stiff and proud, or else shy and reserved; as Queeney was only twelve years old these descriptions are probably interchangeable and equally true.

Hetty and Susan were playing a duet when the great Dr. Johnson came in. Among the hundreds of pages which have been printed on this subject, the Journal's paragraphs of description have appeared so often that this writer apologizes for producing them once again, but Fanny's words are the only right ones to use.

"He is, indeed, very ill-favoured; is tall and stout; but stoops terribly; he is almost bent double. His mouth is almost constantly opening and shutting, as if he was chewing. He has a strange method of frequently twirling his fingers, and twisting his hands. His body is in continual agitation, see-sawing up and down; his feet are never a moment quiet; and, in short, his whole person is in perpetual motion. His dress, too, considering the time, and that he had meant to put on his *best becomes*, being engaged to dine in a large company, was as much out of the common road as his figure; he had a large wig, snuff-colour coat, and gold buttons, but no ruffles to his shirt, doughty [in the original, probably "dirty"] fists, and black worsted stockings. He is shockingly nearsighted, and did not, till she held out her hand to him, even know Mrs. Thrale. He *poked his nose* over the keys of the harpsichord till the duet was finished, and then my father introduced Hetty to him as an old acquaintance, and he cordially kissed her! When she was a little girl, he had made her a present of 'The Idler.' "

In another account of the scene Fanny said that while Dr. Johnson was poking his nose over the keyboard he leaned so low that he interfered seriously with the girls' performance, and they were hard put to it not to laugh aloud. It was probably a technical interest he took in their fingering, for he did not care at all for music. Fanny was lucky to see him for the first time under the softening and cleansing influence of Mrs. Thrale. Before the Thrales took him in hand the doctor had been so careless about his linen that he was sometimes actually offensive.

Having satisfied his curiosity about the harpsichord (perhaps he felt he had been duly courteous to the Burneys, too, in showing interest, and was now free to follow his own inclinations), Dr. Johnson began examining Dr. Burney's books: "He pored over them, shelf by shelf, almost touching the backs of them with his eye-lashes, as he read their titles." Then, like many another absent-minded scholar, he picked out one which interested him particularly and began to read it, standing in a corner away from the company. They were all much provoked by this, as they were anxious to hear the famous conversationalist perform; "but it seems he is the most silent creature, when not particularly drawn out, in the world."

Boswell not being there to sting the doctor to speech, he remained sunk in his book, undisturbed by the concert, which proceeded according to plan. To be sure, he was deaf as well as near-sighted. Mrs. Thrale, who had no more real interest in music than did her pet lion, at least put up a polite pretense; when the next number was finished she asked her host a question about the Bach Concert of the night before. Dr. Burney, hoping to draw Dr. Johnson back into the company, relayed the question to him.

"And pray, sir, *who is Bach?*" asked Lexiphanes, good-naturedly putting up his book. "Is he a piper?"

Amid shocked exclamations, Mrs. Thrale, who was not at all shocked, gave him some explanation of the Bach Concerts.

Gravely, the doctor played up: "Pray, madam, what is the expense?"

"Oh! much trouble and solicitation to get a Subscriber's Ticket; or else, half a guinea."

"Trouble and solicitation I will have nothing to do with; but I would be willing to give eighteenpence."

The flutter and squeals of horror caused by this barbarous statement must have tickled the old man. For the rest of the visit he was sociable and amusing, particularly on one of his favorite subjects, Garrick, his former pupil. "Garrick never enters a room, but he regards himself as the object of general attention, from whom the entertainment of the company is expected; and true it is, that he seldom disappoints them; for he has infinite humour, a very just proportion of wit, and more convivial pleasantry, than any other man. But then off, as well as on the Stage, he is always an Actor: for he thinks it so incumbent upon him to be sportive, that his gaiety becomes mechanical from being habitual, and he can exert his spirits at all times alike, without consulting his real disposition to hilarity."

On the whole it was a very satisfactory party, once the doctor got going. Saying good-by to them, Fanny could have had no premonition of how well she was to know the principal figures of that odd little group. Nevertheless they had stimulated her; with her unfailing particularity for old men, she already felt a warm admiration for the uncouth doctor.

Evelina was practically completed by this time, and the author was fairly certain it would soon make its appearance in print. The guilty secret weighed so heavily on her breast that this good little girl, now twenty-five years old, could no longer support it. Before leaving for Worcester she made a partial confession to her father. ". . . in the fullness of my heart I could not forbear telling him, that I had sent a manuscript to Mr. Lowndes; earnestly, however, beseeching him never to divulge it, nor to demand a sight of such trash as I could scribble; assuring him that Charles had managed to save me from being at all suspected. He could not help laughing; but I believe was much surprised at the communication. He desired me to acquaint him from time to time, how my work went on, called himself the *Pere confident*, and kindly promised to guard my secret as cautiously as I could wish. . . . But, when I told my dear father, I never wished or intended, that even he himself should see my essay, he forbore to ask me the name, or make any enquiries. I believe he is not sorry to be saved the giving me the pain of his criticism. He made no sort of objection to my having my own way in total secrecy and silence to all the world. Yet I am easier in not taking the step, without his having this little knowledge of it, as he is contented with hearing I shall never have the courage to let him know its name."

Protected twice over by anonymity against failure or indifference, and by her father's permission against self-reproach, Fanny Burney set out for Worcester with a light heart. She had made her pie and put it into the oven to bake. There was nothing more she could do.

6. A YOUNG LADY ENTERS THE WORLD

EVELINA, or a *Young Lady's Entrance into the World*
was published at the end of January, 1778. Mr.
Lowndes paid his unknown writer twenty pounds
for possession of all rights to the manuscript. Fanny, like any other
author, went through the preliminary thrill of proofreading, for
Lowndes sent the proofs, as he sent his letters and money, to "Mr.
Grafton," care of the Orange Coffee House.

That was a more leisurely age than ours, and when a book made
its entrance, like *Evelina*, into the world, the world did not exhibit much excitement over the event. The publisher usually announced it in a decorous advertisement which appeared, not too
obviously, in newspapers and magazines, then, having done his
duty, he sat back and waited for the public to demand the book
or to ignore it, as the case might be. Fanny Burney, unlike the
novelist of today, did not huddle in her room on publication day,
nibbling her fingernails or tearing through the newspapers in
search of the book review page. She knew it would take a long time
for *Evelina* to make even a ripple on the surface of London. She
may have been confident of it in her innermost heart, but she
probably believed herself when she said she had no expectations
at all of this, her funny little first effort.

Strictly speaking, *Evelina* was not her first: it was merely the

first since the bonfire in the courtyard. The book was the child
of another novel as the heroine was the child of that other novel's
heroine. In the burned novel Caroline Evelyn, hapless daughter
of a *mésalliance* between a highborn but unscrupulous gentleman
and a vulgar barmaid, died after her secret marriage to one Sir
John Belmont, equally as, if not more highborn than, Mr. Evelyn,
and certainly just as unscrupulous. Wicked Sir John repudiated the
secret marriage, which, like Maria Allen's, had been contracted on
the Continent. Caroline died (both on paper and in the bonfire)
after giving birth to Evelina, but the infant lived on in Fanny's
brain. One can well understand why Maria's elopement should
have thrilled the young novelist. With the memory of her tragic
creation Caroline still fresh in her mind, the predicament in which
Maria might well have found herself, though to be sure she didn't,
must have seemed to Fanny more real than life itself. Secret marriages, possible repudiations, and wicked seducers played a large
part in both *Evelina* and *Cecilia*, Fanny's first two novels.

Evelina, however, is not in the least sensational in any ordinary
sense of the word. The young lady of the title is subjected to a
number of trials imposed on her by the world, but through it all
she remains unchanged, fixed in virtue, untempted by any moral
weakness within her character. Mentally we cannot say as much for
her. The plot, like that of a run-of-the-mill movie, is spun out
tenuously and could be brought to a close half a dozen times if
only Evelina would behave with normal intelligence instead of
like a half-wit. But the same could be said of most romantic eighteenth-century novel heroes and heroines, and *Evelina* possessed
good points which much light reading of the times did not share—
witty characterization, lifelike dialogue, and vivid pictures of fashionable amusements. Evelina's confused family history gave Fanny
the opportunity to bring her heroine into contact with "low"
society as well as "high," so that the story, if not the vapid maiden,
benefits from "the unequal birth by which she hung suspended
between the elegant connexions of her mother, and the vulgar

London Art Service (Photographic) Ltd.

FASHIONABLE HEADDRESS

A VIEW OF THE PARADE AT BATH

ST. DUNSTAN'S, FLEET STREET

ones of her grandmother. . . ." It was a useful device which added much to the slender plot.

In the form of letters between various of the principals, the story runs along in a series of incidents rather than the development of one central theme. Evelina, a beautiful girl of sixteen, has been brought up quietly in Dorsetshire. Every since babyhood she has lived with the Reverend Mr. Arthur Villars, who was tutor to her dissolute grandfather Evelyn as well as to her mother Caroline, the ill-fated Lady Belmont. Mr. Villars has always let her be known to the countryside as "Miss Anville," the daughter of an old friend of his. Until the crisis in Evelina's affairs with which the book opens he has planned to keep her in ignorance of her tragic origin, sheltering her from the world, "bestowing her on one who may be sensible of her worth, and then sinking to eternal rest in her arms." Under these circumstances, good old Mr. Villars, a typical Fanny Burney father-figure, may be excused for the chronic gloom which oppresses his letters. One readily admits the justice of his plaint: "Thus it has happened that the education of the father, daughter, and grand-daughter, has devolved upon me. What infinite misery have the two first caused me! Should the fate of the dear survivor be equally adverse, how wretched will be the end of my cares— the end of my days!"

The barmaid grandmother, twice-widowed Madame Duval, now a woman of substance, precipitates a change in his sorrowful plans by writing from Paris and threatening to take possession of Evelina. Realizing that one way or another his lovely ward must face the world, Villars relinquishes the girl, temporarily and for her own good, to the care of kindly Lady Howard, whose granddaughter is a school friend of Evelina's. With this family group our heroine goes to London to see a bit of life. The following chapters even today are so readable and entertaining that one can easily under-stand why the book attracted people of its own period. Evelina encounters many well-known types of the world of fashion: rakes, gamblers, fine ladies, and silly fops ("macaronis," as they were called in slang). With the fresh enthusiasm of a young country-bred girl, or of a born reporter like Fanny Burney, Evelina describes the complicated ceremonies of high life such as hair-frizzing, shopping in Bond Street, and card parties. She goes to Ranelagh and the Pantheon. She meets the perfect, ideal gentleman, Lord Orville, a character modeled on Sir Charles Grandison, though Orville seems less of a stick, for some reason, than his predecessor.

The trivial complications which arise between Evelina and Lord Orville, due to her ignorance of Society, are well on the way to being conquered when Madame Duval arrives on the scene and spoils everything, at least for the time being and for two volumes. Insisting on her rights as a grandmother, she carries off the hapless girl to live with her, in close proximity to the Branghtons of Snow Hill. Mr. Branghton is a silversmith related to Madame Duval; thus he with his son and daughters, though lowborn, are poor Evelina's kin, and very embarrassing relations they are for a well-bred young lady. Evelina is carried to the Opera by the Branghtons, who haven't the slightest idea how to behave when they get there or how to appreciate the performance; she is forced by Madame Duval to attend a low-class dance, accompanied by pretentious Mr. Smith, the Branghtons' lodger; she must visit Marylebone Gardens with these demeaning companions. Occasionally, thus badly chaperoned, she encounters the rake Sir Clement Willoughby, who has designs on her virtue, and of course he tries to take advantage of these opportunities. Sometimes she is placed in even more appalling situations by running into Lord Orville, who never, never understands; nor is the poor man to be blamed for this slowness of apprehension, as Evelina, overcome with shame and shyness, instead of explaining invariably runs away.

After a succession of these events, which become to our modern taste very tedious, Evelina's father Sir John Belmont returns from his rake's progress through Europe. Sir John must now be persuaded to accept Evelina as his daughter, which is a difficult task to accomplish, as owing to a complicated mistake he has brought up a young pretendress in her place. There follows a strenuous period: melodramatic scenes in blank verse with Belmont and wordy love passages with Lord Orville. Evelina in the end finds herself happily married, surrounded by relatives—a repentant father, a half brother (the illegitimate son of Sir John), and a sister-in-law (the pretendress, settled according to her station by marrying the half brother).

Though often too naïve, and repetitive throughout, the novel *Evelina* deserved the favorable critiques it received. We are startled not by its success but by the large proportion of public notice which it won. In those days almost any book was something to be observed and commented on.

There have been important changes in social philosophy since 1778, and they shift the emphasis of Fanny's humor. Today we would not find the humble aspirations of her lower-class bourgeois characters so screamingly funny as did her readers. It comes as rather a shock, too, that the author of such delicately witty passages as one finds in the Journal should be capable of the brutal schoolboy slapstick to which she subjects Madame Duval and Lovel the macaroni when they are victimized by Captain Mirvan. Of course it was a hearty, full-blooded age, but even so, considering that these paragraphs came from the pen of a languishing young lady . . . The same passages, one is relieved to note, were a bit rich for Dr. Burney's blood even then.

How long after publication, you may possibly ask, was Fanny able to keep her secret? The surprising thing is that her father did not know about it for some months, and even with the rest of her circle, who were not so preoccupied as the doctor, the truth seeped out rather than broke upon them. Some privileged members of the family were initiated before Evelina made her appearance: the two maiden aunts, for example, actually helped the author to read proof, but they held their tongues, and their niece was able to exult at the end of March that her parents were still in ignorance of her literary venture. Yet the book was making headway: it was beginning to be talked about.

"I have an exceeding odd sensation," she wrote, seeing *Evelina* advertised at Bell's circulating library, "when I consider that it is now in the power of any and every body to read what I so carefully hoarded even from my best friends, till this last month or two,—and that a work which was so lately lodged, in all privacy in my bureau, may now be seen by every butcher and baker, cobler and tinker, throughout the three kingdoms, for the small tribute of three pence."

With an intoxicatiing sense of power, humor, whatever one can call it, she hovered about the fringes of the family group while a friend read the book to her Worcester Cousin Richard, convalescent at Brompton after illness. So much comment took place between them on the subject of *Evelina* that Fanny could not trust her self-control; at first she avoided Brompton, but curiosity got the better of her. Reassured by Susan and Aunt Anne, she sat in on one of the sessions and heard what reader and listener had to say.

Richard's opinion was so flattering that Fanny was inclined to suspect he knew her secret. She had expected him of all people, she confessed, to hold it "extremely cheap." But no, Dick was not aware of her authorship. He proved this with one critical comment, "finding great fault with Evelina herself for her bashfulness with such a man as Lord Orville."

"A man whose politeness is so extraordinary," said Dick, "who is so elegant, so refined—so—so—*unaccountably* polite—for I can think of no other word—I never read, never heard such language in my life!—and then, just as he is speaking to her, she is so confused—that she always runs out of the room!"

It was on the tip of Fanny's tongue to come warmly to the defense of her Evelina. A dozen arguments marshaled themselves. But the poor girl had been brought up in strictest retirement, Fanny nearly said; she was too timid to dare hope Lord Orville was serious; Richard couldn't have read the Preface properly: if he had, he would have *understood* Evelina's delicacy of character. Common sense saved the wounded author, as it has saved others of her profession. Upon reflection, the first hot retort to unkind book reviewers is usually throttled. Fanny throttled hers. It could have been much worse, she reminded herself: Richard could easily have been far more severe.

Other opinions were heard. The family friend maintained that the writer must be Christopher Anstey, author of the *New Bath Guide*. Fanny quite rightly called this an extraordinary supposition, yet it was shared by a number of people, perhaps because the *Guide* told a story of a family discovering the delights of life in a fashionable watering place and *Evelina* attended the Hotwells at Bristol. There is no other comparison which suggests itself, the *Guide*, an out-and-out satire, being done in rhyme, whereas *Evelina* is a romantic novel in prose.

An even more amusing game than the mystification of Richard was now beguiling Fanny's days and evenings. She was reading *Evelina* to Mr. Crisp, and Daddy Crisp didn't yet know. His first reaction was awkwardly unrapturous. A novel? He scarcely wanted to bother with a novel, he said.

"Is it reckoned clever?" he asked grumpily. "What do you think of it? Do folks laugh at it?"

Fanny couldn't answer, but Daddy Crisp did not notice her confusion and finally he consented to listen.

"I dared not trust my voice with the little introductory ode," she confessed to the Journal. The ode in question is addressed to Dr. Burney, secretly, thus: "To—— ——." It is very bad poetry, but Fanny's reasons for faltering over it were not aesthetic: she was faltering from pure sentiment. Sooner or later we must reproduce this ode, because Fanny thought a lot of it and often spoke of it or quoted therefrom. It may as well be now.

> Oh author of my being!—far more dear
>   To me than light, or nourishment, or rest,
> Hygeia's blessings, Rapture's burning tear,
>   Or the life blood that mantles in my breast!

If in my heart the love of Virtue glows,
   'Twas planted there by an unerring rule;
From thy example the pure flame arose,
   Thy life, my precept—thy good works, my school.

Could my weak pow'rs thy num'rous virtues trace,
   By filial love each fear should be repressed;
The blush of Incapacity I'd chace,
   And stand, recorder of thy worth, confess'd:

But since my niggard stars that gift refuse,
   Concealment is the only boon I claim;
Obscure be still the unsuccessful Muse,
   Who cannot raise, but would not sink thy fame.

Oh! of my life at once the source and joy!
   If e'er thy eyes these feeble lines survey,
Let not their folly their intent destroy;
   Accept the tribute—but forget the lay.

Fanny skipped this doggerel and kept the book out of Daddy's sight when she wasn't reading to him, for fear he would see it for himself and somehow guess who "—— ——" might be. Even the rest of the book, the impersonal part, was difficult reading, with her darling Mr. Crisp serving as audience and innocent critic. Embarrassment made her performance bad at the beginning, and it grew rapidly worse.

Nevertheless, little by little, she was reassured to observe, the old man began to like the novel. He didn't praise it lavishly, as Richard and some other people had done, but he was certainly interested, "even greedily eager to go on with it," she wrote joyfully. Of all the vignettes one sees in the pages of Fanny's Journal, this is the most striking—the demure little woman, her head bent over her book, reading in a soft glow of candlelight in a country sitting room to the tall old man in his armchair. He grunted appreciatively now and then, or interrupted to make some comment. As her voice grew tired or she finished a chapter, the reading hour would come to an end.

"Not bad," Daddy Crisp probably said, "What do you think, Fanny?"

Fanny evaded the question, merely saying as if to herself, "I wonder who could have written it?"

Then Daddy Crisp would be helped out of his chair, with due deference to his gouty foot, and hobble off to bed.

At last, when *Evelina* had been published six months, Dr. Charles Burney dared face what his daughter had done. Exactly which person let him into the secret, out of the coterie of relations who now knew, isn't clear: most likely Hetty took it upon herself to break the news. One day the *Monthly Review* in its leisurely way deigned to print a critique of *Evelina*. The doctor heard of it abroad. He waited until his wife, Susan, and little Sally had set off for a day at Chesington, and as soon as they were out of the house he called the remaining Burney, seventeen-year-old Charlotte, and told her to bring him the periodical. Charlotte hung about nervously: she knew the game must be up.

Evelina, or a young Lady's Entrance into the World, 12 mo. 3 vols 9s. Lowndes. 1778.

This novel has given us so much pleasure in the perusal, that we do not hesitate to pronounce it one of the most sprightly, entertaining, and agreeable productions of this kind, which have of late fallen under our notice. A great variety of natural incidents, some of the comic stamp, render the narrative extremely interesting. The characters, which are agreeably diversified, are conceived and drawn with propriety, and supported with spirit. The whole is written with great ease and command of language. From this commendation, however, we must except the character of a son of Neptune, whose manners are rather those of a rough, uneducated country 'squire, than those of a genuine sea-captain.[1]

[1]*Monthly Review, Art. 49, p. 316. 1778.*

Charles Burney read the article with great earnestness. He put it down and for a while just sat there quietly. Then he snatched up the paper and read it all over again.

At last he remembered the hovering, palpitating Charlotte; he called her over to his desk. "You know what this is," he said, pointing to the name of the book.

Charlotte admitted that she knew what it was.

Well, then, said Dr. Burney, let the manservant be sent at once to Lowndes's bookshop to buy a copy of *Evelina*. Away went William; back came William with the book. Charles Burney waited until the servant was safely out of the room—with what delicacy the Burneys faced their moments of excitement!—before he opened the first volume.

He opened it upon the *ode!*

He looked all amazement. He read a line or two with great eagerness, and then, stopping short, he seemed quite affected and the tears started into his eyes.

Over at Chesington, reading Charlotte's account of all this, Fanny sobbed aloud.

The scene ended in a manner characteristic of Charles Burney. He couldn't read further: he had to go out to give a music lesson.

For four weeks Fanny kept up the game at Chesington, "smoaking" Daddy Crisp. Sometimes she reported to him that she knew for a certainty who had written *Evelina*, or said mysteriously that the latest rumor attributed it to some young man of their acquaintance. Once Mr. Crisp teased her in return, when she said, "Whoever could it be?" by retorting, "I can't guess: maybe it is you!"

"Pooh, nonsense! What should make you think of me?"

"Why, you look guilty."

This was a nasty shock to Fanny. She neither affirmed nor denied it, but it turned out, much to her relief, that Daddy was only joking, after all. In his next breath he was wondering if the author mightn't possibly be Dr. Burney, or Mrs. Thrale.

In the meantime her proud father had found leisure to finish the novel, though he had to kill a few birds with one stone by sharing his reading hours with two clients. His praise was high. Susan sent what he said straight along to Chesington.

"Upon my word, I think it is the best novel I know excepting Fielding's, and, in some respects, *better* than his! I have been excessively pleased with it." Though he found fault with the broad humor of one of the scenes, he showed what we might justly call a lapse in taste by lavishing compliments on the melodramatic bathos of Evelina's interview with her father—"A scene for a tragedy!" cried Dr. Burney. "I blubbered at it, and Lady Hales and Miss Coussmaker are not yet recovered from hearing it; it made them quite ill; it is, indeed, wrought up in a most extraordinary manner!"

It was now time, he said, to throw off her cloak of anonymity. He vowed that he could see nothing in *Evelina* of which his daughter need be ashamed (especially as the *Monthly Review* had got ahead of him in approving it). There was no suggestion, of course, that the name of the author be announced in the public prints or anything like that, but he did something quite as effective. He told Mrs. Thrale.

Much progress had been made during the past year in the Burney-Thrale *entente cordiale*. Dr. Burney's admiration of Johnson grew with acquaintance, and Mrs. Thrale found the Burney ménage amusing. She was a warmhearted, restless, managing woman, a potential patroness in search of a protégé, and in Burney she found a satisfactory one. She determined to help the Burneys place their youngest son Dick in school in Winchester, for one thing. She kept at Dr. Johnson to use his influence until the old man burst into one of his sudden petulant rages. Mrs. Thrale, saying good-by to him after bringing him home one day, cautioned him not to forget little Dick.

"When I have written my letter for Dick, I may hang myself, mayn't I?" he snarled, and stumped into the house.

These tempers never lasted with Dr. Johnson, who had a warm regard for Dr. Burney and his family. He was quite amenable, therefore, to a suggestion of Charles's a few months before Fanny made her mark. Burney had long wanted to bring Johnson and his old friends and patrons the Grevilles together at St. Martin's Street, and at last this was arranged.

There were many guests who did not belong to the professional-musician class—Mrs. Thrale, Queeney, Dr. Johnson, Mr. Davenant, Mr. Seward, Mr. and Mrs. Greville and their daughter Mrs. Crewe. Those who did were Charles Rousseau Burney, Hetty, and Signor Piozzi, an Italian singer. Susan, Fanny, and young Charlotte were, of course, present.

The party started off stiffly. It would have been strange had this not been so. Greville was a vain man, proud of his powers in social conversation; he had a rich man's conceit of his taste and knowledge. Dr. Johnson among strangers was apt to sink into gloomy silence from which he had to be flattered, coaxed, and drawn out by an admiring audience.

Good-looking and haughty, Mr. Greville stood on the hearth before the fire and waited for Dr. Johnson to be brilliant. He did not intend to put himself out first. He was Greville the superb, Greville who in his time had been the leading spirit at gambling houses and on the turf, Greville who had been known in former days as a talented dabbler in the arts, Greville who did not like to face the uncomfortable fact that his leadership had long been on the wane. Besides, he had heard enough of Johnson's habits in argument not to desire a combat man to man, or rather writer to writer. Against that roaring fury he would soon be discomfited, and he knew it. For the evening, then, Greville resolved to leave off the character of intellectual and fall back on another of his roles, that of patron of the arts. He would "take the field with the aristocratic armour of pedigree and distinction."

Somber in his greatness, his semiblindness, his partial deafness, Dr. Johnson waited, a lion, but a somnolent one. It was definitely not his night to roar.

Mrs. Thrale might have prodded him a bit, but she was a little put out by Greville's airs and graces. Then, too, Mr. Thrale was there, and he usually had a dampening effect on Mrs. Thrale's spirits. Mr. Thrale, in his lethargic way, entertained large expectations of the evening. The rich brewer seldom opened his mouth, but he enjoyed the show when wit and intellect sparkled around him, and he had been assured it would sparkle at the Burneys' party, "between Mrs. Greville, Mrs. Thrale, and Dr. Johnson." Mrs. Greville was still resting gracefully on the laurels which she had won as the author of the *Ode to Indifference*. She had been resting on that spiky bed for a good many years now, and her beauty had sharpened, thinned out, and vanished in the process. Tonight, unfortunately, she seemed to find repose sufficient; like Mrs. Thrale, she preferred to let the men work things out for themselves.

Glumly, then, the company sat there, waiting for somebody to strike the spark. Dr. Burney, a man of sensitivity, decided to get things going one way if he could not the other: he invited Signor Piozzi to sing. Alas, no measure could have been more disastrous. Dr. Burney could never get it into his enthusiastic head that some people simply are not musical. That evening he was unlucky enough to be entertaining the two couples, of all London, most indifferent to music's delights. Neither the Grevilles nor the Thrales, in Madame d'Arblay's words, "heeded music beyond what belonged to it as fashion." Poor Piozzi, therefore, stood up before a cold house when he began his cantata. It was just as cold when he finished.

The atmosphere grew more and more oppressive. Mrs. Crewe may have found some quiet amusement in the situation; Fanny certainly did. Johnson was alone in being truly indifferent. He had a happy faculty for losing himself in abstraction whenever the exterior world bored him. Mrs. Thrale, however, could not bear boredom beyond a certain point. To begin with, she had been miffed by Greville, for she had an ever-present consciousness of her own birth and good blood, a consciousness which at times amounted to an inferiority complex because she was married to a brewer. That singing man bored her; *she* wanted to be showing off. She smoldered, and Mrs. Thrale was not good at smoldering for long stretches of time.

". . . her spirits rose rebelliously above her control; and, in a fit of utter recklessness of what might be thought of her by her fine new acquaintance, she suddenly, but softly, arose, and stealing on tip-toe behind Signor Piozzi; who was accompanying himself on the pianoforte to an animated *arria parlante*, with his back to the company, and his face to the wall; she ludicrously began imitating him by squaring her elbows, elevating them with ecstatic shrugs of the shoulders, and casting up her eyes, while languishingly reclining her head; as if she were not less enthusiastically, though somewhat more suddenly, struck with the transports of harmony than himself."

Johnson sat facing the fire, glooming away in a world of his own with his back turned to the group. He didn't see his "dear Mistress" acting the naughty schoolboy, but the rest of the party naturally began to giggle. Dr. Burney, however, quickly put a stop to Mrs. Thrale's performance. He hurried over to her and whispered, "with something between pleasantry and severity," "Because, madam, you have no ear yourself for music, will you destroy the attention of all who, in that one point, are otherwise gifted?"

Mrs. Thrale saw the justice of the rebuke. Quietly she nodded and resumed her seat, and was a good girl for the rest of the evening. Piozzi, during a duet played by the Burneys, fell asleep.

It was not a gay evening, any way one looks at it. The only other alleviation in the entire dull stretch of it was provided by the indolent lion, who had noticed Greville's behavior, though he gave no hint of it until then. That was always the trouble with Sam Johnson: you could never be sure how blind and deaf and absent he really was. Suddenly he fixed his eye on Greville, who still lounged gracefully before the fire, cutting off its heat from everyone else in the room, as he had done the whole chilly evening. Dr. Johnson spoke.

"If it were not for depriving the ladies of the fire," he said, "I should like to stand upon the hearth myself!"

Greville jerked, stiffened haughtily, smiled faintly, and tried to ignore the remark. But no armor, not even the aristocratic armor of pedigree and distinction, is proof against that sort of thing. After a moment or two, in which he continued to hold the hearth as if against all comers, he rang for his carriage, doing considerable violence to the bell.

Mr. Crisp was still being kept in ignorance, though Mrs. Thrale knew, and that awesome leviathan of literature, Dr. Johnson. It was impossible, Fanny claimed, to bring herself to the point of telling her dear old Daddy. Mr. Crisp must wait until Dr. Burney could come to Chesington and spare her blushes. In the meantime faithful Susan sent a copy of Mrs. Thrale's letter to her father: ". . . Mr. Johnson returned home full of praises of the book I had lent him, and protesting there were passages in it which might do honour to Richardson. We talk of it for ever, and he feels ardent after the dénouement; he 'could not get rid of the rogue,' he said. . . . You must be more a philosopher, and less a father, than I wish you, not to be pleased with this letter. . . ."

Dr. Johnson's approbation! ". . . it almost crazed me with agreeable surprise," wrote Fanny; "—it gave me such a flight of spirits, that I danced a jig to Mr. Crisp, without any preparation, music, or explanation—to his no small amazement and diversion."

But Daddy Crisp was not to wait much longer for enlightenment. Dr. Burney came to Chesington to make a short visit and to escort his daughter home: he himself would break the news to the old man, he said. Any more delay would be awkward.

Fanny on that Sunday evening stopped short at the door of her father's room, for he was talking to Mr. Crisp. "The variety of characters—the variety of scenes—and the language—why, she has had very little education but what she has given herself—less than any of the others!"

A chorus to these ejaculations was Mr. Crisp's voice: "Wonderful!—it's wonderful!"

Heady wine, this, for the dunce, quiet, shy Miss Fanny, the little old lady of the Burney nursery. Not wishing to interrupt such pleasant speeches, she tiptoed away down the hall. When she encountered Daddy Crisp later and he playfully shook his fist at her and began to talk about it, she evaded him. She ran away, holding up her skirts and making as much speed as if she were Evelina herself fleeing from Lord Orville and his compliments. But she was caught at last, like Evelina, and they had it out.

"Why, you little hussy—you young devil!" said her proud Daddy. "An't you ashamed to look me in the face, you *Evelina*, you! Why, what a dance you have led me about it! Young friend, indeed! O you little hussy, what tricks have you served me!"

He vowed that Lowndes the bookseller would have made money on the bargain even if he had paid a thousand pounds for the manuscript; he should not have given less, said Mr. Crisp. But these were statements made in excitement, in understood hyperbole. Mr. Lowndes certainly made a good thing out of *Evelina*; it yielded a big return for twenty pounds. Still, Mr. Crisp was exaggerating. He never thought he would be taken seriously, long years afterward, by Macaulay. He spoke in playful, hopeful spirit. "You have nothing to do now but to take your pen in hand, for your fame and reputation are made, and any bookseller will snap at what you write."

Now for the honor and glory of success!

Fanny on the way to Streatham had the fidgets. She felt as if she were going to meet the Thrales for the first time, and was fearful lest "they would expect a less awkward and backward kind of person than I was sure they would find." She was justified in considering herself a stranger, for it is to be doubted if Mrs. Thrale or Queeney had ever really looked at her before, their attention having always been taken up by her charming father. Mrs. Thrale was to be an important influence in the newly arrived novelist's life, and it seems the moment to describe her background.

Merely to sketch Mrs. Thrale is a difficult job. Few people have been so thoroughly discussed, dissected, and studied under a microscope as has this lady, who served then and still serves today as a football for Johnson enthusiasts. Mrs. Thrale has been overdone, overwritten, certainly overcriticized. One is faced with a task like that of copying a Gauguin, let us say, in pastels, or of giving just a rough idea of the design in a mosaic floor. It seems safest and most fair to use her own records of herself for foundation and to caution the reader to remember that the lively lady was a scatter-brain, prone to exaggeration and to afterthought which led sometimes to censorship. In rougher words, she didn't always tell the truth. Few people do, admittedly, but then few people have been cross-examined by posterity so relentlessly as has Mrs. Thrale.

There has been no argument, at least, that her maiden name was Hester Lynch Salusbury and that she was born in Wales. There has been argument against her statement that "Salusbury" was originally "Salzburg" and that she was descended from Adam of Salzburg, but we do not make such a point nowadays as people used to about these errors once made by the College of Heralds. It is allowed even by her enemies that Hester Lynch Salusbury was born of gentlefolk, as she insisted on distinguishing them from tradespeople such as Thrale's family. Though a gentlewoman, or rather a gentlechild, Hester grew up without much hope of a fortune to supply her with a dowry, in spite of being an only child. Her mother was a worthy lady, rather stiff and stupid; her father, John Salusbury, his wife's cousin, was a man of fantastically difficult temperament. In her earlier years Hester didn't see much of him. With the eager assent of the family, he went off to Nova Scotia with his patron Cornwallis, to found the city of Halifax. His wife and child lived in London, Mrs. Salusbury managing somehow on a slender annuity from her mother. Sometimes, in their role of poor relations, mother and daughter were invited to East Hyde in Bedfordshire where lived Hester's grandmother Cotton. There the little girl had a magnificent time leading a tomboy life and spending most of her time in the stables, but the visit always came to an end.

Happily for Hester, a paternal uncle, Thomas Salusbury, now

took over the responsibility of providing them with a better living. Her new aunt, who was childless, made a pet of her, and though the Salusburys still lived in London, they were usually at Offley Place in Hertfordshire. Hester had the run of the stables, which were stocked with excellent hunters and racers, and she now had the tutelage of Dr. Collier, who was often a guest in the house. Until she died Mrs. Thrale would speak with loving veneration of Dr. Collier. He was a man who inspired a mystic passion in the breasts of at least two young girls, his pupils at different times— Hester Salusbury and Sophy Streatfeild, the beauty who knew Greek.

Dr. Collier taught Hester Latin, logic, and rhetoric. Unofficially he taught her much more, in his own peculiar philosophy, and in adoration for Dr. Collier, though "love had no place in the connection," as she stoutly asserted. She called him "a Man of perfect worth, profound Erudition, and polish'd Manners: a Man who engrossed my whole Heart, & deserved it; he was indeed 64 when I was 16 exactly; so *Love* (as it is falsely called,) had no Share in the Connection:—but nobody ever did feel more fond & true Affection for another, than I did for my dear Dr. Collier, & he for his *Sweetest Angel* as he call'd me."

Perhaps, but Mrs. Thrale's memories of her tutor must have been just a bit sentimental, in spite of these protests. It is significant that she should have exaggerated his age. When she was sixteen Dr. Collier was not sixty-four but fifty.

Besides, Dr. Collier encouraged Hester to discourage her admirers. There were many of these, she said, after her aunt's death, when it was supposed she would come in for a part at least of her rich uncle's fortune. Hester at sixteen was quick of wit, a scribbler of verses, and reasonably proficient in subjects unusual to a girl's education—the aforesaid Latin, logic, and rhetoric. These attributes did not appeal to most of her young men, but her prospects did. In vain; to the accompaniment of Dr. Collier's applause, Hester laughed them off. She must have been attractive in her youth; she was certainly so in maturity, but she was no beauty. Fanny

Burney calls her pretty, but Hester Thrale herself says she was not. Still, her portraits give her the lie. We might think her prettier than her contemporaries did: beauty is to an astonishing degree an affair of fashion, and in the eighteenth century a lady was supposed to be quite plump, whereas Mrs. Thrale, at least between pregnancies, was only slightly so. She was also very small, less than five feet tall. Her features were too large and important for her frame: her portraits show a nose of which the straight line and forward position entitle it to be called Roman, though most ladies would not take this epithet as a compliment. It was definitely an attractive face, though not in any classic style of beauty.

The aunt died, but the Salusburys did not leave Offley. Hunting, flirting, and teasing her suitors, Hester might have gone on indefinitely, growing less and less inclined to marry and more and more fascinated by her tutor. His strange, wry personality still lives in the pages of her *Thraliana*, as it persisted, after his death, in the quirks of nature he encouraged in Hester and Sophy, his pretty pupils. "People generally left the Room with a high Opinion of that Gentleman's Parts and a confirmed Resolution to avoid his Society. . . . To perplex and disappoint was indeed so much his Disposition that he seemed to converse for scarcely any other Purpose," wrote Mrs. Thrale in fond retrospect. ". . . So much for the Character of my earliest, and most disinterested Friend; Ill used by everyone, I also used him ill; and repaid the long and diligent Care he paid to my Improvement, with Slights & Coldness: It was not however easy for me to do better;—my Mother who did not approve of some of his Doctrines nor delight in the Confidence I shewed for him, parted us with Assiduity and Pleasure——"

Mrs. Salusbury was given her chance to accomplish this separation by the return of her husband from Nova Scotia. The wandering prodigal, having quarreled with his colleagues and ruined his chances, now came home to resume quarreling with his family. He had always been a violent, changeable, dueling sort of a fellow, and after a short time everyone at Offley Place was on edge. Hester's young men were sent packing. Mrs. Salusbury was always in tears, and Sir Thomas quietly sneaked off and began to pay court to another lady, intending to marry and rid himself gracefully of his brother's troublesome family. But it was not his intention to cast off his beloved niece completely, without further help.

While John was absent on a trip, Sir Thomas one day brought home a tall young, or youngish, man named Henry Thrale as an eligible match for Hester. From the practical point of view the choice was sensible; Thrale was not, however, a man of good blood, and his future bride was never to forget it.

His connection with Sir Thomas was tenuous, but it was there, his grandfather Thrale having been a cottager on the estate. The laborer's brother-in-law was a highly successful brewer who owned the Anchor Brewery at Southwark. Henry Thrale's aunt, the daughter of the brewer, was thus an heiress, who on the strength of her fortune married Sir Richard Temple. Henry Thrale's father was taken into the brewery and proved himself a capable man; in time he bought the business from the uncle's heir and became an M.P. for the borough and a pillar of society in general. The Thrales were a living picture in little of what was happening to England in large; they grew in importance as the beer and wine trade grew, so that by the time Henry, only son of the third generation, had reached man's estate his family was connected with people of high position, his sisters all made good marriages, and he himself could set up as a gentleman.

Not that he was really accepted by the nobility. Jokes last a long time in England, and the joke about the brewers who run the country is still as exquisite and satisfactory as ever—witness Evelyn Waugh's crack about them in *Vile Bodies*, for example. But English snobbery is almost all in speech, very little in practice. Impoverished nobles like money as much as anyone does, and though Henry Thrale's grand connections snickered at the brewery, they were glad to borrow from him. That taint of labor and trade kept Thrale in a place of secondary importance in the social hierarchy, but what wealth could do wealth did for him, and it is doubtful if the esoteric value of an occasional snub contributed very much to his unhappiness. He was pleasantly free from false shame about his origin, and was eager to claim his "low connections" when he first visited Offley; though his father's birthplace was now used as a dog kennel by Sir Thomas, he made no attempt to play down this fact. Thrale was tall and floridly handsome. He had simple tastes; with one exception, they were brutally simple. He loved to eat, to hunt, and to make love, as it is euphemistically called. The exception was not evident at the time he met Hester, when he was thirty-four, but later, in the company of Samuel Johnson, he developed further his incongruous taste for good conversation. That is to say, for listening to good conversation, for Thrale scarcely ever spoke more than was strictly necessary.

According to Hester, Thrale never spoke to her at all during his courtship, but devoted his attention entirely to her mother. It may not have been tactful behavior, but it was good strategy. His interest in Hester was purely practical: her uncle Tom, in promoting the match, led him to expect that she would bring him plenty of money, if not Sir Thomas's entire estate. With a good dowry and her superior birth, Miss Salusbury was well worth Henry Thrale's attention. His life was already well cushioned: he was master of the brewery, though he never took the intelligent interest in it that his father had expected or hoped for, and he had his houses, his hounds, and his mistress. All he needed now was a wife and—— I had almost written, "a housekeeper," but Hester's experience proved that he did not expect her to keep house: he wanted a wife so that he might breed legitimate children.

Henry Thrale, thus introduced to the Salusburys by Sir Thomas and championed by Hester's mother, was no fly-by-night suitor like the others, to be played with and cast off merely to amuse Dr. Collier and his pupil. He was the official aspirant, and everything seemed to be going well with his suit when Hester's father suddenly came to Offley Place and went into the rage which always seized him when the question of her marriage, or practically any question at all, came up. This time he was worse than usual. He carried off the family to London, roaring about dishonor, exchanging his daughter for a barrel of porter, and God knows what.

"Vain were all my assurances that nothing resembled love *less* than Mr. Thrale's behaviour," wrote Hester.

Scarcely had they arrived in the city when they had news from Dr. Collier that Uncle Tom was going to marry the new lady of his affections. What with all this excitement and disappointment, John Salusbury broke some vital blood vessel and died.

Five thousand pounds were to be scraped from his estate for Hester, and seven hundred a year. Uncle Tom added another five thousand, "with which (and expectations of course)," said Hester with some bitterness, "Mr. Thrale deigned to accept my undesired hand. . . ." Dr. Collier made a last attempt to prevent the match. He wrote his erstwhile pupil, appealing to her sense of duty to her dead father; he reminded her that John Salusbury had objected to her marriage to Thrale. But Dr. Collier at a distance was no match for Mrs. Salusbury on the spot, and besides, as Hester said, "as he rather opposed my marrying *anybody*," his opinion did not now carry so much weight.

Henry Thrale and Hester Salusbury were married in 1763. Mrs. Thrale often harked back to the cold-blooded way in which the match was arranged, but she rendered her husband strict justice and spoke of him with a detachment which is a credit to her self-control. She never hated him. She felt resentment, impatience, and jealousy at times, but she was reasonably fond of Thrale. He always showed her kindness in his own way, she said, and generosity, also in his own way; he was much kinder than he need have been to a *plain girl* with whom he had not bothered to seek as much as five minutes' private conversation before the wedding. Hester neither expected nor got fidelity from him. In the first years of their marriage he treated her with contempt and coldness, but she admitted that this was her own fault, that she was a dull wife, always with her mother and babies. After she took Dr. Johnson's advice and brightened and began to circulate in such society as she found available, Thrale became proud of her, though he never encouraged *too* much freedom. . . . But then Hester, as she cheerfully acknowledged, was a bad bargain, financially speaking.

They lived in Streatham Park the greater part of each year, though sometimes Henry's mildly arduous duties connected with business or his borough took them to his other house at the brewery in Southwark, which Mrs. Thrale detested. She never saw either house, incidentally, until after her marriage, for Thrale had very odd ideas about a wife's place in the world. He would not suffer her to exercise authority in the kitchen; he made her give up horses because they were not a ladylike interest; he seldom took her to the play or opera, though he himself attended regularly, sitting in a box with his mistress of the moment.

"Mr. Thrale's person is manly," wrote his wife in one of the odd little bursts of detached description with which she filled the pages of her *Thraliana* notebook, "his countenance agreeable, his eyes steady and of the deepest blue; his look neither soft nor severe, neither sprightly nor gloomy, but thoughtful and intelligent. . . . He is a man wholly, as I think, out of the power of mimickry. . . . His passions either are not strong, or else he keeps them under such command that they seldom disturb his tranquillity or his friends; and it must, I think, be something more than common which can affect him strongly, either with hope, fear, anger, love, or joy. . . . He has been a most exemplary brother; though, when the house of his favourite sister was on fire, and we were all alarmed with the account of it in the night, I well remember that he never rose, but bidding the servant who called us to go to her assistance, quietly turned about and slept to his usual hour. . . . Mr. Thrale's sobriety, and the decency of his conversation . . . make him a man exceedingly comfortable to live with; while the easiness of his temper and slowness to take offence add greatly to his value as a domestic man. Yet I think his servants do not much love him, and I am not sure that his children have much affection for him. . . . With regard to his wife, though little tender of her person, he is very partial to her understanding; but he is obliging to no-

body, and confers a favour less pleasingly than many a man re-
fuses to confer one. This appears to me to be as just a character
as can be given of the man with whom I have now lived thirteen
years; and though he is extremely reserved and uncommunicative,
yet one must know something of him after so long an acquaintance." The delightful eighteenth-century formality of that last sentence could scarcely be surpassed.

A wife's business, Thrale might have said if he ever said anything, was filling cradles, and he did his best to keep Hester well
employed at that. His worst enemy could not claim that he failed.
In fifteen years of married life before Fanny came to Streatham,
the poor lady gave birth to twelve children. This would have been
a happy state of affairs, given two factors: if Mrs. Thrale had loved
children to a passionate degree, and if they had all, or nearly all,
survived. Mrs. Thrale's attitude toward her children has been
a favorite topic in the eternal Thrale discussion. Baretti said she
hated them, but Baretti has been discredited on many grounds,
and he himself certainly hated Mrs. Thrale when he wrote that
article. She didn't hate the children in their childhood, if her
letters and Children's Book are any criterion. Anti-Thraleites will
not grant that they are. But then the world has always been well
stocked with people who disapprove other people's treatment of
their offspring.

As to the second factor, it is the appalling truth that only four of
her children lived to grow up. One died soon after birth, one in
ten days, one at the age of one year and seven months, one
(Henry) at the age of ten, and so on. Mr. Vulliamy thinks Thrale's
"early history"—i.e., his medical history—may have been responsible for this high rate of mortality, which is probable. The fact which
he quotes as opposite evidence, that the four surviving children
were exceptionally tough and long-living, does not really disprove
his theory. Out of twelve, four might well have escaped inheriting
Sigma Three. But these are matters on which we can only conjecture.

What is not conjecture is the remarkable vitality of Mrs. Thrale,

who was still vivacious, witty, and strong after such a deplorable
history of childbearing and child-losing. She was not a tragic figure.
She would not have expected or welcomed pity. As Thrale's wife
she was wealthy, and she enjoyed being wealthy. In her own right
she had an invincible sort of bounce, a capacity for enjoyment, a
native resistance to any force, natural or social, which tended to
down her. Fortunately for herself, she was not sensitive, in the
usual sense of the word: she was quick enough, even intuitive, but
not thin-skinned or melancholic. Some people, especially male
scholars, resent this quality in Mrs. Thrale. They call it toughness,
vulgarity, abominable flippancy, and other rude terms. One bi-
ographer in particular treats her with a sort of disgusted fascina-
tion, which in spite of a careful disguise seems to imply that if
she were still alive, or if he had lived in 1770 odd, he would have
been in love with her, his teeth would be chronically on edge,
and he would hate himself. A personality which can reach down
through the years to such an extent as that cannot be dismissed
as merely vulgar. Coarse Mrs. Thrale certainly was, but the
eighteenth century in general was not squeamish. She must have
been invincibly good-natured, for she managed to live with Thrale
eighteen years without growing sour, even against him. At the
end she was forced to watch him kill himself by stubborn, unre-
mitting gluttony, a long-drawn-out process during which he entertained a passion for an intimate friend of his wife's. Yet Mrs.
Thrale did not hate her husband unduly. She was not a woman to
harbor a dark passion like hatred. She was a gay creature, a singing cricket, and when she lost her temper she did it all at once
and vented her feelings in a spiteful outburst, and then felt better.

No doubt she loved her children, as children, well enough, as
long as they did not remind her too much of their father.

This was Mrs. Thrale, who was to be Fanny's best friend for the
next five years.

7. THE STREATHAM COTERIE

I WAS shewed a little novel t'other Day which I thought pretty enough & set Burney to read it, little dreaming it was written by his second Daughter Fanny." Mrs. Thrale wrote in her notebook, "who certainly must be a Girl of good Parts & some Knowledge of the World too, or She could not be the Author of Evelina—flimsy as it is. . . ."

Whatever impatience Mrs. Thrale may have felt for Fanny's famous shyness, shyness not being one of her own weaknesses, she had made due preparation to avoid distressing her guest. All the while the mistress was chatting, and showing Miss Burney around, and talking with her upstairs in the bedroom, *Evelina* was not so much as mentioned. When Mrs. Thrale ventured at last to touch on the subject, she had of course nothing but praises for it (after all, would she have dared to attack it?). She quoted Dr. Johnson's praises too. It is rather a shock to discover that Dr. Johnson, in spite of all this, never read the book thoroughly, though Fanny didn't find it out.[1]

[1] "Northcote remarked, that speaking of *Evelina* put him in mind of what Opie had once told him, that when Dr. Johnson sat to him for his picture, on his first coming to town, he asked him if it was true that he had sat up all night to read Miss Burney's new novel, as it had been reported? And he made answer, 'I never read it through at all, though I don't wish this to be known.' Sir Joshua also pretended to have read it through at a sitting, though it appeared to him

Thus gently lured and flattered, she had nearly conquered her tremors when Mr. Seward found her alone in the library and started them up again. Mr. Seward, a bookish young man with an affectedly lightweight manner, was so crude as to begin talking immediately about *Evelina*. "I was actually confounded by his attack; and his abrupt manner of letting me know he was au *fait* equally astonished and provoked me. How different from the delicacy of Mr. and Mrs. Thrale!" Yet it was certainly Mrs. Thrale who had told Seward the secret. Fanny had to accustom herself to that lady's indiscretion.

"Well, the ice is now broke," wrote Mr. Crisp to her, "and your perturbation ought to be in a great measure at an end. When you went into the sea at Teignmouth, did not you shiver and shrink at first, and almost lose your breath when the water came up to your chest? I suppose you afterwards learned to plunge in boldly, over head and ears at once, and then your pain was over. You must do the like now; and as the public have thought proper to put you on a cork jacket, your fears of drowning would be unpardonable."

Mrs. Thrale was what is called a man's woman. More in her century than in ours she was set apart from average females by her literary aspirations. Had she been a "Blue," her intellectual amusements would have been forgiven and expected of her, but Mrs. Thrale was not a member of that august, elegant assembly, though she hovered on its fringes. It was Mrs. Montagu and Mrs. Vesey who were the famous hostesses of the upper circle of wit and fashion. With a lethargic brewer by her side, Mrs. Thrale could seldom enter the lists on equal terms with those ladies. She didn't attempt an all-out rivalry, but contented herself, as far as her restless spirit allowed content, with her own position.

It could have been worse. As the hostess and keeper of Johnson,

---

[Northcote] affectation in them both, who were thorough-paced men of the world, and hackneyed in literature, to pretend to be so delighted with the performance of a girl, in which they could find neither instruction nor any great amusement, except from the partiality of friendship." *Conversations of James Northcote Esq. R.A.*, by William Hazlitt, 1949.

that position was unique. The literary world, the artist's world, the world of Charles Burney and the more discerning patrons, all revered Johnson, and Mrs. Thrale felt the benefit of that reverence. It made up for much that was disadvantageous in the arrangement —the lion's uncouth habits and his dangerous irascibility. Mrs. Montagu, Mrs. Ord, and the others had to take Mrs. Thrale into account as Johnson's friend. They could not have borne with his company in the intimacy of the home, as she did, but they did not deny he was a very wonderful man, and they kept in touch with Streatham, and sometimes, not too often, invited Lexiphanes to dine—and the Thrales as well.

Nevertheless, though Mrs. Thrale still retained a name for respectability in spite of her defiance of small conventions—it would have been difficult even in the eighteenth century to spread much scandal about a wife so constantly and indomitably pregnant —she was not a woman's woman. As a girl Hester had been popular. She was a good fellow and the men still enjoyed her company, but among most women she found little to talk about. She preferred men's society, not perhaps so obviously and avowedly as Miss Bowdler had done, but still the preference was noticeable. No woman but Fanny was a constant member of the Streatham circle. Sophy Streatfeild, the beautiful S.S., was often there, but she never lived with the Thrales as Fanny did, week after week. Most other young ladies already had many interests in "the world," whereas Fanny's emergence into publicity coincided with her capture by the Streatham coterie. Alone and unclaimed until then, she was introduced by Mrs. Thrale; she belonged to Mrs. Thrale. S.S., too, was an unmarried lady, but she was a lady of independent fortune.

According to the innocent Miss Burney, though not to Mrs. Thrale, the two ladies were immensely fond of each other from the very beginning of Fanny's new life. Mrs. Thrale's first partiality was purely due to opportunism; she considered Fanny a piece of luck rarely to be met with, rather than a friend. It was great fun as well as greatly exciting that she, Mrs. Thrale, should have happened to be in Dr. Burney's confidence, so that he naturally deposited this prize in *her* lap—this secret, this sensation of the season! It suited her to have Fanny under her wing, to produce her to the world with a careless flourish at the right moment. A priority claim on her was nearly as much an asset as owning exclusive rights to Dr. Johnson; in many ways it was better, for Fanny was a discreet, quiet little creature, nowhere near as difficult as that turbulent elephantine genius of a doctor.

There is one drawback to the status of a man's woman: she is often lonely. For all Mrs. Thrale's popularity, once she had left the gentlemen to their exclusively manly pursuits she faced a sadly empty world. Either she must return to the hatefully familiar nursery or kill time in conversation with women who bored her, distrusted her, or snubbed her. Fanny was different from these. Fanny was witty, though she took a deal of drawing out. Fanny looked up to her, quite correctly, as a being on a higher social plane than her own. But Mrs. Thrale was not slow to criticize Fanny, even though the younger woman was her own protégée and though she readily championed *Evelina* whenever she had the opportunity. Now and then, feeling the need to assert superiority, she would refer to Fanny's low social status. During the early days of the acquaintance Mrs. Thrale never mentioned it in her diary, though the Burney Journal spoke of nothing else.

". . . his Daughter is a graceful looking Girl," Hester said finally, after a moderated rapture on Dr. Burney, "but tis the Grace of an Actress not a Woman of Fashion—how should it? (The Burneys are I believe a very low Race of Mortals.) her Conversation would be more pleasing if She thought less of herself; but her early Reputation embarrasses her Talk, & clouds her Mind with scruples about Elegancies which either come uncalled for or will not come at all; I love her more for her Father's sake than for her own, though her Merit cannot as a Writer be controverted. . . . She is a Girl of prodigious Parts——"

Fanny, like Boswell, recorded conversations with Dr. Johnson. But Boswell polished his and pointed them up, and kept them in proportion, and cut out extraneous material, whereas Fanny simply remembered and reported everything, good stuff and bad. Boswell knew he was writing for publication; Fanny indulged herself recklessly because she was keeping her Journal as a private exercise.

(That is why it seems unfair to accuse her of conceit, as many people have done. They base their opinions on the Diary, which Fanny never meant us to read any more than she would have meant us to read her mind. Conceit, after all, is simply failure to conceal the ego to the degree demanded by society. Do these critics really believe that they themselves do not have as good an opinion, inwardly, of their persons and talents as Fanny did of herself? Of course she loved praise and reveled in it, and counted over and over the compliments she received. Who in her place would not? But she hid her pride, save from the lynx-eyed Hester Thrale, who resented it, and from her family and Daddy Crisp, who did not. She kept her pride to herself when she was in the world; she exulted only silently, or to her confidential intimates. It is not poor Fanny's fault if we choose to poke and pry among her secrets now that she is powerless to protect them. Nothing could have hurt her worse, in life, than thus to be discovered.

On the other hand, the criticism is a natural, if unkind, reaction to Fanny's twittering protests. We humans are contrary creatures, and when a girl says for the fifteenth time that she is overcome with shyness and timidity, even though we may be eavesdropping, we are apt to make sneering noises of disbelief. Admittedly, Fanny is sometimes tiresome. But, then, whose stream of consciousness is not? Witness Gertrude Stein, or Joyce, or Proust.)

Fanny's picture of Johnson is as sympathetic as Boswell's, though not so forceful. In "little Burney's" presence the old man never flew off the handle in one of his really terrible dudgeons, though he seems to have come near a violent fit once or twice, and certainly never was guilty of mincing a word. Those long conversations at table or in the Thrale library create as pleasant an impression of Lexiphanes as one can find anywhere. At tea one after-

noon "Dr. Johnson was gaily sociable. He gave a very droll account
of the children of Mr. Langton, 'who,' he said, 'might be very
good children, if they were let alone; but the father is never easy
when he is not making them do something which they cannot
do; they must repeat a fable, or a speech, or the Hebrew alphabet;
and they might as well count twenty, for what they know of the
matter: however, the father says half, for he prompts every other
word. But he could not have chosen a man who would have been
less entertained by such means.' "

He would throw his mighty arm around his little Burney and
joke with her about her book; he would scatter broadcast his astonishing, debatable opinions on writers; he would make a good
remark and chuckle with innocent vanity. His light malice when
he talked about friends has not been so well reproduced by Boswell as by Fanny, no doubt because the doctor unbent thus only
with *the ladies*. But often he pouted and sulked because the
ladies went out. When they came home late one night, bringing
company with them, the doctor wouldn't open his mouth.

Mrs. Thrale had long since learned that it is not always unalloyed
bliss to play hostess to great minds and famous people. Her new
guest Fanny, too, caused small ladylike complications in her own
right, and could certainly be irritating. During one of the ladies'
good-night chats, when Fanny ridiculously implored Mrs. Thrale
never, never to tell her secret to anybody, the older woman talked
plainly.

". . . if such a desire does not proceed from affectation, 'tis from
something worse," she declared at the end.

"No, indeed, not from affectation; for my conduct has been
as uniform in trying to keep snug [secret] as my words; and I never
have wavered: I never have told anybody out of my own family,
nor half the bodies in it. And I have so long forborne making this
request to you, for no other reason in the world but for fear you
should think me affected."

Then, said Mrs. Thrale, Fanny was guilty of something worse:
". . . an over-delicacy that may make you unhappy all your life.

Indeed you must check it—you must get the better of it: for why should you write a book, print a book, and have everybody read and take your book, and then sneak in a corner and disown it?"

Fanny eagerly explained. It did look bad to have published at all, she admitted that, but she had never expected to be found out; she had been well persuaded the book would never be heard of—"I really thought myself safe, and meant to be as private, when the book was at Mr. Lowndes's, as when it was in my own bureau."

Now Mrs. Thrale introduced a subject she had been agitating for some time. Fanny must, she really must, write a piece for the stage, a comedy. It was the true style of writing for Fanny: look at her talent for dialogue! Why, the thing was as evident as could be. And a play would bring Fanny out; you could not write and produce a comedy anonymously. ". . . and we will have no more of such sly, sneaking, private ways!" she cried.

Fanny laughed; she neither affirmed nor denied. Actually she was already writing that comedy, slyly, sneakily, and in private.

The new lioness had not been at Streatham more than a month before Mrs. Thrale was able to play her trump card. Mrs. Montagu was coming to dinner, and Fanny would be on view to this indomitable bluestocking. Everyone was impressed, everyone was on tiptoe. When Mrs. Thrale announced it to Dr. Johnson, he "began to see-saw, with a countenance strongly expressive of inward fun, and after enjoying it some time in silence, he suddenly, and with great animation, turned to me and cried, 'Down with her, Burney! —down with her—spare her not!—attack her, fight her, and down with her at once! You are a rising wit, and she is at the top; and when I was beginning the world, and was nothing and nobody, the joy of my life was to fire at all the established wits! . . . and then everybody loved to halloo me on. But there is no game now; everybody would be glad to see me conquered: but then, when I was new, to vanquish the great ones was all the delight of my poor little soul! So at her Burney—at her, and down with her!' "

They chitchatted at length about Montagu: her pedantic style

("She diffuses more knowledge in her conversation," said John-son, "than any woman I know, or, indeed, any man."); her magnif-icent new house which was then a-building and which Johnson was jocosely sure he would not be permitted to enter, since he had once contradicted her; her notorious weakness for finery. Mrs. Montagu may have been feared and respected, but she was not safe from their discreet malice.

The lady arrived early. "She is middle-sized," said Fanny, "very thin, and looks infirm; she has a sensible and penetrating counte-nance, and the air and manner of a woman accustomed to being distinguished, and of great parts." So far so good. "Dr. Johnson, who agrees in this," she adds innocently, "told us that a Mrs. Hervey, of his acquaintance, says, she can remember Mrs. Montagu trying for this same air and manner."

Mrs. Montagu spoke of *Evelina*, the popular new book, which she had not yet been able to get at the bookshop. Mrs. Thrale assured her it was well worth reading. Fanny blew her nose and kept her handkerchief to her face.

"I hope, though," said Mrs. Montagu dryly, "it is not in verse? I can read anything in prose, but I have a great dread of a long story in verse."

No, no, said Mrs. Thrale, nothing like that. It was a remark-able novel, and Mr. Burke had sat up all night to read it, and Sir Joshua Reynolds had been offering fifty pounds to know the author; *Dr. Johnson himself* had declared Fielding never wrote equal to this book.

Fanny stood up involuntarily, on her usual Evelina-like impulse to dart out of the room, but at the thought that Mrs. Thrale would probably start talking about her the minute she was gone, she lin-gered at the window and with passionate interest watched the chickens in the yard.

"But all this time we are killing Miss Burney," said Mrs. Thrale suddenly, "who wrote the book herself."

The sweetness of that moment must have been intense. Seldom was any lady able to get that much ahead of Mrs. Montagu. There is an entertaining echo in a letter which Hester Thrale wrote Dr. Johnson shortly afterward. "Mrs. Montagu cannot bear Evelina—let not that be published—her Silver Smiths are Pewterers She says, & her Captains Boatswains."

The criticism was a common one among Evelina's few detractors. Where most readers marveled at Fanny's wide range of characters, wondering how she could know so much of both high life and low, people who followed the lead of Mrs. Montagu turned up their noses and declared that the chit knew nothing, really, of the true high life: how could she be expected to know? And besides, why had she chosen to be patronized by the Thrale woman instead of by a true Blue?

Mrs. Thrale's dinner party marked the beginning of an elaborate house-party pleasantry which was not quite so much a joke as it appeared. Mrs. Montagu, during Fanny's absence, spoke in her majestically elegant way of arranging a match between clever little Miss Burney and Sir Joshua Reynolds. Such a nice man, so brilliant, she probably said; it would be an excellent thing all round, notwithstanding the difference in their ages. Egged on by Queeney and Dr. Johnson, Hester pounced on the suggestion and elaborated it during the following days. Young man after young man was brought out for inspection. What of Jerry Crutchley, for example? A man of large fortune, a ward of Mr. Thrale (and perhaps his illegitimate son as well); what said Fanny to him? Or Mr. Smith, a second cousin of Mr. Thrale and a modest, pretty sort of young man. Or Sir John Lade, Mr. Thrale's nephew.

Mrs. Thrale in her whirligig way really did try to make a match for Fanny, especially with the last-named entry for the stakes. Thrale was in favor of it, and Sir John had a good fortune, but that was all he had. He was younger than Fanny, and a silly, dissipated fellow. The attempt came to nothing. Fanny much enjoyed her flirts, but she would not try to marry anyone, and it is doubtful if she could have succeeded with Sir John if she had.

But she did like the life at Streatham. She reconsidered her first opinions of Queeney and Mr. Seward, for Queeney was all right once you knew her, and Mr. Seward seemed sorry he had been so foolish that first day: he never repeated his error; *Evelina*, for all he seemed to know, had been written by —— ——. Being lionized was great fun, and stimulating; besides, Fanny was losing her first genuine terror of publicity. She liked publicity now. She didn't admit this to herself, but the repeated shock of being discovered lost its force, little by little. One sees this happening in the Journal. Her shyness was Fanny's own special idiosyncrasy and she clung to it as long as she lived, but more and more it became an act; more and more she learned to enjoy the glow of lavish praise.

In the meantime there was the comedy on which she had begun to work. All the while that Mrs. Thrale was urging her, and Mrs. Montagu was offering, ever so graciously, to help, and Fanny was tremulously protesting that she could never think of attempting a comedy, she was working at it.

Daddy Crisp, that hardened, cynical old one-play man, wrote her a lot of good advice on the subject. His Fannikin was capable of writing a comedy, he was sure, but there were difficulties. In most of the successful comedies of the time, he reminded her, there were frequent lively freedoms that gave a strange animation and vigor to the style, without which it would lose its salt and spirit. "I mean such freedoms as ladies of the strictest character would make no scruple, openly, to laugh at, but at the same time, especially if they were prudes (and you know you are one), perhaps would shy at being known to be the authors of."

Besides, he said, *Evelina's* excellence lay in its "minuteness," in little touches. In novels like *Evelina*, "these little entertaining elegant histories," the writer can take his time to get his effect. The stage is a completely different medium. Dialogue must do the whole thing, and there is almost no scope for that description or narration at which Fanny excelled.

It was good advice, and she promised to be careful. Still, she would have a try.

What with comedies, parties, and flattery, why on earth should

Fanny think of marriage? She laughed away the names of projected candidates. Instead she carried on a violent verbal love affair with Dr. Johnson. That at least was safe and kept her in a pleasant nursery atmosphere. One felt little and young with Johnson; one was still a child; one was happy.

The little Burney's fame was snowballing, faster than her self-possession could keep up with it. It was all very well to be the pet of Streatham and to join in parties where a thousand good things were said in an evening, but it was genuinely distressing to be named in a pamphlet. This was not favorable publicity: it was insinuation verging on scandal. Pamphlets have almost disappeared from the scene nowadays, when "columns" of personalities have taken their place, but in Fanny's lifetime everyone in her circle and other cliques read them. An obscure Mr. Huddisford published a pamphlet in verse dedicated to Sir Joshua Reynolds, and in this verse he referred to Fanny. The thing seems so slight to us that we cannot understand why she made such a fuss about it. All that was said of her was in reference to some plan of Sir Joshua's:

"*Will it gain approbation from dear little Burney?*"

That was all. In spirit, you may say, it was equivalent to a chalked message on a wall, "Sir Joshua likes Fanny," and of course that is not pleasant, especially if Fanny really likes Sir Joshua. But Fanny didn't like Sir Joshua, not that way. He wasn't quite old enough; he was only fifty-seven.

Fanny hid her head in shame.

However, this distress passed, after a good-natured letter of scolding from Mrs. Thrale and general pish-tushing from Daddy Crisp. Dr. Johnson made a special trip to St. Martin's Street to reason with her about it. "To be sure I have been most plentifully lectured of late; and to be sure I have been most plentifully chagrined;" she wrote Susan, "but there is but one voice, and that goes against me. I must, therefore, give up the subject, and endeavour to forget the ideas it raised in me. I will try, my dear Susy, to become somewhat more like other folks, if, as it seems by their reasoning, I am now so different to them."

Among the readers of *Evelina* there was the usual amount of gossiping prattle going on, not all of it as favorable to her as Fanny believed. Through this chitchat Mrs. Thrale stumbled on a Burney skeleton. It was a fresh skeleton, too: what the anthropologists call "green bone."

One of the characters in *Evelina*, a young Scottish poet named Macartney, is saved from despairing suicide by the heroine, who prevents his shooting out his own brains—with a *pair* of pistols, by the way, rather than an ordinary single one. Evelina behaves in a highly creditable manner, though she is overwhelmed with the customary well-bred fainting fit when the danger has passed. Macartney turns out to be her own half brother. Mrs. Thrale told how oddly this passage was brought to her particular attention.

"Mrs. Crewe asked me the other day if the Story in Fanny Burney's Book—Evelina—about Mr. Macartney was not founded on Fact, for said She I heard it was true, and that She had told you so; and that you had told many, how the Anecdote of Circumstance or what you will of Macartney's going to shoot himself actually did happen to her own Brother Charles Burney, who having been expelled the University & forbidden his Fathers house was actually discovered by his Sister Fanny in the desperate State mentioned of Macartney. I protested to Mrs. Crewe that I had never heard a word on't before that moment, so that I never could have related what I never had heard, nor was inclined to invent it.—however said I the Story may be true, tho' tis false that I knew any thing of the matter—and accordingly the next Day when Burney came himself—I gave him a hint that I had heard somebody observe that the Story of Macartney was written with such *feeling*, it must *absolutely* be founded on Fact; at this Discourse he changed Colour so often, and so apparently that tho' I instantly got quit of the Conversation—I left it however well perswaded that all Mrs. Crewe said—or great part of it was but too true. (I have since heard that this Son of the Doctor's this *Charles Burney*

was a *Thief,* and as such expelled the University tho' an eminent
Scholar; if so, & so it certainly was,—the Family might well colour
& fret at the mention of him—I find now that Fanny gave the
Profits of her Book for his Support in ye Distresses to wch Vice
had driven him."

Some of this story is true. About the beginning of 1777, Charles
was expelled from Caius at Cambridge for stealing books from
the university library. Though he was not forbidden his father's
house, there must have been a good deal of distress occasioned the
family by the scandal. Charles redeemed himself in their eyes and
the sight of the world, graduating as Master of Arts from Aberdeen
and gaining a great reputation as a Latin scholar in after years, but
a certain amount of family unpopularity continued to hang round
his name. There exists a letter to Charles written by Fanny after
her father died, when Dr. Burney's children were getting on in
years, and that letter, unlike those of the Burneys which are
published, is anything but loving. Fanny sounds really angry, and
accuses Charles of trying to wangle his father's will so as to cheat
herself and Hetty out of their due. Without knowing Charles's
early history, the reader might be puzzled to understand such
rancor.

Yet Charles's name was so distinguished for scholarship that
Caius, which had cast him forth, had to give him an honorary
M.A. in 1807, by royal command, just thirty years after the old
scandal.

"Fanny Burney has gained such Credit by her Evelina that Mr.
Sheridan invites her to write for the Stage. . . .

"Our Miss Burney is big with a Comedy for next Season; I have
not yet seen the *Ebauche,* but I wish it well: Can I help wishing
well to every thing that bears the name of Burney?"

One might gather from Mrs. Thrale's notebook that the play
was Sheridan's idea, or Arthur Murphy's, or Fanny's: anyone's,
in fact, except Hester Thrale's. Yet it is obvious that the idea of
her doing a play was early suggested by Mrs. Thrale herself, and

most certainly it was Mrs. Thrale who kept the notion constantly in the minds of the Streatham coterie. Murphy, a playwright and general good mixer, had been responsible years before for introducing Johnson to the Thrales; it is for that one social gesture, rather than for all his activities, that posterity now remembers him.

"He may be of use to you," Mrs. Thrale told Fanny, "in what I am most eager for—your writing a play: he knows stage business so well: and if you will but take a fancy to one another, he may be more able to serve you than all of us put together. My ambition is, that Johnson should write your prologue, and Murphy your epilogue; then I shall be happy."

The pattern of *Evelina* was beginning to repeat itself. Fanny had written her play, or a first draft of it, and the knowledge of this guilty secret worried her. At last she spoke privately to Dr. Johnson. "I believe, sir, you heard part of what passed between Mr. Murphy and me the other evening concerning—a—comedy. Now, if I should make such an attempt would you be so good as to allow me, any time before Michaelmas, to put it in the coach, for you to look over as you go to town?"

"To be sure, my dear!—What, have you begun a comedy then?"

Fanny confessed, with hanging head. Dr. Johnson was full of advice. She was not to tell anybody about it, not even to whisper the name of it, to raise no expectations (which were always prejudicial), and she was to have it performed while the town knew nothing of whose it was. At the end he confused his young friend by advising that Murphy should be the last person to see it; i.e., to give the final judgment, rather than the early one. Now Murphy had proffered his services already and was eager to see the first draft, and Fanny did not see how she could in courtesy refuse him. She decided to let Mrs. Thrale figure it out later.

Thus the work in progress, which was to be known to no one and shown to no one, was scarcely begun before Dr. Johnson, Mrs. Thrale, Arthur Murphy, Daddy Crisp, and Susan were all putting in their two cents' worth, and each was cautioning Fanny not to let anybody see it.

"No indeed," said Fanny to each, with humble sincerity.

Callers at Streatham came and went. Johnson, of course, was practically an inmate of whichever house the Thrales occupied: both at Streatham and Southwark he had his room, used the family coach for himself, and spoke as freely as he liked on all occasions. He had a house of his own, occupied by a number of quarreling dependents, and as he was fond of stagecoach traveling he frequently went on trips, but the majority of his time he spent with the Thrales. It was Mrs. Thrale's ambition to keep Fanny as constantly to hand, as a balance to Sophy Streatfeild.

The women were very merry together, twittering and tittering like schoolgirls. Mrs. Thrale was probably only too glad to have someone on her side for a change, since in family disputes Dr. Johnson invariably supported Mr. Thrale. Fanny, though not much of an ally in open combat, was at least a sympathetic listener for Hester. A woman who is bound to lose every argument with her husband is grateful for a comforter, which Sophy was not.

It was this Sophy who shared with Mrs. Thrale the happy status of a Collier alumna; in 1776 Hester had noted in her diary that Dr. Collier after she lost track of him "picked up a more useful friend, a Mrs. Streatfeild, a widow, high in fortune and rather eminent both for the beauties of person and mind; her children, I find, he has been educating; and her eldest daughter is just now coming out into the world with a great character for elegance and literature."

Sophia Streatfeild's pedigree is as romantic as was the young lady herself. "A Mrs. Streatfeild, a widow, high in fortune, etc." is hardly an adequate description of her mother, who had in her time figured in an interesting lawsuit. Her history explains the income which supplied the fair S.S. with the means to wander so beautifully and oddly through life, spreading ruin and scattering ban in the Church of England. It was like this:

The last Earl of Leicester, of the Sidney family, was unhappily married. Lady Leicester was notoriously unfaithful, but since her lover was the Spanish Ambassador, the court quashed the earl's petition for divorce. Angrily Lord Leicester retired with a mistress to Penshurst Castle, to sulk. His daughter by the lady, Anne Sidney, he made his heiress. (Anne was S.S.'s mother.) First his mistress and then the earl himself died, leaving Anne an orphan at the age of ten. Thereupon the two legitimate daughters of Lord Leicester's elder brother swooped down on Penshurst. Claiming to be the rightful heirs, they lost no time in throwing out the child, and even the coffin which held her mother's body.

Happily for her, Anne's father, foreseeing some such eventuality, had appointed two guardians for her: the Duke of Bridgewater and Mr. Henry Streatfeild of Chiddingstone. Streatfeild collected Anne and the coffin, reinterred the latter at Chiddingstone, established the child as his ward, and acted as her guide in the lawsuit between her and the cousins which soon followed. Ultimately the Sidney estate was divided and Anne got as her share some valuable property in Wales.

Finally, Henry Streatfeild, thirty years older than his ward (then twenty), married her. Sophy was the eldest child of the marriage— Sophy in whose arms the tutor Dr. Collier died. Collier had taught his beautiful pupil the Greek which made her remarkable among women, for most of whom even Latin was then a rare accomplishment. He also taught her to prefer his image to that of all other men, just as he had taught young Hester Salusbury, but Sophy was faithful to his memory, in her fashion, where Hester had not been. In the most virtuous way imaginable, the unwed S.S. spread havoc among bishops, doctors, and other unlikely people: she preferred her men old, or at least married.

During her early years in the world, before she became a little monotonous with her *béguins*, Sophy enjoyed a reputation for learning and saintliness to which her beauty added a special piquancy. She must have been an extraordinary creature. The glimpses we get of her through Mrs. Thrale's and Fanny's memoirs are tantalizing: one seems to know so much about her, and yet so little. In many ways she was unlike any other woman of her circle. Hoole wrote in *Aurelia*:

Streatfeild the learned, the gay, in blooming years
Forsakes the dance to dry a widow's tears
When hoary age her tutor's hours o'erspread
And sickness bowed his venerable head,
O'er the pale couch she hung with filial care,
And plucked the thorn disease had planted there.

Mrs. Thrale met S.S. about a year after she came out, and the name of Dr. Collier brought them together immediately. At first they were great friends. "Her face is eminently pretty; her carriage elegant; her heart affectionate, and her mind cultivated," wrote Hester. "There is above all this an attractive sweetness in her manner, which claims and promises to repay one's confidence." She showed her precious notebook *Thraliana* to Sophy; no gesture could have been more trusting.

Alas, seven months later the same notebook says, "Mr. Thrale is fallen in love really and seriously with Sophy Streatfeild; but there is no wonder in that: she is very pretty, very gentle, soft, and insinuating; hangs about him, dances round him, cries when she parts from him, squeezes his hand slyly, and with her sweet eyes full of tears looks so fondly in his face—and all for love of me as she pretends; that I can hardly sometimes, help laughing in her face. A man must not be a *man* but an *it*, to resist such artillery— Marriott said very well

Man flattring Man, not always can prevail,
But Woman flattring Man can never fail."

Near by, just before this entry, is another: "Sophy Streatfeild is adored by her Mother but does not return her Affection: She is dutiful and attentive, but tis done to please God & not herself. (How should she love a silly, drunken, old painted Puss Cat? tho' the best Mother under heaven: . . .)" So much for little Anne Sidney.

"Ev'ry body is gone now [one presumes that *Thraliana* was no longer open to Sophia's perusal], & my poor Master is left to pine for his fair Sophia, till the meeting of Parliament calls him to London, & leaves him free to spend all his Evenings at her House.— it is but five Days till then tho'."

When she wrote her autobiographical memoirs the thought of Sophy was still painful to Mrs. Piozzi, though many years had passed since her first husband had died, and worms had eaten him, but not for love. "No one who visited us missed seeing his preference of her to me; but she was so amiable and so sweet natured, no one appeared to blame him for the unusual and unrepressed delight he took in her agreeable society. I was exceedingly oppressed by pregnancy, and saw clearly my successor in the fair S.S. as we familiarly called her in the family, of which she now made constantly a part, and stood godmother to my new-born baby, by bringing which I only helped to destroy my own health, and disappoint my husband, who wanted a son. 'Why Mr. Thrale is Peregrinus Domi,' said Dr. Johnson; 'he lives in Clifford Street, I hear, all winter'; and so he did, leaving his carriage at his sister's door in Hanover Square, that no inquirer might hurt his favourite's reputation; which my behaviour likewise tended to preserve from injury, and we lived on together as well as we could."

None of this frank treatment of the vexing subject appears in Fanny's Journal, though Mrs. Thrale must have talked freely to her. Either Fanny refrained from writing any of it down or she cut it out later. But every word she does allow herself about the learned coquette has a slightly feline flavor. Fanny was loyal to her Mrs. Thrale at the beginning, whatever happened later; besides, no woman could have loved Sophy very much. The fair S.S. even went after Dr. Burney, ultimately; she got him, too, or as much of him as she wanted.

"I find her a very amiable girl, and extremely handsome," said Fanny; "not so wise as I expected, but very well; however, had she not chanced to have had so uncommon an education, with respect to literature or learning, I believe she would not have made her way among the wits by the force of her natural parts.

"Mr. Seward, you know, told me that she had tears at command,

and I begin to think so too, for when Mrs. Thrale, who had previously told me I should see her cry, began coaxing her to stay, and
saying 'If you go, I shall know you don't love me so well as Lady
Gresham.'—she did cry, not loud indeed, nor much, but the tears
came into her eyes, and rolled down her fine cheeks.

" 'Come hither, Miss Burney,' cried Mrs. Thrale, 'come and see
Miss Streatfeild cry!'

"I thought it a mere *badinage*. I went to them, but when I saw
real tears, I was shocked, and saying, 'No, I won't look at her,' ran
away frightened, lest she should think I laughed at her, which Mrs.
Thrale did so openly, that, as I told her, had she served me so, I
should have been affronted with her ever after.

"Miss Streatfeild, however, whether from a sweetness not to
be ruffled, or from not perceiving there was any room for taking
offence, gently wiped her eyes, and was perfectly composed!"

Mrs. Thrale had come to regret the day she made S.S. her confidante, but Sophy did not choose to recognize the fact that they
were now on a different footing. That spring, ignoring all those
afternoons when Mr. Thrale's carriage waited in Hanover Square,
she confided a tender secret to Mr. Thrale's wife. The peerless
S.S. was in love with a clergyman, Dr. Vyse, chaplain to the Arch-
bishop of Canterbury. "Sophy has suffered her *natural taste* to prevail in her Choice of a Companion for Life," said Hester: "tis a
Happiness Few can enjoy—God send there may be no Obstacle to
her Felicity; I mean no prior Engagement on his side; for the Love
begins on hers: I am a poor Casuist in the *belle Passion*—but I think
the Man shou'd love first—Nature seems to direct it so through all
Animal Life—but surely, surely, there never yet was a Man who
could resist the blandishments of such a Woman as this—& She
does not court him to be sure, but yet——

> She does it with a pudency so rosy
> That her arts are chaste as unsunn'd Snow."

Unfortunately for Sophy, for Mrs. Thrale, and perhaps for Mr.
Vyse, the reverend gentleman wasn't in the running. He did not

spread the fact abroad, but he had an invalid wife living on the continent. Perhaps he hoped she would die before he was brought to the point, but Sophy seems to have been sadly confused about marriage laws. The Vyse-Streatfeild engagement was fated to go on, and on, and on, during which time Miss Streatfeild continued to roam clerical pastures and indulge in her strange hobby of collecting the hearts she found there.

8. MRS. THRALE, PATRON

THE PLAY progressed slowly. Fanny came and went so often that it would be difficult to say in which place lay her real home, St. Martin's Street or Streatham. Streatham provided the stimulus, the petting, the encouragement, everything but the leisure for serious work. For that, she went back periodically to the comparative quiet of the Burney house, though Mrs. Thrale always opposed her departures, and she happened to be in St. Martin's Street when Thrale had his first stroke.

For ten years afterward nobody knew of any particular shock that brought on this catastrophe. Mrs. Thrale-Piozzi found out then from a family document. Her discovery has only lately been published, and so for more than a century and a half it has been the belief of Johnsonians that Thrale's breakdown was due solely to his sedentary habits, his dissipations and gluttony. These were contributory causes, but it was an external force which struck the blow. Poor Thrale has been misjudged all this time.

He was dining that day with his newly widowed sister Mrs. Nesbitt, when he was stricken with a "palsy": his head sank to the table, and though he soon regained enough control to sit up, he talked wildly and was obviously deranged in his wits. They carried him home and duly cupped and bled him, and after a time he made a partial recovery but he was never again quite himself.

"I'm confident he will recover, he has Youth and Strength and general Health on his side;" wrote his wife, "but his Temper is strangely altered; so vigilant, so jealous, so careful lest one should watch him, & so unfit to be left unwatched:—Oh Lord have mercy on us! this is a horrible Business indeed. five little Girls too, & breeding again, & Fool enough to be proud of it! ah Ideot!"

Eleven days later, in more cheerful vein, she noted that her husband was better. "His Head is as good as ever, his Spirits indeed are low, but they will mend: . . ."

Fanny did not delay her return because of her host's illness; on the contrary, she hurried back. Mrs. Thrale would have been mortally offended if she had not. Hester's invariable habit when something went wrong with her husband was to summon all friends and acquaintances to a gathering at the scene of the disaster. She held a grudge against Dr. Burney for weeks because he did not hasten to Streatham as soon as he had word of Thrale's stroke; not until he succeeded in convincing her he hadn't understood the gravity of the affair did she forgive him. Fanny wrote:

"I saw Mr. Thrale fix his eyes upon me with an inquisitive and melancholy earnestness, as if to read my opinion: indeed, his looks were vastly better than I expected, but his evident dejection quite shocked me. . . . At dinner everybody tried to be cheerful; but a dark and gloomy cloud hangs over the head of poor Mr. Thrale, which no flashes of merriment or beams of wit can pierce through; yet he seems pleased that everybody should be gay, and desirous to be spoken to, and of, as usual."

Everybody lived up to Mr. Thrale's desire to such a degree that on the next day we find them strolling, and laughing, and talking, quite as though "my master" were all right. Mr. Thrale's wistful liking for talkative society was to carry through to the end of his life. One of the strangest aspects of the following two years was the restless behavior of the Thrale circle as they moved about and gave their parties, carrying the somnolent figure of their overfed host wherever they went, like a sort of portable idol.

So it is with an unreasonable feeling of remorse, after reading so much to Mr. Thrale's detriment in all the records of his life, that one comes across Mrs. Piozzi's explanation. "Mr. Thrale has been dead now *just* ten Years—and I have *just* now, at the Distance of Time, found out the Cause of his Death."

The cause was that Thrale's brother-in-law Mr. Nesbitt had died a bankrupt, owing Thrale two hundred and twenty thousand pounds. The horrible truth came out when his will was read, which accounts for the palsy at dinner and the dark and gloomy cloud. If he had allowed this news to become public, Thrale would have been ruined. He kept the secret, his widow said, though he lost his wits, "& kept it I do believe even from Sophy Streatfeild."

All honor to Henry Thrale, then, for his heroic secrecy. Heroic it was, though his ethics may have been dubious.

From the beginning of the year 1779, Daddy Crisp had been prophesying a bad time to come, and Daddy Crisp was right. An economic depression had hit England. The Anchor Brewery felt it, other wealthy people as well as the Thrales felt it, and as a result Dr. Burney felt it. Mrs. Thrale, lamenting that the new taxes would cut the family income two thousand pounds a year ("dreadful Times!"), expressed a kindhearted worry. "I fear poor Dr. Burney feels these Times more than he owns to, though Musick is the last Luxury we shall be perswaded to part with; but he will never get paid for his heavy Book upon the Subject I think." A few months later she said, "Poor dear Man! he is sadly pressed for Pelf too I fear, the Times go so hard with him; his Book will never pay its own Expence I am confident, & in two or three Winters more —nothing new happening neither—people will be pretty sick of spending their Money to tickle their Ears, it begins already to grow a grand Thing to have a Concert; and seven Years ago—even the *City* Dames regaled their Company with Italian Musick & elegant Performers. a Harpsichord made by Rucker, & sold six Years ago for sixty five pounds was Yesterday disposed of for *thirty*, Burney says; & the Owners glad to get *that*."

Mrs. Thrale spoke as a rich woman will of her protégés, in a general glow of rather smug charitable pity. Shortly afterward she talked about a bargain in bric-a-brac which had just been offered her, as further proof that the times were dangerously difficult. But Burney, never having felt true security in his busy life, did not despair for himself so readily as his kind friend did for him, it being a familiar paradox that the wealthy fear hard times far more than do the poor. Burney simply went ahead, both with his heavy book and his daily work, and made something out of both. Nevertheless he must have been pleased and hopeful when Fanny finished her play. Mrs. Thrale is witness that he was, at least at first, for she says under the date of May Day, "Fanny Burney has read me her new Comedy; nobody else has seen it except her Father [surely a falsehood, if inadvertent!], who will not suffer his Partiality to overbiass his Judgment I am sure, and he likes it vastly."

Alas for Dr. Burney's judgment: Daddy Crisp was to reverse it for him. There were three months more of hard work for Fanny, revising her comedy, presumably at the advice of Arthur Murphy, who liked it. At the end of July the young playwright felt confident enough of her product *The Witlings* to send it on to Crisp. She wrote a long letter to go with it. In spite of the "general decline of all trade, opulence, and prosperity," and notwithstanding certain warnings which Daddy had voiced from time to time relative to the perils of a theatrical venture in the middle of a depression, she had made up her mind to see the thing through. Mr. Sheridan had been so encouraging that it would seem ungrateful to resist any more. Dr. Burney was bringing a copy to Chesington in person. "I should like to have three lines, telling me, as nearly as you can trust my candour, its general effect. After that take it to your own desk, and lash it at your leisure."

She gave permission for Daddy Crisp's sister Mrs. Gast to read it, so the secret manuscript was now known only to Murphy, Sheridan, Mrs. Thrale, Dr. Johnson, a Dr. Delap, Charles Burney, Susan, and Daddy Crisp's household. There were probably a few more whose names are not mentioned in the Journal, but we must not be captious about trifles.

In a postscript she added, "Let it fail never so much, the manager will have nothing to reproach me with: is not that a comfort? He would really listen to no denial."

So. The two men took *The Witlings* and read it. What next appears with dramatic suddenness is a letter from Fanny to her father.

"The fatal knell, then, is knolled, and 'down among the dead men' sink the poor 'Witlings'—for ever, and for ever, and for ever! . . . You, my dearest sir, who enjoyed, I really think, even more than myself, the astonishing success of my first attempt, would, I believe, even more than myself, be hurt at the failure of my second; and I am sure I speak from the bottom of a very honest heart, when I most solemnly declare, that upon your account any disgrace would mortify and afflict me more than upon my own; . . . I expected many objections to be raised—a thousand errors to be pointed out—and a million of alterations to be proposed; but the suppression of the piece were words I did not expect; indeed, after the warm approbation of Mrs. Thrale, and the repeated commendations and flattery of Mr. Murphy, how could I? . . . Adieu, my dearest, kindest, truest, best friend. I will never proceed so far again without your counsel, and then I shall not only save myself so much useless trouble, but you, who so reluctantly blame, the kind pain which I am sure must attend your disapprobation. . . ."

Her father's rapid about-face need not puzzle us unduly. Dr. Burney's charm consisted to a large degree of what Mrs. Thrale in uncharitable mood called "suppleness." Burney was an agreeable man. He agreed with everybody readily and with sincerity. When Mrs. Thrale and Arthur Murphy told him *The Witlings* was a good piece, bound to succeed, he was thoroughly pro-*Witlings*, and when Mr. Crisp told him it must never, never be produced, he was just as ready to agree with Mr. Crisp that *The Witlings* should be condemned out of hand. In any combined decision of the sort, we must not look to Dr. Burney as the guiding spirit. Daddy Crisp must have put up a convincing argument against Fanny's play: Burney would have been glad enough, poor man, to see her making more money.

Why, one may ask, was Daddy Crisp so downright unflattering to his Fannikin? In a footnote which she added long afterward to her Journal, her explanation sounds to us suspiciously farfetched. *The Witlings* appeared to Crisp, she said, to resemble a vastly superior play, *Les Femmes Savantes*, by Molière, and he did not wish her to court unfavorable comparison or accusations, however unfounded, of plagiarism. She deliberately suppressed the truth.

Mrs. Thrale gives us the true reason, or, rather, the reason Daddy Crisp supplied at the time. "Murphy liked it very well," she wrote, "but her confidential friend Mr. Crisp advised her against bringing it on, for fear of displeasing the female Wits—a formidable Body, & called by those who ridicule them, the *Blue Stocking Club*."

Mr. Crisp knew his Fanny, and knew, too, what argument was best calculated to scare her to death. Nothing could be so effective against all Sheridan's blandishments and Mrs. Thrale's flattery as the threat that she might incur the wrath of those terrible leaders of intellectual society. One hint of such an eventuality and she was ready to disclaim all her sly, witty writings.

Just how sincere was Daddy Crisp in his decision? No doubt he thought he understood his own motives and would not have admitted for one second that they were not purely disinterested. The notion persists, however, that he was oddly reluctant in any case to see his young friend put anything on the stage. Drama was a very special thing to Sam Crisp, author of *Virginia, a Tragedy*. Perhaps it was too special; perhaps he felt himself so much an expert on that one subject that he would not let anyone else come near it. People get that way about their special subjects. They snarl over them like a dog over a much-chewed bone.

Fanny did not insist; she promptly veered off from the bone. She wrote her Daddy a jaunty little letter, accepting all his strictures, and the old dog was appeased and tried to apologize for his snarls. They were due, he said, to his extraordinary sincerity, a sincerity "I have smarted for, and severely too, ere now; and yet, happen what will, (where those I love are concerned), I am deter-

mined never to part with it." All the world pretend to want sincerity, Daddy Crisp complained, but they don't like it when they
get it. They impute it to envy, ill will, and what not. . . .

But Fanny didn't. She was a good little girl, though now she
was twenty-seven; a good little girl, and thoroughly scared. Yet
she was not a perfect angel, or she would have been able to follow
Crisp's suggestion, which he amiably offered in exchange for the
play he had just murdered. Her father had recounted to him, said
Crisp, some story of Fanny's, of a ridiculous family in the neighborhood of Streatham. There now! *There* was a theme for a most
spirited, witty, moral, useful comedy, and she would be stepping
on nobody's toes, either, or at least the toes of nobody who
counted. Like the benevolent Daddy he was, Crisp held out this
new lollipop to his Fannikin, a far, far better lollipop than the
one he had just taken away. "I was delighted with the idea," he
said.

No doubt he was, yet Fanny for some odd reason did not immediately sit down and write it. Still, she must have been duly
grateful.

Mrs. Thrale's latest and last pregnancy drew on toward its climax, influencing to an extreme degree her attitude toward the
world, including the Burneys. Sometimes she rushed to her notebook to record an outburst of fondness toward her dear Burney's
daughter; at other moments she was exasperated against the erstwhile object of her affection. There were never any in-betweens
with Mrs. Thrale.

"Dear Creatures! how earnestly do I wish them Success!" she
said of Fanny and Queeney, as they studied Latin under Dr. Johnson's tutelage—a project which did not last for long. "—what a
Master they have too! Happy Rogues!"

Only a few weeks later, "Fanny Burney has been a long time
from me," she wrote querulously. "I was glad to see her again; yet
she makes me miserable too in many respects, so restlessly and
apparently anxious, lest I should give myself airs of patronage or

load her with the shackles of dependance. I live with her always in a degree of pain that precludes friendship—dare not ask her to buy me a ribbon—dare not desire her to touch the bell, lest she should think herself injured. . . ."

"The Family of the Burneys are a very surprizing Set of People," Hester mused; "their Esteem & fondness for the Dr seems to inspire them all with a Desire not to disgrace him; & so every individual of it must write and read & be literary: He is the only Man I ever knew, who being not rich, was beloved by his Wife & Children: tis very seldom that a person's own Family will give him Credit for Talents which bring in no Money to make them fine or considerable."

In spite of all this preoccupation with the Burney family, however, Hester's nerves finally gave way. She felt ill, and Mr. Thrale's behavior was very odd. It was becoming increasingly odd as his physical health improved. Even in normal times Thrale had never been one to pamper or cosset his wife; when she complained of aches and pains he always said unfeelingly (if he said anything) that no doubt she would feel better next day. Now he was growing more and more brusque toward her, just when she most wanted kindness and attention, and the cruelest cut of all was the discriminating softness he chose to display, with untimely ostentation, to Sophy Streatfeild. Knowing as we do that the poor man was crazed with worry over his financial state as well as his precarious health, we are inclined to make the allowances his wife could not. But even with all the charity and understanding we can muster, it is difficult not to be indignant with him for his behavior at a certain dinner party.

Until then Mrs. Thrale had carefully maintained her detachment. She was always strengthening her pose of ironical observer; I do not love my husband, she told herself; I do not love anyone, and this passion of his for Sophy is therefore merely amusing; it cannot really hurt me. I am jealous, but I am an intelligent woman and I face unpalatable facts with dignity and grace, the more so because such behavior is really the only sensible policy.

"[Murphy] sees Thrale's love of the fair S.S.," she wrote, "& I suppose approves my silent and patient endurance of what I could not prevent by more rough & sincere Behaviour. Men always admire a Woman who tho' jealous does not rave about it—& what shd one rave for!! would raving do anything but drive Mr. Thrale *quite* away from me? No to be sure it would not, I could rave else willingly enough."

This is a very cool, clearheaded attitude, but one which is not easy to maintain when you are ill, misshapen, worried, and sensitive. Mrs. Thrale did not feel passion for her husband, but his illness had rendered her tender and loving toward him, and her jealousy of Sophy Streatfield became proportionately the greater. The larger part of her jealousy before then had been affronted pride: "What can the world be saying of me?" but now it was her emotions, too, which were being hurt. She was not as resilient as usual.

The Thrales and their guests were sitting down to dinner when Henry Thrale did the inexcusable thing. Sophy Streatfeild had a cold, and Thrale was all anxiety about it. The man who always ignored his wife's complaints, the man whose wife was uncomfortably big with his child, fussed over Miss Streatfeild like a hen over her one chick. Miss Streatfeild's chair at table, he noted, was near the door: precious Miss Streatfeild would be in a draft. Henry Thrale told his wife to change places with Sophy.

Hester's defenses suddenly crumbled. She burst into tears and ran from the room.

It is too bad that nobody has had the ill breeding to record what happened then. Did the lovely Sophia feel guilty? Did she blush and try to leave the party, or merely simper and sit where she was put, out of the draft? Did everybody simply pretend nothing had happened? We do not know. We only know that Hester calmed herself and came back to the company in due time, and bitterly took Dr. Johnson to task for not having spoken up for her.

Poor old Johnson was so uneasy that he actually said, "Why, to be sure, you had great provocation." For the anti-feminist doctor those were strong words.

Gloomy forebodings assailed Mrs. Thrale as her time drew near: she was sure she would have a miscarriage and die of it. "Abortions and Profluvia are not easily got through at my Age, & after having had twelve Children," she wrote, adding with vicious satisfaction, ". . . Mr. Thrale would just now too be no *brisk* Widower, & his fair Sophia would find him less a Lover to her mind than before the paralytick Affection."

It is amusing to imagine the effect such talk must have had on Fanny's squeamish nature, for there can be no doubt Mrs. Thrale prattled as airily to Fanny of her sex life as she would have done to a married woman. Even her letters to her daughter Queeney were quite uninhibited. None of all this, not a word of it, ever found its way to Fanny's Journal. Mrs. Thrale's condition and the sad result of it were never mentioned, though Fanny was at Streatham, at intervals at least, throughout this period.

One day a messenger came from Southwark with urgent news from the brewery. Something had gone wrong and the clerks were at odds with each other; it was vitally necessary that Thrale, or someone else with authority, hurry to adjust the matter. The business was in a precarious state, and Thrale's wife appreciated the position, though she knew nothing of the Nesbitt angle. But Thrale would not admit the necessity of haste. His mind could not seem to grasp the affair at all. He simply decided that he would not go. The poor man was in a feeble-minded state more than half the time; what his confidential clerk called "planet-struck." There was nothing else for it, Mrs. Thrale realized, but to go in his stead, and go she did, though her labor pains were almost upon her. She went by coach from Streatham to Southwark, held audience with the clerks, settled the affair, whatever it was, and got back to Streatham by evening, having fainted in the jouncing, jostling coach five times on the way.

"Tis less a Miscarriage after all than a dead Child," she noted sorrowfully a week later, when she had recovered enough to write. "A Boy quite formed & perfect; once I wished for such a Blessing—now if my Life is left me no matter for the rest. . . . I go down Stairs like the Ghost of her who was carried up Stairs a week ago."

What would Mrs. Thrale have said at that moment, one asks oneself, had she been confronted with certain latter-day judgments on her as a wicked, flippant, unnatural, unfeeling, *unmotherly* woman?

Fanny was back, and Mrs. Thrale was glad of it in spite of her ill-tempered outbursts in the notebook. But as the mistress of Streatham regained her never-long-suppressed strength and spirits, the master drooped and wilted. He was not always dazed and stupid, but his demeanor was queer enough to cause his sister Lady Lade, as well as his wife, considerable uneasiness. Another holiday was indicated, change of scene and that remedy which was always advocated by doctors when they weren't sure of their diagnosis, "a change of air." Brighton might do Mr. Thrale good. And it would certainly be good for Mrs. Thrale. "Fanny Burney goes with us," wrote Mrs. Thrale at the beginning of October, "not Johnson, he stays home & writes, & is diligent. Mr. Thrale longs to see his S.S.: *that* makes us go to Tunbridge, I am glad he can think of *anything* externally; & hope her Conversation will dissipate the Gloom which this paralytick Affection has cast over his Temper. Lady Lade thinks too that his head is not even now quite right: bathing in the Sea & flirting with his Sophia may mend it perhaps;—God send it may!"

There is all the difference in the world, you will observe, between the strength of Mrs. Thrale's defenses against Sophy before and after that miscarriage. Fanny described the visit to the Streatfeilds' house at Tunbridge Wells in her customary detailed style; where her friend Hester had called Sophy's mother "a silly, drunken, old painted Puss Cat," Fanny found her "thin, genteel, and delicate . . . very lively, and an excellent mimic . . . as much superior to her daughter in natural gifts as her daughter is to her in acquired ones. . . . She has a kind of whimsical conceit, and odd affectation, that, joined to a very singular sort of humour,

makes her always seem to be rehearsing some scene in a comedy."
Now is that merely a long-winded way of saying Mrs. Streatfeild
was drunk? A small point, I grant you, but Fanny, a prude in a ro-
bust period, sometimes puzzles us sadly.

As a tonic for Thrale, S.S. was a failure this time, Mrs. Thrale
reports. "They met with but little eagerness on either Side, her
Head was pre-occupied with Care I believe, & his with Disease—
they met without Interest, & parted without Pain. . . ." But
Fanny· described a funny farewell scene: Sophy Streatfeild standing in her doorway with a little girl friend by her side, a pretty
child who adored Sophy and copied her in everything; the fair
S.S. wept, of course, as they drove off, and the little girl wept just
as prettily, just as softly, just as meltingly. . . .

Lugging the heavy Mr. Thrale with them, the women paid the
usual calls and attended the usual parties. An influenza epidemic
was going the rounds, and Mr. Thrale developed symptoms of it
just as they planned to go back to Streatham. One of Thrale's inconvenient habits was a disregard for his own health as well as his
wife's; after two days of illness he declared he was well enough to
proceed, so they set out resignedly. On the way, said Fanny,
Thrale "suffered dreadfully from the coldness of the weather; he
shook from head to foot, and his teeth chattered aloud very frightfully . . . when we stopped at Reigate his speech grew inarticulate, and he said one word for another. I hoped it was accident,
and Mrs. Thrale, by some strange infatuation, thought he was
joking—but Miss Thrale saw how it was from the first. . . . Here
the cold returned dreadfully—and here, in short, it was but too
plain to all, his faculties were lost by it. . . ."

With typical divergence of opinion and recollection, Mrs.
Thrale described the Reigate scene: her husband, she says, "had
such a shivering & Torpor come on as shocked me, & set poor Miss
Burney o'crying——"

Cupped, bled, and put to bed at home, the unfortunate man
rallied and scolded everyone for having called the doctor. As usual
when he had an attack, his friends hastily clustered round him in

a manner reminiscent of a Chinese clan gathering. Mr. Seward came; Dr. Johnson came; Dr. Burney came; Fanny, being there already, stood by him and played whist with the invalid, and felt rather a martyr in doing it, because she was sickening for the influenza herself. Mr. Thrale was kept from a heavy and profound sleep only by cards, and like all the Streatham group, she was convinced that Mr. Thrale must not in any event be allowed to go to sleep.

In vain all her self-sacrifice and whist playing: Mrs. Thrale didn't appreciate it at all, for Fanny then committed the unforgivable sin of having the influenza. Just as if there hadn't been enough trouble already!

"Fanny Burney has kept her Room here in my House seven days, with a fever or something that she called a fever; I gave her every medicine and every slop with my own hand; took away her dirty cups, spoons, &c.; moved her tables: in short, was doctor and nurse and maid—for I did not like the servants should have additional trouble lest they should hate her for it. And now,—with the true gratitude of a wit, she tells me, that the world thinks the better of me for my civilities to her. It does? does it?"

There was a brief flare-up of interest in the condemned comedy when Sheridan again approached Fanny and asked her to let him have it. With renewed hope she set to work, "violently fidgeted," but in vain. Daddy Crisp put his foot down again.

"You can't easily imagine how much it goes against me to say anything that looks like discouragement . . . the story and the incidents don't appear to me interesting enough. . . . This, to me, is its capital defect," wrote Crisp, forgetting the several other capital defects he had proffered in the past as good reason for holding down his Fannikin. "Upon the whole," he adds, however, "as he is so pressing to see what you have done, I should almost incline to consent."

This, Crisp's idea of an encouraging letter, is the last we hear of *The Witlings*, and no wonder.

Dr. Burney may well have urged Fanny to get on with it and produce something, no matter what. It was now two years since the advent of his clever daughter's first novel, which had not paid off well in anything but praise and promise. There was the first sum of twenty pounds which was now so famous, and a bonus of ten pounds which Lowndes sent later in tardy recognition of having hit the jackpot with Fanny's book—he was not legally bound to pay anything further. Poor Burney was even more pressed for money than usual. Though in those leisurely days a writer was not expected to turn out a book every year, there was good reason for Fanny to push herself more than she was doing.

On the other hand was the delicate question of Mrs. Thrale and her sensibilities. She had proved herself a valuable friend and patron to the Burneys, and in spite of her shrewish remarks about Fanny she wanted her around all the time. Mrs. Thrale must not be offended. A typical wealthy patron, she could not understand that literary lions cannot roar and yet do their scribbling between parties, as she did. She could give parties and go to parties and yet fill page after page of her notebook when she got home: Dr. Johnson, who had lived in intimacy with her for sixteen years, was seldom too busy to be there when she had guests; why, then, should that young chit Fanny need more time and seclusion? Did she consider herself more important than Johnson? Such airs! It was the age-old struggle between the amateur and the professional point of view, and Fanny was no good in such an unequal combat.

She was trying, all this time, to think out her next novel, *Cecilia*. Yet how could she concentrate on it when so many absorbing affairs called for her attention, when her kind hostess more than ever needed someone in whom to confide?

In April, instead of producing a new book, Miss Fanny Burney accompanied the Thrales to Bath.

When Mr. Thrale hired a house on the South Parade he unwittingly contributed to the upkeep of an artist a century and a half younger than himself, who at Bath in 1948 sells postcard sketches labeled "Fanny Burney stayed here." It was a nice house then, and still is, overlooking the river with its swans. There, in the fashionable watering place, Mr. Thrale sank into his customary lassitude and the ladies threw themselves into their customary whirl of playgoing and visiting. The whirl was a little dizzier than usual, for Mrs. Montagu was at Bath, and Mrs. Thrale dearly loved to meet the Queen of the Blues at a party. Fanny enjoyed it too. As far as we know, she never heard Mrs. Montagu's unflattering comments on *Evelina*, but it was good fun to be catty about the great lady after a meeting, tittering with Mrs. Thrale when they got home. She encountered an old friend of her own at Bath, the daring Miss Bowdler of Tingmouth.

"I was glad to see her, for old acquaintance sake. She does not look well, but is more agreeable than formerly, and seems to have thrown aside her pedantry and ostentatious display of knowledge; and, therefore, as she is very sensible, and uncommonly cultivated, her conversation and company are very well worth seeking." But surely it was not Miss Bowdler's pedantry which had displeased Fanny in the old days?

Many ladies and a few gentlemen idled away the time and met at each other's houses, and chatted, and walked, and went to the play, in a manner which one hopes was more amusing to experience than to read about. Watering places are apt to be dull in any country and in any century.

"Miss Burney was much admired at Bath; the puppy-men said, 'She has such a drooping air and such a timid intelligence'; or, 'a timid air,' I think it was, 'and a drooping intelligence'; never sure was such a collection of pedantry and affectation as filled Bath when we were on that spot," said Hester.

Fanny, as befits the patronized, did not indulge in similar bursts of spleen, nor did she choose to notice them in her patron's behavior. "The kindness of this family seems daily to increase towards me," she wrote Susan; "not indeed that of Mrs. Thrale, for it cannot, so sweetly and delightfully she keeps it up; she has not left herself power to do more;—but Mr. Thrale evidently interests himself more and more about me weekly—as does his fair daughter.

"This morning a milliner was ordered to bring whatever she had to recommend, I believe, to our habitation, and Mr. Thrale bid his wife and daughter take what they wanted, and send him the account.

"But, not content with this, he charged me to do the same. You may imagine if I did. However, finding me refractory, he absolutely insisted upon presenting me with a complete suite of gauze lino, and that in a manner that showed me a refusal would greatly disoblige him. And then he very gravely desired me to have whatever I pleased at any time, and to have it added to his account. And so sincere I know him to be, that I am sure he would be rather pleased than surprised if I should run him up a new bill at this woman's. He would fain have persuaded me to have taken abundance of other things, and Mrs. Thrale seemed more gratified than with what he did for herself. Tell my dear father all this."

Through the detailed records of Fanny's Bath days, if one is not fairly drowned in names, tea drinkings, and vapid talk, one fact begins to make itself evident: Fanny was getting bored with "the world." She never said so, and perhaps did not herself know it, but the bloom was wearing off; the storyteller's zest was ebbing. It was only natural that it should ebb in a place like Bath; the myriad meetings and small busynesses which fill every day without filling the mind are exactly the wrong thing for a reporter's talent like Fanny's. If she had still been living at home in her favorite corner, quiet and observing, it would have been different; she could have picked and chosen her characters and watched them at ease. Now, a celebrity, she was too much in the way of her own light. She was constantly called on to be the novelist, doing her little turn and being acted at by other people doing *their* turns.

Besides, there was the stultifying effect of flattery. A little flattery was very good for Fanny's Muse. Susan always provided just enough, with Daddy Crisp's close watchfulness serving as the sauce *piquante*. Now, though, she was fed with flattery every day, every minute—lavish, indiscriminate banquets of it. She could not digest it all. She tried to laugh it off, and at first her laughter was sincere, but little by little it took on a rather tinny tone, and after a while all smiles stopped together. Fanny began treating flattery in one of two ways; she either swallowed it whole or threw it aside pettishly, in a bad nature. Which may all be merely a roundabout way of saying that she was getting a touch of swelled head. It was not real conceit, either; it was a sort of social, watering-place conceit, bright and light and hollow as a balloon.

Certainly Bath was making her dull, so that it probably came as a relief, however indignantly she would have denied it, when the Gordon Riots shocked the Thrales out of their rut.

Most of us think of the Gordon Riots in the terms of *Barnaby Rudge*, and so vivid is that impression that no amount of chilly factualism will ever dispel it. George Orwell points out in vain that no mob in real life ever behaved as did Dickens's at the burning of Hardcastle's house. The name of Lord George Gordon means much more to us than the dry word "riot" to which we are so unhappily accustomed in newspaper headlines, and Fanny's agitation when the news of the trouble came to Bath does not seem disproportionate.

She wrote her father, anxiously demanding reassurance. Did the martial law confine everybody to the house? Oh, what dreadful times! The bookseller at Bath had secret information that the military had made much slaughter among the mob. But what was it all about? Who, after all, was going to turn papist? There were disturbing hints that the popish chapel at Bath was to be pulled or burned down. . . .

The Roman Catholic chapel and the priest's house had been set on fire, she wrote later, and were in flames. Terrified invalids were being moved to safer places, and all the Catholics in town were trying to get their goods out quietly, and walking on tiptoe, scarcely breathing. "We are determined upon removing somewhere tomorrow; for why should we, who can go, stay to witness such horrid scenes?"

Next afternoon, still from Bath: "I was most cruelly disappointed in not having one word to-day. I am half crazy with doubt and disturbance in not hearing. Everybody here is terrified to death. We have intelligence that Mr. Thrale's house in town is filled with soldiers, and threatened by the mob with destruction. Perhaps he may himself be a marked man for their fury. We are going directly from Bath, and intend to stop only at villages. . . . If it were possible to send me a line by the diligence to Brighton, how grateful I should be for such an indulgence! . . . God bless—defend—preserve you! my dearest father. Life is no life for me while I fear for your safety. . . . Some infamous villain has put it into the paper here that Mr. Thrale is a papist. . . ."

On Sunday night the wandering Thrales reached Salisbury and found it quiet. Word from the Burneys at home came at last.

"Susan will tell you why none of us wrote before Friday," said Charlotte's letter, "and she says she has told you what dreadful havoc and devastation the mob have made here in all parts of the town. However, we are pretty quiet and tranquil again now. Papa goes on with his business pretty much as usual, and so far from the military keeping people within doors . . . the streets were never more crowded—everybody is wandering about in order to see the ruins of the places that the mob have destroyed . . . however, thank Heaven, everybody says now that Mr. Thrale's house and brewery are as safe as we can wish them. . . . To add to the pleasantness of our situation, there have been gangs of women going about to rob and plunder. Miss Kirwans went on Friday afternoon to walk in the Museum gardens, and were stopped by a set of women, and robbed of all the money they had."

Like a homing dove, Fanny flew to St. Martin's Street, and there she was to stay, in spite of all Mrs. Thrale's pleadings and threats of displeasure, for a long time. She had had a bad fright. But oh, what a temper Mrs. Thrale was in!

"Mrs. Byron, who really loves me, was disgusted at Miss Burney's carriage to me, who have been such a friend and benefactress to her," she wrote; "not an article of dress, not a ticket for public places, not a thing in the world that she could not command from me: yet always insolent, always pining for home, always preferring the mode of life in St. Martin's Street to all I could do for her. She is a saucy-spirited little puss to be sure, but I love her dearly for all that; and I fancy she has a real regard for me, if she did not think it beneath the dignity of a wit, or of what she values more —the dignity of Dr. Burney's daughter—to indulge it. Such dignity! . . . I shall if I don't look sharp, be prettily rewarded for fondling the Burneys so. Miss despises me already, & takes little pains to conceal her Contempt; and my second Daughter Susan; (only ten Years old thank God;) declares it her *fixed* and *determinate* Resolution to marry the Doctor's Son Dick, as soon as She is one & twenty, chearful enough!"

One sees her writing in angry haste, slamming the book shut and running off to dress herself for a tea drinking somewhere, her spoiled outburst already forgotten. How much more pleasant it would be, it occurs to her, if Fanny were only there to accompany her!

9. LITTLE BETTER THAN SUICIDE

S T. MARTIN'S Street worked its cure on the jaded author. Home again, with a constant succession of visitors and intelligent talk, Fanny regained her faculty for being amused by the world and so she became again amusing. It was a good enough life, though the news from America was worse and worse, and poor old Daddy Crisp muttered and cursed about the bad times, and dear Mrs. Thrale reported that Mr. Thrale was eating himself into an apoplexy. One day Greville, haughtier than ever, quarreled about America and the war news with the fiery Baretti, Johnson's Italian friend who had been tutor for the Thrales. Fanny reported on it with her old spirit, in her own special style.

"I really expected every moment to hear him [Baretti] exclaim, 'It is that you are an impenetrable blockhead'; . . . the astonishment that seized him [Greville] when he saw the violence and contempt of Baretti was sufficiently comical . . . when he found Baretti stout, and that the more he resisted, the more he bullied him, he could only stare, and look around at us all, with an expression that said, 'Am I awake?' "

Through Johnson's influence Baretti held a pleasant post at Streatham, teaching Queeney, but after a few years his fits of temper and passion for household intrigue became too much for Mrs. Thrale's never very stable nerves. She accused him of turning

Queeney against her—an echo, perhaps, of her own mother's jealousy of Dr. Collier—and after terrible scenes Baretti departed, breathing curses on her head. It is not difficult to imagine what he would have said that night in St. Martin's Street if Fanny had thought to mention the fact that Mrs. Thrale had just acquired a new Italian tutor.

She found him in Bath, whither the Thrales had returned to finish their stay after the Gordon affair quieted down. Hester was making the best of it, but Bath was dull and Mr. Thrale seemed determined to kill himself with gluttony. She could not control him at all, she said in despair, no more could his friends or his physicians. It was now the lamprey season, and Thrale was passionately fond of lampreys.

"Colonel Campbell used four Years ago when we met at Bath to say for Gods Sake Thrale why wilt thou eat so violently?—thou'lt die Apoplectick at last—& tis surely worse than any thing to see you swallowing those *black* Devils so—meaning stewed Lampreys."

While walking out one day she encountered Signor Piozzi, the singer, in the street. She does not seem to have recalled their first meeting at the Burney party, when she made fun of his singing and was scolded by the doctor. The frantic boredom of Bath made Piozzi infinitely more attractive than he had seemed on that first occasion. She said contentedly to her Journal, "I have picked up Piozzi here, the great Italian Singer; he shall teach Hester; She will have some Powers in the Musical way I believe." She scribbled afterward on the margin, "He is amazingly like my Father."

How angry Baretti would have been! He was to be fantastically angry anyway before the matter was ended. In three weeks Mrs. Thrale was raving about Piozzi; he had become a prodigious favorite with her; he was so intelligent a creature, so discerning. Burney would have opened his eyes very wide to hear her discoursing knowledgeably of music and singing. "I made him sing yesterday, & tho' he says his Voice is gone, I cannot some how or other get it out of my Ears,—odd enough!"

It was certainly odd, but Mrs. Thrale often indulged in such little raves when she was alone with her notebook. She had no premonition that someday the singer would be responsible for a juicy scandal in her life, and she had not, after all, too much time to spare just then for soft songs in the Italian language, for Mr. Thrale was becoming acutely troublesome. "My Master is got into most riotous Spirits somehow; he will go here & there, & has a hundred Projects in his Head, so gay, so wild, *I wish no harm may come on't.*"

One of the wild projects was a tour to Italy. Fanny wrote Mrs. Thrale in August, referring to it; Mrs. Thrale must remind "my master" that he had promised to pay Mr. Crisp a visit too. If he didn't keep that promise, she said playfully, *she* certainly would not go to Italy with him, not for any inducement. As a piece of gossip, she reported that Sophy Streatfeild had been in town and had paid the Burneys a long visit. "She looked as beautiful as an angel, though rather pale, but was in very high spirits, and I thought her more attractive and engaging than ever. So I believe did my father."

Somehow, though, the lovely S.S. had ceased to rankle much in the heart of Mrs. Thrale. Her master was far too unlike himself to be the object of jealous accusations. Possessed by this new, ghastly gaiety, he suddenly dragged his worried wife off on a jaunt to the country, and it was her staunch belief that only a last-minute bleeding of thirteen ounces, and "some rough Medicines too," kept him from having another stroke. Then an untimely election brought on another crisis: Mr. Thrale had a stroke the night before he was to canvass for his seat, and in spite of all his wife could do he was outvoted and lost it. "One Day, the last of the Canvass —I worked at Solicitation for ten Hours successively," she wrote, "without refreshment, or what I wished much more for—a *place of retirement.* this neglect, wch was unavoidable, surrounded as I was with *Men* all the Time, gave me an exquisite pain in my Side —wch tho' relieved at my return home of Course, has never quite left me since—& I believe now never will—no matter!"

Piozzi became an intimate of the household. Fanny mentioned his carrying a letter to her from Mrs. Thrale at Brighton, and Mrs. Thrale spoke in her Journal of Dr. Burney's jealousy and resentment of the Italian. Very likely Burney did feel a few twinges, remembering how his own connection with the family had started with teaching Queeney music. He was watchful of his Lady Bountiful and did not wish to share her. It was strange, mused Mrs. Thrale, that even such a good man as Burney should have a flaw. He was, after all, a very jealous fellow, she decided. Look at how he hated Sir John Hawkins, the rival historian of music! As for poor, blameless Piozzi . . .

But if Fanny heard adverse criticism of the Thrale ménage at home, she gave no sign of it in her letters. She spoke instead of a pleasant reunion in St. Martin's Street, when Jem came home. Captain Burney had at last got a command. It was only a temporary one, in lieu of the regular commander, but at least the *Latona* was "one of the best frigates in the navy, of thirty-eight guns," and Jem was ecstatic. The poor fellow's promotions were slow in coming.

"Here is Sophy Streatfeild again," says Hester Thrale; "handsomer than ever, and flushed with new Conquests: the Bishop of Chester feels her Power I am sure. She shewed me a Letter from him that was as tender, and had all the *Tokens* upon it as strong as ever I remember to have seen 'em. I repeated to her out of Pope's Homer—very well Sophy, says I

> *Range undisturb'd among the hostile Crew,*
> *But touch not Hinchliffe, Hinchliffe is my due."*

Hinchliffe was Mrs. Thrale's own pet bishop; she was very proud of that neat joke. It must then have been exceedingly annoying when Mr. Thrale spoiled it. "Miss Streatfeild, (says my Master) could have quoted these lines *in the Greek*: his saying so, piqued me; & piqued me because it was true. I wish I understood Greek! Mr. Thrale's preference of her to me never vexed me so much as my Consciousness—or Fear at least—that he had Reason for his Preference. She has ten Times my Beauty, and five Times my Scholarship—Wit and Knowledge has She none.——"

The last weeks of the year dragged out gloomily, with alarms over Thrale's attacks, unavailing protests from Johnson and Hester against his gluttony, and a growing sense on the part of the Streatham household that their master could not possibly continue much longer at the rate he was going. Fanny and Mrs. Thrale must have been tacitly agreed about this. But Johnson was notoriously averse to discussing death, in the general or in the particular: he had a cantankerous belief that it betokened a desire of someone's end even to mention it. He flew off the handle whenever the dangerous subject was approached and accused his (titular) mistress of hastening Thrale's death. It was a difficult situation, rendered more difficult for Thrale's wife by the psychological schism between her old "inmate" and herself. She had no patience with such mental evasions. She was always downright; she not only faced unpleasant happenings, but flew ahead of herself to greet them. It is a form of impatience which often makes for courageous behavior.

"Fanny Burney has secured my Heart: I now love her with a fond & firm Affection, besides my Esteem of her Parts, & my Regard for her Father. her lofty Spirit dear Creature! has quite subdued mine; and I adore her for the Pride which once revolted me. There is no true Affection, no Friendship in the sneakers & Fawners:——"

This outburst was brought on by the news which had just reached Mrs. Thrale of Susan Burney's engagement to be married. The young man, Captain Molesworth Phillips, had been introduced into the Burney circle by Jem. It was a good match for a dowerless girl: Phillips was heir to a comfortable property. But Fanny could not but feel sorrowful at the prospect of losing her devoted little sister. From Streatham, Mrs. Thrale hurried to send condolences and promises and comfort. "Sweet Susannuccia! I *will* slide into her place, I shall get more of your company, too, and more—is there any more to be had?—of your confidence. Yes, yes, there is a little, to be sure; but dear Mrs. Thrale shall have it all now. Oh, 'tis an excellent match! and he has 700 £ a-year— that is, he *will* have; it is entailed, and irrevocable."

The Streatham coterie received a push upward in the social scale when Thrale suddenly took one of his lavish new notions and moved them to Grosvenor Square. "My Master has taken a ready furnished Lodginghouse there, and we go in tomorrow: He frighted me cruelly a while ago, he would have Lady Shelburne's House— one of the finest in London: he would buy, he would build, he would give 20, 30, Guineas a Week for a House. Oh Lord thought I! the People will sure enough throw Stones at me now, when they see a dying Man go to such mad Expences, & all— as they will naturally think—to please a Wife wild with the Love of Expence." But as her poor master was determined "ay and ten Times more so than ever; since he suspects his Head to be suspected:—" move they did, and she could not honestly say she was sorry, as she had always hated Southwark.

There was all the more reason, now they were in such a fine house and since Mr. Thrale must not be admitted to be dying, to give parties. In February, wrote Mrs. Thrale to Fanny, they had a *conversazione*. "Mrs. Montagu was brilliant in diamonds, solid in judgment, critical in talk. Sophy smiled. Piozzi sung. Pepys panted in admiration, Johnson was good-humoured, Lord John Clinton attentive, Dr. Bowdler lame, and my master not asleep."

"I know I shall always hate this book which has kept me so long away from you," replied Fanny.

The behavior of "my master" grew wilder and wilder, until it reached a climax. Mr. Thrale had made up his mind suddenly to go abroad, reported Fanny, "first to Spa, next to Italy, and then whither his fancy led him! . . . as their journey was without limit either of time or place, as Mr. Thrale's ill state of health and strange state of mind would make it both melancholy and alarming, she [Mrs. Thrale] could not in conscience think of taking me from my own friends and country without knowing either whither, or for what length of time."

Hester was distracted. "Mr. Thrale talks now of going to Spa & Italy again: how shall we drag him thither? a Man who cannot keep awake four Hours at a Stroke, who can scarce retain the Faeces &c."—which throws a more searching light on Mrs. Thrale's difficulties. "Well! this will indeed be a Tryal of one's Patience; & who must go with us on this Expedition? Mr. Johnson! he will indeed be the only happy Person of the party: he values nothing under heaven but his own Mind, which is a Spark from Heaven; & that will be invigorated by the addition of new Ideas—if Mr. Thrale dies on the road, Johnson will console himself by learning how it is to travel with a Corpse—& after all, such Reasoning is the true Philosophy—one's heart is a mere Incumbrance—Would I could leave mine behind. . . ."

The reader must not suppose from this passage that the Thrale house was in any way dull or moping during those anxious times. Fanny described a typical party only a few days before the end: "I spent the whole day again in Grosvenor Square, where there was a very gay party to dinner; Mr. Boswell, Dudley Long, Mr. Adair, Dr. Delap, Mr. B——, Dr. Johnson, and my father. . . . In the afternoon we were joined by Mr. Crutchley, Mr. Byron, and Mr. Selwyn; . . . Sir Richard Jebb and Dr. Pepys have both been consulted concerning this going abroad, and are both equally violent against it, as they think it even unwarrantable, in such a state of health as Mr. Thrale's; and, therefore, it is settled that a great meeting of his friends is to take place before he actually prepares for the journey, and they are to encircle him in a body, and endeavour, by representations and entreaties, to prevail with him to give it up; and I have little doubt myself but, amongst us, we shall be able to succeed."

The master's behavior was not calculated to reassure his friends. Monday, the second of April, a comparatively small bevy of them at luncheon saw their host eating voraciously and heard his wife remonstrate with him. Johnson added, "Sir, after the denunciation of your physicians this morning, such eating is little better than suicide."

But Thrale continued to eat. "Sir Philip said he eat apparently in Defiance of Controul, & that it was better for us to say nothing to him: Johnson observed that he thought so too, & that he spoke more from a Sense of Duty than a Hope of Success."

Glum and full of foreboding, Mrs. Thrale continued to attend parties, telling herself something was sure to happen soon. She broke down while giving Piozzi some money collected for his benefit performance; she had suddenly remembered that Mr. Thrale contributed generously to the fund. This act of "peculiar Tenderness" held poignancy; the thought of it made her weep. So did a harmless letter she received just then from Mr. Pepys. Everything seemed to warn her, to insist on that hovering presence of Death. In vain the picture exhibitions and *conversaziones* and dinner parties which filled the days. In vain her good friend Mrs. Byron, who sat with her as she dressed. Mr. Thrale was dying. It was not so much because of him, but that anyone should be so stricken, that all things come to an end. Hester Thrale wept at her toilette, while Piozzi spoke gentle words to her and sang to comfort her. He used rather too much expression in his singing, she felt; it affected her strongly. She wept while her hair was dressed for dinner. She wept sitting before her glass.

"I suppose that you *Know* that Man is in Love with You," said Mrs. Byron after Piozzi had taken his leave.

"I am too miserable to care *who* is in love with me," sobbed Hester.

". . . and Mr. Thrale came home so well! & in such Spirits; he had invited more People to my Concert or Conversatione or musical party of the next day, & was delighted to think what a Show we should make. He eat however more than enormously;—

six things the Day before, & eight on this Day, with Strong Beer
in such Quantities! the very Servants were frighted . . ."

That afternoon when she went to her husband's room she found
him awake, sitting upright on his bed with his legs up. "Because,"
was all the reason he would give for this strange posture. He asked
who was upstairs in the drawing room but showed no desire to join
them. Later, when Queeney dropped in to visit her father, she
found him on the floor.

"What's the meaning of this?" she cried in alarm.

"I choose it," replied Mr. Thrale firmly; "I lie so o'purpose."

That insane, stubborn, defiant remark, a few hours before his
death, is the most pathetic thing we know of Thrale.

10. NO MERCY IN THE ISLAND

THE SECRECY which destroyed Thrale now stood his family in good stead, for his will left them all well off, and no one knew about the financial crisis which had been weathered. A rush of business kept the executors at Streatham. Fanny Burney was there too, in her role of confidante. Mrs. Thrale was very funny on the subject of Johnson, who was one of the executors: "If an Angel from Heaven had told me 20 Years ago that the Man I knew by the Name of *Dictionary Johnson* should one Day become Partner with me in a great Trade, & that we should jointly or separately sign Notes Draughts &c. for 3 or 4 Thousand Pounds of a Morning, how unlikely it would have seemed ever to happen! . . . Johnson however; who desires above all other Good the Accumulation of new Ideas, is but too happy with his present Employment; & the Influence I have over him added to his own solid Judgment and Regard for Truth, will at last find it *in a small degree* difficult to win him from the dirty Delight of seeing his Name in a new Character flaming away at the bottom of Bonds & Leases."

The pressure was considerable; there were many serious questions to settle, and each executor pulled the widow in a different direction. Mrs. Thrale was anxious to sell the brewery. She was ashamed of it, had always been ashamed of it, and longed to be restored to her "original Rank in Life." Also, not unnaturally, she hated the fatigue and trouble of carrying on with it under her own management, as she had been doing some long months before Thrale's death.

Crutchley, another executor, had been a fairly constant visitor to Streatham and was now there most of the time. All the old friends rallied around the mistress of the house, including S.S., who offered a typically Streatfeild brand of comfort.

"Sophy Streatfeild is an incomprehensible Girl; here has She been, telling me such tender passages of what pass'd between her & Mr Thrale—that She half frights me somehow; at the same Time declaring her Attachment to Vyse—yet her willingness to marry Ld Loughboro.

"Good God! what an uncommon Girl! & handsome almost to Perfection I think, delicate in her Manners, soft in her Voice, & strict in her Principles: I never saw such a Character, She is wholly out of my Reach."

In the early weeks there was nothing for the party to do between meetings with solicitors but walk about, receive condoling visitors, and talk to each other. It was not long before the romance-obsessed mistress detected a new development in her funereal house party, a flirtation dawning between Fanny and Crutchley. Once before, in the old days, she had suggested Jerry Crutchley for Fanny, but that had been a joke. Now she began to wonder.

"Mr Crutcheley lives now a great deal with me; the Business of Executor to Mr Thrale's Will, makes much of his Attendance necessary; and it begins to have its full Effect in seducing and attaching him to the house: Miss Burney's being always about me is probably another Reason for his close Attendance, & I believe it is so—what better could befall Miss Burney? or indeed what better cd befall *him*, than to obtain a Woman of Honour; & Character, & Reputation for superior Understanding—I would be glad however that he fell honestly in Love with her; & was not tricked or trapp'd into Marriage poor Fellow; he is no Match for the Arts of a Novel-writer."

Crutchley had a good deal to recommend him to Mrs. Thrale, aside from the adverse facts that he was ugly and awkward, and that she thought he might be Mr. Thrale's son. (Mr. Thrale, at any rate, had said he was.) He was wealthy, he was devoted to herself in a most respectful way, and, best of all, he had always firmly refused to fall in love with Sophy Streatfeild. She was in favor of Crutchley, ancestry or no ancestry.

And Fanny? Fanny never affirmed or denied, but her Journal was certainly very full of Mr. Crutchley for some weeks. Impetus was given their friendship by a quarrel, a thing which often precipitates friendships. Mrs. Thrale, indiscreet as ever, popped her head out of a window one day when Fanny and Crutchley were strolling on the lawn and said teasingly that Sir Philip had commented on how well their names went together. "I think they can't do better than to make a match of it," Sir Philip allegedly declared. Cheerfully, at the top of her voice, Mrs. Thrale repeated this. Perhaps the remark had never actually been made; she was quite capable of inventing it.

"I leave you to judge if I was pleased at this stuff thus communicated," scribbled Fanny indignantly. She called back dryly, "I am very much obliged to him, indeed!"

As for Mr. Crutchley, he said, *"Thank him!—Thank him!"* in "a voice of pride and pique that spoke him mortally angry." One might ask why Mr. Crutchley's retort should have been considered more offensive than Miss Burney's, but there was not a doubt in her mind that she had been grossly insulted by it. She immediately left him on the lawn and went into the house, not too fast to hear him add to Mrs. Thrale, "So this is Sir Philip's kindness?" and to hear Mrs. Thrale retort, "I wish you no worse luck!"

As a matchmaker Mrs. Thrale had rather a heavy hand.

Fanny brooded for a long time. How had he dared to presume . . . "But these rich men think themselves the constant prey of all portionless girls," she stormed, and made up her mind to speak as little with Mr. Crutchley in the future as she could manage. Fortunately for her *amour-propre,* her cold, offended demeanor brought him quickly to heel, and they somehow made it up. Pages of the Journal are given over to their conversations and her reflections thereon. They sparred, they mocked each other harmlessly, they talked and talked and talked. Mr. Crutchley talked about himself, and Fanny talked about Mr. Crutchley. Mr. Crutchley allowed it to be understood that he suffered from an unrequited passion, or from the memory of one. He went into detail about his peculiar nature. He sighed, and vacillated, and acted in a manner mysterious to behold. But he never declared himself.

Besides, just when everything might have gone according to Mrs. Thrale's plan, Fanny was called away by her father. "What a Blockhead Dr Burney is, to be always sending for his Daughter home so! what a Monkey! is not She better and happier with me than She can be any where else? Johnson is enraged at the silliness of their Family Conduct, and Mrs. Byron disgusted: I confess myself provoked excessively but I love the Girl so dearly—& the Dr too for that matter, only that he has such odd Notions of superiority in his own house, & will have his Children under his Feet forsooth rather than let 'em live in Peace, Plenty & Comfort any where from home. If I did not provide Fanny with every Wearable, every Wishable indeed, it would not vex me to be served so; but to see the Impossibility of compensating for the Pleasures of St. Martins Street, makes me at once merry & mortified.

"Dr. Burney did not like his Daughter should learn Latin even of Johnson who offered to teach her for Friendship, because then She would have been as wise as himself forsooth, & Latin was too Masculine for Misses—a narrow Souled Goose-cap the Man must be at last; agreeable and amiable all the while too beyond allmost any other human Creature."

There was, however, good reason this time for Fanny's presence at home. Susan Burney's love affair was not running smooth, and no doubt Mrs. Thrale's pettishness owed itself partly to her knowledge of this. Dr. Burney was trying to put off the marriage because he felt young Phillips, in spite of his expectations, did not have enough cash in hand. Ultimately the paterfamilias gave in, but

for some weeks St. Martin's Street was the scene of a family
struggle into which Fanny was inevitably drawn. Unfortunately,
her absence from Streatham didn't keep Mr. Crutchley away, and
at last Mrs. Thrale unwillingly admitted to herself that she had
been mistaken as to that moody young man's intentions.

"I begin to wish in good earnest that Miss Burney should make
Impression on Mr. Crutchley; I think She honestly loves the Man,
who in his Turn appears to be in Love with some one else—Hester
I fear! Oh that would indeed be unlucky!"

So there again went her fond hope of settling Fanny in life.
Perhaps some of Fanny's hopes, too, went glimmering, though
she never admitted it. Mrs. Thrale was able later to rejoice for
Fanny's sake that she had not been successful when Crutchley
quarreled with her. Certainly his behavior bore out the theory
that he was in love with Queeney; it was on her behalf that he
was rude, ultimately, to Mrs. Thrale, but he never announced his
passion. He was discouraged, either by the young lady or by a suspicion that he was Thrale's natural son, in which case marriage
with Queeney was of course out of the question. Perhaps that
accounts for his tragic hints and cryptic utterances to Fanny, but
we cannot do more than guess. Mrs. Thrale, bored with the matter,
dropped it, and Madame d'Arblay has left us no further hint.

It was New Year's Day, 1782, and Thrale had been dead nearly
eight months. Hester Thrale started her year's journal with a name
once feared if not hated; she did not love it even now. "Sophy
Streatfeild," she wrote. "Sophy Streatfeild. . . . She has begun
the New Year nicely with a new Conquest—Poor dear Doctor
Burney! He is now the reigning Favourite, and She spares neither
Pains nor Caresses to turn that good Man's head, much to the
Vexation of his Family; particularly my Fanny, who is naturally
provoked to see Sport made of her Father in his last Stage of Life
by a Young Coquet whose sole Employment in this World seems
to have been winning Men's hearts on purpose to fling them away.
How She contrives to keep Bishops, & Brewers, & Doctors, &

Directors of the East India Company all in her Chains so—& all at a Time would amaze a wiser Person than me: I can only say *Let us mark the End!*"

"If nothing of all these Misfortunes however befall me," she mused after a gloomy summary of her affairs, "*if* for my Sins God should take from me my Monitor, my Friend, my Inmate, my Dear Mr Johnson ["Travelling with Mr Johnson *I* cannot bear," she wrote here in one of her marginal after-thoughts, "& leaving him behind *he* could not bear; so his Life or Death must determine the Execution or laying aside my Schemes:—I wish it were within Reason to *hope* he could live four Years."], if neither I should marry, nor the Brewhouse People break; if the ruin of the Nation should not change the Situation of Affairs so that One could not receive regular Remittances from England: and if Piozzi should not pick him up a Wife, and fix his abode in this Country—If therefore & If, & If & If again—All should conspire to keep my present Resolution warm; I certainly would at the close of the four Years from the Sale of the Southwark Estate, set out for Italy with my two or three eldest Girls; and see what the World could shew me. I am now provided with an Italian Friend who would manage my Money Matters, facilitate my Continental amusements, & be faithful to my Interest: I would make it worth his while, & we should live happily together."

"The world" was not yet gossiping unpleasantly about Mrs. Thrale, at least not more than usual, but the time was coming when that close friendship was to undergo a severe trial. The proverbial year of mourning would soon be over. Mrs. Thrale took a house in Harley Street and invitations started coming in again, for quiet affairs which she might with propriety accept. But the lively lady had changed. She had always suffered sudden revulsions against society, but they were short-lived little affairs, mere spats. Now she was showing a sensitiveness which was uncharacteristic. "I had a Letter today, desiring me to dine in Wimpole Street [the house of her friend Pepys] & meet Mrs Montagu & a whole *Army*

of *Blues*: to whom I trust my Refusal will afford very pretty Speculation—& they may settle my character & future Conduct at their
Leisure.

"Pepys is a worthless Fellow at last; he & his Brother run about
the Town spying & enquiring what Mrs Thrale is to do this Winter; what Friends She is to see, What *Men* are in her Confidence,
how soon She will be *married* &c. The Brother Dr the Medico as
we call Him, lays Wagers about me I find—God forgive me, but
they'll make me hate them both; & they are no better than two
Fools for their Pains, for I was willing to have taken them to my
heart."

It was a nasty world, a prying world, withal sometimes amusing.
As a woman not yet old—she was forty—with a good fortune, and
unencumbered of that grotesque brewery, Mrs. Thrale was fully
aware she might reasonably be expected to marry again, but every
hint of it made her flare out angrily. She became ridiculously
touchy. Dr. Johnson was ill too—"if I lose *him* I am more than
undone: Friend, Father, Guardian, Confident! God give me Health
& Patience—what shall I do?"

Still, there was always the gentle Piozzi, with his singing and his
respectful understanding; Piozzi, who never hurt her feelings, or
teased her, or worried her. The three months in Harley Street
dragged on. She had given up reproaching Fanny for staying away:
Fanny was busy on her second novel.

Daddy Crisp sat in Chesington, acting as judge on *Cecilia*. This
time his strictures were not plentiful, as they would have been had
Fannikin dared set foot again on the forbidden territory of the
Drama. She was showing her manuscript to only six people at
this time: Mrs. Thrale, Dr. Johnson, Charlotte, Kitty Cooke, Dr.
Burney, and Daddy Crisp, and of these, only Daddy offered
criticism, constructive or destructive. The rest admired, and
flattered, and cried for more. Dr. Burney assured his talented
daughter that he liked *Cecilia* far better than her first book, though
he thought it would not be so well reviewed. Sometimes this

cheered her up and gave her the spirit to fight Crisp and defend favorite passages which he disapproved, but at other times she was genuinely depressed and fearful. The old terror of public opinion haunted her, though she knew that many people would buy her book simply because of her name.

"Everybody knows that I am about something; and the moment I put my head out of doors, I am sure to be attacked and cate-chized. Oh, that I were but as sure of the success as of the sale of this book! but, indeed, I am now more discomfited and alarmed than I have ever been yet."

June 12, 1782, was the publication date of *Cecilia*, and Fanny need not have worried so much. It was exceedingly well received. Of more complicated structure than *Evelina*, and greater length—*Evelina* had only three volumes and *Cecilia* had five—it lacks the fresh, involuntary quality of the first book, but one can easily see why the public should have greeted more of the same material which had delighted them in *Evelina*. The author was again lavish with her subacid accounts of high life, and she created a number of new characters, of a type familiar enough to be greeted by her readers with applause. Written in narrative form, the story is of another orphan, this time an heiress, but Cecilia is not the romantic orphan child so often met with in Gothic novels. Fanny's realism may sometimes have faltered because of her weakness for melo-drama, but on the whole she maintained, as she set out to do, the attitude of a calm, shrewd observer of everyday life. In a female novelist this approach was still something new, and certainly it was creditable. Readers of Jane Austen should find it easy to detect in *Cecilia* why Miss Austen so admired Miss Burney.

We meet Cecilia some time before she comes of age, when she will be in command of her own fortune. Her father has named three guardians for her, and it is because they are widely dissimilar that Cecilia sees life from many angles when she comes to live in London. The main theme of the plot, Fanny explained to Crisp, is *pride*: the pride of her lover's family stood in the way of Cecilia's marriage and nearly wrecked several lives. In the words of one of

the characters, their troubles were due to PRIDE AND PREJU-
DICE. ("Sense and sensibility" was one of Fanny Burney's phrases
as well.) Most likely the plot did not mean as much to society's
readers as did the embroidery of the scene; the vapidly silent Miss
Leeson, the garrulous Miss Larolles with her up-to-the-minute
slang, the languid Mr. Meadows; Sir Robert Floyer, so satisfyingly
wicked, must have pleased them, as did the major villain, Monckton. One of the important characters was a Mr. Harrel. Fanny
vividly described his extravagance and gambling, his methods of
extracting money from his ward Cecilia, and his scenes of faked
suicide. Harrel is very convincing. It is difficult to believe Fanny
wasn't drawing on personal experience, remembering her troubles
with Brother Charles.

All in all, if Jane Austen did not find the trail clear before her,
she at least found indications of the path she was to follow.

Cecilia was successful, but Crisp wasn't satisfied and was proud
to say so. ". . . to evince my sincerity, and that you may not think
I mean, sycophant-like, to turn about and recant, in order to swim
with the wind and tide that brings you (as I hear) clouds of incense
from every quarter—to avoid this scandalous imputation, I do
declare that I must adhere to my former sentiments on some parts
of the work. . . ."

The most fragrant cloud of this incense, to Fanny's mind, was
a letter from her acquaintance Edmund Burke. "In an age distinguished by producing extraordinary women, I hardly dare to tell
you where my opinion would place you amongst them," wrote
Burke. "I respect your modesty. . . ."

Incense indeed, and it is much to Fanny's credit that she did not
lose patience with old Sam Crisp, prating away in the country and
warning her, like the croaking raven she sometimes called him.

"Now, Fannikin, I must remind you of your promise, which
was to come to your loving daddy when you could get loose. Look
ye, Fanny, I don't mean to cajole you hither with the expectation
of amusement or entertainment. You and I know better than to
hum or be hummed in that manner. If you come here, you come to

work,—work hard—stick to it. This is the harvest time of your life; your sun shines hot; lose not a moment, then, but make your hay directly. . . .

"I talked to your doctor daddy on the subject of disposing of your money; and we both agreed in the project of a well-secured annuity. . . ."

Streatham, though, now claimed Fanny's attention in a way so urgent as to interfere with these prudent plans.

"A serious piece of intelligence has given, does give, and long must give me the utmost concern and sorrow," she wrote to Susan in August. "My dear Mrs. Thrale, the friend, though not the *most* dear friend of my heart, is going abroad for three years certain. . . ."

Her protégée's plaintive concern must have gratified Mrs. Thrale, who liked to be appreciated. Dr. Johnson had disappointed his mistress, and she said so frankly. It was a bit hard, after she had wasted so much of eighteen years fretting over him, had even postponed deciding on her departure for his sake, and had waited until she felt his health was good enough to bear the blow—it was a bit hard that he took it all so coolly.

She had prepared the way carefully, making a little speech about the advisability of going abroad to economize, and adding with careful emphasis that Queeney thoroughly agreed with the plan and was willing to go. And what was Johnson's reaction to this announcement? Was he shattered? Did he weep, and vow he must accompany her, or beg her to change her mind? Not he. "Mr. Johnson thought well of the Project & wished me to put it early in Execution, seemed even less concerned at parting with me than I wished him, thought his Pupil quite right in forbearing to marry Young, & seemed to entertain no doubt of living to see us return rich & happy in two or three Years Time—He told Hester in my Absence that he would not go with me if I asked him——

"See the Importance of a Person to himself! I fancied Mr. Johnson could not have existed without me forsooth. . . ."

Mrs. Thrale wrote several more indignant paragraphs on the subject and boiled over again on the margin. Johnson had *never* cared for her, she said angrily; he had loved Thrale, but looked on Thrale's wife merely as a nurse—"yet I really thought he could not have existed without my *Conversation* forsooth. He cares more for my roast Beef & plumb Pudden which he now devours too dirtily for endurance: and since he is glad to get rid of me, I'm sure I have good Cause to desire the getting Rid of *him*."

It is not the intention of this writer to go too deeply into the complex subject of Johnson and Mrs. Thrale. The story of their relations has already, God knows, a long enough bibliography. We should remind ourselves, however, that Sam Johnson always lived up to his principles, except when absent-mindedness made him slip, and one of his ideals was stoicism. Besides, he was already uneasily jealous of Piozzi, and no doubt he felt sulky. He was too dignified as yet to exhibit spleen, but he sulked. "Mrs. Thrale told me she was going abroad," he wrote in his diary on the day of the interview. That was all. Not for him those long scribbled pages of feminine introspection. Mrs. Thrale was going abroad, was she? Very well, it was Mrs. Thrale's right to go abroad, and if she expected him to show signs of weakness, she was grossly mistaken. A man had always his books. A man had his pride too.

Nervously, unhappily, Hester Thrale went about her preparations. It was upsetting to go away like this from all her old friends, but it was impossible to stay; people were becoming more and more impertinent and pressing; now Sir Philip, too, was paying court to her, though not yet a widower. And Crutchley was definitely set against her taking Queeney away and insisted that Piozzi must not go with them, and he looked disappointed when Mrs. Thrale promptly agreed to give up Piozzi, and he tried to find other excuses. Really, one's only true friends were people like "my sweet Burney, & Mrs Byron. . . ." Piozzi was angelic, though. Piozzi was willing to go if she liked or stay if she liked. He held himself in readiness to do her bidding, whatever it might be.

Evidently Queeney and Crutchley already suspected the true nature of Mrs. Thrale's feelings and were trying to discourage them. Fanny took alarm at the same time, though her Journal is

silent on the subject. If it were not for *Thraliana* and the Queeney
letters, we would be left to believe what Fanny wanted posterity to
believe, that there was nothing in the world at that stage of the
game to make a fuss about. Yet she was as much in her dear Mrs.
Thrale's confidence, at this period, as was the Thrale notebook.
Secret suffering was not one of Hester's indulgences. Fanny
listened, and worried, and disapproved with the hearty concurrence of Dr. Burney, in a rapidly mounting crescendo.

It started mildly enough. "Now!" wrote Mrs. Thrale, "that
little dear discerning Creature Fanny Burney says I'm in love with
Piozzi—very likely! he is so amiable, so honourable, so much above
his Situation by his Abilities," et cetera, et cetera. That was in late
September, when it was still possible to mention the matter half
jokingly to the widow. Fanny had taken a light tone. If she had
not, dear Mrs. Thrale would not have been affectionate as she still
was, as she was not, alas, to remain much longer. Mrs. Thrale's
affection for Piozzi was beginning to cause comment, if not among
the outermost fringes of her set, certainly in such enclosed spaces
as the Burney house.

At last Hester Thrale discussed the topic with herself, in writing. Item one: they said Piozzi was beneath her. In what? Not in
virtue, she only wished she were above him; not in understanding,
she wished his could guard hers; in birth, well, yes, but so was
every other man she was likely to meet; in fortune, yes. But she
had more than enough money for both, and Piozzi had "always
united warm notions of Honour, with cool attention to Oecon-
omy. . . ."

Item two: she had five daughters and must not disgrace their
name and family. Now let us examine this claim, said Hester. Was
Thrale, the man chosen for her by her mother, of better family
than Piozzi, the man she chose for herself? No. He was richer, but
Miss Salusbury had needed money, and Mrs. Thrale does not. "I
am not to think about myself, I married the first Time to please my
Mother, I must marry the second Time to please my Daughter.
. . ." Would her marriage hurt the children in any way, in body,
soul, or purse? Would Piozzi's company or companions corrupt

their morals? Could the marriage injure their fortunes? Could he, even if he wished, impoverish five women to whom their father had left twenty thousand pounds apiece?

"To what then am I Guardian? to their Pride and Prejudice? & is anything else affected by the Alliance?"

There is one fallacy in the argument. Hester referred to her daughters as "five women," whereas actually two of them were still very young children: even Queeney, the eldest, was not yet of age. Hester might reasonably protest that Piozzi's company would not injure anyone, least of all a child; was he not already a trusted music teacher of children? Nevertheless, when a mother of young children was condemned by eighteenth-century society, the children, too, fell under the shadow. But Mrs. Thrale knew how to deal with conscientious scruples. She was no weakling. With one magnificent gesture she simply threw away the years intervening before her baby daughters should reach maturity and independence. "Five women" they were going to be, and so, for her purposes of argument, five women they already were.

"More solid objections" came to her mind, once she had triumphantly banished these obstacles. Piozzi was a foreigner, and as her husband he would have the power to remove her, fortune and all, from her native land. He was perhaps younger than she; what if he should decide he loved her no longer? Supposing he should die before her: what would be her position? Who would look with kindness on Piozzi's widow? And there was his religion; she must enter the Catholic Church and bring up their children, if any, as Catholics.

"These Objections would increase in Strength too, if my present State was a happy one, but it really is not: I live a quiet Life, but not a pleasant one: My Children govern without loving me, my Servants devour & despise me, my Friends caress and censure me, my Money wastes in Expences I do not enjoy, and my Time in Trifles I do not approve. every one is made Insolent, & no one Comfortable. my Reputation unprotected, my Heart unsatisfied, my Health unsettled."

Other, more familiar troubles crowded in on her. The whole

year she had been vexed by rumors. No doubt she exaggerated. She began to see offers of marriage where a man intended merely common civility; sometimes she thought the papers were full of the subject of herself when in truth they were not. Every little slander which was reported to her (and in those lighthearted days there was always slander and always a lady of fashion to report it) struck at her *amour-propre*. She was undergoing a crisis; she was no longer tough little Mrs. Thrale, with the spirit of a cricket and a whirligig tongue. "There is no Mercy for me in the Island—I am more and more disposed to try the Continent. one Day the paper rings with my Marriage to Johnson, one Day to Crutchley; one Day to Seward. I give no Reason for such Impertinence, but cannot deliver myself from it. Whitbread the rich Brewer is in Love with me too. . . ."

Undoubtedly there was some reason for her complaints. It could not have been pleasant, though it was not surprising, that word went round she was to marry Johnson. *Johnson*, who now was so old and ill that he ate at her table "too dirtily for endurance." There went the rounds among the wits a malicious "Ode to Mrs. Thrale, by Samuel Johnson, LL.D., on their approaching Nuptials."

> *If e'er my fingers touched the lyre,*
> *In satire fierce, in pleasure gay,*
> *Shall not my Thralia's smiles inspire,*
> *Shall Sam refuse the sportive lay?*
>
> *My desert lady, view your slave,*
> *Behold him as your very Scrub;*
> *Ready to write as author grave,*
> *Or govern well the brewing tub.*
>
> *To rich felicity thus raised,*
> *My bosom glows with amorous fire;*
> *Porter no longer shall be praised,*
> *'Tis I myself am Thrale's Entire.*

Bitterly Mrs. Thrale recorded that Queeney was being stubborn and opposing her marriage. There was a remarkable scene, brought on, she insisted with guilty fervor, by Queeney, who forced the pace by asking her for an explanation of her unhappy demeanor.

We wonder now why there need have developed so much public feeling about a private matter, and why everyone was so excitedly opposed to the marriage in the first place. On second thoughts, it was quite natural. Even today there is raising of eyebrows and snickering in corners when a wealthy lady marries a music teacher, especially when he has been employed in her household. Perhaps Piozzi was the innocent pioneer: perhaps the headlines in today's tabloids on every occasion of the sort is his humble bequest to posterity. Every newspaper editor knows that a marriage between a "society beauty" and a musician is news. It falls into the category of heiress-actor alliances, or the elopement of a wealthy widow with her chauffeur, or one of those many marriages between a rich girl and a Mdivani. In the conservative Anglo-Saxon mind a musician is by nature a sort of adventurer. Adventurers are fortune hunters. Ergo, musicians are fortune hunters. Mrs. Thrale could have protested until her pen was worn down to the nib that Piozzi was no fortune hunter (which he was not; he made plenty of money for himself, and on one occasion lent her a thousand pounds); her protests made not the slightest difference. The executors were against Piozzi. Queeney, under Crutchley's influence, rejected Piozzi. Johnson, though still ignorant of the full extent of Mrs. Thrale's plans, was already against Piozzi because he was jealous. Whether the jealousy was of an amorous or practical nature, Johnson's friends were up in arms on his behalf, ready to back his attitude with all the arguments at their command. Burney always went with the crowd, so he was against Piozzi, the rival musician. Considering that formidable array of public opinion, it is redundant to say that Fanny as well was against Piozzi.

What? cried the world; marry a fortune-hunting musician, an Italian singer, a man of no more social standing than a servant? *Marry Piozzi?* What of Mrs. Thrale's duty to her daughters, to her social class, to her money, to her husband's memory? A lady of quality, even though the quality of a brewer's wife was admittedly not the highest sort, could not possibly let them all down like that. . . . Echoes of the inevitable chorus rang prematurely but accurately in Queeney's ears, and then, too, her mother was in such an undignified state. She actually declared her matrimonial intentions right there in the parlor, to that man, in the presence of her daughter, or perhaps she declared them to Queeney in the presence of Piozzi—no matter; it was no secret to either of her audience, but the *method* was so crude and distressing.

Queeney, in spite of her cool poise and dignity, was after all a young girl, and any young girl would have been shocked by such a scene. Her mother's relations with her had always been of a capricious sort; whether, as Mrs. Thrale said, the caprices had been Queeney's, or whether, as Mrs. Thrale's detractors say, it was the mother's fault, Queeney had long lived with the mistress of Streatham merely as a dutiful daughter in a family group portrait. She was not a loving or a lovable character, but she had good manners.

Queeney consulted with her guardians and finally announced herself opposed to the whole plan. It was Crutchley who advised this. He held an important card: Mrs. Thrale had just lost a lawsuit and she needed ready money to pay up. Crutchley, with a very bad grace, allowed this money to be borrowed from the girls' estates: after this, he insisted, it behooved Mrs. Thrale to comport herself like a dutiful mother and eschew Italian music masters. "I called into the Room to her [Queeney] my own Bosom Friend, my beloved Fanny Burney," wrote the unhappy lady; "whose Interest as well as Judgment goes all against my Marriage—whose Skill in Life and Manners is superior to that of any Man or Woman in this Age or Nation; whose Knowledge of the World, ingenuity of Expedient, Delicacy of Conduct, & Zeal in the Cause will make her a Counsellor invaluable; & leave me destitute of every Comfort, of every Hope, of every Expectation."

There now arose a situation which nobody at Streatham three

years before could have imagined possible. Fanny Burney leagued with Queeney against Mrs. Thrale.

That is putting it baldly, but prettier words cannot change the facts, though they could, and did, allay the pangs of the Burney conscience. How could Fanny have been such a bitch? The question asks itself, indignantly. Yet, knowing as much as we do of her history, how could she not have been? Fanny's respect for public opinion was almost morbidly intense, and she was excruciatingly squeamish about sex scandals. Today we would not consider as a sex scandal a mere projected *mésalliance*, admitting the Thrale-Piozzi marriage to be that. But Fanny was a prude, and Mrs. Thrale's avowed passion shocked her. Fanny was a good little girl, dwelling in a world where female passion was not supposed to exist. Men felt passion. Even gentlemen felt passion, in a manly way. But ladies felt only esteem, admiration, appreciation of nobility, and, at most, a sort of above-the-waist love. Mrs. Thrale's hysterics, Mrs. Thrale's frank longing for Piozzi, frightened and disgusted Fanny. To turn from her old friend and league herself with Queeney did not seem to her a treasonable performance. The world was on her side; rather, she was on the world's side, which gave her that reassuring consciousness of virtue without which she could not exist. Besides, she was helping, not injuring, her dear Mrs. Thrale. She was trying to save dear Mrs. Thrale from a fate worse than death, from her own evil, crazed impulses, from *social obloquy*. It was not treason, Fanny probably reasoned; it was the highest sort of friendship. It was Duty.

That she thoroughly enjoyed the drama of the ensuing struggle need not brand her as heartless. She did not realize she was enjoying it. She thought she suffered agonies of pity and anxiety, and in all this there was present one very real anxiety, or at least a painful perplexity. How far dared she accompany the Thrales in the matter? Was it going to be a really bad scandal? Would her own reputation suffer, and would her father be involved? No, she would not pursue further that line of thought. She loved dear Mrs. Thrale too much to allow such considerations to stand in the way.

Perhaps, with time, all might yet be saved; she would talk it over some more with Queeney, and if she put any of this exciting affair into her Journal, she expunged it later. It is only her letters to Queeney which give Fanny away.

"I am very, very sorry for you indeed!" she wrote Queeney, "—& too much frightened to do any good by writing. . . . I am glad you applied to me, distressed as I am how to counsel you, for I will think the best I can, & I will, as I ever have, be as honourable in advising you, as I must be tender for your dear unhappy Mother —whom I can hardly think of without crying."

She behaved as though nothing in the world was the matter. She went out regularly with mother and daughter to parties which she reported to Susan and Crisp, with her customary relish. By a coincidence, coming events cast their shadows just now, at this critical period in Fanny's career. The Thrale influence was drawing to a close, but she could not have known, when she heard of the imposing Mrs. Delany reading *Cecilia* with the Duchess of Portland, that she, Fanny Burney, would ever move freely in those circles. She was fluttered and flattered that the Queen had read *Cecilia*, but how could she have guessed what this would ultimately mean to herself? The important matters of the moment were the little satisfactions of her fame and the great satisfaction that Mrs. Thrale had half promised, for the sake of the children, to give up her wild, desperate idea of marrying Piozzi. The hateful affair, as Fanny called it, might yet blow over.

"—sweet Fanny Burney cried herself half blind over it [a passage of passionate grief in *Thraliana*]: said there was no resisting such pathetic Eloquence, & that if She was the Daughter instead of the Friend, she should be even tempted to attend me to the Altar. but that while She possessed her Reason, nothing should seduce her to approve what Reason itself would condemn. . . ."

Then, no doubt, the ladies wiped their eyes, kissed each other, and went out to another party.

11. THIS UNHAPPY INFATUATION

FANNY was not merely a one-book prodigy now, but a full-fledged serious thinker in five volumes, and people treated her accordingly. Her importance was manna to her soul. It was exceedingly pleasant to be looked on as a full-grown lion instead of a cub. When the Blue Mrs. Vesey made a point of her attending a Vesey *salon*, when people clamored for introductions to her at the exclusive house of Miss Monckton, when she arrived at a party with Mrs. Thrale in attendance, as it were, rather than the other way around, it was certainly pleasant. On the other hand, there were drawbacks of a nature peculiarly painful to Fanny Burney. The public seemed to assume that she had outgrown her little-girlness. The public was only being reasonable in making this assumption, Miss Burney having turned thirty, but she sighed for her old childish security nevertheless, and shuddered whenever someone made a fatuous pleasantry about fearing her shrewd novelist's insight. It was disagreeable to be thus reminded that she was shrewd. Little girls should not be shrewd.

Fanny wrote, protesting against this attitude, to her dear old Daddy Crisp, and found comfort in Dr. Johnson's heavy, paternal, imitation love-making, and developed a typically filial sentimental passion for Mr. Cambridge, elderly father of young Mr.

George Cambridge the clergyman. It was young Cambridge with whom Mrs. Thrale thought Fanny was in love, but in her passion for romance Mrs. Thrale leaped to the wrong conclusion. Father Cambridge it was who called on Fanny, who arranged to meet her at the houses of friends, and held long grave talks with her about his principles, his love for his wife, his admiration for her. It was a safe courtship without any culmination: most satisfactory. Miss Burney duly set down their conversations in the Diary as faithfully as she had that other series of half-flirtatious chats, with Crutchley. Young Mr. Cambridge figures scarcely at all in her intimate memoirs, whereas the chaste yet close relationship in which she stood to his father absorbed a large part of her thoughts for some months during the Thrale crisis.

This characteristic behavior was not merely old habit. She was fleeing from the unsavory situation, as she considered it, in which she saw Mrs. Thrale sinking deeper and deeper, as in a cesspool. Nothing could have frightened and discouraged her prudish nature more than the passionate interviews to which she was now subjected whenever she spent a day alone with her dear old friend. She was strongly tempted to drop that old friend, but she could not yet bring herself to such an extremity of disloyalty. Crutchley, too, had become obnoxious to Fanny. Once she had been ready to love him, to marry him if he asked her, and then suddenly the veil was torn from his face and she saw him in his true colors, an enemy to Mrs. Thrale, a man who used unfair methods of battle, an actor playing a principal part in the repulsive Streatham drama. Her second published letter to Queeney is an urgent appeal to the girl to protect Mrs. Thrale from a violent scene with Crutchley.

It was a great relief as well as an honor to be presented to good old Mrs. Delany. Present-day career women might stare at the idea that such an acquaintance could be so raptly desired. Who and what was Mrs. Delany? was she a writer of the preceding generation, with whom Fanny Burney could compare notes on technique? Was she a famous actress, or singer, or beauty, or hostess? She was none of these; she was merely a woman of eighty-two. She was famous, nonetheless, for being, as Burke called her, a woman of fashion—"a truly great woman of fashion, the highest-bred woman in the world, and the woman of fashion of *all* ages." This didn't mean that she dressed well, and we had better put down the phrase "highest-bred" to Irish ebullience, unless Burke meant it in its secondary connotation, "best-mannered." There were other ladies in her set with as good a pedigree as hers, but her manners were perfect.

Mary Granville had been trained for the post of Maid of Honor to Queen Anne, like her mother before her. She never achieved the job, but she went far higher in the end; she became a sort of legend, a Grand Old Lady, an honorary grandmother to George III and his family. Through her second husband she was a friend of Swift, having exchanged with him a series of the elegantly thoughtful sort of letters which were the delight of her age and the admiration of the intellectuals who met in St. Martin's Street. Admiration from the Burney circle was sharpened by awe of Mrs. Delany's social eminence, so Fanny was suitably thrilled when Mrs. Chapone took her to meet the venerable lady.

From our point of view a less thrilling setup could scarcely be imagined. Mrs. Chapone, then known for her book of moral counsel to young girls, is remembered today only for the unsubstantiated rumor that Gilbert White of Selborne once aspired to her hand. Fanny admired her, as suited a younger lady who was not quite a Blue, and credited her with "Good sense, talents, and conversational powers, in defiance of age, infirmities, and uncommon ugliness." She was dull to an extreme degree, but that very dullness was what Fanny wanted and needed after a trying hour with Mrs. Thrale one January afternoon. Fanny's spirit, fluttering in a seamy world, welcomed Mrs. Chapone's heavy worth and purity. Prosing away, the ladies drove to Mrs. Delany's home in St. James's Place.

They found her in her drawing room, herself a museum piece, surrounded by pictures she had painted and ornaments she had devised. Fanny of course fell in love with her on the spot: "She has no remains of beauty in feature, but in countenance I never but once saw more, and that was in my sweet maternal grandmother . . . I almost longed to embrace her. . . ."

There was a good deal of courteous ceremony. The visitors examined the pictures; they dined; they paid their respects to a new art which Mrs. Delany had invented: "It is staining paper of all possible colours, and then cutting it out, so finely and delicately, that when it is pasted on paper or vellum, it has all the appearance of being pencilled, except that, by being raised, it has still a richer and more natural look. The effect is extremely beautiful." A collection of these pieces, *Flora Delanica*, is now in the British Museum, where we can see them for ourselves, an elaborate and pretty invention showing an almost Oriental passion for delicacy in fine detail. Mrs. Delany must have had a remarkable eye for proportion, or a remarkable rapport between eye and hand, since she cut her shapes in exact copy of the object without drawing them first. Because she was such a very old lady when she started her last hobby, some of the *Flora Delanica* show a pathetic shakiness in the final touches of water color and in her signature on the back of the sheet. One feels stirred, looking at these flowers today under the bright twentieth-century lights of the Print Room. One is moved with admiration and also with an affectionate pity which Mrs. Delany would not for a moment have borne with.

Admirers of a more stalwart type of art, of paintings and sculpture, may sniff at an age which cried up such fiddling work in preference to the "bigger" things, but their attitude is without reason. It is the Mrs. Delanys of the world who create tapestries, enamels, lacquerwork, delicate filigree, without which civilized life would be sadly bare. Mrs. Delany retained the eager, catholic intellectual curiosity of her age long after her contemporaries deserted her by dying. Perhaps for this reason she liked young people; certainly young people loved her, and listened to her reminiscences by the hour. She was consistent in wishing to meet Fanny Burney, though one might have thought a new friendship rather too much effort for a lady of her age.

AN ENGRAVING BY WILLIAM HOGARTH, JUNE 25, 1735

Madness, Thou Chaos of ye Brain,
What art? That Pleasure giv'st, and Pain?
Tyranny of Fancy's Reign!

Mechanic Fancy; that can build
Vast Labarynths, & Mazes wild,
With Rule disjointed, Shapeless Measure,
Fill'd with Horror, fill'd with Pleasure!
Shapes of Horror, that would even
Cast Doubt of Mercy upon Heaven.
Shapes of Pleasure, that but seen
Would split the Shaking Sides of Spleen.

O Vanity of Age! here see
The Stamp of Heaven effac'd by Thee
The headstrong Course of Youth thus run,
What Comfort from this darling Son!
His rattling Chains with Terror hear,
Behold Death grappling with Despair;
See Him by Thee to Ruin Sold,
And curse thy self, & curse thy Gold.

THE ENRAGED MACARONI

The Billingsgate with rude and cutting Jokes
The Macaroni to fierce Rage provokes;
Who threatens Blood and Wounds with glaring Eyes;
But she with vip'rous Tongue his Rage defies.

After dinner the Duchess Dowager of Portland came in to pay her daily visit. The duchess, younger than Mrs. Delany by some years, had been her dearest friend since their youth. "Mrs. Delany received her," said Fanny, "with the same respectful ceremony as if it was her first visit, though she regularly goes to her every evening." Here the busy reader of eighteenth-century memoirs is interrupted by a shrill protest from Lady Llanover, who burst out in furious footnotes to her great-great-aunt Mrs. Delany's collected correspondence. Fanny Burney, she says, was an impertinent, pushing, conceited, misrepresenting *novelist* of a female, who could not be trusted for a moment with the sacred subject of Mrs. Delany. "The pert and vulgar dialogue alleged by Miss Burney to have taken place on her first interview," said Lady Llanover, must have been sheer invention. The reader glances again at Fanny's dialogue and rubs his weary eyes. Pert and vulgar it certainly is not. Stately, long-winded, and full of italics, Fanny's version of Mrs. Delany's manner of speech sounds genuine, though we must remember that her style became prolix as she grew older. No doubt she padded, and certainly she need not have repeated *all* those compliments; a good deal of Mrs. Delany's courtesy might have been allowed to pass as court license. Still, all this is a matter of degree, not of fact as opposed to falsehood. Why should Lady Llanover be so fierce? There is good reason, as we shall see.

There is a wide divergence of their reports on the Duchess of Portland's attitude toward Fanny. ". . . the Duchess of Portland," says Lady Llanover, "who Miss Burney describes as *so very anxious to see her* on this occasion, that she came particularly early to secure that gratification." No, that isn't quite fair. The Journal quoted Mrs. Delany, "I am particularly sorry [that her visitors could not stay for the evening] on account of the Duchess Dowager of Portland, who is so good as to come to me in an evening, as she knows I am too infirm to wait upon her Grace myself: and she wishes so much to see Miss Burney. But she said she would come as early as possible, and you won't, I hope, want to go very soon?" There is nothing extraordinarily boastful in repeating a commonly polite speech like that one, which Mrs. Delany may have meant or may not, with equal likelihood. It is an unimportant matter anyway, worth recapitulating only because of Lady Llanover's description of Fanny which follows this outburst of spleen.

"The Duchess of Portland had a prejudice against female novel writers, which *almost* amounted to a *horror of them*, and the Editor's mother often told her that it was with the *greatest difficulty* that Mrs. Delany at last persuaded the Duchess of Portland to see Fanny Burney, whose power of amusing conversation and clever narrations, with exact imitation of the voice and manner of those she described, rendered her very entertaining; whilst her apparent humility, constant deference, and respectful attention in the presence of Mrs. Delany so much pleased and interested her that she was induced, *some time after* she had herself received Miss Burney, to gratify the latter, by obtaining the Duchess of Portland's *unwilling* consent to have the 'authoress of Evelina' presented to her. Mrs. Delany thought that she might thus have an opportunity of diminishing the prejudice of her friend against the class whom she then considered so undesirable as acquaintance in private life, and believing Miss Burney to be as timid and diffident as she was clever, she bestowed upon her that notice and encouragement which at the expiration of half a century appeared in print magnified, misstated, and finally misrepresented by its recipient as *chiefly* conferred by *herself* on *Mrs. Delany!*"

Yet there is certainly no hint of disproportionate patronage on Fanny's part. More enthusiastic reverence for Mrs. Delany couldn't have escaped servility. If Lady Llanover had been of her generation, in a position to feel jealous, it might be some explanation for her enmity, but she was much younger. She published her memoirs of her aunt more than a century after Fanny was born, more than a decade after Fanny died. How is one to account for this bitter attack? Snobbery is not enough of a reason.

The answer is that Lady Llanover inherited her mother's feud with Fanny. Mrs. Waddington, her mother, was Georgina Mary

Anne Port, daughter of Anne Dewes, daughter of Anne Granville, Mary Delany's sister. Georgina Mary Anne Port was a little girl who lived most of the time with her great-aunt when Fanny made friends with the old lady. Miss Port's friendship with Fanny and with Dr. Burney was carried on after Mrs. Delany's death and was a warm and fast one for many years, but in the course of time the fervor of her relations with Fanny ebbed away. When Fanny went to court, Miss Port became acquainted with one of His Majesty's equerries and perhaps fell in love with him, and he with her. Fanny for some reason—probably some older relation of Miss Port's got at her—discouraged the romance, writing long pompous letters of high-flown advice to the girl, and no doubt interfering at the other end as well. Miss Port felt resentment, though she conquered her feelings at the time and allowed Fanny to influence her even further, by approving her prudent marriage with the much older Waddington. Perhaps G.M.A. was not happy with Waddington and sighed all her life after the equerry; perhaps she talked freely about these things, when she was an old lady, to her youngest daughter Lady Llanover. We do not know; we know only that a definite break took place years later, shortly before Fanny's death. The manifest cause was a cold, unimpassioned quarrel over their correspondence. G.M.A. demanded all her letters back, after more than fifty years of corresponding; she may have feared that Madame d'Arblay would publish them, but more likely she was just a peevish old lady, harking back to the grievance of her youth. Whatever it was, she died very angry with Fanny, and Lady Llanover took from her failing hand the torch.

Now let us go back again, a long, long way, to 1783.

There is an obvious disadvantage to living one's entire life, as Fanny attempted to do, in the company of one's elders, for Death he taketh all away. Poor Fanny, who was to outlive even her own generation, was subjected time after time to painful, final partings with people in whom she had invested much of her affection. Old Mrs. Delany, when she selected her companions from the young, chose the better part; the bitterness was left to Fanny, who tasted the first real woe of her life when she lost Daddy Crisp.

"I am much more afflicted than surprised at the violence and duration of your sorrow," wrote Dr. Burney to his daughter at Chesington. She was there when Crisp died; she stayed on to help the housekeeper settle his affairs. Charles Burney felt moved to caution her strongly against too much indulgence in grief. "As something is due to the living," he reminded her, "there is, perhaps, a boundary at which it is right to endeavour to stop in lamenting the dead." But it was two months before Fanny was able to resume the Journal. Crisp had been her chief reason for keeping it, and the adjustment of doing without her favorite audience was difficult. Habit was strong, however, and June 19, 1783, saw the first entry after her loss, with Susan now her sole "auditor." Though it recorded the forecast of another bereavement—Dr. Samuel Johnson had just suffered a severe paralytic stroke—Fanny was back to normal.

This does not mean that she was unchanged. The death of Crisp wrought in Fanny something obscure but important. From that time on she accepted with more resignation the fact that she was a woman, standing, as all adults must stand, alone.

There was always to be a nostalgic longing in her nature for support and advice, but with the disappearance of old Crisp, her staunchest friend and critic, she learned that she must and could, withal reluctantly, make decisions for herself.

For example, the time was coming when an important decision must be made regarding Mrs. Thrale. Crisp's death had followed close on an affecting farewell between the ladies, on the occasion of Hester Thrale's departure from town; that departure was the result of a series of stormy scenes in the Thrale residence. It is necessary here to go back some weeks, before the catastrophe of Crisp's death fell on Fanny.

"Adieu to all that's dear, to all that's lovely. I am parted from my Life, my Soul! my Piozzi: Sposo promesso! Amante adorato! Amico senza equale." These passionate lines were written by a woman who had always boasted that she knew nothing of love.

What happened must be pieced out from the gaps and hints in her record and from Fanny's letters to Queeney, for Mrs. Thrale excised pages of *Thraliana* which referred to this period.

First, Crutchley came "to *conjure me* not to go to Italy: he had heard *such* things he said. . . . The next day Fanny Burney came, said I must marry him instantly, or give him up; that my Reputation would be lost else——"

And yet all this scandal boils down to the fact that Mrs. Thrale had received Piozzi for private interviews throughout the winter, and her servants, in gossiping, had given the most calumnious interpretation possible to these meetings. There was no proof, but eighteenth-century society, like most society, did not ask for proof. At that it was probably not a glaring scandal, not yet. But it was enough to give Crutchley the grounds for grievance he wanted, in his capacity as executor, and it was enough to scare the neurotically conventional Fanny Burney. It also afforded Queeney ample chance to indulge her negatively filial emotions.

Queeney's "cold dislike" of Piozzi had not worn away. "No: her Aversion increased daily, & she communicated it to the others; they treated *me* insolently, and *him* very strangely—running away whenever he came as if they saw a Serpent: . . ." Her mother's hysterics failed to move Miss Thrale. If her mother *would* abandon her children, she said, she *must*. Her father had not deserved such treatment, said Queeney (did she mean his memory?); she said Piozzi in his heart hated Mrs. Thrale and she would live to regret having turned out her children like so many puppies for the drowning. For her own part, said Queeney, she would have to look herself out a place like the other servants, for she would never again see her mother's face.

"Nor write to me?" asked Mrs. Thrale piteously.

"I shall not, madam, easily find out your address; for you are going you know not whither I believe."

The small children burst into tears and lamentations. There was no standing *that*, said the distracted Mrs. Thrale. . . . After a night of weeping and prayers, she flew to Queeney's room to tell her that she would not marry Piozzi.

A sort of compromise was reached. Mrs. Thrale gave up the proposed trip abroad, but insisted, to the executors, upon leaving London and living at Bath, where she could save money to pay off her debt. She would not be her own mistress until she was clear. "They made little or no Reply, and I am resolved to do as I declared. I will draw in my Expences, lay by ev'ry Shilling I can to pay off Debts & Mortgages, and perhaps; who knows! I may in six or seven Years be freed from all Incumbrances; and carry a clear Income of 2500£ a Year, and an Estate of 500£ in Land to the Man of my Heart." All this, of course, in the event that Piozzi should not weary of waiting in the meantime and marry someone else.

"The Newspapers have been Insolent about me & Piozzi, but nobody gave Credit to them; so the Report had I think died away, & his Absence, (for he is going to Italy) will confirm the World in an Opinion that all was Invention."

On April sixth Piozzi and Mrs. Thrale said good-by. "God give me Strength to part with him courageously; I expect him every Instant to breakfast with me for the *last Time*. Gracious Heaven what words are these! Oh No, for Mercy: may we but meet again! and without diminished Kindness—Oh my Love! my Love!"

The Thrale family was leaving London for Bath in a few days' time, and the final interview was carefully chaperoned, at Mrs. Thrale's prudent suggestion, by an Italian friend of Piozzi's. "When all was over I flew to my Dearest loveliest Friend my Fanny Burney, & poured all my Sorrows into her tender Bosom," wrote Mrs. Thrale.

"My dear Mrs. Thrale spent all the morning in my room with me," was Fanny's version. ". . . nothing but the recollection of how narrowly I had escaped losing her for a longer time, and at a greater distance, could have made me bear it with sufficient composure for observation. As it was, however, I took it cheerfully enough, from the contrast of the great evil."

Then Daddy Crisp's death overwhelmed Miss Burney, and for some months she paid little attention to the scorched Mrs. Thrale, put away and left to cool in Bath, as she hoped, like a brand snatched from the burning.

It was at this point that the events occurred which gave rise to the furious controversy about Mrs. Thrale's behavior. Before the exodus for Bath, her two young daughters, Harriet and Cecilia, had contracted whooping cough in their boarding school in Streatham. Their mother realized the illness was serious: she commented spitefully that her three other daughters "who bear every one's Misfortunes (except their own) with Christian Patience; will not break their Hearts at the Accumulation of Fortune such an Event would put them in Possession of." (Thrale's will decreed that if any one of his daughters died her fortune should be divided among the others.) Mrs. Thrale was accustomed to losing her children. Certainly her troubled love affair was much more on her mind than were Thrale's daughters, though why this fact should call down such hot, angry condemnation on her long-dead head is a mystery. We do not command our secret desires. It may be unnatural to prefer one's lover to one's children by an unloved man, but if we accept this tenet, and dub Mrs. Thrale unnatural, surely that should be enough.

Unnaturally, then—but unhappily nevertheless—Mrs. Thrale set up housekeeping in Bath and counted her chances of getting out of debt sooner than she had first reckoned. Two years, perhaps? It might be possible. . . . "My daughter does not I suppose much delight in this Scheme, but why should I lead a Life of delighting her who would not lose a shilling of Interest, or an Ounce of Pleasure to save my Life from perishing? when I was near losing my Existence from the Contention of my Mind, and was seized with a temporary Delirium in Argylle Street, She & her two eldest Sisters laughed at my distress, and observed to dear Fanny Burney— that it was monstrous droll: She could scarcely suppress her Indignation.——"

That last sentence might have been wishful thinking. Fanny

had written to Queeney, "I am sorry too at my very Heart for you,
—I thought you looked pale & miserable—Good God of Heaven
how dreadful in all its circumstances & in all its consequences is
this unhappy infatuation!" But Mrs. Thrale still thought Fanny
staunchly on her side, if not on the Piozzi question, at least in
regard to Queeney. "Would some happy Event might send her
hither," she wrote, "for 'tis dismal to have no one to speak to;
and my Misses have . . . destroyed all friendly Commerce between them and me, who live more on Terms of Politeness than
Affection, agreeing however by a sort of tacit Compact never to
pronounce his Name who caused our disagreement.

"Jealous without Love, they hate even Miss Burney because I
like her Company; tho' I cannot accuse them of desiring to en-
gross mine, for never when they can avoid it do they come within
my sight."

Dr. Johnson was still in ignorance of her love affair, and no one
dared tell him. He was ostensibly on the same intimate terms with
her that had obtained for years, though she admitted that she had
gone to Bath as much to rid herself of her old "inmate" as for
purposes of economy. She was far too disturbed to exercise any
patience at all, and Johnson could try saintly patience, let alone
her limited quantity. The old man, in spite of his stoic principles,
often allowed himself (though not his friends) a considerable
amount of expressed repining. He wrote a petulant letter to Bath,
accusing his mistress of neglect.

At the same time as she got his note she received an urgent
summons to the Streatham school. She had hitherto refused to
visit the girls, fearing to catch their whooping cough. Now the
youngest child, Harriet, had died, and Cecilia's condition was grave.
Mrs. Thrale wrote hastily to Johnson:

"My Children, my Income (of course) and my health are coming to an end Dear Sir—not my vexations. Harriet is dead, and
Cicely is dying; and Mr. Cator writes me word I mustn't sit *philo-
sophically* at Bath, but come to London—(I cannot guess for
what) to see them buried I believe.—I am already so altered that

the people here don't know me—my *Philosophy* has not therefore benefited my Complexion at least—but like Tasso one should learn from it to bear with *them*. I am sorry for you dear Sir with all the Grief I can spare from your much distressed Servant H.L.T. Sat. Morng. I have just taken a Vomit, & just received your Letter; I will set out the first Moment I am able."

Certainly this is a shocking letter. If there are readers who maintain that nature in the raw is never shocking, then we must repeat that Mrs. Thrale was unnatural. She was unnaturally frank as well. She grieved for the living Piozzi; she resented those children who kept her from her lover; a black pot accusing a kettle, she resented Queeney's coldness at the news of her little sister's death. . . . "Harriett is dead, my other Girls Fortunes increased, their Insolence extream, and their hardness of Heart astonishing: When the Baby was to be moved to Streatham for the Air—it will kill her said I—— She will be nearer the Church Yard replied the eldest, coldly.

"My poor Piozzi was ill in Consequence of his Agitation I guess; a sore Throat Pepys said it was, with four Ulcers in it: the People about me said it had been lanced, & I mentioned it slightly before the Girls,—— Has he cut his own Throat? says Miss Thrale in her quiet Manner. This was less inexcusable because She hated *him*, & the other was her Sister: . . ."

Cicely recovered, incidentally, and lived to become one more bone of contention in that unhappy family.

The solace of seeing Piozzi in London, before he left, and of meeting Fanny, was denied Mrs. Thrale. Piozzi was prudent and would not risk fresh scandal; dear Miss Burney was out of town, at Crisp's bedside. Mrs. Thrale returned to Bath and began to urge Fanny, vainly, to come and visit her. She needed solace, she felt; Piozzi was at last gone to the Continent, and the two years of waiting stretched ahead of her, long and barren. Indeed she needed solace . . . For Harriet? After describing her child's symptoms and death, Mrs. Thrale did not again speak of Harriet. An unnatural woman, but no hypocrite.

12. MILD COMPLACENCY

O
H 'TIS a pleasant Situation! & whoever would wish as the Greek Lady phrased it *to teize himself & repent of his Sins:*—let him borrow his Children's money, be in Love against their Interest & Prejudice, forbear to marry by their Advice;—and then shut himself up and live with them.——"

After fuming and pitying herself at Bath for five months, Hester Thrale decided that her troubles had turned her blood "scorbutical." She tried the sea bathing at Weymouth, but in vain; everything was in vain; the times were out of joint, and she kept resenting her daughters and suspecting family plots against her. These suspicions were justified, but she carried them too far: she thought the girls were conspiring with the world to kill her outright.

Again she sighed for Fanny, and wrote a letter urging her to come to Bath. In the meantime Fanny's secret correspondence with Queeney was flourishing.

"You do me but justice in relying upon my inviolable secrecy & discretion, & I have known you too long & too intimately to have the least fear or doubt of yours," she wrote. ". . . Good God! what an infatuation has seized her! how strange, how incurable! Oh how much exultation should I have lost, had I foreseen this

Time when you came to me with the joyful news that *All was over!*——

"You tell me you *know* she is *determined to marry him.* Trusted by her, however much against my will, I must never have told you this, but at the same Time, I cannot deny it: She never writes without confirming it, though I always pretend not to understand her, & have repeatedly entreated that if she will not listen to my advice, she will forbear telling me her designs."

Seward, the old family friend, came to Bath. Though first in sympathy with Mrs. Thrale, he was soon enlisted by Queeney to line up against the projected marriage. He speedily outstripped the girls in his hostility to the notion, and frightened Queeney as well as Mrs. Thrale by his violence. The Piozzi affair is remarkable throughout for the third-party passions it aroused: Seward actually went crazy soon afterward. As for Fanny Burney, she became, purely and simply, hysterical, and her hysteria increased with every letter. "Dr J. *knows* of this horrible affair!" she wrote Queeney. " . . . He does not, however, know its *present* state, but concludes it is all over. O would it were!—The dread this news has given me of his Sight is inexpressible. I am sure I shall feel & look as if a Culprit myself when I appear before him: . . . In what way he will take it, I know not,—Heaven forbid he should examine me upon it!—Is it not terrible that I should now be *ashamed* of being the chosen friend of one in whose friendship I so lately gloried? . . .

"Mr. Seward urges me vehemently to go to Bath—but what can I do there? I have *no* weight in fact, though I seem to have the greatest. Dear, lost, infatuated Soul!—she calls upon me for-ever; & yet never listens to me when called. But come I will, the moment it is in my power, though with no view but to let her open her loaded bosom into my unwilling Ears. . . .

"Her reputation must be utterly gone, if P. should come to England, for this year's scheme, since I am *certain* they would meet eternally; and no innocence in the World could support her character, after all that has passed, if they have any further interviews

. . . let us . . . unite all that we can to save her at least from what so horribly threatens harm—I mean *despair*—as to *ruin*,—I fear it is but the other alternative!"

Hysteria mounted on all sides and infected Thrale's daughter, Sophia, who suddenly began to throw fits. "She will die without a Disease," wailed her mother, "—Fits, sudden, unaccountable, unprovoked; Apoplectic, lethargic like her Father . . . I saved her in the first Attack, by a Dram of fine old Usquebough given at the proper Moment—it reviv'd her, but She only lives I see to expire with fresh Struggles.

"Oh spare my Sophia, my Darling, oh spare her gracious heaven —& take in Exchange the life of her wretched Mother!

"She lives, I have been permitted to save her again; I rubbed her while just expiring, so as to keep the heart in Motion: She knew me instantly, & said you warm *me* but are killing *yourself*— I actually was in a burning Fever from exertion, & fainted soon as I had saved my Child."

In the general turmoil, Queeney and her mother temporarily made up. Possibly, while luxuriating in reconciliation, Queeney was incautious enough to hint at her correspondence with Fanny. Anyway, Mrs. Thrale at last scented something. "I am sometimes ready to think Fanny Burney treacherous," she wrote, "but tis a sinful Thought & must not be indulged——"

Sophia's illness brought triumph to Mrs. Thrale. Queeney withdrew her objections to the marriage. "She now saw my Love of Piozzi was incurable She said, Absence had no Effect on it, and my Health was going so fast She found, that I should soon be useless either to her or him.——"

Happy Mrs. Thrale rushed off to write Piozzi to come and get her, and unhappy Queeney went to her desk with equal alacrity, to inform Fanny.

"Oh Miss Thrale!—" cried Fanny, "what a conclusion to all the scenes of wretchedness we have undergone!" Nothing about the plans gave her any comfort. Even the fact that Mrs. Thrale intended to leave England was blameworthy. "What I now most wish,—*if* she marries him, I should wish her not to leave this Country,—I fear you will object to this,—but indeed it appears to me better than a banishment in her present state of Health. The disgrace to you will in nothing be prevented by her living in Italy,—her sufferings, depend upon it, will be *dreadful*, though she foresees them not . . . if she stayed in England, you could see her *sometimes*, & hear from her often, & know how she was treated, & soften, hereafter, her decline of life. The World believe me, would all *reverence* your *notice* of her by & by, though now it will unite in opinion that she forfeits all claim to it . . . all that you can do for your poor fallen Mother will be all to your own Honour."

The poor fallen mother recovered her health at a speed remarkable to behold. Her indelicate jubilation must have been rather hard for Fanny to take. Could it be that sin and shame were about to triumph? No, no: it was too early to despair. Retribution would surely overtake the wretched woman in good time. One hoped, of course, for friendship's sake, that she would be spared, but still, as a matter of principle and example, it was necessary and inevitable that Mrs. Thrale should suffer horribly, the poor soul. One could only wait and see.

In the meantime one must at all costs avoid going to Bath, though poor Mrs. Thrale's invitations were embarrassingly pressing.

"My Bath journey, my dear Susy, I know not what to say about," wrote Fanny: "could I go for one fortnight nothing could so much rejoice me; for I even languish, I pine to see again my beloved and very—oh, very unhappy Mrs. Thrale! I know well the meeting, as things are at present situated, would half kill her with joy, and me with a thousand feelings I keep off as well as I can; but I cannot tell how to arrange matters for this purpose. The expense of such an expedition, for so short a time, I know not how even to name to my father, who has a thousand reasons against my going, all founded on arguments unanswerable."

A thousand reasons seems excessive when one good one would answer, but Fanny must have felt uneasy in the region of her

conscience, without knowing exactly what ailed her. It is difficult
not to dislike Miss Burney at this crisis in her life, but obviously
she cannot be judged from our point of view. She was born two
hundred years ago, in a caste-ridden age, and throughout her lifetime she was rendered uneasy by having risen out of her caste,
thanks to her father's and her own talents. And it was not only
a slight social maladjustment which troubled Fanny. In a boister-
ous, outspoken age she was out of place, a forerunner of the Victorian ladies who hated and feared the more painful aspects of
nature. Sophy Streatfeild, for all her simpering and her delicate
airs, was tougher than Fanny and more fitted to cope with their
world; she showed her sense of this strength by ignoring society's
opinion in a manner which always took away Fanny's breath and
startled even the insensitive Mrs. Thrale. Fanny dared not thus
ignore the world. Her overwhelming desire was always to conform.
She wanted to be secure as a child in its cradle, or in the womb.
She never cared for financial security as much as she did for the
more primitive safety of the world's approval.

She was a sorely troubled and confused woman as she listened
eagerly to her father's dissuasions and did not go to her friend at
Bath. She poulticed her conscience with long letters in pious vein
to Queeney; she pounced eagerly on all evidence that Mrs. Thrale
was distraite and unhappy at Piozzi's tardy reply to her summons.
There is something very funny in the sight of a music master's
daughter making such a song and dance, on purely snobbish
grounds, about her best friend's engagement to another music master, but she would have talked her way out of the accusation. It
was not merely Piozzi's calling, she would have insisted; it was
that Mrs. Thrale was forgetting her duty to her children; it was
that Piozzi was a foreigner and a Roman Catholic; it was—in sum,
it was that the world would not approve.

Fortunately for the young novelist's general spirits, the world,
that all-powerful world, had lately given two charming proofs of
its complete approval of herself. Young Mr. Hoole in his poem

Aurelia, or the Contest—that same poem which spoke of Sophy Streatfeild tending Dr. Collier's deathbed—gave Fanny these lines:

> I stood, a favouring muse, at Burney's side,
> To lash unfeeling Wealth and stubborn Pride,
> Soft Affectation, insolently vain,
> And wild Extravagance, with all her sweeping train;
> Led her that modern Hydra to engage,
> And paint a Harrel to a maddening age;
> Then bade the moralist, admired and praised,
> Fly from the loud applause her talent raised.

A few years before, Fanny would have been in an agony of self-consciousness over that celebrity; now she was simply proud of it, and did not fly at all from the loud applause her talent raised. Then there was Miss Hannah More's poem, Bas Bleu, with its lines on "Attention," which were perhaps intended to represent Miss Burney: at least so her friends said:

> This charm, this witchcraft? 'tis ATTENTION;
> Mute Angel, yes; thy looks dispense
> The silence of intelligence;
> Thy graceful form I well discern,
> In act to listen and to learn;
> 'Tis Thou for talents shalt obtain
> That pardon Wit would hope in vain;
> Thy wondrous power, thy secret charm,
> Shall Envy of her sting disarm;
> Thy silent flattery soothe our spirit,
> And we forgive eclipsing merit;
> The sweet atonement screens the fault,
> And love and praise are cheaply bought.
>   With mild complacency to hear,
> Tho' somewhat long the tale appear,—
> 'Tis more than Wit, 'tis moral Beauty,
> 'Tis Pleasure rising out of Duty.

What with all this reassurance, the fleeting sensation of being a bad, disloyal friend to Mrs. Thrale did not overpower our heroine. Anyway, Bath was out of the question. She was happily far too busy these days in London, with new friends, to go away. First there was Mrs. Delany, at whose home she met Miss Hamilton, a niece to Sir William Hamilton; her pedigree and ladylike ways impressed Fanny very much. "Miss Hamilton, formerly companion to the Princess Royal, but lately resigned, on account of disliking the confinement of the Court," wrote Fanny to Queeney, when discussing the future establishment of the Thrale girls, "has joined her income with that of three ladies, the Miss Clarkes, & they all live together in Clarges Street. . . . They are all acquainted with people of the first fashion, Miss Hamilton, indeed, being nearly related to Sir William, to Lady Stormont, & several families of distinction. . . . Something of this sort I should think might be very eligible to you. . . ."

This highborn young lady was practically always with Mrs. Delany. Fanny prized the acquaintance and sought successfully to improve it. By the time she ate her second dinner *chez* Delany, Miss Burney had learned to take a rather lofty view of her companions. "Lady Dartmouth . . . seems a very plain, unaffected, worthy woman," she said artlessly. Her attitude was less humble than Dr. Burney's approach to glittering circles, which was just as well, for in good time Fanny was to climb higher than any of his patrons.

Other new friends were the Lockes of Norbury Park. Locke was a wealthy art amateur. His wife "Fredy" took Mrs. Thrale's place in Fanny's heart, and his house, similarly, was adopted as a substitute for Streatham. Norbury Park was not very far from Chesington. Norbury was much more convenient, after all, than Bath. And Mrs. Thrale was becoming even more awkward, if possible, than before; she had now actually announced her intention of staying on in Bath after marrying Piozzi. This was another sad shock to Fanny, whose suggestion that the sinful woman remain in England had been based on quite other hopes: the Piozzi couple should in all propriety hide themselves, she felt, in some quiet out-of-the way place like, say, a Devonshire village. For all the love Fanny felt for Mrs. Thrale, she never seems to have understood that lady's character very well.

The awful day was drawing near. Piozzi had at last shown life, in spite of all the Thrale well-wishers' hopes that he would let her down, and the wedding was scheduled for June. Long and agitated were the letters Fanny wrote to Queeney; the correspondence was not interrupted by the fact that Queeney's mother came to London for a visit in May and saw her dearest Fanny every day. "She looked far better than I expected,—but the accounts she gave me of her past agonies made her recovery from them no inducement to risk renewing them. Her passions are, indeed, too strong for control unless she voluntarily undertook to govern them herself."

Dr. Johnson knew. One day the Burneys, father and daughter, called on the sick old man in Bolt Court, and the very minute Dr. Burney went away, leaving the tremulous Fanny alone with the sage, it happened. There was an awful silence, and what followed, even in Fanny's worst old-lady style, even in her Memoirs, has a tremendous effect. "The Doctor, then, see-sawing violently in his chair, as usual when he was big with any powerful emotion whether of pleasure or of pain, seemed deeply moved; but without looking at her, or speaking, he intently fixed his eyes upon the fire: while his panic-struck visitor, filled with dismay at the storm which she saw gathering over the character and conduct of one still dear to her very heart, from the furrowed front, the laborious heaving of the ponderous chest, and the roll of the large, penetrating, wrathful eye of her honoured, but, just then, terrific host, sate mute, motionless, and sad; tremblingly awaiting a mentally demolishing thunderbolt.

"Thus passed a few minutes, in which she scarcely dared breathe: while the respiration of the Doctor, on the contrary, was of asthmatic force and loudness; then, suddenly turning to her, with an air of mingled wrath and woe, he hoarsely ejaculated: 'Piozzi!' "

At last the marriage took place. Fanny, feeling she must make some public gesture of disapproval, returned to Norbury and wrote her new friend Miss Hamilton to underscore her actions: ". . . as she [Miss Hamilton] knew the uneasiness which dampt all my pleasure, even in the charming party at Hampton, I hope when she hears that the fatal termination of that suspence made me wish for nothing but to hasten into the country to recruit both my health and spirits, she will forgive my silence . . ."

The inevitable break was not long in coming. Miss Burney's conventional wedding letter did not satisfy the bride, who detected a lack of enthusiasm. She wrote Fanny to say so, but there was something else she refrained from mentioning: that she was still smarting from her recent discovery of the Fanny–Queeney correspondence. "She has played a false and cruel part towards me I find—stimulating my daughters to resist their natural Tenderness, & continue the steady refusal of a Consent wch alone cd have saved my Life:—Very severe in Miss Burney, & very unprovok'd— I wd not have serv'd her so."

Fanny said not a word in her Journal about having been found out. She merely quoted her dignified reply—her carefully considered, gently hurt, above all dignified reply. Mrs. Piozzi wrote again in more friendly terms, but after another exchange the correspondence stopped altogether.

With the departure of the Piozzis to Italy, the last vestige of the Streatham coterie disappeared and Hester's onetime intimate friends went their ways. Seward, gone mad, was confined. Crutchley never married. The lovely S.S. waited many long years for her clergyman, but Mrs. Vyse would not die, and Sophy waited in vain. Like Crutchley, she never married. She became a nervous wreck in her old age, who had made nervous wrecks of so many dignified churchmen. The Streatfeild family has a story that she had to cut short a visit she was making to a cousin in the country because the nightingales kept her from sleeping.

Queeney the cold and proud became colder and prouder as the

years went by. She continued to quarrel with her mother; an unedifying lawsuit of theirs dragged on for many months. At well past forty she married an admiral and became Lady Keith. Sophia——

But never mind Sophia and the others: what of Mrs. Piozzi? Did she do the proper thing and slip into oblivion, living the rest of her life in miserable obscurity? No, she didn't. Mrs. Piozzi bounced. She published, she traveled, she wrote lively letters to her friends, though not to Fanny, and she bounced continually.

"I hear of her often, & always of her happiness," Fanny wrote to Queeney. "Do you think it can be sincere? she used always to say she *knew* she must not complain, happen what might: & this recollection makes me always fear she is only flourishing."

Alas, though, for principle. Regrettable it may be, but Piozzi made a very good husband, and his wife really was happy. It was enough to confuse any moralizing novelist, but Fanny continued to hope. She had plenty of company. They waited a long time for vindication. At last they grew tired of waiting and turned to fresh scandals, and the name "Piozzi!" no matter how much scorn and hatred may once have been poured into it, was forgotten in London. Johnson died, and so after a long time did Piozzi, and so after another long time did his whirligig-tongued wife. They are dust with Fanny and Fanny's own foreign Roman Catholic husband. Only the letters remain, and the ancient, grotesque quarrel, which still smolders under the ash and leaps anew to flaming life with every publishing season.

December 20, 1784. "This day was the ever-honoured, ever-lamented Dr. Johnson committed to the earth. Oh, how sad a day to me!"

A quiet little extra on the outskirts of Dr. Johnson's deathbed scene—she waited hours on the staircase in his house the day before his death, in the vain hope of seeing him—Fanny asked herself why the good old man had such an extraordinary fear of dying. Had he known what lay in store for his reputation he might have been reconciled.

The next few years saw a Johnson boom. First there was Boswell's *Tour to the Hebrides*, and then there was Mrs. Thrale-Piozzi's *Anecdotes*, and it was soon common knowledge that Bozzy planned to bring out a complete *Life*—what would be called today a *definitive Life*—of the great man. Long before these literary offerings were out, the wits were rubbing their hands and chortling in glee at the prospect of so much flying fur and feathers. The uproar even reached Mrs. Delany's quiet little drawing room, although, as Lady Llanover put it, "Mrs. Delany never associated with Mrs. Thrale or Dr. Johnson, having a disinclination to make the acquaintance of the one and a *horror* of the occasional bursts of rudeness of the other: though as a moralist she honoured Dr. Johnson."

However, the old lady was not above a wicked chuckle at the doctor's expense. At least her friend Mrs. Boscawen did not scruple to copy down and send to Mrs. Delany an epitaph which was going the rounds, attributed to that senile wit and dandy, Soame Jenyns:

Here lies poor Johnson—Reader, have a care,
Tread lightly, lest you rouse a sleeping bear!
Religious, moral, gen'rous and humane
He was—but self-sufficient, rude, and vain;
Ill-bred and overbearing in dispute,
A scholar and a Christian, yet a brute.
Would you know all his wisdom and his folly,
His actions, sayings, mirth and melancholy,
Boswell and Thrale, retailers of his wit,
Will tell you how he wrote, and talk'd, and cough'd and spit!

Then the incomparable Peter Pindar produced a ridiculous *Town Eclogue*, in which he depicted Boswell and Mrs. Piozzi, the rival authors, fighting bitterly.

MADAME PIOZZI

. . . Good me! you're grown at once confounded tender
Of Doctor Johnson's fame a fierce defender:
I'm sure you've mentioned many a pretty story
Not much redounding to the Doctor's glory.
Now for a saint upon us you would palm him—
First murder the poor man, and then embalm him!

BOZZY

Well, Ma'am! since all that Johnson said or wrote,
You hold so sacred, how have you forgot
to grant the wonder-hunting world a reading
Of Sam's Epistle, just before your wedding;
Beginning thus, (in strains not form'd to flatter)
    "Madam,
        If that most ignominious matter
        Be not concluded"—

                                    Farther shall I say?
No—we shall have it from yourself some day,
To justify your passion for the Youth,
With all the charms of eloquence and truth.

MADAME PIOZZI

What was my marriage, Sir, to you or him?
He tell me what to do!—a pretty whim!
He, to propriety, (the beast) resort!
As well might elephants preside at court.
Lord! let the world to damn my match agree!
Good God! James Boswell, what's that world to me?
The folks who paid respect to Mistress Thrale,
Fed on her pork, poor souls! and swill'd her ale,
May sicken at Piozzi, nine in ten—
Turn up the nose of scorn—good God! what then? . . .

Mrs. Piozzi probably didn't mind that one. The cruelest cut of all this comment, for her, must have been Sayer's caricature called *Johnson's Ghost*, where a shadowy Sam says to Mrs. Piozzi:

> When Streatham spread its pleasant board,
> I opened learning's valued hoard,
>   And as I feasted, prosed.
> Good things I said, good things I eat,
> I gave you knowledge for your meat,
>   And thought th' account was closed.
>
> If obligations still I owed,
> You sold each item to the crowd,
>   I suffered by the tale.
> For God's sake, Madam, let me rest,
> No longer vex your quondam guest,
>   I'll pay you for your ale.

There is little or no Diary from Fanny's pen and very few letters left from the first half of 1785. Not that she was busy on a new novel or play, but she was spending more and more time with Mrs. Delany, interspersing her town program with visits to Norbury Park. She was surfeited with the old round, which reminded her of Mrs. Thrale. Besides, there was now fresh reason for going to Norbury. Her sister Susan Phillips, after living a year at Boulogne for the sake of her health, had been pronounced well enough to return to England. The Lockes never did things halfway: after adopting one Burney they were eager to get on with the job and adopt the whole family. The Phillipses, therefore, were now installed in a cottage at Mickleham, in the Locke pocket. Dr. Burney was another regular visitor to Norbury Park. During the past year the doctor had obtained the sinecure of a post as organist in the chapel of Chelsea Hospital; not particularly well paid, but it was a regular salary and the duties were not arduous.

Among new Burney acquaintances was the then celebrated Madame de Genlis, author of books which are now forgotten. As an important Frenchwoman of letters, Madame felt that she should become a close friend of Miss Burney, that important English-woman of letters. Lively Madame had arrived at her rather stuffy eminence (as tutor and counselor to the young ladies of the Orleans family) through a roundabout career, the history of which Fanny didn't know in the early days of their acquaintance. Later Miss Burney heard the story, or at least a highly embroidered part of it, and she was not only astonished, but terrified.

"I am indeed surprised," she wrote Queeney, "at your intelligence concerning Me de Genlis, though it has reached me from other quarters. I met with great & uncommon civilities from her, . . . I thought her wise, sagacious, unassuming & quiet: & when I saw her in private, I found her strikingly amiable, caressing & engaging."

The Diary editor gives the final comment, ". . . such tales, whether true or false, were forced into the unwilling ears of Miss Burney, that, to use her own words, 'notwithstanding the most ardent admiration of Madame de Genlis' talents, and a zest yet greater for her engaging society and elegantly lively and winning manners, she yet dared no longer come within the precincts of her fascinating allurements.' "

Madame de Genlis's reactions to this decision are not, unfortunately, on record. It would be interesting to know what a French lady of her background thought of such priggish behavior on the part of an eminent authoress no longer in the first blush of youth. We do know, however, what another eminent Frenchwoman said about Fanny eight years later; Madame de Staël and Madame de Genlis, without a doubt, would have agreed on that subject to the last word. Utterly fantastic, we can hear them saying; where, one asks oneself, could such a thing happen except in England?

Washing her hands of Madame de Genlis, Fanny hurried back to dear Mrs. Delany's exclusive little drawing room. Even Mrs. Delany, it must be admitted, was no prude, but then she was so very, very old that her reminiscences of a freer day took on an antiseptic quality, like Shakespeare's bawdy jokes today. The broader humor and franker speech of Queen Anne's reign must be excused in Queen Anne's contemporaries. . . . Besides, dear Mrs. Delany was perfect. Everybody knew it. The King and Queen themselves knew it, and thereby hung a tale.

Nearly a decade before, King George III and Queen Charlotte his wife had fallen into a pleasant intimacy with the Duchess Dowager of Portland and her old friend and crony Mrs. Delany. Anyone who, like Mrs. Delany, could remember the dowdy immorality of the earlier Georges might well have been amused by the spectacle of dowdy morality afforded by the present court. But if either the duchess or her friend entertained such irreverent thoughts, they never admitted it. The habit of awed respect which a royal George could command in court-trained ladies was far too strong to be broken at their venerable age. A king was a king, and if life at court was not very gay nowadays, well, it had not been exactly gay under George's grandfather either.

The royal family, with a generous handful of their enormous assortment of children, called at Bulstrode, the duchess's country seat, in full panoply; admired the duchess's china and shellwork and the chenille upholstery which Mrs. Delany had designed and executed, showed enthusiastic interest in the *Flora Delanica*; made the old ladies sit down now and then instead of keeping them constantly standing at attention; were charmed and charming. King George in surroundings like this was at his most likable. Though that year of his first visit—1776—he had just plunged his country into a disastrous war through stubborn bad judgment, he could put aside his worries, and those of the nation, in the family circle. They were grave worries. The unfortunate man lived under the tragic threat of insanity, and he knew it. He had already undergone one bad spell, and his life and diet were carefully ordered to avoid the risk of another attack. He ate simply, and the pleasures he permitted himself were those of an uninspired, respectable farmer—hunting, surveying good crops, listening to sweet but not too excitingly sweet music, playing with his children, and talking in platitude with his mental equals or inferiors, if any.

"He loved mediocrities," said Thackeray. "He was a dull lad brought up by narrow-minded people." Yet he was also courageous, conscientious, kindly, and in the last analysis pathetic. Grim terrors haunted his mind, and to avoid them he sought the company of genial extroverts among his equerries, or of horses, or of women too old or bovine to be disturbing.

His wife Charlotte's chief virtue in his eyes was probably that she was not like his mother. He had loved Lady Sarah Lennox but he had meekly married this obscure German princess instead, and in a way the marriage was successful: comfortable if not rapturous. They had a huge family and they always put on a gratifying show of propriety and homeliness. Charlotte's only claim to fame was her ugliness, but even that ugliness was not fantastic. There was nothing fantastic about Charlotte. She was completely commonplace.

Both King and Queen were stingy, and the capricious British public disliked them for that. It is true that the same public would have been the first to decry lavish extravagance on the part of their rulers. The nation was more accustomed to criticizing that sort of thing than this, yet perhaps the national heart would genuinely have preferred more glamour and a trifle less of the other extreme. It would be too much to say that George III and Charlotte cast a blight over the royal house of England which has lasted until today, but it is a fact that since the end of the eighteenth century the crowned heads of England have evaded beauty and chic, as if with deliberation. Any native prettiness which may impertinently make itself seen in a British queen or princess is ruthlessly suppressed, by tradition. The original sin is probably Charlotte's. Not that she tried to suppress her beauty, poor lady, she really had none to suppress, and she had a groping desire for it too; she manifested this in her love of jewels, which she wore in profusion and without the slightest taste. But Nature was against Charlotte. There is an old story in Weymouth, George III's favorite watering place. In his day there was a bathing woman, one of those whose duty it was to attend the bathing machines used by summer visitors, and this woman was notoriously ugly. One day the King, during the early stages of his final catastrophic mental breakdown, encountered her in the streets of Weymouth. She was wearing a broad-brimmed hat, and the King, whose well-known habit it was to walk about quite alone, suddenly leaned close to her face and pulled the hat up, peering at her features.

"Good God!" he cried. "Even uglier than the Queen!"

A description given by Mrs. Delany of her first expedition to take tea with the royal household at Windsor is a fair picture of the daily life and amusements of the royals at home. The Queen and two of the youngest princesses entertained the guests, in a drawing room of the castle, while music was played outside, under the window. At dusk the King and his seven sons came in and chatted for a bit, after which all the royals went out on the terrace for their daily walk of half an hour, when the public was free to come and watch the pageant, the guests staying indoors with ladies and gentlemen of the court. Afterward they all had tea, and the princes and princesses danced, until the King decided the musicians under the window—performers on hautboys and other wind instruments—were too tired to go on. Thereupon the party moved to the Queen's house across the great court, where a concert was given. "The Prince of Wales [then sixteen] and the Bishop of Osnaburg [a younger Prince, Frederick] began the ball, and danced a minuet better than I ever saw danced. Then the Prince of Wales danced with the Princess Royal, who has a very graceful agreeable air, but not a good ear. . . . The *delightful* little Princess Mary, [two years old] who had been a spectator all this time, then danced with Prince Adolphus [four] a dance of *their own composing*, and soon after all were dispersed."

Mrs. Delany had since become well acquainted with the young royals, and watched them grow, until by the time she made a friend of Miss Burney she knew most of the household problems, of which the Prince of Wales was an outstanding one. The King and Queen loved her for herself alone, not merely as the duchess dowager's friend. They showed this when the duchess died.

No one, Mrs. Delany included, had expected her to outlive her friend. That is one reason why she was not named in the will, and the omission left her considerably embarrassed. She had had to manage on little income all her life. Her first husband, Pendarves, had cheated her people by breaking his promise to leave her his money, and her second husband, Delany, was not rich. The widow kept up appearances, but her custom of spending six months of every year at Bulstrode with the duchess had saved her a good deal of expense, and now that assistance was gone. She was proud, though; she refused any help from her friend's family, though the Duke of Portland quite properly offered to do whatever he could and begged her to continue to use Bulstrode as a country residence. Then the King and Queen took a hand.

Soon after Mrs. Delany rallied from the first shock she received a message that the King owned a house near the castle gate at Windsor which he wished to give Mrs. Delany as a country residence. To help support the expense of two establishments, he also bestowed on her a pension of three hundred pounds a year.

Until the move should be accomplished, Fanny Burney moved into the town house in St. James's Place to take care of the old lady, for the invaluable Miss Hamilton had departed to be married, and Mrs. Delany's great-niece, Miss Port, was still too young to be much of a mainstay. "At first I slept at home," said Fanny, "but going after supper, and coming before breakfast, was inconvenient, and she has therefore contrived for me a bed-room."

She was thus plunked down in the middle of all the preparations for Mrs. Delany's debut in a new role at the age of eighty-five; that of royal household pet. There were thousands of little things to do. Mrs. Delany spent a good deal of time with Fanny, as she had done with Miss Hamilton before, sorting out all the correspondence and souvenirs she had collected in her long life. It was a formidable task and did not go quickly, for many a letter or scrap of paper (first examined by the old lady with a magnifying glass if she had any doubt about showing it to Fanny) called forth its reminiscence or started a lengthy discussion. Those were the days when people spared plenty of time for sentiment, and Fanny wrote, "Just now we have both of us been quite overset. In examining some papers in a pocket-book, she opened one with two leaves dried in it; she held them a little while in silence, but very calmly, in her hand, yet as something I saw she highly prized: she then bade me read what was written on the envelope;—it was, I think, these words—'Two leaves picked at Bolsover, by the Duchess of Portland and myself, in September 1756, the 20th year of our most intimate and dear friendship.' I could hardly read to her the last words, and, upon hearing them, for a little while she sunk."

The King threw himself with delight into the sort of pastime he preferred to all others. Bustling about, hurrying the workmen in Mrs. Delany's house and discussing the furnishings with the Queen, was a pleasant relief. George III brooded dangerously over the American Revolution and his unsatisfactory sons; knowing the danger that lay in wait for his weak mind, he had practically retired to Windsor to live. His life, always dull and monotonous, was even more safely so here; he hunted or rode in the mornings, in the long afternoons he read to the Queen while she worked on her tasteless embroidery, and in the evenings there was always the solemn little family parade on the terrace, followed by a concert of Handel's music. Now his program was gently varied, by the benevolent puttering little jobs involved in preparing Mrs. Delany's house. The old lady was to bring nothing to her new home, said her royal patrons, but herself and her clothes. Everything else—plate, china, glass, linen, wine, sweetmeats, even pickles —was provided, with careful attention to detail, by King George and Queen Charlotte.

It was very kind of them, and also very funny, though nobody said so. Perhaps if George III had been allowed to keep a hotel instead of a kingdom, he would have been a sane man until his death. Certainly he would have been a good hotelkeeper.

Fanny Burney heard all about his kindness until Mrs. Delany was safely embarked for Windsor and the royal pickle jars. Then she departed on a modest round of visits, having promised eagerly to come soon for a sojourn in the Windsor gatehouse with her dear old lady. The prospect of coming within the royal orbit abashed her somewhat. Had she known what schemes on her behalf Mrs. Delany was hatching in her courtier's brain, Miss Burney would have been less precipitate in keeping her promise.

13. NEITHER MORE NOR LESS THAN A BELL

Miss Burney was later to declare solemnly that in her position at court she considered herself married, so it is quite in order to call Mrs. Delany the matchmaker, or go-between. Cleverly she contrived it, telling the King and Queen how intelligent her little friend Miss Burney was, and how sweet and helpful, and how virtuous, then telling Fanny how often the royal pair spoke of her and how they said at last that they must have a look at this paragon. Fanny, arriving at Windsor, found the Delany household well settled in, living in a permanent haze of grateful awe. Little Miss Port whispered, to thrill her, that all the princesses intended to come and see Fanny; Mrs. Astley, maid to Mrs. Delany, walked around beatified with gratification, and the mistress herself might have given some special sign of happy awareness of all this glory had she not been ill. Being the royal pet was a strenuous task for a frail old lady. Even when she took to her bed she could not relax. She had to be very ill before the King or Queen were dissuaded from dropping in and being kind. As soon as she could get up after an illness one of the royal couple, or both, would immediately come in to drink tea for two hours. According to her reports to Fanny afterward, the royals talked either about the health of the children—one princess or another was usually ailing—or about Miss

Burney's works, this latter subject being introduced with regularity by the wily matchmaker.

It was some weeks before an introduction between the royals and Fanny was effected, which was Miss Burney's fault. It was no use for Mrs. Delany to reassure her palpitating guest, and give expert directions on how to behave with royalty, and extract Fanny's promise not to be an Evelina and run away when the dread moment arrived. As soon as the Queen was announced, Fanny ran away just the same. Mrs. Delany became a little irritable about it and reminded her that if this kept up the august pair would soon make a point of *sending for* Miss Burney. Sobered by this threat, Fanny promised to be good.

"I do beg of you," Mrs. Delany added, "when the Queen or the King speaks to you, not to answer with mere monosyllables."

Fanny was in the middle of a Christmas game next afternoon with a nephew of Mrs. Delany, his little daughter, and Miss Port. The venerable lady had just arrived among them in the drawing room from her after-dinner nap, when a large man dressed in mourning quietly walked in, shutting the door behind him without speaking. A star glittered on his black chest. Fanny stood silent, in terror. It was the King!

"Every one scampered out of the way: Miss Port, to stand next the door; Mr. Bernard Dewes to a corner opposite it; his little girl clung to me; and Mrs. Delany advanced to meet His Majesty, who after quietly looking on till she saw him, approached, and inquired how she did. . . .

"I had now retreated to the wall, and purposed gliding softly, though speedily, out of the room; but before I had taken a single step, the King, in a loud whisper to Mrs. Delany, said, 'Is that Miss Burney?—and on her answering 'Yes, sir,' he bowed, and with a countenance of the most perfect good humour, came close up to me."

Fanny gave a profound reverence; His Majesty asked how long she had been back; Fanny whispered the reply, which he didn't hear, and the first dread moment was over. While the King talked

The Parker Gallery, London

QUEEN CHARLOTTE OF GREAT BRITAIN
AND THE PRINCESS ROYAL

ROYAL HUNT IN WINDSOR PARK

THE PROMENADE IN ST. JAMES'S PARK

with Mrs. Delany, Fanny, in a rush of high spirits, due to relief, began whiling away the time with fancies. They looked, frozen in their places, as if they were playing puss in the corner, she reflected, or as if they were acting a play. She began assigning a part to each person in the room, and was suddenly brought back to herself by the King, who good-naturedly referred to the famous secret of *Evelina*. Dr. Burney had told of it, said the King:

"But what?—what?—how was it?"

"Sir?"

"How came you—how happened it—what?—what?"

Now Fanny had often been warned of the monarch's odd manner of speech, but the warning probably worked the wrong way around and tickled her risibilities rather than quieted them. She could not keep out of her mind "those vile *Probationary Odes*," amusing poems which had been anonymously published.

> *What?—what?—what?*
> *Scott!—Scott!—Scott!*

"But your publishing—your printing—how was that?" insisted the King.

Fanny mumbled something. She dared not speak aloud. She knew she was going to burst out laughing.

"What?" repeated His Majesty.

"I thought—sir," gasped Fanny, "it would look very well in print!"

"I do really flatter myself," she wrote later, "this is the silliest speech I ever made!"

Then the Queen arrived. Fanny's talent for remembering conversation, important or unimportant, had never served her so well. Every trivial word spoken by either of the royals on that occasion has been preserved in the Journal, and there was a good deal to report, for the King was in a chatty, gay mood and the Queen may possibly have been stimulated by the presence of a genuine novelist: at any rate she made wise, virtuous remarks and asked Fanny if she was never again to publish. It seemed a pity not to, she said, when one had such a power for doing good to young people. This was a surprising thing for Queen Charlotte to say, because she was usually inimical to novels, but Miss Burney and her works were admittedly exceptional. Mrs. Delany had laid her foundations carefully.

On a second meeting the King made a valiant effort to be literary. He spoke of a recent published biography, and of Madame de Genlis, who had just visited England, and of Voltaire. "I think him a monster," cried the King; "I own it fairly."

Rousseau was not quite such a monster, but the philosopher did not possess the King's favor. He was accused of "savage pride and insolent ingratitude." Here Fanny tried to spread a little oil on troubled waters, for "I know he had had a pension from the King, and I could not but wish His Majesty should be informed he was grateful to him . . .

" 'Some gratitude, sir,' said I, 'he was not without. When my father was in Paris, which was after Rousseau had been in England, he visited him, in his garret, and the first thing he showed him was your Majesty's portrait over his chimney.'

"The King paused a little while upon this; but nothing more was said of Rousseau."

His Majesty was more at ease on the subject of the drama. He spoke warmly in praise of Mrs. Siddons, though Fanny could not bring herself to agree, as she thought this famous actress slow and stately and stiff. Not being able or willing to argue with the King, she remained silent and let him continue his disjointed delivery of opinions. There were not enough good modern comedies, he complained, and most of the old ones were extremely immoral. (The royal family went often to the play, and preferred farces.)

" 'Was there ever,' cried he, 'such stuff as great part of Shakespeare? only one must not say so! But what think you?—What?— Is there not sad stuff? What?—what?'

" 'Yes, indeed, I think so, sir, though mixed with such excellences, that——'

" 'Oh!' cried he, laughing good-humouredly, 'I know it is not to be said! but it's true. Only it's Shakespeare, and nobody dare abuse him.'

"Then he enumerated many of the characters and parts of plays that he objected to; and when he had run them over, finished with again laughing, and exclaiming,

" 'But one should be stoned for saying so!' "

The Queen's conversation was more determinedly on the side of books. She discussed Madame de Genlis's *Adele,* and the *Sorrows of Werther,* which she couldn't bear, she said, because it was as Fanny suggested a "deliberate defence of suicide" and, what was worse, suicide done by a bad man for revenge. There followed the well-known remark by the Queen to the effect that she often picked up bargains from the bookstalls. "Oh, it is amazing what good books there are on stalls. . . . I don't pick them up myself; but I have a servant very clever; and if they are not to be had at the booksellers, they are not for me any more than for another.'

The subject of Klopstock's *Messiah* carried Her Majesty to a discussion of sacrilege, and of "the Roman Catholic superstitions."

" 'Oh, so odd! Can it signify to God Almighty if I eat a piece of fish or a piece of meat? And one of the Queen of France's sisters wears the heel of her shoe before, for a penance; as if God Almighty could care for that!' "

Fanny agreed: "It is supposing in Him the caprice of a fine lady."

Miss Burney was charmed with the discovery that she was not after all a complete deaf-mute and nitwit in the presence of such august personages. Such was her relief that she allowed herself some of the Burney humor of her girlhood. In a letter to her sister Hetty she gave lessons in court etiquette, which she entitled "Directions for coughing, sneezing, or moving before the King and Queen."

"In the first place, you must not cough. If you find a cough tickling in your throat, you must arrest it from making any sound; if you find yourself choking with the forbearance, you must choke —but not cough.

"In the second place, you must not sneeze. If you have a vehement cold, you must take no notice of it; if your nose-membranes feel a great irritation you must hold your breath; if a sneeze still insists upon making its way, you must oppose it, by keeping your teeth grinding together; if the violence of the repulse breaks some blood-vessel, you must break the blood-vessel—but not sneeze.

"In the third place, you must not, upon any account, stir either hand or foot. If, by chance, a black pin runs into your head, you must not take it out. If the pain is very great, you must be sure to bear it without wincing; if it brings the tears into your eyes, you must not wipe them off; if they give you a tingling by running down your cheeks, you must look as if nothing was the matter. If the blood should gush from your head by means of the black pin, you must let it gush; if you are uneasy to think of making such a blurred appearance, you must be uneasy, but you must say nothing about it. If, however, the agony is very great, you may, privately, bite the inside of your cheek, or of your lips, for a little relief; taking care, meanwhile, to do it so cautiously as to make no apparent dent outwardly. And, with that precaution, if you even gnaw a piece out, it will not be minded, only be sure either to swallow it, or commit it to a corner of the inside of your mouth till they are gone—for you must not spit."

Mrs. Delany, with all her courtier's art, advocated some sign of royal favor for her talented young friend. The Queen, though willing, was not sure how to help. Fanny hoped for a pension, the customary form of recognition from the country's rulers to an outstanding writer. The King had granted a pension to Dr. Johnson, Whig though he was, and to that almost-monster, Rousseau the freethinker. But Fanny Burney was a different proposition; they had never yet given a pension to a young lady novelist, and the King and Queen must have discussed such an innovation at length before other circumstances changed the trend of their ideas. Would it not be better to make her the Queen's reader, perhaps? The Queen at one time said in Fanny's presence that she had no

English reader. Or a governess of some sort, for one of the many princesses? Miss Burney was a virtuous person, and in addition she was pious, well-behaved, and all other things one would want a royal governess to be, except one: she was not well-born.

It is indeed difficult when one is Queen to satisfy everybody and to award places at court to all the people who clamor for them, especially when one happens to be a queen of very thrifty habits. How could Charlotte satisfy dear old Mrs. Delany and yet somehow make a profit from the transaction? Some advantage was necessary to counterbalance the envious complaints such an appointment would stir up. The affair continued to hang fire while the Queen talked to Fanny in Mrs. Delany's drawing room and the King addressed the little writer with his customary bluff, ejaculatory manner. It is a compliment to Fanny's tact that George III should have liked her, in spite of her very real intelligence. He wasn't afraid of her at all. Like any sporting squire, he went through the hasty ceremony in her presence of mentioning her work:—Are you writing anything these days? How do you get your ideas? Now don't you put me in a book!—and then it was clear sailing; obviously he felt it would be arrant nonsense to suspect such a demure little woman of possessing an awkward amount of brain power.

One May day after she was at home again, Fanny's father heard a piece of interesting news. The master of the King's band had just died. Charles Burney recollected that he had been promised the next vacancy for that position, but he didn't know how to go about reminding the powers of this promise. He asked the advice of his friend Mr. Leonard Smelt (unfortunate name!), the deputy governor to the young princes. Mr. Smelt told Burney he should go immediately to Windsor and be there on the south terrace in time for the evening walk of the royal family. He was not to speak to the King; that would be too direct an approach; "Take your daughter in your hand," said Mr. Smelt, "and walk upon the terrace."

Miss Port wrote Fanny on the same day, urging her to come to see Mrs. Delany, as the Queen expressly desired it. The Burneys were overjoyed at what they considered a strong hint that Dr. Burney's appointment was secure.

That evening Fanny and her father took tea at Mrs. Delany's and went with a party of acquaintances to the terrace. "The King and Queen, and the Prince of Mechlenburg, and Her Majesty's mother, walked together. Next them the Princesses and their ladies, and the young Princes, making a very gay and pleasing procession, of one of the finest families in the world. Every way they moved, the crowd retired to stand up against the wall as they passed, and then closed in to follow."

Fanny, like her father, felt uneasy, with the guilty embarrassment of a petitioner. She would have hidden herself in the crowd by pulling her wide-brimmed hat over her face, if Lady Louisa Clayton, a friend of Mrs. Delany, had not kept her close to herself in a prominent position in the crowd. The Queen stopped to speak to Lady Louisa and then had a few words with Miss Burney; the King followed and did the same. The publicity of the encounter made it an ordeal. Fanny blushed and stammered. "His condescension confuses, though it delights me," she said.

Alas for Dr. Burney's hopes; though his daughter was singled out for such honors, neither King nor Queen spoke to him at all. The King, it is true, bowed every time he passed, and the Queen curtsied; their silence, however, boded no good for the mastership. Any solicitation is hateful for the solicitor even when successful; it is worse when it fails. Sure enough; when they got home at eleven o'clock it was to find the news arrived ahead of them, that the Lord Chamberlain had promised the place to another man. "This was not very exhilarating," confessed Fanny.

The King and Queen probably realized that a shabby trick had been played on Charles; all the more reason, then, for doing something for Miss Burney. Then occurred an idea which relieved them of the expense of a pension, and perhaps also spared them public outcry for pensioning such a young woman. In their haste to be kind and economical, they never stopped to see that it was a grotesque notion. One of the Queen's Keepers of the Robes, an old lady, resigned in order to return to Germany, whence she had come with her royal mistress when Charlotte married. George and Charlotte resolved to bestow her place on Fanny Burney.

Mr. Smelt carried the preliminary offer to her at Mrs. Delany's house, and Fanny wrote an account of the proceedings afterward, in a letter to a friend. "You cannot easily, my dear Miss Cambridge, picture to yourself the consternation with which I received this intimation. It was such that the good and kind Mr. Smelt, perceiving it, had the indulgence instantly to offer me his services, first, in forbearing to mention even to my father his commission, and next in fabricating and carrying back for me a respectful excuse. And I must always consider myself the more obliged to him, as I saw in his own face the utmost astonishment and disappointment at this reception of his embassy."

As the modern reader might well wonder why even the missish Fanny should be so overcome by an offer like this, a few explanations are in order. Going into service to the Queen was the equivalent of taking the veil in some particularly strict religious order, without the compensations of the true *dévouée*. As a "Keeper of the Robes," or, as Lady Llanover persisted in calling her, a mere "dresser," Fanny would do the work of a lady's maid, but she would not have a maid's freedom to take an occasional holiday or to retain relations with the outside world. Once in the royal service, she would be cut off from all her old life. ". . . the confinement to the court continual;—I was scarce ever to be spared for a single visit from the palaces, nor to receive anybody but with permission,— . . . what a life for me, who have friends so dear to me, and to whom friendship is the balm, the comfort, the very support of existence!"

One might expect Mr. Smelt to have understood these hesitations, but Fanny was evidently ahead of her time in being aware of any disadvantages to glory. Mr. Smelt "expatiated warmly" on the sweetness of the royal character and begged her to consider what a very peculiar distinction was being shown an obscure, lowborn lady like herself. Unsolicited, unsought, this favor had been bestowed by the Queen herself. It was really, he urged, incredible. Merely because the Queen liked Fanny she intended to settle her with one of the princesses "in preference to the thousands of offered candidates, of high birth and rank, but small fortunes, who were waiting and supplicating for places. . . . Her Majesty proposed giving me apartments in the palace; making me belong to the table of Mrs. Schwellenberg, with whom all her own visitors—bishops, lords, or commons—always dine; keeping me a footman, and settling on me £200 a year. 'And in such a situation,' he added, 'so respectably offered, not solicited, you may have opportunities of serving your particular friends,—especially your father,—such as scarce any other could afford you.' "

Fanny was in a cleft stick. She deferred at last to her father's judgment, but he was simply overwhelmed with joy; he had no misgivings at all. Their fortunes were made, he felt sure: the disappointment of the mastership was completely wiped out.

Then the Queen sent for Fanny, desiring a personal interview, and the poor young woman gave up hope. The word "permanent" rang prophetically in her ear. Would the Queen propose a term of years? It was her last, forlorn hope. Anything that has a period is endurable, she reflected, but . . . "Could I but save myself from a lasting bond,—from a promised devotion!"

Macaulay's account is too sweeping: he said Fanny's whole world united in shoving her into court. Most people, though, did think it a good thing, as in many ways it certainly looked to be. The same arguments which had been used by Daddy Crisp to further Fanny's marriage with Mr. Barlow now applied even more strongly to a job at court. What else could possibly be done with Miss Burney? She was thirty-four and unmarried. She had made, all told, something less than three hundred pounds with her two astonishingly successful books—three hundred pounds in eight years. Scarcely a remunerative career, so far, and Fanny showed less and less signs of producing more books rapidly. For all her fame, she was dependent on her father, who was still grinding away, spending money as fast as he made it. Two hundred a year and all found, with a footman to herself, and high social position, and a chance of getting favors for all the other Burneys, though admittedly these favors were only vaguely sketched in the prospectus—it wasn't too bad.

Fanny was not a fool for accepting, and Dr. Burney was not a fatuous old snob for encouraging her to accept the offer, as Macaulay said. She couldn't very well have done anything else, anyway. It would have meant grievously hurting Mrs. Delany's feelings, offending the King and Queen, ruining any further chances of advancement, and probably estranging her father. There was no way out. The woman who had allowed the world to come between her best friend and herself was not the woman to stand out against the worldliest of temptations.

Reluctantly Fanny Burney went to see the Queen; less reluctantly, after that interview, she prepared for the great change.

"I rise at six o'clock, dress in a morning gown and cap, and wait my first summons, which is at all times from seven to near eight, but commonly in the exact half-hour between them.

"The Queen never sends for me till her hair is dressed. This, in a morning, is always done by her wardrobe-woman, Mrs. Thielky, a German, but who speaks English perfectly well.

"Mrs. Schwellenberg, since the first week, has never come down in a morning at all. The Queen's dress is finished by Mrs. Thielky and myself. No maid ever enters the room while the Queen is in it. Mrs. Thielky hands the things to me, and I put them on. 'Tis fortunate for me I have not the handing them! I should never know which to take first, embarrassed as I am, and should run a prodigious risk of giving the gown before the hoop, and the fan before the neck-kerchief.

"By eight o'clock, or a little after, for she is extremely expeditious, she is dressed. She then goes out to join the King, and be joined by the Princesses, and they all proceed to the King's chapel in the Castle, to prayers, attended by the governesses of the

Princesses, and the King's equerry. Various others at times attend; but only these indispensably.

"I then return to my own room to breakfast. I make this meal the most pleasant part of the day; I have a book for my companion, and I allow myself an hour for it. . . .

"At nine o'clock I send off my breakfast things, and relinquish my book, to make a serious and steady examination of everything I have upon my hands in the way of business—in which preparations for dress are always included, not for the present day alone, but for the court-days, which require a particular dress; for the next arriving birthday of any of the Royal Family, every one of which requires new apparel; for Kew, where the dress is plainest; and for going on here, where the dress is very pleasant to me, requiring no show or finery, but merely to be neat, not inelegant, and moderately fashionable.

"That over, I have my time at my own disposal till a quarter before twelve, except on Wednesdays and Saturdays, when I have it only to a quarter before eleven.

"My rummages and business sometimes occupy me uninterruptedly to those hours. When they do not, I give till ten to necessary letters of duty, ceremony, or long arrears;—and now, from ten to the times I have mentioned, I devote to walking.

"These times mentioned call me to the irksome and quick-returning labours of the toilette. The hour advanced on the Wednesdays and Saturdays is for curling and craping the hair, which it now requires twice a week.

"A quarter before one is the usual time for the Queen to begin dressing for the day. Mrs. Schwellenberg then constantly attends; so do I; Mrs. Thielky, of course, at all times. We help her off with her gown, and on with her powdering things; and then the hairdresser is admitted. She generally reads the newspapers during that operation.

"When she observes that I have run to her but half dressed, she constantly gives me leave to return and finish as soon as she is seated. If she is grave, and reads steadily on, she dismisses me, whether I am dressed or not; but at all times she never forgets to send me away while she is powdering, with a consideration not to spoil my clothes, that one would not expect belonged to her high station. Neither does she ever detain me without making a point of reading here and there some little paragraph aloud. . . .

"I find her then always removed to her state dressing room, if any room in this private mansion can have the epithet of state. There, in a very short time, her dress is finished. She then says she won't detain me, and I hear and see no more of her till bed-time.

"It is commonly three o'clock when I am thus set at large. And I have then two hours quite at my own disposal: but, in the natural course of things, not a moment after! . . .

"At five, we have dinner. Mrs. Schwellenberg and I meet in the eating-room. We are commonly *tête-à-tête*: when there is anybody added, it is from her invitation only. Whatever right my place might afford me of also inviting my friends to the table I have now totally lost, by want of courage and spirits to claim it originally.

"When we have dined, we go upstairs to her apartment, which is directly over mine. Here we have coffee till the *terracing* is over; this is at about eight o'clock. Our *tête-à-tête* then finishes, and we come down again to the eating-room. There the equerry, whoever he is, comes to tea constantly, and with him any gentleman that the King or Queen may have invited for the evening; and when tea is over, he conducts them, and goes himself, to the concert room.

"This is commonly about nine o'clock.

"From that time, if Mrs. Schwellenberg is alone, I never quit her for a minute, till I come to my little supper at near eleven.

"Between eleven and twelve my last summons usually takes place, earlier and later occasionally. Twenty minutes is the customary time then spent with the Queen: half an hour, I believe, is seldom exceeded.

"I then come back, and after doing whatever I can to forward my dress for the next morning, I go to bed—and to sleep, too, believe me: the early rising, and a long day's attention to new affairs and occupations, cause a fatigue so bodily, that nothing mental stands against it, and to sleep I fall the moment I have put out my candle and laid down my head."

The more one thinks this program over, the more extraordinary it becomes. In her wildest dreams Miss Frances Burney, talented novelist, daughter of a talented musician, could not have imagined herself spending every day in such fashion. Some other female novelists might reasonably be expected to cope with domestic tasks of this sort, but Fanny Burney—Fanny Burney who was so nearsighted she could never recognize acquaintances in the street, who was supremely disinterested in clothes, unique among her sex and her colleagues for never describing a heroine's attire nor so much as mentioning the look of a shawl or bonnet! Her appointment was a masterpiece of royal misjudgment, and the only explanation for the rejoicing of her friends at the bungle lies in their ignorance of the true conditions under which she was to live. We can forgive them, for the general public had always thought of court appointments in fairy-tale terms, all gold and diamonds, no real work at all. Under some monarchs this may be a true description of a courtier's life, but Queen Charlotte, like the careful German housewife she was, worked her attendants hard.

We must also excuse the King and Queen for their mistake, which was based on ignorance as deep as that of Fanny's circle. The royal pair had not the faintest conception of any life pattern but their own. They had always dwelt among attendants; they had always distributed places at court to eager, clamoring candidates. Such a life as Fanny's in St. Martin's Street, with its liberty of movement and constantly changing list of visitors and free-and-easy conversation, was totally foreign to their limited experience. Nor had they a notion of a writer's methods of work or his occupational peculiarities of temperament. One can imagine Charlotte's kind plans for her new Mistress of the Robes—"Between the short hours when she waits on me she will have all the time in the world to do her writings."

There was another important point. Had Charlotte not been a queen she might have discovered what queens are never supposed to notice, though housekeepers always know—that life among underlings is a tangle of intrigue, a jungle existence where the biggest bully comes out on top. In the Queen's Lodge the biggest bully, Mrs. Schwellenberg, retained her position by virtue of the Queen's favor. Charlotte demanded loyalty and blind devotion, and she repaid such offerings with a similar, if less absorbing, sentiment of loyalty in return. She was deliberately blind in her loyalty to Mrs. Schwellenberg. Had she wished to open her eyes, the Queen could easily have seen that Mrs. Schwellenberg made life miserable for everyone under her in the lodge. Mrs. Schwellenberg was stupid, jealous, spoiled, and sadistic. Sometimes these facts were delicately brought to Charlotte's attention, but the Queen would not understand the hints. She didn't want to see or to understand: it made for trouble. She found it far easier to remain ignorant.

Two ladies in waiting had accompanied the Princess Charlotte on that important marriage journey from Germany. Both had remained in faithful attendance all this time—Mrs. Schwellenberg, or Schwellenbergen, and Mrs. Haggerdorn. But Mrs. Haggerdorn at last fell by the wayside, her eyes hopelessly impaired by years of service and cruel treatment by Mrs. Schwellenberg. (Both ladies were unmarried. It was by reason of court etiquette that they were called "Mrs.")

Nobody who knew had the heart to warn Fanny in advance against this Mrs. Schwellenberg, the chief stumbling block to her comfort at court. The day she moved in—July 17, 1786—was painful enough without any such friendly warnings to add to her agitation. Walking from Mrs. Delany's house to the Queen's Lodge, a distance of only fifty yards, accompanied by her father, Fanny wept to such an extent that the happy man became alarmed, and for the first time, evidently, wondered if the appointment was such an unalloyed blessing after all. He stayed at the lodge in his daughter's apartments until she came back, reassured and quieted, from her interview with the Queen, and then it took all her powers of argument to cheer *him* up. She succeeded without undue effort, for Burney was always an optimist. He went away quite gay again.

"Everybody so violently congratulates me," Fanny wrote her sister Charlotte, now Mrs. Francis, of Norfolk, "that it seems as if *all* was gain. However, I am glad they are all so pleased. My dear father is in raptures; that is my first comfort."

The Reverend Mr. Twining, a very old friend of her father and herself, wrote a most amusing letter, quite bubbling over with merriment and hope. "Heaven bless you, for I am so pleased!" he said. Only one thing disturbed him a little—she might not have leisure, now, to write. Mr. Twining knew more about writing than did his Queen. "Another thing I am afraid of: when I come to town I shall never get a peep at you in St. Martin's Street, you will be so taken up with reading or talking to your royal mistress, or handing jewels, and *colifichets*, and *brimborions* [i.e., baubles], baubles, knick-knacks, gewgaws, toys, etc. . . . Lawk! that I could but see you handing the brimborions! Shall you be frightened? . . .

"P.S.—What a fine opportunity you will have of studying 'the philosophy of the human capacity,' in the highest *spere* of life!" There was one passage in this letter which expresses the hope most of Fanny's circle held: ". . . as for the satisfaction of other folks, for other reasons which I will tell anybody but you, I have no doubt of it; and I see, or think I see, a heap of pleasant circumstances and pleasant consequences, etc. etc."

In due course the other ladies of the court—ladies of the bedchamber, governesses, wives of preceptors, paid their duty calls on Miss Burney, and she found wry amusement in their badly disguised wonder at her appointment. They all had their own candidates for the post, and though some of them knew their starters hadn't a chance, not one had expected that the author of *Evelina*, of all people, would be the lucky one, or that she had even been considered.

The first courtier to meet with her liking was the King's equerry Major William Price, who knew the Worcester Burneys well.

These equerries were not confined like the Queen's ladies to a life-time of servitude: they took their turns and went out of waiting regularly, for a spell at home, looking after their own interests. Because court etiquette forbade that any man should sit in the Queen's presence, all her male dinner guests were relegated to Mrs. Schwellenberg's table, and this company, with that of the equerries, was Fanny's chief contact with the outside world. Otherwise her life was quite as circumscribed as she had feared: even more so, because the inflexible Mrs. Schwellenberg demanded constant company and attention.

By the Queen's permission, Fanny was allowed to call on Mrs. Delany or receive her in her rooms, and if the Queen sent her on errands she paid extra curricular calls on other inhabitants of the court. Aside from these small dispensations and a very occasional big one—a visit home was a great and most infrequent occasion—Fanny had no liberty to do anything but take her walk near the palaces. It may appear to our modern eyes that an unmarried woman of Fanny's class in the eighteenth century led a sufficiently circumscribed life even at home; she was not supposed to travel about alone, and Fanny hated to go unescorted even to a friend's party. But in comparison with most of her contemporaries she had been remarkably free. In retrospect the house in St. Martin's Street seemed to the poor glorified lady's maid a very heaven, without park palings or restrictions or Mrs. Schwellenberg. There was one thing in especial which galled her about the Queen's Lodge:

"My summons, upon all regular occasions—that is, morning, noon, and night toilets—is neither more nor less than a bell. . . . At first, I felt inexpressibly discomfited by this mode of call. A bell! —it seemed so mortifying a mark of servitude, I always felt myself blush, though alone, with conscious shame at my own strange degradation. But I have philosophised myself now into some reconcilement with this manner of summons, by reflecting that to have some person always sent would be inconvenient, and that this method is certainly less an interruption to any occupation I may be employed in, than the entrance of messengers so many times in the day. It is, besides, less liable to mistakes. So I have made up my mind to it as well as I can; and now I only feel that proud blush when somebody is by to revive my original dislike of it."

We must remember how proud Fanny was, as witness Mrs. Thrale's exasperated remarks, and how proud Fanny also was of her pride, an attitude natural to a woman who had spent all her life among people better off than she. Demure and shy though she appeared, there was nothing really humble about Miss Burney, and that bell must long have rankled bitterly in her heart.

The princesses, at least, never gave her cause to feel offended or slighted. They all had good manners, and from the princess royal, who was about twenty years old when Fanny first met her, to the three-year-old Princess Amelia, her father's favorite, Fanny met with the most courteous treatment. In that harem atmosphere she saw little of the princes, but the princesses were always about the lodge running small errands for their parents or paying calls on the ladies. Whatever their enemies had to say about the royal children after they had grown up, and however dull life was in the lodge, there is always something pleasant in a large family group like that of George III. They were nice-looking children and nicely behaved. Until they were old enough to be bored, they were happy. They had never known anything other than stilted routine, and they were not cursed by inheritance with a lively intelligence which might have made them kick against the pricks. It is to be supposed that they were happy as puppies in a kennel or as small chicks in a well-fenced farmyard. We know what happened once they sniffed liberty, but that is another story. Unfortunately for Fanny in the same enclosure, she was no ignorant child, no matter what she pretended. She was intelligent and she had already grown up outside the bars.

Life was so dull! There was a sort of break on court days when they went to London—Fanny was allowed to receive friends at St. James's because she had a private staircase straight to her apartments. At Kew there was less freedom than at Windsor, because the royals moved about informally, and one had to step lively to keep out of the way. But it all slipped into routine, and was dull. Sometimes Mrs. Delany helped Fanny make a break, to get a few hours off for paying some call. Sometimes the princesses dropped in, in assorted sizes, with commissions from the Queen; Fanny learned to mix snuff for her royal mistress and became adept at it, a trivial fact which assumed enormous proportions in that life of stagnant placidity.

There was nothing out of the way about this prodigious lack of excitement: it followed a long-standing pattern set down by George III in his youth. Augustus Hervey had written twenty years before, of life at St. James's: "The few people that are there act their parts so well, that in all the solitude of privacy one finds oneself at the same time in all the dangers of eminence, and beset with all the in-conveniences of a public life without the advantages of the social part of it; there are constant avocations without any employment, and a great deal of idleness without any leisure; many words pro-nounced, and nothing said; many people smiling, and nobody pleased; many disappointments and little success; little grandeur, and less happiness."

The royal family dwelt in less comfort than did many of their wealthy subjects. The gifts which Mrs. Delany and other favorites received from time to time from the Queen, which they exhibited with loyal rapture, were trumpery, frugal affairs in truth. At court such an opinion was never breathed aloud, but outside the Whigs were not so kind. Like the others, Fanny suffered from strange little austerities in regard to fires and even food. Then that salary of hers, that munificent two hundred pounds a year, did not go so far as one might think. Fanny had to dress herself according to her station, and she was required to make herself extra fine for the birthday of every prince and princess, no small order for a family like Char-lotte's. It was a duty particularly galling for Miss Burney, who had been accustomed before she went to court to arrange herself with little expenditure. Those days were over, and for all she knew, they were gone forever. Oh, it was endlessly dull.

Yet there were some excitements. There was, above all, the attempted assassination of the King, soon after Fanny entered the court. Margaret Nicholson, a lunatic, tried to stab him with a knife one day when he had just alighted at the garden door of St. James's. "A decently dressed woman"—Nicholson was a housemaid—stepped up to present him with a petition, a form of communication then common enough between the King and his subjects. As he bent forward to take it she brandished a knife, rather awkwardly and slowly because she was using her left hand. The King drew back, and before her second thrust could do any harm an attendant wrenched the weapon from her hand. Telling the story to his suitably horrified family afterward, George said, "Has she cut my waistcoat? Look! for I have had no time to examine." No, she had not. "Though nothing could have been sooner done," he said cheerfully, "for there was nothing for her to go through but a thin linen, and fat."

The King had plenty of courage: when the mob was hustling Nicholson away he called, "The poor creature is mad!—Do not hurt her! She has not hurt me!"

Margaret Nicholson was afterward put into Bedlam and lived to a ripe old age. In a way one might consider her as a benefactor to the entire court, for she brought liveliness and color to them. The incident pleased and excited the King, and made a most satisfactory scene among the princesses, the Queen, and all their ladies. They wept violently: Fanny had what was nearly a *crise de nerfs*. What with keeping the truth from Mrs. Delany, sending agitated notes to Miss Port, and reassuring the Queen, who was being worked up by Mrs. Schwellenberg's dark hints of national conspiracy, she was in a pleasant flutter for days. The Queen didn't take her usual airing: she shut herself up, and the princess royal went out in the carriage in her place, driving quickly through the town so that people wouldn't suspect the substitution. The crisis must have been awfully good for everybody.

Miss Burney had been at court a month and was well in train. She had refused to invite Major Price in when he escorted Mrs.

Delany to her door, though she admired him. She discouraged
other gentlemen of the court who wanted to call: doubtless none of
them had ulterior motives, but one must think of appearances. She
had run foul of Mrs. Schwellenberg by taking charge, during an
attack of that lady's recurrent illness, and making tea for the company. Mrs. Schwellenberg took it badly, but then she was bound to
take badly whatever Fanny did; it couldn't be helped.

". . . I shall do for you what I can; you are to have a gown,"
announced Mrs. Schwellenberg one morning, with a benevolent air.
What could she mean? A *present?*

"I stared, and drew back," wrote Fanny, "with a look so undis-
guised of wonder and displeasure at this extraordinary speech, that
I saw it was understood, and she then thought it time, therefore, to
name her authority, which, with great emphasis, she did thus: 'The
Queen will give you a gown! The Queen says you are not rich.' "

That familiar pride rose hotly to Fanny's cheeks. She said, "I
have two new gowns by me, and therefore do not require another."

Mrs. Schwellenberg was astonished. "Miss Bernar, I tell you
once, when the Queen will give you a gown, you must be humble,
thankful, when you are Duchess of Ancaster!"

Mrs. Schwellenberg was quite in the right, though perhaps her
mistress would have disapproved her manner of conferring the gift.
It was in order for the Queen to give one of her ladies a gown; any
of the others would have accepted it without feeling at all squeamish. But Fanny was different: Fanny was not used to such favors, or
did not wish to admit it: she forgot the Thrales. However, peace
was made that night; Mrs. Schwellenberg was again violently ill,
and Fanny felt sorry for her and deigned to suggest playing cards
with her. Cards was a pastime Mrs. Schwellenberg loved above all
else. The affair was forgotten, and face was saved for both ladies.
Fanny received the gown in time, and conquered her repugnance:
the garment, a "lilac tabby," served her in one form or another for
many years.

"Mr. Fairly," as Fanny and Susan spoke of him to avoid awkwardness in case their letters went astray, was really Colonel Ste-

phen Digby, the Queen's vice-chamberlain. Fanny liked him from the start of their acquaintance. "He is a man of the most scrupulous good-breeding, diffident, gentle, and sentimental in his conversation, and assiduously attentive in his manners. His wife was a Fox-Strangways,"—daughter of the first Earl of Ilchester—"and I am told [he] is a most tender husband to her."

Colonel Digby was brought in to tea with the Ladies of the Wardrobe during a court drawing room, when the whole town was flocking to congratulate His Majesty on his recent escape. It was about the time when the newspapers were full of attacks on Mrs. Warren Hastings: Hastings was soon to be tried for the East India Company affair and the papers had pounced on the fact that Mrs. Hastings was a divorced lady when he married her. Digby innocently made some stuffy remark to the effect that he was sorry to see her name associated in the paper with Her Majesty's. Unfortunately, Mrs. Schwellenberg took umbrage at this, for Mrs. Hastings was a friend of hers; she leaped violently and ungrammatically into the breach. There was the most tremendous row, mostly one-sided. Fanny felt compelled to speak up and clear the air, being herself a friend of the Hastingses: divorce laws in Germany, she explained, were not so strict as English laws, and as Mrs. Hastings hadn't been divorced for infidelity she couldn't be put into the same class as Lady Di Beauclerk. Lady Di's divorce was at that time a cause célèbre in society.

Though she was on the other side of the argument, Digby was no doubt favorably impressed by her calm propriety. The storm was stilled only for a moment, however; Mrs. Schwellenberg flew at him again, and only Major Price's determined tact put a final stop to the stupid discussion.

Fanny decided that she liked Colonel Digby. So much sanctimony, she felt, betokened a kindred soul.

14. DARLING OF VIRTUE

THE COURT appointment was not good for Fanny's character. A situation more encouraging to her peculiar faults could scarcely be contrived. Aside from the influence of Mrs. Schwellenberg, who did not contribute to her original failings but managed to stimulate a few new ones, the position now held by the novelist forced her to revert to nursery mentality. She was expected to feel complete trust in and loyalty to her King and Queen. Being Fanny Burney, she went further than this and imagined herself completely dependent morally on Charlotte. It was the compensation she unconsciously demanded for the loss of her freedom. Cut off from the world, was she? Spiritually married, or at any rate consecrated to the sacred task of handing the Queen every morning her collar and gloves? Then it was the Queen's moral obligation in turn to take on the responsibility for Fanny's soul. Fanny, left alone and unprotected without her Daddy Crisp and her dear father, sought another parent in Charlotte. (She was too canny to extend the filial relationship to George.)

Soon after her installation she asked the Queen for advice on a point of extreme delicacy: only Fanny Burney could have spun the matter so fine. It was a question which had arisen before—whether or not to maintain friendship with Madame de Genlis. Fanny had never replied to the French writer's letters; now another French-woman who was at court, a Madame la Fite, reader and French teacher to some of the princesses, began to press her to do so. Madame la Fite was a friend of Fanny's dear intimates the Lockes, but the bond between them did not obviate the awkwardness of this matter. With Latin enthusiasm and a certain pertinaciousness not necessarily Latin, Madame la Fite called on Fanny every day and every day brought up the name of Genlis. She had two reasons for this persistence: a genuine desire to see literary ladies chums together, and a hope of working Madame de Genlis into a good position with the Queen through Fanny's influence. But when it came to exerting influence for the countess, Miss Burney was determined to be a broken reed.

"I think of her as one of the first among women—I see her full of talents and of charms—I am willing to believe her good, virtuous, and dignified;—yet, with all this, the cry against her is so violent and so universal, and my belief in her innocence is wholly unsupported by proof in its favour, etc. etc."—that she was unwilling, in short, to espouse her cause, especially as Madame la Fite would be indiscreet enough to shout such a favor from the housetops. Cornered, Fanny went to the invaluable Mrs. Delany for advice, and Mrs. Delany said she should go and ask the Queen direct: should Fanny, or should she not, write letters to Madame de Genlis? "Madame de Genlis is so public a character, you can hardly correspond with her in private, and it would be better the Queen should hear of such an intercourse from yourself than from any other."

This acutely unimportant matter occupied pages and pages of the Diary. Fanny described her shyness, her fear the Queen would think her presumptuous in daring to ask for direction, and her hesitations at great length: we can well afford to be more brusque. Charlotte said that if Fanny hadn't yet answered the letter, then she had better not. The Queen had already been "tormented" into giving the lady a private audience, which she regretted. Not surprisingly, she wasn't offended by Fanny's daring; "she looked the whole time with a marked approbation of my applying to her." It was a rare and subtle flattery which even a spoiled queen could appreciate.

The Journal account of the royal Oxford expedition of 1786 has been often cited, and there is good reason for this: Fanny's sharp eye and tenacious memory, added to the novelty of the proceedings, which made her more than ever careful and detailed, is a valuable contribution to history. It was not a picture of unalloyed discomfort, though some of the secondhand reports would lead one to think so. Fanny was indignant enough at times, and must have made a nuisance of herself with her airs and sulks, but she was diverted too; she admitted that where the experienced Miss Planta almost fainted under the strain, her own fresh interest in the proceedings sustained her, keeping her tough and alert. Her *amour-propre* was badly wounded at Nuneham, where the party spent the first night. Their hostess, Lady Harcourt, kept passing the buck of entertaining Fanny to her sisters the Misses Vernon, who neglected her because they were dazzled by more important guests. Invitations to Nuneham meals were not delivered with what Fanny considered the right degree of ceremonial courtesy. Her pride was further lacerated by the fact that the overworked court hairdresser didn't get around to doing her comparatively insignificant coiffure until very late in the day. But she built her vanity up again by refusing to laugh when Colonel Digby tried to make a joke of her grievances, and she rebuked the Misses Vernon, ever so gently and indirectly, for getting so excited by royalty that they forgot what was due Miss Burney. She had the satisfaction of seeing them blush, and faced the next day at Oxford in a really pleasant, appeased state of mind.

Sight-seeing with a king and queen is even more arduous than sight-seeing by oneself. The party was treated to all sorts of ceremonies and tributes of loyalty, and thanksgiving prayers for the King's recent escape, and organ-playing, and hand-kissing by the professors and doctors, in the university theater. Fanny particularly enjoyed the spectacle of the hand-kissing: many of the worthy scholars were awkward at kneeling, and worse at walking backward out of the King's presence. Some of them simply got rattled, turned their backs, and walked off normally. But the walking about, and polite chatting, took so much time that it was three o'clock before the party reached Christ Church, where a cold lunch was spread for the royal family. Everyone felt famished, but, alas, only the family could sit down to lunch.

The "untitled attendants"—Fanny, Miss Planta, the Misses Vernon, Digby, an odd clergyman or two—stood at the far end of the room in a respectful, hungry semicircle, and the titled ladies and gentlemen stood near their masters' chairs at the table, equally hungry. It was unheard of to eat in the presence of the royal family, explains Fanny; as unheard of as sitting down. Nevertheless some of the kind professors secretly laid a table with snacks for the untitled attendants; by lining up in a double row, front shielding back during this indelicate operation, everybody had a chance to gobble something unobserved. They ate standing up: chairs would have been too much to expect. The veteran courtiers commiserated with poor Miss Burney, who was as yet so unused to such exercise that she didn't know, as they did, what it was to stand for five hours on end, but Miss Burney had not yet been on the job long enough to get a martyr complex and was having the time of her life. During the afternoon she saw "a performance of courtly etiquette, by Lady Charlotte Bertie, that seemed to me as difficult as any feat I ever beheld . . ."

This unlucky Lady Charlotte had sprained her ankle and complained at intervals throughout the day that she must stand on it for so long a stretch of time. (Her relative, Lord Macartney, was England's first Ambassador to China, the man who refused as a loyal Briton to "kowtow" to the Emperor of China. One wonders whether the worthy Englishmen of his embassy, as they marveled at the quaint Oriental customs of the Emperor's court, saw any parallel between Chinese and Manchu nobles on their knees and British nobles on their tired, aching feet.) Suddenly, because of a reshuffle in the exits of the family, the suffering Lady Charlotte found herself high up in a long room near the King, who was on his way out, strolling along deep in conversation with a professor.

"Had I been in her situation, I had surely waited till His Majesty went first; but that would not, I saw, upon this occasion, have been etiquette;—she therefore faced the King, and began a march backwards,—her ankle already sprained, and to walk forward, and even leaning upon an arm, was painful to her: nevertheless, back she went, perfectly upright, without one stumble, without ever looking once behind to see what she might encounter; and with as graceful a motion, and as easy an air, as I ever saw anybody enter a long room, she retreated, I am sure, full twenty yards backwards out of one. . . .

". . . I was also, unluckily, at the upper end of the room. . . . However, as soon as I perceived what was going forward,—backward, rather,—I glided near the wainscot (Lady Charlotte, I should mention, made her retreat along the very middle of the room), and having paced a few steps backwards, stopped short to recover, and, while I seemed examining some other portrait, disentangled my train from the heels of my shoes, and then proceeded a few steps only more; and then, observing the King turn another way, I slipped a yard or two at a time forwards; and hastily looked back, and then was able to go again according to rule, and in this manner, by slow and varying means, I at length made my escape. . . .

"Since that time, however, I have come on prodigiously, by constant practice, in the power and skill of walking backwards, without tripping up my own heels, feeling my head giddy, or treading my train out of the plaits—accidents very frequent among novices in that business; and I have no doubt but that, in the course of a few months, I shall arrive at all possible perfection in the true court retrograde motion."

Miss Burney and Miss Planta at last took a secret, sit-down rest in the master's parlor at one of the colleges, and began to eat some bread and apricots which he produced from his pocket. In the middle of their scratch meal the Queen and a lot of attendants suddenly marched in. "Up we all started, myself alone not discountenanced; for I really think it quite respect sufficient never to sit down in the royal presence, without aiming at having it supposed I have stood bolt upright ever since I have been admitted to it."

One reason Miss Burney remained lighthearted in spite of her weary legs, and was able to write amusingly about the journey afterward, was that Mrs. Schwellenberg stayed home, being too old and ill to undergo such rigors. But such escapes were exceptional, and it is quite appalling to trace the swift progress of Fanny's capitulation to the annoyances of everyday life with the difficult old woman. Miss Burney had been at Windsor only about six weeks before she gave way to a sulkiness which she expressed by maintaining silence in the presence of Mrs. Schwellenberg, a protest she carried to the pitch of absurdity. This behavior was Major Price's fault, one suspects, the major having given her, in vulgar parlance, an earful. ". . . he frankly told me that there was not a man in the establishment that did not fear even speaking to me, from the apparent jealousy my arrival had awakened; and after a little longer talk, opening still more, he confessed that they had all agreed never to address me, but in necessary civilities that were unavoidable.

"How curious! I applauded the resolution, which I saw might save me from ill-will, as well as themselves. Yet he owned himself extremely surprised at my management, and acknowledged they had none of them expected I could possibly have done so well.

" 'Nay,' cried I, 'I only do nothing; that's all!'

" 'But that,' answered he, 'is the difficulty; to do nothing is the hardest thing possible.' "

Because of that ill-advised compliment Fanny went to the furthest extreme she could reach, sitting in conspicuous modesty and absolute silence in Mrs. Schwellenberg's presence, night after night when the equerries came to tea. There can be no doubt she was thoroughly tiresome. The equerries must have wanted to choke her, unless she really got the effect she was aiming for and became the pitiable, oppressed object of their sympathies. But this is doubtful: the world seldom lives up to our hopes. Mrs. Delany, at any rate, was a satisfactory audience of Fanny's "sitting dumb and unnoticed. To me, as I have explained, this was no hardship; but to Mrs. Delany, when she joined the set, it was quite afflicting.

Accustomed to place me herself so high, to see me, now, even studiously shunned, had an effect upon her tender mind that gave me uneasiness to observe; and indeed, she told me it was so painful a scene to her, that she would positively come no more, unless I would exert and assert myself into a little more consequence.

"I have promised to do what I can to comfort her for the apprehensions she conceives of my depression; but in truth I like the present state of things better than at present I should any reform in them."

Yes, one gathers that.

A book of memoirs is often very good fun to read, but the pleasure of this is as nothing compared with reading two books of memoirs which occasionally cover the same subject. Thus just when the reader begins to regret the loss of Mrs. Thrale from Fanny's sphere of influence, or vice versa (for even Fanny, excellent Memorialist as she is, cannot be more than a unilateral power), it is a true thrill to discover the Journal of Sophie de la Roche, or von la Roche, as she was called at home in Germany.

Maria Sophia Guterman was born twenty-two years earlier than Fanny, in Swabia. At the age of twenty she was romantically involved with her young cousin, Christoph Wieland, who later became a famous poet. Perhaps it was Wieland's influence which turned Sophie to writing, but her romantic nature predisposed her to this career in any case. She married La Roche instead of Wieland, and bore five children to him, but in spite of family cares she kept producing novels, travel diaries (she loved to travel), solemn social treatises, and edifying books of counsel for young people, these last being expected of every serious female writer of that day. She was a woman full of what we call "personality," that is, she was vital and attractive in a way which cannot be fully expressed either in her writings or her portraits. She was warmhearted, full of good health, and enthusiastic. She was also, if one wishes to carp, a gusher, a yearner, and a weeper, all qualities which seemed then, as they still seem, more ludicrous in England than they do in Germany. Intense emotion brought tears to Sophie's eyes, and as Sophie was subject at all times to attacks of intense emotion, her progress through life was moist. She enjoyed the moisture, however. She enjoyed most of her experience, and no doubt this was the secret of her attraction.

In 1786, past middle age, Sophie visited England with her eldest son and had a wonderful time. Through her tearful eyes we see London in a fresh light. Nobody else has painted for us so vividly the dazzlingly lamplit width of Oxford Street, by that time the most important shopping quarter in the city. No one else presents in such detail the Zoo which flourished in its mangy way at the Tower. Sophie gives us a new view of the "color bar" in the eighteenth century. She was an ardent humanitarian, always on the watch for poor downtrodden natives to champion. In London the sight of a "Moorish" funeral stimulated her to write several pages of moral reflection on this subject, from which we must conclude that the black and brown races were not accepted in the mass by whites with any more kindliness than they are today, however courteous an occasional Lord Sandwich may have been to novelties such as Omai.

Indefatigable, uncritical, gushing all the time, Sophie visited the usual temples of the sight-seer and a few new ones. At Westminster Abbey she was, quite rightly, shocked by the bedizened waxwork statues of some of England's great. She viewed with impartial admiration Sir Ashton Lever's museum in Leicester Fields, the market at Covent Garden, a clockmaker's workshop, Hatchett the saddler's premises, a pastry cook's shop, a tea auction at East India House, the Bank of England (where nobody looked happy, she observed with the customary moral reflections), the works of Benjamin West, and the court at Windsor.

It was Madame la Fite who gave Sophie her chance to visit Windsor. For years the two intellectual ladies had been corresponding, and at last they met. Immediately Madame la Fite put to work all her talents for intrigue. Such a brilliant woman as Madame la Roche must procure an audience with the Queen. A lesser *must* was an introduction to the famous Miss Burney, but that was comparatively simple: the Queen was difficult, because she had a prejudice against novel writers. However, Miss Burney, if she possessed the right feelings toward a sister colleague, would no doubt do all in her power to help. So reasoned the ever-hopeful Madame la Fite, though her project of bringing together Madame de Genlis and Fanny had just fallen flat.

We can detect no hint in Sophie's journal that she had any idea of the tortuous processes of court etiquette regarding her introduction to such high circles. According to Sophie's memoirs, it all went like clockwork, but she must have realized to some extent that Madame la Fite did not find the task of presenting her plain sailing. The Frenchwoman was not one to keep her efforts hidden under a bushel. Perhaps Sophie simply ignored the preliminary mechanics as unworthy the attention of an intellectual; her account of her meetings with Fanny and other ladies of the court, and finally with the Queen (no thanks to Fanny), makes it all sound as easy as rolling off a log. Not so with poor Fanny's version, one of the most diverting passages in the D'Arblay Diary.

From her usual excess of cautious modesty, Miss Burney first tried to get out of meeting the lady, because the Queen didn't approve of novelists, because Fanny was afraid of Mrs. Schwellenberg's comments, and because she didn't want to be let in for any new complications. But Madame la Fite persisted, and at last Fanny went to her apartments, and Madame la Roche was presented. Such embraces! Such continental cries of joy! "*La digne Miss Borni!—l'auteur de Cécile?—d'Evelina? non, ce n'est pas possible! —suis-je si heureuse!—oui, je le vois à ses yeux!—Ah! que de bonheur!*"

"Madame la Roche, had I met her in any other way, might have pleased me in no common degree; for could I have conceived her character to be unaffected, her manners have a softness that would render her excessively engaging. She is now *bien passé*—no doubt fifty—yet has a voice of touching sweetness, eyes of dovelike gentleness, looks supplicating for favour, and an air and demeanour the most tenderly caressing. I can suppose she has thought herself all her life the model of the favourite heroine of her own favourite romance, and I can readily believe that she has had attractions in her youth nothing short of fascinating. Had I not been present, and so deeply engaged in this interview, I had certainly been caught by her myself; for in her presence I constantly felt myself forgiving and excusing what in her absence I as constantly found past defence or apology.

"Poor Madame la Fite has no chance in her presence; for though their singular enthusiasm upon 'the people of the literature,' as Pacchierotti called them, is equal, Madame la Fite almost subdues by vehemence, while Madame la Roche almost melts by her softness. Yet I fairly believe they are both very good women, and both believe themselves sincere. . . .

". . . At the chapel this morning, Madame la Fite placed Madame la Roche between herself and me, and proposed bringing her to the Lodge, 'to return my visit.' This being precisely what I had tried to avoid, and to avoid without shocking Madame la Fite, by meeting her correspondent at her own house, I was much chagrined at such a proposal, but had no means to decline it, as it was made across Madame la Roche herself.

"Accordingly, at about two o'clock, when I came from the Queen, I found them both in full possession of my room, and Madame la Fite occupied in examining my books. The thing thus being done, and the risk of consequence inevitable, I had only to receive them with as little display of disapprobation of their measure as I could help; but one of the most curious scenes followed I have ever yet been engaged in or witnessed.

"As soon as we were seated, Madame la Fite began with assuring me, aloud, of the 'conquest' I had made of Madame la Roche, and appealed to that lady for the truth of what she said. Madame la Roche answered her by rising, and throwing her arms about me, and kissing my cheeks from side to side repeatedly.

"Madame la Fite, as soon as this was over, and we had resumed our seats, opened the next subject, by saying Madame la Roche had read and adored *Cecilia*: again appealing to her for confirmation of her assertion.

" 'O, oui, oui!' cried her friend, 'mais la vrais Cecile, c'est Miss Borni: digne, douce, et aimable! Coom to me arms! que je vous embrasse mille fois!'

"Again we were all deranged, and again the same ceremony being performed, we all sat ourselves down.

"*Cecilia* was then talked over throughout, in defiance of every obstacle I could put in its way.

"After this, Madame la Fite said, in French, that Madame la Roche had had the most extraordinary life and adventures that had fallen to anybody's lot; and finished with saying, 'Eh! ma chère amie, contez nous un peu.'

"They were so connected, she answered, in their early part with M. Wieland, the famous author, that they would not be intelligible without his story.

" 'Eh bien! ma tres-chère, contez nous, donc, un peu de ses aventures; ma chère Miss Burney, c'étoit son amant, et l'homme le plus extraordinaire—d'un vous recontre? ou est-ce qu'il a commence a vous aimer? contez nous un peu de tout ça.'

"Madame la Roche, looking down upon her fan, began then the recital. She related their first interview, the gradations of their mutual attachment, his extraordinary talents, his literary fame and name; the breach of their union from motives of prudence in their friends; his change of character from piety to voluptuousness, in consoling himself for her loss with an actress; his varied adventures, and various transformations from good to bad, in life and conduct; her own marriage with M. de la Roche, their subsequent meeting when she was mother of three children, and all the attendant circumstances.

"When she had done, and I had thanked her, Madame la Fite demanded of me what I thought of her, and if she was not delightful? I assented and Madame la Roche then, rising, and fixing her eyes, filled with tears, in my face, while she held both my hands, in the most melting accents, exclaimed. '*Miss Borni! la plus chère, la plus digne des Angloises! dites-moi—m'aimez vous?*'

"I answered as well as I could, but what I said was not very positive. Madame la Fite came to us, and desired we might make a trio of friendship, which should bind us to one another for life.

"And then they both embraced me, and both wept for joyful fondness! I fear I seemed very hard-hearted; but no spring was opened whence one tear of mine could flow.

"The clock had struck four some time, and Madame la Fite said she feared they kept me from dinner. I knew it must soon be ready, and therefore made but a slight negative.

"She then, with an anxious look at her watch, said she feared she was already late for her own little dinner.

"I was shocked at a hint I had no power to notice, and heard it in silence—silence unrepressing! for she presently added, 'You dine alone, don't you?'

"'Y-e-s,—if Mrs. Schwellenberg is not well enough to come downstairs to dinner.'

"'And can you dine, ma chère Mademoiselle—can you dine at that great table alone?'

"'I must!—the table is not mine.'

"'Yes, in Mrs. Schwellenberg's absence it is.'

"'It has never been made over to me, and I take no power that is not given to me.'

"'But the Queen, my dearest ma'am—the Queen, if she knew such a person as Madame la Roche was here.'

"She stopped, and I was quite disconcerted. An attack so explicit, and in my presence of Madame la Roche, was beyond all my expectations. She then went to the window, and exclaimed, 'It rains!—*Que ferons nous?*—My poor littel dinner!—it will be all spoilt!—*La pauvre Madame la Roche! une telle femme!*'

"I was now really distressed, and wished much to invite them both to stay; but I was totally helpless; and could only look, as I felt, in the utmost embarrassment.

"The rain continued. Madame la Roche could understand but

imperfectly what passed, and waited its result with an air of smiling patience. I endeavoured to talk of other things; but Madame la
Fite was restless in returning to this charge. . . .

"At length John came to announce dinner.

"Madame la Fite looked at me in a most expressive manner, as
she rose and walked towards the window, exclaiming that the rain
would not cease; and Madame la Roche cast upon me a most tender smile, while she lamented that some accident must have prevented her carriage from coming for her.

"I felt excessively ashamed, and could only beg them not to be
in haste, faithfully assuring them I was by no means disposed for
eating.

"Poor Madame la Fite now lost all command of herself, and
desiring to speak to me in my own room, said pretty explicitly, that
certainly I might keep anybody to dinner, at so great a table, and
all alone, if I wished it.

"I was obliged to be equally frank. I acknowledged that I had
reason to believe I might have had that power, from the custom of
my predecessor, Mrs. Haggerdorn, upon my first succeeding to
her; but that I was then too uncertain of any of my privileges to
assume a single one of them unauthorized by the Queen; and I
added that I had made it the invariable rule of my conduct, from
the moment of my entering into my present office, to run no risk
of private blame, by any action that had not her previous consent
or knowledge.

"She was not at all satisfied, and significantly said:

" 'But you have sometimes Miss Planta?'

" 'Not I; Mrs. Schwellenberg invites her.'

" 'And M. de Luc, too,—he may dine with you!'

" 'He also comes to Mrs. Schwellenberg. Mrs. Delany alone, and
her niece, come to me; and they have had the sanction of the
Queen's own desire.'

" '*Mais, enfin, ma chère Miss Burney*,—when it rains,—and when
it is so late,—and when it is for such a woman as Madame la
Roche!'

"So hard pressed, I was quite shocked to resist her; but I assured her that when my own sisters, Phillips and Francis, came to Windsor purposely to see me, they had never dined at the Lodge but by the express invitation of Mrs. Schwellenberg; and that when my father himself was here, I had not ventured to ask him.

"This, though it surprised, somewhat appeased her; and we were called into the other room to Miss Planta, who was to dine with me, and who, unluckily, said, the dinner would be quite cold. . . .

"Again she desired to speak to me in my own room; and then she told me that Madame la Roche had a most earnest wish to see all the Royal Family; she hoped, therefore, the Queen would go to early prayers at the chapel, where, at least, she might be beheld; but she gave me sundry hints, not to be misunderstood, that she thought I might so represent the merits of Madame La Roche as to induce the honour of a private audience.

"I could give her no hope of this, as I had none to give; for I well knew that the Queen has a settled aversion to almost all novels, and something very near it to almost all novel-writers.

"She then told me she had herself requested an interview for her with the Princess Royal, and had told her that if it was too much to grant it in the Royal apartments, at least it might take place in Miss Burney's room! Her Royal Highness coldly answered that she saw nobody without the Queen's commands.

"How much I rejoiced in her prudence and duty! I would not have had a meeting in my room unknown to the Queen for a thousand worlds. But poor mistaken Madame la Fite complained most bitterly of the deadness of the whole court to talents and genius.

"In the end, the carriage of Madame La Roche arrived, about tea-time. . . . And thus ended this most oppressive scene. You may think I had no voracious appetite after it."

Sophie merely says with simple innocent pleasure that Madame la Fite gathered to meet her "ladies of very high standing, others of noble rank or court circles, and a very delightful member of the scholarly world. . . . Miss Burney, daughter of Mr. Burney, who made the great musical tour and criticisms, is herself famous as authoress of *Miss Evelina* and *Cecilia*. Your brother and I thought her a true ideal in figure, culture, expression, dress and bearing. I do not think the fine mind and gentle disposition for which she is conspicuous can ever be surpassed. . . . Mme. la Fite and I went to Miss Burney's; she has a very choice book collection, from which I should steal Samuel Johnson's *Dictionnaire* of the best thoughts and passages from English poets. . . . My whole discussion with Miss Burney was extremely pleasant, and it is certainly doubtful whether her personal grace, her mental accomplishments or her modesty merit first place, but all noble-minded rational beings would delight in her acquaintance, and feel at home with her. As I was thinking about her, despite my small amount of English, I discovered an expression which fits her qualities excellently: 'Darling of virtue,' that is, 'Liebling der Tugend.' "

Nevertheless, it was in spite of virtue's darling, not because of her, that the sentimental Sophie did at last get her coveted interview with Queen Charlotte.

15. THE SORROWING WIDOWER

Pᴇᴏᴘʟᴇ have commented in surprise on the fact that Fanny, on going into waiting, failed to express one particular regret. She lamented her losses, it is true: she often enumerated them—her family, her friends, her freedom. But we seek in vain any reference to her greatest sacrifice, that of her *work*. Why was this? How could it be? Macauley put it down to sheer intoxication of snobbery, which made her ready and willing to give up her birthright. Austin Dobson merely pointed to the fact in quiet wonder. George III himself mentioned it, when Fanny resigned from court: he spoke of five years which had passed by without Fanny's using her pen. The obvious truth did not occur to any of these people. Macauley read her Diary page by page, but he never counted the hours which each day's entry must have consumed in the writing; he evidently never knew that he had the answer, concrete and heavy, in his hands. Fanny didn't give up her work for so much as a week. She was writing, solidly writing, all the time, with all the leisure at her command.

But that doesn't count, someone will probably say; that's only letters or her Diary: Fanny Burney never wrote a novel all the while she was in waiting on the Queen. Yet why should diary-keeping be counted as nothing and the writing of novels considered the only serious work? Fanny was a born writer, and all her life the true substance of her writing lay in her Journal. The novels were merely third- or fourth-degree adaptations of her experience, which she produced in a form remote from autobiography because convention demanded such disguise. She would have been agonized at the suggestion that she write a private Journal for publication. She never forgot her father's early lesson about leaving such writing about; as for publishing one's private life, that was in the worst of taste. Even the uninhibited Mrs. Thrale edited and bowdlerized her memoirs. But the novel form took off the curse, giving Fanny a chance to use what she knew about life, as long as she was careful to transmute it.

Fundamentally, she didn't write for money or fame. She wrote, as she recognized when she was fifteen, simply because she couldn't help it. There were subsidiary motives; she did indeed think her work would "look very well in print"; and certainly it must have been pleasant to earn money and thus help her father. But the true, primary urge was to write, whether or not it was published and whether or not she was paid for it. At court, where she shrank from publicity and felt less necessity to earn by writing, Fanny still clung to her original outlet, the Journal. It was her first love: now, when there were few enjoyments in life, the Journal was the gainer.

Fourteen years were to elapse between the publication of *Cecilia* and that of Madame d'Arblay's next novel *Camilla*. But to say this was the Queen's fault, or that Fanny wrote nothing in all that time, is sheer nonsense: three volumes of the Diary prove it nonsense. During her stay at court Fanny recorded the most stirring account of George III's lunacy which exists, and how can we say the time and effort would have been better spent on a five-volume tale of some genteel young lady's premarital adventures?

Miss Burney celebrated the New Year with an attack of rheumatism and fever. She decided to use the rare leisure thus gained taking stock of her soul's condition. On the whole, things were not too bad. She was inclined to say they would not be bad at all were it not for Mrs. Schwellenberg, and Mrs. S. was in such bad health that her company did not always have to be borne. Aside from Mrs. Schwellenberg, then, what did life hold? Very little, pleasant or unpleasant; all was dead and tame. There was her consciousness of doing well by her father, who had lately been for a visit and was most kindly treated by His Majesty. There was the Queen, whose favor became more and more marked. There were the princesses, always sweet and pleasant, especially little Princess Amelia, who had developed a strong partiality for Fanny. Sometimes the Queen asked Fanny to read to her, but the writer was not good at these performances: her nearsightedness and self-consciousness made her falter over the print.

There was the work—the actual attendance, and the consultations with tailors and embroiderers and seamstresses and milliners; boring enough to a confirmed dress-hater. Then the odd duties on special occasions such as the Queen's birthday, when Fanny had to dress in splendor, with towering hair ornaments, to appear for an hour or two in the ballroom before she must flee to the royal dressing room to help put her mistress to bed.

She paused in her summary to recall and describe the high spots of that festival. For a space she had held the Queen's train and was suddenly overwhelmed by a feeling of unreality that she of all people should be taking such part in such pageantry. In getting back to the Queen's apartments from the ballroom she had encountered great difficulties, difficulties which are well-nigh inconceivable to us. She actually got lost between doors. The whole problem centered around the fact that she had to go out of doors on foot and around St. James's Palace, the interior way being blocked off because the state apartments were in use. Outside, in ordinary times, she would be carried in her chair from the ballroom entrance to her own door. That was how she had arrived. But her footman and chair attendants had disappeared and could not be found in the crowd, and Fanny willy-nilly entrusted herself to a hackney chair. The chair carriers asked her where she wanted to go, but she couldn't tell them: all she knew was that her destination was another door of the palace. When they pressed her for more information she said, "Mrs. Haggerdorn's rooms." Mrs. Haggerdorn's name meant nothing to a couple of drunken chair-bearers, and the palace guards knew no more than they.

It was raining, Fanny had no cloak, and she was in mortal terror of being late for her work. She had been late once before, and the Queen had not been pleased. . . . Terrified by the magnitude of this problem, the poor helpless eighteenth-century woman dashed about in the rain, sometimes in the chair, sometimes out, a few hundred yards from her own door and absolutely incapable of getting there until a kind clergyman forced her to accept his guidance. He was a stranger, it was most improper, it was unheard of, but Fanny at last took his arm and was led the few steps necessary to her own door. She was just in time. More terror and suspense went into the writing of that adventure than we are likely to find in many accounts of today's military campaigns. Drunken chair bearers, wind and rain, prowling clergymen, impending disgrace, mazes in the palace grounds—who dares say that Fanny Burney led a sheltered life? Think of what *might* have happened! Yet when we look today at St. James's Palace we can only shake our heads over poor Evelina.

Aside from such extraordinary alarms and excursions, the day-by-day excitements were chaste and gentle. Mr. and Mrs. Smelt were always at hand when the court went to Kew: Fanny adored Mr. Smelt and took so many walks with him in the gardens that the princesses teased her for flirting; she was allowed to invite the Smelts to dinner. There was Mrs. Delany, of course: Mrs. Delany had asked her to help rearrange the scraps of autobiography which she had written years before to amuse the Duchess of Portland, and every evening after tea Fanny and Mrs. Delany would spread out their papers and get to work, and every evening the King would swoop down and spoil it by carrying off his dear old pet to join the exalted family circle. Miss Planta, Mrs. Delany, Mr. Smelt: Mr. Smelt, Mrs. Delany, Miss Planta—an endless round of solid, virtuous time killing. The equerries provided a dash of excitement which was pleasant if you liked equerries. Fanny did, rather, but she hated to admit it. Middle age was stalking Miss Burney and changing her habits; where once she had neither affirmed nor denied, she now took to denying everything, constantly and vigorously.

The pattern of social intercourse among the attendants had become rigid under the reign of Mrs. Schwellenberg and Mrs. Haggerdorn, and among other customs there was one which Fanny was not sure she need observe—giving tea to the equerries after dinner. The King's gentlemen expected to come every day after their meal to Mrs. Haggerdorn's, or Fanny's, room, for half an hour or so. Fanny didn't know who had started the tradition, but when Mrs. Schwellenberg was not presiding she resented the necessity of carrying on with it alone. She felt compunctions about being alone with Men, and besides she would rather have been free at that time; not really free, of course, but at any rate free to run down to the gatehouse and visit with Mrs. Delany. Days and pages of Diary were given over to Fanny's futile, fluttering little intrigues to break away from the equerries at tea. Mr. Smelt advised strongly against any change, on general principles: when in doubt, stay put, was the general rule of the court. Of course the equerries themselves may not have liked the custom either, but that was neither here nor there; it was the custom and it must be followed.

However, while Colonel Goldsworthy was in waiting, there were compensations. He amused Fanny. She liked him. So did Miss Port like him. Possibly Colonel Goldsworthy was the indirect cause of Lady Llanover's inimical attitude toward Madame d'Arblay when all the court party were dust in their graves. Maybe Colonel Goldsworthy wanted to marry sixteen-year-old Georgina Mary Anne Port, and maybe G.M.A. would have liked to marry the colonel, and maybe Miss Goldsworthy, who was the princesses' governess and the colonel's sister, did not approve the match, and maybe Fanny, at Miss Goldsworthy's request, helped put a spoke in the wheel. There's no record of her interference, but it's the sort of thing she liked to do.[1] Lady Llanover's relentless spite fairly glimmers in this passage: "[Miss Burney] lived in an ideal world of which she was, in her own imagination, the centre. She believed herself possessed of a spell which fascinated all those she approached. She became convinced that all the equerries were in love with her, although she was continually the object of their ridicule, as they discovered her weaknesses and played upon her credulity for their amusement."

This is too brutal to be fully credible, but there's a grain of truth in it. The gentlemen must have found Miss Burney rather funny, with her exaggerated fears and her preoccupation with appearances. But she couldn't have been outstandingly eccentric; the court was full of such mild insanities.

Miss Port had good taste. Of the equerries, Colonel Goldsworthy shows up by far the most charming; he was humorous and crotchety. One evening he came in with a doleful air of weariness after a day's hunting with the King; it took all G.M.A.'s coaxing to make him talk. But when he did talk it came in a flood.

"After all the labours of the chase, all the riding, the trotting, the galloping, the leaping, the—with your favour, ladies, I beg pardon, I was going to say a strange word, but the—the perspiration,—and—and all that—after being wet through over head, and soused through under feet, what lives we do lead! Well, it's all honour! that's my only comfort! Well, after all this, fagging away like mad from eight in the morning to five or six in the afternoon, home we come, looking like so many drowned rats, with not a dry thread about us, nor a morsel within us—sore to the very bone, and forced to smile all the time! and then after all this what do you think follows?—'Here Goldsworthy,' cries His Majesty: so up I comes to him, bowing profoundly, and my hair dripping down to my shoes; 'Goldsworthy,' cries His Majesty. 'Sir,' says I, smiling agreeably, with the rheumatism just creeping all over me! but still, expecting something a little comfortable, I wait patiently to know

[1]"A Georgian Friendship"—George Paston, *Sidelights on the Georgian Period*, 1902.

his gracious pleasure, and then, 'Here, Goldsworthy, I say!' he cries, 'will you have a little barley water?' "

Then there was Major Price, helpful and very knowledgeable; he was one equerry who could speak just as he liked to the King. When Major Price during his liberty came back to court on a visit, the King was overjoyed, as nobody else played backgammon so much to his taste. One afternoon when the equerries were at tea, just as it was being poured out, the King came in and hovered about, as he did when he meant to make a raid on the company. At last he came over to the tea table and said, "How far are you got?"

"I knew he meant to know if he might carry off Major Price," said Fanny, "but while I hesitated, the Major, with his usual plainness, said, 'Sir, we had not begun.'

"His Majesty then went away, without giving any commands to be followed; and Major Price had the thanks and compliments of the company for his successful hardiness."

The pleasant Colonel Digby was sentimental, and at this time he was more than ever soft and sighing, because his wife was dying of cancer.

The equerries all knew Fanny's troubles regarding Mrs. Schwellenberg and were disposed to help her out whenever they could. There was another gentleman at court, however, not an equerry, who ruffled her plumes a little. This was the Reverend Charles de Guiffardière, French reader to the Queen and Prebendary of Salisbury. It will save time if we call him by the pseudonym Fanny bestowed on him in her Journal, Mr. Turbulent. Mr. Turbulent was connected in some way with the family Guiffardière where Maria Allen Rishton stayed in her youth.

The Queen was fond of her French Protestant clergyman, and one can understand why. Turbulent, unlike most of her attendants, was full of spirits. He was six feet tall and had remarkable eyes. He talked back to her, he cheeked the princesses, he was a *beau garçon* and a bad boy who knew just where to stop. He was not exactly a court jester, but he was not exactly an ordinary clergyman either. While fully conscious of his good fortune in holding his appointment at court, he found life there just the tiniest bit dull. He was a solid citizen; he must have been, to have survived the "screening" which all Her Majesty's attendants were put through. He was duly married, as befitted a man who saw so much of the princesses, and he was a clergyman. But he was also witty, vital, and mischievous, and something about Fanny Burney raised the devil in him.

It was probably Fanny's inflexible virtue combined with a piquant attraction which still existed. He went out of his way to shock her, perhaps in the belief it would be good for her and perhaps merely out of a natural human desire to give so much complacency a good shake. Besides, they were thrown together a good deal, the Queen having recommended Mr. Turbulent warmly to her new protégée and signified her desire that he travel in the Schwellenberg-Burney coach between Kew and Windsor whenever there was a place for him. One day at dinner in Fanny's rooms he began the campaign, during a discussion on morality. The majority of the company had declared themselves much in favor of completely impeccable "character" in females. "Miss Planta declared her opinion that it was so indispensable to have it [female character] without blemish, that nothing on earth would compensate, or make it possible to countenance one who wanted it. Mrs. Smelt agreed that compassion alone was all that could be afforded upon such an occasion, not countenance, acquaintance, nor intercourse. . . . I spoke little, but that little was, to give every encouragement to penitence, and no countenance to error."

At this point Mr. Turbulent broke out into warm argument, holding that many females of easy virtue, or anyway of bad reputation, were the most amiable of their sex. What was more, he said, the ladies he was addressing at that very moment never lived up to these severe strictures they were quoting. They, even they, had friends who had been touched by scandal.

Fanny was furious that he should dare accuse her of ever showing mercy to sinners. The others of the party backed her up and insisted they kept themselves properly aloof from all such tarnished creatures. Mr. Turbulent stuck by his guns; they all knew at least one lady with a bad reputation, he said: Miss Burney knew, visited, received, caressed, and distinguished a lady in this very class. "I think her one of the most charming women in the world!" he added, "—amiable, spirited, well-informed, and entertaining, and of manners the most bewitching! . . . And with all this, ma'am, she has not escaped the lash of scandal; and, with every amiable virtue of the mind, she has not been able to preserve her reputation, in one sense, unattacked."

After a lot of coaxing, he consented to tell them the name of that lady, and who should it be but Madame de Genlis! Fanny was speechless. Certainly she had lately cut off the acquaintanceship; she could have said this in her own defense. But that would have meant going back on all her former asseverations that Madame de Genlis was innocent though misunderstood, and that she had merely taken the Queen's advice. She could not do it. Fanny was severe, but not habitually dishonest. Mr. Turbulent retired with the honors of the battle, and he must have got a lot of wicked fun out of them.

Some time later, traveling in Fanny's coach from town to Windsor, he took advantage of three hours and a half alone with her to bring up that awkward question again. He spoke the names of other frail ladies. More seriously and less violently than before, now that he had Fanny completely at his mercy, he cited their sweetness, their amiability, their general excellence. Would Miss Burney not admit that perhaps these very qualities had contributed to their sacrifice of character? Fanny, all of a tremble from the shock of some of his disclosures, was too confused by the tone of the conversation to disagree with her customary spirit, but she did wish he would change the subject.

She had her wish, but the new topic of conversation was almost as embarrassing, for Mr. Turbulent now turned his attention to religion. Gentlefolk didn't discuss religion outside the church. "There is no topic in the world upon which I am so careful how

I speak seriously as this," wrote Fanny. "By 'seriously' I do not mean gravely, but with earnestness; mischief here is so easily done, so difficultly reformed. I have made it, therefore, a rule through my life never to talk in detail upon religious opinions, but with those of whose principles I have the fullest convictions and highest respect. It is therefore very, very rarely I have ever entered upon the subject but with female friends or acquaintances, whose hearts I have well known, and who would be as unlikely to give as to receive any perplexity from the discourse. . . ."

Mr. Turbulent pursued; Fanny fled him down the labyrinthine ways. "When, in order to escape, I made only light and slight answers to his queries and remarks, he gravely said I led him into 'strange suspicions' concerning my religious tenets; and when I made to this some rallying reply, he solemnly declared he feared I was a 'mere philosopher' on these subjects, and totally incredulous with regard to all revealed religion.

"This was an attack which even in pleasantry I liked not, as the very words gave me a secret shock. I therefore then spoke to the point, and frankly told him that subjects which I held to be so sacred I made it an invariable rule never to discuss in casual conversations.

" 'And how, ma'am,' said he, suddenly assuming the authoritative seriousness of his professional character and dignity, 'and how, ma'am, can you better discuss matters of this solemn nature than now, with a man with whom their consideration peculiarly belongs?—with a clergyman?' "

He accused her of being either a Roman Catholic or an esprit fort. They were both opprobrious terms in 1786—fighting words. Fanny was considerably unsettled by the time they reached Windsor and simply didn't know how to reply to the Queen when that lady asked her if her trip had not been very pleasant. "Nobody converses better than Mr. Turbulent," declared Charlotte, "nobody has more general knowledge, nor a more pleasing and easy way of communicating it."

Fanny, fearing not to assent, assented, "but faintly however, for indeed he had perplexed far more than he had pleased me."

Hard upon this journey, the irrepressible Turbulent began to pester Miss Burney with another new idea. He was determined to introduce to her tea-drinking circle an equerry who had just come into his turn in the cycle of waiting—Colonel Fulke Greville. Though the equerry was a connection of Dr. Burney's first patron, Fanny had never met this scion of the family, and she protested she had no desire to do so, as she wished to make a break from the tea hour after dinner. Like a naughty schoolboy, Turbulent kept pressing upon her the threatened introduction, and Miss Burney had all too good reason for believing he was urging the presentation in the same way on the equally reluctant colonel. In the end, by cajolery and trickery, he brought them together, and she was forced to admit that "Colonel Welbred," as she dubbed Fulke Greville, was indeed a pleasant fellow. Nevertheless, the maneuver called for revenge, and Fanny evolved a sly scheme.

She administered a stab in Turbulent's back, and in his own fashion: she suggested to the Queen that Turbulent travel thereafter in the equerries' coach instead of hers. Mr. Turbulent much preferred their company, she explained to the surprised Charlotte; yes, yes, he was a charming companion, but at least while Fulke Greville was at court it was kinder to leave him to the company he preferred. A man liked better to be with men.

The Queen consented, and a radiant Fanny was able to show Mr. Turbulent that two could play at his game. He was very angry, or pretended to be. He made a scene. After traveling with apparent content six years with that oyster Mrs. Haggerdorn, he said, and now that traveling was become really agreeable in that coach, to be turned out of it . . . All of a sudden the astonishing man threw himself at Fanny's feet and made a lot of extravagant speeches. She was beginning to be alarmed by his vehemence when he relieved her by calling on all the pagan gods to witness his oath. It was all a joke, after all. . . . But was it? How the man worried her!

For a while after that he was quiet, and managed to please her by expressing pity for her position with Mrs. Schwellenberg. Whoever would have thought Fanny Burney would have such a companion? he asked rhetorically, and that time Fanny could not find it in her heart to snub him. Yet, though in a friendly way, she had to turn him out of her room as much as two or three times a day. He could not resist coming in on the slightest pretext, just to annoy, because he knew it teased.

Some of her severity melted after she witnessed a scene between Turbulent and the Princess Augusta. The clergyman teased Augusta quite as if she had been Fanny Burney. He twitted her about her rumored engagement to the Danish prince, standing before her in the doorway; he wouldn't let her leave the room until he had made her blush.

"Miss Burney," she cried, angry yet laughing, "pray do you take him away!—Pull him!"

"Indeed, ma'am, I dare not undertake him! I cannot manage him at all."

"I had not imagined any man," confessed Fanny later, "but the King or Prince of Wales, had ever ventured at a *badinage* of this sort with any of the Princesses; nor do I suppose any other man ever did."

Mr. Turbulent made faces at Fanny in the royal presence. He wiggled his eyebrows at her, he mimicked her expression, until she was terrified the Queen would notice and ask for an explanation. He made scenes bordering on gallantry when they were alone, and she could never be quite sure if he were *really* joking. He still insisted on traveling in her coach, though as Miss Planta usually came along he had to behave himself. He threatened to come and breakfast with the ladies every morning. They were gratifyingly scandalized at the very idea. Perhaps this success went to his head, because soon after this he made such a violent scene in Fanny's room that she lost her temper completely and frightened him into good behavior that lasted for several weeks.

His company was confusing, distressing, and bewildering, yet not quite painful. Somehow the days did seem to pass a bit more quickly because of Mr. Turbulent.

Queen Charlotte's staff gave her just as much trouble as any staff gives any housekeeper, though royal domestics' grievances and rewards loom the larger from being in the public eye. In no home but a king's or a president's are these matters so full of interest. Yet when one comes to examine them, they are all of the same homely stuff. A housemaid or a maid of honor gets into trouble; a common or royal footman tells fibs; a page is aggrieved because he does not get what he considers his rightful perquisite of wax candles from his commoner mistress or the princess's table. The Queen was chronically criticized by her underlings, for taking the "wrong type" of person into her service cheap, and thus letting down the tone of the whole establishment, or for failing in generosity. Most decidedly she does seem to have failed in that respect. The necessity of providing in a suitable manner for fifteen growing princes and princesses, especially when princes had such extravagant habits, gave her an excuse to be frugal.

By the time Fanny joined the household the Prince of Wales had already become the bad boy he was to remain. His parents regretfully decided that he was an enemy, and his visits home were few. When they passed off without trouble everyone drew a sigh of relief. One by one the younger brothers made their exit in turn from the close family circle, and they were all very glad to go. The dull, stiff routine of the palace, the unexciting company such as Mrs. Delany's, a flock of clergymen for preceptors, and quarreling musicians and painters, could not vie with the attractions of the lively, raffish society which existed outside the charmed circle. What man of the Prince of Wales's age would have hesitated between a stuffy evening at home with Papa, Mamma, and Mrs. Delany or a night in the town where there were all the delights of gambling, drinking, flattery, and pretty women? The prince was genuinely fond of music, but Handel's sweet sounds were not enough for a young man whose tutors were dissipated rakes like Hulse, Lake, and St. Leger.

Fanny was aware of the distress this situation caused her royal mistress. She was always there to hear the household gossip. The Queen confided in her, and she could not have chosen a safer ear. Miss Burney never did more than hint darkly at these sinful things in the Journal: she had enough to write about without being tempted to such indiscretion. These were only vicarious thrills, whereas she had troubles of her own, due mostly to the terrible Mrs. Schwellenberg.

The old woman possessed far more power than she should, considering her narrow, ignorant brain. She usually had her own way with the Queen, and rumors of her influence increased it enormously, most people not daring to test it with defiance. Fanny, by a process of reasoning which remains obscure, determined to avoid trouble at any cost. She, too, had the Queen's ear and could have fought Mrs. Schwellenberg with her own weapons, but she didn't. At least she said she didn't; it would merely make trouble, she argued, for the dear Queen. But at one period she did almost give in to temptation and resolve to hit back at the tyrant no matter what the consequences—a row, perhaps resignation of her post.

They shared a coach, and the incident occurred there, in the wintertime. Mrs. Schwellenberg, who liked fresh air, insisted on the glass window by Fanny's elbow being kept open to the breeze. Fanny's eyes, never very strong, caught cold and were badly inflamed. They were still in such a bad state during the next journey that the court naturalist Mr. de Luc, who was with them, leaned over and closed the window. The action put Mrs. Schwellenberg into a dreadful temper, so that Fanny hastily opened the window again. "Miss Burney might sit there, and so she ought!" cried the old demon, referring to the opposite seat of the coach.

Fanny said she was always sick riding backward.

"Oh, ver well! when you don't like it, don't do it. You might bear it when you like it! what did the poor Haggerdorn bear it! when the blood was all running down from her eyes!"

Indignantly Miss Burney reminded herself—and was obligingly reminded by the servants as well when she got home—that Mrs.

Haggerdorn had gone blind. No doubt Mrs. Schwellenberg's window had caused it. She fumed, and when her father came to pay her a visit he agreed that it was too much. She must resign without hesitation, he said, if it came to such a point.

We may take leave to doubt if Fanny would really have submitted to going blind, failing this parental permission, but that is what she said. However, her father in his infinite mercy *had* given permission; she felt appeased and didn't resign after all. A milder revolt was set in motion. Miss Burney avoided Mrs. Schwellenberg's company whenever possible, in a marked manner. She replied briefly to the old woman's remarks, in a "dry" tone of voice. She circumvented routine more often, going straight to the Queen for permission for her innocent outings to the gatehouse. Mrs. Delany was pressed into service and ceased to visit the tearoom, but with her niece went to Fanny's private apartments instead. It was the sort of cold war that often takes place in isolated communities like lonely huts at the North Pole, and royal courts.

It didn't last long, though. Miss Burney couldn't keep it up; the pressure was too much. She suddenly did a rightabout and began being extra nice to Mrs. Schwellenberg. She made the supreme sacrifice and played piquet. A species of peace descended on the ladies' dining room.

The Queen, realizing something was wrong, treated Miss Burney with tact. Our diarist claims never to have complained, but it is impossible to believe she didn't give Charlotte some hint of her state of mind. By a coincidence a newspaper printed a story just then that Fanny Burney was resigning her position at court . . . or had Dr. Burney inspired the rumor? Next day the paper followed up the item, saying Miss Burney was being promoted from the Queen's service to a position "near one of the Princesses."

The royal family kept up pretty faithfully with the news, and the Duke of York called his mother's attention to these paragraphs. They disturbed the Queen. She demanded Fanny's reassurance and denial of any intent to leave.

It may seem strange that a Queen of England should take

such interest in housekeeping trifles, especially if Miss Burney was as poor a hand at her job as Lady Llanover later alleged, but Charlotte, within her narrow limits, was shrewd and sensitive to public opinion. Fanny's much-admired Miss Hamilton had resigned recently enough to make the Queen touchy. Her reputation as a kind employer was at stake; she felt guilty and apprehensive in any case, because of Mrs. Schwellenberg. Fanny Burney was a prominent person, and her resignation so soon after Miss Hamilton's would give the Whigs a good chance to make capital. Charlotte must have thought it expedient to be more than ever gracious to her caged novelist, however unsatisfactory the woman was as a dresser. Maybe Dr. Burney knew all this and passed the word to the newspapers. . . .

The Queen might have spared herself those few minutes of uneasiness. Miss Burney was too tame to fly away. She made a vow to herself, after the coach affair. Until her father called her away from court, or her feeble frame sank under the strain, she would stay.

Why did she insist upon this martyrdom? To resign was not impossible. In her position, Fanny was more free to quit than was any ordinary lady's maid. Admittedly the laws of those days had been framed for the convenience of employers, so that it was a legal offense, for instance, to tempt a woman's servant away from her with promise of higher wages or better conditions. But Fanny was not a domestic, in spite of that hateful bell. She could resign, if she insisted on so doing. Why, then, since life there was so dead and tame, and Mrs. Schwellenberg impossible, and her father had given her permission, did she not leave the court?

She did not really want to leave. At court there was still a heavy balance in favor of security, and glory, and hope of advancement for her relatives. Dr. Burney would have been deeply disappointed. The Queen would have been grieved. Out in the world, as Fanny expressed her idea of the rest of England, what was there for her to do? Now it seemed a chancy life, without Daddy Crisp and, since the royals had so completely adopted her, without Mrs.

Delany. Besides, what would everyone have said? One did not lightly give up a royal appointment.

The weeks dragged on. Mr. Turbulent's wife was gravely ill, so for a time the ebullient clergyman mended his ways and was satisfactorily grave and gloomy. Colonel Fulke Greville came into waiting again and spent pleasant evenings drinking tea with Miss Burney, to whom he talked openly, disregarding Mrs. Schwellenberg's jealous displeasure. Colonel Digby's wife died; Colonel Digby ("Mr. Fairly") came back, sadder and more sentimental than ever, and more attractive, though he had aged under the strain. He too spent much time talking about life with Fanny. How much better it was, she reflected, to talk about life with Colonel Digby than with Mr. Turbulent! Turbulent wasn't serious. Turbulent was like quicksilver, a substance Fanny was temperamentally incapable of liking. But Colonel Digby adored being serious. He could be serious for hours. "All his sentiments," she sighed, "seem formed upon the most perfect basis of religious morality." Both gentlemen spoke about life in general with disfavor, but in how different a fashion! Where Turbulent was, well, turbulent, Colonel Digby was soft, and gentle, and resigned; he murmured like wind in the willows.

It was rumored about the court that Colonel Digby might solace his sorrowing heart with a second wife, Miss Charlotte Margaret Gunning. "Miss Fuzelier," as Fanny called her, was a maid of honor and a famous beauty—"pretty, learned, and accomplished; yet, from the very little I have seen of her, I should not think she had heart enough to satisfy Mr. Fairly, in whose character the leading trait is the most acute sensibility. However, I have heard he has disclaimed all such intention, with high indignation at the report, as equally injurious to the delicacy both of Miss Fuzilier and himself, so recently after his loss."

An advance copy of *Letters to and from the Late Samuel Johnson, LLD.*, Vol. I., by Mrs. Piozzi, was lent by the Bishop of Carlisle to Mr. Turbulent, who lent it to the Queen, who lent it to Mrs.

Schwellenberg, who handed it to Fanny. We can imagine how eagerly and fearfully she riffled the pages looking for her family name, but she found it only once, where Dr. Johnson mentioned a visit with Mrs. Thrale to St. Martin's Street—that first, unforgotten concert. Not knowing that in the second volume Mrs. Piozzi was to call her a "female infidel," Miss Burney had a field day discussing the book. She was offended by Mrs. Schwellenberg's attacks on Mrs. Thrale—she could not yet bring herself to use the hated name "Piozzi"—but Queen Charlotte was different. The Queen was not anxious to condemn, only curious. She kept asking Fanny to explain references in the letters and to describe the people named therein. Thus at last was the little Burney's rankling pride assuaged. To be able to forgive Mrs. Thrale from her new eminence was a great luxury; to defend Mrs. Thrale's name before her Queen was a greater. She need no longer feel uneasily that she had done wrong to her friend and been well and truly snubbed for it. Mrs. Thrale could scarcely, even in memory, snub Miss Burney, Assistant Keeper of the Robes and confidante of the Queen of England.

The Warren Hastings trial had begun. No one realized then that it was going to drag on for more than seven years. The Queen decided that Fanny out of all the household could best report on its progress, so Miss Burney had a ticket to Westminster Hall for most days during the opening weeks. Fanny never disappointed her royal mistress, her phenomenal birdlime memory serving better on some of the important speeches than did the notes kept by professional reporters.

The early days of the trial made a break in her dull routine. Sitting in the Great Chamberlain's Box with her brothers Charles or James, being greeted by famous men, and arguing at length with Mr. Wyndham, who was on the wrong side—for Fanny, like the royal family, staunchly supported Hastings—she felt once more like a living part of the world, instead of an inmate of a monastery. She glowed with passionate indignation on behalf of Hastings, not that she really knew anything about the East India Company's affairs, but she knew the Hastingses, and she could tell from his personality that he could never be guilty of all those crimes. She saw Sheridan, and he reminded her that she still owed him a comedy. It was an impossible suggestion nowadays, of course, and yet somewhere in her mind a window blew open and a refreshing breeze ruffled the hangings in a room which had long been sealed.

Mr. Crutchley was there too; Fanny was unaffectedly glad to meet him again. It was good to talk of Streatham and the old days. Together they shook their heads over Mrs. Thrale's mad impropriety in publishing the *Letters*.

Altogether, the spring of 1788 would have been a happy one, except for a calamity which had long been dreaded but was none the less tragic when it arrived. Mrs. Delany died, quietly and in good taste, as might be expected of the venerable lady. Weeping, Fanny swore eternal friendship for Miss Port. The two women, who had knelt together at the side of the deathbed for Mrs. Delany's last blessing, melted in tears in each other's arms, quite as if the seed of an enmity which was to outlive both of them had not already been sown.

Fanny's difficulties were now enormously increased, since there was no sympathetic Mrs. Delany to fly to. Though sometimes in her higher flights of fancy she pretended that she concealed her trials and pains from her dear old friend to spare her feelings, the truth was that Mrs. Delany had known all about it and was always ready to proffer the wise advice of a courtier born and bred. She in turn told Fanny her own troubles. They had comforted each other: now Mrs. Delany was dead, and Fanny must brave Cerbera alone. But Cerbera for the time being was not so fierce as she had been before the affair of the coach window. God tempered the wind.

His Majesty was not well, so it was decided in the middle of the year that he should have a course of the waters at Cheltenham Spa. The house taken to accommodate him, called either Faucon-

berg Hall or Bays Hall Lodge, was so small that the usual royal
party was much curtailed. No man but the King slept there; the
other males were quartered in the town. Fanny and Miss Planta
had to go without their maids; the ladies reckoned themselves
lucky to have footmen. But this informality, and the tiny rooms
in which Fanny was lodged, and the crowded conditions, led to a
new experience. Fanny was happy at Fauconberg Hall. If we were
not speaking of the composed Miss Burney, we would say that
she was even wildly happy. Though she did not quite commit herself, and never wrote the betraying word, Fanny fell in love. There
is no possible doubt whatever.

Colonel Stephen Digby asked on the first evening if he could
drink tea for once with the ladies, as all the house was still upset.
He promised in the same breath that thereafter he would leave
Miss Burney to her privacy. How unusual, she reflected, and what
true delicacy Mr. Fairly possessed, to understand her desire for
solitude! Almost, he made her willing to relinquish that solitude.

During the following days Colonel Digby spent all his spare time
sitting in Fanny's room. Such behavior would have attracted
attention in a court anywhere; in a small house like the lodge it was
glaringly noticeable. The King made a comment reminiscent of
Fanny's stepmother, exclaiming with arch surprise when he walked
in on them, "What! only you two?" At which Colonel Digby
laughed a little, and Fanny, instead of sinking through the floor
with Evelina shame, only smiled.

The colonel wrote letters in Fanny's room, sometimes asking
her help, but until they began reading poetry together they spent
most of the time in discourse. "Highly cultivated by books, and
uncommonly fertile in stores of internal resource, he left me nothing to wish, for the time I spent with him, but that 'the Fates, the
Sisters Three, and such like branches of learning,' would interfere
against the mode of future separation planned for the remainder
of our expedition." For Fanny, those are strong words. Before, she
had expressed herself so warmly only when the subject of her
gushing was Mrs. Delany or some superannuated clergyman.

Everything conspired in her favor against the dreaded separation. The King directed that his gentlemen were to breakfast with Miss Burney and Miss Planta every morning. They were to take tea in the same room and to sup there whenever they had time to sup. Every day, as soon as they were left alone, Colonel Digby started on his favorite subject, "participation," the necessity of it to every species of happiness. Life single and unshared seemed a mere melancholy burthen to the colonel. "Alas! thought I, that a man so good should be so unhappy!"

It was amazing how many poets Fanny had never read, whom the colonel now brought to her attention. There was a poem by William Falconer, *The Shipwreck*, which he read to Fanny while she busied herself with her work on morning caps or dress trimmings. "One line he came to, that he read with an emotion extremely affecting. 'Tis a sweet line—

He felt the chastity of silent woe.

He stopped upon it, and sighed so deeply that his sadness quite infected me."

Another evening the colonel stayed behind after the other gentlemen departed to the town in quest of acquaintance or amusement. Fanny said, "Mr. Fairly has not spirit for such searches; I question, indeed, if ever had taste for them. . . . How unexpected an indulgence—luxury, I may say, to me, are these evenings now becoming! While I listen to such reading, and such a reader, all my work goes on with an alacrity that renders it all pleasure to me. I have had no regale like this for many and many a grievous long evening! . . . And how little could I expect, in a royal residence, a relief of this sort!"

Colonel Gwynn asked Fanny if she thought Digby would ever marry again. She said she thought it doubtful but she hoped he would for the sake of his own happiness.

"And what do think of Miss Fuzilier?"

"That he is wholly disengaged with her and with everybody."

"Well, I think it will be, for I know they correspond. . . ."

This correspondence, if it were truly going on, should have convinced Fanny, but she was very sure of her ground. If Miss Gunning and Digby did correspond, she argued, they must have begun doing it when Digby's wife was a party to it, and it was merely carried on now as a matter of friendship. A man like the colonel would never, never think of a second connection at so early a period, not a year after his wife's death! In proof of this sensibility, Colonel Digby soon afterward confided to Miss Burney that he was much troubled, as the royal party intended to take an extra week for their outing. He was expected to remain in waiting until they returned to Windsor, and this would mean he would not be home on August sixteenth, the anniversary of his wife's demise. At the very best he would be on his way home, *traveling*. Pious people did not travel on Sunday, or on other spiritually important occasions, and the colonel was deeply worried. He wished to dedicate the day in some peculiar manner with his four children. "Her Majesty must know what the 16th is to me," he said, with feeling. "And then," said Fanny, "almost immediately, he wished me good morning, and went away; leaving me so much touched by the mournful state of his excellent mind, and so gratefully impressed by the kind confidence he seemed to feel that he spoke to a safe and a sympathising well-wisher, that I could not, for the whole day through, turn my thoughts to any other subject."

Sometimes she feared that with her backwardness and silence she seemed insensible, or at least insipid, but she dreaded to seem forward. She wished her dear friends were near, to give her advice. As they were not, she could only go on as things seemed to indicate; tremulous, fearful, but very happy and for once gloriously careless of appearances. Not once did she give an anxious thought to gossip. It was an extraordinary lapse, a veritable transformation, which can only be explained in one way: Fanny had met her match. Mr. Fairly's prudery outdid even hers. A more decorous, delicate courtship has never been recorded. It was all soul and sentiment.

Colonel Digby, after being unwell of some mysterious complaint that swelled his face, developed a bad gout in his foot. This kept him from going off with the King on his daily expeditions, but allowed him to hobble over to Miss Burney's room to read poetry with her. There was a good deal of suspense connected with his visits now; the King would not be pleased to think Digby was well enough for Miss Burney but not for his service, and people might not understand, said Digby—it was his thought, not Fanny's. The world would call the pair of them bluestockings, said the colonel humorously, if they were found reading poetry and serious literature; such an accusation would be most unpleasant. Another reason for shyness was the title of the book they were perusing: *Original Love Letters between a Lady of Quality and a Person of Inferior Condition*. In spite of the injudicious title, which put Fanny off for days, the book turned out to be most improving. There wasn't a word in it which was not elevated, even lofty, in sentiment. Still, other people might not understand. One knows what other people are—evil-minded.

When the colonel, still on sick leave, dared to come and dine with Fanny, however, it could not be hoped that the news would not get around. That evening was particularly memorable. The weather was so fine that Miss Burney assented when Digby, because he could not walk, suggested standing on the steps of the hall in the sweet air. "And here, for near two hours, on the steps of Fauconberg Hall, we remained; and they were two hours of such pure serenity, without and within, as I think, except in Norbury Park, with its loved inhabitants and my Susan, I scarce ever remember to have spent."

"Sunday, July 27.—This morning in my first attendance I seized a moment to tell Her Majesty of yesterday's dinner. 'So I hear!' she cried; and I was sorry any one had anticipated my information, nor can I imagine who it might be.

" 'But pray, ma'am,' very gravely, 'how did it happen? I understood Mr. Fairly was confined by the gout.'

" 'He grew better, ma'am, and hoped by exercise to prevent a serious fit.'

"She said no more, but did not seem pleased. The fatigues of a

Court attendance are so little comprehended, that persons known to be able to quit their room and their bed are instantly concluded to be qualified for all the duties of their office."

The King twitted Colonel Digby, saying he and his gout were only fanciful. The colonel was displeased. "Fanciful, sir?" he repeated, so that the King took back his words, saying, "Why, I should wonder indeed if you were to be that!"

Then, when the colonel had recovered, it was Fanny's turn. She felt so ill (it was influenza) that it was all she could do to attend at the Queen's toilettes, and after the second one she tried to sleep but could not. She went down to the parlor, and there was Colonel Digby, reading sermons all by himself. "How could this man be a soldier? Might one not think he was bred in the cloisters?" He read a sermon to Fanny, so feelingly, forcibly, solemnly, that it was almost too much for her. She had some difficulty behaving with proper propriety. . . .

On August ninth the Queen surprised Fanny by gravely asking her what were Colonel Digby's designs with regard to his going away? Poor Fanny experienced a painful sensation. To answer promptly would be an admission that she was better informed than the Queen, and it would also betray his confidence, yet—"I understand, ma'am," she faltered, "that he means to go to-morrow morning early."

A little more cross-questioning, and the Queen's displeased remark, ". . . he has not spoke to me of his designs this great while," left Fanny gasping for inspiration. Suddenly she got it. The colonel had intended to leave that very day, she said, but as Her Majesty was going to the play, he had postponed his departure so that he could have the honor of attending her thither, as usual. It was a happy thought, and the Queen seemed appeased.

Colonel Digby came next day to take his leave. After a little impersonal chat about the children, he said some very significant things. "There is no happiness without participation; no participation without affection. There is, indeed, in affection a charm that leaves all things behind it, and renders even every calamity that does not interfere with it inconsequential; and there is no difficulty, no toil, no labour, no exertion, that will not be endured where there is a view of reaping it."

Fanny's concurrence was too perfect to require many words.

"And affection there sometimes is," he continued, "even in this weak world, so pure, so free from alloy, that one is tempted to wonder, without deeply considering, why it should not be permanent, and why it should be vain."

"Here I did not quite comprehend his conclusion," confessed Fanny, "but it was a sort of subject I could not probe, for various reasons. Besides, he was altogether rather obscure."

After more melancholy moralizing, Fanny grew quite daring. She said, "I will say—for that you will have pleasure in hearing—that you have lightened my time here in a manner no one else could have done, of this party."

". . . He said not a word of answer, but bowed, and went away, leaving me firmly impressed with a belief that I shall find in him a true, an honourable, and even an affectionate friend, for life."

Two days later Fanny received a letter from Colonel Digby. "Her Majesty may possibly not have heard that Mr. Edmund Waller died on Thursday night. He was Master of St. Catherine's, which is in Her Majesty's gift. It may be useful to her to have this early intelligence of this circumstance, and you will have the goodness to mention it to her. Mr. W. was at a house upon his estate within a mile and a half of this place.—Very truly and sincerely yours,

S. Digby."

This may sound obscure, but it was really plain to the eye of a sovereign. Colonel Digby wanted that job as Master of St. Katherine's by the Tower; it was a sinecure worth something between four and eight hundred pounds a year. By being first with the news, he had put in a good claim. None of this was a mystery to Fanny, but the informal tone of the letter made her feel squeamish about handing it over to the Queen. In those verbose days only an intimate would sign his letter thus simply, "very truly and sincerely yours," and Fanny was hard put to give the news to the Queen without the letter. She sent it at last by word of mouth, via Princess Elizabeth whom she happened to encounter, and that might have been the end of it, but the Queen was inquisitive. She sent for Fanny herself and interviewed her in the presence of the princesses.

As to Mr. Waller: "Pray have you known him long?" said Charlotte.

"I never knew him at all, ma'am."

"No? Why, then, how came you to receive the news about his death?"

"I heard of it only from Colonel Digby, ma'am."

The Queen looked surprised. "From Colonel Digby?—Why did he not tell it me?"

"He did not know it when he was here, ma'am; he heard it at Northleach, and, thinking it might be of use to your Majesty to have the account immediately, he sent it over express."

There was a dead silence, so uncomfortable that Fanny plunged ahead. "Colonel Digby, ma'am, wrote the news to me, on such small paper, and in such haste, that it is hardly fit to be shown to your Majesty; but I have the note upstairs."

No answer; again all silent. At length Princess Augusta said, "Mamma, Miss Burney says she has the note upstairs."

"If your Majesty pleases to see it——"

"I shall be glad to see it," said the Queen, much more pleasantly.

Poor Fanny! Charlotte read the letter aloud, and when she came to that telltale signature her voice changed noticeably. Poor Fanny . . . Yet, observe, the incident had its advantage. It pointed to something; it planted ideas in the Queen's mind; it almost compromised the colonel. Could Miss Burney have realized this? Did she exult in her secret soul? She didn't say so.

Colonel Digby got the place of master.

16. JOY OF A HEART UNBRIDLED

WE APPROACH two crises, one of national magnitude and one which was to Fanny much more important, being a private matter of her own. Back at Windsor, without Digby's company, she found Mrs. Schwellenberg a bad substitute. For all that, she was unusually lighthearted, and this part of the Diary is remarkable for a unique entry—Miss Burney actually made a risqué joke! At any rate she repeated one.

The explosive Colonel Goldsworthy, in protest against spending his tea hour with Mrs. Schwellenberg when Fanny was not present, had taken to the most open rudeness permitted within his code. Every evening, as soon as he came in to tea, he pretended to go to sleep, sitting back in his chair with his eyes closed, and perhaps he even went so far as to give an occasional snore. Mrs. Schwellenberg was not quick on the uptake, but after some evenings of this she began to realize it could not be mere coincidence that the equerry always became drowsy the minute he saw Miss Burney wasn't there. She said to Fanny, very gravely:

"Colonel Goldsworthy always sleeps with me! sleeps he with you the same?"

" 'In the midst of all my irksome discomfort, it was with difficulty I could keep my countenance at this question which I was forced to negative.

"The next evening she repeated it. 'Vell, sleeps he yet with you—Colonel Goldsworthy?'

" 'Not yet, ma'am,' I hesitatingly answered.

" 'Oh! ver well! he will sleep with nobody but me! Oh, I von't come down.'

"And a little after she added, 'I believe he vill marry you!'

" 'I believe not, ma'am,' I answered."

October 17, 1788. "The King is not well; he has not been quite well some time, yet nothing I hope alarming, though there is an uncertainty as to his complaint not very satisfactory."

His medical advisers, always on the alert since the King had gone temporarily insane twenty-seven years before, were convinced that he was again heading for trouble. Three days later, Fanny said, he was taken very ill in the night, but recovered. Nevertheless the Queen was much alarmed. She had seen him in the same terrifying state soon after their marriage.

What must have been especially nerve-racking for all the household was the embarrassment of the situation. They had been so carefully drilled in their routine that they had come to depend completely on their countless small rules of etiquette. It would be hard to conceive of a group of people less fitted to cope with such an emergency; all potential initiative had long since been crushed out of them. There was simply no precedent for it. What is the proper thing for a lady of the bedchamber to do when her King suddenly babbles nonsense? Nobody knew. Everyone was confused and frightened, and the word "everyone" includes the royal physicians, for treatment of mental disease had not gone further than the methods of Bedlam, that model lunatic asylum and show place, where the cells were at least kept clean and violent cases were simply put into strait jackets.

Things would have been simpler if the wretched staff had been permitted to use the word "insane" or "mental." But the Queen and all the others felt the horror which still attaches to those words, a horror much amplified because the patient was the King. They would not admit it at first in the medical reports; they did not dare speak of it aloud to each other. The King was ill, he was in a fever. . . . One did not even say he was ill, at first.

"I had a sort of conference with His Majesty, or rather I was the object to whom he spoke, with a manner so uncommon, that a high fever alone could account for it; a rapidity, a hoarseness of voice, a volubility, an earnestness—a vehemence, rather—it startled me inexpressibly; yet with a graciousness exceeding even all I ever met with before—it was almost kindness! . . .

"The King was prevailed upon not to go to chapel this morning. I met him in the passage from the Queen's room; he stopped me, and conversed upon his health near half-an-hour, still with that extreme quickness of speech and manner that belongs to fever; and he hardly sleeps, he tells me, one minute all night; indeed, if he recovers not his rest, a most delirious fever seems to threaten him. He is all agitation, all emotion, yet all benevolence and goodness, even to a degree that makes it touching to hear him speak. He assures everybody of his health; he seems only fearful to give uneasiness to others, yet certainly he is better than last night. Nobody speaks of his illness, nor what they think of it."

That was October twenty-sixth, after which deterioration was rapid. The poor King grew weaker and walked like a gouty man, but he kept talking, until he talked away his voice and grew so hoarse it was painful to hear him. Even then nobody dared use coercion. He actually went hunting November first. That night Fanny found him still in the Queen's dressing room when she went to attend her mistress. "He was begging her not to speak to him when he got to his room, that he might fall asleep, as he felt great want of that refreshment. He repeated this desire, I believe, at least a hundred times, though, far enough from needing it, the poor Queen never uttered one syllable! He then applied to me, saying he was really very well, except in that one particular, that he could not sleep."

By November fifth nothing more definite had occurred, though the Royal Lodge was all uneasy and alarmed. Residence seemed fixed at Windsor; the usual drawing rooms had been put off; the

Duke of York had come to see his father. Still there was no real change in procedure. At noon the King went out for an airing with the princess royal in his chaise. Fanny saw him go, from the window; "he was all smiling benignity, but gave so many orders to the postillions and got in and out of the carriage twice, with such agitation, that again my fear of a great fever hanging over him grew more and more powerful."

The *Morning Herald* had printed some news of the King's "indisposition" which angered the Queen. She was all for punishing the printer severely, and had just done talking about it with Fanny when the Prince of Wales was announced. An undefined chill seems to have settled over the apartment. The prince had come from his favorite place, Brighthelmstone. His mother did not seem at all glad to see him and asked ungraciously if he shouldn't go back. Yes, he said, he would return next day; first he had something to say to her, however. They retired.

Oppressed with gloomy forebodings, Fanny returned to her room and saw from her window a joyous sight: Colonel Digby arriving. He must have been sent for, she reflected with mixed feelings of hope and apprehension; he was still limping and had not intended to come back so soon. But of course she could not run to meet him. She must wait. . . . Her lonely dinner with Miss Planta was nearly silent. That evening an unwonted stillness reigned over the house, and the footman told Fanny that the musicians had been ordered away. No *music?* Why not? Fanny was astonished. Might not his usual concert have soothed His Majesty?

It was not until a dreadfully gloomy tea hour had ended and Colonel Digby was left alone with Fanny that she discovered "the whole of the mysterious horror!" The King had grown violent at dinner, irritated beyond control by the presence of his eldest son. Fanny contents herself with a refined version of the affair: George III had broken forth into positive delirium, she said, "and the Queen was so overpowered as to fall into violent hysterics. All the Princesses were in misery, and the Prince of Wales had burst into tears." In actual fact, His Majesty had suddenly leaped at the prince, seized him by the collar, and bumped his head against the wall, something he had probably been longing to do for many years. There is no doubt the prince did burst into tears. Indeed he nearly fainted, and the princesses had to rub his temples with "Hungary water," and he was bled. What with the Queen screaming, the prince weeping, and his sisters contributing to the general uproar, it is to be hoped the poor King had another few moments' gratification after all those years of restraint and good manners.

In Fanny's mind the horror of that agonizing thrill when "Mr. Fairly" told her the story must have made up for the shocked disappointment she felt when they met in the tearoom: "How grave he looked! how shut up in himself! A silent bow was his only salutation; how changed I thought it,—and how fearful a meeting, so long expected as a solace!"

Now, cozy together in their common worry, all seemed healed though the atmosphere was depressed. And after talking so much about the royals and expressing himself warmly for the principal sufferers, Digby kindly examined Fanny herself. "How are you? Are you strong? are you stout? can you go through such scenes as these? you do not look much fitted for them."

Truthfully she assured him that she could stand a good deal in behalf of other people. It is a fact that during the whole ordeal of the King's attack Fanny stood up to it amazingly well, and the Queen had reason for commending her when the worst was past.

After that dramatic dinner party the household was hastily rearranged; it was feared the King might next attack the Queen or some others of his children, and this danger must be avoided somehow without annoying him or showing disrespect. The courtiers told him that the Queen was ill and should not be disturbed, but that night, just after the scene with the Prince of Wales, he went in to her room to make sure she was there in her bed, and the unexpected visit frightened her terribly. One of the Queen's ladies had to sit on guard by her bed every night after that incident, until apartments were arranged for her at a distance from the King's chamber. The anteroom of the royal sufferer's bedroom afforded an amazing spectacle, with great numbers of his attendants, equerries, and one or two of the less offensive sons sitting there solemnly all night, every night, waiting until they should be needed. Whether or not it was really necessary to separate him from the Queen, any continued stay in his neighborhood would have been unbearably painful to her. The poor King talked without stopping, except when sleep overtook him; once he went on talking without a break for sixteen hours—"his voice was so lost in hoarseness and weakness, it was rendered almost inarticulate."

To add to the discomfort and anxiety of the gentlemen in waiting, no fire was permitted in the King's apartments, for fear he might again grow violent and set the palace or himself ablaze. It was already very cold; the weather that winter was more severe than it had been for years. No one could bear to remain in the royal bedroom for more than half an hour at a time. And all the time, except in fitful bouts of sleep, the King talked—about the Duke of York, who should not have come without permission from Hanover and who must go back immediately, like a dutiful son; of his dear dead little boy Octavius; of the wicked Prince of Wales; of the loss of the American colonies.

". . . the tears rolled down his cheeks in a manner pitiful to behold," wrote Mrs. Papendiek, daughter and wife of court pages, in her Memoirs. "His Majesty used to inquire who called, and on wishing to be told if Lord North had ever been, was answered in the affirmative. Then the King said, 'He might have recollected me sooner. However, he, poor fellow has lost his sight, and I my mind. Yet we meant well by those Americans; just to punish them with a few bloody noses, and then make bows for the mutual happiness of the two countries. But want of principle got into the Army, want of energy and skill in the First Lord of the Admiralty, and want of unanimity at home. We lost America. Tell him not to call again; I shall never see him.' "

According to the fond Fanny, her Colonel Digby was the hero of the hour. He took charge of the King one day when he was wandering about and nobody else dared try to manage him; Digby cleverly persuaded him back to his bed. The Queen placed great trust in Digby and was always calling him to her side.

Suddenly the Prince of Wales decided that the household must not be left free to talk outside, in the world; he dropped a sort of iron curtain on the lodge. The first hint of this decision was strangely unpleasant, and typical of the prince. Old Mr. Smelt, in an agony of loyal grief, had been hovering about the place. Should he or should he not live there at Windsor during the crisis? He thought he might have influence with the King, but would the princes approve of his staying?

While discussing this point with the sympathetic Miss Burney and Mr. de Luc, he noticed the doctor in the courtyard. He went out to speak to him, and the watching Fanny saw the Prince of Wales join them. She was pleased with the way the prince took Mr. Smelt's arm and paced up and down with his old teacher, chatting in the friendliest manner. Smelt came back to her gratified and flattered because the prince had himself suggested that Smelt stay, in order to comfort the Queen. Off went the bustling old man to write to his wife and arrange for a room at the inn. . . . When he came back to the lodge the porter handed him his greatcoat at the door and would not let him in, by express order of the Prince of Wales.

"The condition of the Queen was pitiable in the extreme," wrote Mrs. Papendiek. "The first few days of her terrible grief she passed almost entirely with her hands and arms stretched across a table before her, with her head resting upon them, and she took nothing to eat or drink except once or twice a little barley water. . . . The conduct of the Prince of Wales was . . . very heartless. He came constantly to the Lodge and assumed to himself a power that had not yet been legally given to him, without any consideration or regard for his mother's feelings . . . after being most severe, and knocking his stick several times on the floor, while condemning the whole of what had been done, [he] bowed and retired without kissing the Queen's hand according to the usual custom."

Nobody was permitted to go out of the house, and nobody was allowed to communicate with anybody in the outside world or even with anyone else in the lodge itself, though of course the last regulation was impossible to enforce. At least all tea drinkings in company were suspended, by order of the prince. Nevertheless, Colonel Digby called on Miss Burney, dined with Miss Burney, and gave Miss Burney the day's report, and nobody stopped him. Certainly Miss Burney didn't attempt to.

The King was a little better for a few days, then he was worse. Sir Lucas Pepys was called in; he came to see his friend Miss Burney, and Colonel Digby encountered him in her room and was not pleased. (But Miss Burney was.) The King was again better. Rambling on in his usual way, he suddenly twitted Colonel Digby for neglecting him: "He's so fond of the company of learned ladies, that he gets to the tea-table with Miss Burney, and there he spends his whole time."

"I know exactly," added the colonel, after repeating this to Fanny, "what it all means—that the King has in his head—exactly what has given rise to the idea—'tis Miss Gunning." He hurried on, as Fanny stared; he spoke of Miss Gunning very highly and mentioned her learning: a report of their attachment probably had reached the ears of the King before his illness; but this report was completely false, said the colonel. "And this in the present confused state of his mind is altogether, I know, what he means by the learned ladies."

After she was left alone, Fanny pondered. Was this perhaps becoming a major scandal? Should she not put a stop to Colonel Digby's visits? But, mused the ex-prude, what after all had been said? There had been no hint of flirtation; she had merely been called a learned lady, and Digby had been accused of liking learned ladies . . . no scandal at all. Nothing, in fact, for anyone to feel embarrassed about. Why should she give up Colonel Digby's friendship? It was her only solace in her troubled loneliness. No, she would not give up the colonel: she would meticulously forget that remark of the poor King's.

The King was worse, and continued worse. It was decided he must be moved to Kew, and his unhappy family as well, because at Windsor the gardens and rooms were always within view of the public. The King could not take exercise there without being spied on, and it was important that the public should not see him now. There was his beard, for one thing. He could not be trusted with a razor, said the physicians, but he violently resented the attempts of his attendants to shave him, for he realized the imputation. For days he wasn't shaved at all. Mrs. Papendiek described proudly how her husband persuaded His Majesty to allow him to do it at last.

"Twice only was the King shaved between November and some time in January. My father [Albert] though 'principal barber' . . . was too nervous to undertake it. Mr. Papendiek, however, was ready. He begged the Queen to have Palmer, the razor-maker, down, that there might be no flaw or hitch in the instruments, and the razor well sharpened. This was done, and Mr. Papendiek succeeded in clearing the two cheeks at one sitting, which, with the King's talking in between, was nearly a two hours' job. The Queen, out of sight of the King sat patiently to see it done, which was achieved without one drop of blood.

"Everyone complimented the poor barber, who in a few days cleared the mouth and throat, by hitting upon a pleasant conversation to amuse his Majesty while the operation was proceeded with, and this was repeated after a few weeks' interval." But this happy experiment could not be repeated often, and the King, emaciated and unshaven, with his wild expression and ceaseless chatter, was not a soothing spectacle. His people must not see him.

The buildings at Kew were isolated; large gardens, well railed, separated the houses from the public. But the King strongly opposed any move. He said he was quite comfortable at Windsor. At last he was coaxed into his coach by means of the doctors' promise that he would see the Queen as soon as he got to Kew. When they broke their promise, his disappointment and rage were overwhelming. He should have been allowed the interview with his wife, mused Miss Burney; surely this treatment couldn't but be bad for him? But the gentlemen and physicians were convinced that such a course was too dangerous to risk. Uncomfortably, the court settled into Kew Palace.

Papendiek had another story for his wife one night when he came home from duty. The King, fulminating in his bedroom against his people, who had, he declared, all turned against him, suddenly crawled under a sofa. Still talking away in this uncomfortable position he vowed he would remain there, communing with his Maker. Papendiek, thinking quickly, promptly crawled under the sofa and sprawled there on the floor next to His Majesty. After a short pause he directed the servants to lift the sofa straight up into the air, leaving the King exposed: then with a gigantic effort he picked up George III and carried him bodily to his couch. In doing it Papendiek injured himself for life, George being no featherweight, but the story made good telling.

The King was worse. Life at Kew was really uncomfortable. The palace had never been intended for more than a summer residence, and the rooms were bitterly cold, underfurnished, carpetless, and drafty. To make things more sinister, a regency was rumored. The Prince of Wales's party was trying to push it through quickly, as the prince was eager to get control of all the power and money—especially the money—that would be his. Under the strain, Mrs. Schwellenberg's temper became so nasty that Miss Burney felt she really could not, would not bear it much longer, though of course for the moment, while her mistress needed her . . .

The King was better. How pleasant life could be, after all! The Queen permitted Colonel Digby, at his tactful suggestion, to buy six tiny carpets, and she gave one to Fanny for her bedroom. Mrs. Schwellenberg was only an unpleasant old woman, thought Fanny: she was not important.

The King was worse. Now Miss Burney was given the interesting job of receiving the first news every morning of how he had passed the night, and hastening to the Queen with the report. When it was a good one she flew on wings of happy eagerness, and when it was bad she softened the message a little. Mrs. Schwellenberg, jealous of this new duty, tried to scuttle Fanny's popularity with the Queen. Mrs. Schwellenberg was really quite impossible. But Mr. Smelt had once more gained access to the Queen's house (the Prince of Wales having apologized to him for the incident at Windsor) and he sometimes called on Mrs. Schwellenberg and drew off her fire from Fanny.

The King was a little better—a little worse—a little better—one could not swear that any of the changes amounted to much. It was common knowledge that the Queen had consented to call in Dr. Willis, a clergyman with a hobby for curing mental disorders. This Dr. Willis held novel theories of treatment and had gained considerable reputation in his line. It was exactly because of this reputation that the Queen had been reluctant to call him in, for he was known throughout England as a specialist in mental diseases: would not his name then be an admission of the dreadful truth? Left to herself, the Queen would probably have acted like any ignorant poor woman of the parish—hidden her husband away in some dark room and kept him a dreadful secret shame which the Law must never find out. But she was the Queen, at the mercy of the government and their committees, and so Dr. Willis was called in. He was presented to George III, with many recommendations. "Will he let me shave myself," asked the King, "cut my nails, and have a knife at breakfast and dinner, and treat me as his Sovereign, not command me as a subject?"

When Dr. Willis promised, the King immediately tested his good faith: he announced that he wished to shave. Under the anxious eyes of the court attendants, Willis calmly called for the shaving materials and let his patient go to it. "It now took the King a long time to complete the task," said Mrs. Papendiek, "and he was glad not to repeat it. The nails were cut the next day with the same permission."

There was hope for a cure, pronounced Dr. Willis after this interview; of course the royal patient had not been treated properly, and the disease had had a long time to get under way, but there was still hope. Indeed, Willis was confident he *could* work a cure. In the meantime a fire must be provided immediately in the King's room.

Beneath the lowering clouds of the threatened regency the distracted household pulled itself together, and fearfully, with timid longing for a miracle, watched Dr. Willis.

Now at last did the King make definite progress toward recovery. At least if he didn't show improvement from the very beginning, the court did. The new treatment was vastly reassuring. On December eleventh His Majesty took a walk in Kew Garden. "Still amending," wrote Miss Burney, "in all but my evenings; which again, except one hour under pretence of drinking tea, are falling into their old train."

Mrs. Schwellenberg had never forgiven Colonel Digby his remarks on Mrs. Hastings. One evening when he was absent she attacked his name, accusing him casually, in passing, of spite, disloyalty, calumny and an unfeeling heart. Miss Burney could not listen quietly to such dreadful statements; she spoke up indignantly on behalf of the colonel. And what, asked Mrs. Schwellenberg, could Fanny know of the subject, thus to set herself up as an expert?

"I know you can't not know him; I know he had never seen you two year and half ago; when you came here he had not heard your name," she said.

Fanny replied haughtily, "Two years and a half, I [do] not regard as a short time for forming a judgment of anyone's character."

"When you don't not see them? You have never seen him, I am sure, but once, or what you call twice."

No, said Miss Burney, she had seen him much more often than that.

"And where? when have you seen him?"

"Many times; and at Cheltenham constantly; but never to observe in him anything but honour and goodness."

Mrs. Schwellenberg remained stubbornly scornful and incredu-

lous, so after a little more childish argument Miss Burney let the
matter drop. Next day she had a cold and in the evening went early
to her room, leaving Mrs. Schwellenberg to entertain at tea. To her
room, as she perhaps expected, the colonel too soon repaired. Mr.
Smelt came along after a while to call on Miss Burney, and to his
surprise he encountered Colonel Digby there. For a while the two
gentlemen were under some constraint in their conversation, and
Fanny, not ill pleased by this awkwardness, sat quietly sewing until
it wore off. Each bit of evidence added to the Digby-Burney scandal made her feel more secure. She was very sure, now.

Two weeks passed. As Christmas drew near, the King's improvement became marked, though his regular physician, Dr. Warren,
jealously denied it. And it was high time for improvement, for on
December twenty-second the regency was to come up for discussion
in the House; it was a race between Willis and the Whigs.

That day, December twenty-second, Colonel Digby took his
leave for a while, just when Fanny was beginning to feel that the
time had come for something more definite in their relationship.
She took matters into her own hands; she almost announced an
enagagement to Mrs. Schwellenberg. The Journal entry describing
her encounter with Cerbera must have been erased and rewritten
by Madame d'Arblay long years after, for Miss Burney never per-
petrated such writing, and Madame d'Arblay did, all too often:
". . . in looking forward to a friendship the most permanent, I saw
the eligibility of rendering it the most open," she wrote. "I therefore went back to Mrs. Schwellenberg; and the moment I received
a reproach for staying so long, I calmly answered, 'Mr. Fairly had
made me a visit, to take leave before he went into the country.'"
The old lady was perfectly furious and made Fanny pay in full for
her triumph. But it wouldn't be for long, said Miss Burney to herself; not long.

On New Year's morning the report on the King was excellent,
but ten days later there was a relapse, and among other rearrange-
ments Colonel Digby was again summoned back before his leave
was up.

Fanny could not be sorry, save for the cause of the summons. She and Digby resumed their literary discussions. They also exchanged personal views, including those on the interesting subject of "learned ladies." Colonel Digby spoke with uncommon liberality on the female powers and intellects, but he doubted whether any woman he had ever seen might not have been better without the learned languages than with them, one woman only excepted. Miss Gunning? No, replied the colonel; his mother. As a girl she had got on very well with Latin until her brother interfered and righteously burned all her books.

Fanny hastily assured him that she knew no Latin. She had once begun to study under the great Dr. Johnson, but her father objected and that was the end of it.

These delectable conversations and agreements were constantly menaced by Mrs. Schwellenberg, who complained to the Queen that she was being neglected. So Charlotte spoke to Fanny about it, dwelling on the sad lot of Mrs. Schwellenberg, her illness, her loneliness. Should not the colonel pay his respects to Mrs. Schwellenberg, instead of retiring to another room with Fanny and leaving the invalid alone as he did night after night?

At this point the Queen met with a surprise. The mouselike Miss Burney did not, as Charlotte expected, immediately and eagerly offer to make good Colonel Digby's defections. Miss Burney remained stubbornly silent. The good child had gone on strike.

Later Charlotte returned to the attack, this time speaking more plainly. On Christmas Day poor Mrs. Schwellenberg had been left alone for two whole hours! "With you Colonel Digby was," said Charlotte, "and the Schwellenberg was alone."

Fanny was silent. No protests, no promises to be a good girl—it was amazing.

"I believe—he comes to you every evening when here?" asked the Queen.

That, said Fanny, she did not know. She knew only that she was always very glad to see him, as his visits made all the little variety she had. Since October she had not seen one human being who did not live there in the palace except Mr. Smelt, Colonel Digby, and Sir Lucas Pepys.

Such complaints from so unexpected a source astonished the Queen. Fanny standing up for her rights must have looked rather like a ruffled canary, but she was not ineffectual. The situation remained suspended.

Dr. Willis had brought his two sons to assist him.

"*Kew Palace*, Monday, February 2.—What an adventure had I this morning! one that has occasioned me the severest personal terror I ever experienced in my life. . . .

"This morning, when I received my intelligence of the King from Dr. John Willis, I begged to know where I might walk in safety. 'In Kew Gardens,' he said, 'as the King would be in Richmond.'

" 'Should any unfortunate circumstance,' I cried, 'at any time, occasion my being seen by His Majesty, do not mention my name, but let me run off without call or notice.'

"This he promised. Everybody, indeed, is ordered to keep out of sight.

"Taking, therefore, the time I had most at command, I strolled into the gardens. I had proceeded, in my quick way, nearly half the round, when I suddenly perceived, through some trees, two or three figures. Relying on the instructions of Dr. John, I concluded them to be workmen and gardeners; yet tried to look sharp, and in so doing, as they were less shaded, I thought I saw the person of His Majesty!

"Alarmed past all possible expression, I waited not to know more, but turning back, ran off with all my might. But what was my terror to hear myself pursued!—to hear the voice of the King himself loudly and hoarsely calling after me, 'Miss Burney! Miss Burney!'

"I protest I was ready to die. I knew not in what state he might be at the time; I only knew the orders to keep out of his way were universal; that the Queen would highly disapprove any unauthorized meeting, and that the very action of my running away might deeply, in his present irritable state, offend him. Nevertheless, on I ran, too terrified to stop, and in search of some short passage, for the garden is full of little labyrinths, by which I might escape.

"The steps still pursued me, and still the poor hoarse and altered voice rang in my ears:—more and more footsteps resounded frightfully behind me,—the attendents all running, to catch their eager master, and the voices of the two Dr. Willises loudly exhorting him not to heat himself so unmercifully.

"Heavens, how I ran! I do not think I should have felt the hot lava from Vesuvius—at least not the hot cinders—had I so run during its eruption. My feet were not sensible that they even touched the ground.

"Soon after, I heard other voices, shriller, though less nervous, call out 'Stop! stop! stop!'

"I could by no means consent: I knew not what was purposed, but I recollected fully my agreement with Dr. John that very morning, that I should decamp if surprised, and not be named. . . .

"Still therefore, on I flew; and such was my speed, so almost incredible to relate or recollect, that I fairly believe no one of the whole party could have overtaken me, if these words, from one of the attendants, had not reached me, 'Dr. Willis begs you to stop!'

" 'I cannot! I cannot!' I answered, still flying on, when he called out, 'You must, ma'am; it hurts the King to run.'

"Then, indeed, I stopped—in a state of fear really amounting to agony. I turned round, I saw the two Doctors had got the King between them, and three attendants of Dr. Willis's were hovering about. They all slackened their pace, as they saw me stand still; but such was the excess of my alarm, that I was wholly insensible to the effects of a race which, at any other time, would have required an hour's recruit.

"As they approached, some little presence of mind happily came to my command: it occurred to me that, to appease the wrath of my flight, I must now show some confidence: I therefore faced them as undauntedly as I was able, only charging the nearest of the attendants to stand by my side.

"When they were within a few yards of me, the King called out, 'Why did you run away?'

"Shocked at a question impossible to answer, yet a little assured by the mild tone of his voice, I instantly forced myself forward, to meet him, though the internal sensation which satisfied me this was a step the most proper to appease his suspicions and displeasure, was so violently combated by the tremor of my nerves, that I fairly think I may reckon it the greatest effort of personal courage I have ever made.

"The effort answered: I looked up, and met all his wonted benignity of countenance, though something still of wildness in his eyes. Think, however, of my surprise, to feel him put both his hands round my two shoulders, and then kiss my cheek!

"I wonder I did not really sink, so exquisite was my affright when I saw him spread out his arms! Involuntarily, I concluded he meant to crush me: but the Willises, who have never seen him till this fatal illness, not knowing how very extraordinary an action this was from him, simply smiled and looked pleased, supposing, perhaps, it was his customary salutation!

"I believe, however, it was but the joy of a heart unbridled, now, by the forms and proprieties of established custom and sober reason. To see any of his household thus by accident, seemed such a near approach to liberty and recovery, that who can wonder if should serve rather to elate than lessen what yet remains of his disorder!

"He now spoke in such terms of his pleasure in seeing me, that I soon lost the whole of my terror; astonishment to find him so nearly well, and gratification to see him so pleased, removed every uneasy feeling, and the joy that succeeded, in my conviction of his recovery, made me ready to throw myself at his feet to express it.

"What a conversation followed! When he saw me fearless, he grew more and more alive, and made me walk close by his side, away from the attendants, and even the Willises themselves, who, to indulge him, retreated. I own myself not completely composed, but alarm I could entertain no more.

"Everything that came uppermost in his mind he mentioned; he seemed to have just such remains of his flightiness as heated his imagination without deranging his reason, and robbed him of all control over his speech, though nearly in his perfect state of mind as to his opinions.

"What did he not say!—he opened his whole heart to me,—expounded all his sentiments, and acquainted me with all his intentions.

"The heads of his discourse I must give you briefly, as I am sure you will be highly curious to hear them, and as no accident can render of much consequence what a man says in such a state of physical intoxication.

"He assured me he was quite well—as well as he had ever been in his life; and then inquired how I did, and how I went on? and whether I was more comfortable?

"If these questions, in their implication, surprised me, imagine how that surprise must increase when he proceeded to explain them! He asked after the coadjutrix, laughing, and saying, "Never mind her!—don't be oppressed—I am your friend! don't let her cast you down!—I know you have a hard time of it—but don't mind her!"

"Almost thunderstruck with astonishment, I merely curtsied to his kind 'I am your friend,' and said nothing.

"Then presently he added, 'Stick to your father—stick to your own family—let them be your objects.'

"How readily I assented!

"Again he repeated all I have just written, nearly in the same words, but ended it more seriously: he suddenly stopped, and held me to stop too, and putting his hand on his breast, in the most solemn manner, he gravely and slowly said, 'I will protect you!—I promise you that—and therefore depend upon me!'

"I thanked him; and the Willises, thinking him rather too elevated, came to propose my walking on. 'No, no, no!' he cried, a hundred times in a breath; and their good-humour prevailed, and they let him again walk on with his new companion."

The King chattered on. He made grave accusations against his pages and asked Miss Burney's help against the lying world. He skipped to the subject of her father and spoke of Handel. "Then he ran over most of his oratories, attempting to sing the subjects of several airs and choruses but so dreadfully hoarse that the sound was terrible.

"Dr. Willis, quite alarmed at this exertion, feared he would do himself harm, and again proposed a separation. 'No! no! no!' he exclaimed, 'not yet; I have something I must just mention first.'

"Dr. Willis, delighted to comply, even when uneasy at compliance, again gave way.

"The good King then greatly affected me. He began upon my reverend old friend, Mrs. Delany; and he spoke of her with such warmth—such kindness! 'She was my friend!' he cried, 'and I loved her as a friend! I have made a memorandum when I lost her—I will show it you.'

"He pulled out a pocket-book, and rummaged some time but to no purpose.

"The tears stood in his eyes—he wiped them, and Dr. Willis again became anxious. 'Come sir,' he cried, 'now do you come in and let the lady go on her walk,—come, now you have talked a long while,—so we'll go in,—if your Majesty pleases.'

" 'No, no!' he cried, 'I want to ask her a few questions;—I have lived so long out of the world, I know nothing!'

"This touched me to the heart. . . . "

To the embarrassment of everyone there, he showed her the list of the new establishment he intended to form. He was getting rid of the men he had, he said; they had betrayed him. He vowed her father had been badly treated in the matter of the King's Band. He would fix all that too, when he got loose again.

" 'I shall be much better served, and when once I get away, I shall rule with a rod of iron!'

"This was very unlike himself, and startled the two good doctors. . . .

"Finding we now must part, he stopped to take leave, and renewed again his charges about the coadjutrix. 'Never mind her!' he cried, 'depend upon me! I will be your friend as I live!—I here pledge myself to be your friend!' And then he saluted me again just as at the meeting, and suffered me to go on."

The news of this interview was greeted with the wildest excitement by everyone from the Queen down to the smallest domestic. The regency bill had been fought, point by point, to completion, and would soon be put to the vote. If the committee was satisfied that the King was mending, this bill would be defeated. Dr. Willis and his sons had to battle constantly against jealousy and prejudice, and even against what would nowadays be called sabotage.

The King's recovery was now complicated by an embarrassing development, probably common enough to his kind of derangement but nevertheless exceedingly awkward under the circumstances. When his physicians told him joyfully that he would soon be allowed to see his Queen, he retorted that he didn't want to. He absolutely refused the honor. The Queen had deserted him in his hour of need, he said, and from thenceforth his only right true mate was "Queen Esther"—Lady Pembroke, a young woman who had come to court two years previously. Fanny must have heard of this scandal, since Mrs. Papendiek did, but she was far too much of a lady, and far too loyal a Robe Keeper, to breathe a word of it even to her Journal.

Another, slighter inconvenience was caused by the King's elated spirits. Just as he had with Fanny, he began promising everything in the world to his attendants and everyone else around him. He wrote a letter to Mr. Papendiek bestowing on him a very nice house; unfortunately for the Papendieks, Queen Charlotte pounced on a flaw in the document as soon as she saw it. "Incoherent," said the Queen, and the Papendieks' house went glimmering. (It was later given to the Duke of Cambridge by his fond mamma.) The family were quite busy for a while, checking up on the King's blithe promises and checking their fulfillment.

In spite of these eccentricities, George III continued to improve. He began teaching his physicians how to treat him. According to an anecdote of Hannah More's, when walking one day in the garden with Dr. Willis he objected because Willis sent a few workmen off from his proximity. "Willis," he said, "you do not know your own business, let the men come back again; you ought to accustom me to see people by degrees, that I may be prepared for seeing them more at large."

His enemies were frustrated in their knavish tricks. On February nineteenth, by a motion from the chancellor in the House of Lords, the regency was put off. That day the King went upstairs to drink tea with the Queen and princesses for the first time since his illness began. Four days later Fanny encountered him in the Queen's dressing room. There he stood when she entered. "He smiled at my start, and saying he had waited on purpose to see me, added, 'I am quite well now,—I was nearly so when I saw you before—but I could overtake you better now!'"

In the midst of all this rejoicing, Fanny felt an undercurrent of unpleasantness regarding her status. Perhaps she was already self-conscious, sensitive to the pangs of guilty conscience, but the Queen did indubitably snub her when Miss Burney asked leave to invite the Lockes to call. The Lockes could come, said Charlotte grudgingly, as long as they promised to remain in Miss Burney's room. And when, Fanny indignantly demanded of herself, had they ever desired to wonder about the palace? She resolved to put off her invitation, since permission had been so unpleasantly granted. Then the princess royal, hitherto so sweet and amiable, was acting cold and stiff to Fanny: that awful Mrs. Schwellenberg had been at her, no doubt. One day the argument of the coach window cropped up again. Fanny was taking an airing with Mrs. Schwellenberg. The old lady was rude to Digby, whom they chanced to meet. Then she lowered the glass on Fanny's side and was frightfully cross when Fanny ostensibly held up her muff before her face. Miss Burney caught a violent cold which nearly put her out of action for five days. She dutifully attended at the toilettes, and the Queen noticed her sniffling and asked her what had happened.

"I told the simple fact of the glass,—but *quite* simply, and without one circumstance. She instantly said she was surprised I could catch cold in an *airing*, as it never appeared that it disagreed with me when I took it with Mrs. Delany.

" 'No, ma'am,' I immediately answered, 'nor with Mrs. Lock; nor formerly with Mrs. Thrale:—but they left me the regulation of the glass on my own side to myself; or, if they interfered, it was to draw it up for me.'

"This I could not resist. I can be silent; but when challenged to speak at all, it must be plain truth.

"I had no answer. Illness here—till of late—has been so unknown, that it is commonly supposed it must be wilful, and therefore it meets little notice, till accompanied by danger, or incapacity of duty. This is by no means from hardness of heart—far otherwise; there *is* no hardness of heart in any one of them; but it is prejudice and want of personal experience."

Mark the fraying temper, the lack of angelic sweetness, the failure of her unquestioning loyalty. Our heroine was in a dangerous state of mind.

17. *IT LOOKS NOT WELL*

ARCH ninth was decreed a day of general rejoicing, and the court went to London on the
tenth to see all the illuminations. Fanny,
whose eyes were always letting her down, contented herself in her
Diary with describing Rebecca's beautiful "transparency" at the
palace, in which the King, Providence, Health, and Britannia were
displayed "with elegant devices," but we must turn to Mrs. Papendiek, who saw everything, for a more general description.

"From Strand-of-the-Green we proceeded through the back lanes
of Chiswick and part of Hammersmith into the high road, where
there was not a house, large or small, not a cottage nor the hum-
blest dwelling of the poor, but what showed some sign of lighting
up, even to a rushlight. The Assembly House in the Broadway,
Hammersmith, was very splendid, as was also Hatchett's, the coach-
builder, who had emblematical devices of his trade in coloured
lamps placed in each window . . . All the houses in Kensington
Gore were beautifully illuminated also, and at the turnpike an
arch of great height was thrown over the road from Hyde Park
Gate to the opposite side, above the two toll-houses, the barrier
gates being removed. The arch was made in sort of steps meeting
in the centre, and on the two sides, one facing Piccadilly and the
other the western road, were devices in coloured lamps of the
crown, star, initials, etc. arranged with flags. . . . The India House

was covered with transparencies, very well done, showing every article that the Company imported, with a whole-length portrait of George III at the top, with the crown etc., and lower down a portrait of Pitt, with his crest and arms. . . ."

All the ladies wore bandeaux on their heads, white or purple, with the gold letters "God Save the King" embroidered on them. At all the parties the ladies wore purple, gold, and white exclusively. A costume is described by Mrs. Papendiek: "The façon or make was new. The dress round, with a small train prettily sloped from the sides; the bodice had the cape with the handkerchief under, and the three straps as before. The capes were edged with purple and gold cord, and the body was laced with gold over a purple stomacher. The words 'God Save the King' were worked in purple and gold on the white satin bandeau. Shoes purple satin."

As far as we can judge today, the public rejoicing was sincere. Favorable feeling for George never ran so high before or after this period in his life. Everyone was happy to see the good, kind, moral King once more up and about, walking arm in arm with his virtuous wife and his lovely daughters. Everyone was happy—everyone, that is, but the wicked princes. Like their prototypes in the fairy tales, they gnashed their teeth and muttered imprecations. "The conduct of the Prince of Wales and the Duke of York was extremely heartless," said Mrs. Papendiek. "At their first interview with the King after his recovery, they showed no emotion whatever, unless the mortification at the loss of power which was so evidently depicted on their countenances may be termed emotion."

In the continued absence of Colonel Digby, Fanny regained both her standing at court and her spirits. She was merry in a letter she wrote to Mrs. Locke.

"My Dearest Friends—I have her Majesty's commands to inquire—whether you have any of a certain breed of poultry?

"N.B.—*What* breed I do not remember.

"And to say she has just received a small group of the same herself.

"N.B.—The quantity I have forgotten.

"And to add, she is assured they are something very rare and scarce, and extraordinary and curious.

"N.B.—By *whom* she was assured I have not heard.

"And to subjoin, that you must send word if you have any of the same sort.

"N.B.—How you are to find that out, I cannot tell.

"And to mention, as a corollary, that, if you have none of them, and should like to have some, she has a cock and a hen she can spare, and will appropriate them to Mr. Lock and my dearest Fredy.

"This conclusive stroke so pleased and exhilarated me, that forthwith I said you would both be enchanted, and so forgot all the preceding particulars.

"And I said, moreover, that I knew you would rear them, and cheer them, and fondle them like your children.

"So now—pray write a very *fair answer*, fairly, in fair hand, and to fair purpose."

The court went to Weymouth for the King's health, on a magnificent triumphal tour. Everywhere the King was received with acclamation. At Winchester, said Fanny, the town was *one head*. At Romsey there was a band to play "God Save the King" and the multitude joined in (that was the first time; thereafter it happened *ad nauseam*). As he entered the lovely New Forest, His Majesty was presented, according to tradition, with two milk-white greyhounds, and a party of green-clad foresters with bugle horns welcomed him and escorted him all the way to Salisbury. The court spent five nights at Lyndhurst, in Charles II's hunting seat, and the villagers followed them everywhere, crowding on the lawn, peering in the windows, and singing "God Save the King" without surcease.

It was all the same; at Salisbury where the green foresters left them the clothiers and manufacturers took over the escort, "dressed out in white loose frocks, flowers, and ribbons, with sticks

or caps emblematically decorated from their several manufactories."
At Blandford there was nearly the same ceremony. "At Dorchester
the crowd seemed still increased. The city has so antique an air,
I longed to investigate its old buildings." Girls with chaplets
strewed the entrance of various villages with flowers, and there was
noise and joy all along the road to Weymouth.

Gloucester House, now the Gloucester Hotel, was their living
place there. (The hotel still exhibits George III's bathtub.) Fanny
was lodged in the attic—"Nothing like living at a court for exalta-
tion," she commented—and she had a parlor with a dull aspect,
which may have accounted for her moderate raptures over Weymouth. Nothing but the sea, she said, afforded any life or spirit,
though the bay was very beautiful after its kind.

However, the royals fell in love with the little town, and vice
versa. The first night when the family took their walk abroad with
their suite they were attended by an immense crowd—sailors,
bargemen, mechanics, countrymen, all united in so vociferous a
volley of "God Save the King" that the noise was stunning. The
town was illuminated, of course. Every child had a bandeau round
its head or cap or hat of "God Save the King," all the bargemen
wore the legend in cockades, even the bathing women had it in
large coarse girdles round their waists. It was printed in golden letters upon most of the bathing machines, and in various scrolls and
devices it adorned every shop and almost every house in the towns
of Weymouth and Melcombe Regis.

The King bathed daily, from a "machine" on wheels, as was the
custom. Another machine always followed his into the sea; it was
filled with fiddlers who played "God Save the King" as His Majesty
took his plunge. In a letter to her father Fanny went into detail
about these bathing women, whose work it was to hitch the horses
into the shafts of the bathing machines, lead them into water
sufficiently deep for plunging, and lead them out again. "Those
bathers that belong to the Royal dippers wear it ["God Save,"
etc.] in bandeaus on their bonnets, to go into the sea; and have it
again, in large letters, round their waists, to encounter the waves.

Flannel dresses, tucked up, and no shoes nor stockings, with bandeaus and girdles, have a most singular appearance; and when first
I surveyed these loyal nymphs it was with some difficulty I kept
my features in order."

With excursions, boating parties, plays, and healthy exercise the
royals gaily disported themselves. They visited Lulworth Castle,
the ancient seat of the Welds, which held a certain grim interest
for them because it had been the temporary home of Mrs. Fitz-
herbert, the Prince of Wales's wife. They went to look at Sherborne Castle. They sailed near Portland Island and admired its
steep cliffs. Altogether, Weymouth more than lived up to George
III's expectations. He took such a liking to it that he returned,
year after year, making it a resort as popular as the longer-estab-
lished Bath. It was in Weymouth years later that the usually cir-
cumspect King showed the first signs of a returning attack of the
old complaint. Weymouth residents still talk about it. One day
when he was walking along the front alone, as was his amiable
habit, the monarch came upon a beach donkey trotting across the
road ahead of him. Just as he passed by, one of the court ladies
rapturously fell on the little animal's neck, crying, "Oh, what a
pretty little ass!"

That evening as the King walked up the steps of Gloucester
House he encountered the same lady, who didn't see him because
her back was turned. George III paused and to the astonishment
of all beholders solemnly patted the lady on the rump, saying, in
imitation of her voice, "Oh, what a pretty little ass!"

It was at this time, they say, that the court reluctantly decided
His Majesty was in for it again. . . .

A week before they left Weymouth, Colonel Digby presented
himself. He seemed disgruntled about something, and though he
spoke to Miss Burney respectfully of Their Majesties, he said,
"Nothing could be so weak as to look *there*, in such stations, for
such impossibilities as sympathy, friendship, or cordiality!" And he
finished with saying, "People forget themselves who look for
them!"

Miss Burney, shocked by this treasonable sentiment, wondered in what matter her friend had been disappointed, but he didn't explain. He never did explain.

The court left Weymouth in a happy medley of ship salutes and cheers. They went back by way of Bruton, Sherborne, Longleat where Mrs. Delany was married, and Tottenham Court. Digby didn't accompany them.

And here the Journal changes abruptly. The aged Madame d'Arblay admitted that she rewrote her entries for that November into condensed accounts of what she called "the days and circumstances essential." No doubt she first put down whatever her outraged spirit dictated, and in after years she regretted having done so but couldn't quite wipe out the whole story. She was an author, after all. Though it was her own life, she couldn't take liberties with a well-rounded drama, and anyway, she must have felt, there ought to be a record, however secret, of the man's perfidy; a hidden account of that dreadful period of shame and heartbreak. . . . Writers are odd animals.

Colonel Gwynn came to court one day, reporting that Digby on his way to Windsor had been stopped by an attack of gout. Miss Burney was just asking anxiously for particulars when Major Garth interrupted. "The gout? nay, then, it is time he should get a nurse; and, indeed, I hear he has one in view."

Gwynn smiled triumphantly at Miss Burney. Hadn't he been right after all about Miss Gunning? He didn't say this, but he meant it. Fanny refused to take him seriously; she had heard the same rumor many times and Digby had always denied it. But she wasn't permitted to remain in this comfortable state of mind. Next morning while she was in the royal dressing room her mistress began to speak of Digby, saying she was very angry with him for some mistake he had made about the court program. Fanny ventured to offer a word in his defense, as she always did at such moments, but the Queen interrupted. She said severely, "He will not come here! For some reason or other he does not choose it! He cannot bear to come!"

"How was I amazed!" wrote Fanny, "and silenced pretty effectually!"

Charlotte added, "He has set *his heart* against coming. I know he has been in town some considerable time, but he has desired it may not be told here. I know, too, that when he has been met in the streets, he has called out, 'For Heaven's sake, if you are going to Windsor, do not say you have seen me.'"

This was not pleasant. Miss Burney could not now refuse to realize something was wrong. She lived in a state of acute uneasiness until next day, just as the court was preparing to go to town, when Miss Planta flew into her room, eagerly exclaiming, "Have you heard the news?"

Miss Burney saw instantly, by her eyes and manner, what news was meant; she answered as calmly as possible, "I believe so."

"Colonel Digby is going to be married! I resolved I would tell you."

"I heard the rumour the other day, from Colonel Gwynn."

"Oh, it's true! he has written to ask leave; but for Heaven's sake don't say so!"

"I gave her my ready promise," added Fanny, "for I believed not a syllable of the matter; but I would not tell her that."

Her last stubborn hope was killed two days later, when after some idle conversation about court business the persistent Miss Planta said, "Oh! à propos—it's all declared, and the Princesses wished Miss Gunning joy yesterday in the drawing-room. She looked remarkably well; but said Colonel Digby had still a little gout, and could not appear."

One wonders if Miss Planta noticed anything—a pause, perhaps.

"Now first my belief followed assertion;" said Fanny, "—but it was only because it was inevitable, since the Princesses could not have proceeded so far without certainty."

There follows here a long deletion. Poor Fanny had evidently continued her Diary for a considerable distance in her notebook and then thought better of it. We are relieved, on the whole, not to know more about her innermost thoughts. She has left for our perusal only one word of emotion: "We returned to Windsor as usual, and there I was, just as usual, obliged to finish every evening with picquet—and to pass all and every afternoon, from dinner to midnight, in picquet company."

Did Mrs. Schwellenberg rub it in? Or was she silent, only peering now and then into Miss Burney's face with her beady eyes? Miss Burney must have been unusually meek and silent over the cards. . . . No, we don't really want to know.

A week had passed since Fanny was forced to believe. She was with the Queen that day when the princess royal came in with a message; Colonel Digby would like to see his royal mistress for a moment. Charlotte received the message coldly.

"I am very sorry, but I am going now to dress."

"He won't keep you a moment, mamma, only he wants to get to St. Leonard's to dinner." (Miss Gunning was at St. Leonard's, reflected Fanny.)

"Well, then, I'll slip on my powdering-gown, and see him . . . How melancholy he looks!—does not he, Princess Royal?"

"Yes, indeed, mamma!" The ladies then broke into German, which Miss Burney couldn't understand. As the princess went to summon Digby, Fanny hurried into the next room, ostensibly to inspect some caps: no doubt the Queen knew why and approved.

At tea everyone was talking about the wedding, which would take place in a fortnight. They were all surprised that the colonel had been and gone again without attempting to see any of his friends. Many of the courtiers were incensed.

"For what not stay one night?" demanded Mrs. Schwellenberg. "For what not go to the gentlemen?—it looks like when he been ashamed.—Oh fie! I don't not like soch ting. And for what always say contraire?—always say to everybody he won't not have her!— There might be something wrong in all that—it looks not well."

Miss Burney took no part in the discussion; she had nothing now to say in defense of her acknowledged friend. The equerries, too, were offended with him. Only General Harcourt tried to vindicate his behavior: "Digby is not the thing—not at all—very unwell: an unformed gout—the most disagreeable sensation I suppose a man can have. . . ."

Nobody replied; nobody seemed at all distressed by Colonel Digby's gout.

"To forget is soon to be forgotten!" mused Miss Burney. "—he has dropped them till they now drop him."

On the other hand, they may have been tactfully silent because Miss Burney was there.

18. IT WON'T DO, MA'AM!

Miss Burney contemplated a change. The Hastings trial gave her a welcome chance to get away from court and ponder the question. She had lived through the worst of the aftershock; she had controlled herself; she had saved her pride from disaster. But court was repugnant to her.

The Digby-Gunning wedding was over; even the little flurry of nuptial gossip was dying. Fanny listened avidly for remarks on the subject and took a bitter, morbid pleasure in writing them down. They said it was a strange wedding, with the ceremony taking place in the Gunning parlor; not, as one would suppose, in church. Odd, was it not, when Colonel Digby had always been so particular about religious observances? They said the honeymoon was quickly ended. They said—— But then the false Fairly arrived, bringing his bride to court, and speculation ceased, all whispering ceased while the world watched curiously.

He paid his respects to Miss Burney, quite properly and politely. Mrs. Digby called on her a few days later and the women had a nice long chat. The bride seemed very happy. . . . So that was that, and now Fanny was considering the question of resigning her appointment.

When she visited home, Brother James had approached her in his bluff sailor way, asking her to get him a ship, as if she could get anything she wanted at court merely by asking. She, who had failed to get her heart's desire! James wanted a frigate of thirty-two guns, he said, and when Fanny asked for it she was not to say just a *frigate* and get him one with twenty-eight. On second thought, said James, he would come to court himself; that way there would be no mistake about the guns.

His horrified sister persuaded him to wait, but sitting in the hall at the trial, she pondered this matter too. Was it such an outrageous request? After all, she had never got anything but her salary out of this job, in spite of Mr. Twining's happy prophecy. She had not even got Colonel Digby. She suddenly made up her mind, and at the next opportunity she asked the Queen for James's ship. But though Charlotte wasn't offended, she said she could do nothing of that sort; James could be proposed for a ship only by a superior officer.

There were no other loose ends to tie up. When Colonel Digby had been married five months, Fanny asked her father's permission to resign. Fortunately she proposed it at a most propitious moment; Charles Burney had just been discussing his daughter with some French noblewomen, *émigrées* from the Revolution. They had wanted to meet the talented Miss Burney, and when he explained why this could not be done, one of them cried, "But, monsieur, that can't be possible! Do you mean to say your daughter never has a holiday?"

The enormity of this fact seems never to have struck Dr. Burney until then. He listened thoughtfully to Fanny's speech, and one confession led to another. At last, "If you wish to resign," he said, "my house, my purse, my arms, shall be open to receive you back."

There the matter rested for a space.

Mrs. Piozzi was back in England! The meeting so long awaited and dreaded took place without unseemly behavior on the part of either lady. Neither of them wept; there was no quarreling or embracing. "All ended, as it should do, with perfect indifference," wrote Mrs. Piozzi. The ladies met again by chance at Windsor

Church, and then they met again, without warmth or rancor, until embarrassment was over.

In many ways the old life out in the world began to creep into the palace in advance of Fanny's liberation. She hadn't yet mustered up the courage to resign, but the world was pushing her at it. People were talking, stirring up dissatisfaction on her behalf. Dr. Burney had only to confide her plans to half a dozen of his best friends and they did the rest. Sir Joshua was one of the malcontents; busy Boswell was another.

In the interests of literature, declared those gentlemen, Fanny Burney must be freed. The bird could not sing in that gilded Windsor cage.

The only thing wrong with this statement was that it wasn't true: Miss Burney had written a tragedy. She had started it during the King's illness, when the days were long and dull and the Queen made no elaborate toilettes; she finished it in August 1790, and proudly noted that it was "an almost spontaneous work, and soothed the melancholy of imagination for a while. . . ." Then she started another.

There was still that matter of the resignation. For months she played with the idea, dandling it, fondling it, doing everything in fact but putting it into action. At the back of her mind was her vow never to leave the Queen's service until her father should ask her to come to him, or until her health broke down. Perhaps she could not really feel right in her conscience until she fulfilled both alternatives. Therefore, in October, Fanny Burney's health began most obligingly to break down.

Just what ailed her is difficult to discover. "I was ill the whole of this month, though not once with sufficient seriousness for confinement, yet with a difficulty of proceeding as usual so great, that the day was a burthen—or rather, myself a burthen to the day. A languor so prodigious, with so great a failure of strength and spirit, augmented almost hourly, that I several times thought I must be compelled to excuse my constancy of attendance, but there was no one to take my place, etc. etc. . . . ."

". . . one morning at Kew, Miss Cambridge was so much alarmed at my declining state of health that she would take no denial to my seeing and consulting Mr. Dundas. He ordered me the bark. . . ."

"Mrs. Ord spent near a week at Windsor at the beginning of this month. I was ill, however, the whole time, and suffered so much from my official duties, that my good Mrs. Ord, day after day, evidently lost something of her partiality to my situation, from witnessing fatigues of which she had formed no idea, and difficulties and disagreeabilities in carrying on a week's intercourse, even with so respectable a friend, which I believe she had thought impossible.

"Two or three times she burst forth into ejaculations strongly expressive of fears for my health and sorrow at its exhausting calls. I could not but be relieved in my own mind that this much-valued, most maternal friend should receive a conviction beyond all powers of representation, that my place was a sort to require a strength foreign to my make."

This was gratifying and satisfactory; the good little girl was not going to annoy too many powerful adults, after all. Mr. Wyndham added his voice to the swelling chorus. "It is resolution, not inclination, Dr. Burney wants," he said to Charlotte Francis. "I will set the Literary Club upon him! Miss Burney has some very true admirers there, and I am sure they will all eagerly assist. We will present him a petition—an address."

Meeting her at the chapel of St. George at Windsor, Mr. Boswell spoke strongly to Fanny about it. "I am extremely glad to see you indeed, but very sorry to see you here. My dear ma'am, why do you stay?—it won't do, ma'am! you must resign—we can put up with it no longer. I told my good host the Bishop so last night; we are all grown quite outrageous!"

November was a month of mental struggle. Fanny's health, still obliging, turned worse again; "languor, feverish nights, and restless days were incessant." Still she could not quite bring herself to present that "memorial," or resignation. The war was over, she hadn't got a ship for James after all, her health was bad . . . But she could not. The Queen had never been more gracious, which made everything much worse. How could one give her an unpleasant surprise when she was so wholly unprepared?

"It is true, my depression of spirits and extreme alteration of person might have operated as a preface; for I saw no one, except my Royal Mistress and Mrs. Schwellenberg, who noticed not the change, or who failed to pity and question me upon my health and my fatigues; but as they alone saw it not, or mentioned it not, that afforded me no resource."

December came in, and Fanny's bad health was more and more persistently obvious—"notorious," was her word for it. ". . . no part of the house could wholly avoid acknowledging it; yet was the terrible picquet the catastrophe of every evening, though frequent pains in my side forced me, three or four times in a game, to creep to my own room for hartshorn and for rest. And so weak and faint I was become, that I was compelled to put my head out into the air, at all hours, and in all weathers, from time to time, to recover the power of breathing, which seemed not seldom almost withdrawn.

"Her Majesty was very kind during this time, and the Princesses interested themselves about me with a sweetness very grateful to me; . . ." But the desired offer of release didn't arrive, even so. Still, after all this spadework, her resignation could not now be a complete surprise. ". . . a general opinion that I was falling into a decline ran through the establishment," Fanny wrote with simple pride. "Miss Planta was particularly attentive and active to afford me help and advice; Mdlle. Montmollin's eyes glistened when we met; Miss Goldsworthy declared she thought my looks so altered as scarcely to be known again; Lady Elizabeth Waldegrave enjoined me earnestly to ask leave for respite and recruit, lest the Queen should lose me entirely by longer delay; Miss Gomme honestly protested she thought it became a folly to struggle on any longer against strength and nature; Mr. de Luc was so much struck with the change as to tell the Queen herself that a short and complete retirement from attendance seemed essential to my restoration; and even Mr. Turbulent himself called one day upon me, and frankly counselled me to resign at once, for, in my present state, a life such as that I led was enough to destroy me."

One would think that all this turmoil was bound to have the desired effect at last. It did—but only on Dr. Burney. When he saw Fanny he told her to hurry up and quit once for all; even then her heart failed her, "for though I was frequently so ill in her [the Queen's] presence that I could hardly stand, I saw she concluded me, while life, remained, inevitably hers."

Obviously it was useless to hope for any results from these gentle advertising methods; Charlotte was not a Queen to meet trouble halfway. She suspected Miss Burney would soon ask for sick leave, that was all, and until Miss Burney asked, the Queen didn't feel called on to notice anything wrong. Fanny and her father took counsel together and concocted a fresh memorial, which the Keeper of the Robes boldly presented to her mistress.

Cornered, Charlotte refused to read it. She gave the paper to Mrs. Schwellenberg. But she could defy destiny no longer; Mrs. Schwellenberg must in the end bring its contents to her attention, though the old lady put up a good fight first, accusing Fanny of lèse-majesté and various other crimes.

While her fate was discussed in the royal boudoir, the royal physician called on Miss Burney, having been sent as a desperate last-minute gesture by Charlotte. He prescribed opium, three glasses of wine daily, and temporary retirement from the palace. Seeing him off, Fanny gave silent thanks that all was so nearly finished, and she eagerly greeted Mrs. Schwellenberg's return.

The old lady did not, however, bring complete release. Instead she had a proposition to make. What about a leave of absence? A nice long leave of absence—six weeks, if necessary—to spend visiting friends. What about that?

Charlotte was a notoriously tenacious employer. Fanny was not the only woman to be caught in her clutches: Lady Aylesbury had a similar experience, and so, later, did Cornelia Knight. Cornelia described her affair in her memoirs, with full explanation and self-vindication. Her crime lay in wishing to change posts and become companion to young Princess Charlotte, daughter of the Prince of Wales. The Queen was cruelly stubborn, said Cornelia. "I could not find it in my heart to devote myself till death to the Queen's service, sacrificing the pleasing idea of rendering happy the life of a persecuted young creature . . . I will not say that I had not some wish for a more active and more important employment than that which I held at Windsor, dull, uninteresting, and monotonous. Every year more and more confined, and, even from the kindness of the Royal Family, condemned to listen to all their complaints and private quarrels."

What was the explanation of this unpleasant streak in a lady otherwise soft and kind? Sheer conceit, probably. Her best friend could never have called Charlotte a clever woman, and stupidity can't be expected to withstand the flattery a queen receives. At the best, too, she was completely untrained for her position. One day while she was still a child, living in her stuffy obscure German home, her brother had said, "Come on now, don't be a baby; you're going to be Queen of England," and shoved her headlong into a ceremony of marriage by proxy. It was as sudden as that. Immediately people had begun bowing down to the girl, besieging her with flattery, devotion, and pleas for favors. No wonder that her normal ego swelled and flourished in that fertile soil. No wonder she felt an ever-increasing desire to own people body and soul.

Some of her ladies—Mrs. Schwellenberg, Miss Planta, and others —kept the peace by not getting in her way, always being there when they were wanted, and never trying to go against her wishes. Charlotte forgave them many faults because they were devoted. Fanny couldn't have been a good wardrobe mistress, but as long as she so evidently and assiduously adored Charlotte it was enough. Mrs. Schwellenberg made life hell for the court, but she was a faithful old slave, so Mrs. Schwellenberg stayed in spite of everyone's efforts to dislodge her, including the King's. Charlotte took care of her own.

But let a court lady once try to strike out for herself, let her admit that her own happiness or health meant more to her than Charlotte's vanity, and the Queen was merciless. Cornelia Knight, for daring to show preference for Charlotte's granddaughter, was banished forever from the implacable old lady's good will. Fanny barely managed to wriggle out of her job without leaving all her skin behind.

Charlotte simply refused to accept Fanny's resignation: she would not even face the fact that it had been presented. If she acted very kind, she seemed to think, and gave Miss Burney a nice present, and rode her on an easy rein for a bit, everything would be all right. So she made a feeble attempt to relieve Miss Burney of her duties at the Twelfth-night ball, telling her not to sit up in order to help undress her. But as things turned out, Fanny had to sit up anyway . . . and so it went.

Miss Burney had another weapon, however, which even a queen could not oppose—passive resistance. She became seriously ill, on the most inconvenient day she could have chosen, just before the Queen's birthday. And she stayed triumphantly ill for four months, four long months, during which time Charlotte had to manage without her services and Mrs. Schwellenberg wasted her venom in a vacuum. Four months is a long time, long enough to convince the stubbornest Germanic queen. "She deigned to consult with me openly upon my successor," said Fanny.

Even then the day of departure wasn't settled. In May she ventured to speak to her royal mistress about it.

"She was evidently displeased at again being called on," said Fanny, "but I took the courage to openly remind her that the birthday was Her Majesty's own time, and that my father conceived it to be the period of my attendance by her special appointment. And this was a truth which flashed its own conviction on her recollection. She paused, and then, assentingly, said 'Certainly!' " It took a little time after that for the Queen to forgive her all over again, but after a while she did.

Nevertheless she hung on to her victim. Fanny fell ill again, but the King's birthday was not celebrated until June fourth, and the Queen was determined to get her contract's worth. She also decreed that Fanny's departure must be kept a secret until it took place: she was probably ashamed of what she considered her defeat.

The Duke of Clarence provided an unusually colorful interlude at the birthday celebration by coming to visit Mrs. Schwellenberg's dinner party in a happy state of intoxication and making the company drink champagne with him.

"Is not your Royal Highness afraid," said fatuous Mr. Stanhope, "I shall be apt to be rather up in the world, as the folks say, if I tope on at this rate?"

"Not at all! you can't get drunk in a better cause. I'd get drunk myself if it was not for the ball. Here, Champagne! another glass for the philosopher! I keep sober for Mary." (The duke had promised his sister Mary to dance the minuet with her.) When he called for yet another round of wine, Mrs. Schwellenberg ventured to protest.

"Your Royal Highness, I am afraid for the ball!"

"Hold you your potato-jaw, my dear," cried the duke, patting her; but, recollecting himself, he took her hand and abruptly kissed it. At the ball he did make rather a mess of the minuet with Mary. Next day, laughing, he said to her, "You may think how far I was gone, for I kissed the Schwellenberg's hand!"

Yet one more fortnight of service, said the Queen, before Fanny could go. In spite of the Assistant Robe Keeper's gloomy fears that she could not possibly bear that long a postponement, she must have felt some invigoration that the end was in sight, for she actually began work on a third tragedy.

"I come now to write the last week of my Royal residence," she said in July. "The Queen honoured me with the most uniform graciousness, and though, as the time of separation approached, her cordiality rather diminished, and traces of internal displeasure appeared sometimes, arising from an opinion I ought rather to have struggled on, live or die, than to quit her,—yet I am sure she saw how poor was my own chance, except by a change in the mode of life, and at last ceased to wonder, though she could not approve."

At last, at last, Miss Burney's successor arrived—Mlle. Jacobi from Germany. With the effort of a quicksand releasing a victim who has nearly gone under, Charlotte bade farewell to her tame novelist. She did something very important into the bargain. With an apologetic "You know the size of my family," she bestowed on Fanny a pension of a hundred pounds a year.

Fanny wept, saying good-by to the court. Miss Planta wept, Mlle. Montmollin wept—everybody wept, except perhaps Mrs. Schwellenberg. Drowned in tears, Miss Burney was carried off by the coach.

"Here, therefore, end my Court Annals; after having lived in the service of Her Majesty five years within ten days—from July 17, 1786, to July 7, 1791."

19. NEVER MORE BLESSED

ENGLAND in 1792 was filling with French *noblesse*, who found it wisest to stay away from home until they could be sure which way the wind would settle down to blowing. The Burneys were all staunchly Royalist on general principles, for France as for England. They admitted that the French aristocracy probably had much to answer for, but the idea of complete republicanism horrified them, especially when the Revolutionists began executing people. Burke, sharing their horror, went so far as to announce that he was after all in favor of kings. One must have kings, within their limits, he said; if a monarchy meant slavery for the people, very well then; slavery forever! This was a tremendous change in tune for Burke the Whig, but most of the intellectual English "pinks" followed his example, for they were really frightened by what had happened over the water. Under a pseudonym, Hannah More published a tract, *Village Politics*, which was designed to counteract the revolutionary ideas supposedly infiltrating the British lower classes, and it had a tremendous success—among the upper classes, at least. It was bought and distributed in thousands.

Fanny spent the year recuperating and being luxuriously idle. Mrs. Ord took her on a long, leisurely tour, and when she returned she lived in Chelsea College with her father, occasionally paying visits to various relatives.

Then Sister Susan one day wrote a letter announcing news of great interest from Mickleham, where the Phillipses were living near the benevolent Lockes of Norbury Park. "We shall shortly, I believe, have a little colony of unfortunate (or rather, fortunate, since here they are safe) French noblesse in our neighbourhood. Sunday evening Ravely informed Mr. Lock that two or three families had joined to take Jenkinson's house, Juniper Hall. . . . I long to offer them my house, and have been much gratified by finding Mr. Lock immediately determined to visit them . . . At Jenkinson's are—la Marquise de la Châtre, whose husband is with the emigrants; her son; M. de Narbonne, lately Ministre de la Guerre; M. de Montmorency; Charles or Theodore Lameth; Jaucourt; and one or two more, whose names I have forgotten. . . . I feel infinitely interested for all these persecuted persons."

Susan's French was as good as her English, if not better. She was passionately interested in France's fate and reminded herself constantly of her own Huguenot blood. She wrote at great length to Fanny about her new neighbors, growing more and more Latin and ejaculatory as time went on. In November she reported excitedly that she had met them all, or at least all then in residence; they were naturally, she observed, a shifting, restless crowd, forever greeting new arrivals or saying farewell to adventurous souls returning to the Continent.

"Madame de la Châtre received us with great Politeness . . . A gentleman was with her whom Mrs. Lock had not yet seen, M. d'Arblay. She introduced him, and, when he had quitted the room, told us he was adjutant-general to M. Lafayette, *Maréchal de camp*. . . . He is tall, and a good figure, with an open and manly countenance; about forty, I imagine."

One morning Susan heard someone in the parlor, talking to her husband. "Je ne parle pas trop bien l'Anglois, monsieur." She recognized the general's voice and hurried in to greet him. He stayed a long time: she was charmed with him; he was charmed with the children; they all adored him. To think he was a friend of Susan's hero, Lafayette! Together they lamented Lafayette's fate. Susan spoke of the sacrifices made by the French nobility; d'Arblay spoke warmly of his particular friends among them.

"For himself, he mentioned his fortune and his income from his appointments as something immense, but I never remembered the number of hundred thousand livres, nor can tell what their amount is without consideration. 'Et me voilà, madame, reduit à rien, hormis un peu d'argent comptant, et encore très peu. . . .'"

For months Susan wrote to Fanny about this refugee colony which brought so much color and excitement into her quiet life. Every day was filled with their discussions, hopes, and disappointments. The Phillipses dined at Juniper Hall and the Juniper inmates dropped in on the Phillipses, and the Lockes kept watch over all. Then early in '93 Mrs. Locke urged Fanny to come and join them, and so Miss Burney went to Norbury Park, which had become much Gallicized since her last appearance there.

She was in time to share in their tragic lamentation for "the dreadful tragedy acted in France," the execution of Louis XVI. M. de Narbonne and M. d'Arblay were almost annihilated, she said; they were breaking their hearts with the humiliation they felt for having been born in that guilty country. ". . . M. de Narbonne has been quite ill with the grief of this last enormity, and M. d'Arblay is now indisposed. This latter is one of the most delightful characters I have ever met, for openness, probity, intellectual knowledge, and unhackneyed manners."

The French newcomers made a great fuss over Miss Fanny Burney; the most enthusiastic among them was Madame de Staël, who was a sort of leader. She welcomed Fanny as a sister in the bonds of literature; she wrote quaint notes in bad English to her dear friend and begged her to correct them; she invited her to Juniper Hall for a visit, before Miss Burney should return to London.

She was impossible to resist, Fanny said in a letter to her father. "She exactly resembles Mrs. Thrale in the ardour and warmth of her temper and partialities." If he permitted, therefore—and of course he would—she would accept the invitation. Then Miss

Burney turned to the subject of Susan's Chevalier d'Arblay. "M. d'Arblay is one of the most singularly interesting characters that can ever have been formed. He has a sincerity, a frankness, an ingenuous openness of nature, that I had been unjust enough to think could not belong to a Frenchman . . . he is passionately fond of literature, a most delicate critic in his own language, well versed in both Italian and German, and a very elegant poet. He has just undertaken to become my French master for pronunciation, and he gives me long daily lessons in reading. . . . In return, I hear him in English. . . ."

Did Dr. Burney see the danger? Did he reflect on the possible effect of a visit by Fanny to Juniper Hall, under the same roof as the singularly interesting M. d'Arblay? At any rate he replied in words nicely calculated to scare his daughter to death. "I am not at all surprised at your account of the captivating powers of Madame de Staël. It corresponds with all I had heard about her. . . . But as nothing human is allowed to be perfect, she has not escaped censure. Her house was the centre of revolutionists previous to the 10th of August . . . and she has been accused of partiality to M. de Narbonne. But perhaps all may be Jacobinical malignity. However, unfavourable stories have been brought hither, and the Burkes and Mrs. Ord have repeated them to me. . . . I know this will make you feel uncomfortable, but it seemed to me right to hint it to you. If you are not absolutely in the house of Madame de Staël when this arrives, it would perhaps be possible for you to waive the visit to her, by a compromise, of having something to do for Susy, and so make the addendum to your stay under her roof."

The good little girl, who was now, by the way, nearing her forty-first birthday, eagerly replied to her father, arguing away to the best of her superior knowledge the scandal he had repeated. "I would, nevertheless," she said, repeating the old, old pattern, "give the world to avoid being a guest under their roof, now I have heard even the shadow of such a rumour; and I will, if it be possible without hurting or offending them. . . . She wants us to study

French and English together, and nothing could to me be more desirable, but for this invidious report."

The explanation and excuse offered Madame by Fanny did not quite go down. Miss Burney was spared the necessity of being associated with the tainted couple under their own roof, but she hurt Madame de Staël's feelings. Susan reported after Fanny had gone back to town: "Poor Madame de Staël has been greatly disappointed and hurt by the failure of the friendship and intercourse she had wished to maintain with you,—of that I am sure; I fear, too, she is on the point of being offended . . . She asked me if you would accompany Mrs. Lock back into the country? I answered that my father would not wish to lose you for so long a time at once, as you had been absent from him as a nurse so many days."

Madame de Staël at this point asked a question which some of Fanny's circle must often have wished to pose. "But is a woman a schoolgirl for life in this country?" she demanded. "Your sister seems to me like a fourteen-year-old girl."

"This enchanting M. d'Arblay," Fanny called him. Soon she was speaking of him as "my master of language."

It wasn't a courtship like Digby's, all sighing and insinuating, nor did Miss Burney react to him as she had done to Digby. With the colonel one has the feeling that she was always conscious of his suitability—a widower for a spinster no longer young. She had approved of Colonel Digby, who read sermons and expressed exemplary sentiments. M. d'Arblay wasn't suitable, and as far as we can make out he didn't read sermons. He was fascinating, that's all. He wasn't suitable; he was only handsome, and charming, and romantic, and courageous, and in love with her.

He had nothing to offer in marriage but his name and himself. But these, after a long struggle with conscience and pride, he offered, in the presence of all their intimate circle, incidentally, at the Lockes'. How can we say now that she wasn't in luck? Aging and bitter, fast becoming a neurotic, with nothing to look forward to but more of the life she had always known, she suddenly came upon this love.

Miss Burney decamped to Chesington, where she could be alone to think things out. She fled, like Evelina. What would Daddy Crisp have said? She knew all too well what her father would say if she made up her mind to accept this imprudent, delightful offer. Dr. Burney would have to be faced later; for the moment she must explore her own desires.

To Chesington came her lover in pursuit, like Lord Orville. Daddy Crisp's kindly ghost must have approved the chevalier; the visit was a success, and Kitty Cooke, with Mrs. Hamilton, thrilled at sight of the handsome French nobleman. If Fanny had needed a sign, this was enough.

When he had gone she turned again to practical matters. Mr. Locke, the benevolent Croesus, had given it as his considered opinion that the couple, if they were to become a couple, that is, could live on Fanny's hundred pounds a year. He pointed out that many a married curate managed on less. Nobody knew better than Fanny how to manage on little; her wants were few, by temperament and training. But would the Queen continue giving the hundred-pound pension if Fanny should make a marriage of which she disapproved?

Dr. Burney didn't like the idea at all, and said so in a long letter. He felt he must "beg, warn, and admonish" his daughter not to entangle herself in a wild and romantic attachment, "which offers nothing in prospect but poverty and distress, with future inconvenience and unhappiness." M. d'Arblay was perfectly charming, no doubt, but he was "a mere soldier of fortune, under great disadvantages." Suppose the Queen should stop the pension? A hundred wasn't enough, anyway. . . . Fanny was so attached to her family that even if d'Arblay had money, Dr. Burney would be against her marrying a foreigner and living out of England. He said so flatly. The friends she had in England were of the highest and most desirable class; to quit them and go to a place like France where such awful things could happen seemed wild and visionary.

No, said Dr. Burney, he couldn't encourage it. Definitely.

The crisis had come. Just after her forty-first birthday, Fanny stood with reluctant feet where the brook and river meet. To be happy, or to go on being good? Never yet had she defied her father openly. Never yet in their infrequent disputes had her father displayed so much reason on his side. Yet never had she been so tempted to disobey him, to cut the bonds which grew stronger every year; no, not even at the time her two fathers commanded her to give up her comedy.

What was she to do? Trying to decide, she must have reviewed her life, as one does at such times. . . . Mr. Barlow. Daddy Crisp and all those other father-figures who had harmlessly played the gallant. Mr. Crutchley and the few days when she may possibly have thought of him as a husband. The dreadful marriage of Mrs. Thrale, which made Fanny resolve to keep herself clear of passion and all that sort of thing. The immolation at court. Mrs. Delany, whose first marriage, arranged by her family, was such a dreadful mistake. And Mrs. Delany had married again for love, not for money. . . . The companionship of Colonel Digby, the happy days of false hope, the ultimate shock. . . . Why had Digby done it? No doubt he had acted on impulse all the way. Away from the court and Fanny, under Miss Gunning's family roof, an old attraction revived: doubtless, too, he had reminded himself that Miss Burney had no fortune.

No fortune: that was always the crux of the matter. It was Fanny's lack of fortune which had led Daddy Crisp and Dr. Burney to urge her into a loveless marriage with Mr. Barlow. She had stood out against them, and never once had she regretted it. Now here was her father again urging her to outrage the dictates of her heart, and for the same prudent reasons. For forty-one years Fanny Burney had been a dutiful daughter. The thought may have stirred in her mind that though forty-one years is a long time, life is longer.

Other things may have occurred to her. Charles Burney had himself made an imprudent marriage for love.

Did she wonder about Mrs. Piozzi's probable opinion? Here was Miss Burney contemplating marriage when she was past forty; yet she had considered Mrs. Thrale at forty long past her marrying time. Miss Burney, too, was thinking of marrying a foreigner, a Roman Catholic, a portionless fellow; she would be taking far more of a risk, doing so, than had the wealthy Mrs. Thrale. Dr. Burney called d'Arblay a "soldier of fortune." Yet no doubt Fanny did not seriously consider a comparison of d'Arblay with Piozzi. D'Arblay was no music master. In spite of her father's gibe, he was an aristocrat. It made all the difference to the music master's daughter.

Besides, the world, that all-powerful world, was not opposed to d'Arblay; only Fanny's father was. Everyone else favored the match. Mr. Locke offered the couple a piece of land in Norbury Park where they could build a cottage. Susan volunteered to make peace with her father. The Queen could be won round, at Fanny's own pace; Fanny knew from long practice how to manage the Queen. Surely a woman could write more novels now that she had an incentive. They would manage. Someday, perhaps, the chevalier might even recover his fortune.

Once and for all, then: to marry or not to marry? Fanny looked again at her lover and knew that she had never really hesitated.

Dr. Burney was not at the wedding, he would not come, but on July 31, 1793, Fanny Burney and the Chevalier d'Arblay were married.

". . . and never, never was union more blessed and felicitous; though, after the first eight years of unmingled happiness, it was assailed by many calamities, chiefly of separation or illness, yet still mentally unbroken."

—F. d'Arblay, May 7, 1825.

20. *THE LAST WORD*

ERE, if I were writing after Fanny Burney's style, I would leave her. All her heroines finished with adventure when they went to the altar. It would be only justice to treat her in the same way, but Charles Burney's daughter will not be disposed of in so summary a fashion. Fanny, like the doctor, was wiry, vigorous, and long-lived. Like him, she allowed her habit of scribbling to grow with the years. In spite of everything she destroyed, reams of Burney papers remain. We know something of the rest of the long story.

At first it looked like a typical Fanny Burney ending—a cottage in the country (though their poverty wasn't like a Burney heroine's circumstances), and in due time a little boy named Alexander. Fortunately Queen Charlotte graciously approved the marriage and didn't cut off her pension. Fanny dedicated her next novel, *Camilla*, to the royals: this time she earned two thousand guineas, publishing it by subscription, as many writers did then. It is characteristic of the publishing game and of the power of a name that she made a lot of money out of this bad book when she made so little out of her good ones. *Camilla* is really awful. It's easy to see in its pages how involuted and tortured the Burney style was growing.

All went very well with the d'Arblays for a while. The cottage, which was built from the proceeds of the book and called Camilla

Cottage, was near Norbury Park. There the chevalier grew vegetables, Fanny wrote hundreds of letters and did a little work, and
baby Alexander learned to walk and talk. Then over in France,
which d'Arblay watched closely, politics took a turn to the Right.
He hurried back as soon as it was considered the proper time for
his party. His little family followed, and so Dr. Burney's sad
prophecy was fulfilled, for Fanny, who had never before been
abroad and who needed, he said, the constant companionship of
her relatives, was cut off from home for ten years, by the Napoleonic
Wars.

It is tempting to use the customary cliché at this point and say
that what happened there would make a book in itself, but this
wouldn't be true. On the whole, Fanny's life in France was dull,
or she makes it sound dull, which amounts to the same thing. The
d'Arblays lived like others of the French aristocracy, huddled in
little communities, never in acute want but never in security. The
chevalier went out gallantly and marched with the campaigners,
and behaved well, and received an injury, not in action but behind
the lines, when a horse kicked him in the knee and crippled him for
life.

Then the English won at Trafalgar, and Fanny came back to
England at last, in 1812. The astonishing woman (not aged, but
actually much improved in looks, according to a friend) found
her astonishing father still working, still writing, and still going to
parties, though he was eighty-four years old.

Alex d'Arblay won a scholarship for Cambridge. His mother,
who needed money as much as ever for his extra expenses, ground
out The Wanderer, quite her worst book. The strange indirection
which had long afflicted her style buried every semblance of original
talent beneath tons of fancy phrase.

The years rolled on until Dr. Burney surrendered at last and
went with them. By dying at the age of eighty-seven he missed
an event which would have made him very proud and happy: his
daughter was given a title. Louis XVIII, when he came to England, announced to Fanny, whose husband was then in France,

that he was ennobling the chevalier as a reward for loyal services rendered to the Crown. But M. le Comte and Madame la Comtesse Piochard d'Arblay quietly agreed that they couldn't afford to support such grandeur, and they left the matter in abeyance. Ultimately young Alex formally renounced all claim to French nobility: that day his grandfather the music master must have turned completely over in his grave.

The d'Arblays settled in Bath, where living was cheap and they could save money for their son. Alex had developed into a mathematical genius, one of those chess wizards who bloom young, but as mathematics could not provide him with a career he studied for the ministry. Fanny saw the Queen every year, when Charlotte came to Bath to take the waters.

It was during such a royal visit that General d'Arblay died. He was cut off in his prime, a mere youth according to Burney standards; he was only sixty-five. After her loss Fanny went to live in London.

She spent the last twenty-two years of her life there, still writing —letters and then more letters, as well as a Memoir of her father. Among her correspondents was Mrs. Piozzi. Hester's liveliness had never been stifled; she had lived for a time in Italy and then brought Piozzi back to the British Isles, where he died after quiet years with his wife in Wales. His widow was of stronger stuff. At eighty she still had the spirits and vivacity which had made Mrs. Thrale so outstanding. The two old ladies exchanged memories and bits of gossip about their old friends, and if either of them remembered the bitterness of the past, she avoided speaking of it.

"How changed is the taste of verse, prose, and painting! since *le bon vieux temps,* dear Madam!" wrote Hester. She added, further down in her letter, a news item which could not fail to interest Fanny almost as much as it enthralled herself. "Fell, the Bookseller in Bond Street, told me a fortnight or three weeks ago, that Miss Streatfeild lives where she did in his neighbourhood,— Clifford Street, S.S. still."

Clifford Street, not far from Hanover Square where Thrale used to leave his coach so no one would talk. . . .

Alex died in 1836, a year after he became Minister of Ely Chapel, Holborn. He was unmarried. As his mother was nearly blind from cataract, we have few letters that tell us of her last years. She was deaf as well, and suffered from coughs and fever; nevertheless she tried to rally at the end. The woman who had always considered herself delicate still held Death firmly at bay, protesting all the while that she was ready to go.

On January 6, 1840, at the age of eighty-seven, Fanny Burney died, and was buried at Bath, lying with her husband and son. She had outlived fame and success, she had outlived her only child, she had even outlived her spiritual descendant, Jane Austen.

BIBLIOGRAPHY

d'Arblay, Madame (Frances Burney)—*Camilla,* 1796.
———*Cecilia,* 1782.
———*Diary & Letters,* edited by Charlotte Barrett, 4 vols., 1892.
———*Diary & Letters,* edited by Austen Dobson, 6 vols., 1904.
———*Early Diary,* edited by Annie Raine Ellis, 2 vols., 1889.
———*Evelina,* 1779.
———*The Wanderer,* 1814.
———*Memoir of Dr. Burney,* 1832.
Calthrop, Dion Clayton—*English Costume,* 1907.
Chapman, R. W.—*Jane Austen's Novels,* 1923.
Cook, Captain James—*An Account of a Voyage Round the World,* et cetera, 1809.
Delany, Mary—*Autobiography and Correspondence,* edited by Lady Llanover, 1861–62.
Dobson, Austen—*Fanny Burney,* 1903.
———*Four French Women,* 1896.
Fitzmaurice (The Marquis of Lansdowne)—*The Queeney Letters,* 1934.
Guttmacher, M. S.—*America's Last King,* 1941.
Ham, Elizabeth—*Elizabeth Ham, by Herself, 1768–1778,* edited by Eric Gillett, 1945.
Hazlitt, William—*Conversations of James Northcote, Esq., R.A.,* 1949.

330   Bibliography

——Review of Camilla, English Comic Writers, 1819.

Hill, Constance—Juniper Hall, 1904.

——The House in St. Martin's Street, 1907.

Hoole, Samuel—Aurelia, 1783.

Johnson, R. Brimley—Bluestocking Letters, 1926.

——Fanny Burney and the Burneys, 1926.

Knight, Ellis Cornelia—Autobiography of Miss C. K., 1861.

La Roche, Maria Sophie von—Sophie in London, 1933, translated and edited by Clare Williams.

Lloyd, Christopher—Fanny Burney, 1936.

Macaulay, Thomas Babington—Essays; Review of Diary and Letters of Madame d'Arblay and Samuel Johnson (any edition).

Manwaring, G. E.—My Friend the Admiral, 1938.

Masefield, Muriel—The Story of Fanny Burney, 1927.

Moore, Frank Frankfort—The Keeper of the Robes, 1911.

Overman, A. A.—An Investigation into the Character of Fanny Burney, 1933.

Papendiek, Mrs.—Court & Private Life in the Time of Queen Charlotte, 2 vols., 1887.

Paston, George—Sidelights on the Georgian Period, 1902.

Pindar, Peter (John Wolcott)—Choice Cabinet Pictures, 1817.

——The Bath Pump Room, 1818.

——The Contest of Legs, 1817.

——The Cork Pump, 1815.

——Works, 1794–1796.

Piozzi, Hester Lynch (Mrs. Thrale)—Anecdotes of the Late Samuel Johnson, LLD., 1786.

——Autobiography, Letters & Literary Remains, 2 vols., 1861.

——Thraliana, edited by K. Balderston, 1942.

Scholes, Percy—The Great Dr. Burney, 1948.

Seeley, L. B.—Fanny Burney and Her Friends, 1895.

Stuart, D. M.—The Daughters of George III, 1939.

Thackeray, William Makepeace—The Four Georges, 1903.

Tourtellot, A. B.—Be Loved No More, 1938.

Trevelyan, C. M.—*English Social History*, 1944.

Turberville, A. S.—*English Men and Manners in the Eighteenth Century*, 1929.

Vulliamy, C. E.—*Mrs. Thrale of Streatham*, 1936.

——*Royal George*, 1937.

——*Ursa Major*, 1946.

Wheeler, E. R.—*Famous Blue-Stockings*, 1910.

INDEX